Praise for *Household Gods*

"Turtledove and Tarr both know that the past is a different country and that they do things differently there. We come to care both about the fallible, far-from-omniscient but tough and determined protagonist, and the Romans among whom she lives, who are a brilliant combination of the alien and the familiar. This is a page-turner that makes you think, long after the last page is turned."

—S. M. Stirling

"Judith Tarr and Harry Turtledove both have a storytelling instinct, and in this happy instance, it seems to have multiplied rather than just added."

—Gordon R. Dickson

"Turtledove and Tarr make a fine team, and they bring a past era—with all its terrors, joys, humanity, and brutality—to remarkable life."

—Michael F. Flynn

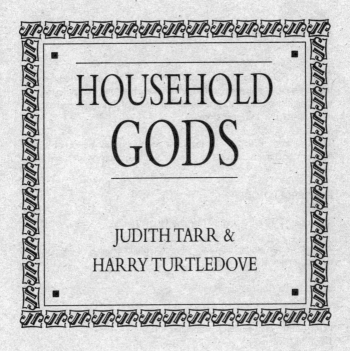

HOUSEHOLD GODS

JUDITH TARR &
HARRY TURTLEDOVE

TOR®
fantasy

A TOM DOHERTY ASSOCIATES BOOK
NEW YORK

HOUSEHOLD GODS

Copyright © 1999 by Judith Tarr and Harry Turtledove

Edited by Patrick Nielsen Hayden

A Tor Book
Published by Tom Doherty Associates, LLC
175 Fifth Avenue
New York, NY 10010

www.tor.com

Tor® is a registered trademark of Tom Doherty Associates, LLC.

ISBN: 0-812-56466-9

First edition: September 1999
First mass market edition: July 2000

Printed in the United States of America

0 9 8 7 6 5 4 3 2 1

ACKNOWLEDGMENTS

No book is wholly original. This one springs from an idea that Fletcher Pratt (1897–1956) died before he could use. The authors hope he would approve of what they have done with and to it.

Thanks to Jim Brunet, whose suggestion sparked this collaboration.

Very special thanks to Brian N. Burg, who practices family law, for advice on matters legal.

1

NICOLE GUNTHER-PERRIN ROLLED over to turn off the alarm clock and found herself nose to nose with two Roman gods. She nodded a familiar good morning to Liber and his consort Libera, whose votive plaque had stood on the nightstand since her honeymoon in Vienna. Maybe they nodded back. Maybe she was still half asleep.

As she dragged herself up to wake the children and get them ready for daycare, her mouth twisted. Liber and Libera were still with her. Frank Perrin, however . . .

"Bastard," she said. Liber and Libera didn't look surprised. They'd heard it every morning since her ex-husband took half the assets, left the kids, and headed off for bluer horizons. She doubted he thought about her except when the child support came due (and not often enough then), or when she called him with a problem. She couldn't help thinking of him a dozen times a day—and every time she looked at Justin. Her son—their son, if you wanted to get technical—looked just like him. Same rough dark hair, down to the uncombable cowlick; same dark eyes you could drown in; same shy little smile that made you feel you'd coaxed it out of hiding.

Justin smiled it as she gently shook him awake. "Mommy!" he said. He was only two and a half. He hadn't learned to wound her yet.

"Come on, Tiger," she said in her best rise-and-shine, mommy-in-the-morning voice. "We've got another day ahead of us." She reached inside his Pull-Ups. "You're dry! What a good boy! Go on and go potty while I get your sister up."

He climbed onto the rail and jumped out of bed. He landed with a splat, of course, but it didn't hurt him. It made him laugh. He toddled off sturdily toward the bathroom. Watching him go, Nicole shook her head. Kimberley never jumped out of bed. *Testosterone poisoning,* Nicole thought, and almost smiled.

Kimberley not only didn't jump out of bed, she didn't want to get out of bed at all. She clutched her stuffed bobcat and refused to open her eyes. She was like that about every other morning; given her druthers, she would have slept till noon. She didn't have her druthers, not on a Tuesday. "You've got to get up, sweetie," Nicole said with determined patience.

Eyes still resolutely closed, Kimberley shook her head. Her light brown hair, almost the same color as Nicole's, streamed over her face like seaweed. Nicole wheeled out the heavy guns: "Your brother is already up. You're a big four-year-old. You can do what he does, can't you?" If she'd used such shameless tactics in court, counsel for the other side would have screamed his head off, and the judge would have sustained him.

But she wasn't in court, and there was no law that said she had to be completely fair with a small and relentlessly sleepy child. She did what she had to do, and did it with a minimum of remorse.

It worked. Kimberley opened her eyes. They were hazel, halfway between Frank's brown and Nicole's green. Still clutching her beloved Scratchy, Kimberley headed for the bathroom. Nicole nodded to herself and sighed. Her daughter wasn't likely to say anything much for the next little while, but once she got moving, she moved pretty well.

Nicole got moving, too, toward the kitchen. Her brain was running ahead of her, kicked up into full daytime gear. She'd get the kids' breakfasts ready, get dressed herself while they ate, listen to the news on the radio while she was doing that so she could find out what traffic was like (traffic in Indianapolis had not prepared her for L.A., not even slightly), and then . . .

And then, for the first time that day, her plans started to unravel. Normally silent Kimberley let out a shrill screech:

"Ewwww!" Then came the inevitable, "Mommmmy!" Ritual satisfied, Kimberley deigned to explain what was actually wrong: "Justin tinkled all over the bathroom floor and I stepped in it. Eww! Eww! Eww!" More *ewws* might have followed that last one, but, if so, only dogs could hear them.

"Oh, for God's sake!" Nicole burst out; and under her breath, succinctly and satisfyingly if not precisely accurately, "Shit."

The bathroom was in the usual morning shambles, with additions. She tried to stay calm. "Justin," she said in the tone of perfect reason recommended by all the best child psychologists and riot-control experts, "if you go potty the way big boys do, you have to remember to stand on the stepstool so the tinkle goes in the potty like it's supposed to."

Children raised in psychologists' laboratories, or rioting mobs, might have stopped to listen. Her own offspring were oblivious. "Mommy!" Kimberley kept screaming. "Wash my feet!" Justin was laughing so hard he looked ready to fall down, though not, she noticed, into the puddle that had sent Kimberley into such hysterics. He thought his big sister in conniptions was the funniest thing in the world—which meant he'd probably pee all over the floor again sometime soon, to make Kimberley pitch another fit.

Nicole gave up on psychology and settled for basic hygiene. She coaxed the still shrieking Kimberley over to the tub and got her feet washed, three times, with soap. Then, with Kimberley hopping on one foot and screeching, "Another time, Mommy! I'm still dirty! I smell bad! Mommy, do it again!" Nicole got the wriggling, giggling Justin out of his wet pajama bottoms and the pulled-down Pull-Ups he was still wearing at half mast. She washed his feet, too, on general principles, and his legs. He'd stopped giggling and started chanting: "Tinkle-Kim! Tinkle-Kim!"—which would have set Kimberley off again if she'd ever stopped.

Nicole's head was ringing. She would be calm, she told herself. She must be calm. A good mother never lost her cool. A good mother never raised her voice. A good mother—

She had to raise her voice. She wouldn't be heard otherwise. "Go out in the hall, both of you!" she bellowed into sudden, unexpected silence, as Kimberley finally stopped for breath. She added, just too late: "Step around the puddle!"

Something in her face must have got through Justin's high glee. He was very, very quiet as she washed his feet again, his big brown eyes fixed on her face. From invisible foot-washer to Mommy Monster in five not-so-easy seconds. She took advantage of it to send him out to the kitchen. Unfair advantage. Bad parenting. Blissful, peaceful quiet.

"Guilty as charged, Your Honor," she said.

While she was cleaning up the mess, she got piss on one knee of her thirty-five-dollar, lace-trimmed, rose-printed sweats—Victoria's Secret called them "thermal pyjamas," which must have been a step up the sexiness scale from sweats, but sweats they were, and sweats Nicole called them.

She emerged somewhat less than triumphant and wrapped in the ratty old bathrobe that hung on the back of the door, to find Kimberley, who still hadn't had a chance to go to the bathroom, hopping up and down in the hallway. At least she was quiet, though she dashed past Nicole with a theatrical sigh of relief.

Ten minutes wasted, ten minutes Nicole didn't have. She popped waffles in the toaster, stood tapping her foot till they were done, poured syrup over them, poured milk (Justin's in a Tommee Tippee cup, so he'd have a harder time spilling that on the floor), and settled the kids down—she hoped—for breakfast. Justin was still bare-ass. He laughed at the way his bottom felt on the smooth vinyl of the high chair.

As she turned on *Sesame Street,* Nicole muttered what was half a prayer: "Five minutes' peace." She hurried back past the study into her own bedroom to dress. About halfway into her pantyhose (control tops, because at thirty-four she was getting a little round in the middle and she didn't have time to exercise—she didn't have time for anything), Kimberley's

voice rose once again to a banshee shriek. "Mom-meeeee!
Justin's got syrup in his hair!"

Nicole felt her nail poke into the stockings as she yanked
them all the way up. She looked down. Sure as hell, a run,
a killer run, a ladder from ankle to thigh. She threw the robe
back around herself, ran out to the kitchen, surveyed the
damage—repaired it at top speed, with a glance at the green
unblinking eye of the microwave-oven clock. Five more
minutes she didn't have.

Once back in the dubious sanctuary of her bedroom, she
took another ten seconds of overdraft to stop, breathe, calm
down. Her hands were gratifyingly steady as she found and
put on a new pair of hose, a white blouse, and a dark green
pinstripe suit that not only looked professional but also, she
hoped, played up her eyes. The skirt was a bit snug but
would do; she'd go easy on the Danish this morning, and
leave the sugar out of her coffee—if she got the chance to
eat at all. She slid into mocha pumps, pinned on an opal
brooch and put in the earrings that went with it, and checked
the effect. Not bad, but she was late, late, late. She still had
to get the kids dressed, put on her makeup, and maybe even
grab breakfast for herself. She was past morning mode by
now, past even Panic Overdrive, and into dead, cold calm.

Kimberley knew she didn't want to wear the Magic Mountain sweatshirt Nicole had picked out for her, but had no idea
what she did want. Nicole had hoped to hold onto her desperate calm, but that drove her over the edge. "You figure it
out," she snapped, and left Kimberley to it while she went
to deal with Justin. He didn't care what he wore. Whatever
it was, getting him into it was a wrestling match better suited
to Hulk Hogan than a working mother.

After Nicole pinned him and dressed him, she went in
search of Kimberley. Her daughter hadn't moved. She was
still standing in the middle of her pink-and-white bedroom,
in her underwear, staring at a tangled assortment of shirts,
pants, shorts, and skirts. Nicole felt her hands twitch in an
almost irresistible urge to slap. She forced herself to stop and
draw a breath, to speak reasonably if firmly. "We don't have

any more time to waste, young lady." In spite of her best efforts, her voice rose. "Here. This shirt. These pants. Now."

Sullenly, Kimberley put them on. "I hate you," she said, and then, as if that had been a rehearsal, found something worse: "Daddy and Dawn never yell at me."

Only four, and she knew just where to stick the knife.

Nicole stalked out of her daughter's bedroom, tight-lipped and quivering with rage she refused to show. As she strode past the nightstand on her way into the master bathroom, she glared at Liber and Libera—especially at Liber. The god and goddess, their hair cut in almost identical pageboy bobs, stared serenely back, as they had for . . . how long?

She grasped at that thought—any straw in a storm, any distraction before she lost it completely. The label on the back of the limestone plaque said in German, English, and French that it was a reproduction of an original excavated from the ruins of Carnuntum, the Roman city on the site of Petronell, the small town east of Vienna where she'd bought it. Every now and then, she wondered about that. None of the other reproductions in the shop had looked quite so . . . antique. But none of the Customs men had given her any grief about it. If they didn't know, who did?

As a distraction, it was a failure. When she stood in front of the makeup mirror, the modern world came crashing back. Fury had left her cheeks so red, she almost decided to leave off the blusher. But she knew what would happen next: the blood would drain away and leave them pasty white, and she'd look worse than ever. When she'd done the best she could with foundation and blusher, eyeliner and mascara and eyebrow pencil, lip liner and lipstick, she surveyed the results with a critical eye. Even with the help of modern cosmetology, her face was still too round—doughy, if you got right down to it. Anyone could guess she was a schnitzel-eater from a long line of schnitzel-eaters. She was starting to get a double chin, to go with the belly she had to work a little harder each year to disguise with suit jackets and shirtdresses and carefully cut slacks. And—what joy!—she was getting a pimple, too, right in the middle of her chin, a sure sign her period was on the way.

"Thirty-four years old, and I've got zits," she said to nobody in particular. God wasn't listening, that was plain. She camouflaged the damage as best she could, corralled the kids, and headed out to the car.

The Honda coughed several times before reluctantly kicking over. If Frank had got the last child-support check to her, or the one before that, she'd have had it tuned. As things were—as things were, she gritted her teeth. She was a lawyer. She was supposed to be making good money. She was making good money, by every national standard, but food and daycare and clothes and insurance and utilities and the mortgage ate it all up and then some.

House payments in Indianapolis hadn't prepared her for Los Angeles, either. With two incomes, they were doable. Without two incomes . . .

"Yay! Off to Josefina's," Kimberley said when they pulled out of the driveway. Apparently, she'd forgotten she hated her mother.

Nicole wished she could forget as easily as that herself. "Off to Josefina's," she echoed with considerably less enthusiasm. She lived in West Hills, maybe ten minutes away from the splendidly multicultural law offices of Rosenthal, Gallagher, Kaplan, Jeter, Gonzalez & Feng. The daycare provider, however, was over in Van Nuys, halfway across the San Fernando Valley.

That hadn't been a problem when Nicole was married. Frank would drop off the kids, then head down the San Diego Freeway to the computer-science classes he taught at U.C.L.A. He'd pick Kimberley and Justin up in the evening, too. Everything was great. Josefina was wonderful, the kids loved her, Nicole got an extra half-hour every morning to drink her coffee and brace herself for the day.

Now that Frank didn't live there anymore, Nicole had to drive twenty minutes in the direction opposite the one that would have taken her to work, then hustle back across the

Valley to the Woodland Hills office. After she got off, she made the same trip in reverse. No wonder the Honda needed a tuneup. Nicole kept wanting to try to find someone closer, preferably on the way to work, but the kids screamed every time she suggested it, and there never seemed to be time. So she kept taking them to Josefina's, and the Honda kept complaining, and she kept scrambling, morning after morning and evening after evening. Someday the Honda would break down and she'd scream loud enough to drown out the kids, and then she'd get around to finding someone else to take care of them while she went about earning a living.

She turned left onto Victory and headed east. Sometimes you could make really good time on Victory, almost as good as on the freeway—the freeway when it wasn't jammed, of course; the eastbound 101 during morning rush hour didn't bear thinking about. She hoped this would be one of those times; she was still running late.

She sailed past the parking lots of the Fallbrook Mall and the more upscale Topanga Plaza. Both were acres of empty asphalt now. They wouldn't slow her down till she came home tonight. Her hands tightened on the wheel as she came up to Pierce College. Things often jammed there in the morning, with people heading for early classes. Some of the kids drove like maniacs, too, and got into wrecks that snarled traffic for a mile in either direction.

Not today, though. "Victory," Nicole breathed: half street name, half triumph. Victory wasn't like Sherman Way, with a traffic light every short block. Clear sailing till just before the freeway, she thought. She rolled by one gas station, apartment house, condo block, and strip mall with video store or copy place or small-time accountant's office or baseball-card shop or Mexican or Thai or Chinese or Korean or Indian or Armenian restaurant after another, in continual and polyglot confusion. They had a flat and faintly unreal look in the trafficless morning, under the blue California sky.

Six years and she could still marvel at the way the light came down straight and white and hard, with an edge to it that she could taste in the back of her throat. Good solid Los

Angeles smog, pressed down hard by the sun: air you could cut pieces off and eat. She'd thought she'd never be able to breathe it, gone around with a stitch in her side and a catch in her lungs, till one day she woke up and realized she hadn't felt like that in weeks. She'd whooped, which woke up Frank; then she'd had to explain: "I'm an Angeleno now! I can breathe the smog."

Frank hadn't understood. He'd just eyed her warily and grunted and gone to take over the bathroom the way he did every morning.

She should have seen the end then, but it had taken another couple of years and numerous further signs—then he was gone and she was a statistic. Divorced wife, mother of two.

She came back to the here-and-now just past White Oak, just as everything on the south side of the street turned green. The long rolling stretch of parkland took her back all over again to the Midwest—to the place she'd taught herself to stop calling home. There, she'd taken green for granted. Here, in Southern California, green was a miracle and a gift. Eight months a year, any landscape that wasn't irrigated stretched bare and bleak and brown. Rain seldom fell. Rivers were few and far between. This was desert—rather to the astonishment of most transplants, who'd expected sun and surf and palm trees, but never realized how dry the land was beyond the beaches.

There was actually a river here, the Los Angeles River, running through the park. But the L.A. River, even the brief stretch of it not encased in concrete, would hardly have passed for a creek in Indiana. She shut down a surge of homesickness so strong it caught her by surprise. "Damn," she said softly—too softly, apparently, for the kids to hear: no voice piped up from the back, no "Damn what, Mommy?" from Justin and no prim "We don't use bad words, Mommy," from Kimberley. She'd thought she was long past yearning for Indiana. What was there to yearn for? Narrow minds and narrower mindsets, freezing cold in the winter and choking humidity in the summer, and thousands of miles to the nearest ocean.

And green. Green grass and bare naked water, and air that didn't rake the lungs raw.

Just past Hayvenhurst, everything stopped. A red sea of brake lights lay ahead, and she had no way to part it. She glared at the car radio, which hadn't said a word about any accidents. But the traffic reports seldom bothered with surface-street crashes; they had enough trouble keeping up with bad news on the freeways.

"Why aren't we going, Mommy?" Kimberley asked from the backseat, as inevitable as the traffic jam.

"We're stuck," Nicole answered, as she'd answered a hundred times before. "There must be an accident up ahead."

They were stuck tight, too. With the park on one side of Victory and a golf course on the other, there weren't even any cross streets with which to escape. Nothing to do but fume, slide forward a couple of inches, hit the brakes, fume again.

People in the fast lane were making U-turns to go back to Hayvenhurst and around the catastrophe that had turned Victory into defeat. Nicole, of course, was trapped in the slow lane. Whenever she tried to get into the fast lane, somebody cut her off. Drivers leaned on their horns (which the Nicole who'd lived in Indianapolis would have been surprised to hear was rare in L.A.), flipped off their neighbors, shook fists. She wondered how many of them had a gun in their waistband or pocket or purse or glove compartment. She didn't want to find out.

Ten mortal minutes and half a mile later, she crawled past the U-Haul truck that had wrapped itself around a pole. The driver was talking to a cop. "Penal Section 502," she snarled, that being the California section on driving under the influence.

She had to slow down again as cars got onto the San Diego Freeway, but that happened every day. She bore it in resigned annoyance as a proper Angeleno should, but with a thrum of desperation underneath. *Late-late-late* . . .

Once she got under the overpass, she made reasonably

decent time. Thoughts about locking the barn door after the horse was·stolen ran through her mind.

Parts of Van Nuys were ordinary middle-class suburb. Parts were the sort of neighborhood where you wished you could drive with the Club locked on the steering wheel. Josefina's house was right on the edge between the one and the other.

"Hello, Mrs. Gunther-Perrin," Josefina said in accented English as Nicole led her children into the relative coolness and dimness of the house. It smelled faintly of sour milk and babies, more distinctly of spices Nicole had learned to recognize: cilantro, cumin, chili powder. The children tugged at Nicole's hands, trying to break free and bolt, first into Josefina's welcoming arms, then to the playroom where they'd spend most of the day.

Normally, Nicole would have let them go, but Josefina had put herself in the way, and something in her expression made Nicole tighten her grip in spite of the children's protests.

Josefina was somewhere near Nicole's age, several inches shorter, a good deal wider, and addicted to lurid colors: today, an electric blue blouse over fluorescent orange pants. Her taste in clothes, fortunately, didn't extend to the decor of her house; that was a more or less standard Sears amalgam of brown plaid and olive-green slipcovers, with a touch of faded blue and purple and orange in a big terracotta vase of paper flowers that stood by the door. Nicole would remember the flowers later, more clearly than Josefina's face in the shadow of the foyer, or even the day-glo glare of her clothes.

Nicole waited for Josefina to move so that Kimberley and Justin could go in, but Josefina stood her ground, solid as a tiki god in a Hawaiian gift shop. "Listen, Mrs. Gunther-Perrin," she said. "I got to tell you something. Something important."

"What?" Nicole was going to snap again. Damn it, she was late. How in hell was she going to make it to the office on time if the kids' daycare provider wanted to stop and chat?

Josefina could hardly have missed the chill in Nicole's

tone, but she didn't back down. "Mrs. Gunther-Perrin, I'm
very sorry, but after today I can't take care of your kids no
more. I can't take care of nobody's kids no more."

She did look sorry. Nicole granted her that. Was there a
glisten of tears in her eyes?

Nicole was too horrified to be reasonable, and too astonished to care whether Josefina was happy, sad, or indifferent.
"What?" she said. "You what? You can't do that!"

Josefina did not reply with the obvious, which was that
she perfectly well could. "I got to go home to Mexico. My
mother down in Ciudad Obregón, where I come from, she
very sick." Josefina brought the story out pat. And why not?
She must have told it a dozen times already, to a dozen other
shocked and appalled parents. "She call me last night," she
said, "and I get the airplane ticket. I leave tonight. I don't
know when I be back. I don't know if I be back. I'm very
sorry, but I can't help it. You give me the check for this part
of the month when you pick up the kids tonight, okay?"

Then, finally, she stood a little to the side so that Kimberley and Justin could run past her. They seemed not to
know or understand what she'd said, which was a small—a
very small—mercy. Nicole stood numbly as they vanished
into the depths of the house, staring at Josefina's round flat
face above the screaming blue of her blouse. "But—" Nicole
said. "But—"

Her brain was as sticky as the Honda's engine. It needed
a couple of tries before it would turn over. "But what am I
supposed to do? I work for a living, Josefina—I have to.
Where am I supposed to take the children tomorrow?"

Josefina's face set. Nicole damned herself for political in-
correctness, for thinking that this woman whom she was so
careful to think of as an equal and not as an ethnic curiosity,
looked just now like every stereotype of the inscrutable and
intractable aborigine. Her eyes were flat and black. Her features, the broad cheekbones, the Aztec profile, the bronze
sheen of the skin, were completely and undeniably foreign.
Years of daycare, daily meetings, little presents for the children on their birthdays and plates of delicious and exotic

cookies at Christmas, reciprocated with boxes of chocolates—
Russell Stover, not Godiva; Godiva was an acquired taste if
you weren't a yuppie—all added up to this: closed mind and
closed face, and nothing to get a grip on, no handhold for
sympathy, let alone understanding. This, Nicole knew with
a kind of angry despair, was an alien. She'd never been a
friend, and she'd never been a compatriot, either. Her whole
world just barely touched on anything that Nicole knew. And
now even that narrow tangent had disappeared.

"I'm sorry," Josefina said in her foreign accent, with her
soft Spanish vowels. "I know you are upset with me. Lots
of parents upset with me, but I can't do nothing about it. My
mother got nobody else but me."

Nicole made her mind work, made herself think and talk
some kind of sense. "Do you know anyone who might take
Kimberley and Justin on such short notice?"

God, even if Josefina said yes, the kids would pitch a fit.
She was . . . like a mother to them. That had always worried
Nicole a little—not, she'd been careful to assure herself, that
her impeccably Anglo children should be so attached to a
Mexican woman; no, of course not, how wonderfully free of
prejudice that would make them, and they'd picked up Spanish, too. No, she worried she herself wasn't mother enough,
so they'd had to focus on Josefina for all the things Nicole
couldn't, but should, be offering them. And now, when they
were fixated like that, to go from her house to some
stranger's—

Even as Nicole fussed over what was, after all, a minor
worry, Josefina was shaking her head. "Don't know nobody,"
she said. She didn't mean it the way it sounded. Of course
she didn't. She couldn't mean, *It's no skin off my nose, lady.*
Josefina loved the kids. Didn't she?

What did Nicole know of what Josefina felt or didn't feel?
Josefina was foreign.

Nicole stood on the front porch, breathing hard. If that
was the way Josefina wanted to play it, then that was how
Nicole would play it. There had to be some way out. She
would have bet money that Josefina was an undocumented

immigrant. She could threaten to call the INS, get her checked out, have her deported . . .

Anger felt good. Anger felt cleansing. But it didn't change a thing. There wasn't anything she could do. Deport Josefina? She almost laughed. Josefina was leaving the USA on her own tonight. She'd probably welcome the help.

"I'm sorry, Mrs. Gunther-Perrin," Josefina repeated. As if she meant it. As if she even cared.

Nicole didn't even remember going from the house to the car. One moment she was staring at Josefina, hunting for words that wouldn't come. The next, she was in the Honda, slamming the driver's-side door hard enough to rattle the glass in the window frame. She jammed the key in the ignition, shoved the pedal to the metal, and roared out into the street.

Part of her wanted to feel cold and sick and a little guilty. The rest of her was too ferociously angry to care how she drove.

She might not care, but with the luck she was running, she'd pick up a ticket on top of being drastically late. She made an effort of will and slowed down to something near a reasonable speed. Her brain flicked back into commuter mode, cruising on autopilot. The main part of her mind fretted away at this latest blow.

I can't worry about it now, she told herself over and over. I'll worry about it after I get to the office. I'll worry about it tonight.

First she had to get to the office. When she came out onto Victory, she shook her head violently. She knew too well how long tooling back across the western half of the Valley would take. Instead, she swung south onto the San Diego Freeway: only a mile or two there to the interchange with the 101. Yes, the eastbound 101 would be a zoo, but so what? Westbound, going against rush-hour traffic, she'd make good time. She didn't usually try it, but she wasn't usually so far behind, either.

Thinking about that, plotting out the rest of her battle plan, helped her focus; got her away from the gnawing worry about Josefina's desertion. It was good for that much, at least.

As she crawled down toward the interchange, she checked the KFWB traffic report and then, two minutes later, the one on KNX. They were both going on about a jackknifed big rig on the Long Beach Freeway, miles from where she was. Nobody said anything about the 101. She swung through the curve from the San Diego to the 101 and pushed the car up to sixty-five.

For a couple of miles, she zoomed along—she even dared to congratulate herself. She'd rolled the dice and won: she would save ten, fifteen minutes, easy. She'd still be late, but not enough for it to be a problem. She didn't have any appointments scheduled till eleven-thirty. The rest she could cover for.

She should have known it wouldn't be that easy. Not today. Not with her luck.

Just past Hayvenhurst, everything stopped. "You lying son of a bitch!" Nicole snarled at the car radio. It was too much. Everything was going wrong. It was almost as bad as the day she woke up to a note on her pillow, and no Frank. *Dear Nicole,* the note had said, on departmental stationery yet, *Dawn and I have gone to Reno. We'll talk about the divorce when I get back. Love, Frank.* And scribbled across the bottom: *P.S. The milk in the fridge is sour. Remember to check the Sell-By date next time you buy a gallon.*

Remembering how bad that day was didn't make this one feel any better. "Love, Frank," she muttered. "Love, the whole goddamn world."

Her eye caught the flash of her watch as she drummed her fingers on the steering wheel. Almost time for the KNX traffic report. She stabbed the button, wishing she could stab the reporter. His cheery voice blared out of the speakers: "—and Cell-Phone Force member Big Charlie reports a three-car injury accident on the westbound 101 between White Oak and Reseda. One of those cars flipped over; it's blocking the number-two and number-three lanes. Big Charlie says only the slow lane is open. That's gonna put a hitch in your get-

along, folks. Now Louise is over that jackknifed truck on the
Long Beach in Helicop—"

Nicole switched stations again. Suddenly, she was very,
very tired. Too tired to keep her mad on, too tired almost to
hold her head up. Her fingers drummed on the wheel,
drummed and drummed. The natives, she thought dizzily,
were long past getting restless. Her stomach tied itself in a
knot. What to do, what to do? Get off the freeway at White
Oak and go back to surface streets? Or crawl past the wreck
and hope she'd make up a little time when she could floor
it again?

All alone in the passenger compartment, she let out a long
sigh. "What difference does it make?" she said wearily. "I'm
screwed either way."

She pulled into the parking lot half an hour late—twenty-
eight minutes to be exact, if you felt like being exact, which
she didn't. Grabbing her attaché case, she ran for the entrance
to the eight-story steel-and-glass rectangle in which Rosenthal, Gallagher, Kaplan, Jeter, Gonzalez & Feng occupied the
sixth and most of the seventh floors.

When she'd first seen it, she'd harbored faint dreams of
L.A. Law and spectacular cases, fame and fortune and all the
rest of it. Now she just wanted to get through the day without
falling on her face. The real hotshots were in Beverly Hills
or Century City or someplace else on the Westside. This was
just . . . a job, and not the world's best.

Gary Ogarkov, one of the other lawyers with the firm,
stood outside the doorway puffing one of the big, smelly
cigars he made such a production of. He had to come outside
to do that; the building, thank God, was smoke-free. "Nicole!" he called out in what he probably thought was a fine
courtroom basso. To Nicole, it sounded like a schoolboy imitation—Perry Mason on helium. "Mr. Rosenthal's been
looking for you since nine o'clock."

Jesus. The founding partner. How couldn't he be looking
for Nicole? That was the kind of day this was. Even knowing
she'd had it coming, she still wanted to sink through the

sidewalk. "God," she said. "Of all the days for traffic to be god-awful—Gary, do you know what it's about?" She pressed- him, hoping to hell he'd give her a straight answer.

Naturally, he didn't. "I shouldn't tell you." He tried to look sly. With his bland, boyish face, it didn't come off well. He was within a year of Nicole's age but, in spite of a blond mustache, still got asked for ID whenever he ordered a drink.

Nicole was no more afraid of him than the local bartenders. "Gary," she said dangerously.

He backed down in a hurry, flinging up his hands as if he thought she might bite. "Okay, okay. You look like you could use some good news. You know the Butler Ranch report we turned in a couple of weeks ago?"

"I'd better," Nicole said, still with an edge in her voice. Antidevelopment forces were fighting the Butler Ranch project tooth and nail because it would extend tract housing into the scrubby hill country north of the 118 Freeway. The fight would send the children of attorneys on both sides to Ivy League schools for years, likely decades, to come.

"Well, because of that report—" Gary paused to draw on his cigar, tilted his head back, and blew a ragged smoke ring. "Because of that report, Mr. Rosenthal named me a partner in the firm." He pointed at Nicole. "And he's looking for you."

For a moment, she just stood there. Then she felt the wide, crazy grin spread across her face. Payoff—finally. Restitution for the whole lousy morning, for a whole year of lousy mornings. "My God," she whispered. She'd done three-quarters of the work on that report. She knew it, Gary knew it, the whole firm had to know it. He was a smoother writer than she, which was the main reason he'd been involved at all, but he thought environmental impact was what caused roadkill.

"Shall I congratulate you now?" he asked. His grin was as broad as Nicole's.

She shook her head. She felt dizzy, bubbly. Was this what champagne did to people? She didn't know. She didn't drink. Just as well—she had to be calm, she had to be mature. She couldn't go fizzing off into the upper atmosphere. She had a reputation to uphold. "Better not," she said. "Wait till it's official. But since you are official—congratulations, Gary." She thrust out her hand. He pumped it. When he started to give her a hug, she stiffened just enough to let him know she didn't want it. Since Frank walked out the door, she hadn't wanted much to do with the male half of the human race. To cover the awkward moment, she said, "Congratulations again." And hastily, before he could say anything to prolong the moment: "I'd better get upstairs."

"Okay. And back at you," Ogarkov added, even though she'd told him not to. She made a face at him over her shoulder as she hurried toward the elevators. She almost didn't need them, she was flying so high.

When she'd floated up to the sixth floor, her secretary greeted her with a wide-eyed stare and careful refusal to point out that she was—by the clock—thirty-three minutes late. Instead, she said in her breathy Southern California starlet's voice, "Oh, Ms. Gunther-Perrin, Mr. Rosenthal's been looking for you."

Nicole nodded and bit back the silly grin. "I know," she said. "I saw Gary downstairs, smoking a victory cigar." That came out with less scorn than Nicole would have liked. She had as little use for tobacco as she did for alcohol, but when you made partner, she supposed you were entitled to celebrate. "Can he see me now, Cyndi?"

"Let me check." The secretary punched in Mr. Rosenthal's extension on the seventh floor, where all the senior partners held their dizzy eminence above the common herd, and spoke for a moment, then hung up. "He's with a client. Ten-thirty, Lucinda says."

Cyndi down here, Lucinda up above. Even the secretaries' names were more elevated in the upper reaches.

Nicole brought herself back to earth with an effort. "Oh," she said. "All right. If Lucinda says it, it must be so."

Nicole and Cyndi shared a smile. Sheldon Rosenthal's secretary reckoned herself at least as important to the firm as

the boss. She was close enough to being right that nobody
ever quite dared disagree with her in public.

Something else caught Nicole's eye and mind, which went
to show how scattered she still was after her morning from
hell. She pointed to the photographs on her secretary's desk.
"Cyndi, who takes care of Benjamin and Joseph while you're
here?"

"My husband's sister," Cyndi answered. She didn't sound
confused, or wary either. "She's got two-year-old twins of
her own, and she stays home with them and my kids and her
other sister-in-law's little girl. She'd rather do that than go
back to work, so it's pretty good for all of us."

"Do you think she'd want to take on two more?" Nicole
tried to make it sound light, but couldn't hide how hard Josefina's desertion had hit.

Cyndi heard the story with sympathy that looked and
sounded genuine. "That's terrible of her, to spring it on you
like that," she said. "Still, if it's family, what can you do?
You can't very well tell your mother not to be sick, you have
to stay in the States and take care of other people's kids."
She hesitated. Probably she could feel Nicole staring at her,
thinking at her—wanting, needing her to solve the problem.
"Look," she said uncomfortably. "I understand, I really do.
You know? But I don't think Marie would want to sit any
kids who aren't family, you know what I mean?"

Nicole knew what she meant. Nicole would have felt the
same way. But they were *her* kids. She was left in the lurch,
on a bare day's notice. "Oh, yes," she said. She hoped she
didn't sound as disappointed as she felt. "Yes. Of course. I
just thought . . . well. If my family were here, and not back
in Indiana . . . Oh well. It was worth a try." She did her best
to make her shrug nonchalant, to change the subject without
giving them both whiplash. "Ten-thirty, you said? I'll see
what I can catch up on till then. Lord, you wouldn't believe
how long it took me to get here this morning."

"Traffic." Cyndi managed to make it both a four-letter
word and a sigh of relief. *Off the hook,* she had to be thinking.

Lucky Cyndi, with her sister in town and not in Bloomington, and no chance of her disappearing into the wilds of Ciudad Obregón. Nicole mumbled something she hoped was suitably casual, and retreated to her desk. She was still riding the high of Ogarkov's news, though the bright edge had worn off it.

The first thing she did when she got there was check her voice mail. Sure enough, one of the messages was from Sheldon Rosenthal, dry and precise as usual: "Please arrange to meet with me at your earliest convenience." She'd taken care of that. Another one was from Mort Albers, with whom she had the eleven-thirty appointment. "Can we move it up to half-past ten?" he asked.

"No, Mort," Nicole said with a measure of satisfaction, "you can't, not today." It was just as satisfying to have Cyndi make the call and change the schedule—the pleasure of power. Nicole could get used to that, oh yes she could. Even the little things felt good today. *Tomorrow,* she thought. Tomorrow she'd be doing them as a partner. Today—her last day as a plain associate—had a bittersweet clarity, a kind of farewell brightness. She answered a couple of voice-mail messages from other lawyers at the firm. She wrote a memo, fired it off by e-mail, and printed out a hard copy for her files. Frank would have gone on for an hour about how primitive that was, but the law ran on paper and ink, not electrons and phosphors—*and to hell with Frank anyhow,* she thought.

It was going to feel wonderful to tell him she was a partner now. Even if—

She quelled the little stab of anxiety. He had to keep paying child support, as much as he ever did. That was in the divorce decree. She was a lawyer—a partner in a moderately major firm. She could make it stick.

The clock on the wall ticked the minutes away. At ten twenty-five she started a letter, hesitated, counted up the minutes remaining, saved the letter on the hard drive and stood up, smoothing wrinkles out of her skirt. She checked her pantyhose. On straight, no runs—thanks to whichever god oversaw the art of dressing for success. She took a deep breath and squared her shoulders, and forayed out past Cyndi's desk. "I'm going to see Mr. Rosenthal," she said— nice and steady, she was pleased to note. Cyndi grinned and gave her a thumbs-up.

Nicole took the stairs to the seventh floor. Some people walked all the way up every day; others exercised on the stairs during breaks and at lunch. Nicole never had understood that, not in a climate that made you happy to go outside the whole year round—even on days when the smog was thick enough to asphyxiate a non-smog-adapted organism. People who'd been born in L.A. didn't know when they were well off.

She stood in the hallway for a minute and a half, so she could walk into Sheldon Rosenthal's office at ten-thirty on the dot. It was an exercise in discipline, and a chance to pull herself together. She thought about ducking into a restroom, but that would have meant heading back down to the sixth floor: she didn't—yet—have the key to the partners' washroom. Her makeup would have to look after itself. Her bladder would hold on till the meeting was over.

Then, after what felt like a week and a half, it was time. She licked her dry lips, stiffened her spine, and walked through the mock-oak-paneled door with its discreet brass plaque: *Sheldon Rosenthal, Esq.*, it said. That was all. No title. No ostentation. Noble self-restraint.

That restraint was, in its peculiar way, as much in evidence inside as out. Of course the óffice was a lot more lavishly appointed than anything down on her floor: acres of deep expensive carpet, gleaming glass, dark wood, law books bound in red and gold. But it was all in perfect taste, not overdone. It was a perk, that was all, a symbol. Here, it said, was the founding partner of the firm. Naturally he'd surround himself with order and comfort, quiet and expense, rather than the cheap carpet and tacky veneer of the salaried peon.

Lucinda Jackson looked up from the keyboard of—of all things—an IBM Selectric. Not for her anything as newfangled as a computer. She was a light-skinned black woman, the exact shade of good coffee well lightened with cream.

She might have been fifty or she might have been seventy. One thing Nicole did know: she'd been with Mr. Rosenthal forever.

"He still has the client in there, Ms. Gunther-Perrin," she said. Her voice was cultured, soft, almost all traces of the Deep South excised as if by surgery. "Why don't you sit down? He'll see you as soon as he can."

Nicole nodded and sank into a chair so plush, she had real doubts that she'd be able to climb out of it. Her eyes went to the magazines on the table next to it, but she didn't take one. She didn't want to have to slap it shut all of a sudden when she received the summons to the inner office.

Twenty minutes slid by. Nicole tried to look as if she didn't mind that her life—not to mention her day's work—had been put on hold. When she was a partner, she would be more careful of her schedule. She wouldn't keep a fellow partner waiting.

At last, with an effect rather like the parting of the gates of heaven in a Fifties movie epic, the door to the inner office opened. Someone her mother had watched on TV came out. "Thanks a million, Shelly," he said over his shoulder. "I'm glad it's in good hands. Say hi to Ruth for me." He waggled his fingers at Lucinda and walked past Nicole as if she'd been invisible.

She was almost too bemused to feel slighted. Shelly? She couldn't imagine anyone calling Sheldon Rosenthal *Shelly.* Certainly no one in the firm did—not even the other senior partners.

"Go on in, Ms. Gunther-Perrin," Lucinda said, at the same time as Rosenthal said, "I'm sorry to have kept you waiting."

"It's all right," Nicole said, carefully heaving herself up and out of that engulfing chair. It wasn't all right, not really, but she told herself it was—the way hazing is, a kind of rite of passage. And after all, what could she do? Complain to his boss?

Rosenthal held the door open so that she could enter his sanctum. He looked like what he was: a Jewish lawyer—thin and thoughtful type, not fat and friendly—in his mid-sixties, out of the ordinary only in that he wore a neat gray chin beard. He waved her to a chair. "Please—make yourself comfortable." Before she could sit down, however, he pointed to the Mr. Coffee on a table by the window. "Help yourself, if you like."

The mug on his desk was half full. Nicole decided to take him up on his offer—a show of solidarity, as it were; her first cup of coffee as a partner in the firm. She filled one of the styrofoam cups by the coffee machine. When she tasted, her eyebrows leaped upward. "Is that Blue Mountain?" she asked.

"You're close." He smiled. "It's Kalossi Celebes. A lot of people think it's just as good, and you don't have to rob a bank to buy it."

As if you need to rob a bank, Nicole thought. Her office window looked out on the street, and on the office building across it. His offered a panorama of the hills that gave Woodland Hills its name. He had a mansion up in those hills; she'd been there for holiday parties. Serious money in the Valley lived south of Ventura Boulevard, the farther south, the more serious. Sheldon Rosenthal lived a long way south of Ventura.

He made a couple of minutes of small talk while she sipped the delicious coffee, then said, "The analysis you and Mr. Ogarkov prepared of the issues involved in the Butler Ranch project was an excellent piece of work."

There. Now. Nicole armed herself to be polite, as polite as humanly possible. Memories of Indiana childhood, white gloves and patent-leather shoes (white only between Memorial Day and Labor Day, never either before or after), waylaid her for a moment. Out of them, she said in her best company voice, "Thank you very much."

"An excellent piece of work," Rosenthal repeated, as if she hadn't spoken. "On the strength of it, I offered Mr. Ogarkov a partnership in the firm this morning, an offer he has accepted."

"Yes. I know. I saw him downstairs when I was coming in." Nicole wished she hadn't said that; it reminded the founding partner how late she'd been. Her heart pounded. *Now it's my turn. Let me show what I can do, and two years from now Gary will be eating my dust.*

Rosenthal's long, skinny face grew longer and skinnier. "Ms. Gunther-Perrin, I very much regret to inform you that only one partnership was available. After consultation with the senior partners, I decided to offer it to Mr. Ogarkov."

Nicole started to say, *Thank you.* Her tongue had already slipped between her teeth when the words that he had said— the real words, not the words she had expected and rehearsed for—finally sank in. She stared at him. There he sat, calm, cool, machinelike, prosperous. There was not a word in her anywhere. Not a single word.

"I realize this must be a disappointment for you." Sheldon Rosenthal had no trouble talking. Why should he? His career, his life, hadn't just slammed into the side of a mountain and burst into flames. "Do please understand that we are quite satisfied with your performance and happy to retain you in your present salaried position."

Happy to retain you in your salaried position? Like any attorney with two brain cells to rub against each other, Nicole knew that was one of the all-time great lies, right up there with *The check is in the mail* and *Of course I won't come in your mouth, darling.* If you weren't on the way up, you were on the way out. She'd thought she was on the way up. Now—

She knew she had to say something. "Could you tell me why you chose Mr. Ogarkov"—formality helped, to some microscopic degree—"instead of me, so that . . . so that I'll be in a better position for the next opportunity?" Rosenthal hadn't said anything about the next opportunity. She knew what that meant, too. It was written above the gates of hell. *All hope abandon, ye who enter here.*

He coughed once, and then again, as if the first time had taken him by surprise. Maybe he hadn't expected her to ask that. After a pause that stretched a little longer than it should have, he said, "The senior partners were of the opinion that, with your other skills being more or less equal, Mr. Ogarkov's very fluent writing style gives the firm an asset we would do well to retain."

"But—" Nothing Nicole could say would change Sheldon Rosenthal's mind. That was as clear as the crystal decanter that stood on the sideboard in this baronial hall of an office. Nicole could do the mathematics of the firm, better maybe than anybody in it. She was five times the lawyer Gary Ogarkov would ever be—but Gary Ogarkov had ten times the chances. All it took was one little thing. One tiny fluke of nature. A Y chromosome.

They all had it, all the senior partners, every last one of them. Rosenthal, Gallagher, Kaplan, Jeter, Gonzalez & Feng, and most of the junior partners, too. A precise handful of women rounded out the firm, just enough to keep people from raising awkward eyebrows. Not enough to mean anything, not where it counted.

Class action suit? Discrimination suit? Even as she thought of it, she looked into Sheldon Rosenthal's eyes and knew. She could sue till she bankrupted herself, and it wouldn't make the least bit of difference.

Men, she thought, too clear even to be bitter. They would not give a person her due, not if she was female: not as a woman, not as a partner, not as a professional. All they wanted to do was get on top and screw her, in bed or on the job. And they could. All too often, they could. In the United States at the end of the twentieth century, in spite of all the laws, the suits, the cases piled up from the bottom to the top of an enormous and tottering system, they still had the power.

Oh, they paid lip service to equality. They'd hired her, hadn't they? They'd hired half a dozen other peons, and used most of them till they broke or left, the way they were using Nicole. Hypocrites, every last one of them.

"You wished to say something, Ms. Gunther-Perrin?" Rosenthal probably didn't get into court once a year these days, but he knew how to size up a witness.

"I was just wondering"—Nicole chose her words with enormous care—"if you used anything besides the senior partners' opinions to decide who would get the partnership."

However careful she was, it wasn't careful enough. Sheldon Rosenthal had been an attorney longer than she'd been alive. He knew what she was driving at. "Oh, yes," he said blandly. "We studied performance assessments and annual evaluations most thoroughly, I assure you. The process is well documented."

If you sue us, you're toast, he meant.

Performance assessments written by men, Nicole thought. Annual evaluations written by men. She knew hers were good. She had no way of knowing what Gary's said. If they were as good as hers . . . *If they're as good as mine, it's because he's got the old-boy network looking out for him. There's no way he's as good at this as I am.*

But if Rosenthal said the process was well documented, you could take it to the bank. And you'd have to be crazy to take it to court.

"Is there anything else?" he asked. Smooth. Capable. Powerful.

"No." Nicole had nothing else to say. She nodded to the man who'd ruined her life—the second man in the past couple of years who'd ruined her life—and left the office. Lucinda watched her go without the slightest show of sympathy. Woman she might be, and woman of color at that, but Lucinda had made her choice and sealed her bargain. She belonged to the system.

The stairway down to the sixth floor seemed to have twisted into an M.C. Escher travesty of itself. Going down felt like slogging uphill through thickening, choking air.

A couple of people she knew stood in the hallway, strategically positioned to congratulate her—news got around fast. But it was the wrong news. One look at her face must have told them the truth. They managed, rather suddenly, to find urgent business elsewhere.

Cyndi's smile lit up the office. It froze as Nicole came in clear sight. "Oh, no!" she said, as honest as ever, and as inept at keeping her thoughts to herself.

"Oh, yes," Nicole said. She almost felt sorry for her secretary. Poor Cyndi, all ready and set to be a partner's assistant, and now she had to know she'd landed in a dead-end job. Just like Nicole. Just like every other woman who'd smacked into the glass ceiling. "They only had one slot open, and they decided to give it to Mr. Ogarkov." She felt, and probably sounded, eerily calm, like someone who'd just been in a car wreck. Walking past Cyndi, she sat down behind her desk and stared at the papers there. She couldn't make them mean anything.

After a couple of minutes, or maybe a week, or an hour, the phone rang. She picked it up. Her voice was flat. "Yes?"

"Mr. Ogarkov wants to talk to you," Cyndi said in her ear. "He sounds upset."

I'll bet, Nicole thought. She could not make herself feel anything. "Tell him," she said, "tell him thanks, but I really don't want to talk to anyone right now. Maybe tomorrow." Cyndi started to say something, but Nicole didn't want to listen, either. Gently, she placed the handset in its cradle.

2

NICOLE SAT STARING AT the phone. After a while, when it didn't ring, she picked it up. Work was a lost cause even if she'd given a damn. But the kids weren't going to go away, the way her partnership had, and Josefina, and Frank, and most of the rest of her life. She had to do something about them, find someone to take care of them tomorrow.

She paused with the receiver in her hand, ignoring its monotone buzz. No, she could not quit. She could not go tramping back upstairs and tell Sheldon Rosenthal to take his crummy little salaried job and shove it. She could not take the kids, the Honda, and the assets she didn't have, and run back to Indianapolis. The world didn't work that way. She didn't work that way. She had to do it right. She'd hunker down, grit her teeth, and let them put it to her here, till she could find something else somewhere else. Never mind where.

Meanwhile, Josefina was off to Mexico tonight, and Kimberley and Justin weren't going to take care of themselves. There wasn't any help for it. She had to talk to Frank.

She dialed the UCLA number. She didn't expect to get him, not right away. Frank had always despised phone calls. They interrupted. They disrupted. They interfered with the thinking of wise thoughts.

Horny thoughts, more likely, Nicole thought sourly. But he wasn't too bad about answering his voice mail—when he got around to it.

She had the message all ready in her mind, set to give to the machine. But the phone cut off at the first ring, leaving her wondering briefly if she'd dialed a wrong number. Then Frank's voice said cheerily, "Hi, Dawn, darlin', how you doin'?"

"This isn't Dawn darlin'," Nicole said, cold as black ice in a Midwest February. "Sorry to disappoint you. It's your ex-wife."

"Oh. Nicole." Frank Perrin's voice dropped about forty degrees. "I didn't think it would be you."

"Obviously. 'Dawn darlin'.'" Nicole imitated his eager tone again, as nastily as she could. Goddamn blond California bimbo, fresh out of college and raring to go after the prof. Dawn—Dawn Soderstrom, how was that for a nice sexy Nordic name?—had been Frank's editor at the University of California Press. She'd been just wild, like totally jazzed, she said, about his book on industrial espionage and the Internet. In Nicole's day, busty blondes had got the hots for cuter topics, volumes of deeply angst-ridden poetry, say, or passionate monographs on Derrida or Thomas Pynchon. Dawn's hots were the wave of the future.

She hadn't been the only one, either. Frank had got lucky. After he turned in the book but before it saw print, the topic caught fire. To everybody's surprise—most of all Nicole's, but obviously not Dawn's—*Spy by Wire* took off, and even made a couple of nonfiction bestseller lists. And then, a few weeks later, Frank took off, too—with Dawn.

Frank couldn't have been aware of Nicole's train of thought, but he couldn't have missed the direction it was going in. He exhaled through his nose the way he always did when he was angry. "Just tell me what you want, okay?"

"What do I want?" Nicole shot back. "This month's check would be nice. Last month's check would be even nicer." The other thing Nicole wanted, the thing she couldn't say, was to understand what Frank saw in an airhead more than ten years younger than he was. She'd seen enough of Dawn both before Frank left that note on her pillow and in the time since, dropping off and picking up kids on weekend visitations, to be sure her only visible asset (aside from the nicely rounded ones in her bra) was the ability to listen to Frank go on about encryption algorithms for hours at a time without her blue, blue eyes glazing over.

Frank snorted again. He sounded like an irritated mule. "Is that why you called? To nag me again? I'll get 'em to you as fast as I can. I'm not made of money, you know."

Thanks to *Spy by Wire,* he had a very nice little pile. If he thought Nicole didn't know that, he was bone stupid. Stupider than somebody who'd run off with a twenty-two-year-old golden girl when his son was just starting to crawl. Nicole had been listing all the payments he'd been late on or skipped. One day, in court . . .

But she didn't need the list now. She needed cash—cash and a place for Kimberley and Justin to stay.

Her grip on the telephone tightened. If only it were his neck. But she couldn't afford to lose her temper. She couldn't afford anything right now, least of all an ex-husband more annoyed with her than he already was. "No, that isn't why I called." She didn't apologize—she never apologized when she was right. "I called to ask if you could take the kids tomorrow. Your hours are a lot more flexible than mine. If you could just—"

"What's the matter with Josefina?" Frank broke in. "Immigration finally catch up with her?"

Nicole took a deep breath and counted to five—counting to ten, right then, was beyond her. When she could trust her voice, she said "No" and explained in words of one syllable, with a minimum of sarcasm, about Josefina's mother. "I know it's impossibly short notice"—for that, she could apologize; her pride wasn't so sticky—"but she didn't give me any warning at all, just hit me with it when I dropped the children off this morning. I'll find somebody else as fast as I can. I'm sure it won't be past this weekend. By that time I'll—"

Frank interrupted again: "I can't." She'd always had a knack for knowing when he was lying—except, of course, about Dawn, but that wasn't the issue now. She was sure, down in her bones, that he was telling the truth. "It *is* impossibly short notice," he said. "I've got way too much stuff going on to take 'em now. I'm sorry, Nicole. I wish I could."

He was telling the truth about that, too. She could feel it much too clearly for comfort. Dammit.

"Please, Frank," she said—never mind if she had to get down on her knees and beg, this was critical. "Have I ever asked you for anything like this before?"

"No, you haven't," he admitted, but there wasn't any give in his voice. "It doesn't matter. I can't do it."

Nicole rolled all her frustrated fury into a bullet—rage at Josefina, rage at Sheldon Rosenthal, years' worth of rage at Frank—and sighted it dead center on her ex-husband. "Why not? They're your children, too, in case you've forgotten."

"I can't take them tomorrow," Frank said again. He not only snorted like a mule, he could dig in his heels like one. He wasn't budging now.

Nicole didn't care if he grew roots to China. "Why not? What are you doing that's so important?"

"Nicole . . ." There it came, the tone of sweet reason driven to desperation, with the edge of temper that threatened but hadn't quite, yet, blown up. "Look, I'm not on the witness stand. You don't get to cross-examine me anymore."

"What do you mean, 'anymore'?" Nicole couldn't manage sweet reason, or desperation, either. She was plain, flat angry.

"Just what I said," Frank said. "If you're done, will you kindly get off the line? I'm expecting a call."

"Go to hell," she said crisply, and hung up.

The rush of gratified fury died away, leaving her shaking too hard to do anything more useful than stare at the telephone. It wasn't supposed to happen like this. It had been her idea to move to L.A. from Indianapolis. She'd always been the dynamic one, the go-getter, the one who'd make her mark on life in capital letters, while he'd messed around in grad school playing with computers because they were easier for him to deal with than people. And now, somehow, he was happily shacked up with Ms. Youngblonde, with a big name that was likely to grow bigger, while her life and her career headed the wrong way down a one-way street, head-on into a phalanx of trucks.

She swiveled her chair to glare at the framed law degree on the wall. Indiana University Law School. In Indianapolis, it would have stamped her forever as second-rate: if you weren't Ivy League, you weren't anybody. In Los Angeles, she'd found, it was unusual, even exotic. That still bemused her, after half a dozen years.

"There ain't no justice," she said to the wall. The wall didn't deign to answer.

Nicole was still sitting there, still glowering at the diploma, when Cyndi came into the office and plopped the day's mail on the desk. "Doesn't look like anything you have to handle right away," she said. She was trying to sound normal—trying a little too hard.

Nicole didn't snap at her for it. Much. "Good," she said. "The way this day is going, I'm not up for handling much of anything anyway."

Cyndi bit her lip. "I'm sorry," she said, and hesitated, visibly wondering whether to go on. At last she decided to go for it: "It should have been you, Ms. Gunther-Perrin."

"It wasn't." Nicole's voice came out flat. "That's all there is to it."

Cyndi couldn't say anything to that. She shook her head and left for the relative safety of her desk.

Nicole hardly noticed. Opening envelopes gave her hands something to do but let her mind stay disengaged: perfect. If she worked hard enough at it, she might just disconnect altogether. Once the envelopes were open, she shuffled the papers they'd held, looking busy without doing much till she could escape to lunch.

Yang Chow, over on Topanga Canyon, was hands down the best Chinese place in the west half of the San Fernando Valley. That wasn't why Nicole drove there. The restaurant was also a couple of miles away from her Warner Center office building, far enough that, with luck, she'd be the only one from the firm there today. Shop talk and gossip were the last things she wanted.

She sat alone at a table in the casual elegance of the restaurant—no storefront fast-food ambience here—eating soup, drinking tea, and going after chili shrimp with chopsticks. Yang Chow's were of hard, smooth plastic, and didn't give as good a grip as the disposable wooden kind. She counted herself lucky not to end up with a shrimp in her lap.

That's what my luck's come down to, she thought, splashing soy sauce onto steamed rice: *I don't spill food on myself.* All around her, businessmen chattered happily in English, Chinese, Spanish, and some other language she didn't recognize.

Why shouldn't they be happy? They were men.

One of them caught her looking. She saw what she'd come to call The Progression: widened eyes, Who-Me? glance, broad come-hither grin. He was wearing a wedding ring, a broad gold band. He didn't bother to hide it. Without that, she would simply have ignored him. As it was, the look she sent suggested he had a glob of snot in his mustache. He hastily went back to his pork chow mein.

Nicole took her time finishing her lunch. Going back to the office had all the appeal of a root canal. She stared out the window at the traffic whooshing past on Topanga. She was aware, rather remotely, of the busboy taking her dishes. Only after the waiter came by to ask for the third time, in increasingly pointed tones, whether she wanted anything else did she admit to herself that she couldn't stay there all afternoon. She threw a five and a couple of singles on the table and walked out to her car.

When she drove into the lot, she had to park a long way from the building. She'd expected that; most people had been back from lunch for half an hour, maybe more. As she trudged wearily across the gray asphalt, someone called, "Nicole!"

She looked around a little wildly, wondering if she was having a flashback to the morning. But it wasn't Gary Ogarkov this time, smoking his blasted cigar and blowing up her hopes till they couldn't do anything but explode. Tony Gallagher, who'd just got out of his Lincoln Town Car a few spaces away from where she'd parked, waved and called her name again. When she paused, he caught up with her at a ponderous trot, belly lapping over the waistband of his slacks.

She didn't have much gladness to spare for anyone, but, thanks to that Midwestern upbringing, she could still be polite. "Hello, Mr. Gallagher," she said. Of all the senior partners, she liked him best—not that that said much right now. But Gallagher had more juice in him than the rest of them put together. He was a vigorous sixty, his hair dyed a red close to the color it must have been when he was younger. He'd probably grown his bushy muttonchops when they were cool, back about 1971, and then never bothered shaving them off. Whoever had made his jacket had killed and skinned a particularly repulsive plaid sofa for the fabric. Nicole doubted it had ever been cool, but Gallagher didn't care. He wore it with panache.

"I just want to tell you, I personally think you got a raw deal today," he said, breathing whiskey fumes into her face. Half of her wanted to hug him for even such a small kindness. The other half wanted to run. When she was little, her father had come home from the factory—or rather, from the bar after the factory—reeking just like that. Then he'd stopped coming home at all. Then, in very short order, her mother had divorced him. One, two, three. Nicole still hated the smell of alcohol on a man's breath, the strong sour-sweet reek that, her mother had told her, signified everything bad about a man.

Now that Nicole thought back on it, her father hadn't kept up with his child-support payments, either. He'd poured them down his throat instead, one shot at a time. Frank didn't do that. *No,* Nicole thought—*he spends the money on Dawn. Some improvement.*

"Like I say, Nicole," Tony Gallagher said, just a little unsteady on his feet, "I did what I could for you." He held the door of the office building open so she could go in to the lobby ahead of him. "I got outvoted. You know how it is with some people—can't see the nose in front of their face. It's a goddamn shame, pardon my French."

A couple of paces away from the elevator, she turned toward him. "Thank you for what you tried to do. Believe me, it's nice to know someone here thinks I've been doing a good job. I guess it just didn't work out." It sounded lame, but it was the best she could manage. She felt she owed it to him.

"Damn shame," Gallagher said again, vehemently. The odor of stale Scotch came off him in waves. What had he had, a six-drink lunch? He patted her on the back, heavily: between her shoulderblades at first, but slipping lower with each pat, till his hand came to rest a bare inch above her panty line.

When the hand didn't move after that, Nicole did, away from Gallagher and toward the elevator buttons. She punched UP with unnecessary violence. Was he being sympathetic or trying to feel her up? Did he know the difference? With that much Scotch sloshing around in him, did he even care?

The elevator door slid open. Nicole got on. So, of course, did Tony Gallagher. She eyed him with more than a little apprehension as she pressed the button for the sixth floor. But, as etiquette demanded, he took his place on the opposite side of the elevator after hitting the seventh-floor button.

With a thump, the car started up. Gallagher said, "Why don't you come up to my office with me, Nicole? We ought to talk about ways to make sure this doesn't happen the next time the opportunity rolls around."

She didn't answer for a second. And he said he'd been on her side. Was he thinking of closing the door to his office and trying to get her clothes off? If he did, she'd scream and knee him in the nuts. Then she'd sue him and the firm for every nickel they had. Which added up to a lot of nickels.

She shook her head a tiny fraction. No. He might be a lush, but he was still an attorney.

She grasped at the one straw he'd offered—and if that was desperate, so be it. So was she. He'd talked about a next time—about another partnership. Sheldon Rosenthal had been notably silent on the subject. "All right," she said, hoping he hadn't noticed the length of her hesitation. "I'll come up."

The elevator stopped at the sixth floor. Nicole let the door open and close, but didn't get off. On the seventh floor, Gallagher stood back with courtly manners, and held the door for her to get off. Somewhat encouraged, holding her breath against his effluvium of Scotch, she walked with him down the long carpeted hallway. His secretary didn't look up from her computer when the two of them went by into his inner office.

He did shut the door behind him, but, instead of trying to grope her, he went over to a coffee machine like the one in Mr. Rosenthal's office. Next to it he had a little refrigerator, atop which stood several bottles and a neat row of crystal tumblers. "Coffee?" he asked. "Or can I fix you a drink? Sounds like you've earned one today."

You don't know the half of it. But Nicole said, "Coffee—black, please. I don't use alcohol."

The frost in her voice only made him grin disarmingly. "You know what they say. Drink—and die; don't drink—and die anyway. But suit yourself." He poured her the coffee, then splashed a good jolt of Johnnie Walker Black over ice for himself. He carried it to his desk and sat down, leaning back in the big mahogany leather chair: leopard on a tree branch, Nicole caught herself thinking, or lion on the veldt, waiting in lordly ease for his wives to bring him dinner. "Sit down," he said. "Make yourself at home."

Nicole sat. This wasn't the sort of place that she'd have wanted for home or office, not with those gaudy LeRoy Neiman prints—a redundancy if ever there was one—on the wall, but it fit the flamboyant Gallagher perfectly. The only thing missing was a lava lamp.

He knocked back the Scotch, then held up a well-manicured forefinger. "Cooperation," he intoned, giving the word the same mystic emphasis with which the fellow in *The Graduate* had informed *plastic.* "That's what we've got to see."

Nicole tensed. "Mr. Gallagher," she said, "I've been co-operative in every way I know how. I've worked as hard as I can for this firm. The Butler Ranch report is only one example. I've also—"

Gallagher waggled that forefinger. "Not exactly what I meant." He wasn't looking at her face as he spoke. He was, she realized, trying to look up her skirt, which was a little above the knee when she stood and a good deal shorter than that when she sat down. She crossed her legs as tight as she could, and hooked one ankle behind the other for good measure.

Cooperation? *Sleep your way to the top,* he meant. He couldn't mean anything else, though he hadn't been so blatant as to leave himself in trouble if she wanted to make something of it. Nicole damned herself for having been right the first time—and also for having been so stupid as to miss the fact that there was another way than the obvious and actionable.

Here it was, almost the turn of the millennium, and a woman couldn't get a damned thing on her own merits. Why not forget about degrees and credentials and qualifications? Why not just demand that every female applicant submit her bra size and her body measurements, and never mind pretending that anything else mattered?

Her teeth were clenched so tight her jaw ached. Outrageous, unjust, hypocritical—*When was any society so unfair? Not in any time I ever heard of. Not in any, ever, I'd bet.*

While she stewed in silence, Gallagher got up and made himself another drink. "More coffee?" he asked. Nicole shook her head stiffly. Gallagher's Adam's apple worked as he swallowed half the Scotch he'd poured into the tumbler. He filled it again and set the bottle down on the refrigerator with a sigh of regret. He wobbled a bit as he walked back to his desk. "Where was I?"

Halfway to Skid Row. Nicole's thought was as cold as the ice in his glass. *More than halfway, if you can't remember what you're saying from one minute to the next.*

Well then, she thought, colder yet—the kind of coldness she imagined a soldier must feel in battle, and she knew a lawyer felt in a bitterly fought case: an icy clarity, empty of either compunction or remorse. In that state of mind, one did what one had to do. No more, not a fraction less. Maybe she could take advantage of his alcoholic fog to steer him away from the line he'd been taking and toward one more useful to her. "We were talking," she said, "about ways to improve my chances for the next partnership that becomes available."

"Oh, yeah. That's right." But, even reminded, Tony Gallagher didn't come back at once to the subject. At least, for the moment, he wasn't leering at her. He was staring out the window instead; he had a view as splendid as Mr. Rosenthal's, as emblematic of both eminence and power.

Nicole began to wonder if he'd forgotten she was there. She pondered slipping quietly away while he sat there in his semistupor, but she couldn't be sure if he was drunk enough to let her get away with it. She stirred in her chair. As she'd half hoped, half feared, the motion drew his attention back to her. He wagged his forefinger in her direction again, as if it were something else, something not symbolic at all. "Say, I heard a good one the other day."

"Did you?" Nicole said. Gallagher told jokes constantly, both out of court and in. He insisted he'd caught several breaks from judges and juries over the years because of it. Nicole could believe it. Not that she'd have cared to try it herself, but with his personality and his—well—attributes, he could carry it off.

"Sure did," he said now. "Seems this gorgeous woman walked into a bar and asked the bartender for a six-pack of Budweiser. She . . ." From the very first line, Nicole hadn't expected she'd care for the joke, but she hadn't expected the disgust that swelled up in her as Tony Gallagher went on telling it. When he finished, he was grinning from ear to ear: "—and so she said, 'No, give me a six-pack of Miller instead. All that Budweiser's been making my crotch sore.' "

He waited, chortling, for her to fall over laughing. No, she thought. Not even for a senior partner. "Mr. Gallagher," she said with rigid deliberation, "that was the most sickening, sexist thing I've ever heard in my life." She could have stopped there—should have, if she'd started at all. But something in her had snapped. "Nobody," she said, shaking with the force of her disgust, "nobody should tell a joke like that, under any circumstances, to anybody. If that's what it means to 'cooperate,' to be 'one of the boys'—if I have to crawl down in the gutter with all the rest of you, guzzling pricey liquor and laughing at sick jokes—then frankly, Mr. Gallagher, I don't want to play."

There was an enormous silence. Nicole knew with sick certainty that he'd erupt, that he'd blast her out of her—his—chair.

He didn't. His eyes went cold and hard, like green glass. He was, she realized with dismay, much less drunk than she'd thought. "Ms. Gunther-Perrin," he said with perfect and completely unexpected precision, "one of the complaints leveled against you by your peers and by the senior partners was that you did not get along with people as well as you should. I took the contrary position. I see now that I was mistaken."

"What exactly do you mean, I don't get along?" Nicole asked. Maybe he would give her enough rope to hang him. She should have known he wouldn't. He was a lawyer, wasn't he? "I mean what I said," he snapped. "No more, no less." But even while he played the lawyer's lawyer, his eyes slid down to her hemline again. Maybe—and that was worst of all—he didn't even know he was doing it. He straightened in his chair. "Good afternoon, Ms. Gunther-Perrin."

"Good afternoon," Nicole said, with the starch of generations of Midwestern schoolmarms in her voice and in her spine.

She left with her head high. Oh, he wanted her to cooperate, no doubt about it—in bed and naked, or more likely wearing something vinyl and crotchless from Frederick's of Hollywood.

So now she'd offended not only the founding partner but the one senior partner who'd even pretended to be on her side. At least, she thought, she still had her self-respect. Unfortunately, it was the only thing she did have. She couldn't eat it, put it in the gas tank, or pay the mortgage with it. She'd shot her chance for a partnership right between the eyes.

On the other hand, if she'd read Sheldon Rosenthal right, she'd never been in line for a partnership. She'd been a blazing fool from start to finish.

"Thank you so much, Mrs. Gunther-Perrin," Josefina said when Nicole handed her a check that afternoon. "You are the last one. I got to cash this, then run for the airport." Nicole's nod was grim. She'd have to get a cash advance from her MasterCard to keep the check from bouncing. She was buying groceries, gasoline—everything—on plastic till she got paid again. The MasterCard was close to maxing out. So was the Visa. Her whole life was on the verge of having its charging privileges revoked.

Kimberley and Justin hugged Josefina so tightly when she bent to say good-bye to them that she laughed a little tearily and said something half reproving, half teasing, in the Spanish that they understood and Nicole never had. At that, Kimberley, who professed loudly and often that "only babies cry," wept as if her heart would break. Nicole's own heart was none too sturdy, either. Damn it, it pulled her apart to see her baby hurt.

"Oh." Josefina straightened, wiping her eyes and sniffing. "I got to tell you, Mrs. Gunther-Perrin, we got a virus going around the kids. I had to call two mothers this afternoon."

Great, Nicole thought. Why not? The way this day had been going, all she needed was a nice round of the galloping crud. "Thanks," she managed to say to Josefina, though the last thing she felt was gratitude. She fixed Kimberley with a mock-severe look, one that usually made her erupt into giggles. There were no giggles today, just tears. "Don't you dare get sick, do you hear me?" Nicole said—as if by simply saying it she could make the virus sit up and behave.

Kimberley had stopped sobbing, at least. "I won't, Mommy," she said, sounding stuffy and forlorn. "I feel fine."

"Me, too," Justin declared, not wanting to be left out.

Then why were you wailing like that? Nicole thought uncharitably as she buckled her daughter into her car seat and got Justin into his. It wouldn't be much longer before Kimberley outgrew the one she was in. Another milestone. These days, Nicole measured time by how her children changed. First step, first time dry through the night, first dirty word . . . Her mouth twisted. Her own life was on the downhill slide. First abandonment, first divorce, first partnership lost—first firing next, probably, if things didn't get better fast.

On the way home, Victory was slow. Sherman Way would have been slower. The 101 would have been slowest. Nicole had got past White Oak and was heading for Reseda Boulevard—halfway back, more or less—before Kimberley gulped. "Oh, baby," Nicole said in despair—she knew what that sound meant. "Don't be sick. See if you can hold it till we get there."

"I'll try." Kimberley gulped again. She wasn't saying she was fine now. Nicole tried, too: tried to go faster. She didn't have much luck.

Just past Reseda, Kimberley threw up. "Corny dogs!" Justin said gleefully. Nicole hadn't wanted to find out quite that way what the kids had had for lunch.

There was a medium-sized shopping center at the corner of Victory and Tampa. Nicole pulled in there among the people stopping for milk and groceries on the way home from work. None of them, she was sure, had to stop to mop up a pool of puke. She fished an old towel out of the trunk and, holding her breath against the acrid reek, cleaned off Kimberley and the car seat and the upholstery under it as best she could, and flung the towel into a trash can. She probably couldn't afford to replace it. "Who gives a damn?" she said to the trash can.

Kimberley had the thousand-yard stare of a sick child. Her forehead was hot. A virus, sure as hell. "It still stinks, Mommy," she said as Nicole buckled her in again.

"I know it does," Nicole said, as gently as she could. "I'll put that goop on it after we get home." Odo-Clean, the stuff people used to get the smell of dog and cat pee out of rugs and chairs, also worked wonders on making cars livable when kids puked in them. Frank had taught her about it; it was an old family trick of his. At the moment, Nicole was not inclined to give him any credit for it.

Home came none too soon. Justin had stopped holding his breath and started making imitation retching noises of his own. Kimberley was mute, which said something worrisome about how sick she was. Nicole got her out of the car and cleaned her up properly and threw her soiled clothes in the washing machine, then settled her in front of the VCR in her pajamas with *Toy Story* and some water to rinse out her mouth, and fed her a little Tylenol liquid to make her feel better. Nicole hoped it would stay down. In case it didn't, she equipped her daughter with a red plastic bucket and a roll of paper towels, and went back outside with rags and the bottle of Odo-Clean. *Fine way to work up an appetite before dinner,* she thought as she held her breath and scrubbed.

It wasn't till she'd made it back into the house again that she noticed the smear of vomit on her suit jacket. She shed it with a muffled curse. The tag inside said *Dry Clean Only.* Of course.

Justin was waiting for her in the kitchen, perched in his high chair with the tray table up. "Hungry," he announced, patting his tummy.

"Nice to know somebody is," Nicole said dryly. She wondered if he'd get sick tonight, or if he'd wait till tomorrow or the next day. He'd been massively exposed to whatever bug Kimberley had. But, she conceded to herself, he'd also been good while Nicole took care of his sister and cleaned up the car. She took a package of chicken nuggets and french fries out of the freezer.

When Justin recognized the box, he slid down out of his high chair and hopped with glee. Chicken nuggets and french fries had no nutritional value whatsoever. So, of course, he loved them. So, also of course, his father fed them to him all the time. Frank was a devout believer in the four basic food groups: sugar, fat, salt, and chocolate. Nicole, cast by default in the role of Health-Food Ogre, often wondered why she even tried.

Tonight, just for this once, she stopped trying. One meal of solid fat and sodium wouldn't kill the kid, and he'd earned a little reward for being so good for so long.

Slacker, her conscience chided her. She shut it down and clamped the lid on it.

She thrust the tray in the microwave, set the timer, and pushed the button. Nothing happened. The light inside didn't go on, either. She gave the door a push, thinking—hoping— she hadn't closed it all the way. It was closed. She opened it and closed it again. Still no light. When she pressed the button, still no action. One dead microwave. "Oh, for God's sake," she said.

"Hungry," Justin repeated. He watched Nicole take the chicken nuggets out of the microwave; his eyes went huge with dismay as she shoved them into the regular oven and twisted the temperature knob up as high as she dared. "Hungry!" he screamed, and started to cry.

God, Nicole thought, prayed, maybe cursed, *give me patience. Give Justin some, too, please, while you're at it.* "You can still have them," she said. "They have to cook longer in this oven, that's all." Half an hour longer. Getting the idea of a half-hour delay across to a hungry two-year-old who was already feeling betrayed made everything she'd gone through at the office seem like a walk in the park.

In the end, she broke her own rule. She gave him some chocolate Teddy Grahams and milk to shut him up. That killed any chance he'd have of eating a good dinner, but chicken nuggets and fries weren't a good dinner to begin with, so who cared?

Absently, Nicole slid a frozen dinner in the oven for herself, too. It was healthier than the one she'd pulled out for Justin, that much she could say for it. Frozen food was all she had time for, all she ever had time for. Sometimes she dreamt of cooking lavish gourmet meals full of vitamins and minerals, fresh vegetables and quality ingredients, then freezing portions and heating them up for all those nights when she had neither time nor energy to spare for feeding herself once the kids were fed and bathed and tucked away in bed. But who had time to cook anything, even on weekends? Who had the ambition to even start? So she lived on Lean Cuisine and Healthy Choice and Thrifty Gourmet, and pitched fits when Frank fed the kids hot dogs and frozen chicken nuggets.

"It's a wonderful life," she said to Justin, who ignored her. He was playing happily on the kitchen floor with his cup of milk and his Teddy Grahams.

In the front room, Kimberley stared through Woody and Buzz, not at them, but she hadn't thrown up again. That was something. Not much, but something. Patting her daughter on the head, Nicole went into the bedroom to call Frank at his place. She liked that even less than calling him at UCLA, but didn't see that she had a choice. She'd have to replace the microwave, and for that she needed money—money he owed her.

Someday, she swore to herself, she'd be in a position to pay for everything without the humiliation of calling Frank. Until that day came, she'd just have to bite the bullet and do what she had to do.

The phone sat on the nightstand. As she reached for it, the plaque with Liber and Libera caught her eye. There they stood, god and goddess together, equal, as they were supposed to be. She'd never known any Latin that wasn't strictly legalese—she'd been a business administration major before she got into law school—but what their names meant was clear enough. Liberty, liberalism, liberality. She didn't have enough of any of those things.

She dialed the number to Frank's condo so seldom, she had to look it up. The phone rang once, twice, three times, four. Then, with a faint but distinct click, a sweet—gooey-sweet, Nicole thought—voice came on the line. "Hi, this is Dawn. Frank and I can't come to the phone right now, but if you'll leave your name and number, we'll get back to you as soon as we can. Remember to wait for the beep. 'Bye."

"Frank, this is Nicole," Nicole said, ignoring Dawn even in recorded form. "I just want to let you know Kimberley is sick, the microwave is dead, and I need the child support you're late with. Pay up, dammit. Good-bye."

It wouldn't do much good. She knew that too well. Frank would take his own sweet time answering a message like that, but she'd been too frazzled to come up with anything kinder or gentler. She had a sudden, horridly vivid picture of him and Dawn screwing when she called, and laughing like a couple of loons when they heard who it was.

The front of the house was quiet when she emerged from the bedroom. Kimberley hadn't moved since she left. Nicole bent to feel her forehead, then to kiss it. Kimberley was still warm, but maybe a touch less. The longer the Tylenol stayed down, the better. "How's your tummy feel?" Nicole asked. Kimberley shrugged and subsided back into immobility.

Loud stomping noises sent her running to the kitchen. Justin had scarfed down most of the Teddy Grahams, then dumped the rest of them on the floor and spritzed them with milk from the three little holes in the Tommee Tippee cup. Now he was having a high old time smashing them up. "Mud!" he told Nicole, delighted.

"No, not mud," she barely managed not to scream at him.

"Mess. Naughty. No-no!" Her hand itched to give him a good solid spanking.

No. She wouldn't do it. She didn't believe in it. A good parent had no need to strike a child to make it behave.

Not that she was a perfect parent, either. She'd smacked Justin and Kimberley once or twice, more because she was at the end of her rope than because they had done anything extraordinarily hideous. Each time she'd felt horrible, and each time she'd thanked heaven she hadn't seemed to do them any lasting harm.

She pried Justin's Reeboks off him and carried them over to the sink. Their soles, though formed in miniature, had as many gripping cups and ridges and grooves as those on the shoes she wore on weekends. Milk-smeared chocolate crackers had got into all of them, and refused stubbornly to be scrubbed out. Finally, she found an old toothbrush that did the job—bristle by bristle, crumb by crumb, and ridge by ridge.

The floor was just as delightful. Paper towels and Formula 409 disposed of most of the mess, but, sure as hell, some of the sodden Teddy Graham crumbs had slithered down between the tiles. She had to rout them out with the toothbrush, too. She couldn't just let them go. Teddy Grahams were worse than mud. A lot worse, all things considered. If she didn't scour out every speck, by morning the kitchen would be swarming with ants.

By the time she was through cleaning, the chicken nuggets and french fries and her own Lean Cuisine shrimp-and-boring-vegetables were ready. She carefully cut the chicken and potatoes into bite-sized bits for her son and let him practice impaling them with a fork. After four or five bites, he was picking, not eating: the Teddy Grahams had taken their toll on him along with his shoes and the floor.

She'd managed two bites from the tray in front of her (too much sodium, and low-fat only by comparison to some of the other frozen food out there) when the telephone rang. She got up so fast, she almost overturned her bottle of Evian.

Maybe Frank would come through after all. Stranger things had happened.

"Hello?" she panted, breathless from the dash to the bedroom.

"Hello, is this Nicole?" asked a friendly and completely unfamiliar male voice.

"Yes," Nicole said warily. "Who is this, please?"

"My name's Bob Broadman, Nicole." Too friendly. "Now, I know that a busy homemaker like yourself doesn't have a lot of time, so I'll make this quick for you, all right, Nicole?" *Way* too friendly. "Would you be interested in trying in your own home—"

Nicole slammed the receiver into its cradle. She hated telemarketers. She particularly hated telemarketers who, hearing a female voice, assumed the person who owned it was a housewife. She most particularly hated telemarketers who did all that and—insult on top of injury—called at dinnertime.

Her gaze fell again on Liber and Libera. She could have sworn they looked back at her with sympathy in their stony eyes. The thought wasn't so absurd as it might have seemed before she went through this day from hell. Nobody in their time could have had to put up with what she'd just put up with. Just look at them, god and goddess side by side, equal and anything but separate. No repressive patriarchy. No fat plaid-jacketed lawyers leering up an employee's skirt. "And, by God," she said, "no telemarketers."

Times were simpler then. They had to have been better. How could they possibly have been worse?

She trudged back to the kitchen. Justin, gymnast extraordinaire, had succeeded in standing up on the seat of his high chair. Just as she caught sight of him, he set himself up for a swan dive to the floor. Nicole caught him with a grab that would have made a big-league center fielder jealous.

"I think you're done," she said. Amazing how calm she sounded—she had to be numb. "Go play quietly in your room and let me finish eating my dinner." Maybe that would buy her the five minutes' peace she'd prayed for in the morning. She hadn't got it then. She didn't honestly expect to get it now.

No more than a minute and a half later, Justin was in the front room pestering Kimberley. Most of the time, Kimberley could take care of herself, but not when she was laid flat with a virus. Nicole charged to the rescue, to find her daughter halfway toward falling asleep, and Justin trying to wake her up by shoving a toy truck in her face. Nicole laid down the law to him, which wasn't easy when she was trying to be quiet and not disturb Kimberley. She doubted it was sinking in. Two-year-olds paid even less attention to the laying down of the law than some juries did.

By the time the credits rolled on the *Toy Story* tape, Kimberley had dozed off. She hardly stirred when Nicole picked her up and carried her to bed. It was well before her usual bedtime, but Nicole didn't worry about that. If her daughter got a long night's sleep, she might be close to her old self in the morning. Kids got sick in a hurry, but sometimes they got well in a hurry, too.

Justin wasn't used to being up when his big sister was asleep. He took one of Kimberley's Barbies and tried to fracture its skull on the coffee table. Nicole looked on with benign approval. She would never have given Barbies to Kimberley: they sent all the wrong messages. The damn dolls were Frank's fault. What was worse, and what worried Nicole most, was that Kimberley liked them far too much to make it worth her mother's while to confiscate them.

"The minute they're born, they're trapped in gender roles," Nicole muttered.

Justin looked up from his mayhem, distracted by the sound of her voice but not curious to know what she meant. Nicole smiled at him. Justin whacked happily away at the coffee table. "Wham! Wham!" he shouted.

"Beat her brains out, kid," Nicole said. The doll, she thought with malicious glee, looked a little like Dawn.

After he'd worked out all of his hostility and some of Nicole's, too, Justin went to bed with no more than a token protest. Nicole took a shower, pulled on a clean pair of designer sweats—Neiman-Marcus this time, with blocks of pure strong color, blue and hot pink and acid yellow, as if she could brighten her mood forcibly by livening up her color scheme—and scowled at the telephone. She didn't think Frank had classes on Wednesdays this quarter. If he didn't, he could take the kids, and she wouldn't have to burn a vacation day riding herd on them.

When the hour crawled past nine o'clock ¬and he still hadn't called, she called him again. Again, she got Dawn on the answering machine. This time, she tried to be more civil. She didn't know how well she succeeded.

Ten o'clock rolled by. The telephone stayed obstinately silent. Shaking her head, Nicole went into the study and turned on the computer. She used America Online just often enough to keep from quitting the service. One reason she hadn't quit was times like this. Frank might take too long to answer telephone messages, but he was religious about replying to e-mail the minute he saw it.

As soon as she logged on to AOL, a bright electronic voice announced, "You've got mail!" Nicole blinked. People didn't send her e-mail all that often; the ones who knew she was on-line also knew the mail might sit in her box for a couple of weeks before she saw it.

What the hell, she'd read it before she sent her own.

There was only one letter. It was from Frank, from his UCLA Internet address, and sent that afternoon. In the way of e-mail, it was short and to the point: *The reason I can't take the kids tomorrow is that Dawn and I are leaving for three weeks in Cancún tonight, so you might as well stop bugging me for a while, all right? I won't be around to listen to it.*

Nicole stared at the screen. "You son of a bitch," she said. "You can't pay child support, but you and Ms. Dumbblonde can bop off to Mexico any time you feel like it? You *son* of a bitch."

She logged off in controlled fury and shut down the computer. No point to sending e-mail now. Frank was off to sunny Mexico, Frank and Dawn and—god damn her—

Josefina, though even in a well-nurtured rage Nicole couldn't imagine Josefina doing the sights in Cancún with a pair of irredeemably Anglo tourists. Frank didn't give a damn what happened back here in smoggy L.A. That was Nicole's job. Women's work. Sit at home mopping up puke and scouring Teddy Grahams out of kitchen tiles, while the big brave man went gallivanting off to play.

She trudged back into the bedroom. Time was when it had been a sanctuary, a place she'd made for herself after Frank left. She'd hauled the curtains and the comforter and the rest of the bedroom accessories off to Goodwill, got the dresser and the bedside tables refinished, dumped the king-sized waterbed that took sheets the size of Alaska, and bought herself a nice brass bed with a queen-sized mattress. She'd even painted the walls, got rid of the old ugly peach enamel in favor of a nice flat oyster white. She'd been proud of it then, determined to make it a new beginning: Nicole Gunther-Perrin, independent woman.

Now the bold Aztec print of the comforter was crumpled and dingy and flung half on the floor. The sheets still matched, but hadn't been changed in a week. Justin had tried to climb the drapes and pulled the whole thing down, double rod and all. The window was naked but for the venetian blinds that she'd used to open to let the daylight in, but she hadn't done that since she could remember.

Not that, at the moment, there was any daylight to let in. If she bothered to look out, she'd see a dark stretch of yard and the fence that divided it from the neighbors' swimming pool. She was glad the fence was good and strong and high, to keep the babies safe. She hadn't had to have it built; just about all L.A. backyards were fenced, which still struck her as strange.

Both of Nicole's babies were as safe as they could be, when their father had walked out on them and their mother had just been bilked of a partnership. She and Frank had planned to put in a pool themselves later, when the kids were past the drowning stage. Now they'd never do it. The yard was a nondescript patch of dirt with a sunburnt swingset and a sandbox that Kimberley and Justin could turn into a battlefield. These days, they never got to use it. They were always either at daycare or doing weekend visitations with Frank and Dawn.

It was all dark now, invisible. Nicole turned back to the disheveled bedroom. An impulse struck, to straighten up, make the bed, dust the tables and the dresser, pick up the scattered clothes and the pile of assorted shoes. Before she could start, a glance at the bedside clock changed her mind for her. Ten thirty-eight at night was no time to make her bed for the day.

She settled for shaking out the sheets and the blanket and pulling the comforter straight. It was an absurd thing to do, anal and rather pathetic, but at least she'd crawl into a more or less orderly bed. Sleep didn't enter into it. She was wide awake, almost painfully so.

Well, and who cared? With Kimberley sick, with Josefina off to Mexico, and with her louse of an ex-husband off to Mexico, too, she could sleep as late as the kids would let her. Rosenthal, Gallagher, Kaplan, Jeter, Gonzalez & Feng would have to do without her services tomorrow—not that they'd shown much enthusiasm for said services. The kind they really wanted, the bend-over-and-take-it kind, she would not provide.

Her eye fell again as it so often did, on the one thing in the room that wasn't Yuppie Eclectic Chic. Liber and Libera stood in their stone calm, clasped hand in hand, staring gravely out at a world they couldn't ever have imagined, let alone created. They wouldn't have stood for the crap that had landed on her today. How could they, with names like theirs? Nothing in their world or time had been as purely awful as this one she lived in.

She rested her hand on the votive plaque. It felt cool and smooth, inert but somehow subtly alive, the way carved stone can be when it's very old. "I wish I'd lived then," she said. "It would have been a good time to be alive, not so . . . artificial as it is now. Not so hateful."

She squeaked in surprise. Her hand jerked itself away from

the plaque. She stared at the palm. It couldn't be—of course it couldn't—but it felt as if it had been blessed with a pair of tiny kisses.

Had Liber and Libera smiled quite so broadly before? Of course they had. They must have. She was tired. She was stressed out. She was imagining things wholesale.

She shook out the comforter again, for luck as it were, and to clear her own head; then climbed into bed. She hesitated as she reached to turn out the light. The lamp's glow fell softly on the gods' smiling faces. Her palm itched a little, and stung a little, as if it had had a tiny—doubled—electric shock. She shook her head firmly, steeled herself, and flicked out the light. Dark came down abruptly. Sleep came down with it, too fast almost to perceive. The last thing she remembered was a kind of dim astonishment.

In the dark, quiet bedroom, on the old, old plaque, Liber turned his head and smiled at Libera. She smiled back. Excitement sang between them. True, it was true. A prayer at last; a votary; a wish so strong, it had roused them from their sleep. How long had it been? Hundreds of years—a thousand, and half a thousand more. Bacchus, that simpering Greek, had never lacked for either prayers or devotees. Liber and Libera had been all but forgotten.

And such an easy prayer to answer, though not—they admitted to each other—as strictly usual as most. Most prayers were for wealth or fertility or escape from the morning-after price wine inevitably exacted. Such a wish as this: how wonderfully novel, and how simple, too. Nicole had traveled to Carnuntum. This plaque, on which Liber and Libera's power was now so singularly focused, had come from that ancient city. And, best of all, when the plaque was made, a woman of Nicole's blood and line had been living in Carnuntum. *Is it not wonderful?* they said to one another. *Is it not meant? Is it not a beautiful symmetry, as beautiful as we are ourselves?*

What pleasure, too, in granting the prayer; what divine and divinely ordained ease. This woman's spirit was as light as thistledown, for all its leaden weight of worry. Purest simplicity to waft it out of the flesh, to send it spiraling down the long road into that other, kindred body.

Such lovely days, those had been, so much more delightful than these, which were nothing if not dull. How perceptive of this woman to comprehend it, and how ingenious of her to utter a prayer they could grant.

Because she was so clever a child of men, and because they were, in their stony hearts, as generous as gods can sometimes choose to be, they granted her spirit a gift. As it spun backward through the years, they instructed it in the language that mortal men had spoken then, the beautiful Latin that was so little like the harsh barbaric rattle of its native English. It had not thought, silly thing, to ask; but how else could it share fully in those lively times, those vivid and brightly sunlit years before the world grew gray and old?

After all, they assured each other, they were granting her every wish, both expressed and unexpressed. They could do no less for their first worshipper in so many hundreds of years. *Our blessing on you,* they called after the swiftly flitting spirit. *May all gods keep you, and prosper you, and give you joy.*

Nicole's dreams were strange. She rode a spiral through the dark. Spiral dance? Spiral galaxies? —No: a helix, for she went down, backward, as well as round and round. Damn, what did that remind her of? It was dim, shadowed, fluxing in and out of her perception. And yet . . .

There. She grasped it and held on tight, before it slipped away again. She'd seen it on TV. Watson and Crick. The Double Helix.

DNA—that was it. Building block of life. Ascending chain of being. Descending stair of existence. She could feel the rungs under her feet, the gravity that drew her down and down, round and round.

She'd never dreamt such a dream before. She'd never been so aware of dreaming, either. Would she remember when she woke? Usually, she didn't want to. This wasn't frightening, nor particularly weird as dreams went. It was interesting. Words flitted past her, whispers, murmurs in a language she didn't know, yet felt—strangely—that she did. *How odd,* she thought in passing. *How wonderful. How deliciously strange.*

Maybe after all it was the waking she wouldn't want to remember. Maybe she wanted to stay inside the dream. She'd dream it to the hilt. She promised herself that, far down the spiral stair, the endlessly turning helix of her own and only self.

3

STILL DREAMING BUT STARTING to swim out of the long spiraling dark, Nicole rolled over in her bed.

The mattress was lumpy. Her eyelids were still asleep, but her brain roused slowly, taking count of the individual senses. Yes—there were lumps under her. Hard ones. She hissed. Damn those kids! They knew the rule. No hiding toys in Mommy's bed. Whichever one had done it, it was going to cost. Early bedtime for Kimberley, no Teddy Grahams for—

She drew in a deep, would-be calming breath. Her eyes flew open. She gasped, gagged, almost puked all over the bedclothes. Jesus Christ! What a stink! The last time she'd smelled anything even close to this bad, the septic tank had backed up at Cousin Hedwig's house in Bloomington. But this was a richer, more complex odor, compounded of sewage and barnyard and city dump and locker room and apartment-house fire. It was a stench with character, a stench to be respected and admired, even a stench to be savored. If you were going to build a stench to order, these were the specs for the very finest, luxury model.

It was such a stench, in fact, that for a couple of seconds her nose overwhelmed her eyes. Even as she decided that a

garbage truck must have overturned on the front lawn, she
realized something more immediately important.

This wasn't the room she'd gone to bed in, or any room
she remembered, anytime, anywhere.

Wan daylight seeped in through a wood-framed window.
There was no glass, only wooden shutters thrown back. Flies
danced in the shaft of pale light and buzzed through the
room: the window had no screen, either. An enormous hairy
black fly landed on the wall near the bed and perched there,
rubbing its hands together. The wall was roughly plastered
and even more roughly whitewashed. Dark spots here and
there suggested that a good many flies had met their death
on it.

Aside from the bed, the room was sparsely furnished. A
battered chest of drawers stood against one wall, its yellowish pine looking as if it had been the victim of an amateur
refinisher. There was no chair, only a pair of stools like—
well, like milking stools; they were more or less that shape
and about that size. No TV. No photos of kids, no radio, no
alarm clock, no lamp on the nightstand. For that matter, no
nightstand. No closet, either. Just the bare box of a room and
narrow lumpy cot of a bed and the chest and the stools.

On the chest sat a pitcher, a two-handled cup, and a bowl,
all of pottery glazed the same gaudy red as the sticks of
sealing wax Nicole had affected in her brief but passionately
romantic phase, between thirteen and thirteen and a half.

Terra sigillata, she thought. The words shouldn't have
made any sense to her; she knew she'd never known them
before. And yet she knew what they meant: sealing-wax
ware. That was the name for the crockery on the chest.

A lamp squatted next to the bowl. Another sat on a stool.
She'd seen the genie emerging from one just like them in
Aladdin. But Aladdin's lamp had been bronze or brass or
something like that. These were plain unglazed clay.

Nicole sat up carefully, as if her head might rock and fall
off her shoulders. She wasn't hung over: she didn't drink.
She wasn't on anything—no drugs, prescription or otherwise. She might be dreaming, but she could never have

dreamt that monumental stink. Which only left—

"I've gone crazy," she said.

Sitting up, she could see the floor. It was no more reassuring than any of the rest of it. No beige shag carpeting here, only bare, well-rubbed boards. Carefully, almost fearfully, she ventured to look up. Boards again. Rough boards, and low, too.

She couldn't, quite, touch the ceiling, but she could brush her hand across the blanket that covered her. She remembered vividly, distinctly, the touch and feel of her own comforter, its soft down-filled thickness, the faintly wilted but crisp and brightly printed cotton. Its pattern was called Cinnabar. She'd admired the colors when she bought it, deep green to match her eyes, rich dark purple, terracotta, and a touch of red and gold. This wasn't her comforter. It was a blanket, rough wool worn thin and threadbare, dyed a sad, faded blue.

She itched just looking at it. She scrambled it away from her, thrusting it aside with a hand that—

A hand that—was not her hand.

The fingers twitched when she told them to twitch. The arm lifted when her mind said lift. But it was not her arm. She knew what her arm looked like. How could she not know what—?

She throttled down hysteria. *Look,* she thought. *Look at it. Study it. Make sense of it.*

It wasn't her arm. It was thinner—a great deal thinner. There were muscles on it, hard ropy muscles, no softness, no deskbound flab. Her arm was smooth-skinned and round and dusted with pale blond hairs, not these rougher and thicker dark ones. The skin was darker, too; not the darkness of a California tan but a warmer olive tone that had to be its natural shade. There was a scar above the wrist, a good two inches long. She had no scars, not on her arms.

This was not her arm. Nor her hand. Her hands were smooth, the nails filed and rounded and painted a light and unobtrusive shell-pink.

This was—these were, as the right emerged from the blan-

ket to join the left—battered, callused. The nails were short
and ragged. They had black dirt ground in under them. If
these hands had ever seen a nailfile or an emery board, let
alone a bottle of nail polish, it hadn't been in years.

Hysteria yammered still, not far under her hard-fought
calm. She looked around, not wildly but not what you'd call
calmly either. No mirror on the wall. *Mirror, mirror,* she
thought dizzily. *Who's the craziest of us—?*

Calm. Be calm. She raised those stranger's hands, those
hands that answered when she called, and laid them shaking
against her cheeks. Like a blind woman, she explored the
face that, it seemed, she had come to live behind. Not her
face, of course not. No soft, faintly sagging curves. No blunt
German nose. This was leaner, longer, with cheekbones
standing sharp in it, and a nose with a pronounced arch. She
had to look—God, she couldn't giggle, she'd break down
completely—she had to look something, maybe a little more
than something, like Sheldon Rosenthal.

Calm. Calm. Focus. Explore. Make this make sense. She
ran her tongue over her—someone's—teeth. They weren't
hers, any more than the rest of it. No years of orthodontia
here. No caps, no crowns, no carefully cleaned and regularly
brushed and flossed tributes to modern dentistry. These are
crooked. One in front was broken. Two uppers and one
lower, a molar, were gone, long gone, the gaps healed over,
no sign of a wound.

One of those that hadn't vanished still made its presence
felt. It was broken, too, and ached, not horribly but persist-
ently, as if it had settled in and meant to stay. She prodded
it with a finger. It twinged. Her finger jerked away. *Dentist,*
she wrote in a mental file. *Find. Make appointment. Soonest.*

Find where? Find how? Where was she?

Here. She was here. Wherever here was. She had to keep
going. She had to take inventory. Right now she had two
choices. She could fret about tiny details, or she could fall
down in a screaming fit.

She wiped her finger on the blanket, shuddering a little at
the scratchy wool, and reached up to touch her hair. It felt

greasy, dirty between her fingers. It was shorter and curlier than her own—what she remembered as her own. Her scalp itched, too. *Dandruff,* she thought.

She pulled a strand forward to peer at it out of the corner of her eye. It was dark, dark brown, almost black—nothing like her own light brown shoulder-length professional woman's cut with its faded blond rinse. The name of the rinse was as clear as if she'd read it on the wall: Amber Essence. She'd chosen it as much for its name as for what it did for her hair.

Nicole lowered the hand with care, folded back the blanket, and rose gingerly to feet that had not, till now, belonged to her. They were filthy, black with grime, hard-soled and ragged-nailed. They were—and this was almost a pleasure—both smaller and narrower than her own broad Austrian farmer's feet. Cleaned and pedicured, they might have been something to look at.

They protruded from beneath the hem of a garment as completely unlike her Neiman-Marcus sweats as this body was unlike her own. Wool again—no wonder she wanted to scratch—dyed much the same color as the blanket. The rasp of her legs against it told her what her eyes confirmed as she pulled it up: they were desperately in need of shaving, though not grown out as full and shaggy as if they'd never been shaved at all. Under the furze of dark hair they were, like her arms, leaner, narrower, finer-boned, than the ones she'd always owned, with long ropes of muscles in the calves. The ankles were fine, finer than hers had ever been; her legs went to thunder thighs at the drop of a plate of strudel. No thunder thighs here. These were lean but shapely, muscled and strong, as if she—this body—worked out on the stair-stepper every day.

Her foot brushed something under the bed. She reached down and pulled out a pair of sandals that, for fancy leatherwork, would have run into three figures at a boutique on Ventura Boulevard—if they were new. These were anything but. The leather was faded and filthy and sweat-stained, and patched here and there.

For a moment, as she reached for the sandals, she'd touched something else. She hesitated, shutting down visions of skulls and bones and monsters under the bed. Go on. Find out everything.

She stooped and got a grip on the thing and pulled it out. Her nose wrinkled. Bigger than a skull, than two skulls, wide-mouthed, unglazed like the lamps, sloshing with acrid liquid: no doubt about it. She'd found the facilities. A chamber pot. A real, live chamber pot.

She wasn't dreaming. Dreams didn't take care of every last detail. Even fantasy gamers didn't do that—and she'd seen a few when Frank was in his Multiple-User Dungeon phase. Dreams slid over the essentials of life: an unshaved leg, a half-full chamber pot, a bladder that told her in no uncertain terms it would like to finish filling the pot.

So she'd gone crazy, yes? Gone right around the bend. She'd never had such a detailed dream in her life.

She'd never heard of anyone going crazy quite like this. Delusions could come only from your own experience. She knew that. She'd seen it on TV, one night when she'd actually had time to watch, some shrink show or other, or maybe one of those movies, disease of the week, delusion of the decade, whatever. Maybe it was the shrimp she'd had for dinner. No, they'd been frozen. The ones from lunch at Yang Chow? God, shrimp twice a day. Not only was she in a rut; she was repeating herself from one meal to the next.

This sure wasn't any repetition of anything she'd done before. She was feeling punchy again. She couldn't get a grip on anything. This body she was in, this room, these things that were all completely and unmitigatedly strange— this was insanity. Had to be. The shrink show had talked about that, too. "Things aren't real," some thin intense person had said, rocking back and forth, talking to her—his—its knees pulled up to its chest. "Things don't connect. The world isn't there, not the world. You know? Just all this not-realness."

This was not real, it could not be real, but it was as real as a stink in the nose, a prickle of wool, a taste of sour

morning mouth and bad teeth and something she couldn't
identify and didn't want to.

She got hold of what she could get hold of, which was an
increasingly urgent need to use the bathroom. Except that,
according to the chamber pot, there was no bathroom.

She glanced at the door. A bar lay across it, a heavy
wooden thing lying on dark metal hooks. She had no desire,
none whatsoever, to lift that bar and open that door and see
what was on the other side of it. Even if it was her bedroom,
or a nice safe insane asylum—because it might not be. It
might be blank nothingness, or worse: it might be the world
that went with this room.

She pulled up the tunic to identify the garment underneath:
linen, she recognized that, though it was rougher than her
linen suits, and undyed. It looked more like a loincloth than
panties, and had no elastic to hold it up. She tugged at it. It
came down over hips narrower than her own were—had
been. What it had covered . . .

Her ears flamed. Her pubic hair was shaved as well, or as
badly, as the hair on her legs. Awkwardly, she squatted over
the pot. Damn, she'd hated doing that on camping trips, or
on long drives when her father wouldn't stop for anything
but immediate, screaming emergency—and when he did,
there'd only been bushes by the side of the road. He would
never stop at someplace civilized, like a gas station.

As she squatted there, she knew the half-angry, half-
sinking sensation she'd had on those drives. No toilet paper.
None hiding under the bed among a jostling herd of dust
bunnies. The stains on the loincloth told her what she didn't
want to know. Grimacing, struggling a bit as it passed the
curve of her hips, she pulled it up.

There was no tent to go back to, no car, no impatient
parents and squabbling sisters and hours more of travel before she could get clean again. Only the room she'd trapped
herself in, the chest she hadn't explored, the window she
hadn't dared look out of. Chest or window? Window or
chest? The lady or the tiger?

After a moment, she walked over to the window. The light

that came through was as strange as everything else. It wasn't the harsh, uncompromising desert glare of Los Angeles, or the gray-gold wash of morning in Indiana. It was softer, moister than either. It reminded her of something. But where? When? The memory wouldn't click.

She looked out, east, toward the strongest of the light. She couldn't see the sun. Most of her horizon was the wall of another building across a narrow, muddy alley. It was as tall as the one she stood in, two stories, more or less. If she craned down the alley she could see what must be the front of it, where it shrank to a single story. The first floor of each building was stone, with whitewashed plaster above. The red tile roof on the building across the alley made her think of California houses, the ones she called pink palaces, by Taco Bell out of a Spanish hacienda.

She leaned out the window to peer north—left—up the alley. It opened on another street that ran perpendicular to it. Some of the buildings along it and across the other, wider street were of stone and plasterwork like the one she was in. One or two had front porches supported by stone columns. Others were built of wood, with thatched roofs. *Picturesque,* she thought, as if she were a tourist and could relish the quaint and the twee. But even as she thought the word, she discarded it. There was nothing cute or touristy about the muscular stench assaulting her nostrils. She was getting used to it, enough at least not to gag and choke, but it never came close to disappearing.

The alley was amazingly narrow; she could almost touch the house on the other side. The street beyond it was broader but equally unpaved, and no wider than a California alley. It didn't look as if two cars could slip past each other in it. Not that she saw any try. There were no cars parked on it, either, the way there surely would have been anywhere in the Los Angeles area.

The thought slipped away before she grasped it. She didn't see any cars. She didn't hear any, either. A mournful cry close by nearly startled her out of her skin. It sounded like a train whistle crossed on a car horn and mismated with a flat trumpet. A human voice growled in the wake of it: "Come on, curse you!" The sound brayed out again. A sharp whack cut it short. The man snarled, "There, that'll shift you, you dirty bugger."

Nicole gasped. Automatically, as if in her own bedroom, she looked around for the telephone book, to find the number of the SPCA. No phone book. No phone. God, what if there was no SPCA?

She leaned out the window again, half sagging on the rough wood of the sill. Her knees weren't so steady as they might be. Two figures came down the street, the man who had spoken and the thing that had made that braying sound: a small gray long-eared donkey.

The man looked as strange as everything else in this world, dream, hallucination, whatever it was. He wore a belted tunic of undyed wool, a little shorter than hers, with a hood shrugged down over his back. In one hand he held a rough rope knotted to the donkey's halter, in the other a stout stick, no doubt the weapon with which he'd abused the poor beast. The donkey tottered along under a massive load, four huge clay pots strapped to its back with a complicated set of leather lashings. The pots all together stood higher than the donkey, and looked hideously heavy.

The man caught her eye and waved without letting go of the stick, a bit of bravado that made her think of Tony Gallagher. "Good morning to you, Umma," he called. His smile showed a couple of missing teeth. The molar in Nicole's mouth twinged in sympathy. "Looks like a nice day, doesn't it?"

"Yes, I think so," she answered—and ducked back into the room in astonished confusion. He'd spoken to her—and to the donkey, for that matter—in a language she'd never heard before. And she, worse, had answered in the same tongue.

If she let it, that other language came to her lips as readily as English. When she thought *What in God's name is going on?* it came out as *Qui in nomin' Dei fit?* It sounded something like the Spanish that made sizable parts of Los Angeles seem a foreign country, but that wasn't quite right, either.

When her mind groped for the name of the language, she felt a shift and a click, a sensation somewhat like opening a program that someone had installed on her computer's hard drive without bothering to tell her. Frank would do a thing like that. But did Frank know Latin?

"Sed non possum latine loqui," she protested, and stopped. She wanted to scream, or to giggle crazily. Could you say *But I can't speak Latin* in Latin? Of course you could. She'd just done it.

As if opening that one file had opened another cross-referenced to it, her memory came clearer than it had since she awakened in this strange place, in this body that wasn't hers. She remembered the wish she'd made just before she went to bed in West Hills, California. Or maybe it had been a prayer, to Liber and Libera, the gods with the names that to her had always meant both freedom and sympathy. To go back to their time. To live in their world.

"I don't believe it," she said, deliberately making herself speak English. Odd, came the fugitive thought, that the language hadn't vanished with all the rest of her, subsumed in strangeness.

She didn't believe it. But she'd felt the gods' kisses on her palm—could feel them now, like the memory of a static shock. She looked down at the rough, callused, workworn hand and the arm it sprang from. That was not the hand that had felt the touch of those stony lips, or that small and doubled snap of divine energy.

Once more Nicole turned to the window, half hoping that it would look down on something she knew. The street was still there, the house next door, but the man and the donkey were gone. Other people had taken their place, a morning rush of people. Rush hour in—where? Ancient Rome? Most of them wore tunics and kept their heads down. A few men strutted along importantly in what looked like enormous beach towels wrapped around their bodies and tucked over one shoulder. Togas, those had to be togas.

Something creaked and squeaked—the axle of a cart, she

saw as it trundled past. The wheels, solid slabs of wood without spokes, sent up a cloud of dust. So did the hooves of the oxen drawing the cart. One of the oxen lifted its tail and dropped a trail of steaming green dung down the middle of the alley. No one came rushing out with a pooper-scooper. The cart creaked down the street and groaned round a corner and out of sight.

Once more she looked up, straining to see northward. More buildings, a gray stone wall, and beyond them a blue curve of hills. Those hills . . . she knew them. She remembered . . .

"The hills on the other side of the Danube," she whispered, not noticing or caring whether in English or Latin. She remembered those hills. They hadn't been so thickly forested when she saw them, but she'd promised herself never to forget their shape, the way they rose and swelled under the soft blue-gray sky. She hugged herself. She was cold and warm, both at once: awed, astonished, terrified, overjoyed.

"Carnuntum!" In Latin, with this body's accent, it had a sweeter, stronger rhythm than she'd known before, and a lilt to it like the refrain of a song. "I'm in Carnuntum! This is the Roman Empire, and I'm in Carnuntum, and the year is— the year is—"

That, she didn't know. It hadn't been uploaded, or installed, or whatever the word was. As if her brain had hit a bad sector, the lawyerly part of her clicked awake, looked around, and said a flat, *No*. And, when the rest of her tried to argue with it: *This isn't real. This isn't Carnuntum. You're hallucinating.*

Really, counselor? the rest of her asked a little too sweetly, the same tone she'd taken in court more than once, just before she moved in for the kill. *So it's not Carnuntum, and this isn't the Roman Empire. How do I know enough about either of them to hallucinate anything this elaborate?*

The lawyer-self couldn't answer that. Nicole turned in the room, all the way around, from window back to window again. After awe, fear, hysteria, panic, disbelief, all the wild mishmash of shock and realization, she settled on the best of all, the one she should have had from the first: dizzy, singing joy.

"Thank you," she said in a voice almost too full for sound. Then, louder: "Thank you, god and goddess! Thank you!" She danced across the room in a country-western step that wouldn't be invented for—how long?

She paused before she spun right out of the window, and forced some small calm. So—what did she know? The Roman Empire had gone on for a long time, then declined and fallen. The label on Liber and Libera's plaque, which she'd read often enough to have memorized it, said it dated from the second century A.D. She could reasonably suppose that that was the time she'd come back to, at least till she had a chance to ask. If that was when she was, the Achy-Breaky Shuffle wouldn't be born for another eighteen hundred years.

Good thing, too, probably.

Still whirling with delight in her discovery, she pulled open a top drawer of the chest. She hesitated an instant, with a completely silly attack of guilt—this wasn't her room, after all. These weren't her clothes.

This wasn't her body, either, but she was using it. She had to cover it somehow.

The drawer she opened held three or four loincloths like the one that clung clammily to her hips and buttocks. She pulled it off with a hiss of relief and put on a clean one.

Under the loincloths on the drawer lay a small and carefully made wooden box. It was not too heavy, not too light, longer than it was wide, about half as deep as the breadth of her hand. She lifted it out and set it on top of the chest. It wasn't locked or latched. Its lid yielded easily to the pressure of her fingers.

A scent of dust and old wood wafted out of the box as she opened it, overlaid with a strong, musky perfume. A small pot lay inside the box. When she opened it, she found it half full of white powder. Two more, smaller yet, held a greasy salve the color of—"Sunset Blush," Nicole said in English. She used Touch of Dawn herself. Sunset Blush was for serious occasions and for old beauties with fading eyesight, who thought its strong carmine red could trick people into thinking they were young again.

Nicole knew what this box was, then. A makeup set. Jumbled in with the pots were a wooden comb with very fine teeth; a pair of tweezers of bronze or tarnished brass; a thin and pointed piece of the same metal, about as long as her little finger, that might have been a toothpick; and another implement that looked like nothing so much as a coke spoon. She didn't think the Romans had known about cocaine. Maybe it was the Romans' answer to a Q-tip: not stylish, except perhaps in a campy way, but practical. Did they even have cotton here? she wondered. And what did they use for paring nails, if they didn't have nail scissors or clippers?

She was losing herself in detail again. She had to stop doing that. She had to accept, to absorb. She had to be part of this world.

She contemplated the makeup jars, the implements, the block of what must be eyeliner—kohl?—and the little brushes, and thought of her makeup kit at home—at what used to be home. She drew a shuddering breath. She couldn't be either stylish or practical, not by the standards of this place and time. Not till she could see other women, could know how they did it. That meant going out. That meant appearing in front of people, talking to them as she'd talked to the drover. Her hands were cold, the palms damp. The gods' kisses itched and stung.

Shakily, she returned the jars and implements to the makeup box. She'd paid no particular attention to the square of polished bronze that she'd found on the bottom, except to take it out and see if something else lay underneath. As she went to put it back in, she caught her hand's reflection in it, and the reflection of the box's lid, and realized, with a little shock of recognition, what the thing was for.

"Speculu'!" she said, then repeated herself in English: "A mirror!" She snatched it out. Her hand was shaking almost too hard to hold the mirror, but she stilled it with a strong effort of will, and stared avidly at the face reflected in the bronze. It wasn't clear, not like the silvered mirrors she re-

membered, but dark and faintly blurry. Still, it was enough
for the purpose. It bore out what her hands had told her:
whoever this was, it wasn't Nicole Gunther-Perrin, West
Hills, California, USA.

This face—long, strong-nosed, strong-chinned—looked to
be about the same age as the one she'd left behind. The eyes
were dark, as she'd more than half expected. When she
smiled, the broken tooth was visible, but it wasn't as bad as
it had felt. A corner out of an incisor, that was all. It didn't
disfigure her. It made her look rather interesting.

Not bad, she thought, deliberately striving for objectivity—
like a lawyer, think clearly, see all the angles, don't involve
the self if at all possible. This body she wore was no great
beauty, but neither would it make people look away in the
street. She considered it with some satisfaction. Beauty
would have been too much. This was a good-looking woman,
attractive without being too much so, and those cheekbones
were everything she'd ever dreamed of when she was growing up. Her—other—face hadn't had any to speak of.

She smiled at the face in the mirror. It smiled back, dark
eyes sparkling—no muddy catty green; and those black-
brown curls framed it quite nicely indeed. "I'll do," she said.
"I'll definitely do."

She laid the mirror carefully in the makeup case and put
it away. The odd feeling of trespass faded as she explored
the rest of the drawers in the chest. They held several pairs
of thick wool socks, not too unlike the ones you could order
from L. L. Bean for winter weekend wear, and tunics of
about the same style as the one she was wearing. Some were
of wool, others, lighter, of linen. A couple were dark blue,
one a rusty brown, and the others not only undyed but not
particularly clean. There was a definite limitation to the color
scheme here, and not too much regard for hygiene, either.
With the tunics she found a pair of woolen cloaks, one old
and growing threadbare, the other so new it still smelled
powerfully of sheep.

The last drawer, on the bottom, opened less easily than
the rest. She had to set her back to it and pull, and hope she

didn't break something. When it gave way at last, she found the drawer crammed full of rags. Dustrags? Cleaning rags? She frowned. They were all clean, but the stains on the ones she pulled out were hard to mistake. Even modern detergents couldn't always remove the stain of blood.

Bandages, then? *Yes,* she thought, *in a way.* Clearly, the Romans had never heard of tampons.

That could be a nuisance. She hadn't thought about such things when she'd prayed to Liber and Libera to snatch her out of her own place and time. She should have asked them for a stopover at a drugstore. The things she could have brought with her if she had—

Obviously, that wasn't how it worked. She told herself she didn't care. She didn't. She hadn't prayed for physical comfort or material wealth. She'd asked for equality; for justice. For a world that gave a woman a fairer chance, and a better quality of life. They'd brought her here, hadn't they? Then they must have given her the rest, too. If a price came with it, if she had to resort to rags for a week a month, then that was a price worth paying. After all, she couldn't be the only one. Every other woman in this place—in Carnuntum—had to do the same. That was equality, after a fashion.

She couldn't help thinking that it would be even more equal if the men had to do it, too. But she doubted even gods had the power to change the world as profoundly as that.

She pulled the blue tunic off over her head and picked up the brown, which seemed the cleanest of the lot. Before she put it on, she paused, looking down at herself. It felt strange, like being a voyeur, but she was inside the body she stared at.

It wasn't a bad body. The Nicole who'd lived in West Hills would have killed to be as slim as this. The breasts did sag a bit, more than her own—her others—had. They were a little larger, too. No bras here, or none that she'd found. The nipples were wide and dark, with the look she'd come to know in her other body, that with the stretch marks on her belly told her that this body had borne at least one child.

She stood briefly frozen. Children? That meant—

No. If she'd had a husband, she would have found his clothes and belongings in the room, and him in her bed, too. This was the room of a woman who lived, or at least slept, alone.

Her mouth twisted. Bless Liber and Libera. After all she'd gone through with Frank, the last thing she either wanted or needed was a husband.

She shrugged into the brown tunic, stooped and picked up the sandals, pulled and wiggled them onto her feet. The straps puzzled her a bit, with their bronze eyelets, but her hands seemed to know how they went. After a few moments she stopped trying to guide them and let them do what they wanted to do. The fingers worked deftly, lacing and fastening.

Then at last they were on and she was standing straight, ready to face the world. "Ready or not," she said to it, "here I come."

Unbarring the double door was easy, but it didn't open. What to do next? When she pushed against the handles, nothing happened. She pushed harder. Nothing. With a hiss of annoyance, she braced her back and pulled. The doors flew inward, nearly sweeping her off her feet. They were not hinged, she saw, but hung on pegs that fit into holes in the lintel and sill. How odd. How unusual. How—primitive? No. Just different.

This whole world would be different, more differences than she had ever known. She had to stop, to swallow the surge of panic. Culture shock didn't begin to describe it. She groped for the remnants of her former dizzy joy. Most of what was left was simply dizziness. It was still better than the black horrors. She was glad to be here. She had prayed to be here. The gods had given her the language and, it seemed, a little body-knowledge. Surely they'd have given her enough other skills to get by.

The hall was only a hall, if rather dark: no electric lights here. One or two doorways opened on either side. Only hers had an actual door. In the others, curtains hung from rod-

and-ring arrangements, like shower curtains in a bathtub—if shower curtains could be made of burlap.

People might be sleeping behind those curtains, or eating or using the chamber pot or doing whatever people did in curtained rooms in the morning. Nicole didn't want to look in—to disturb them, she told herself. But some of it was fear and a kind of crippling shyness. She wasn't ready to see what those people looked like.

At the end of the short hallway, wooden stairs descended in unlit gloom. She drew a breath so deep, she coughed— the stink of this whole world was concentrated here, overlaid with a sharp tenement reek—and squared her shoulders and girded her loins, metaphorically speaking. "Let's see what we've got," she said a little breathlessly, and set foot on the topmost step.

The stairs opened into an expanse of near-darkness. It felt wider and more open than the area above, and the air, as a consequence, was easier to breathe. It had a new sharpness here, a pungency that wasn't unpleasant. It reminded her of a student café at Indiana, dark and shut up and quiet in the morning before anyone came to open it.

She groped her way along the wall to a glimmer of light that seemed to mark a line of shuttered windows. Shutters, yes. She worked the rawhide lashings free and flung them back, blinking in the sudden glare of daylight. As she turned back to the room, she clapped her hands in delight that was only about three-quarters forced. "A restaurant!" she said. How wonderful of Liber and Libera—not only a nice body, no husband, and a simpler world, but a direct line to the best food, too. No more frozen dinners. No more Lean Cuisine. No more Thrifty Gourmet, not ever again.

The room was wider than it was long, and higher than the rooms and hallway above. It held half a dozen tables, no two of them identical—all handmade by human beings, no soulless mass production here—and a small forest of similarly various stools. Toward the rear was a long counter that looked like something out of Rancho Santa Fe: it was made of stones cemented together, with a flat slate top. Arranged on it in rows were baskets of things to nibble on: walnuts, raisins, prunes, faintly wilted green onions.

Nicole let the joy well up again, till she laughed with it. "No Fritos, no Doritos, no Cheetos, no Pringles." It was a litany of delight.

Set into the countertop were several round wooden lids with iron handles. She passed them by to explore what must, here, do duty for stove and microwave. Just past the wooden lids was an iron griddle over an open fireplace set into the counter. Another fireplace opened farther down. A complicated arrangement of chains hung over it. From several hung a row of pots on hooks.

There didn't seem to be a chimney. There was a hole in the roof above each fireplace—so that was why the second floor was set back like that, this must be like a walled and covered porch—and the window was open, unglazed and unscreened. That was all the venting there seemed to be. Soot stained the roofbeams and the plaster of the walls.

"You would think," she said to the nearer fireplace, "someone here would have thought of the chimney."

That was a deficiency, and disappointing, nearly as much so as the absence of tampons, but Nicole had to make the best of it. The oven helped. It stood past the farther fireplace, and it was wonderful. Beehive-shaped and made of clay, it could have been the prototype for every pizza oven she'd ever seen . . . except that, like the fireplaces, it had no proper venting. She would have to see if she could do something about that.

Next to the charming oven stood a large pot full of grain, and what she recognized after a moment as a mill. She fed a few grains of—wheat, she supposed it was—into the opening of the upper stone, then turned it. A sprinkling of flour sifted out of the bottom. She lifted a pinch of it between thumb and forefinger and tasted it. It wasn't Gold Medal quality, coarse and a little gritty, but it hadn't come from a factory the size of a city block, either. She'd made it with her own hands. She knew exactly where it came from, and how it got there, too.

She smiled proudly at it. How wonderful. How beautifully natural.

She walked across the rammed-earth floor to the front door, which was made the same way as the one in her room. This time, she opened it without hesitation or fumbling. Learning this first trick of living in Carnuntum made her as proud as if she'd just passed the bar exam.

The view from the doorway was a wider version of the one she'd had from her upstairs window. A building or two down from hers, several large stones were set crosswise in the street, sticking up several inches above the unpaved dirt. An oxcart rolled and squeaked past them without trouble. She saw that its wheels fit into deep ruts in the dirt, evidently a standard width apart.

So why the stones?

Dust. Dirt. Rain—of course, she thought. The stones would help a pedestrian cross from one side of the street to the other without sinking up to her knees in mud.

While she was congratulating herself on having solved yet another mystery of this brave new world, the fellow in the oxcart waved in friendly fashion and said, looking straight at her, "Good morning, Umma! I'll have some lettuces to sell you next week."

Nicole felt the heat rise to her cheeks, the hammering in her breast—panic again. She fought it as she'd learned to do at moot court in law school: by turning her back on it and concentrating on her response. "That's good," she said, carefully speaking in Latin. The man waved again and went on. She sagged against the doorframe, weak with relief. He hadn't noticed anything odd.

While she got her wits back together, a woman came past walking an ugly little dog on a leather leash. She nodded to Nicole. People knew this Umma, and apparently liked her, or at least respected her. Nicole was a stranger here, but Umma wasn't. How in the names of Liber and Libera was she supposed to find her way with people whom she'd never seen before in her life, but who expected her to know everything about them?

She could do it. She knew she could. This wasn't Los Angeles. This was a simpler world, a purer world, brighter and more innocent, if not exactly cleaner. It couldn't be as sexist as the world she came from, and it certainly couldn't be so rampantly unjust. People would accept her because they were conditioned to accept her. She wouldn't have to fight constant paranoia and mistrust, gender-bashing and racism and discrimination and all the rest of it. Here she could be what she fundamentally was: not a pair of boobs and a skirt, not a gringa, not a yuppie, but a plain and simple human being.

Her hand, she discovered, had risen to the side of her jaw. Damn that tooth. Tylenol would take care of it, but they wouldn't have that here. They probably didn't even have aspirin.

"I'll just have to make the best of it," she said to herself. "I can do that. I can."

Someone opened the front door of the building across the street: a stocky, balding man with a dark beard going gray. The sign above the door read, TCALIDIUSSEVERUSFULLOETINFECTOR, all the letters run together. Nicole needed a moment to separate one word from the next in her mind—T. CALIDIUS SEVERUS, FULLO ET INFECTOR—and another to read in Latin instead of English. It came to *Titus Calidius Severus, fuller and dyer*—after a moment's alarm at *infector,* which meant different things in English and Latin.

The man stabbed the pointed bottom of a large amphora into the dirt just to one side of the doorway. He waved and grinned at her. The grin showed a gap here and there. "Morning to you, Umma," he called. "You look pretty today. But then," he added, "you look pretty every day."

"Er—thank you," she said. Exactly how well did Umma and this—Calidius?—know each other?

Well, she thought with an inner headshake, that didn't matter, not anymore. She was her own person here. She would make up her own mind.

The fuller and dyer retreated into his shop. Nicole had barely begun to relax before he came out again carrying another amphora, which he thrust into the ground on the other side of his doorway. He waved again, this time without the grin and the greeting, and went back inside. His building looked like hers: one story in front, two in the back, living quarters set over a shop. From the look of the buildings up and down the street, this whole district was much the same.

A man in a dirty gray tunic paused in front of Calidius' shop. He hiked up the tunic. Nicole, staring in blank astonishment, saw that he wore no drawers, or loincloth either. He took himself in hand, casual as if he did this every day, and urinated into one of the amphorae. A strong yellow stream arced out and down, dwindled, dribbled, and gave out. He shook himself once or twice, let the tunic drop, and went on his way with a sigh of relief and a nod for Nicole.

It took all she could do to nod back. Every instinct of Midwestern upbringing and Los Angeles survival training was yelling in outrage. But there was no mistaking what the two tall jars were for, or that the man had simply been doing what was, for this place and time, his civic duty.

So did the next one who came by, a man of much higher social status from the look of his crimson tunic and halfway clean toga. He was as casual as the first one had been, as coolly matter-of-fact, and as unconcerned by the presence of a spectator—and a female spectator at that.

Wonderful, she thought. *I've got a public* pissoir *across the street from my restaurant. That should do wonders for business.*

Nicole Gunther-Perrin would have marched straight off to complain to Calidius. But Nicole Gunther-Perrin was wearing the body of a woman named Umma. Should she, shouldn't she? What could she get away with?

While she dithered, she became aware, distinctly and unmistakably, that someone had come up behind her. Whoever it was was silent, and she certainly couldn't see through the back of her head, but for the first time in her life she realized someone was nearby solely by smell. With a gasp she regretted as soon as it was out, she spun.

The woman who'd come up behind her gasped, too, in

evident alarm, and ducked her head so low that she seemed to be babbling into the loose fold of tunic over her ample breasts: "I'm sorry, Mistress Umma, I'm sorry, I'm sorry! I didn't mean to startle you. Please believe me."

"It's all right," Nicole said automatically. She was shaking, not so much from startlement now as from the proximity of another human being from this world, this time. People passing by, people across the street, were distant enough that she could, if she had to, pretend that they didn't count. There was no pretending this woman was anything but real. Every sense said so: sight, sound, smell so strong she could taste it—and, if she dared reach out, she could touch, too. She kept her hand in a fist at her side, and, as she'd done when she first woke, took refuge in the recording of details.

The woman was younger than she was, somewhere in her twenties, maybe, and half a head taller than Nicole—than Umma. However tall that was. Her skin was fairer than Umma's, almost like Nicole's own. Her eyes were gray, her hair neither blond nor brown and very, very dirty, rudely hacked into a bob like those of Liber and Libera on their votive plaque.

Her hands and face were clean enough, but her bare feet were black, not simply dirty like Nicole's—Umma's, Nicole reminded herself. She wore a stained, shabby tunic, shabbier than any of those Nicole had found in the chest of drawers. The body under that tunic was ripe, with wide hips and full breasts whose nipples thrust against the wool, but the odor that came off it went far past ripeness.

"I'm sorry I slept so late that you were up before me, Mistress." The young woman's words still tumbled over one another, as if she had to get them all in before someone stopped her. "It won't happen again, I promise it won't."

Nicole recognized that nervousness, though it seemed exaggerated. Employee in front of employer when employee was noticeably late. She knew the feeling herself.

With sympathy came a rush of relief. If this woman worked for her, then she had a guide, somebody to walk her through the things she needed to live in this world. She hadn't known how badly she wanted something like this till she had it. She wanted to fall on the woman's neck and thank God—or gods—for the gift.

Common sense kept her where she was, and made her say, "It's all right. No harm done."

Nicole had just, not entirely advertently, observed the cardinal rule of any lawyer or executive in a new job: make friends with the staff. Do that and they'll do your job for you, show you the ropes without your having to ask.

It seemed to work with this—what? Waitress? Cook? Hired girl? Her face lit up. "Oh, thank you, Mistress! What a kind mood you're in today." She was almost beautiful when she smiled. With the stink that came off her, though, who would want to get close enough to her to notice? She went on eagerly, almost too fast to understand: "Shall I make breakfast for you, Mistress? Still plenty of bread from yesterday. Or I could—"

"No," Nicole said before she fell over herself trying to please. "No, that would be fine." The body she wore was suddenly, ferociously hungry. It wanted to be fed now.

The—employee, Nicole guessed she could call her— smiled happily. She was as simple as a child, it seemed— nerves and shakiness one moment, puppy-eagerness the next. "Good! Good, then. The children should be down any time now. I'll see they're fed, too, Mistress. Everybody's sleepy today—everybody but you, Mistress Umma." She ventured another smile.

Nicole smiled back. It seemed unkind not to. The result was mildly startling: another of those wide, delighted grins. As the younger woman turned and went back toward the counter, she was humming under her breath.

Damn, thought Nicole, *she's easy to please.* Men might think so, too, the way she walked. Dawn Soderstrom had swiveled her hips like that, but she'd needed heels to do it. Anyone who could manage it barefoot had determination, and one hell of a limber spine.

Once the woman was gone about her business, backfield in motion, odor, and all, Nicole could focus on what she'd said. She—Nicole—Umma—was mother to—two? three? how many?—children she'd never seen before.

And what about Kimberley and Justin, back in West Hills, back in the twentieth century? It hit her with a force so strong it knocked the breath out of her. All the while she'd been veering between panic and selfish delight, she hadn't spared a moment's thought for her own children. It might almost seem she was glad to be shut of them—to escape the daily drag of responsibility, the interruptions, the disruptions. Had she been hoping she'd be spared that here? Was she so terrible a mother?

God. What had happened to her own body, back in West Hills? Was it just . . . unoccupied? Had it gone into some kind of coma? What would happen to the kids? She hadn't even gone in to kiss Kimberley good night, to see if her fever had gone down, or checked in on Justin and made sure he had his teddy beside him in case he woke up in the middle of the night. She'd been so tired, so fed up, so far over the top, that she'd put herself to bed and said her prayer and gone to sleep without a thought for her children.

No. No, something must have happened, the same way something had happened to make sure she spoke Latin. Somebody or something would look after Kimberley and Justin, at least till morning. Then—

Oh, God. They'd find her in a coma or worse. Would Kimberley know to dial 911? Would Justin—

She couldn't think about that. She had to hope—to pray—they'd be all right. Her last prayer had been answered. Why not this one, too?

"Liber," she whispered, "Libera, if you're listening, do this one last thing for me, will you please?" Damn, she sounded like Nicole-in-the-office, asking Cyndi to do her a favor. Good legal secretaries sit at the right hand of God, every lawyer knows that, but it might not be strictly kosher to address a pair of gods as if they were the original administrative assistants.

She shook herself. It didn't matter. "Just take care of them, okay?"

If she'd hoped for some sign, some feeling at least that she'd been heard, she didn't get it. She caught herself smiling slowly, widely, and not at all nicely. If Nicole Gunther-Perrin wasn't home anymore, there was no doubt at all who would inherit the kids. Frank and Dawn wouldn't get much of a vacation. And Frank would finally, after all this time, be left holding the baby—literally. Twice over.

"There is justice in the universe," Nicole said to the reek-rich air.

Her—servant, whatever, came back out of the shop carrying a chunk of bread, a small bowl, and a cup on a wooden tray. "Thank you," Nicole said as the young woman set the tray down on a table just inside the door, where the light from outside was brightest.

"You're welcome, Mistress." The woman, whose name Nicole was going to have to learn soon or be in trouble, smiled another of those wide smiles. "Oh, you are kind today! Have the gods blessed you, then, Mistress? Is this a white day?"

Nicole stared blankly at her. The part of her that knew Latin knew that a white day meant a lucky day, marked in white on the Roman calendar. It still didn't explain why the woman should be so transparently delighted to get a simple thank-you. Either Umma had been an ogre or something else was going on, something Nicole didn't know enough to catch.

Her stomach growled loudly, drowning out the rattle of her thoughts. It wanted breakfast, and it wanted it now.

She pulled a stool over to the table, sat down, and examined her breakfast. The bread made her want to giggle. Had it been served in slices instead of a slab half a dozen slices thick, it would have done for Roman Meal: same medium-brown color, same coarse flour. She'd eaten a lot of bologna sandwiches on Roman Meal, growing up in Indianapolis. She tore off a piece and bit into it. It was fresher than any Roman Meal she'd ever eaten, and had a slightly smoky taste from being baked over a wood fire.

It was also grittier than any Roman Meal she'd ever eaten.

She glanced at the stone quern beside the oven. Was that
what had broken her front tooth, and what set the back one
to aching whenever she wasn't busy thinking about something else?

So she'd chew carefully. She was hungry.

When she'd taken the edge off her hunger with a good
portion of the bread, she took time to explore the rest of the
tray. The shallow earthenware bowl was full of thick, shiny,
green-yellow liquid. She sniffed. Her eyebrows rose. Remembering dinners in fancy restaurants before Frank stopped
taking her and started taking Dawn instead, she twisted off
another piece of bread and dipped it in the bowl. She tasted
again. Yes, she'd called it. Olive oil. They were still eating
bread that way in Italian restaurants, eighteen centuries from
now.

Olive oil was a fat, but God knew it was better than butter.
This body didn't look as if it needed to worry much about
its weight. Even so, a lifetime of habit persuaded Nicole to
push the bowl of oil away and investigate the cup. Again
she sniffed. Again her eyebrows rose, but this time they rose
higher. Wine? At breakfast? What was she supposed to be,
an alcoholic?

Dammit, she needed to know her employee's name. Rather
than sing out *Yo!* or *You there!* she coughed. That did it: the
young woman looked up from the two trays she was filling
as she'd filled Nicole's. Her eyes were wide, her face a mask
of apprehension. All her emotions seemed to be broad, car-
toonish, as if she were playing a role, and not too well, either.

Those emotions were real. Nicole would have been willing
to bet on that. They were just . . . exaggerated. For effect?
Or because she'd never learned to tone them down? "Is
something wrong, Mistress?" she asked anxiously.

"Yes," Nicole said, and the woman's face went white. Terror? *Good Lord,* Nicole thought. *Umma must have been a
raving tartar.* She smoothed her voice as much as she could,
though she couldn't rid it of all the disapproval. That was
too deeply ingrained, for too long, in Nicole's other—

future—life. "I don't think I'll be having wine this morning. Would you bring me some water instead?"

"Water?" The other woman's eyebrows flew up almost to her hairline. She was as astonished as if Nicole had asked for—well, wine. Or Scotch. Or creamed angleworms on toast. "Mistress, are you sure?"

"Yes, I'm sure." Nicole hadn't meant to snap so hard. She hadn't meant to crush the servant—just to shake her loose from her incredulity and set her to fetching the water. The young woman looked as if she expected to be fired without a reference. More gently, as gently as she could, Nicole said, "I may stop drinking wine altogether. Water's more healthy, don't you think?"

"Healthy?" The servant's eyebrows went up even higher this time. She was easy to reassure, at least; soften the tone even a little and she forgot she'd ever been snapped at.

Or else she really was too incredulous to watch her step around an employer she so evidently feared. Nicole had to be acting completely and shockingly out of character.

"Healthy?" she repeated. "Water? Mistress, your customers won't think so, if you try to tell them such a thing."

"What do you mean?" Nicole said.

Her employee stared at her. She had, she realized, just asked her first truly stupid question here in Carnuntum. The young woman retreated to the long stone counter, as if it represented some kind of refuge. Something in the way she walked, and in the things she'd said, made Nicole see it suddenly for what it was. It wasn't a counter. It was a bar.

Not caring for an instant what the other woman might think, she hurried over to it and lifted the wooden lids she'd ignored before. Under each of them rested an amphora with a bronze dipper. The strong alcoholic smell of wine floated up to her nose.

Umma wasn't running a restaurant. She was running a tavern. Nicole startled herself with the intensity of her revulsion and anger. How many men of Carnuntum would stagger home drunk to abuse their spouses and children because of this place? Any one of them could have been her

father: face red with drink and rage, mouth open wide as he
bellowed at his wife, hand swinging up to hit whatever, or
whomever, got in its way.

"I will not," she said tightly, "sell—this—"

The employee didn't understand. "Mistress, most of it's
not Falernian, but it's all the best we can get for the price.
Why, you said—"

Nicole cut her off. She had to understand. It was very,
very important that she understand. "I will not sell wine."

Her expression must have been alarming. The young
woman started to babble again. "Mistress, are you ill? Have
you lost your senses? You know we have to sell wine. If
you don't, nobody will come here. We'll all go hungry."

"I could serve—" Nicole started to say *coffee,* only to
discover that the Latin she'd acquired had no word for it.
She used the English instead.

"Coffee?" The young woman's accent did strange things
to the vowels. "I don't know what that is, Mistress. Where
would you get it? How would you serve it?"

Nicole started to answer, but stopped. Blue Mountain coffee came from Jamaica, Kalossi Celebes from Indonesia,
Kona from Hawaii, good old unexciting Yuban from Colom-
bia. She didn't know much about Roman history, but she
was pretty sure those weren't places the Romans had ever
heard of.

Her employee seemed absolutely convinced she couldn't
make a go of a restaurant that didn't serve wine. Nicole had
no way of knowing whether she was right, not on her first
morning in Carnuntum.

This was the only guide she had, the only hope of getting
through without being labeled insane or worse. She'd seen
it in movies, how the alien landed on earth with a head full
of data but missing a few of the most important. He was
always found out, and then he had to suffer. Did the Romans
have police? Government agencies? Whatever they'd call the
CIA?

She had to fit in, at least at first. She had to act normal,
or people would ask too many questions, questions she

couldn't answer. "Very well," she said grudgingly. "We'll keep on serving wine. For now. But," she went on, and that was firm, "I will drink water."

The servant sighed deeply, the kind of sigh that said, *You may be crazy, but you're still the boss.* "Yes, Mistress," she said, meekly enough, and poured her a cup from a pitcher on the bar.

Because the cup was earthenware and not glass, Nicole couldn't admire its crystal clarity as she would have liked. But when she sipped, she let out a sigh of pleasure. Now this was water, water as it ought to taste. What came out of the tap in Los Angeles was as full of chlorine as a swimming pool, and full of God only knew what all other chemicals. None of those pollutants here—just good, pure H_2O.

"See?" Nicole set down the empty cup. "This is what's good for you."

"Yes, Mistress." The young woman sounded even more resigned, and even more dubious, than she had before.

A clatter from upstairs distracted them both from what might have been an uncomfortable pause. The servant smiled. "Here come the children, Mistress. They were sleepy today, weren't they?"

"Weren't they?" Nicole echoed. Her employee, fortunately, didn't seem to notice how hollow her voice sounded. How in the world was she going to convince—how many?—children she'd never seen before that she was their mother? She had no idea what to do or say—no time to think, either, before they were on her.

4

IT WENT, THANK GOD, better than she'd dared hope. It still wasn't easy, not for her, but the kids, like the servant, seemed prepared to take her on faith. Why not? She looked like their mother. She sounded like their mother. Who else could she be?

By now she took in data as automatically, and almost as effortlessly, as she had when she was studying for the bar exam. As she had then, she shut out emotions that wouldn't immediately serve her purposes, simply recorded them and filed them away to deal with later.

She had—Umma had—two children: a son named Lucius, who looked about eight years old, and a daughter called Aurelia, a couple of years younger. Aurelia reminded Nicole of Kimberley. It wasn't just that they were near enough the same age, and it certainly wasn't that they looked alike—Aurelia, naturally enough, looked like a smaller version of Umma. But the way she carried herself, the turn of her head when she looked at her mother, the prim little purse of her mouth, were all strikingly like Kimberley.

It struck Nicole rather strongly, if belatedly, that Umma might be one of her ancestors. The dream she'd had, the double spiral ladder of DNA, could have been the way she'd traveled here. Almost all of her great-grandparents had come to the United States from Austria. Carnuntum was—had been—would be—in Austria. Suppose their several-dozen-times-great-grandparents had come from here, from this town?

What a chain of coincidences if it was true: that she should have honeymooned in Carnuntum, that she'd found the votive plaque, that it had become the constant occupant of her nightstand, even long after it stopped being a symbol of her marriage to Frank Perrin. And after that marriage had gone sour beyond all repair, when her job imploded on her and her whole life was falling apart, a prayer expressed as a wish had done the impossible, had brought her down through the long chain of genes into this one of all her myriad ancestors.

Another thought trod on the heels of the first. If Umma was her ancestor, then so was either Lucius or Aurelia—or, for that matter, so were both of them. She swallowed a sudden, nearly hysterical giggle. They were children, half her size. Hard to imagine that they'd grow up, have children of their own, and those would have children, and . . .

Right now, at this moment in the long skein of time, they were children, as real and unmistakable as Justin or Kimberley. They tore into breakfast as if, if they ate it fast enough, they'd grow into adulthood between the first bite and the last. She kept her mouth shut when they soaked their bread in olive oil and ate it greasy and dripping. They were growing children. They could get away with it.

At least, she thought, they aren't swilling down cholesterol with the fat. Did people in the Roman Empire even know what cholesterol was?

The children's table manners could have been better, but she kept quiet about those, too. For now. Lucius wolfed down every crumb of his bread, licked lips glistening with oil, and snapped to the young woman, "Julia! More bread."

"Yes, young sir," Julia said, and dropped her own breakfast to rise and do as he ordered. She smiled a trifle sadly at Nicole. "Doesn't he sound just like his father, Mistress? He tries so hard to be a little man—so good of him, and so well done, with your poor husband gone among the shades so young. We've need of a man about the house."

Nicole reined in her first response, which was to demand to know what was so good about a man underfoot. So she was a widow, was she? Well, good for the late Mr. Umma, whatever his name had been. At least he'd had the courtesy to die instead of running off with the cute young thing next door.

Lucius snatched the bread that Julia brought him and sopped it in oil, without so much as a word or a glance. Nicole frowned. Table manners were one thing. Courtesy was another altogether. "Lucius," she said sternly, "that was impolite. I didn't hear you say 'please' to Julia. And what should you have said when she brought you your bread?"

Lucius looked at her as if she'd gone off her head. "What should I have said, Mother?"

He didn't sound as if he was sassing her, though the words could hardly mean anything else. Nicole took a deep breath and counted to five before she answered. "What about 'thank you'?"

Lucius' straight black brows went up. " 'Thank you'? To a slave?"

Nicole's mouth was open. She shut it. She looked at Julia in a dawning horror. She couldn't be a slave. Slaves were something out of—

Something out of old dead history. This was old dead history. This, right now, this world she was living in.

Julia didn't even blink at what Lucius had called her, or at his tone. She sat back down in her place—a little apart from the others, Nicole saw as if for the first time, and on a lower stool, so that her head was a little below theirs. She kept it bowed even lower as she tucked into her own bread and oil and, with a sort of cautious defiance in the glance she shot at Nicole, her wine.

When Nicole thought of slavery, she thought of African-Americans and cotton fields and the Civil War. She vaguely recalled a movie or two about Rome, and something about slaves. Slave revolts? Chariot races? Charlton Heston? Frank would have known, damn him. Frank had a thing for Fifties movie epics. She'd ignored them when he had them on, except to notice that there was a lot of noise and bare skin, and costumes that made her think of a slow night in a Vegas casino. She'd forgotten all that when she prayed to come back to Roman days. She'd never imagined that she'd come back as a slaveowner. No late-twentieth-century minds thought like that.

Neither did they think of traveling back in time at all, not seriously. Not unless they were heavily into fantasy and gaming and all the rest of that unreal nonsense.

This was real enough. So was Julia, sitting there drinking the last of her wine with a little too clearly evident enjoyment.

While Nicole sat speechless, Aurelia held out her cup to Julia and said, "Get me some more wine." Her eyes flicked to Nicole. She added, "Please." Her smug little smile was the image of Kimberley's. *Look how good I'm being*, it proclaimed to the world, *and look what a nasty brat my brother is.*

Nicole had always detested that smugness in Kimberley. It didn't look any better in Aurelia, or do her any more good, either. Nicole snatched the cup from her hand before Julia could take it. She raised it to her nose and sniffed. The odor was unmistakable. "You are giving the children wine?" Her voice was quiet, dangerously so.

Julia understood her. "Yes, Mistress," she said, as quietly, but without the deadly edge. There was a suggestion of great patience and of indulging a preposterous fancy, but it was too faint to do more than bristle at. "Of course I am, Mistress. I watered the wine half and half, just as I always do. I'd never give it to them neat. You know that, Mistress."

Nicole didn't care what excuses she made, nor listen to her beyond that first, damning yes. "You gave them wine," she said again, incredulous. "What are you trying to do, turn them into—" She groped in her new Latin vocabulary, hunting for the word that was so clear in English: alcoholics. There wasn't any such word. The best she could wasn't quite good enough: "Are you trying to turn them into drunkards?"

"I said," Julia said with an air of shaky determination, "I watered it exactly as I should, as I was supposed to—as you, Mistress, always told me to—till now."

She thought she'd done right, Nicole realized. She was so sure of it that she'd even held her ground against her—her owner. Nicole shuddered. Julia, oblivious, went on, "Mistress, by all the gods I don't know why you've taken so against wine today. Are you feeling well? Are you ill? Should I fetch you some poppy juice?"

Poppy juice? Opium? *One can of worms at a time,* Nicole thought. "I am not ill," she said, with taut-strung patience. "And you are not to give my children wine for breakfast."

"Then," said Julia, still defiant, "what am I supposed to give them?"

"Milk, of course," Nicole answered sharply. Didn't she know that? Didn't anybody?

Apparently not. "Milk?" the children and Julia said in chorus, all three; and in the same shocked tone, too. Lucius and Aurelia hacked and gagged and made disgusted faces. You'd have thought she'd just tried to feed them a plate of lima beans.

"Milk?" Aurelia repeated. "It's slimy!"

"It tastes horrible," Lucius said. They looked at each other and nodded in perfect, and horrified, agreement. Nicole didn't think they agreed like that very often.

"It's expensive," Julia said, making it sound like a clincher. "And besides, Mistress, you can't keep it fresh. It's even worse than fish. You waste what you don't use, because it's sure to be sour the next day, especially this time of year. Please pardon me for telling you, but really, Mistress, what in the world makes you want to feed them milk?"

"Because it's full of—" Nicole found she couldn't say *calcium* in Latin, either, even though it sounded like a Latin word to her. This time, her circumlocution was clumsy: "It helps make bones strong."

"Barbarians drink milk," Lucius said, as if that settled everything. "The Marcomanni and the Quadi drink milk." He stuck out his tongue. Not to be outdone, Aurelia stuck out hers, too.

Some arguments you just couldn't win. This looked like one of them. Religion, politics, divorce—on some things, people's minds locked themselves shut and lost the key. If she tried to force it, she'd get into a fight; and that wouldn't gain her anything.

Sidestep, then. "If you won't drink milk, will you drink water?" she asked. The children didn't look happy, but they didn't screw up their faces and make puking noises, either. Neither did Julia, though her expression was eloquent. Nicole threw an argument at the kids to bolster her case: "I drank water this morning, and it hasn't hurt me."

"You did?" Lucius sounded as if she'd just told him— well, as if she'd told him that she'd traveled in time from the twentieth century and she wasn't his mother at all.

What joy, she thought. *A whole family of alcoholics in training, from the baby on up—and their mother is in busi-*

ness selling wine. She'd fix that, maybe not all in a day considering how Julia and the children had reacted to her suggestion that wine maybe wasn't the best thing for a human to drink, but by Liber and Libera she would show them how a healthy person ought to live. "I certainly did drink water this morning," she said to Lucius. "Ask Julia if you don't believe me. She watched me do it. She even fetched the pitcher and poured me a cup."

Lucius laughed. It was a distinctly and viscerally unpleasant sound, a Beavis-and-Butthead snigger. "Huh! That's funny, Mother. You can't believe a slave about anything. Only way they can testify is if you torture them." He made a horrible face at Julia, a twisted devil-snarl, and jabbed his finger at her, with indescribable boy-type sound effects: hissing and bubbling and an abrupt, blood-curdling shriek.

He was making it up. He had to be. But Julia's white face and the sudden change in her silence, the way her shoulders went tight and hunched under her sad bag of a tunic, ate away at Nicole's disbelief.

She'd never taken legal history. It hadn't been required, and she hadn't been interested, and she hadn't had time even if she had been interested. Now, with piercing intensity, she wished that she had.

Legal history she might have missed, but she'd been a parent long enough to know how to shut down a thread of discussion that was going in a dangerous direction. Briskly, she said, "We're not talking about court right now, young man. Are you saying Julia and I would both lie to you about what I drank?"

Lucius shrank suddenly, startling her: flinched into himself, as if he'd expected a slap. "No, Mother," he said. "I'll drink water after this, Mother. I promise I will."

God, what had he expected? That she'd clobber him, just because he'd been obnoxious? What kind of mother had this Umma been? Not just alcoholism—abuse. Her stomach, even as full of breakfast as it was, felt small and tight and cold.

It knotted even tighter when Aurelia hastened to agree

with her brother. "I'll drink water, too," she said. "I'll drink
it right now. Julia, get me some water!"

Julia glanced at Nicole. Nicole nodded sharply. Julia
sighed just audibly, poured Aurelia's wine into her own cup,
and filled Aurelia's again with water.

Nicole's triumph, such as it was, was evaporating fast.
Julia had just manipulated herself into a double ration of
wine. Umma's children were flat-out terrified, and their fear
had given Nicole the victory. What kind of mother raised her
children to be afraid of her? *Not any kind of mother I am,*
Nicole resolved grimly. And Julia—tricky bits aside, Julia
obeyed her mistress, oh, sure. But she did it with slow sul-
lenness, neither too slow nor too sullen to be caught and
punished, but just enough to make her feelings clear.

Just what did Julia think wine was? Or was it water she
was afraid of? Nicole knew about not drinking the water in
Third-World countries, but that was for Americans traveling
away from their chlorinated, fluoridated, homogenized, pas-
teurized, all-clean-and-sanitized local water companies. People who actually lived in those countries did perfectly well
on the water there. Wasn't she—in Umma's body—still
standing up and not crouched groaning over a chamber pot?

So much ignorance. So much misunderstanding of what
was best for people's health. Maybe Liber and Libera had
sent her back to make life better for these people, to teach
them about sanitation and hygiene and healthy food and
drink. Surely they hadn't given her her wish just because she
wanted it. There had to be something they meant her to do
in return.

If she was to do any good, if that was what she was here
for—and never mind if she wasn't; she'd do it anyhow—she
had to learn much more of this world and place than she
knew. Knowing Latin, for instance, didn't seem to let her
know where anything was in Carnuntum.

Still, how hard could that be? Social mores and mental
attitudes were rough, and she was working her way gingerly
through those. Carnuntum itself was much simpler. If she'd
found her way around Los Angeles, all hundreds of square

miles of it, and even learned to drive its freeways without going catatonic with terror—she could learn what she needed to know about this much smaller, much less complicated town.

She didn't know the date, either. Well, she could ask that, and she did, casually, as if it had slipped her mind.

"It's four days before the Kalends of June, Mistress," Julia said, and then added, "I think." At least she wasn't surprised to be asked.

May 28, Nicole thought after a moment of going back and forth between what she knew in Latin and what she knew in English. It was only half an answer, and the smaller half. "Everything's going out of my head this morning," she said with what she hoped was a light little laugh. "What year is it?"

"It's—what?—the ninth year of the reign of Marcus Aurelius," Julia said. Her voice held a little of the tone Nicole knew well: *The boss is an idiot,* it meant. But only a little. It was, oddly, maybe deceptively reassuring. Maybe Umma wasn't a brutal slavemaster after all.

Or maybe it meant a slave didn't dare step too far over the line. Nicole had seen that in offices with tyrannical bosses, or in houses where the parents were too strict. Employees, and kids, learned just how far they could go, and went that far and no further.

Lucius broke in on her thoughts with the air of the know-it-all proving he really did know it all: "The consuls for the year are Marcus Cornelius Cethegus and Gaius Erucius Clarus."

Nice, Nicole thought. And no help at all. She might have heard of Marcus Aurelius once upon a time, but no way in the world did she know when he'd reigned. The other two names had a fine and ringing sound, but they meant exactly nothing. And what difference did it make, anyway, who or what a consul was? Were they like President and Vice President? King and queen? Lord Mayor of London?

Careful; she was getting sarcastic. She tried one more time, and hoped the strain didn't show in her voice: "I wonder what year this would be by the Christian calendar?"

Lucius and Aurelia gaped, then made gagging noises—
exactly as they'd done when she'd suggested they drink milk.
Julia said with prim firmness, "I didn't even know those
nasty people had a calendar. I don't have anything to do with
them. They're all crazy, or so you'd think, the way they act.
Even I know better, and I'm only a slave. They don't respect
the gods. They won't worship the Princeps—why, they
throw themselves on legionaries' swords if anyone tries to
make them. If you ask me, they deserve whatever they get."

That was more than Nicole had bargained for. She thought
of herself as a Catholic, though she'd gone to church only a
handful of times since she got married, and not at all since
the divorce. Visions of catechism class, crucifix on the wall
and sappy long-faced Jesus, Christians and lions and legionaries dicing in front of the Cross, swirled in her head, fast
enough to make her dizzy. All that, and Victor Mature standing up to Peter Ustinov in a purple gown, while the choir's
voices swelled in the background.

She'd gone back that far? God. Or Jesus. Or somebody.
And she hadn't come back as a Christian, either. Somehow
it had never occurred to her that that could happen, that she'd
be—a pagan. Or something. It was startling how that struck
her, that same twisting in the stomach she'd had when she
was seven years old and had learned that not only were some
people not Catholic, some people didn't even believe in Jesus. "Will they go to hell?" she'd asked her mother.

She didn't remember what her mother had said. Something
impatient, probably: "Shut up and eat your dinner." Her
mother didn't like answering hard questions. Her catechism
teacher, when she asked the same question, had gone on
about sincere belief, tolerance for other religions, and differing views of the afterlife. It had been more than she'd been
ready to swallow, at that age. In a lot of ways, it still was.

Even worse than being a pagan, than being surrounded by
pagans, was hearing one of them scorn the religion she'd
grown up in. Never mind that she'd fallen away from it.

Maybe political correctness had something in it after all. For that matter, so did simple politeness.

She drew breath to begin a reprimand, but let it out again without saying anything. What good would it do? She'd learned long ago never to get into arguments over politics or religion. People's minds were always made up.

She glanced at Lucius and Aurelia. Was Aurelia named for Marcus Aurelius? Did they do things like that here?

For that matter, weren't the children supposed to be getting ready for school? Did they even go to school? If they did, they weren't showing any signs of it. Or was today Saturday? Sunday? Did Saturday or Sunday matter in Carnuntum in the ninth year of the reign of Marcus Aurelius, whenever that was? How could she find out without looking like an idiot again?

Before she could find an answer to any of those crowding questions, Julia said, "Oh! Mistress, here's Ofanius Valens. He's early today." She leaped up and ran busily about, as if the boss had come into the office and found the secretaries in the middle of a kaffeeklatsch.

Nicole leaped up, too, but, once she was up, had no idea what to do. *Christ!* she thought in panic. *A customer!* At least Julia had given her his name. She scrambled to remember what a proper restaurant owner would say to a regular. "Good day to you, Ofanius Valens," she said as smoothly as she could manage—fund-raisers were good practice; so were jury selections. "What can we get for you?"

He sat down on a stool: a thin fellow a few years younger than she, not too clean but not too dirty, either. He'd had horrible acne in his youth, which couldn't be that long ago; his beard didn't hide all the scars. "First time you've even asked in a while," he said with a familiar chuckle. "My usual will do fine, thanks."

And thank *you*, Ofanius Valens. I'll remember you in my nightmares. Umma, no doubt, had known what his usual was. Nicole hadn't the faintest idea. But maybe, she thought with a stab of relief, someone did. "Julia," she said, "take care of him."

"Yes, Mistress," Julia said, and did. Along with his bread and oil, Ofanius Valens favored walnuts and green onions and the wine from under the second lid from the left. As he ate, the eye-watering pungency of the onions moved in around him and settled to stay.

He seemed content enough to have Julia deal with him rather than Umma in person. Nicole congratulated herself for escaping unscathed, for once, from yet another difficult situation. What she'd done didn't dawn on her for a few moments. She'd ordered Julia about as a mistress would order a slave.

No, she told herself. *I'd have handled it the same way if she were free and working for me.* Maybe that was true. She thought it was true. She devoutly hoped it was.

She shivered, though the room was warm enough. Every word she spoke to Julia, every gesture she made, couldn't be a normal human interaction. Not as long as Julia was her property. Everything she did, as long as she knew that, was a political act.

As soon as Nicole knew how it was done, if it could be done, she'd have to free Julia. She couldn't go on living like this, owning another human being, treating her like an object. Pretending Julia was a hired servant didn't cut it. The truth remained, insurmountable.

Should she free the rest of the slaves, too? For of course there had to be more. Lots of people had to have them, if Umma, who wasn't particularly wealthy or powerful, could own one. But Nicole couldn't start right this instant. She didn't know enough—and reality, in the person of Ofanius Valens, intervened. He fumbled in the pouch he wore attached to his belt. "An *as* for the bread," he said, and slapped a copper coin about the size of a quarter on the table in front of him. "An *as* for the oil." He brought out another copper coin.

Nicole was glad he knew what everything cost, because God knew she didn't. "Two *asses* for the nuts and onions." Two more of the copper coins. "And two *asses* for the wine. Here, I'll give you a *dupondius,* because I'm running out of *asses*." This coin was bigger and brighter, yellowish instead of dirty-penny brown. It couldn't have been gold, not if it was worth only two of the copper ones. Brass, maybe? Julia, watching him count up the bill, nodded at the amount. Nicole breathed a faint sigh of relief. She wasn't being ripped off, then.

"Here," Ofanius Valens said with a wink, "I've got one lonely *as* left in my purse. If I give it to Julia, you will let her spend it on herself?"

For an instant, Nicole didn't understand why he'd asked her that. Julia was an adult, wasn't she? Then realization smote. Legally speaking, Julia wasn't an adult. Probably, she wasn't even a person. Which had to mean that, technically, that *as* belonged to her owner. Before Julia could accept it, Nicole had to assent. "Yes," she said, trying not to let anger at the system show. "Yes, of course."

Ofanius Valens nodded and smiled. He hadn't intended her to refuse, nor given her much room to do it, either, by the signs. Nicole might have lousy taste in men, but she could read them perfectly well—too well, maybe, if you asked any one of a number of male lawyers whom she'd shown up in front of a judge. Men didn't like to know how transparent they were.

"Thank you very much, Mistress," Julia said. If Ofanius Valens had expected Nicole to say yes, she probably had, too. Her gratitude had a hint of calculation in it, the calculation of the extremely disadvantaged. If she didn't grovel enough, she might be thinking, then maybe next time she wouldn't be allowed to keep the money she got. Children could think like that. So could employees. But there was an edge to it, a hint of ugliness. More than anyone else, a slave had to keep her mistress sweet, or who could say what might happen? If a slave wasn't considered human, how could she have human rights?

Women still got treated like that in the twentieth-century world—some even in the United States. People in the Third World lived like that. But not like this. Not quite.

And what, Nicole wondered, did this slave really think of

her mistress? What was going on, deep down, when she bent her head and said the words she judged it best to say? Nicole shivered. The likely answer wasn't comfortable. In fact, it was scary.

Ofanius Valens couldn't know, any more than anyone else in this world and time, what Nicole was thinking—or even that Nicole was there; that it wasn't Umma standing by him, waiting for him to get up and go on his way. He obliged with a cheerful air, oblivious to any undercurrents. "Tomorrow, then, Umma," he said. "Then maybe I'll order something different. Wouldn't that be a jolt?"

He went off whistling and laughing to himself at what was evidently a great joke. Well, Nicole thought a trifle wryly, there was a rarity: a man who knew how much a creature of habit he was.

She shook her head and forgot about him—until tomorrow. Julia was still standing there, the coin clenched in her fist as if she feared her mistress would take it away after all. Nicole tried to reassure her with a smile. "What will you do with your *as*, Julia?" she asked. She hoped she didn't sound too patronizing, or too much like an adult talking, uncomfortably, to a child.

Julia didn't seem to notice anything wrong with the tone, or, if she did, it was a wrongness she was used to. She answered readily enough: "When things slow down this afternoon, Mistress, if you'll let me, I'll go over to the baths— it's a ladies' day today—and get clean. Is that all right? I'll work hard all morning, I promise, so I won't put you to any trouble. Please?"

A grown woman shouldn't have to beg like that. Nicole's anger at Julia's condition heated up again. She should not have to ask permission for every little thing, as if she were a small child.

There was nothing Nicole could do, not right this instant, except give Julia what little she had to give, which was her permission. "Yes," she said. "Yes, that's all right."

Julia smiled in pure happiness. Considering how rank she was, it had to be excruciating to have to be herself, and smell herself. Nicole wasn't quite willing to admit that she was surprised. She'd let herself think nobody minded smelling bad—but if that was the case, why did the Romans have baths at all? Lord knew the ruins she'd seen here on her honeymoon were the biggest building in town.

Now she was here, in the time when Roman baths were whole and in use, and she'd passed a milestone. She'd survived her first customer. That was worth a pause, and a gathering of forces. If one had come in for his breakfast, another couldn't be far behind.

Another customer did come, a few minutes after the first; and two more after that, and then a whole flood of them. Most were men, all hungry or thirsty or both—hungrier in the morning, thirsty as the day went on, hungry again toward evening. Without a clock, Nicole couldn't know how many hours were passing. She was too busy most of the time to care.

What with one thing and another, talking fast and ducking faster and calling on Julia to do the honors whenever she was caught up short, she survived the rest of the day. By the time the sun went down, she was wondering if she would go down, too: down for the count. In spite of Julia's promise that things would slow down in the afternoon, Nicole was hopping every moment of the day.

The first crisis came early, when someone bought two cups of wine, some bread, and a piece of smoked pork. Nicole hadn't even noticed that the tavern boasted smoked pork; Julia used a forked pole to get it down from a hook in the ceiling. The hook was secured in a beam next to a hole through which smoke from the cookfires—or some of it, at least—escaped. As the smoke dribbled out the hole, it happened to preserve the meat. Nicole watched the middle-aged man happily devour the pork—ham, she supposed she should call it—and tried not to think about the carcinogens he must be ingesting with it.

"That'll be a *sestertius* altogether," Julia said. She'd been giving out all the prices this morning, readily enough but with a glance at Nicole each time as if she expected Nicole to do it instead.

After he'd fished in his belt pouch for what seemed like a very long time, the man confessed that he didn't have enough small copper and brass coins to make up the value of a large—silver-dollar-sized—brass *sestertius*. His expression was sour. "I'm going to have to give you a *denarius,* curse it. Jupiter! I hate paying out silver for trifles, when I know cursed well I'll get back nothing but base metal. Say whatever you like, but you know as well as I do, three bloody brass *sesterces* don't come near being worth three-quarters of a silver *denarius*."

Four *sesterces* to a *denarius*. Nicole filed that away. And two *asses* made a *dupondius,* and two *dupondii* a *sestertius*.

What was even worse, considering how unhappy her customer already was, she was still an *as* short of being able to give him the right change. He'd already complained about shelling out silver—real money—for fiat-currency pocket change. He'd be even less delighted to come up short of what he was supposed to be owed. It wasn't just that he was getting toy money for his fifty-dollar bill—that toy money didn't even equal the amount of his change.

Julia saw the same thing at the same time. She looked around, seemed not to find what she was looking for, and turned back to Nicole. "Mistress, didn't you bring the cash box downstairs with you this morning?"

Nicole's stomach clenched, as it had been doing at intervals since she woke in a strange bed. If it did much more of that, she'd end up with an ulcer. She shook her head in reply to Julia's question.

Julia made a noise that hadn't changed between whenever this was and the 1990s: a small sigh that meant, *I may be stuck working for you, but which one of us is the dummy?*

Nicole sighed herself and prayed for calm—never mind whom she prayed to; it didn't matter. "Go and get the box," she said. And added, probably not wisely: "Please."

For the first time Julia didn't go running to do her mistress' bidding. "Oh, no, Mistress," she said. "You can't trick me that way. I don't spy on you, no I don't." She folded her arms and set her lips thin and made herself a picture of triumphant virtue. It was so exaggerated, so downright stagey, that Nicole almost laughed and told her come off it—but she didn't dare. This was worse than dealing with the secretarial pool, and much worse than knowing what to do with all the flocking servers in an upscale restaurant. She didn't own the secretaries, and she certainly didn't have the power to torture or kill the maître d' at Spago.

"Well," she said to cover the pause, which was stretching a little too long. "I certainly am glad that I can trust you." If she could. But she wasn't going to think about that. She nodded to the customer, who was starting to twitch with impatience, and almost fled up the stairs. If a slave had to get permission from her owner to receive even an *as* of her own, it made a horrid kind of sense that she wouldn't be allowed to know where the cash was stashed. Unfortunately, neither did Nicole.

It seemed logical that the money should be somewhere in the room where she'd awakened. But when she stood in the doorway, the little bare box of a place didn't look as if it offered a hiding place for one *sestertius,* let alone a box full of them. She dropped to one knee to peer under the bed. Only the chamber pot there, as she'd seen earlier in the morning. Fear rose to choke her. If the box was lurking behind a loose board or in some kind of hidden compartment, she'd never find it—and her customer was waiting. Everyone was waiting for Nicole to give herself away, to prove she wasn't Umma.

She rummaged hastily through the drawers of the chest. The only box there was the one she'd found earlier, with its pots and jars of makeup. More out of desperation than anything else, she pulled the chest away from the wall—and nearly fell down in relief. There where it must have rested between chest and wall sat a wooden box. She picked it up, and grunted a little with surprise. It was heavy—and it rattled, a lovely, faintly sweet sound, the sound—she hoped— of coins sliding against one another.

The dizziness of relief went briefly dark. She'd crowed too soon. This had to be the cash box, and that was wonderful—but the box was locked.

The lock, broader and deeper than a regular padlock, was of shiny brass like a *sestertius*. So were the hasps holding it to the cash box. Those hasps looked stout. Nicole tugged hard at the lock. No give at all. No way she'd pull that lock off, or break it either, not without tools. She had to find the key.

And if she wanted to keep people downstairs from suspecting that she wasn't Umma, she'd have to find the key pretty damn quick. "Where the hell did she put it?" she muttered in English. The words felt strange on her tongue after so many hours of speaking Latin.

She knew what was in the drawer with the makeup case. She'd emptied that one out most thoroughly. She shuffled through the others one at a time, with rapidly receding hope. Last of all and reluctantly, with the same sensation she'd had when she had to change a loaded diaper, she opened the drawer filled with stained rags. She tossed them on the floor, trying to touch them as little as possible. Close to the bottom, tangled in a knot of ill-washed scraps, something caught at her fingers. She pulled at the rags. The thing inside them slipped free. She'd been afraid it would be a brooch or a buckle or a bit of useless jewelry, but her luck had finally turned. A brass key gleamed in the shadow of the drawer. It was an odd-looking thing, the teeth cut perpendicular to the shaft instead of along its edge as on the keys she knew.

When she thrust the key into the lock, it refused to turn. "Oh, come on!" she snapped at it. She twisted and jiggled. Nothing. Her fingers clenched till they began to ache.

She hissed at them and at the intractable lock—*God, don't tell me that's not the key, it's got to be the key.* Just as she was about to scream in frustration, the lock clicked and, grudgingly, ground open.

She held her breath as she opened the box. If it proved to be full of buttons or bangles or something equally worthless, she really was going to scream.

Her breath rushed out in a groan of relief. The box was filled nearly full: copper, bronze, even a little silver, coins of all sizes and states of wear, from dim and almost illegible *asses* to silver *denarii* like the one she had to make change for, and quickly too. It would be just her luck if the customer had cursed her and her fool of a slave, taken his change and his *denarius* too, and left in a snit.

She hurled the rags all anyhow back into the drawer, slammed it shut, shoved the chest against the wall, and fairly fell downstairs. The man was still there, for a miracle. He'd fallen into conversation with another of the customers, she hoped not about how strangely Umma was acting today; he broke it off in his own good time, and took the three *sesterces* that she handed him, scowling at their brassy gleam. "Took you long enough," he growled. "What did you have to do, fetch them from the mint?"

"Was that lock giving you trouble again, Mistress?" Julia asked with an air of great solicitude. Turning to the customer, she went on, "You should hear all the things Mistress Umma calls that lock. Anybody would think she'd been in the legion herself, not just married to a veteran—may he rest in peace among the shades."

"Heh," the man said: one syllable's worth of laughter. He tossed the change into his purse and stalked off jingling.

When he was gone, Nicole lifted her brows at Julia. "Am I really as bad as that about the lock?" she asked.

Julia nodded, wide-eyed: another of her exaggerated stage effects. "Worse, Mistress, since you're the one who wants to know," she replied. Lucius and Aurelia mirrored her nod, big eyes and all. So were they in it together, or was Nicole—Umma—as paranoid as that?

It paid to be paranoid in Los Angeles, but here? What could there be to be afraid of, that anyone from the twentieth century should worry about—except being discovered for what she was?

It was midmorning, as best Nicole could determine, and the children still showed no sign of going off to school. Either this was a weekend (did the Romans have weekends?), or they didn't go. Nicole could read and write, of course, and she'd seen that she was literate in Latin, too. Had Umma been as well? She hadn't seen any books in the bedroom, but that didn't prove anything. There hadn't been any in her bedroom in West Hills, either, only the latest issue of *Cosmo*. Most of the books in the house, and all the bookcases, had gone with Frank. If Nicole ever had time to read at all, she read legal briefs that she'd brought home from the office.

These children of Umma's weren't completely idle. They seemed to have their chores: cracking nuts, chopping scallions, sweeping out between waves of customers. They played, too, at headlong speed, till the inevitable happened: Aurelia screeched, Lucius whooped, they were on each other like cats and dogs. Nicole, as much amused as not—children, it seemed, were the same in every place and time—waded in and separated them. "There now," she said, "you know that's not nice. Lucius, be good to your little sister. Aurelia, don't poke your brother, it's rude. Now be good. Mother's busy."

Nicole went back to grinding wheat into flour. It was hard work: her shoulder had already started to ache. Lucius and Aurelia watched her for a little while in silence, as if fascinated; then they were at it again, Aurelia poking, Lucius thumping with his fist, one screeching, the other jeering, till it escalated into honest violence.

Nicole hissed between her teeth, left the mill for the second time and pulled them apart again, not quite so gently as before. Sore shoulder, toothache that never went away, and now children who refused to yield to reason, left her very little patience to spare. She held them apart in a firm grip, and glared into their flushed faces. "Didn't the two of you listen to a word I said?"

"Well, yes, Mother," Lucius answered seriously, "but you didn't hit us, so you couldn't have really meant it." Aurelia nodded as if she thought exactly the same preposterous thing.

Nicole stared at both of them. She understood the words they said—as words. The thoughts behind them were as strange to her as the far side of the moon. Umma must beat them, she thought, for them to talk that way. Hadn't Lucius flinched earlier when he'd thought she was going to wallop him?

At the same time, they didn't act the way abused children were supposed to act—the way she'd learned in law school they acted. There weren't any marks on them, bruises or evident broken bones. They didn't cringe when she lifted a hand, not unless they'd done something they thought deserved a spanking, or go mute when she spoke. There was nothing subdued about them. Lucius spoke of being hit calmly, as if it were something he was used to, and nothing exceptional at all.

What kind of world was this, where children expected to be beaten, and weren't obviously traumatized by it? That it wasn't a world without violence, she'd certainly known, between Frank's old movies and her own Sunday-school lessons: the Crucifixion, the persecution of Christians. But she'd never expected it to be as violent as it had turned out to be—or, what was worse, quite so easy about it. Her own century, after all, was the century of mass destruction, but life in America was sacred, and abuse, particularly abuse of children, was anathema. She'd thought better of this older, simpler age, and hoped for more than she was apparently going to get. Her jaw set in determination. These children were hers, it seemed, for the duration. Surely she had an obligation to teach them how civilized people should behave.

She approached the problem obliquely: "If you don't hit each other, I won't have any reason to want to hit you. Why don't we try that for a while and see how it works? Doesn't it make sense?"

By their expressions, Lucius and Aurelia didn't just wonder about the wisdom of what she proposed, they wondered about her sanity. They didn't say anything, which was probably a good thing. Nicole found herself mortified at her ancestress' habits: starting on wine when the sun came up, slapping the children around . . . What else did Umma do that would embarrass and worse than embarrass anyone who knew anything about health, hygiene, or progressive parenting? And when, and in what mortifying ways, would Nicole find out about it?

Lucius and Aurelia went off about some business of their own that, at least, did not involve fighting. Nicole went back to the flour mill. Before too long, she wondered how Umma found time to be any kind of mother, even a bad one. Grinding grain into flour was slow, dull work. "How many loaves do you think we'll need today?" Nicole asked Julia.

"Doesn't look like a fast day," the slave said thoughtfully. "Doesn't look like a slow day, either. Maybe we'll get away with twenty-five; we have a good bit left over from yesterday. But thirty would be better, don't you think?"

"I'm afraid I do," Nicole said with a sigh. Baking thirty loaves from scratch was a long day's work when scratch meant store-bought flour. When scratch meant wheat that needed to be ground before it could even be used, it was worse than that.

She'd made bread a few times, back in West Hills, before Frank walked out on her—when she'd had time, or made time, to cook her own, healthy meals. There was a wonderfully sensuous pleasure in mixing the flour and the yeast, adding the water or milk or buttermilk, honey or eggs or butter, mixing them in with strong slow strokes, then heaping the rich-scented elastic dough on the floured board and working it, kneading and rolling and kneading it again till it was just exactly right to let rise and bake. Later on, Frank had bought her a bread machine, but even before she realized it was a guilt-gift—a kind of material apology for his affair with Dawn—she'd put it away to gather dust. There just wasn't any tactile pleasure in dumping ingredients into a plastic box and letting it do all the kneading and rising and baking for her.

No bread machines here. No KitchenAid, either, with its miracle of a dough hook. Her own fingers did the kneading now, hers and Julia's and, after they'd been washed and washed again, Aurelia's. Lucius was off somewhere else by then, or she'd have put him to work there, too.

She had to keep stopping for customers, too, which didn't

make things any easier. Most wanted something from the unwritten menu, whose contents everyone seemed to know. A few brought in meat or fish and expected her to do the cooking—that took her aback the first time, and nearly blew her cover. Luckily Julia took the fish and slapped it on the grill without a word or a look of surprise, giving Nicole the cue for her own reaction. Everyone, whether he ate or not, drank wine: plain for an *as,* better for a *dipondius,* and the best she had for a *sestertius* a cup. People didn't seem to have heard of distilled liquor. Wine was all there was here. It was enough, and bad enough. The smell of it would stay with her, she was sure, even if she were transported back to West Hills in an instant.

Since she was unfamiliar with the oven, she had Julia bake the first batch of bread, eight loaves' worth, so she could learn by watching. It wasn't so simple as setting the heat control at 350 and coming back in half an hour. The slave had to keep the fire burning evenly, and to go by guess when it came to timing. She had a knack, or the ease of long practice. She did it right the first time, and then a second, as casual about it as if she'd done nothing special at all. And maybe, in this world, she hadn't.

After that, she popped the *as* Ofanius Valens had given her in her mouth, since there wasn't a pocket anywhere in Carnuntum that Nicole had seen, and her tunic lacked a belt and therefore one of the ubiquitous pouchlike purses. With that, and with a grin and a wave to her mistress, she went off to the baths.

Nicole had a not very brief, completely cowardly thought of forbidding her to go. Julia's departure left Nicole in charge of the *taberna.* Umma must have been able to do it on her own, or Julia would never even have offered to leave. Nicole felt overwhelmed as soon as the slave got out of sight. She had to bake the bread, cook for her customers, serve them, rinse their dishes in water that started out clean but didn't stay that way—no lemon-scented dishwashing liquid here, and no dishwasher, either—and keep half an eye, or a quarter of an eye, or an eighth, on the children. Her children, she reminded herself. If she didn't look out for them, nobody would.

She burned her hand getting her own first batch of loaves out of the oven. She plunged it into the dishwater, which, if not cold, was at least cool. The only soothing thing she could find to put on the burn was olive oil. It seemed to help a little. She would never have used it back in West Hills, but this was Carnuntum. No Aloe-Heal here. Not even an aloe plant. *The price I pay for freedom,* she thought.

Freedom, at the moment, looked suspiciously like drudgery. She was too busy even to notice how busy she was.

There were compensations. The loaves she'd turned out weren't quite perfect; she'd let the crust get browner and thicker than Julia had done. But they were damn good, she thought, for a first try. The customers certainly didn't object. If they said anything at all, it was to demand another piece hacked off the loaf.

The rest of her cooking passed the test, too, though a couple of people noticed her style wasn't the same as Umma's. "Next time I bring you a sow's womb," a plump fellow said, "I'll want it seethed in honey and vinegar, the way you usually do it, not just grilled with garlic. This wasn't bad, but I like the other better."

She nodded, gulping a little. She hadn't known what to do with the odd-shaped lump of meat she'd been handed. For that matter, she hadn't known what the odd-shaped lump of meat was. Now that she did, she wished she didn't.

She struggled for objectivity, the same mental distance she'd cultivated in the courtroom or in dealing with clients who weren't quite the kind of people she'd want in the same room with her kids. What the plump man had suggested didn't actually sound too bad, though she wouldn't have chosen that particular cut or recipe for sweet-and-sour pork.

Just as Nicole was taking the last batch of loaves out of the oven, Julia came back at last from the baths. The slave smelled much better than she had before, and her skin was several shades lighter, closer to the milky white that Nicole would have expected with her fair coloring and Germanic features. She still wasn't as fresh as Nicole would have been coming out of the shower. That newly milky skin smelled potently of olive oil. That, Nicole realized, was one of the many rank perfumes that impregnated the tunic Julia still wore. Not only hadn't she had it cleaned, Nicole didn't think it ever had been cleaned, not in the months—maybe years—Julia had been wearing it.

Still, thought Nicole, the bath had been an improvement. Julia carried herself a little straighter, hunched her shoulders a little less. She examined the new-baked bread with a judicious eye. "A little underdone," she judged, "but no one will complain about it." She beamed at Nicole. "I hope it wasn't too much trouble, Mistress. The bath was wonderful."

She punctuated that with a happy wiggle that caught the eye of every male in the place. There all too obviously wasn't anything between her body and the much-worn tunic. Equally obviously, she hadn't been quite dry when she put the tunic back on after her bath. A wet T-shirt it wasn't, but it left precious little to imagination.

Nicole couldn't match Julia's happy tone, not with the thoughts she was thinking. "All right," she said a bit more roughly than she'd intended. "Get back to work."

Julia obeyed her with evident contentment. From the way she was acting, she'd expected nothing gentler, and probably something a great deal more harsh. Even in her depths of disgust for the male half of the species, Nicole couldn't seem to match Umma for ferocity.

Some time in the late afternoon—Nicole kept glancing at her left wrist, at a watch that wasn't there—Titus Calidius Severus strode briskly into the restaurant with a pair of plump trout. "Hello, Umma," he said cheerfully. "Thought I'd wait till things thinned out over here before I brought you these to fry."

He smelled worse than the fish would have if he'd left them in the sun for three days. Nicole's nose had tuned out most of the background stink of Carnuntum, but the fuller and dyer might have had a chamber pot spilled over his head. As she dipped the trout in an egg-and-flour batter she'd made

up not long before, Nicole approached that by—she hoped—
easy stages: "Do you have to have those jars out in front of
your shop for—for men to—to piss in?"

"You've teased me about that often enough," he said with
a chuckle. She had, had she? Or Umma had. Nicole wasn't
teasing. Not in the least. He went on, "They're not wagging
their prongs at you, dear, even if it looks that way." He
reached across the counter and chucked her under the chin.

No one, not here, not anywhere, had ever done that to her.
Even as a child, she hadn't been the kind of little girl who
invited such an insult. She certainly didn't either invite or
accept it as an adult. She slapped his hand down. To her
utter fury, he only laughed and said, "Ai, pretty lady! I've
had mates in the legion who weren't as fierce as you."

Nicole sucked in a breath, nearly choking on it. Her voice
when it came was almost too tight to be audible. "Don't
you—ever—do that to me again. Or you won't eat these fish,
you'll wear them."

Somewhat to her surprise, he seemed to realize that she
meant it. "All right," he said willingly enough, if with a hint
of puzzlement. "You never said you didn't like it before—
but what's a woman if she can't change her mind, eh?" He
shrugged, grinned rather ruefully at himself, and went on
more seriously, "Right. So. Pisspots. Don't like them either,
do you? Look at it this way. They're neater than pissing
against the wall—and I'd be out of work without them.
There's nothing like stale piss to get the grease out of wool
so it'll hold the dye. If rosewater would do the trick, I'd use
it. But alas, pretty lady, it doesn't."

Nicole finished frying the trout in silence. She hadn't
thought whether Calidius Severus might actually need the
urine he collected. She hadn't wanted to think about it. Not
to put too fine a point on it, she'd been too busy being
grossed out.

She was supposed to be glad that this was a more natural,
more organic world than the one she'd left: no plastics, no
polyester, no coal-tar dyes. Urine was natural, all right; anyone who'd ever changed a baby knew that. But Carnuntum

was rubbing her nose in the fact that natural and pleasant weren't necessarily synonyms, no matter what the commercials for Quaker 100% Natural said.

As Calidius began to eat his fish, he set a *dupondius* on the counter. Nicole started to give him back an *as*. He waved for her not to bother. "Call it a peace offering," he said.

"All right," she said after a pause. "A peace offering. Thank you."

"These trout are good," he said after he'd taken a bite or two. "I don't think you ever did them quite like this before. Tasty." He ate another mouthful. He used his fingers. They were a peculiar color, like nothing human: mottled blue and green and muddy brown, as if in dyeing cloth he had dyed his skin with it.

As for his table manners, nobody here had any better. Nicole had found spoons and a few knives in a pot by a stack of plates, but no forks. She wondered if Calidius had washed his hands before coming over with the fish. Then she wished she hadn't. He said, "I don't want you angry at me, you know."

"I'm not angry," she answered, more or less sincerely.

"Good." He studied her. "Are you not-angry enough for me to come over tonight?" The meaning of that was unmistakable—and, as plainly, he expected her to say yes. Her face froze.

He saw. His own face stiffened in response. He stood up abruptly, grimaced, and shoved the plate at her. There was no meat left, only bones, neatly picked and pushed into a pile. Without a word, he stamped out of the restaurant.

Julia was gaping. So were all three of the remaining customers. Nicole sighed. So Umma and Calidius had been an item, had they? Why on earth the woman whose body Nicole was wearing would want a man who smelled like an outhouse was beyond her.

Whatever the reason for it, Julia obviously thought Umma and Titus Calidius Severus had had a good thing going. Well, to hell with what Julia thought. Nicole had come back here for herself, not to play bedwarmer to the piss merchant across the street.

She would have told Julia so, in no uncertain terms, but two more men and a woman came into the place just then, and set her to running about again. She stayed busy till sundown, which came late this time of year.

As soon as it began to get dark, business didn't just fall off: it died. Nicole didn't fully understand that till she lighted a lamp. Matches she didn't have; she had to use a twist of straw from a basket by one of the cookfires, and light it from the fire. The oil-soaked wick sputtered and guttered before it came alive. The flame did next to nothing to push back the gathering gloom. Not for the first time, and very probably not for the last, she missed the daily magic of electric power.

The *taberna* was empty. So was the street. The children had come in not long before, devoured a supper of bread and cheese and a little of the smoked pork, and gone upstairs with Julia. They hadn't insisted that she kiss them, though they'd stood in a line, slave and children alike, and said a polite good night. Nicole hadn't tried to keep them downstairs, or tried to persuade them to eat a few vegetables with their bread and protein. She was too tired to fight that battle tonight. Tomorrow, she'd promised herself, on the children's behalf. Even as she thought it she'd been struck with a memory of older guilt: Justin and his chicken nuggets and french fries, eating a meal that couldn't possibly be good for him, because his mother was too tired to fix a proper dinner.

She missed him suddenly, so fiercely that for a moment she couldn't breathe. She missed Kimberley. She missed the house in West Hills. She even—

No. She didn't miss Frank. Not for one split second.

She took the lamp with her to the front door and stood in it, peering out. Good Lord, she thought: she hadn't set foot outside all day. She looked across the street, then up and down. A few torches and lamps flickered, but only a few. Above the flat black line of roofs, a piercingly bright star—

Venus?—hung in the western sky, at the edge of the skirts of twilight.

After work back in West Hills, she would have watched TV or read a magazine or put a CD on the stereo. No TV here, no magazines, no stereo or CDs.

Even if she'd had the energy for them, she'd have been too exhausted to bother. She pulled the solid weight of the door shut and barred it, then shuttered the windows. Picking up the feeble lamp again from where she'd set it on the table by the door, she retrieved the cash box and carried it upstairs. The stairs seemed steeper than ever in that bare hint of light, narrow and precipitous and ripe for a fall. But she managed them without even tripping, let alone breaking her neck.

The curtains were drawn in the other rooms. She ventured to look in. Two were empty, though one had a bed in it. The third was full of the sound of quiet breathing. Something large lay across the door. The rasp of a snore sent Nicole starting back, even as she realized what it was. Julia, sleeping on the floor, being a living obstacle to anything that tried to come in and get at the children. It was touching, in its way, though Nicole made a mental note to give Julia permission to sleep in one of the unused rooms. Whatever those were for. Guests? Storage? In the morning, or whenever she could, she'd have to look and see.

But not tonight. She was swaying on her feet. If Julia hadn't been in the way, she might have gone in and tucked the children in as she would have done with Justin or Kimberley, but she wasn't at all sure she could do it without waking the slave. Best to let them be.

In the room that she'd begun to think of as hers, she set the lamp on the chest and the cash box beside it. She had no energy at all for wrestling the heavy chest and hiding the box. What could happen to it, after all? The door was locked below, and she'd barred the door up here. She used the chamber pot—a luxury she'd had too little of in that long full day—and let herself sink down on the bed. Before she could even rise to blow out the lamp, she was deeply and soundly asleep.

5

NICOLE WOKE EARLIER THAN she'd intended. The lamp had gone out. It was pitch-black outside, though the moon had climbed over the roof of the house, the shop, whatever it was, next door and sent a thin strip of wan gray light through the bedroom window. She hadn't bothered to shutter it: this was the second floor; what could get in?

She noticed the light only peripherally, in that it helped her find the chamber pot. The one advantage of having the damned thing right there under the bed was that she didn't need to race down the hall to the bathroom. That was as well, for she didn't think she would have made it. The next couple of minutes were among the most urgently unpleasant she'd known for as long as she could remember.

"Stomach flu!" she groaned when the worst of it was over. What awful luck!

It was even more awful than she'd thought at first. There wasn't any toilet paper. She used one of the rags from the drawer in the chest, and threw it into the chamber pot afterwards. And regretted instantly and powerfully that it wasn't a toilet after all. A toilet you could flush. A pot just sat there, stinking. She lay back down with another groan. Even without the stink, she didn't think she'd have gone back to sleep again in a hurry. She could tell she wasn't done yet. A herd of buffalo with iron hooves was stampeding through her guts.

Just as she finished the second bout—almost as bad as the first, and no promise more wasn't coming—somebody knocked on her door. "What is it?" she said weakly, amazed she'd remembered to use Latin. If it wasn't the end of the world, she had no intention of getting up for it.

It was worse than the end of the world. "Mistress," Julia said through the door, "Aurelia is puking something fierce,

and Lucius has the trots." She sounded as if she was afraid
she'd be killed for bringing the bad news.

Who knew? Maybe in Carnuntum, a slave would be. "I'm
coming," Nicole groaned. She got out of bed and stood swaying. These were, in effect, her kids. If her guess was right,
they really were her relatives. They were her responsibility,
that was certain. *Single mother then,* she thought in weary
disgust. *Single mother now.* She hadn't figured on that when
she came back to Carnuntum.

She unbarred the door. Julia was standing in the hallway
holding a wan and flickering lamp. She looked like a ghost
with her sleep-disheveled hair and her pale face.

Her voice was real enough, shakily stern—almost smug.
It reeked of *I told you so.* "Mistress, it really wasn't very
wise of you to give them water to drink all day. You know
perfectly well—" She paused to inhale, which must have
given her a good whiff of the chamber pot. "Oh, dear, Mistress—you've got it, too!"

"Yes, I've got it, too," Nicole said. "Happy day." A piece
of limerick ran through her head: *Her rumblings abdominal
were simply phenomenal.* And wasn't that the sad and sorry
truth? Any minute now, dogs would start barking at the
noises her insides were making.

But that had nothing to do with anything. She was on
mommy duty now. "Come on," she said as brusquely as her
queasy innards would allow. "Take me to the kids."

As they walked down the hall, Julia picked up where she'd
left off. "Drinking water all the time isn't healthy," she insisted. "I did try to tell you, but you didn't want to hear,
Mistress, even though everybody knows it."

A lot of what everybody knows was nonsense. That had
been so in Los Angeles, and was bound to be so in Carnuntum. Still, Nicole thought, what if the water really was bad,
the way it was in Mexico? She hadn't had any trouble drinking it in Petronell or Vienna on her honeymoon.

Her mouth twisted. That was the twentieth century, not the
second. Evidently chlorine had something going for it after
all.

But wine? Her frown deepened. People here drank like fish. If they weren't alcoholics, it wasn't from lack of trying.

There was no way she was taking that route herself. She'd watched her father crawl into a bottle and pull the stopper in after him. She'd never touched a drop of alcohol, and she was damned if she was going to start now.

Her belly tied itself in a knot and yanked hard. She gasped and doubled up. God! She hadn't felt this bad since she went into labor with Justin. Whatever this was, it was nasty.

This time, it let her go. She straightened and made it the rest of the way down the hall, where Julia was waiting beside one of the curtained doorways. Her nose told her it was the right place. It smelled even worse in there than in her bedroom: between the two of them, Lucius and Aurelia had been sick from both ends.

Nicole took the lamp from Julia. Its flame was low. "Go fetch another one," she said. "This one's almost out of oil."

Julia didn't seem to mind the errand. The air would be fresher where she'd been sent, that was certain. "Yes, Mistress," she said with suspicious good cheer.

As Nicole listened to her thump her way downstairs, it struck her that she hadn't even bothered to say please. She'd treated Julia like a . . . like a slave again.

No time to waste in feeling guilty. Both children were groaning, a sound she knew too well. At the same time, the lamp guttered and went out. There was no moonlight on this side of the house, no way to see anything. She tracked the kids by their moans and their heavy breathing, and a little catch that must have been a sob. She barked a shin against the hard side of a bed, swallowed a curse—damn, that hurt!—and bent to feel for a forehead. She found one, and another next to it. Hot. Hers was probably hot, too, not that she had time to care. Kids first.

The lamp Julia brought was marginally brighter than the one Nicole had left by the door after it burned out. It still shed about as much light as a nightlight back in West Hills.

Julia set it down on a stool and stepped back against the wall and waited.

That was what guards did in Frank's pet old movies. The gesture must mean the same here as there. It was Nicole's show. She looked around a little desperately. So now what?

In West Hills, she had known what to do. Here—Here, her own toothache, which hadn't gone away, which as far as she could tell would never go away, had already taught her Latin didn't have a word for Tylenol. It didn't have a word for aspirin, either. By unpleasant but perfect logic, no word meant no thing.

Back in West Hills, she wouldn't have thought of giving aspirin to kids with fever anyhow, because of the small but real risk of Reye's syndrome. Back in West Hills, she'd had other, better choices. Her mother, who hadn't, and who hadn't known about Reye's syndrome, either, had given Nicole aspirin plenty of times. Nothing bad had happened. Nicole would have given it to Lucius and Aurelia—and taken some herself—without a qualm, if only she'd had any.

Julia stirred, probably deciding Nicole wasn't thinking straight because she was sick. "Shall I get the willow-bark decoction, Mistress?" she asked.

Oh, joy, Nicole thought. *A folk remedy.* In West Hills, she'd have laughed it off. In Carnuntum, without any other useful choice, she grasped at it almost eagerly. It might not do any good, but it might not hurt, either. Folk remedies weren't supposed to kill, were they?

Julia was waiting for her to say something. "Yes," she said more impatiently than she'd meant. "Yes, go on, go get it— please," she added a bit belatedly.

Julia seemed almost relieved to be snapped at, though the politeness of the last word made her eyes roll briefly before she darted back down the stairs.

The children might be sick, but they weren't too sick to make a whole range of revolted noises. "Willow bark!" said Lucius, who seemed the livelier of the two. "Ick! Ick ick ick!"

"Be quiet," Nicole said to him. No, snapped at him. She was too blasted sick herself to be nice about it. Somewhat to her surprise, he shut up, though he kept making horrible faces.

Julia came back none too soon with a bottle and a tiny cup. The stuff she poured out looked horrid and smelled worse, but Nicole held her nose and gulped it down regardless. Its taste was even worse than its smell—gaggingly, throat-wrenchingly bitter.

The kids were staring at her as if she'd done something ridiculously brave. Taking medicine, it seemed, was no more popular in Carnuntum than it had been in California. That might have been funny, had she felt less like dying.

She'd expected the stuff to be nasty. It was. It was also familiar, which she hadn't expected. When she'd had a sore throat, her mother had made her gargle with a couple of aspirins dissolved in warm water. God, she'd hated that! This taste wasn't far from it.

Nicole made the kids take the decoction anyway. If it tasted like aspirin, maybe it had something like aspirin in it. Hadn't she heard or read somewhere that aspirin came from some folk remedy or other? Maybe it came from this one.

"Julia, you're feeling all right," Nicole said tiredly, "and I'm not." Even in the dim lamplight, she saw how smug Julia looked. She lacked the energy to call her on it. "Would you take care of the chamber pots in here and in my room, please?"

"Yes, Mistress," Julia said. Her method of taking care of a pot was to pick it up, carry it to the window, and dump it out on the ground below. She went back to Nicole's bedroom and did the same thing with the one in there, or so the second wet splat declared.

The words were shocked right out of Nicole's head. If there'd been any to be found, they would have come out in a shriek. No toilets was one thing. No sewers—but Rome had sewers! She'd seen a documentary. Where were Carnuntum's sewers? Didn't these people know anything about sanitation?

No wonder flies buzzed in through her window. And no

wonder at all that Carnuntum smelled the way it did—and the water wasn't fit to drink.

The willow-bark decoction made her feel better—not a lot better, but some. And the kids' foreheads were cooler. They'd stopped groaning and subsided into a fretful doze. She hugged them and, after a little hesitation, kissed them. They didn't object. She felt strange: half like a babysitter, taking care of children not her own; half like a mother. If these had really been her own—

She didn't know any Latin lullabies. On sudden inspiration, and because she couldn't think of anything else, she hummed "Rockabye Baby." Even without the English words, maybe the tune would do the trick. Apparently it did. First Aurelia's breathing, then Lucius', slowed and deepened into the cadence of sleep.

"That's a nice song, Mistress," Julia whispered as they tiptoed out of the children's room. "Has it got words?"

"If it does, I don't know them," Nicole answered, with a small stab of guilt at the lie—or maybe it was her gut clenching again. "I'm going to go back to sleep now myself, or try. If I do, you'll be on your own for a while in the morning. I hope you can—"

"I understand," Julia said. "I've managed before. Rest if you can, Mistress."

Lumpy mattress. Scratchy blanket. Leftover stink from the dregs in the pot. Nicole didn't care. Her belly wasn't churning so hard. Next to that, nothing else counted. She yawned, stretched, wiggled . . . slept.

When Nicole woke up, daylight was streaming in through the window. She still didn't feel good, not even close, but, after she used the chamber pot a little less explosively than she had in the nighttime, the buffaloes decided to end their stampede through her insides and head off somewhere to graze.

There was nowhere to dump the chamber pot except out the window. "Sewers," she muttered. "This town needs sewers." She gritted her teeth and dumped the pot as Julia had the night before.

She dressed quickly in a fresh loincloth and tunic, and looked at herself in the mirror in the makeup kit. She looked like a chimney sweep. Most of the smoke that hadn't gone through the hole in the roof the day before had clung to her.

She washed her face with water from the *terra sigillata* pitcher, careful now not to get any water in her mouth, the way she would have been in a shower south of the border.

The water was bad, no arguing with that—or with the reek that lingered around the emptied chamber pot. So what was she supposed to drink? Wine? She could water it, she supposed—wouldn't the alcohol kill germs as easily as it slaughtered brain cells? She'd get a lower dose then, too. Maybe she could work out a formula as to how little wine she could get away with before the water went toxic.

She still didn't like it. She liked even less that the kids had to drink the stuff in any proportion. Maybe she could talk them into drinking milk after all, and never mind the Marcomanni and the Quadi, whoever they were.

She studied her newly washed face in the mirror. Not a chimney sweep, not anymore. Now she just looked like hell. "That," she said to nobody in particular, "is why God made makeup."

Women here, she'd observed, powdered and painted themselves as heavily as a geisha in full regalia—and into much the same dead-white mask. The makeup Umma had used was less finely ground than the pricey Clinique that Nicole had held onto even when money got tight, as her one by-God extravagance. Its texture and color made her think, rather disjointedly, of quite another white powder, one that had been distressingly common in L.A. Rome might lack flush toilets and bathroom tissue—but it was also blessedly free of cocaine.

It was free of powderpuff and makeup brushes, too. She smoothed the powder on as best she could with a bit of rag— no cotton balls, either. Who'd have thought there'd be a world without cotton balls? Or swabs? Or—

Or eyebrow pencils, or lipsticks. Her finger had to do for both, and the rag growing grubbier with each step in the ritual. No cold cream, either, to remove mistakes or clean her fingers. If she could figure out how all those things were made, she'd be willing to bet there'd be a market for them.

It was enough, for the time being, that she'd armored her face against the world. She'd understated the effect—probably people would think she was trying for a little too much of the natural look—but she still looked, to her own eyes, clownish and overdone. "Tammy Faye Does Carnuntum," she said to her reflection. A smile, she noticed, cracked the paint just a little. No wonder geishas never seemed to wear an expression, just the blank white mask.

It did what it was supposed to do, at least. It kept the world from guessing how lousy she felt.

"Cash box," she reminded herself, and scooped up that and the key before she headed out the door. She didn't go straight downstairs, but paused at the curtain to the children's room. No sound came from inside. She peered in. Enough of the early light seeped through their shuttered window to show them both still sleeping. Their faces were quiet, neither flushed nor pale. Aurelia had taken all the covers, but Lucius didn't seem to mind. He slept on his stomach with his black hair all in a tousle. He looked nothing at all like either of Nicole's in the way he slept, but the soft baby-cheeks, the nub of nose, caught at her throat.

That was why children looked the way they did, wasn't it? So their mothers wouldn't throw them out before they could walk. Not just their mothers, either. Whoever found herself in charge of them.

Aurelia stirred and kicked off the covers. Nicole froze, but neither child woke. Aurelia was clutching a cloth doll the way Kimberley would have hung onto Scratchy the bobcat. Other toys lay on the floor: another doll or two, a toy cart, a wooden sword.

Nicole frowned at the sword. No children of hers were going to play with war toys—even if they weren't, strictly speaking, her children.

Her frown changed, darkened. Lucius' father had been a soldier, from what she'd heard. Titus Calidius Severus was a veteran, too; he'd made that plain. Several of her other customers, from snatches of overheard conversation, also must have served in the legions. A legion had been based around here—she remembered that from her honeymoon day trip to Petronell. Hadn't Rome had a Vietnam, then? Didn't they understand what a horror war was?

She shook herself, shrugged. War was far enough away from this here and this now, that there was no point in worrying about it. She slipped backward as quietly as she could, let the door-curtain fall back into place, and trudged down to her work. She was her own boss, after all. Nobody else was going to do it for her. No secretarial pool, no janitorial staff. Just herself—and Julia.

Julia had the tavern open already, the fires going, everything in order and ready to start the day. She greeted Nicole almost too brightly, though her words were solicitous enough: "Good morning, Mistress! How are you doing now? Are you well?"

Nicole caught herself wondering just how smug Julia felt. She quashed the thought and answered as civilly as she could manage, which wasn't very, without coffee and with none in sight for the next however many hundred years. "I'm all right. I may even live."

Julia smiled one of her wide halfwit smiles. "Oh, Mistress! The last couple of days, you've had such a funny way of putting things."

Nicole's heart thudded. God—what if Julia had guessed—what in the world was she going to—

But Julia's smile had turned conspiratorial. "And here you put your paint on, and you didn't even bother with it yesterday."

"Right," Nicole said a little too quickly. "Yes, that's right. I didn't need it yesterday. Today—"

Julia nodded, woman to woman now instead of slave to mistress. "I know just what you mean. There's nothing like a nice coating of white lead to keep people from guessing

you aren't right underneath it." She stopped. Her voice rose
in surprise. "Mistress! Where are you going?"

Nicole was already halfway up the stairs. "To wash it off!"
she flung back. *My God,* she thought, over and over. *My
God!* Had she swallowed any? Had any gone up her nose?

My God. Even the makeup was poisonous. And hadn't
she thought it looked a little like cocaine? It was worse than
cocaine—a more certain, a more deadly killer than cocaine
had ever been. Had she got any in her eyes? Could the blood
vessels in her eyes absorb it? God, what was she supposed
to do? She didn't know a thing about lead poisoning, except
that it was bad—and she was a prime candidate for it.

At the top of the stairs, she almost bowled over Lucius,
who obviously had felt well enough to get out of bed.
"Mother!" he called as she rushed past him. "What's the
matter? Are you all right?"

She didn't answer. She dived into her bedroom, slammed
and barred the door, and leaped on the washbasin. No face-
cloth, no towel, but rags—rags! She yanked a fistful out of
the drawer and dunked them, and scrubbed at her face, over
and over, till the skin stung and burned. Every time she
splashed herself with water, she made herself blow out
through her mouth and nose, to keep from getting any more
of the lead into her system. Once she had it all off, or hoped
to heaven she did, she took the little pot of makeup over to
the window and dumped it out, as she had with the chamber
pot not long before. This time, she watched the cloud of
white powder drift down to the ground. No one was passing
below, to be startled by the small deadly snow. Nothing
moved but the flies, seething in the noisome mess that, she
could see, lined every house-wall. There'd be a few million
fewer, she thought, thanks to her latest contribution.

She was calm again—or calm enough, at least, to face the
world. She took a deep breath and braved the stairs again.

Lucius and Aurelia were both down below and both eating
breakfast: a little bit of bread without oil, and something in
a cup that was probably watered wine. Nicole couldn't find
the energy to make an issue of it.

Julia, of course, wasn't about to leave well enough alone. "Why did you get rid of your makeup, Mistress?" she asked. "You looked nice with it on."

Nicole caught herself wondering if Julia was a little slow in the head—or if it was a game slaves played, to ask questions that sounded wide-eyed innocent but were calculated to catch a person in the raw.

If that was a game, Nicole could play one of her own. "Can I get face powder that doesn't have lead in it?" she asked. And held her breath, hoping she hadn't come too close to sounding like the foreigner she was.

Julia didn't seem to find the question that far out of the ordinary. Maybe she was slow; or maybe slaves learned to expect any kind of oddity from their masters. She frowned, as if in thought. "Some people use white flour, but I don't like it myself—you don't either, much, do you? No matter how tight you close it up, sooner or later it gets bugs in it. That never happens with white lead."

"I should hope not!" Nicole said. "Lead's poisonous."

"Oh, it can't be, Mistress." Julia sounded absolutely sure of herself. "If it were, they wouldn't use it for water pipes."

Nicole started to say *They do?* but stopped before the question was out of her mouth. They did, and she didn't need Julia's word for it. The Latin for lead was *plumbum.* She and Julia had said it close to a dozen times between them. What was a plumber but somebody who messed around with *plumbum?* It was a lead-pipe cinch that was how plumbers had got their name.

What she did say was, "They shouldn't."

"Mistress," Julia said in a tone that reminded Nicole rather too strongly of her mother trying to be very, very patient with her father when he came home—because he'd said or done something right out of line, but if she called him on it too soon or too strongly, he'd take a swing at her, "Mistress, really, haven't you been complaining an awful lot, the past day or two?" *And about things like wine and water that made you nice and sick, too,* Nicole could almost hear her thinking, *and look where that got you.* "What are they supposed to use for pipes, Mistress? Clay breaks too easy, and wood rots."

"Copper—" Nicole began.

"And how expensive would that be?" Julia asked. Impossibly so, her tone said. "Besides, copper's no good for you. Cook vegetables in copper and you'll see the verdigris right away, and taste it, too." She made a face. "And it'll sicken your stomach faster than drinking water will. That's why they put lead on the inside of copper kettles, for goodness' sake."

"It is?" Nicole said faintly. "They do?"

Yesterday morning, she'd looked around the restaurant with delight. Now she looked again, with growing horror. Some of her cooking pots were lead-lined? Her eye fell on a jar of olive oil, which was made of glazed pottery. What was in the glaze? Every so often, the TV news would report that batches of stoneware from China or someplace were being banned from the USA because their glazes had too much lead. The amphorae of wine under the counter were glazed, too, all but the one that held the cheapest local stuff. You couldn't even put lead foil over the corks on wine bottles anymore, not in California you couldn't.

God knew, this wasn't California. This wasn't anyplace fit or healthy for human occupation, from the looks of it.

What about the *terra sigillata* pitcher and bowl in her room? How was she going to know? How could she find out?

God. God, God, God. What was that book she'd seen in a used bookstore once, with the day-glo pink cover? *Future Shock,* that was it. So what was this? Past shock? Culture shock? Pure unadulterated shock? Nothing here was safe. Everything could poison you. Every little taken-for-granted thing.

Julia was happily oblivious to Nicole's confusion. She seemed to think they were still playing some kind of game, a game of wits maybe, a test of her cultural literacy. Or was it literacy, if it had nothing to do with reading?

Julia spoke again as the voice of sweet reason, as if that

were the role she'd decided she was cast in. "Besides, Mistress, if lead were poisonous, we'd all be dead, wouldn't we?" She laughed at the absurdity of the notion, the same way people in the twentieth century had laughed at the notion that DDT might hurt the environment.

Lead poisoning was insidious, Nicole knew that. It took a long time to build up. But she couldn't explain that here, even if there were words to express it. Julia wouldn't listen, any more than people had listened about DDT, or fluorocarbons, or the hole in the ozone layer.

Julia seemed to have decided the game was over; that it was time to go back to work. Her tone had changed, and even the way she held herself. She was the slave again, carefully submissive; no more arguments, no thinly veiled rebukes. "What would you like for breakfast, Mistress?" she asked.

Nicole wasn't pleased to note how glad she was that Julia had gone back to being servile again. "Bread and watered wine, same as the children," she said—and that was a capitulation, too, but she couldn't see any way out of it. Except possibly one. "The one-*as* wine," she added, "nothing fancy." That was the one that came in the unglazed amphora. If it was bad wine, so much the better. Then maybe she could keep from growing too fond of it.

Even if it didn't have lead—she hoped it didn't have lead—it still had alcohol in it. The odor rising from the (unglazed, thank God) cup made her shiver. She could all but hear her father downstairs yelling at her mother, while she lay in bed with the covers pulled up over her head and tried not to listen. She had to will herself to sip.

Diluted, the wine tasted like watery, half-spoiled grape juice. It had a tang to it, a sharpness and a kind of dizziness in back of it, that had to be the alcohol. She'd never tried any before, to know. She'd refused.

Her heart was thumping again, as it had when she discovered her face was armored in lead. She'd thought, somehow, that the first taste would do it: would hit her hard enough to make her stagger. Apparently, that wasn't how it worked.

She sipped again, deeper, and again, till the cup was empty. Did she feel anything? Was there anything to feel? Maybe she was a tiny bit more detached from the world than she had been before. Maybe she wasn't. She'd been in varying degrees of fog since she woke up in Carnuntum—and for certain sure she was detached; she was a complete stranger to this whole world and time.

Julia was watching her, nodding sagely, as if she could see an effect Nicole couldn't feel. "That will do you good, Mistress," she said.

"I doubt it," Nicole said. Her belly was rumbling again, knots and snarls that were more nerves than sickness. The wine hadn't made it worse, at least. She was grateful for that.

Medicine. She could think of it as medicine. Even her mother had had a stash of medicinal brandy, that her father had never managed to find.

Julia's voice broke in on her thoughts, as so often before: as if it were a kind of lifeline, an anchor to this world. "Are you feeling well enough to go out and buy things today, Mistress, or will you send me?"

Nicole focused abruptly and too sharply, though the edges of things still wavered just a little. Julia was watching her alertly, with a look she'd seen on a dog hoping for a portion of the humans' dinner. So was this a new game, then? A gambit to get hold of some money, to do God knew what with it?

Nonsense, Nicole thought. Julia could get at the till either way, whether she stayed to mind the tavern or went out shopping. Maybe she just wanted to get out of the house.

If that was it, too bad. Nicole hadn't gone out since she got here, either. Her insides still felt very uncertain; and even though Imodium looked like a Latin word, it surely wasn't, or she'd have found a bottle of it by now. Maybe if she could get out, breathe relatively fresh air, see more of Carnuntum than she could from window or doorway, she'd forget her indisposition for long enough to make it go away.

"I'll go," she said. Julia's face fell, but she didn't argue. After all, her expression said, she wasn't the boss. Nicole did her best to sound brisk. "Let's see—what do we need?"

Julia visibly swallowed her disappointment to focus on the duties at hand. "That amphora of Falernian in there"—she pointed to the bar—"will last the day out, I think, but not tomorrow. And we're out of scallions and raisins, and we could use some more mutton."

"I'll get some fish, too, if I see any worth buying," Nicole said. She had to say something, if she expected people to think she was staying on top of things.

"All right, Mistress." Julia sounded vaguely dubious, but then she nodded. She'd dropped her façade of submission again, Nicole noticed. It seemed to go up when Nicole was giving orders, but to go down when they were working to-gether—as if a slave could think for herself, sometimes, if her mistress gave the signal. Had Nicole been giving the right signals after all?

Maybe it was all those years of dealing with secretaries—pardon, administrative assistants—and paralegals. They hadn't been much more than slave labor either, not at the pay they got and with the workload they carried.

Julia had gone right on talking, in a tone that reminded Nicole almost poignantly of a paralegal invited to voice an opinion on a case: "Fish spoils fast, so there's always that risk, but we can eat it ourselves tonight if no one else does. And people will probably order it. You were doing some interesting things with it yesterday when they brought it in for you to cook. Word will get around."

"I suppose so," Nicole said, though she wondered how. No TV, no radio, no telephones, no e-mail. How did people find out what was going on in the world, or even in Car-nuntum?

She wasn't going to find out by staying cooped up here. Under Julia's eye, she unlocked the cash box and chose a selection of coins, picking them out with care, as if she knew to the *as* how much she was leaving behind. Julia's glance didn't flicker; her brow didn't wrinkle. Nicole drew in a breath of relief, and escaped out the door.

She turned left more or less at random. She'd gone several

steps before she realized: she didn't know where to buy any of the things on her mental list. Nothing in sight looked like a supermarket, or even like the corner grocery stores the supermarkets had forced out of business. A vague memory of her honeymoon brought to mind tiny shops, boucheries and boulangeries and something with a horse's head out front that she'd found very pretty till she learned it was a horsemeat butcher. She didn't see anything like that, either.

A voice called out behind her. She stopped and turned, expecting it to be Julia, calling out that she'd gone the wrong way. But it was someone from the next house down, a little bony bird of a woman with an extraordinary crown of curled and frizzed hair, waving and calling, "Umma! Oh, Umma! Good morning!"

Nicole almost didn't respond. But the woman was looking straight at her, looking so delighted that Nicole wondered if Umma and she were long-lost sisters. She raised her hand and waved back, trying to put a little enthusiasm in it, so as not to seem suspicious.

"Off to market then?" the woman asked. "And isn't it a lovely morning? Do come over later, will you please, dear? It's been ages since we had a good gossip!"

Nicole hoped her expression didn't betray what she felt, which was a kind of horror. Neighbors in West Hills didn't lean out of upstairs windows—if they had any—and yodel at passersby. This neighbor obviously thought she was a friend, too. Or else she really was a relative.

"Later," Nicole managed to say. "Yes, I'll come over later." In about ten years. She put on a bright company smile, and wished she had a watch to glance at significantly. "Well. I'm off, then. Good morning."

"Good morning!" the stranger caroled, and mercifully ducked back inside.

She hadn't said Nicole was going in the wrong direction, either. Nicole decided to take that as an omen. She strode on out, feeling better already, though she had to be careful where she stepped; and she kept a wary eye on the windows above. Some of her original sense of adventure was coming

back. She felt like a brave explorer—Montezuma's Revenge
and all.

Pigeons strutted in the streets of Carnuntum, arrogant and
brainless and half tame, just as they did in Los Angeles. Life
here was riskier for them, however. A fellow tossed a fine-
meshed net over a couple, scooped them up before they could
let out more than one startled coo, and ran back inside his
house, shouting, "I've got supper for today, Claudia!"

Nicole wouldn't have wanted to eat them. Living in Los
Angeles, she'd come to despise the automobile for the pollution it caused, even while she worshipped at its shrine. No
cars in Carnuntum. But that didn't mean no pollution, as
she'd thought it would. The streets were packed deep with
ox droppings, horse droppings, donkey droppings. The pigeons mined them for any number of treasures: seeds, in-
sects, the unmistakable and nauseating pale wriggle of a
worm.

One good look at what they were pulling out of the heaps
of ordure, and Nicole knew she wouldn't touch one of those
birds if a waiter from Le Bistro brought it.

She'd hated the air she'd had to breathe in the San Fernando Valley, back in the twentieth century: thick, stinking,
and the color of filthy old chinos. It had stung her eyes and
caught at her lungs with every breath she took. The air in
Carnuntum stank worse than the air in the Valley ever had.
It was clogged with smoke. It stung her eyes and caught at
her lungs with every breath she took.

It was also full of flies. Every time someone walked past,
they rose in buzzing clouds from the dung that beasts of
burden had left behind, and from the occasional dog turds in
the street. At least, Nicole hoped that was what those were.
Some of them seemed on the large side for that.

The flies didn't all go back to their suppers, either. Some
decided to take the long way home, pausing to snack on
passing animals or, better yet, people. Slapping while walking looked to be as automatic as breathing.

It wasn't so easy or mindless for Nicole, nor apparently

so effective, either. In the first few minutes after she'd left the restaurant, she took at least three powerfully annoying bites. These weren't little itching mosquitoes, either, like the ones that had made the summer evenings miserable in Indiana. These were horseflies—B-52s, people had called them when she was little. Their bites stabbed like a red-hot needle.

Slapping, cursing, wishing in vain for a vat of Woodsman's Fly Repellent, she turned off her own street onto a larger one. A block or two down, that one ran into a bigger one yet, one big enough to boast a cobblestoned paving. At the intersection sat a fountain from which water splashed lethargically into a stone tank. Women stood around chatting and filling jugs from the tank.

They can't use all that for cooking or washing, Nicole thought. *They must drink some of it.* She shuddered, wondering how often it made them sick. And that was just the water itself, without help from lead pipes and lead-glazed jars. She shuddered again. If the galloping trots didn't get you, lead poisoning would.

A block farther down the cobblestoned street stood a marble statue, half again life size, of a nude, bearded man. The Getty Museum, twenty minutes from West Hills, had a marvelous collection of ancient statuary; the couple of times Frank dragged her there on one of his cultural-literacy jags, Nicole had admired the cool white elegance of the stone.

This statue was neither cool nor white nor elegant. It had been painted to look as lifelike as possible, down to eyeballs, nipples, and pubic hair. It was, in Nicole's opinion, one of the tackiest things she'd ever seen. Hadn't they run a Saudi sheik out of Beverly Hills for painting the statues on the grounds of his mansion like this?

Seeing her astonished stare, a woman in a grimy linen tunic mistook its meaning. She pointed to the marble penis—also half again life size—and said, "I wish my husband got that hard. How about you, dearie?" The woman didn't wait for or seem to expect an answer. She bustled on down the street, chortling at her own bawdy wit.

The statue had to be just as bad a joke as the one the

woman had made. Nicole wondered if some civic-minded person would come along and sandblast the paint off the marble to make it decently pure again.

Then, as she rounded a corner, she came on the next one. This was of a woman, mostly and graphically nude. It had been painted with the same loving attention to detail and the same total lack of taste as the male statue.

If that physique represented Carnuntum's ideal of beauty, Umma's body was on the skinny side by local standards. At least half of the old wheeze, *You can't be too thin or too rich,* didn't apply here. Somehow, Nicole suspected the other half was still in force.

Distracted by the statue, she almost jumped out of her skin as a nightmare of teeth and glaring eyeballs lunged out of a shop almost into her face. Just as her scattered wits identified the thing as a dog, a stout iron chain brought it up short. Nicole's yelp of alarm was lost in its yelp of surprise.

A roar from the shop reduced them both to silence: "Hercules! Blast you to Hades, you fornicating thing!"

The owner of the voice burst into the street, armed with a stout stick and a glare as red-eyed and wild as the dog's had been. The glare reduced the dog to a whimpering puddle, but the owner never seemed to notice. The stick slashed the dog across the nose; a foot armed with a hobnailed sandal booted it in the ribs. The dog whined piteously and slunk back into the shop, chain rattling behind it.

The shopkeeper tucked the stick in his belt and shook his head. "Damn, Mistress Umma, I'm sorry for that. You know why I got the miserable beast—three break-ins in six months, and the last time the bastards got as far as the cash box before I drove them off. But even with the sign, the blasted dog's scared off half my customers." He tilted his head toward the wall, where a neatly painted inscription read, CAVE CANEM: *Beware the dog.*

Nicole was still shaking with reaction and a surprising, unexpected surge of anger. "I don't care if you do have a sign," she said. "If that dog had bitten me, I'd have sued."

The sentence came as naturally in Latin as it would have in English.

It had the same effect it would have had in English, too. The shopkeeper turned a chalky white, stuttered something she couldn't make out, and scuttled back inside the shop. Thumps and anguished barks told her he was beating the dog again. Mean or not, no animal deserved that. But what could she do about it? There was no SPCA in this world. For the first time, Nicole really understood what the phrase "dog-eat-dog" meant.

As if the CAVE CANEM sign had flicked a switch in her head, Nicole found herself sharply aware of other signs and scribbles than the ones that announced a shopkeeper's name and business. The Romans might not have spray paint, but they knew about graffiti. They wrote in chalk on dark walls and, more often, in charcoal on light ones.

MARCUS LOVES LYDIA, someone had scrawled in charcoal now faded. Nicole wondered if Marcus had done it, or if some of his friends were giving him a hard time. Either way, the graffito had a modern ring to it. Two doors farther down the street she found another, fresher, charcoal scrawl: BAL-BUS SCREWED LYDIA AGAINST THIS WALL. Was he boasting? Was he teasing Marcus? Was he talking about a different Lydia?

Nicole didn't usually wonder about things like that, questions she might never answer, things she'd likely never know. Somehow, here, now, time seemed more flexible.

Across the street, somebody had drawn an elaborate sketch of a man with a donkey's head, hanging from a cross, with a normal man standing below, lifting up his hands. Scribbled under it she read, ALEXANDER WORSHIPPING HIS GOD.

"What's that supposed to mean?" Nicole murmured in absent-minded English. It hit hard when it hit, as the painfully obvious can do, taking her straight back to Sunday school. So when was this, the age of Christians and lions? Someone here obviously didn't think much of the Christians.

A scribble like that would have brought Sunday school down around everybody's ears. No one here seemed to take the least notice of it. Maybe people agreed with it. Maybe it honestly didn't matter to them. No wonder Julia had thought Nicole was acting strangely when she'd asked about the Christian calendar.

Just down the street from the shop with Alexander's portrait on its wall stood an enormous building, by far the largest Nicole had seen in Carnuntum. *City hall?* she wondered. *State capitol?* Whatever it was, it was busy. People—all men, she noticed with a reflexive feminist sting—bustled in and out of several side entrances. Smoke poured from the slits of windows and out the doors as people came and went. In Los Angeles, she'd have been sure the place was on fire. In Carnuntum, where chimneys hadn't been invented, smoke seemed ubiquitous and, for all she could tell, harmless.

Nicole walked along beside the building for what had to be 150 yards before she came to a corner. Around that she found what she'd been hoping for: the main entrance. It was even more floridly ornate than she'd started to expect. An inscription ran above it in the spiky and portentous Roman capitals, proclaiming that Marcus Annius Libo, to celebrate assuming the consulship for the second time during the reign of the august Emperor Hadrian, had erected for the city of Carnuntum these . . . public baths.

Nicole laughed out loud. "That's right!" she said, remembering the ruins again. Any town whose grandest building was a bathhouse was her kind of place. She wondered if it was as fancy on the inside as its white-marble, columned elegance suggested. On impulse, she started up the low stairs. She hadn't bathed the day before, and couldn't remember the last time she'd missed before that.

But, at the top of the stairway, a bored-looking attendant held up a hand to stop her. "Gents today," he said. "Ladies yesterday, ladies tomorrow, gents today." He sounded like a broken record.

"Oh." Nicole felt like an idiot. Hadn't Julia said yesterday was a ladies' day? So men and women alternated. How bloody inefficient. Couldn't they have had separate sections? Alternating half-days? Coed facilities? What if someone needed a bath now and it was the wrong day? What was she supposed do then?

Damn it, her skin was crawling just thinking about two days without a hot shower, let alone an all-over bath.

She opened her mouth to say something of that, but shut it again. She wasn't, at the moment, feeling quite up to fighting weight. As she turned on her heel, letting that be her whole expression of temper, she stopped short. Two women strolled out of the baths, laughing and chattering and jingling coins in little dyed-leather pouches. Nicole forgot the flutter in her belly and the ache in her head. She rounded on the doorman, porter, whatever he was, and jabbed an indignant finger in their direction. "What about them?"

The attendant sneered. She'd seen that look back in L.A., once or twice, when her clothes weren't fancy enough to suit a maître d'. "They didn't go in to *bathe,* lady," he said.

Nicole snapped her mouth shut on a retort, and looked again at the women. Even for women in Carnuntum, they were heavily made up. Their faces looked like the masks she'd seen hanging over the stage in every theater she'd been in. And every inch of it, she had no doubt, the same deadly white lead that she'd thrown out the window this morning. Their tunics seemed made of gauze, wafting in whatever breeze happened to blow, and leaving exactly nothing to the imagination. Their pubes, she couldn't help but notice, were shaved as—she blushed inside herself, and snarled at herself for it—as her own was. Their nipples appeared to be rouged or painted. The scent that wafted from them was so strong she nearly gagged. Rosewater and musk and something oddly . . . culinary? Was that cinnamon? Even as strong as it was, its sweetness was welcome amid the smoke and stench of the city.

It was also, she realized, advertising.

"Oh!" she said again before she could catch herself. She wasn't supposed to feel what she was feeling, which was all the indignation of the Midwestern matron at being brought face to face with a pair of hookers. Umma was a respectable woman; no one had indicated otherwise. And yet these two prostitutes sashayed past her in their waft of perfume and their flutter of inadequate draperies, acting as if they had just as much right to promote their business as she did hers.

So what was she supposed to feel? As a feminist, she should deplore the reduction of her fellow women to mere commercial sex toys—and be dismayed to realize that the so-called oldest profession probably was that ancient. As a liberal, she should approve the lack of hypocrisy of a culture that allowed the same freedom from persecution to hookers as to johns.

It was the good old liberal feminist's dilemma, as insoluble now as it had ever been. The two contrary notions jangled together uneasily in her mind as she hurried down the stairs.

Just past the baths lay a large open square with colonnades on all four sides. Rows of stalls filled it and spread out under the colonnades. It reminded Nicole of the Farmers' Market in Los Angeles, only more so. Nothing had a price tag. Buyers and sellers haggled with loud shouts and frantic gesticulations. Some of them grinned, enjoying the game. Others tackled it with grim determination, as if dickering were a matter of life or death.

Nicole could understand the grim ones a fair bit better than the grinning ones, just then. Her head was aching again, and not just with the aftermath of the trots. She'd been in supermarkets bigger than this. Hell, she'd been to the Mall of America.

In the Mall of America, she knew the rules. What to expect, what to look for, where the maps were if she couldn't find her way. Here there was nothing to guide her. No nice little map on a pillar with a pink dot labeled, "You Are Here." Nothing but a churning mass of people and things. Far too many of those things were alive. No shrink-wrap or cold cases here. Dinner came on the hoof or just recently killed, with head and feet still on.

Nicole took a deep breath that didn't steady her quite so much as she'd have liked it to, and set out around the edge of the cobblestoned square. She'd look things over, she told herself, before she tried to buy anything.

She'd got about halfway round when a man called out to her: "Hello, Mistress Umma! Look at the lovely raisins I've got for you today."

As far as Nicole was concerned, raisins were raisins. These could have come straight out of a red SunMaid box. She looked down her nose at them, as if they were a legal brief she intended to tear to pieces. She'd learned to do that in Mexico, and found there that she liked it. A little of the thrill started to come back through cranky stomach and culture shock. She let it build up. She was going to need it, if she expected to get out of here with any cash left over.

Focus, then. Forget the bellyache, the headache, the over-taxed brain. Think of it as an exercise, like moot court in law school: up all night and running on caffeine, briefcase full of illegible notes and brain full of irrelevant data, but everything coming to one single, all-important point.

Raisins. Never act as if you really want what you intend to buy, she'd learned south of the border. That was easy enough now. She never had cared much for raisins. But Julia had said the restaurant needed them. Therefore, the restaurant was going to get them.

"Go on, taste a few," the seller—dealer? huckster?—urged her. "You'll see how fine they are."

She took one, examined it on all sides, ate it. She shrugged. "Yes, it's a raisin. How much?"

"Eight *sesterces* for a *modius*," he answered, not quite promptly.

A *modius* was a lot; the image that sprang into her mind at the sound of the word was of a jar that had to hold a couple of gallons' worth. The idea of getting that many raisins for a few brass coins was mind-boggling. Still, the dealer had hesitated the least little bit before he replied. Maybe that didn't mean anything. Maybe it did. "And what did you charge me for them last time?" she asked in her best cross-examination voice.

It wasn't quite *Where were you on the night of the fourth?*

but it did the job. The raisin-seller winced. "All right, six *sesterces*," he said sullenly. "That's not any higher than Antonius is charging—you don't need to go trotting over to him the way you did the last couple of times."

"Oh, you think I should?" she said as if that were a brilliant idea, and shifted as if to turn away from the stall.

"Don't you move!" the raisin-seller shrilled at her. "I just heard him sell a *modius* of rabbit droppings to Junia Marcella for seven and an *as*. What makes you think he'll give you any better deal?"

Nicole shrugged again. The shrug was the buyer's best weapon in these Third-World markets—except that this wasn't the Third World, was it? It was a completely different world altogether. "I suppose I believe you," she said. "This time."

He beamed. "Good!" he said. "Good!" Then he waited. She fumbled in her purse and counted out the six *sesterces*, but he wouldn't take them. "Not yet, not yet! Where's your basket? Didn't you bring anything to put them in?"

Of course I didn't! Nicole started to say, but stopped herself in time. Everywhere she looked, people were carrying baskets and bags, bundles and parcels. No plastic bags—that, she didn't miss at all. But no paper, either. Nothing that resembled it.

No wonder Umma hadn't had any books on the chest of drawers or by her bed. How did the Romans run their empire without paper? Nicole wished she knew how to make it. It would be like getting in on the ground floor of Microsoft.

Unfortunately, she didn't. And, even if she had, she wouldn't have had time to do it while the raisin-seller waited. She had to stand watching and feeling foolish while he borrowed a *modius*-sized pot from the bean-dealer next door, filled it full of raisins, then poured the raisins into a big pile on a grimy linen sheet and tied it around them with what looked like a leather bootlace. He charged her an *as* for the packaging, too, and sounded as if he had every right in the world to do it. She gave him the little copper coin without a murmur.

She wandered on down the line of stalls, finding in them a bewildering variety of things in no discernible order: fruit next to sandals next to bolts of cloth next to the kind of beads and bangles she'd expect to see on the street in San Francisco.

When she came to a butcher's stall, she wondered if she'd ever eat meat again. No neat, clean packages wrapped in polyethylene film here. Some of the meat lay on platters. Some—she peered, doubting her eyes—was nailed to boards. All of it was crawling with flies. Once in a while, the butcher swiped halfheartedly at them, but they came back in buzzing swarms.

What was it some friend of Frank's had said after spending a semester in Africa? All about picturesque markets and the African equivalent of hotdog stands: kabob-sellers. "They're called fly kabobs," Frank's friend had said. Nicole had thought he was exaggerating.

Not anymore, she didn't.

There was blood everywhere—literally. As Nicole moved closer, drawn as much by revulsion as by curiosity, she realized the butcher was hawking it. "Pig's blood for blood sausages! Three *asses* for a *sextarius!*" He held up a small pot, about the size of a one-cup measure in West Hills. "One more *as* buys you the gut to case it in."

His eye caught Nicole's. Before she could back away, he put down the pot and scooped up a wriggling, pink-and-gray mass that had to be pig intestines, and thrust them in her face. They stank of pig, and of the pig's last meal. Garbage, from the smell of it, and other things even less savory.

She recoiled. Her stomach, which had forgotten its complaints, abruptly remembered them. She swallowed bile. It burned going down, and made her voice even tighter than it would have been to start with. "I don't want pig guts," she said through clenched teeth. "I want a leg of mutton."

He never even blinked. "I've got a nice one with the hide still on," he said. "You can get it tanned with the wool, if you want, or do the shearing and spin yourself some nice thread." He reached under his counter and rummaged, mut-

tering to himself. With a grunt that sounded excessively satisfied, he pulled something out from below and slammed it
down in front of her. "Here you go," he said.

She stared at it. It was a sheep's leg. No doubt about it.
It had been hacked right off the body, hide and all. She
gulped down a new rush of bile. The leg was bloody at the
top, with the pink knob of bone showing through. The hoof
was still on it. It wasn't a particularly clean hoof, either.

The butcher grinned at her. "It'll go about twelve pounds,
I'd say. How does twenty-five *sesterces* sound? Buy it for
that, and I'll throw in the head for another, mm, seven. Brain,
tongue, eyeballs—all sorts of good things in a sheep's head."
He pointed. There it was, nailed to a board, staring at Nicole
with idiot fixity.

The mouth hung open. A big fly walked across the sheep's
tongue. It paused to nibble on some dainty or other, washed
its face fastidiously, walked on. Nicole watched in sick fascination. Another fly buzzed down beside the first one.
Calmly and without any fuss, the second climbed on top of
the first. They began to mate.

"No, not the head." Her voice came from far away; she
was trying not to lose her breakfast. Good God, how did any
Romans ever live to grow up? "I'll give you fifteen *sesterces*
for the leg."

They ended up splitting the difference. By the butcher's
smirk, she knew he'd ripped her off, but she didn't care. She
only wanted to get away. Magnanimously, the butcher tied
a strip of rawhide around the leg of mutton above the hoof
and looped it into a carrying handle. Even more magnanimously, he didn't charge her for it.

By the time she found two men and a woman selling scallions within twenty feet of one another, she'd recovered . . .
somewhat. She wasn't quite *compos mentis* enough to do any
haggling of her own, but an inspiration saved her the effort:
she let them do it for her. She went to the first, got his price,
went on to the next for a better offer, challenged the third to
top it. By the time she was done, she'd got the green onions
for next to nothing. She left the three vegetable dealers shout-

ing and shaking their fists at one another. The woman's curses were most inventive. The smaller, thinner man had, surprisingly, the most impressive voice.

She decided to get out of there before they started a riot. She tucked the bunch of onions into the top of her bundle of raisins, got a grip on the leg of mutton, and beat a prudent retreat.

There were lots of fishmongers in the market, what with Carnuntum lying on the bank of the Danube. Nicole went from stall to stall in search of the one that smelled least bad. It wasn't easy. The fish peered up at her with dead, unblinking eyes: bream and pike and trout and carp that looked amazingly like ornamental koi except for their dull gray scales.

She couldn't move fast, not weighted down as she was. While she strolled, she let the gossip from other strolling shoppers wash over her. She'd done that every so often at Topanga Plaza, too; people-listening could be as interesting as people-watching. A lot of the stories could have come from her time as readily as this one: So-and-so had found her husband in bed with her friend (Nicole's lips tightened), one partner was supposed to have cheated the other in a real-estate deal, Such-and-such had got his brother-in-law drunk and buggered him.

But there were differences. When a boy of six or seven started crying and wouldn't stop, his mother whacked him on the bottom, hard. He kept crying. His mother whacked him again and bellowed, "Shut up!"

He shut up. In Topanga Plaza, that would have been a minor scandal, with people rushing to the child's defense. Nicole might have done it here, if she'd been a little closer and a lot less loaded down.

Nobody else even offered to try. Nobody seemed to want to. Quite the opposite, in fact. Three different people congratulated the mother. "That'll teach him discipline," growled a grizzled fellow who carried himself like a Marine. Heads bobbed in agreement.

Nicole gaped. So it wasn't just Umma abusing Lucius and

Aurelia. Everybody abused children, and expected everybody else to abuse them, too. That was . . . appalling, that was it. That was the word she wanted.

The little Roman boy's filthy face and snot-dripping nose struck Nicole with a powerful memory of Kimberley and Justin as she'd seen them last, clean and sweet-smelling and tucked up in bed. Nobody had ever laid a hand on them in anger; not Nicole, and no, not Frank, either. Frank had never been abusive. Absent, yes; abusive, no. Dawn? Who could say? Stepmothers were wicked by definition. There wasn't a fairy tale that didn't say so—and some of those were pretty horrifying.

Everything was suddenly horrifying. Even the bit of gossip she heard, one woman to another, cool and matter-of-fact as if it were nothing out of the ordinary: "Just got news my husband's brother died down in Aquileia."

"Ahh," her friend said, sounding just as calm about it. "That's too bad. What was he doing down in Italy, anyway?"

"Didn't you know Junius? I thought you did. He was a muleteer."

"I never met him, though you've told me about him before. What happened to him? Did the Marcomanni get him?"

"No, he didn't have any trouble with the barbarians. Anyhow, they got driven out of Aquileia—was it year before last? I forget. No, it was this pestilence that's going through Italy. It's very bad, they say. The gods grant it doesn't come here." At that, for the first time, the woman sounded less than nonchalant. This wasn't gossip. This was honest fear.

Wonderful, Nicole thought. An epidemic. Of what, flu? She remembered only too vividly the sound of Kimberley losing her corn dog in the backseat of the Honda.

She also, after a moment and with a chill that had nothing to do with the temperature of the air, remembered another kind of epidemic, one much deadlier, that people might speak of with the same fear she heard in the women's voices. She'd known three people who'd died of AIDS. Two gay men, and a woman friend from law school, who hadn't known till too late that the man she'd had a brief affair with was bisexual.

Resolutely, she shut that out of her mind. It would happen on the other side of the world, eighteen hundred years or so from now. There was nothing she could do about it. Nor, frankly, could she do anything about this "pestilence" that had taken a life hundreds of miles from here. This wasn't the twentieth century. People couldn't travel that far that fast. What had they said about the Ebola virus? If it hadn't been for air travel, it might never have left Africa.

No air travel here. Of that she was absolutely sure.

What she could do now, and what she was going to do, was buy fish. She bought some trout that didn't look too flyblown: she'd already seen they were popular in Carnuntum. She bought some bream, too, partly in the spirit of experiment, partly because a couple of them were so fresh they still quivered a little. The fish were cheaper than the meat. In Los Angeles, it would have been the other way round.

The fishmongers strung their catch on the leather thong that the butcher had given her to help carry the leg of mutton. Nicole felt like a comic-page fisherman who'd hooked a sheep along with the rest of his catch. She was glad by then of the wool that still wrapped the mutton: it let her sling the thing over her shoulder with the fish dangling, and carry it a little less awkwardly than if she let the whole lot hang. With the meat and fish balanced on her shoulder and the bundle of raisins and onions under her arm, she paused to run through her mental shopping list.

A stall nearby reminded her of one item that she couldn't get out of. "Wine," she said reluctantly to herself. The dealer in the stall she'd seen first wasn't the only one with wine to sell. They were all ready, no, eager, to sell it to her. Every one of them wanted her to taste his particular brand, too, "To be sure it's the genuine article," one said in a voice as fruity as his wine. She couldn't get out of it, but neither could she tell one wine from the next, except that they were all darker and sweeter than the cheap stuff she'd drunk with breakfast.

Of course she wasn't about to admit that. She remembered how she'd seen people in restaurants and on TV, sniffing and making portentous faces and tasting tiny bits from crystal goblets. Here she was given a whacking big ladle—God knew where that had been or how many people had put lips to it before her—and invited to taste, taste!

She tasted, for what that was worth, and settled to the inevitable haggle. Meat and fish might be cheap here compared to L.A., but wine cost the living earth.

She didn't have nearly the luck beating them down that she'd had with the scallion-sellers. "Mistress Umma, it's real Falernian," said one who recognized the body she was wearing. "That means it has to come all the way from the middle of Italy on muleback, so you can't wonder that it's not cheap. I can't go any lower, or I lose money." Something about his tone, the mixture of patience and exasperation, overcame her court-trained skepticism. He was telling the truth as he saw it.

Nicole hadn't had to worry about transportation costs, except at the office when she had to decide whether to throw something in the mail or FedEx it. No trucks here, she reminded herself. No trains, either. She wondered how long the wine had taken to get here, and what problems it had had along the way.

Once she'd bought an amphora, she had a transportation problem of her own: how to get home with a big clay jug, some dead fish, a leg of mutton, a makeshift sack of raisins, and, for good measure, the green onions. She wished she'd brought Julia after all, even if that meant bringing the children, too, and closing the tavern while everybody was gone. For that matter, she wished she had one of the pack mules that had brought the Falernian wine from Italy.

While she tried to figure out how not to have to make more than one trip—and kept coming up with the answer, *No way, José*—someone at her elbow spoke in a dry voice: "Want me to give you a hand with some of that?"

She whirled. There stood Titus Calidius Severus, one eyebrow raised in an expression of sardonic amusement. All he carried were half a dozen dead thrushes, their scrawny yellow legs bound together with twine. *How could he want to eat them?* she thought in faint disgust. *They're too cute to eat.*

But that wasn't what he'd asked her. "Thank you, Calidius," she said with as much grace as she had to offer, and a good bit of relief. "I'd love a hand."

His mouth tightened. She'd said something wrong, and she didn't even know what. Nor did he say anything that might give her a hint. He simply picked up the amphora and the raisins, leaving her with meat, fish, and scallions, and strode off through the market. Nicole followed, not least because she was sure he knew how to get back. She wasn't at all sure she did.

As they were leaving the market square, four men tramped past them. They weren't Romans; they were speaking a guttural language Nicole didn't understand. It reminded her somehow of the German she'd heard on her honeymoon. She didn't think it was—didn't think it could possibly be—the same language, but she couldn't have proved it, not with only a dozen or so words of German to call her own.

Even if the men had been speaking Latin, she would have tagged them for foreigners. They were taller, thicker through the chest, and ruddier than most of the locals. They let their beards and hair grow longer than the Romans did, and—Nicole's nose wrinkled—used rancid butter for hair oil. They wore the first trousers she'd seen in Carnuntum—baggy woolen ones, tied tight at the ankles—and short tunics over them. Each of them wore a long sword on his left hip.

They stared around the square as if they owned it, or perhaps as if they planned on robbing it. People stared at them, too, in fear and alarm, and muttered behind their hands. Nicole had seen exactly the same reaction in Topanga Plaza when a pack of gangbangers walked into the Wherehouse or Foot Locker.

"Mithras curse the Quadi and Marcomanni both to the infernal depths," Calidius Severus growled. He was eyeing the strangers as a cop might eye gangbangers at the mall. He'd made it plain he was a veteran. Had he fought these Quadi or Marcomanni? Maybe he had, from the bitterness in his tone. "Miserable barbarians have their nerve, coming into town to buy this and that when they invaded the Empire three years ago not far west of here."

"Invaded?" Nicole said, and then, hastily, "Yes, of course." Odd bits of gossip began to fit together like pieces of evidence. The Marcomanni had conquered Aquileia in Italy, and been driven back from it. She didn't know where in Italy Aquileia was, but nowhere in Italy was particularly close to the Danube. She shivered a little, though the day was fine and mild. "It must have been quite an invasion."

"That it was." To her relief, Calidius didn't notice the odd phrasing; he was intent on his own thoughts. "Some officers I've talked with—educated fellows, you know—say it was the worst since the Cimbri and Teutones came down on us, and that was—what?—almost three hundred years ago."

Longer than the United States has been a country, Nicole thought, and shivered again. On her honeymoon, she'd caught glimpses of the sense of history that filled Europe but was so conspicuously absent from America. She hadn't expected to find that sense in second-century Carnuntum. After all, this was ancient history, wasn't it? Not so ancient, evidently, that it didn't have history of its own. She hadn't gone back to the beginning of time, as she'd sometimes felt—never more urgently than when her belly griped her. She was stuck somewhere in the middle.

She stayed close to Titus Calidius Severus. He hadn't been afraid of the Marcomanni or Quadi or whoever they were. He'd been angry at them. From the way he stamped resolutely ahead, he was still angry. But that anger might not all have been aimed at the men he called barbarians: after a while, he said, "Umma, if you tell me what you think I've done wrong, I may decide to be sorry for it. If it's something I ought to be sorry for."

Nicole couldn't quite suppress the twitch of a smile at his careful phrasing. He could have been a lawyer, with that kind of mind. "I don't think you've done anything wrong," she said.

She was glad he was in front of her, so he couldn't see

her wince. Something she hadn't expected to deal with when she traveled in time: the past life of the body she wore. People made assumptions about her. They expected things of her, things she was supposed to do or think or say, because Umma had always done or thought or said them. Sometimes, as with Lucius and Aurelia, it came in handy. Sometimes . . .

The fuller and dyer stopped and looked back at her then. Fortunately, she'd managed to pull her face straight. Calidius was nothing if not forthright: "Then why didn't you want me to come over last night?"

"Because I didn't feel like it," she answered, not angrily but without any hesitation, either. If he made a habit of coming on by whenever he felt like a roll in the hay, he was going to have to get himself some new habits.

He grunted. "All right. Can't expect a woman to know her own mind from one day to the next, I guess." Before she had a chance to bridle at that, he redeemed himself, at least in part, by adding, "Women likely say the same about men. I've known enough who'd give you cause to, anyhow."

If he was in the habit of mocking everyone impartially, she could deal with that. All the cops she'd ever known, in Indiana and California alike, were the most cynical people on the face of the earth. Maybe soldiers were the same way. Because of that, and because she felt, for a moment, as if she could almost like him, she said, "Besides, it wouldn't have mattered either way. I was sick last night."

"Belly, I'll bet." Calidius grunted again, apparently a noise that indicated his brains were working. "Julia told me you and the kids were drinking water all day yesterday. What got into you, Umma? One of your new ideas? Water's handy if you haven't got anything else, but if you do, forget it. Kids all right?"

"Not too bad," Nicole answered. The amphora of Falernian he was carrying for her was glazed. God only knew what was in the glaze, but she could make a pretty fair guess that lead was part of it. But he wouldn't believe lead was poisonous. Even if he did, so what? If lead killed you, it killed you a little bit at a time. Drinking the water, she'd discovered, was liable to be lethal in a hurry.

"That's good," he said. "I'm glad they're all right. They're pretty fair kids, they are."

His stock jumped several points in Nicole's book. She'd gone out only a couple of times after Frank broke up with her. She might have done it more often if so many men, on learning she had children, hadn't reacted as if they were a dangerous and possibly contagious disease. *I still don't want to go to bed with him,* she thought. She didn't want to go to bed with anyone.

She started down the street away from the market, back toward the tavern, but Titus Calidius Severus held up a hand. "Wait. You still haven't told me what you're angry at."

Nicole gritted her teeth. He was losing points again, and fast. "I did tell you, Calidius: I'm not angry at you. I will be, though, if you keep pushing at me like this."

"There—you did it again," he said.

And there it was again: the prickle of alarm. *What have I done? What's wrong?*

Thank God, finally—he went on in a growing heat, spelling it out in terms even a time-traveler from West Hills could understand: "How can I help thinking you're mad at me when you haven't called me by my praenomen since day before yesterday? If you can't be that familiar with someone who knows you've got a little mole halfway down from your navel, what in Ahriman's name is a praenomen good for?"

Nicole bit her tongue. Good God! He knew her body— no, knew *this* body—better than she did. How had she managed to miss a mole in *that* spot?

Because, she told herself with tight-drawn patience, she'd been too busy overdosing on her new reality—and freaking at the shaved parts south of the mole. But if she did start calling him Titus, would he take it as a signal and assume she was open for business again? She'd been formally polite, and he'd taken it for displeasure. If she didn't go back to the intimate use, he'd be convinced she really was mad at him. Except she wasn't. Except probably she was, because he was a man and she was a woman and it was all too clear that relations between the sexes were no easier to figure here than they'd been in Los Angeles.

She couldn't take all day making up her mind, not with him standing there studying her. Finally, with an exhalation that wasn't quite a sigh, she said, "I'm sorry, Titus. I just haven't been myself the last couple of days." *And you don't know how true that is.* But, instead of the truth, she opted for the simple, the rational, and the practical: "Too much to do, not enough time to do it."

"Well, that's so twelve months a year, and an extra day on leap year," Calidius answered. He too hesitated, as if looking for something else—he couldn't remember what— that needed saying. Then, as if he'd found it, he grinned. "And I won't chuck you under the chin anymore, either. I really didn't know you didn't like it."

He was trying. She could say that much for him. Of course, he had an ulterior motive. What male didn't, in whatever century she found herself in? Nicole nodded, but said simply, "Let's get on back."

Titus Calidius Severus started walking. She followed again, with one pause to set down the leg of lamb and scratch her head. *No Head and Shoulders,* she thought with more sadness than she'd ever expected to feel. *No Selsun Blue. No Denorex.* Still, there was a bright side. No idiotic commercials for them, either.

They passed the two graffiti about Lydia, in reverse order this time. Pointing to the one and then, a bit farther along, to the other, Nicole said, "Put those two together and they're pretty funny."

"I think so, too, but I'll bet you Marcus doesn't," Calidius said wryly. He walked on a couple of paces, then stopped so abruptly, Nicole almost ran into him. "You read them." He sounded almost accusing.

Uh-oh. "Yes, I read them." If Nicole stayed cool, kept it light, maybe he wouldn't fuss about it.

No such luck. "All these years I've known you, and I never knew you had your letters." When he frowned, his face looked absolutely forbidding. "Mithras, I can think of plenty of times when you've had me read things for you."

"I've been studying lately," Nicole said. It was weak, but it was the only explanation she could come up with on the spur of the moment. "Not knowing how always seemed such a lack."

Muscle by muscle, he relaxed; he'd gone as tense facing her as he might have before a battle. "Well, I've heard you say that before," he allowed. *Thank you, Umma,* Nicole thought. Calidius went on, "But why didn't you tell me you wanted to learn? I'd have helped."

"For one thing, I wanted to surprise you," she said: again, the path of least resistance.

"You did it, all right," he said, and chuckled. "And now that you can read a little, you'll think you can read everything. Isn't that just like a woman?"

He'd been doing so well for himself. Now he'd pressed the wrong button—no, he hadn't just pressed it. He'd stomped on it. "I *can* read anything," she said in the frosty voice she used to reserve for asking Frank why the check was late. Titus Calidius Severus started to say something. She overrode him. "And I'll show you."

And she did. She read every sign, every graffito, every inscription between MARCUS LOVES LYDIA and her restaurant and Calidius' shop across the street from it. She didn't stumble once. She made no mistakes. After she'd read the sign above his door, she added, sweetly, "And thank you very much for carrying the wine and the raisins all this way . . . Titus."

His sour expression proved she'd done that just right. He looked as if he wished he'd been born without a praenomen, let alone been so rash as to make a big deal of it. But under that, and rapidly swelling through it, he looked astonished. "How did you do that? I don't think I ever heard anyone read that way, not even men who called themselves philosophers. You didn't mumble the words at all to see what they were. You just . . . read them straight out. That's amazing. How do you do it?"

Nicole's astonishment couldn't have been much less than his, though she tried to keep it buried underneath her courtroom mask—the one with the faint, superior smile and the slightly lifted eyebrow. She'd gone to a public school in Indianapolis that was no better than it had to be, and then to a medium-good university. That had landed her a job at a medium-good law firm in Los Angeles, which had not even been a medium-good job by the time it was done with her.

Here . . . Here, if what Calidius was saying was right, simply being able to read without moving her lips set her above the local equivalent of a Ph.D. He had to be exaggerating. He knew more about it than she did, didn't he? Anybody who'd grown up here knew more about it than she did.

And if it was true, if literacy was as rudimentary as that, it didn't promise much for the rest of civilization, either. This wasn't what she'd expected when she'd wished herself to Carnuntum.

She needed to think. There was never time to think. That was just as true here, since she'd wakened in Umma's bed, as it had been when she went to sleep in West Hills.

Calidius was still waiting for an answer. Simplest, again, seemed best: "I don't know how I learned to read like this. It's how I taught myself, that's all."

"Amazing," he repeated, and stabbed the amphora's pointed tip down into the dirt of the street, as he'd done with the empties he used for urinals outside his shop. He set down the raisins beside the jar and, still shaking his head, carried the songbirds back toward his door. On his way he stopped at one of the jars and pissed in it, as unself-conscious as any of the other men who paused there. Seeing that Nicole's gaze had followed him, he grinned and let his tunic fall. "My own private stock, from my own privates."

She didn't know why she smiled. It was a godawful joke. *Face it,* she told herself. *Face the way things are.* The way things were was plain. He took it utterly for granted that a man would piss in a pot in a public place. There was nothing either shameful or prurient about male nudity here—that was obvious. Female nudity . . .

Best not get into that. So: nothing shameful. Even noticing that he wasn't circumcised, or calling to mind that no one else she'd seen pissing in front of his shop was, either. Like the doors that swung on pegs rather than hinges, it wasn't any better or worse than what she'd known before. It was just different.

Titus Calidius Severus went inside his shop, leaving Nicole to look after herself. He hadn't even said good-bye. She didn't know why that should matter, but it did.

6

S HE GRITTED HER TEETH, picked up the leg of mutton with its pendant fish, and lugged them into the odorous dimness of the tavern. The scent of wine and sweat, must and hot oil, garlic and herbs and unsubtle perfume, struck her like a wall. She clove her way through it.

Julia materialized out of it, imperturbably cheerful as ever, and fetched in the wine and the raisins and the scallions. As she came back in, Nicole asked her, "How are the children?"

"They haven't been too bad, Mistress," Julia answered, as willingly as always. If she'd been a babysitter in West Hills, Nicole thought, she'd have been booked from one end of the week to the other. "They're using the pot more than they should, but I think they're getting better. Are you all right?"

Nicole's stomach rumbled alarmingly. She set her teeth and ignored it. "I'm not too bad, either."

"You were lucky," Julia said. "A lot of times, when people's bellies gripe them like that, they keep on shitting and shitting till they die. That's what happened to Calidius' wife a few years ago, remember?"

"Of course I remember," Nicole said. Of course she didn't, but from now on she would. Titus Calidius Severus hadn't been two-timing anybody when he came visiting her, then—

no, when he came visiting Umma. A point in his favor. Did it balance off that rude remark he'd made about women? *Not even close,* Nicole thought. That was exactly the attitude that she'd fled in the twentieth century. She'd prayed for a place that was free of it. *Liber, Libera—what were you thinking? Couldn't you understand what I meant?*

They didn't blast her where she stood, but neither did they answer. She was left where she'd been before, face to face with a monumental wall of male chauvinist piggery.

And he'd seemed so decent, too. A pleasant man. A nice man, as her mother in Indiana might have said.

"There ain't no such thing," Nicole snarled to nobody in particular. Nobody answered, or even seemed to notice that she'd spoken.

Snarl though she might, fact was fact. And men, it seemed, were men. Nicole dug fingers into a sudden fierce itch in her scalp. Damn, it was getting worse. She needed a shower, shampoo—even a bath would do. All over. In hot water.

Tomorrow was ladies' day in the baths. She'd live till then. Maybe.

Julia's voice startled her out of her funk. "Business was good while you were gone, Mistress," Julia said brightly, "and I got a couple of *dupondii* for myself. May I keep them?"

Had she slipped her hand in the till? Had she sneaked out a good deal more than a couple of *dupondii* and claimed the smaller amount, hoping Nicole wouldn't notice? Listening to her, looking at her, Nicole didn't think so. Her tone was eloquent. She'd asked because she might get in real trouble if she kept the *dupondii* without asking, but she didn't think Nicole could possibly say no.

Nicole couldn't see any good reason to refuse. "Yes, go ahead. That's more than you got from Ofanius Valens yesterday morning. How did you do it?"

"Usual way," Julia said with a smile and a shrug. The smile had an odd edge to it, but nothing Nicole could lay a finger on. "Customers thought I was nice."

"All right," Nicole said. "Here, will you take the hide off

this leg of mutton while I tend to the rest of the things I bought?"

"Of course, Mistress," the slave replied.

I have to set her free as soon as I can, Nicole thought again. *The Romans don't have paper, right? So how bad can the paperwork be?*

As Julia went to get a knife for the mutton, she said over her shoulder, "Oh—Mistress, I almost forgot. Your brother stopped by while you were gone to market. He said he'd come back another time."

"Did he?" The words were entirely automatic—they didn't have anything to do with any rational thought processes on Nicole's part. Up till this moment, she hadn't known she, or rather Umma, had a brother. Up till this moment, she'd never had a brother. Two sisters, yes; a brother, no. She supposed she had to make the best of it. "If that's what he said," she said, she hoped not too lamely, "that's what he'll probably do."

Julia nodded vigorously. "Oh, yes. Brigomarus is always very reliable." Now Nicole not only had a brother, she knew what his name was. That helped. If only she'd be able to recognize him when he walked through the door. . . .

Julia skinned the leg of mutton with nonchalant competence. Nicole was sure she couldn't have done it half so neatly. She'd never had to try anything like that before—but she was going to have to learn. Another survival skill in this world without supermarkets, like pissing in a chamber pot and haggling in the market. *Next time,* she decided, *I do it myself.*

While Julia worked, Nicole checked the cash box, doing her best not to be too obvious about it. Julia saw her doing it even so. The slave went right on with her task. Even as an ordinary employee, she wouldn't really have had any grounds for complaint. As a slave, she doubtless could land in very hot water if she got out of line.

Nicole didn't like the small stab of relief—almost of approval—that accompanied the thought. It was the same less than laudable gut reaction and the same tardy pang of guilt that she'd felt when she saw a police car patrolling a Latino neighborhood while she was driving through it. She didn't want to be glad the cops came down harder on poor minorities than on affluent whites—but just at that moment, she couldn't help it. She was glad.

Lucius came running down the stairs, pulling a toy cart on the end of a leather thong. It squeaked almost as much as a real one. By the way he squealed with laughter, he wasn't at death's door or anywhere close. All the same, Nicole asked, "How are you feeling?"

"I'm fine, Mother, thanks," the boy answered, as carelessly as if he hadn't had the galloping trots in the middle of the night. *Kids,* Nicole thought, half in amazement, half in envy. Lucius was kind enough to add, "Aurelia's fine, too."

"That's good," Nicole said. Even so, she snagged him as he loped on by, and felt his forehead. Normal. He was grubby, too, but there wasn't much she could do about that on short notice. "If you are feeling fine," she said, "I have a job for you. Would you help me put the groceries away? Here, I got some raisins, and some scallions. Put them where they belong, will you please?"

As clever stratagems went—Nicole had no idea where either item belonged—it was about as successful as she might have expected. "Oh, Mother," Lucius said with the indignation of a child in any country, in any time, faced with the adult insistence on doing something useful instead of running around making a nuisance of himself. Nicole armed herself for battle, but he amazed her: once he'd registered his complaint, he did as he was told. Maybe he was afraid he'd get whacked if he didn't. Maybe he was just a good kid.

By what Nicole had seen here, anybody in Carnuntum would have loudly maintained that those last two notions had something in common. She didn't care what anybody in Carnuntum would maintain. She didn't believe it, not for a minute.

Lucius scratched his head. The gesture was as contagious as a yawn. Nicole gave in to the irresistible urge to scratch. Her scalp—no, Umma's scalp: it wasn't her fault—never stopped itching, any more than her tooth stopped aching or her heart stopped beating.

Lucius stopped suddenly and let out a very grown-up grunt of satisfaction. He reached up and squished something between the fingernail of one hand and the thumbnail of the other. Nicole's stomach did a slow lurch that had nothing to do with the water she'd drunk the day before. "Lucius!" she said sharply. "What was that?"

He grinned. "Louse," he said, wiping his hands on his tunic. He sounded insufferably pleased with himself. "I've been trying to catch the miserable thing all day. And look, I finally did."

"Oh . . ." Nicole bit her tongue before she burst out in a flood of English swearwords. Latin still felt strange to her, like a made-up language; something she'd learned in school and recited by rote. She couldn't cut loose in it. If she started screaming in English, people would think she'd gone round the bend. Did they burn witches here? No English, then. Latin wasn't enough. She clamped down hard on the most satisfying option of all: a plain old wordless shriek.

Once, about a year before, Kimberley and Justin had come home from Josefina's with head lice. That had been a nightmare: washing the kids' hair with Nix, using the Step 2 rinse to help loosen the nits—the eggs—from the hair shafts, and washing everyone's bedding and spraying the mattresses and the furniture with Rid to kill any nits the children might have shed.

She'd used enough chemicals to exterminate a couple of endangered species. That had been bad enough, but it hadn't been the worst part: not even close. The worst part was going through Justin's hair, and especially Kimberley's, which was both longer and thicker, one strand at a time, looking for the nits the fine-toothed comb that came with the Nix hadn't been able to free.

The only difference between her and a mother chimpanzee was that chimps had to worry about hair all over the bodies of their offspring, and she didn't. From then on, she'd understood how and why searching for tiny details got to be known as nitpicking.

"Come over to the window here," she told Lucius. He rolled his eyes but obeyed. She shifted him around till his head was in the light, and started going through his hair. He didn't ask what she was doing, which meant he knew. "Oh . . ." Nicole muttered again, in lieu of anything stronger. Umma might have done this for him before, but she hadn't done much of a job. His hair was full of telltale white specks. They were so small, they disappeared if you looked at them from the wrong side of the hair shafts, but they were there, all right. They were all too evidently there.

He yelped more than once as she yanked and tugged, pinching nits one by one, sliding her fingers along each laden hair till she could crush them. She wasn't gentle. Her revulsion was too strong. Each time she crushed a nit, she wanted frantically to wash her hands.

She didn't do that. What good would it do? She had no soap. Nothing but water.

Every time she thought she'd found the last of them, a dozen more turned up. And there—oh, God, there was a live one, pale and slow and small, like a piece of dandruff with legs. It scuttled away from her questing fingers. Lucius wiggled as she pursued it. "Hold still!" she snapped. Her tone froze him in place. She barely noticed, except that he'd stopped moving. "Got it!" she said, and squashed the thing with a horrid mixture of delight and revulsion. It expired with a faint, crisp pop.

Just as she was about to go on playing mommy ape, a pair of customers wandered in. Her grip on Lucius slackened as she turned to take care of the man and woman. He escaped before she could tighten her hold again, scampering gleefully past the customers into the freedom of the street.

She could hardly go after him, not with both customers settling noisily at a table and calling out their orders. She fed them wine from the middle-range jar, and bread that Julia must have made while she was out, and honey and nuts. They scratched at themselves as they ate and drank, casually and without shame, as if it were something everybody did all the time. Had people been doing that to excess the day before? Had they been doing it in the market square? There'd been so many things to see, so much to absorb, that she hadn't noticed.

She'd notice now. Oh, Lord, wouldn't she just?

Her fingers clawed at her own scalp. Something . . . squished under one of them. She wanted to scream again. She wanted to throw up. She had to stand there while the customers finished and paid her and left, her head throbbing with Excedrin Headache Number Six Hundred and Sixty-six, and one thought beating over and over. Lousy. Lousy. Lousy . . .

No Nix here. No Step 2. No Rid. She couldn't have cared less now about what was in them. She just wished she had them. Oh, God, she wished she had them.

Back before Nix and the rest, people had killed lice and nits with kerosene. Some people still did, because it was cheap or because it was what they'd used before they came to the United States. Once a year or so, there'd be a news story about an immigrant child whose head caught fire while her mother was delousing her.

Kerosene seemed like ancient history to Nicole. Unfortunately for her here and now, it wasn't ancient enough. The Latin vocabulary she'd acquired from wherever she'd acquired it didn't even have a word for the stuff.

"Julia," she said, "what do I do about these horrible lice?"

Even in her misery, she'd framed the question with a lawyer's precision. As she'd hoped, Julia took her to be complaining about the ones she'd just found on Lucius and on herself—oh, Christ, and on herself—rather than about lice in general.

"They are annoying, aren't they, Mistress?" the slave said with a sigh. *Annoying* was not the word—was not a tenth the word—Nicole would have used. Julia went on, "I don't know what you can do except what you did: pick nits, comb hair, and wash it, too, I suppose, though nothing seems to do much good. Just about everybody has 'em."

Nothing seems to do much good. Just about everybody has 'em. Nicole hated bugs of any sort. She could deal with them, but she hated them. The idea that she had bugs living on her would make her scalp crawl if it hadn't been crawling already. She'd felt dirty before. Now she felt unclean. She'd never known what that meant before, or how much worse it was than merely being filthy.

"Lice carry disease," she said. She knew she shouldn't have. It wouldn't get her anywhere. But she couldn't stop herself.

Sure enough, Julia looked at her as if she'd gone around the bend again, and said what she'd expected, as predictable as a sitcom script: "I never heard that before. Bad air or evil spirits or getting your humors out of line some way, yes, but lice? Beg pardon for saying so, but you sure have been coming up with some funny ideas lately, Mistress."

"Ha," Nicole said in a hollow voice. "Ha, ha." Convincing Julia she was right wasn't the most important thing in the world—and that was lucky, too, because she could tell at a glance she wasn't going to convince Julia, any more than she'd convinced her lead was poisonous. Julia had that everybody-knows look on her face again, the one impenetrable to everything this side of a baseball bat.

And there it was again, the script according to Julia: "How could lice carry disease? Like I said, almost everybody has 'em. If they carried disease, people would be sick all the time, wouldn't they? And they aren't. So lice can't carry disease." The slave hugged herself with glee. "Listen to me, Mistress! I'm reasoning like a philosopher."

Nicole sighed and went back to grinding flour. Julia's logic was as good as she thought it was—if all lice carried disease all the time. If some lice carried it some of the time, no. But how could Nicole show that? She couldn't, not by mere assertion, which was all she had going for her here.

It didn't matter anyhow. Lice weren't bad only because they carried disease. They were bad because they were disgusting. They were bad because they were lice. And she had them in her hair. In her hair. Every time she itched, she scratched frantically. Sometimes she drew blood. Every once in a while, she squashed something. She wiped her hands on her tunic, again and again.

When she found half a moment, she yelled for Aurelia. The little girl fidgeted more under her hands than Lucius had. She was just as lousy as her brother. As she had with Lucius, Nicole plucked nit after nit from her hair, and killed a couple of live ones for good measure.

But she didn't have time to do anything even close to a proper job, not with baking and cooking and dealing with customers. It wouldn't have mattered even if she had had time, because the children's bedding was sure to be full of nits—and probably full of lice, too. Julia's, too. And her own. Dear God in heaven, her own too.

Scratch, scratch, scratch. Squish—a chitinous yielding under her fingernail. *Got* one. Five minutes later . . . Scratch, scratch, scratch.

No matter how she scratched, no matter how she picked through the kids' hair, she couldn't keep up. Long before sunset, she understood why Umma hadn't been able to keep the kids' heads even halfway clean. She went on anyhow, with the kids getting more and more fractious every time, till she had to light a lamp to see the nits; then even the lamp wasn't enough. The kids went up to bed in visible relief—there, they probably figured, they'd be safe from her pinching, prodding fingers.

She followed them not long after, tired to the bone. She thought seriously of stripping the bed—but there was still the mattress under the sheets. And the floor wasn't clean either. Nothing short of a house fire was going to get rid of every louse in the place.

She undressed and washed up as best she could, missing toothpaste the most—her teeth felt as if they were coated in flannel. She rubbed them, and tried not to think of lice. The bed waited for her, deceptively tidy, as she'd made it in her innocence, just this morning. How many newly hatched baby lice would crawl onto her, once she lay down?

She couldn't sleep propped up against the wall. For that

matter, she couldn't live if she went on like this. She'd been walking the edge of hysteria since Lucius found the louse in his hair. She had to stop. She had to stop now—or go straight screaming out of her mind.

Nicole hated nothing so much as a silly, screaming woman. Snakes, spiders, scorpions, two-inch roaches in the kitchen—no, she didn't like them, but she could handle them. She'd never known anything but contempt for women who couldn't handle the crawly things in life. What was a louse but another damned crawly thing?

But it was on her. It was laying eggs on her. It was—

"Enough," she said, so harshly it made her throat ache. She took three deep breaths, each held a few seconds longer than the last. She made herself calm down. It wasn't completely effective—she was still shaking, and her stomach was tied in a raw and painful knot—but it held her steady enough to lie on the bed. She couldn't quite bring herself to pull the covers up over herself. She'd work up to that gradually. For now, just lie there. Just let the muscles relax one by one. Forget the worst blow this world had struck her. With everything else, untreated sickness, raw sewage in the street, rampant animal and child abuse, slavery—a few million lice were awesomely trivial.

"It's the small things that get you," she mumbled. Sleep had seemed light-years away, but, once she was horizontal, it crept inexorably up on her. It wasn't just her body that was tired. Her mind was exhausted, wrung out and hung up to dry. Sleep was wonderful. Sleep was beautiful. Sleep would let her forget everything—even the myriad small live things that hatched and crawled and bred and died—but not soon enough—right on her body.

Wine the next morning at breakfast seemed oddly welcome, not a poison to be drunk in slight preference to a different poison. Did it make her feel a little easier about the likelihood—no, the certainty—she was walking around with six-legged company? Maybe. Did it make her want to scratch a little less? Maybe. If it did, was that bad or good? For the life of her, Nicole didn't know.

She had two cups with her bread. *I'm thirsty,* she told herself. When she finished the bread and that second cup of—after all—well-watered wine, she declared, "I'm going to the baths. Aurelia, you're coming with me." She sounded very loud and sure, even to herself.

"Oh, good!" Aurelia squealed with glee. No fights here, not like getting Kimberley into the tub. But this wasn't just getting into the tub. This was an outing, which made it special.

Nicole wanted her to come for two very good and useful reasons. First and foremost was the chance to scrub Aurelia's hair as well as she could, to get rid of as many lice and nits as possible. While she did that, she'd get an answer to a question that had occurred to her as soon as she remembered baths, ladies' day, and the kids' vermin: how would she go about taking care of that with Lucius? Could she bring a boy eight years old to the baths with her on a ladies' day? Maybe, but it didn't seem likely. She'd have to see if she spotted any boys his size there today. If she couldn't, could she ask Brigomarus, the brother she hadn't met? Or would Titus Calidius Severus let Lucius go with him when he went to the baths? Did he go to the baths? The way he smelled, it was hard to tell.

Second, and not the least important of matters, either, Aurelia knew the ropes at the baths and Nicole didn't. Nicole had learned how to run the tavern by watching Julia. Now she would learn how to take a Roman bath by watching . . . her daughter? She still didn't think of Aurelia that way. How long did parents who adopted need to start thinking of their new children as if they were actual, blood relations? Aurelia, now—Aurelia was a blood relative, had come from this body, this blood and bone, these genes.

But Aurelia was not Nicole's child in the spirit, where it mattered; not fully, not yet. Kimberley and Justin, who were . . . they were farther away than children had ever been from their mother; as far away as if she had died and not gone spiraling down through time. She hoped they were all right. She prayed they were all right, prayed to the deaf God in whom she'd almost given up believing and whom the Romans mocked, and prayed also to Liber and Libera. *Let my children be all right.* They'd listened to her once. Why not again?

She took a couple of *asses* out of the cash box, then scooped out a random handful of coins. Maybe she'd shop a little on the way home, or buy Aurelia a treat, or maybe there would be extras at the baths over and above the price of admission. Julia didn't act surprised: Umma must have found some way to make those *dupondii* and *sesterces* disappear.

Poor Julia. She'd had to depend on the kindness of a customer or on Nicole's generosity—on her owner's generosity, a notion that still gave Nicole the cold grues—for even the small change that let her into the baths. She'd got a couple of *dupondii* while Nicole was out, but that wasn't much, not set against the copper and brass and silver in the cash box.

My owner gets to take as much money as she wants, whenever she wants. That thought, or one like it, had to be echoing in Julia's mind. How did everyone who owned a slave escape being murdered in her bed? It was evil, that was all. Just purely evil.

"Come on," Nicole said to Aurelia. "Let's go get clean." That was cowardice, but she didn't care. As long as she was in the baths, she wouldn't have to look at Julia. She wouldn't be reminded of the injustice she was still perpetrating.

Aurelia knew the way to the baths. Nicole thought she could have found them again by herself—not finding them would have been like mislaying an elephant—but letting the little girl scamper ahead and then catching up every fifty yards or so worked very well. Aurelia paid no attention whatever to the anatomically correct statues. Nicole shouldn't have been surprised, not with men casually pissing in a jar right across the street from the tavern. Nonetheless, she was. It was all too different. She had to take it in a piece at a time, and pray she could put it together before she made a fatal mistake.

As men had the day before, women trooped up the steps and into the baths. The only men now in evidence around that enormous place were half a dozen burly types in ragged tunics, each of them bent under a load of wood that looked almost as enormous as the baths.

Off to one side of them marched a self-important little man who was obviously their boss. His tunic was not only fairly new but dyed the rust brown of the one Nicole was coming to think of as her best dress. More important than that, however, the only wood he carried was a single, straight, peeled stick.

"Keep moving, you lazy bastards, keep moving!" he shouted. "Got to keep the fires fed, so we do, so we do. Ladies' day today. Ladies want their water nice and hot, that they do. Ladies want lots of nice steam, too. Ladies want hot air going through the hypocausts, yes indeed. Can't let their pretty little feet get cold, oh no." What the workmen no doubt wanted was for the overbearing little twerp to shut up and let them do their job.

Suddenly, not ten feet from the little door they were approaching—Nicole looked for but didn't see an AUTHORIZED PERSONNEL ONLY sign—one of the workmen tripped and fell. The leather lashings of his bundle parted. Twigs and branches and hacked chunks of treetrunk spilled over the paving stones.

"You oaf! You cocksucking idiot! You dingleberry hanging off the ass of the city of Carnuntum!" The straw boss literally hopped with rage. Nicole had never seen anybody do that before. He kept right on cursing while he did it, too. Aurelia giggled. Nicole's hands flew up to cover the child's ears, but the fellow was yelling too loudly for that to do any good.

Slowly, the workman shook himself free of lumber and climbed to his feet. Both knees and one elbow dripped blood on the cobbles. "I'm sorry," he said in gutturally accented Latin. "I pick it up and—"

"Sorry!" the nasty little straw boss screamed. "Sorry? You think you're sorry now? I'll have 'em sell you to the mines. That'll make you sorry, by Jupiter's great hairy balls!"

The workman quailed. Nicole didn't fully understand the threat, but he did, and it terrified him. She did understand that he wasn't just a workman. He was a slave. He would have to be, to get stuck with a job like the one he had. His abject manner said so as loudly as the threat to sell him.

And the boss' stick wasn't only for show. He swept it whistling up over his head, then down, again and again, beating the workman as cruelly—and, worse, as casually—as that man whom Nicole had seen whipping his poor over-burdened donkey the morning she came to Carnuntum.

And the slave let him. He stood there and took it with the air of a man who knew he'd get worse later if he tried to do anything about it now.

Inside Nicole, something snapped. "Stop that!" she shouted at the straw boss. "You stop that this instant!"

"Ah, butt out, lady," he said, sounding barely even annoyed. "I ain't gonna hurt him so bad he can't work." He hardly paused to talk to her, but kept right on whaling the slave. He was only doing his job, his manner said. No point in getting upset. If it was nasty—well, that was life, wasn't it?

The guards at Auschwitz had been like that, Nicole had heard somewhere. Just doing their job. "Leave him alone," she said. "You've got no business abusing him that way."

"Who says I don't?" the boss retorted. "I'm supposed to get work out of him, ain't I? How's he supposed to feed the fires if he's out here picking up all this crap? His skull's so thick, the only way to get anything in is to beat it in." As if to prove his point, he laid into the slave again.

"Stop that!" Nicole's voice held itself just on the edge of a scream.

"You don't like the way I do my job, take it up with the town council. I'll tell you, though, they like it fine." The straw boss' stick went right on flaying the poor man's hide, rising and falling, rising and falling.

But the worst part was that the slave didn't even bother to cower, except when the stick cut a little too close to an eye or an ear. By all the signs, he'd been through it before. While the blows rained down on his back, he gathered up his burden again and mended the lashings till they'd hold without snapping. While Nicole stood gasping for breath and coherence, he looked up and snarled, "Shut up, lady, why don't you? You're just making it worse."

Where nothing else had, that stopped Nicole cold. She didn't want to make trouble for the poor fellow. She wanted to save him from it. But she couldn't, dammit. That was the worst thing she'd seen about slavery yet. An instant later, she shook her head. No. The worst thing about it was the way the slave himself accepted it.

Aurelia plucked at her tunic. "Mother, are we going to have a bath, or are we going to quarrel all day?" By the way she said it, she was ready for either, but would have preferred the bath, probably because it was more unusual.

Nicole drew a slow, careful breath. "All right." As tight-lipped with fury as she'd been since—*since Frank's e-mail,* she thought—she stalked past the straw boss, Aurelia skipping at her side. The look she gave the man should have scorched him to a cinder. He leered back, running his eyes over her as if he were stripping her naked under her tunic.

Her back stiffened. He laughed, impervious to the heat of her glare. Testosterone: it gave a man all the tact and sensitivity of a rhinoceros.

He laid off the slave, at least, and let him make his way wincing and stumbling through the side door to the baths. Nicole was a little bit glad of that.

The attendants at the top of the stairs today were women. Nicole eyed them with horrified fascination. Were they slaves, too? If she'd grown up here, she'd know as automatically as she breathed. Since she hadn't, she couldn't tell. Things weren't so cut-and-dried here as they had been in the South before the Civil War, where if you saw an African-American you knew she was a slave.

How did the Romans keep all their slaves from walking

off and settling down two towns over as free men? She couldn't for the life of her see. There were rules, obviously; but no one had bothered to give her a rulebook. It was like walking cold into a game of bridge, being handed a pack of cards, and told to play—without even knowing what trumps meant. And if she asked, or was too blatant about not knowing, all the other players would think she'd gone insane.

No time to worry about it, not now. She'd be here for the rest of her life. It hit her hard, thinking that—knowing it as surely as, say, Julia knew she was a slave. Right behind it came a stab of real pain, a pang of longing for Kimberley and Justin, so strong that she almost couldn't go on.

She put it down. There was nothing she could do for them but pray. She'd done that. For the rest of it . . . sooner or later, she'd have to sit down, take a deep breath, and do some serious sorting out. For now, for this moment at least, she gave one of the women an *as* for herself and another for Aurelia, then walked into the baths. She was getting good, perhaps too good, at segueing in and out, alternating between near-horror at her situation and a somewhat desperate determination to cope with it. Coping was all she could do— unless she broke and ran screaming into the Danube.

Though the sun streamed in through many windows, her eyes needed a moment to adapt from the brighter light outside. As her vision cleared, she had to work hard not to burst into a torrent of helpless giggles. When, back in the twentieth century, she'd thought about the Romans at all, which wasn't often, what came to mind was cool white marble, as at the Getty. She'd learned in the street that that wasn't exactly accurate, but she hadn't realized, till just now, how very far off the mark it was.

They had cool white marble here—had it and painted it. Or, even better, plastered it over, then painted it. Statues decorated the antechamber, every one of them painted in the same disturbingly lifelike and gaudy style as the ones at street corners. The plastered walls were painted with garden scenes, each individual flower or shrub rendered realistically in itself but without perspective, so that everything was on the same flat, oddly dreamlike plane. The ceiling, lost in lofty dimness, showed a glimmer that might have been gilding and probably was. And as if all that had not been enough, the floor under her foot was a riot of reds and greens and golds, browns and bronzes and blues, hundreds, maybe thousands of vividly glazed tiles arranged into a mosaic of hunters and hounds, stags and wild boar.

The room beyond that was unroofed, a courtyard open to the sky. Something about that, about the transition from enclosed space to outer air, the shape and placement of entry and courtyard, reminded Nicole of something, as if she'd seen them before. Of course: on her honeymoon in Carnuntum, she'd walked in the ruins of this place. She looked around, taking it all in, trying to keep it in memory so that she could come back here and know where she was.

The flowers in this courtyard weren't painted on the wall. They were real, planted in orderly rows, the bushes near the walls trimmed with geometric severity. Women exercised in the middle of the yard, some with dumbbells, others tossing around what looked like green balloons. "Pig bladders!" Aurelia was jumping up and down with delight. "Mother, may I? Pig bladders are so much fun!"

"Pig . . . bladders." Nicole had already seen that the Romans used every part of the pig except the squeal. One more proof here. They had to paint or dye the bladders that interesting shade of green: it didn't look like anything one would find inside of a pig.

Most of the women who were exercising had rounder, fleshier bodies than Umma's—they were built more as Nicole had been back in twentieth-century California. They had to be exercising to lose weight, Nicole thought, as in a health club in that other world and time. She had a moment's sensation almost of relief—at last, something that resembled the things she'd known before.

Then she overheard two women sitting on a bench, watching the show and offering commentary. One pointed to a woman who to Nicole's eyes was somewhat on the beefy side. "What's Pollia doing hefting those weights? Her fig-ure's perfect as it is. Her husband never complains about sticks and bones."

Her friend, whom Nicole would have called nicely if not overly slim, sighed in clearly evident envy. "Doesn't he now? Nor," she added with a flash of malice, "her boyfriend either."

"Do tell!" the first woman said. "So who is it now? Faus-tus still? Or is she creeping around in corners with that pretty young Silvius instead?"

"Why, both!" her friend declared.

They laughed together, rocking back and forth on the stone bench, clinging to each other as if they'd never heard a better joke. When they were under control again, the second woman said, "It's chic, that's why she does it. Run around, show off your nice breasts and your firm buttocks, let every-body admire your technique. What's it to her how much meat and oil she needs to scarf up, to keep the weight on? Every-body knows she married old Aulus for his money—and his handsome slaves."

Nicole moved past them before they could guess she was eavesdropping, taking a second, longer look at the women playing what looked like a cross between volleyball and soc-cer.

Their rings and earrings and bracelets were gold, most of them. They're the rich ones, she realized with yet another shock to the tottering structure of her assumptions: the ones who can eat enough to put on weight, and who don't do enough real work to take it off again. She thought of her own new body, and how she'd admired its slimness. A sigh—half rueful laugh—escaped her. Wasn't that just like her luck? Thin was not In in Carnuntum. The body that had been on the chunky side in California would have been per-fect here—and this one, which would have been a killer in the latest in short, tight, and Spandex, was too skinny by local standards. "You can't win," she said to herself.

Aurelia was tugging at her tunic again. "Mother! Mother, can I play?"

"No," Nicole said absently. Then, with more focus: "No, there's no one else your age playing. Come on inside."

Aurelia didn't protest too loudly. She was too excited by the whole adventure to quibble over every detail of it. Nicole didn't need to do anything clever to get her to lead the way. She aimed unerringly toward one of several doorways on the far side of the colonnade, into a room whose function was unmistakable. Two of the walls were bristling with pegs, some draped with items of clothing, others empty. While she stood just inside the doorway, letting her eyes adapt again from sunlight to indoor dimness, a woman slipped out of her tunic and drawers and hung them with her sandals on a peg. A clothed attendant sat on a stool nearby. She was probably supposed to be keeping an eye on things, but she looked half asleep.

Nicole hadn't been nude in public since she'd escaped her last high-school p.e. class, for which she was heartily glad. No choice now—and the woman who'd just stripped off wasn't anything special, either. Defiantly, she pulled her tunic off over her head and yanked down her loincloth. The roof didn't fall in. The walls didn't shake with laughter and jeers and cries of *Skinny Minnie!* and *Hey, Horseface!* No one took any notice of her at all.

Aurelia got out of her clothes in one fluid motion. She took it altogether for granted. *When in Rome . . . ,* Nicole thought, and grinned to herself. She wasn't sure how amused she was, but the irony of the situation was hard to escape.

She looked down at herself. Sure enough, halfway between her belly button and the edge of her indifferently shaven bush was a nondescript brown mole. No doubt about it: Calidius Severus had seen this body naked—and paid attention to what he'd seen.

She sighed. Well, so had she, now. *And isn't it about time? Now everybody's happy.*

Once her eyes adapted, she saw the room was larger than she'd thought at first, and more crowded. A counter stood along the wall at the far end. A second attendant sat there, looking as bored as the first. When Nicole and Aurelia came up to her, she did as she'd done for the woman just ahead of them: she handed Nicole a small, cheap earthenware jar without a stopper and a bronze tool resembling a half-scale sickle.

What am I supposed to do with this? Nicole wondered. She looked around for the answer. Women sat naked on benches rubbing the stuff from the jars over themselves and then scraping it off with the sickle-like tools. She didn't see any boys Lucius' age, or any other age either. A soft murmur of conversation filled the room. A few women sat in pairs and threes, oiling and scraping one another, but most seemed to be there alone and comfortable with it.

While Nicole took it all in, Aurelia spotted an empty bench and dashed over to lay claim to it. "Come on, Mother!" she called. "You're so slow today. Will you do me first, Mother, please? I want to go swim in the pool!"

Nicole picked her way past the benches full of preoccupied women. None of them looked up. Nobody stared or even seemed to notice her. She sat on the bench. Aurelia presented her narrow back and shoulders with an air of someone who knows very well what she is in for.

Nicole poured a little of the liquid from the jar into the cupped palm of her hand. It was olive oil, as she would have guessed by Julia's odor fresh from the baths—not so good and, by the scent, not so fresh as what she used in the tavern, but unmistakably olive oil. *This is going to get anybody clean?*

One thing was certain: Aurelia had plenty of dirt on which to experiment. Nicole rubbed the oil over her. Aurelia was still at the age where she made a perfect figure one—all vertical lines, no curves whatever. But, though she was slim enough for her ribs to show, she wasn't scrawny; her arms and legs had plenty of flesh on them.

"Mother!" she squeaked when Nicole began to scrape off the olive oil. "The strigil tickles!"

That gave Nicole the name of the tool she was awkwardly wielding. Amazing, how much dirt it took off with the oil. It wasn't as good as soap would have been, but it wasn't bad. And she only had to tell Aurelia to stop wiggling about half a dozen times.

After she'd finished with Umma's daughter—her daughter now—she swallowed a twinge of revulsion and rubbed oil into her own skin, all over. It had a slimy, slippery feel, like cold cream gone bad, or rancid baby oil. Aurelia begged to help. Nicole handed her the strigil. "Here, you do my legs." Aurelia was happy to oblige. She did as good a job as one might expect, but grew bored with it and wandered off, humming to herself. Nicole finished the rest, twisting awkwardly to do her back and buttocks. It was truly astonishing how well the oil lifted dirt. Her skin was a couple of shades lighter, and it hadn't even seen water yet.

A man's voice sent her into a purely reflexive jump-and-curl, one arm over her breasts, the other over her privates. The owner of the voice sauntered in beside and a little behind one of the women who'd been exercising in the courtyard, the one who looked astonishingly like Elizabeth Taylor and seemed to have about the same fondness for gold and out-sized stones. No diamonds, Nicole was rather disappointed to note. The jewels were huge, but looked rough and barely polished; they ran heavily to garnets and amber.

The woman skinned her tunic over her rigidly curled and plaited head and strolled, unconcernedly naked, to a vacant bench. She lay on her belly and rested her head on her folded arms, sighing and wriggling her ample buttocks as if to get comfortable on the well-worn wood.

Her escort was a type Nicole would have recognized in L.A. He'd have been showing off his buff pecs on the beach and trying out for roles on *Baywatch,* back where Nicole came from. Here he seemed to have settled into the life of a kept studmuffin. He bent over his—mistress? that could be taken several different ways—and began to rub her back. She purred with pleasure. Nobody could miss the sound: it echoed through the room.

Was he a slave? Was he her slave? Did the baths provide a masseur if you paid extra? Nicole didn't know the answers to any of those questions. Another one occurred to the lawyerly side of her, one that made her laugh to herself: how many masseurs figured in divorce actions in Carnuntum?

Aurelia was hopping up and down with impatience. "Mother! Are you asleep? I asked you. Shall we go in the hot plunge now, or the cool one?"

Nicole shook herself back into line. "The hot one," she answered promptly. The man's muscles hadn't aroused her a bit, but her insides went all soft and quivery at the thought of hot water.

She'd chosen right for Aurelia, too: the child clapped her hands and danced. She skipped ahead through one of two doorways at the far side of the stripping-off room. More women had been going through that doorway than through the other. So it wasn't just Nicole's twentieth-century sensibility. In a world in which hot water wasn't simply to be had at the turning of a tap, people valued it all the more.

The hot plunge was a small swimming pool, although Nicole had never before gone into a pool with a mosaic of voluptuously naked women on the bottom. Their hair was green—sea nymphs? She sighed as she lowered herself into the water: the temperature was just what she would have wanted in her own tub.

Some of her pleasure died abruptly. This water hadn't come from a nice safe heater in a corner of the laundry room. Slaves had hauled wood to feed the fires that heated the pool. There was human sweat in it, and human blood, too.

She couldn't wallow in liberal guilt every time she made a new move. This whole world looked to be a liberal's nightmare. Too much of it would have been her nightmare if she'd known what it was really like.

Well, she hadn't. And she was here, and she was staying here, and that was that. She shut off the corner of her mind that niggled her with guilt, and went back to reveling in the feel of hot water on her skin.

Aurelia had slid into the plunge a little way down. Now she came paddling up to Nicole, sleek as a fish. "Come here," Nicole said. "We're going to do your hair."

Aurelia didn't like getting dunked, not even slightly. She

spluttered and squawked and wiggled, none of which did her
any good. Nicole was all for empowering children, but not
when they had heads full of lice and nits. She did the best
job she could with hot water and no shampoo, and had to
hope it would be enough.

When she'd finished tormenting Aurelia, she worked at
her own hair and scalp with fingers and nails till she could
feel the sting of water in scrapes and scratches. Maybe she'd
managed to unload the current cargo of vermin. But even if
she had, how long would that last? She'd have to boil all the
bedding and all the clothes in her house to have a prayer of
banishing them for good—and she had next to no chance
that they'd stay banished, not with customers bringing in a
whole new shipment five minutes after she'd killed off the
last one.

She could get used to stuffing her underwear with rags
several days a month, because the other women in Carnuntum had to do the same. She supposed she could get used to
chamber pots, because everybody in Carnuntum used chamber pots. Could she get used to being lousy, because everybody in Carnuntum was lousy? Not—bloody—likely. She
scrubbed at her scalp again.

A woman a few feet away from her stopped trying to rub
dirt off an arm that was hardly more than skin wrapped
around bones and started coughing: long, wet, racking
coughs that made her ladder-thin body shudder and her face
turn dusky purple. When at last she seemed able to pause
for breath, Nicole saw flecks of reddish froth in her nostrils
and the corners of her lips, as if she'd literally coughed up
bits of lung.

Tuberculosis, Nicole thought with a frisson of horror. The
horror that followed was too big for a frisson: the woman
spat the bloody foam into the water, as casual as if there
were no harm in it at all, and went back to trying to get
clean.

Nicole stared transfixed at the swirling, turbid water. The
foam had melted right into it. In her mind's eye, she saw the
bacilli floating there, spreading through the plunge, multiply-

ing in that wonderful warm, wet medium. But the germs
were too small for her physical eyes to see—for anyone to
see. And there were no microscopes here. She remembered
that from some class or other, history of science or some
such: what a world-shaking discovery that had been. It was
still centuries in the future.

And, because germs were too small for human eyes to see,
no one in Carnuntum would believe they were there. Everything she'd seen in the city made her sure of that.

But that didn't mean they weren't there, or that she didn't
know they were there. She grabbed Aurelia, who was doing
her best to imitate an otter. "Time to get out," Nicole said
firmly.

"Oh, Mother! Do you want to go to the sweating room
already?" Aurelia sounded like every kid ever born, in any
corner of the world.

It did her no good whatever. "Yes, that's where we're
going," Nicole said, though she hadn't known it was till Aurelia mentioned it. All she'd known was that they were getting out of this pool, and they were doing it this instant.

Reluctantly, Aurelia did as she was told. Reluctantly, she
led the way down a dim stone passageway to the sweating
room, though Nicole wasn't about to let her know she was
doing that.

Outside the room, an attendant stood holding a tray. She
held it out as Nicole came up. Half a dozen leaf-shaped iron
blades lay on the tray. "Razor?" she asked.

Nicole took a razor. She held it cautiously; in California,
she'd used an electric shaver, not least because she kept slicing herself with blades. This wasn't just a slicing tool; if you
weren't careful, you could kill somebody with it. Yourself,
for instance.

Nevertheless, and in spite of her misgivings, she took it.
She'd already seen that nobody in Carnuntum went around
au naturel. If she wanted to blend in, she had to do what
everybody else did.

And, having seen how bad the lice problem was, she
thought she knew why women here shaved everything but

their heads. It was a wonder they didn't shave their heads, too. Maybe she should do that, and start a fashion?

She wasn't feeling quite so radical just then. She had chances enough for mayhem as she shaved tender places she'd never tried shaving before with any razor at all, let alone one as potentially lethal as this. The razor was dull, too, and scraped and pulled, and altogether it was not a pleasant process.

Women might shave everywhere, and for good sanitary reasons, too, but Nicole had already seen that men didn't even shave their faces. So what was fair about that? *Not one thing,* she thought with a familiar smolder of anger.

Hot air hissed and wheezed through pipes in the walls and floor of the sweating room. Nicole wasn't the only woman shaving there; the sweat that poured from her helped soften the hair and made it easier for the razor not only to cut the hair but to slide across the skin. Nicole still cut herself three or four times, but she wasn't the only one doing that, either. Small bloody nicks and muttered curses marked other victims of fashion and hygiene.

Aurelia, being small, was thoroughly baked before Nicole had started to brown. Just as Nicole scraped the last wiry black fuzz from her shin, Aurelia tugged at her free hand. "Let's jump in the cold plunge now, Mother. I'm melting!" Sweating room . . . Cold plunge . . . *Sauna,* Nicole thought happily. She slid down into the cold pool with a sigh of bliss. Aurelia jumped in, splashing water everywhere. None of the women in the pool complained. Maybe they were willing to let kids be kids. Maybe, like Nicole, they felt too good to complain.

When the water started feeling chilly instead of wonderful, Nicole climbed out. Aurelia's lips were blue, and her teeth chattered. Nicole looked around for a towel, but there didn't seem to be one. The air of the baths at least was warmer than the water they'd been in. They dried as they walked down the hall back to the stripping-off room, and warmed up, too. Aurelia paused halfway down the hall. "I have to go to the latrine," she said, and ducked through a doorway.

Nicole, and Umma, too, thank God—or gods—wasn't one of those women who had to go every ten minutes, or she'd have been in bad shape by now; but her bladder was a little full, and she was curious as to what, if anything, Romans had besides chamber pots. She was envisioning a row of stalls, and in each a malodorous earthen pot, as she stepped from the dim passage into a slightly brighter and much wider space. It was larger than she'd expected, as big as the biggest public restroom she could remember from the twentieth century. It was public, too, no doubt about that. No stalls or partitions separated one hole from another on the long stone bench. You sat down and did what you did in front of everybody, and everybody did her business in front of you.

Nicole's bladder clamped up tight and wouldn't let go. Bashful bladder syndrome sounded like a joke, but it wasn't. It was as real as this giant privy and the dozen or so women squatting and chattering and doing their business with no more trouble than the men had had pissing in Titus Calidius Severus' urn.

Closing her eyes helped. So did the gurgle of flowing water beneath her: houses might not boast running water, but the baths and fountains did. The latrine even had the equivalent of toilet paper: a sponge on a stick in a jar of water. The water was murky. Nicole picked up the sponge with some misgivings, wondering who'd used it last. Nobody else seemed to wonder about that, or care.

The latrine wasn't all it might have been, but it was bliss compared to squatting over an earthenware jar. In spite of the sweating room and the cold plunge, the baths weren't all they might have been either; but again, compared to being filthy they were heaven.

Aurelia obviously agreed. "That was nice, Mother," she said as they got back into their clothes, "even if you did scrub my hair too hard."

Nicole nodded. "It was nice," she said. She probably hadn't got all of Aurelia's nits, or her own, but she didn't want to think about that. She didn't want to think about going back to work, either, not after this lovely lazy morning. She sighed and squared her shoulders. "It was nice," she repeated, "but we've got to go home."

7

NICOLE WAS SURPRISINGLY GLAD to see the street she'd come to think of as her own, and the tavern that technically was her own, even after the pleasure of a bath and a romp through the market and the rich indulgence of sticky buns. She'd even got the baker to throw in a basket with a broken handle, no good for displaying his wares but more than good enough for bringing a sampling home. She'd eaten one, too, and Aurelia had had two and was sulking slightly at being denied a third.

Aurelia scampered through the door ahead of her. She paused, licking sticky fingers and letting her eyes adjust. "Hello!" she sang out to the dark within. "I'm—"

She stopped. Her eyes made out shapes that came clearer the longer she stared.

"Oh, hello, Umma," Ofanius Valens said. He was sitting on a stool. Julia was sitting on his lap. His right arm circled her waist. His left arm had hiked her tunic up to her knees so his hand could slide between her legs. Her tongue was doing something monstrously lewd to his ear.

Lucius rampaged up and down behind them, joyfully oblivious, or else so used to the sight that he didn't even think it was worth noticing. He swept his toy sword hither and yon, leaping and stabbing the defenseless air. "Take that, you miserable barbarian! Ha!" He whooped and brandished the sword. "By Jupiter! Right in the guts!" What Julia was doing with Ofanius Valens didn't bother Lucius.

It bothered Nicole. It bothered her a lot. "What's going on here?" she demanded.

Aurelia ran right past the two of them, sparing a giggle that told Nicole she knew exactly what was going on, she thought it was mildly amusing, but it wasn't half as interesting as the game her brother was playing. She sprang into that with a whoop and a cry, not even needing a toy sword to become a fearless warrior maiden. Still whooping, they rollicked and scrambled up the stairs.

Julia didn't move from Ofanius Valens' lap. His hand went right on rubbing and fondling. Nicole watched it move rhythmically up and down, up and down, raising and lowering her filthy tunic. "Now, now, don't worry," he said easily. "I wasn't going to cheat you." He tilted his head toward the table. "See, there's your two *sesterces,* and Julia'll get her *dupondius* once we've gone upstairs, if she's as lively as she usually is."

"I'll do my best," Julia purred. The purr and the smile that followed were polished to a hard, clear—professional— gloss. Ofanius Valens' hand pumped harder. She rocked with it, still smiling, with little, audible catches of breath that Nicole would have bet were as calculated as the rest.

They both took the whole thing completely for granted. Nicole didn't. Julia had been pleased with herself yesterday: she'd made a couple of *dupondii* for herself. How had she made them? *The usual way,* she'd said. Was this the usual way? Prostituting herself? Umma must have—no, not looked the other way. Where Julia might get a *dupondius* for herself if the customer—if the john, mincing no words—liked her, Umma raked in two *sesterces* every time her slave walked up those stairs. That was good money: more than she took in for some meals. Of course, it also made her a small-time madam. Umma obviously hadn't cared about that. Nicole did.

Every time she began to have the shaky beginnings of a feel for the way Carnuntum worked, something like this slapped her in the face. Julia was at Ofanius Valens' ear again, flicking her tongue down the curve of it. "Stop that!"

Nicole burst out, her voice thick with revulsion. Ofanius
blinked at her through a visible haze of horniness. Julia
blinked in the exact same way, through the exact same haze.
They honestly, incontestably did not understand what Nicole's problem was. "Stop that," she repeated a little more
quietly. "Julia, get off him."

Julia did as she was told, automatically, like a child or a
well-trained animal. The haze retreated, though enough of it
lingered that she kept a hand on Ofanius Valens' shoulder,
kneading it absently as she frowned at Nicole. "What's the
matter, Mistress?" she asked in the tone that had become too
familiar, that didn't quite dare ask, *What's wrong with you?
You're acting weird again!* "You see he's already paid. Like
he says, we weren't going to steal from you. Or are you
worried about yesterday? I put the two *sesterces* in the box
each time, just like always. Didn't you find them when you
reckoned up the accounts?"

Nicole hadn't known how to reckon up the accounts, or
how much to look for, either. She couldn't say so. She concentrated on the other thing, the more important thing. "Julia,
look at me." Julia was already doing that. Her expression
made it clear that she knew it and was refraining from com-
menting on it. Nicole took a steadying breath and went on
with the speech she'd prepared: "You don't have to go to
bed with him, Julia. You don't ever have to go to bed with
anybody for money again. That's all done now." She glared
at Ofanius Valens. "Food is one thing. Wine is another." It
wasn't anything she wanted, but it also didn't seem to be
anything in which she had a choice. Here . . . "This is something else altogether. It's over, done, finished. Not in this
place, ever again. Do you understand me?"

Ofanius Valens scratched his head. Nicole flinched inside
for reasons that had nothing to do with the business at hand.
He couldn't possibly know about those reasons, or the flinch,
either.

He seemed to decide, after a moment's puzzlement, that
argument would get him nowhere. *Smart man,* Nicole
thought. Smarter than most twentieth-century males. He was

still a male, however, and he wasn't any happier than any other male who'd ever been born about being told no, he couldn't have what he wanted. "I don't know what you're getting yourself in an uproar about, Umma. Whatever it is, I guess I'll just take myself someplace else from now on." He scooped up his two *sesterces* from the tabletop, dumped them in his belt pouch, and stalked past Nicole and out the door.

"And good riddance." Nicole turned to Julia, a smile at the ready, to receive the slave's thanks for freeing her from that sordid transaction.

Julia gave her no such thing. Julia, in fact, looked furious. Her nostrils flared. Her blue eyes glittered. She hissed, a sharp, furious sound.

Her words were an anticlimax, her tone studiedly mild, but her expression gave away how angry she was. "That wasn't very nice, Mistress. Now he won't come back."

She doesn't know anything about freedom. How can she? She's never had it. Nicole chose her words with care, to soothe Julia's temper and get her thinking rationally. "Don't worry about him," she said. "We don't need his business, or business like his." As she spoke, she advanced into the room, till she was close enough to lay a hand on Julia's shoulder. It was stiff, set against her. "I told you: you're never going to bed with another man for money. Never again—I promise."

Julia's eyes widened. It still wasn't gratitude—it was somewhere between dismay and horror. Worse yet was the gleam of tears. "Mistress, why can't I go to bed with men anymore? What did I do? Why are you so angry with me? Just tell me and I'll fix it. You can beat me all you like, if that will make you feel better."

Nicole's head shook. Good Lord. Titus Calidius Severus had thought she was angry with him, too. That had been a misunderstanding. What was there to misunderstand here? "I'm not angry," Nicole said, just as she had to Calidius Severus. "I don't want you to have to suffer like that, that's all."

"Suffer, Mistress?" Julia tossed her head in amazement. "What is there to suffer? Ofanius Valens knows how to make a woman hot." Her hips twitched a little; Nicole didn't think she knew she was doing it. "And even the ones who aren't very good usually give me something for myself afterwards, because I make them hot. Now that you've taken another of your strange new notions, how am I supposed to get any money of my own? That was all I had, Mistress: taking men upstairs. I *liked* taking men upstairs."

Nicole stared. Julia stared back, for once not lowering her eyes in submission. She was shocked enough, and indignant enough, to show for once what must have been her real self. She wasn't slow at all, or simple either. That was a mask she wore, like the hooker's mask she'd put on for Ofanius Valens.

"Ofanius Valens gave you an *as* at breakfast the other day," Nicole said. "You didn't do anything for him then but wait on him and be pleasant to him."

"Oh, yes, a whole *as*," Julia said scornfully. "And that wasn't just on account of breakfast, either. He was being nice to me so I'd be nice to him later."

An as *for a piece of ass,* Nicole thought, but she didn't say it—it only worked in English. What she did say was, "Sleeping with men for money is degrading."

Julia shrugged, still sullen and not about to let Nicole forget it. "I've heard people say that," she said. "Usually women who don't have what it takes. They're jealous, that's all. Can't get any fun, so don't want anybody else to get any either."

"Fun?" Nicole said incredulously. "You call it fun?"

Julia did a creditable bump-and-grind, with a wild, mirthless grin in it for Nicole. "Sure it is. What else is there in the world that's anywhere near as much fun?"

She wasn't just saying it to be obnoxious, Nicole realized. She meant it. In Los Angeles, there had been any number of things to do besides hop between the sheets. Anything from aerobics to pottery classes to nightclubs to fancy restaurants to biker bars to mall-crawling to . . . She stopped the mental recitation before it threw her into a funk. None of those things existed in Carnuntum. Nicole had been here only three days, scrambling every minute to keep afloat in a sea of totally new and strange details. She hadn't had time to be bored. Julia had lived her whole life here, without television, without radio, without movies, without recorded music, without newspapers, books, magazines . . . without much of anything when it came to entertainment. Nicole remembered when she was a kid in Indiana, when a tornado would roar through, or a blizzard, and the power would go out, in rural areas sometimes for days or weeks; and nine months later the maternity wards in the hospitals would be doing a boomtown business. When there was nothing else to do, people just naturally turned to sex.

"I mean," Julia said, sounding like a Latinate Valley girl, "I could get drunk all the time, but you wouldn't like that, either, because then I wouldn't be able to work."

"No," Nicole said, "I wouldn't like that." Considering how she felt about alcohol, there were few things she would have liked less. But this was one of them. She might have descended from lawyer to tavernkeeper, but by God, she hadn't descended from lawyer to procurer. "You're not going to prostitute yourself just to get a little spending money."

"Mistress," Julia said with an air of desperate patience. "It's not just for the money. You don't sleep by yourself every night. Or at least," she added after a pause, "you didn't till you quarreled with Calidius Severus the other day." When Nicole didn't erupt at that—Nicole was momentarily unable to think of anything to say—Julia went on, "Oh, Mistress! I know I'm a slave and you can do whatever you want and I can't say a thing about it, but you've never been as bad as you've been in the past few days. If you've got it into your head that I'm suffering—how about the pain I feel when I don't have any money to call my own?"

Her expression was piteous, but Nicole didn't budge. Mothers of teenagers heard the same arguments in pretty much the same tone. It didn't mean a thing, and she was not about to let it sway her. "You will not make money by selling yourself," she said. Julia dropped her wounded-kitten pose and glared. Nicole glared right back.

The moment stretched. Nicole drew in a deep breath, then let it out in a long sigh. "I've been thinking about this for a long time"—ever since her spirit came to Carnuntum, even if that was only two days—"and now I'm sure the time is right. I'm going to set you free."

This time, she was sure Julia would fall on her neck in gratitude. She waited for it, expected it. But, as before, Julia seemed anything but glad to get such a gift. If anything, she looked upset. "But," she said, "Mistress, what would I do if I was free?"

Nicole reminded herself again that this was a slave, and probably born a slave. The concept of freedom was alien to her. Therefore Nicole kept her voice light, encouraging. "What will you do? Why, anything you want to. You'll be free."

Julia eyed her warily. "Could I go on working here?"

"For wages, do you mean?" Nicole asked.

Julia nodded. She was still wary, with a hint of apprehension, but Nicole had noticed that if Julia got a thought in her head, she couldn't help but pursue it to its logical conclusion. "Yes, Mistress. Or at least, some wages. Room and board and a little money for myself."

Which was exactly what she got now—except for the money part, which had just evaporated. Julia was canny, Nicole thought. Behind that open face and simple, forthright manner lay a sharp intelligence.

Intelligence, maybe, but no ambition. Nicole was a little disappointed. "If that's what you want to do," Nicole said, "yes, I suppose so." *And God knows I need you to help me get through all the things I still don't know.* "Or you could go to school and—"

Julia looked at her as if she'd gone around the bend again. "School? Mistress, what good would that do?"

Now that Nicole had rather expected. "It would give you more kinds of work to choose from," she answered. "After all, you can't read or write, can you?" Umma hadn't been able to, so it was safe enough to assume that her slave couldn't either.

Julia didn't seem to feel the lack. She shrugged indifferently. "What if I could? There aren't many jobs that need it. Clerk for the city, I suppose, or bookkeeper—but even if I could learn enough or fast enough, I wouldn't want to be locked up all day making birdtracks on papyrus. Besides, those are men's jobs. Who ever heard of a lady bookkeeper?" She laughed and shook her head, as if the notion were too absurd for words.

Those are men's jobs. Nicole heard the words with sick dismay. *Who ever heard of a lady bookkeeper?* She'd fled California not only for its sexism but for its hypocrisy. Carnuntum was every bit as sexist—and not the least bit hypocritical about it. "What about Liber and Libera?" Nicole asked, a little hoarsely.

"The wine god and his wife?" Julia asked as if puzzled. "What about them, Mistress? They're gods. They aren't bookkeepers."

"The—wine god and goddess?" Nicole felt as if she'd been slugged in the gut. What had she done to herself? Of all the deities she would have picked to help her . . .

But they had helped her, snickering at her ignorance, all too likely, but helping her nevertheless. And here she was, in the world they'd chosen for her, and she was damned if she knew what to do about it.

Maybe she was damned. Sunday school had included a long rant on sin and damnation, and a scenic tour of hell. Wine and drunkards had warranted a whole separate dissertation, along with fornicators, whom Nicole had thought of then, in her eight-year-old innocence, as people who had been put to work stoking the furnaces.

It wasn't particularly warm in Carnuntum, but there was plenty of heat inside Nicole's skull. It felt as if her brains were boiling. "Liber and Libera," she managed to say. "Aren't they—" She softened what she'd been about to say: "Aren't they also the gods of liberty?"

Julia thought about it briefly, then nodded. "Yes, I suppose so. Liberty from care—isn't that what wine does? Frees your soul from worry, lets you forget for a while that life isn't going the way you want it to?"

"Liberty—from care?" Again, Nicole's echo was hesitant and filled with a dismay she tried to hide from Julia. That fit too well with what the god and goddess had done, her last night in West Hills. She'd been filled with care then. Liber and Libera had taken her out of it, had sent her back to their time, back to their town, where she'd thought—where they must have thought—she would be carefree.

She didn't know whether to laugh or to cry. Carefree? Wine, lice, slavery—and now sexism, too? Some freedom this was—all the new worries of this time and place, and a whole set of old ones from California, too. It was more than she could take.

She almost prayed to Liber and Libera to ship her back to California. But she wasn't giving up yet, even for Kimberley and Justin. She'd asked for this. She had to make the best of it.

"Mistress?" Julia said. Nicole nodded to show she'd been paying attention, even if she hadn't. "Mistress," Julia said again, "I was thinking. If I work here as a freedwoman, not as a slave, I'll be able to take men upstairs and keep all"—Nicole's expression gave her pause, but she misinterpreted it—"all right, not all, but more of what they pay, for myself."

"If you work here as my freedwoman," Nicole said through clenched teeth, "you will not prostitute yourself."

"But why not," Julia asked, "if I'm free and if I want to?" She searched Nicole's face as if she could find an answer there. "Mistress, I don't understand."

Nicole opened her mouth, then closed it again. Here was an issue she'd never imagined she'd have to face. If a woman wanted to go on selling herself, did another woman have the right to forbid it? She couldn't face that, not on those terms. She sidestepped instead, as she had with Lucius and Aurelia: "Isn't there anything else you'd rather do?"

Julia raised her hands and let them fall. "Mistress, you

keep saying that, but what else can I do? I can cook some and bake some, so maybe I could work at another tavern, but it's hard to find one that doesn't already have its own slave—and slaves work for free. Remember that woman you wouldn't hire last year because you owned me?"

Again, Nicole made herself nod. *Because you owned me.* Julia said it so calmly. She took it for granted. However unhappy she might be as a slave, she never blinked at slavery itself.

"I'm good at something else, too," she said, "or the men say I am. But I don't want to do that for a living, either. I'd have to take on men I didn't want at all, and I wouldn't much care for that."

Nicole lowered her aching head into her hands. Had she really expected life here to be simple? In California, she'd always known how to react, what to think, what was right and what was wrong. In Carnuntum, there was no such thing as simplicity—not to her twentieth-century mind.

She settled on the one thing that was simple, the thing she had decided on. "Let's do what we have to do to get you free," she said, "and then we'll worry about everything else. How does that sound?"

"All right, Mistress." Even now, Julia sounded more dutiful than delighted. "Brigomarus won't like it, I'll bet."

"Brig—?" Nicole needed a moment to recall the name of Umma's brother—now, effectively, her brother. "Don't you worry about Brigomarus. Just leave him to me."

"Yes, Mistress." Julia still sounded dutiful. She sounded, Nicole supposed, very much the way a slave was supposed to sound. The contrast with Julia's usual, freer manner was strong enough to bring Nicole up short, and to stab her with guilt—which was probably what Julia intended.

Slaves and children, Nicole thought. *They're powerless—but they can manipulate the ones in power, to get what they think they want.* And hadn't she done the same thing herself more times than she could count, growing up and going to school and working in a law firm that took equity so far and not an inch further?

*   *   *

Two afternoons later, Brigomarus breezed into the tavern. Luck was looking after Nicole again. She didn't need to wonder who this casual type was who blew in as if he owned the place. Lucius, who'd been cracking walnuts, shouted "Uncle Brigo!" and tried to tackle him.

He swept the boy up, tipped him upside down, and bonked his head on a tabletop. Lucius squealed in delight. Brigomarus tipped him back upright and set him bouncing on his feet, and pulled a handful of candied figs from his belt pouch. Lucius snatched them as eagerly as if he hadn't been eating as many walnuts as he dropped into the bowl, and danced around the room while Aurelia, who'd heard the uproar and come downstairs to see what was happening, fell on her uncle and held him hostage till he surrendered a second handful of figs.

"Greedy kids," he said affectionately, planting himself on a stool and thumping the table with a fist. "Let me have some wine, would you, sister? I'd have been back sooner, but . they've had us making shields from dawn to dusk. The war with the tribes across the river isn't anywhere near over yet, you mark my words."

Nicole dipped a cup of Falernian for him, figuring family deserved the best. Maybe Umma hadn't been that generous: Brigomarus' eyebrows rose and he smacked his lips. He downed the cup with as much pleasure as thirst.

She studied him while he drank. He looked like one of Umma's relatives, sure enough. He was, she suspected, a younger brother, though not by much. He was a little fairer than Umma, his eyes hazel rather than brown, but they shared long faces and prominent noses and sharp cheekbones. His beard obscured the shape of his chin, but she supposed it was narrow and rather pointed, like her—Umma's—own. He was rather good-looking, in a lean and hungry way. If she'd been her California self, she might not have wanted to know him; he looked hard and a little dangerous, though his ready smile and easy manner tended to conceal it.

Lucius pestered him, tugging at his arm, voice escalating into a whine: "Wrestle me, Uncle Brigo! Come on, let's wrestle, come on, Uncle Brigo!"

"No," Brigomarus said. Lucius kept at him, tugging harder, ignoring Brigomarus' frown and reiterated, "No!" Brigomarus casually hauled off and smacked him upside the head, harder than Nicole had ever hit a child in her life. "Cut it out, kid," he said. "I want to talk to your mother."

Lucius rocked with the blow, but he didn't start crying or screaming. "Oh, all right, Uncle Brigo," he said, disappointed but evidently undamaged.

If he had started to cry, Nicole would have been on Brigomarus like a tiger. As it was, she wanted to yell at him anyhow. It was hard to hold herself back, to be sensible, to keep from giving herself away. Julia was inclined to take Nicole's odd moments in stride. Somehow, Nicole didn't think Brigomarus would be so accommodating.

"What's on your mind?" she asked him, and hoped she sounded enough like his sister to pass muster.

Evidently she did. He answered a question with a question: "What's this I hear about you wanting to set Julia free?"

Nicole's heart jumped, but she held steady. "It's true," she said. "I do." She'd had time enough over the past couple of days to frame a response that, from what Julia had said, a person from here and now could legitimately have made: "I decided that I didn't want her to have to sleep with customers to get a little spending money." She kept wanting to say pocket change, but nobody in Carnuntum knew about pockets.

Brigomarus raised his eyebrows. "What? That never bothered you before." He sucked on a front tooth, as if it helped him get his thoughts in order. "I hate to lose the money she cost, too—and if one of those customers knocked her up, the brat would bring a nice piece of change." By his tone, he might have been trying to talk his sister out of a real-estate deal he thought foolish. Like Julia and everyone else Nicole had seen in this place, he had not the slightest sense that anything was wrong with or about slavery itself.

It drove Nicole crazy. The casual way in which Brigomarus spoke of selling a child for profit made her belly go tight and cold. "Setting Julia free is what I want to do," she said with unshaken determination, "and I'm going to do it."

Brigomarus scowled. "Listen, you know it's not that simple." He paused as if to control his temper, or maybe to come up with an argument a silly woman would understand. "Look, Umma, if you're bound and determined, I don't want to fight over it. Life is too short as it is. Let's do it like this, if you've got your mind set on it." He waited for Nicole's emphatic nod, then went on, "Let her earn more money and keep more money, so she can pay back what she cost."

Julia's face fell. Nicole could make a pretty good guess what that meant: with what Julia could make, she'd never be able to pay for herself—unless she sold her body, and sold it and sold it. . . . That was partly why Nicole shook her head even more violently than she'd nodded, but only partly. She could not stomach owning a slave for one more instant. And there was no way in hell she was going to compromise with the system by taking money from Julia in return for Julia's freedom. "No," Nicole said. "I'm going to emancipate her, and that's that."

"I say you're not going to do anything of the sort." Brigomarus sounded as revoltingly sure of himself as any senior partner at her old law firm.

"You may be my brother"—*and then again, you may not*—"but you're not my master, so don't treat me as if you think you are," Nicole snapped. Brigomarus stared at her as if she, or rather Umma, had never spoken to him like that before. If Umma hadn't, she'd probably wasted a lot of good chances. "She's not your slave, she's mine, and I'm going to do with her as I think best."

"As you think best?" Brigomarus' eyebrows had climbed to his hairline in an expression of comic incredulity—but there was nothing comic about his tone. "And what does that have to do with it? You have a family, Umma, and you seem to have forgotten about it."

"I haven't forgotten!" Nicole said hotly—and honestly

enough. She never forgot Kimberley or Justin, either, even in the deep throes of life in Carnuntum.

She knew what he meant, nevertheless, and couldn't help a stab of guilt at the actual, if not technical, falsehood.

"Oh, you haven't?" Brigomarus drawled. "Not that I'd blame you for wanting to forget dear Mother and our snotty sisters, after they've married up and you've stayed where we came from, and I know they never waste a chance to remind you of it, either. But even so, Umma, and even if you don't care what this does to the rest of the family, I never imagined you, of all people, throwing away good money for no good reason."

Nicole stiffened her back and lifted her chin. "I'm going to do what's best for me and what's best for Julia, and that's all I'm worried about," she said.

She'd shocked Brigomarus: she saw it in his eyes. And she'd shocked Julia, which shocked her in turn.

Well, she thought, *if the second century isn't ready for a little twentieth-century assertiveness*—and only a little, because she'd soft-pedaled it as best she could—*too damn bad.*

Stiffly, Brigomarus said, "We'll speak of this further when you've come to your senses. The gods grant it be soon." He looked into his cup, saw he had a swallow of wine left, and gulped it down. Then he stalked out of the tavern, shaking his head and muttering under his breath. He hadn't, Nicole noticed, said good-bye, even to the kids.

"Mistress—" Julia looked and sounded deeply worried. "Mistress, are you really sure you want to quarrel with your family over me? A family's the most important thing in the world. If you don't have a family you're on good terms with, who's going to nurse you when you're sick? Who's going to take care of your children if you die? Who's going to help you if you go into debt? If I had a family, I'd never get them angry at me."

Nicole looked at Julia as if seeing her for the first time. She was all alone in the world. As a slave, she was more thoroughly isolated from everyone around her than anyone in the twentieth century could be. That, thought Nicole, no doubt made her look at family with a wistful longing only distantly connected to anything real. You needed to be in a family to know how horrible it could actually be.

Umma apparently knew. "Dear" Mother and a couple of upwardly mobile sisters, was it? Then they probably didn't just drop in to visit, the way Brigomarus felt free to do; and that was a relief. It was enough of a tightrope walk to keep Umma's image going in this tavern and in the neighborhood, without trying to fool Umma's own mother into believing that Nicole was Umma.

So where was Umma? Back in West Hills trying desperately to cope? Floating somewhere in limbo? Or—with a jolt that made her gasp—dead? Dead and . . . gone?

For now, Nicole focused on a simpler problem. "Don't you worry about it," she said to Julia. "Everything's going to be fine, and Brigomarus will figure out he'd be smart to keep his nose out of things that are none of his business."

"How can you say they're none of his business?" Nicole hadn't pegged Julia as a worrier, but neither had she presented Julia with a problem that pertained directly to her. "You're part of his family. They'll all be up in arms when they hear what you want to do, mark my words."

In the United States of the late twentieth century, family was a pallid thing—so pallid that Frank, damn him, could abandon his with hardly a backward glance, and abandon it without disapproval from anyone but Nicole. If anything, his colleagues were jealous he'd latched on to a new, young, sexy girlfriend. And Nicole herself, while she liked her sisters well enough, lived two thousand miles away from them and didn't call as often as she should, let alone write. She'd hardly thought of them at all in the week before she came to Carnuntum, except to wish she could palm the kids off on them for a couple of days after she found out Josefina was heading for Ciudad Obregón.

On the whole, Nicole had liked things that way. She hadn't cared for it when Frank bugged out, not even a little bit, but she'd enjoyed being free herself, ever since she'd got big enough to tell her mother no and make it stick. If she didn't have to kill herself over money and her job, she liked responsibility, liked being, from day to day, the only one who really took care of the house, the kids, her life in general.

Julia sounded as if family disapproval in Carnuntum was like being shunned in an Amish community—Nicole had seen something on television about that, and been caught by the intensity of reaction to something that amounted to the silent treatment. Silence was lovely, she'd thought. So was being left alone. She could have used a lot of that when she was growing up, stuck sharing a bedroom with a sister she could barely stand the sight of, who'd grown up into a reasonably decent person but with whom Nicole had next to nothing in common.

It seemed Umma had about the same relationship with her sisters as Nicole had—but The Family meant far, far more.

Well. So it did. She'd weathered infidelity, she'd weathered divorce. She could weather family disapproval, too. She was her own person, first, last, and always.

She said so, loudly and emphatically. She had no real hope of raising Julia's consciousness, but maybe, over time and with repetition, some of it would stick.

Right at the moment, Julia didn't look enlightened. She looked horrified. Nicole was used to working hostile audiences; it was what a lawyer did for a living. But Julia had a look that warned her to go slow or she'd lose the case. She tried one more time, regardless: "I am my own person. You can be your own person. Family doesn't have to dictate every breath you take. It isn't even your family! I'm not worried about it. Why should you be?"

Julia's chin was set, her face closed. She wrapped herself in a cloud of flour, slapping together another batch of bread for the evening crowd, immersing herself in work to keep from listening—or perhaps to keep from screaming at her mistress to shut up.

She visibly relaxed when Nicole dropped the subject. Nicole sighed. "Rome wasn't built in a day," she murmured in English, and started, painfully, to laugh. Julia's startled expression only made her laugh the harder.

*   *   *   *

Family you could escape, but even in West Hills it was
sometimes hard to escape the neighbors. Not that, there, they
dropped by and wanted to borrow a cup of oil and stay on
for a chat; it was more like hard rock at three A.M. and dog
poop in the front yard.

In Carnuntum, there wasn't anything at three A.M. but
maybe an early rooster crowing, but during the day plenty
went on. The day after Brigomarus came to pull his sister
into line, Nicole looked up from chopping scallions to find
herself face to face with a vaguely familiar figure. It was the
voice that jogged her memory, high and rather thin, with a
touch of what people in Indiana used to call adenoids.

The owner of the voice, Nicole realized, was rather obviously pregnant. She didn't seem to be blooming, but rather
the Rosemary's Baby type: wan and hollow-cheeked, but in
this case irrepressibly cheerful. She held up a cup and said
brightly, "Good morning, Umma! It's been absolute days
since I saw you. Here, look, I have an excuse. I'm out of oil
and my dear woollyhead of a husband has gone off all day
drumming up clients, and it's such a long walk to the market."

Nicole was no recent expert in cup-of-sugar diplomacy,
but she'd seen plenty of it when she was growing up. If it
wasn't sugar, it was coffee, or maybe, in extremity, a cigarette: a transparent excuse to come by, camp in the kitchen,
and chatter the morning away. Housewives did it to lighten
the monotony, or to get out of washing the ceilings, or to
drum up sympathy for this or that husbandly stunt.

In Carnuntum, apparently, the medium of exchange was
olive oil. Nicole spared a half-instant to wonder if Umma
actually gave away what she sold to regular customers, then
shrugged and dipped the cupful. Her neighbor, as she'd expected, didn't just thank her and leave, but perched on a stool
near the counter where Nicole was working. It was a slow
time of day, as she must have known and calculated. She
looked as if she was a regular occupant of that same stool,
easy and comfortable—surprisingly so for someone whose

pregnancy didn't seem to be treating her well.

"So," she said. "How is everything, then? Do you believe what Valentia got up to with that traveling eye-doctor? Why, I hear her husband whipped her black and blue—then she made him feel so guilty he gave her a new necklace! Imagine that!"

Nicole hadn't known she was tense till she felt the muscles of her back and shoulders relax. This was the easy kind of neighbor, then, the one who never let you get a word in edgewise. She didn't appear to notice anything odd about Nicole, nor did she expect any answer to her rapid-fire questions—just rattled right on through them. There was something strangely soothing in the endless flow of her voice, names and events that were as alien to Nicole as the far side of the moon, but so many of them were familiar, too: this couple married, that one divorced ("And he tried to pretend her dowry was his own family money, can you believe that? Got slapped good and proper for that one, you can be sure!"), a third blessed with a son, "and about time, too, after six daughters—they had to expose the last four, they just couldn't feed them."

The woman sighed. Her face, for a moment, was almost somber. "Some people have children and don't want them. Me, I want them and neither of my first two saw even one birthday." Nicole heard her with grim astonishment. Things like that didn't happen in California. No—they did, but rarely enough that they put you on the talk-show circuit with your anguish. Well, Nicole's neighbor was on the talk-show circuit, too. She sighed and patted her belly. "This time, by Mother Isis, everything will be fine. It will."

On and on it went. Somewhere in the middle, Julia came down from cleaning upstairs, greeting the visitor with a smile of honest pleasure and a delighted, "Fabia Ursa! How good to see you. You're looking well." Which gave Nicole a name and a respite, while they chattered at each other for a while—till Julia seemed to remember her status and excused herself to take the heap of soiled bedding and filthy clothes across the street to Titus Calidius Severus, who would trample them in a tub full of water and fuller's earth. No washing machines or laundromats here. No Tide, either, worse luck.

Nicole realized as the morning went on that she liked Fabia Ursa. She also realized she couldn't say that of anyone else she'd met in Carnuntum, even Lucius and Aurelia. It was odd, because back in the twentieth century she'd cordially despised the kaffeeklatsch queens, as she'd liked to call them. Fabia Ursa was a cheerful soul, happily married to a somewhat feckless but much beloved husband, whose foibles she was not shy about sharing. She had two slaves who did everything, as she professed, and had not much to do, it seemed, but trot about and discover who was doing what to whom. She did it with such relish, and with such a clear sense of vocation, that it was impossible to dislike, still less despise her.

Yes, Nicole liked Fabia Ursa. She was not so sure at all that she liked Titus Calidius Severus. Sometimes she did. Then he'd say something, or do something, to set her off again.

He waved to Nicole whenever they saw each other outside their front doors. She always answered politely, and she remembered to use his praenomen. Past calling him Titus, however, she gave him nothing he could take for encouragement.

Although Julia clucked like an unhappy mother hen, Nicole wasn't altogether unhappy when the fuller and dyer stayed out of the restaurant for a few days after her trip to the market. She hoped that meant she'd made him stop and think. No one, she told herself fiercely—not Umma's brother, not Umma's lover, no one—was going to take her for granted here.

Despite that determination, her nerves twanged like a Nashville guitar string when, two or three days after she and Brigomarus had got nowhere, Calidius Severus walked in with a man about half his age who otherwise looked just like him—and, unfortunately, smelled just like him, too. They sat down together like an identical-twin act, exact same stoop, exact same turn of the head, even the same shift and hitch on their respective stools. Nicole, watching them, felt a small, distinct shock, a *Why didn't he tell me?* shock, much the same as if she'd found a wedding ring on Calidius Severus' finger. But he couldn't be married, could he? No. Julia had said he was a widower.

She'd tangled herself in a brief knot, and he was speaking, ordering dinner with perfect and not perceptibly strained casualness. "Wine and bread and onions for both of us, Umma," he said, "and what else have you got that's good?"

"Snails fried with garlic in olive oil?" she suggested. She'd been holding her breath, she discovered, but she'd had to let it out to play the polite proprietor. "I had Lucius bring me back a basketful of snails this morning." And Lucius, no doubt, had had as much fun catching them as an eight-year-old boy could. An incongruous bit of English doggerel went reeling through her head: *Snips and snails and puppy dogs' tails.*

"Those do sound good," Titus Calidius Severus said. Nicole had to clamp down hard on a giggle. His son, whose name Nicole resigned herself yet again to having to pick up from conversation, licked his lips and nodded, smiling widely. The smile, at least, was different from his father's. Titus Calidius Severus was much too sure of himself to indulge in such a goofy grin.

Nicole would sooner have done the snails in butter herself. They had butter in Carnuntum—had it and looked down their noses at it. It was their last resort when they couldn't get olive oil. *No accounting for taste,* Nicole thought, the phrase forming in her mind in English and Latin at the same time. *De gustibus non disputandum.*

"Two orders of snails," she called to Julia. "I'll get the rest."

"All right, Mistress," Julia said from behind the counter. She dropped the snails and chopped garlic into the fierce hiss of hot oil. A wonderful smell wafted out from the pan: oil, garlic, the fishy-sweet scent of snails. Butter would have smelled even better, in Nicole's opinion, but she was, as far as she could tell, a minority of one. Olive oil was healthier, she consoled herself—until she remembered that the oil, like most of the wine in Carnuntum, was imported in glazed amphorae. She'd never imagined worrying about whether lead was more likely to be dangerous than cholesterol. She'd never imagined living in a place where nobody worried about either one.

Calidius Severus' son kept watching Julia while she fried the snails. She'd glance at him every now and again, too, and preen a little. If that didn't mean he'd gone upstairs with her a few times, Nicole would have been astonished.

As Nicole brought them the wine and bread and onions, Titus Calidius Severus whispered something to his son. The younger man frowned. "Is what my father says true?" he demanded.

"I don't know," Nicole answered evenly, arranging food and drink, cups and bowls, on the table in front of them. "What does your father say?"

"That you aren't letting Julia screw for money anymore," he said.

She couldn't say she was startled, though shocked was another matter. From everything she'd heard, Romans charged through the bushes instead of beating around them.

"Yes, it's true," Nicole said, in a tone that couldn't mean anything but, *Want to make something out of it?*

Before his son could make anything out of it, Titus Calidius Severus said, "Why in Ahriman's name would Ofanius Valens lie to me, Gaius? Why would he lie about something like that, anyhow? No money in it." He glanced up at Nicole. His expression was honestly curious. "Why aren't you letting her screw for money anymore?"

"I decided I would sooner have a little less money than be a part-time madam," she replied as starchily as she knew how.

Gaius Calidius Severus still looked miffed. His father grunted the way he did when he was thinking about something that, in his opinion, bore thinking on. "All right, that's not a bad answer," he said at last. "It will likely do your soul good when judging time comes."

Titus Calidius Severus looked to be on the point of saying something more, but just then Julia sashayed between Nicole and the table, accompanied by a powerful odor of garlic. She carried two dishes of snails and a pair of spoons, which she set down with a flourish. Nicole couldn't help but notice that the movements showed off her full breasts in the slightly snug tunic, and the fine curve of her hips and buttocks as she turned and sauntered back to the cookfire. The two Calidii pried their eyes off her long enough to pry the snails out of their shells with the handles of the spoons. No doubt about it, when it came to a choice between food and sex, food had at best an even chance.

They ate with lip-smacking relish. They both, obviously, appreciated Nicole's recipe, if not her social ideas.

Julia didn't appreciate those, either. As she took her place again by the fire, she put in a bump and a wiggle that would have led to a vice-squad bust on any L.A. street. Gaius Calidius Severus had eaten a couple of snails—enough to take the edge off his hunger for food. The third one stopped halfway to his mouth, forgotten in the glory of the scenery. His eyes reminded Nicole pointedly of the sheep's eyes she'd seen in the market.

His father watched, too, not without admiration. Men did that. A lot of the time, they didn't even seem to know they were doing it. It was the way they were made, the kaffeeklatsch queens had said to one another, back in Indiana. Fabia Ursa said it, too, when she came round for a morning's gossip. So what, Nicole wondered, might Umma have said if she'd caught her boyfriend ogling her slave? Something interesting, she hoped. Something memorable. Something better than Nicole's tongue-tied silence.

Or maybe the fuller and dyer was checking Julia out for a different reason. Turning back to Nicole, he said, "Do I hear rightly that you're thinking about manumitting her?"

"Yes, it's true," Nicole repeated in the same truculent tone as before. But curiosity got the better of her defiance; she couldn't keep from asking, "Where did you hear that?"

His smile was on the crooked side, and matched his lopsided shrug. "Somebody who talked to somebody who talked to your brother—you know what gossip's like. If I heard it straight, your brother isn't any too happy about it, either."

"No, he's not." Nicole tossed her head. "He'll get over it—or if he doesn't, too bad for him. It's not his business; it's mine."

Titus and Gaius Calidius Severus stared at her with the same deeply shocked expression Julia had inflicted on her when she'd said that before. In damned near comic chorus, they echoed Julia word for word: "It's family business." *And that,* their tone said, *should most certainly be that.*

Not for me, Nicole thought stubbornly. *Not now, and not while I'm alive to say so.* "I'm not going to let that smother me," she said aloud. "I'll do what's best for me and what's best for Julia. If that's not what the family wants—then too bad for the family. They can just learn to live with it."

"Well," said Calidius Severus after a long pause, clicking his tongue between his teeth. "I suppose that's one way of looking at it." It was not, his expression said, how he would have looked at it. "Families can be a pain, no two ways about it. But you do hate to throw out the connections. You never can tell how things will go—only the gods know that. We mortals, well . . . it never hurts to have something to fall back on."

Good, sound, sensible advice. Even if he did smell like an outhouse on a hot summer day, Titus Calidius Severus was a good and sensible man. But Nicole hadn't got to Carnuntum by being sensible. "I'll take my chances," she said.

He shrugged again. "Hey, I'm not your family. You're not stuck with me." He smiled that crooked smile again, too, which did the oddest—just this side of annoying—things to her middle. "Like I'm telling you something you didn't already know."

Oh, she could read him perfectly well. *You used to want me and now you don't, and I can't figure out why.* That was what he meant. Still, he didn't say it, not out loud. He didn't sound angry, either, just perplexed. When you got down to it, that was a pretty . . . civilized way of going about things.

It was a hell of a lot more civilized than the come-ons she'd suffered through in California. The guys who'd made those hadn't even been to bed with her, and they were assuming rights she damned well didn't want to give them. Calidius Severus had slept with her, or thought he had; and he was letting her decide just how to handle this thing between them.

Damn, she was starting to like him again. Worse; to sympathize with him. She wasn't used to sympathizing with a man. Men were pains, every last one of them. Except—this one didn't seem to be, nor did he seem to be pretending. He really was a decent sort. She should have hated him for it. Instead, she hated herself either for letting down the side so far as to actually like a member of the Y-chromosome set, or for being such a bitch that she couldn't see a decent human being when he stood in front of her face.

He had to make it worse, too, when she wouldn't rise to his bait. He shrugged one last time, reached into his belt pouch, didn't push or lecture her, but just said, "I know what I owe you for everything but the snails. You don't do those often enough for me to remember."

"A *dupondius* a plate," she said. It came out clear enough, after all, through a throat just a little tight.

Calidius Severus didn't complain. No one else had, either. He paid the bill, then put down an extra *as*. "Give this to Lucius. The hunter deserves his reward."

Gaius Calidius Severus set down an *as*, too. "Can Julia have it?" he asked, adding, "She did cook them up very nicely."

Nicole looked at Titus Calidius Severus. The fuller and dyer pursed his lips and looked up at the sooty ceiling. He didn't say anything. He very loudly didn't say it. Watching him not saying it, watching his son thinking he'd been subtle and not given away what was really on his mind, or perhaps on his crotch, made Nicole want to laugh—or snarl.

All right. Titus Calidius Severus had given her one victory. She could give him this other, minor one. As she was expected to, she said, "Yes, Julia can have the *as*."

Gaius Calidius Severus looked as if he would have clapped

his hands and bounced up and down, if he hadn't remembered his manly dignity. "Oh, good!" he said with another of his goofy grins.

His father pursed his lips again. This time, instead of looking at the ceiling, he glanced at Nicole. They shared a moment of silent amusement.

Yes, shared it. It felt . . . good. Dammit, it felt good.

Titus Calidius Severus ended it with ease that Nicole could envy. He got to his feet, moving briskly but comfortably, and said, "Come on, son. We'd better get back. No matter how much you wish it would, the work doesn't do itself." He nodded to Nicole. "See you soon."

"All right," she answered automatically, and a little more warmly than she'd expected.

Both women watched the Calidii Severi walk back across the street, the son a slighter, paler copy of the father. Nicole didn't know what expression Julia wore, nor did she care to glance at her, to find out.

Julia came up beside her, a redolence composed of garlic and wool and unwashed body—the same as ever, but somehow more bearable than it had been just a few days ago. She picked up the copper coin the younger Calidius Severus had left for her. "I think Gaius is very nice," she announced.

"Of course you do," Nicole said. And caught herself too late. Her tone was snide, and worse than snide.

It didn't offend Julia, or Julia didn't admit to being offended. She nodded, that was all, and slipped the coin into her mouth till she could go up to her room. She accepted Nicole's meanness as plain truth. Compared to that, Nicole would sooner have seen her offended.

Slaves accept such things, she thought. *Free women rebel against them.* But she didn't say anything—which was a cowardly thing, and a sensible thing, and a thing she didn't admire herself for; but she did it nevertheless. This place was getting under her skin. The next thing she knew, she'd be deciding to keep Julia a slave, because The Family objected to the waste of such valuable property. Giving herself to herself—what a horrible thing.

Nicole was comforted, a little. She still had most of her irony intact. She was safe enough—for now.

A woman left the tavern looking less happy than she might have. Julia said, "Tsk, tsk," a sound that hadn't changed much when Nicole dropped back in time.

"What's wrong?" Nicole asked, a bit distracted: she was taking the latest batch of bread out of the oven.

"I'm afraid you might have offended your cousin Primigenia, Mistress," Julia said, which, given the care slaves had to use when speaking, meant Nicole sure as blazes had offended Cousin Primigenia. Julia went on, "You treated her like you'd never set eyes on her before in your life."

Nicole lifted out the last of the loaves and set it on the counter to cool—carefully, because the bread was hot and the action kept her from hitting the wall that she could see rushing toward her at freeway speed. With Brigomarus, she'd lucked out. With other people, she'd either been given enough clues to go on with, or she'd been able to cover for her ignorance—most often because of Julia.

Nicole slid a glance at the slave. Julia was wearing one of her blander expressions. Was she figuring things out? Had she kept quiet deliberately, to see what would happen?

Of course not, Nicole thought. How could she know Umma wasn't Umma anymore? Nicole had been scrambling as fast as she could, as hard as she could, to keep up with things. She'd been doing well, she'd thought. Till now.

She had to say something. Julia was starting to shuffle her feet. She put on a kind of frantic nonchalance, straightening up, dusting her hands, making a show of inspecting the row of nicely browned loaves. "Well," she said. "that's done. As for Primigenia . . . I must have had too much on my mind. I swear I didn't even see her. I'll make it up to her next time, that's all."

That was only about half true. Nicole had seen Primigenia. The woman was a little hard to miss: she had the beginning of a harelip. A surgeon in the twentieth century would have repaired it while she was a baby. Here, she had to live with it. Nicole remembered thinking, *What a shame. She's not bad-looking otherwise.*

At the moment, she hoped Julia hadn't seen her looking. Or had taken her stare for abstraction, figuring the accounts, maybe, or making a mental shopping list for tomorrow's trip to the market.

Julia didn't appear to have seen, or else had decided to play the game by Nicole's rules. In a way. "I hope she doesn't take it too hard," she said. "Your brother's angry at you as it is. You don't want to get your whole family up in arms."

"That's the last thing I want." Nicole paused. That was it; she'd had it. She had to say it, and never mind what Julia thought. "No, the next to last thing. The last thing I want is for people to think they can tell me what to do."

Julia sighed. People had been telling her what to do since she was born. That thought, and the thought of a family row on the horizon, crystallized the timing of the decision Nicole had already made. "Come on, Julia. We're going over to the town-council building and do what we have to do to set you free."

"Right now?" Julia said. Nicole nodded. Julia still looked as if she didn't believe it. "You're going to close the place down and everything?"

"That's right," Nicole said with the crispness of a decision well and firmly made. It felt wonderful. "Fabia Ursa can keep an eye on the children while we're gone." Fabia Ursa was by now a fixture of Nicole's morning routine. Nicole had learned in the course of her chatter that she and her husband owned the house-shop combination next door to Nicole's, the one she'd seen across the alley the first morning she'd awakened in Carnuntum. They were brassworkers and tinkers: they made and repaired pots and pans. Or rather, the husband did; Fabia Ursa had the skill and the craft, she said, but with this baby coming after she'd lost two, she was taking things slower than usual. Hence her mornings in Umma's tavern.

She'd just left a while before, in fact, saying that she

needed to see to something in the shop. If Nicole strained, she could hear that clear, somewhat strident voice chattering to a customer as it chattered in her own ear every morning.

Lucius and Aurelia didn't raise a ruckus about having Fabia Ursa watch them; they had someplace less familiar in which to get into mischief. Nicole overheard Aurelia reminding Lucius, quite seriously, "We do have to be a little bit careful. Fabia Ursa will wallop us if we're naughty."

Nicole stiffened—a reaction she had much too often in this world and time. What was she supposed to make of that? Should she tell Fabia Ursa not to hit them even if they misbehaved? Fabia Ursa was a gentle soul, as people went in Carnuntum, but she was completely unsentimental—and Nicole had heard her, more than once, approve of a woman who spanked her children. If Nicole tried to force her to lay off the kids, she'd smile, pat Nicole's arm, and say kindly, "Oh, very well, dear, if you insist—but since I can't possibly keep from hitting a child who's being a brat, I can't possibly look after your children for you, now, can I?"

It wasn't easy, understanding these people. Worse: Nicole was starting to think they might have a point. Children were, as a species, better behaved here than she remembered them being in L.A. They said *please* and *thank you.* They called women *ma'am.* If they ran around yelling and being a pain in the ass, somebody smacked them, and that was that.

So. Should she tighten up herself? Even her own—well, Umma's—children thought her soft. They were used to being smacked and brought up short. It hadn't damaged them that she could see.

No. She shook her head. She couldn't hit them; she just could not. It was too much like her father coming home drunk and slapping his wife around, or one of the kids if they were closer. Her hand, upraised to strike a blow, mutated into her father's hand in her mind's eye, and she froze.

She'd pretend she hadn't heard. Better that than trying to explain everything to a pair of children who couldn't imagine equating a well-earned slap or two with abuse.

If the tavern was going to be closed for the morning, she

needed a sign to say so—but there wasn't any paper, no
cardboard, nothing. Here was a world without scrap paper or
Post-its, empty of anything handy to write with or on.

But people still did write, and wrote on things. Walls, for
example. A piece of charcoal on the whitewashed wall in
front of the house did as well as could be expected. It looked
like a graffito but it said what she needed it to say, which
was the important thing.

Julia watched in wide-eyed wonder. "Calidius Severus was
right!" she said. "You don't just know how to read, you
know how to write, too. How did you ever learn that?"

Nicole started to answer, then caught herself. She'd told
the fuller and dyer she'd studied on her own, but could she
have studied so secretly her own slave didn't know about it?

A lawyer learned when to talk fast—and when to say nothing. Julia was expecting something; Nicole gave her the barest minimum. "I managed," she said, and let it go at that.

It seemed to work. Julia looked greatly impressed. Even
better, she asked no more awkward questions. Her calm acceptance of the stranger things in life had to be a side effect
of her slavery; an art of not seeing what she wasn't supposed
to see, and keeping quiet when silence was the safest course.

Not for much longer, Nicole thought with satisfaction—
and the barest hint of guilty apprehension. Julia, free, might
ask questions that Julia the slave had never dared to think
of.

Then again, she might not. At the moment, she was full
of Nicole's hitherto unsuspected ability. She walked along
beside Nicole as if she'd had a whole new world opened to
her, pointing to this sign or that bit of graffiti, then listening
in awed delight as Nicole read it off to her.

Nicole didn't mind. It was a lot like going for a walk or
a drive with Kimberley or Justin, when they played Read the
Sign, Mommy, and tried to figure out what it said before she
read it.

Remembering that made her throat tighten a bit. She put
the memory aside, focused on this world she'd wished herself into, and worked herself up to enjoying the game. In

Carnuntum, after all, you made your own fun, or you didn't have any. You couldn't turn the car radio on or dump the kids in front of the TV when you or they got bored. This was all there was: people, imagination, and, at the moment, bits of Latin scribbled on walls.

It was men's day at the baths. As Nicole and Julia walked by, clots of freshly bathed and barbered men whistled and called and made propositions that would have made a twentieth-century construction worker blush. One even flipped up his tunic to show what he was offering.

Nicole bristled. Julia slid eyes at the merchandise and sniffed. "I've seen better," she said with a toss of her head—and a sway of the hips that made a whole row of yahoos moan in unison.

"Stop that," Nicole hissed. "You're encouraging them."

"Of course I am," Julia said, and giggled. "Why not?"

You made your own fun, or you didn't have any. Nicole's thought of a moment before rose up and bit her. These grunting pigs were committing blatant sexual harassment. Julia was having a grand time encouraging it. If she wasn't harassed, in fact wasn't bothered at all, was it harassment?

"What if they do more than just ogle you?" Nicole demanded. "What if one of them tries to rape you?"

"I'll stick a knee in his balls," Julia answered equably. "I've done that a time or two. Didn't take much doing. Word gets around, you know. 'That one's tough,' they say. 'Look, but don't touch.' "

Nicole found that hard to believe. No way men were ever that reasonable. Before she could say so, one of the rougher-hewn types on the steps called out, "Hey, girls! Yeah, the two of you! Come up here to papa. I'll make you think you died and went to Elysium." As if that weren't explicit enough, he grinned and pumped his pelvis, showing off a decent-sized erection under the grubby tunic.

Julia looked him up and down, good and long, tilting her hips and thrusting out her breasts till his tongue was hanging halfway to the ground. Her eye came to rest at last on the bulge under his tunic. Her lip curled. "Will you now?" she said in ripe scorn. "You and what legion?"

Nicole didn't think that was very funny, but the whole crowd roared with laughter. The would-be superstud flushed crimson and slunk away—back to his wife and sixteen snotty-nosed children, Nicole rather devoutly hoped.

The market square was as loudly frenetic as it had been when Nicole went shopping. From everything she'd gathered, it was like that from sunup to sundown every day of the year. Not far beyond it lay the building where the town council met. Despite a fine display of fluted columns and an entranceway cluttered with statuary, it wasn't nearly so splendid as the baths—and it seemed to know it. As if embarrassed to be left behind, it tried to make up for its deficiencies with an excess of gaudy paint. One of the statues, a Venus, boasted a pair of gilded nipples. They looked like pasties in a Vegas strip joint. Bad taste, evidently, was a universal constant.

Nicole hadn't quite figured out how Carnuntum's city government worked. She knew there was a town council, and a pair of magistrates called duovirs above it. Both duovirs had to approve council measures, she thought; if one vetoed them, they didn't become law.

Veto, she realized suddenly, working back and forth between English and Latin, meant *I forbid.* Chunks of this legal system lay embedded in the one she'd studied, maybe not so much in the law itself as in the language in which it was framed. It was an obvious discovery, she supposed—but she'd never thought of it before. It hit her with the force of a revelation, a piece of historical knowledge that she'd never have conceived to be remotely relevant . . . until she found herself in a place where Latin was a living, and lively, language.

How Carnuntum's city government stacked up against that of the province of Pannonia, or against that of the Roman Empire as a whole, she didn't know yet. Nor was she going to worry about it. She wasn't going anywhere. She had time to learn.

She and Julia walked between the central pair of columns, past the striptease Venus and a statue of someone male, pinch-faced, and heroically proportioned—it looked as if someone had taken the head of a skinny little nerd and stuck it on the body of a Rambo clone.

Once past these monuments to kitsch, however, and once her eyes had adjusted to the dimness of a building without electric lights, she saw that she was in a more familiar place than any she'd found since she came to Carnuntum. There was no mistaking what kind of place this was. For a moment, she had a potent feeling of home—of standing in one of the interminable lines at the Department of Motor Vehicles office on Sherman Way.

What was it they used to write on the old maps? *Here be Dragons,* yes. *Here,* she thought, *be Bureaucrats.*

Oh, there were differences. The clerks wore tunics instead of suits; some of the snootier-looking ones even wore togas. They sat behind folding tables rather than desks, each flicking the beads of an abacus rather than the keys of a calculator—fingers flying, beads clicking, narrow-mouthed faces screwed up and sour.

None of the differences mattered. Bureaucrats were bureaucrats, it seemed, in every age of the world: bored, crabby, and studiedly insolent. As if to prove the point, one of them yawned in her face.

They were all men. The other differences hadn't bothered her. This one did. A lot. This was exactly why she'd come— why she thought she'd come to Carnuntum—to get away from sexism, covert and overt, and find a world where men and women lived as equals. There was nothing she could do about it now. She could whine and carry on and get herself nowhere, or she could make the best of it—and do what she could to make things better.

When yawning in her face didn't make her disappear, the clerk said, "May I help you?" With a faint but elaborately long-suffering sigh, he shoved to one side the sheet on which he'd been writing. It wasn't paper; it was thicker and grainier, as if made from pressed leaves. A word came into her head: *papyrus*. A thought followed the word: *No paper, but paperwork after all*. A moment later, another thought: *Damn*.

She suppressed it all, even the mild but heartfelt curse, and said briskly, "Yes, you can help me." She pointed at Julia. "I want to emancipate my slave."

The clerk was the first person Nicole had said that to, who didn't react in the slightest. "And you are . . . ?" he said.

"My name is Umma," Nicole answered—congratulating herself that she'd remembered.

"Oh," the clerk said, as deadpan as ever. "Of course. The widow of Satellius Sodalis." And a good thing he knew that, too, because Nicole hadn't. Were Liber and Libera looking after her after all, making sure she didn't stumble more often than she had to? "Now, then, since you've come here, I suppose you'll want formal manumission, not just the informal sort you could get by emancipating her in front of a group of friends."

"Yes, that's right," Nicole said, and then, with trained caution, "Remind me of the differences between formal and informal manumission."

The clerk smiled. It was not at all a pleasant smile. It was, in fact, more of a leer. "Well," he said. "Of course. One can't expect a woman to know how the law works, now, can one?" It took all of Nicole's years of legal training and dealing with good-ole-boy judges and sleazy lawyers to keep from braining him with his own bronze inkpot. He went on in blind complacency, reciting as if by rote, in just about the same tone she would have used for explaining torts to a four-year-old: "Formal manumission is more complicated, of course, and grants a slave higher status. It makes her free, and it makes her a Roman citizen. She'd still be your client, of course, and you, or rather your guardian, her patron. She won't be able to hold office"—he smiled that nasty smile again, as if to show how unlikely that was in any case—"but her freeborn children, if she should have any, will be."

Julia nodded as if she'd known that all along. Her expression was eager, but there was wariness underneath, like a dog that accepts a bone but looks for a kick to follow.

Nicole made herself ignore Julia and concentrate on what the clerk was saying. "And informal manumission?" she asked.

"As I said," the clerk replied with a little sniff of scorn, "for that you needn't have come here. She'd be free then, but not a Roman citizen. Junian Latin rights, we call it." And anyone but an idiot or a woman, his expression said, would know as much. "When she dies, whatever property she's acquired while she's free reverts back to you."

That didn't seem like much of a choice to Nicole. "We'll do it the formal way," she said.

"The other difference," the clerk said, "is the twenty-*denarius* tax for formal manumission: five percent of her approximate value."

Nicole winced. "That's a lot of money."

"One gets what one pays for," the clerk said: a bureaucrat indeed, and no mistake. "For your twenty *denarii* you receive full and proper documentation." He paused. His eyebrows rose slightly. "I gather you haven't brought the proper fee?"

Nicole had an all but irresistible urge to ask if he took MasterCard or Visa. "No, I haven't," she said a little testily. No credit cards here, either—not even a bank, that she'd seen or heard of. And what would people write checks on? The walls?

Meanwhile, there was the issue of the fee, and the fact that twenty *denarii* would lighten the cash box by a significant degree. So Julia was worth about four hundred *denarii*. That was a lot of money. No wonder Julia hadn't thought she could save it on her own—and no wonder Brigomarus had been so upset. Nicole was, in effect, giving away the family Mercedes.

The clerk was no kinder and certainly no pleasanter, but he seemed—for whatever reason—to have decided against the usual bureaucratic obstructionism. "Well then," he said. "You can get the money, I suppose."

Nicole nodded. She had practice in looking sincere—it

was a lawyer's stock in trade—but she wasn't lying, either.

The clerk seemed to know it, or else it was the one hour a day when he cut his victims an inch of slack. "Very well. I'll draw up the documents. You go, collect the money, and come back with your guardian."

"My guardian?" Nicole said. That was the second time he'd used the term. So what was she, a minor child? Or did the word have another meaning?

"That would be your husband, of course," the clerk said, unsurprised by what had to look to him like female imbecility, "but your husband is dead. Let me see." The clerk frowned into space, mentally reviewing family connections he knew better than Nicole did. "He was his own man, not in anyone's *patria potestas*, which means that you no longer come under the legal authority of any male in his family. Which returns responsibility to your own, birth family. Father's dead. Brothers—you have a brother, yes? Britomartis—Brigomarus. We'll need his signature, or failing this his witnessed mark, before the documents are legal and binding."

"Why?" Nicole demanded. "I can sign for myself."

The clerk laughed, a strikingly rich and full sound to have come from so pinched and small a mouth. "Why, Madam Umma, of course you can! You can write your name wherever you like, if you can write it at all. But if this transaction is to be legal, it must have a man's name attached to it."

"What?" Nicole veered between fury and horror. First, to have to ask Brigomarus to agree to Julia's manumission, after what he'd said and implied when Nicole informed him of it—fat chance. And second, and worse, her own approval wasn't enough—because she was a woman, she had no right or power to sign a legally binding contract. That—by God, that was positively medieval.

But this wasn't even the Middle Ages yet, she didn't think. It was a long and apparently unenlightened time before that.

And there was Julia, shocked out of her awe at the place and the proceedings, blurting out with a rather remarkable lack of circumspection, "Didn't you know that, Mistress? Brigomarus knows it, I'm sure he does."

"To the crows with Brigomarus," Nicole snarled. "It's outrageous. It's unjust, it's immoral, it's unequal, it's unfair, it's absurd, it's impossible." Her voice had risen with every word. In fact, she was shouting. People were staring. She didn't care. Was she any less a human being because she couldn't piss in one of Calidius Severus' amphorae?

The clerk was signally unimpressed by her vocabulary or her volume. "It's the law," he said primly.

"To the crows with the law, too," Nicole snapped. Now there was a hell of a thing for a lawyer to say. And she didn't care. She didn't care one little bit. She got a grip on Julia's arm, swiveled her about, and stalked off in high indignation.

8

"MISTRESS!" JULIA CALLED FROM the street just outside the tavern, where she'd gone to peer at something or other outside. "Look at the sunset. Isn't it beautiful? The sky is turning all those clouds to fire. I'll bet you an *as* it will rain tomorrow."

Nicole didn't gamble, but she didn't say so. Julia seemed unperturbed by the setback to her manumission. In fact, as they'd walked home, Nicole slamming her feet down furiously with every stride, Julia trotting along behind her, Julia had said, "Ah well. Isn't that just like fate?"

Julia the slave might be a fatalist, but Nicole was damned if she'd sit around blathering about kismet or whatever else you wanted to call it. The idea that a man's signature was required to make a document valid told her loud and clear where women stood in Carnuntum—and, no doubt, in the rest of the Roman Empire. In Los Angeles, at least the letter of the law had been on her side. There, hypocrisy had got her so frothing mad she'd wished herself centuries back in time to get away from it. Well—she'd succeeded. No hypocrisy here, oh no. Just pure naked oppression.

"Rain would be nice," Julia was saying. "I heard the farmers saying in the market yesterday that it's been too dry for too long—the crops are suffering. Much more drought and we'd be in trouble. You know what they say: *dry summer, winter famine.* Rain now would mean we eat well come winter."

"I hope it's a cursed flood," Nicole said sullenly.

Julia pulled out the neckline of her tunic and spat down onto her bosom. Nicole stared at her. "What on earth did you do that for?"

"To turn aside the evil omen, of course," the slave—still a slave—answered. "Drought's bad, but floods are really and right-there bad."

Spitting in your bosom was, Nicole supposed, like knocking on wood or crossing your fingers for luck. But in the twentieth century, most people who knocked on wood didn't really believe it would do any good. Julia sounded as serious about averting the omen as Nicole's grandmother had been when she made the sign of the cross.

Not a fair comparison, Nicole thought. *Grandma was doing something religious. This is just superstition.*

So? said the lawyerly part of her mind. *Would you be so kind as to define the difference?*

Well: religion got higher ratings than superstition. But that, she admitted to both sides of herself, was a less than useful distinction.

She'd had two cups of wine with her supper. They combined with the undercurrent of burning outrage to make her discontented with the idea of trudging upstairs and falling asleep. She'd done that every night since she'd come to Carnuntum, and it looked to be what everybody did every night, without variation and without exception.

"Julia," she said suddenly, "I want some fun tonight."

"Why are you telling me, Mistress?" Julia asked. "Go

across the street." She pointed toward the shop and house of
Titus Calidius Severus.

Nicole's face grew hot. "That's not what I meant!" she
said a little too quickly. "I meant someplace . . . oh, someplace to go: to a play, or to listen to music, or to go out
dancing." Yes indeed: no TV, no movies, no radio, no
stereo—she was starting to go stir-crazy. It wasn't quite like
living in a sensory-deprivation tank—some of her senses,
especially smell, got a bigger workout here than they ever
had back in the United States—but it wasn't far removed,
either. If she didn't do something besides get up and get to
work and get hit over the head with culture shock and collapse into sleep, she was going to scream.

"Mistress," Julia said, "you know daytime is the time for
things like that." She shrugged. Nicole, even through her
haze of fury, thought Julia might just have decided that her
mistress was intermittently simpleminded and needed to be
humored. "Of course," Julia went on, "the daytime is when
we're busy, too. But there'll be plays and beast shows in the
amphitheater all summer long."

"Beast shows," Nicole said, distracted almost out of her
mood. So what were those? A traveling zoo, maybe? That
would make sense, with no planes or trains or automobiles,
and not much chance to go much of anywhere. It stood to
reason that enterprising types might think to bring the zoos
to the people, rather than the other way around.

That didn't help her immediate predicament. "What do I
do *now?*" She sounded like a bored four-year-old, she knew
that, but she couldn't help it.

"I still don't know why you're mad at Calidius Severus"—
Julia shrugged again, as if to say she wasn't and wouldn't
be responsible for Nicole's vagaries—"but since you are,
there isn't much else *to* do but get drunk."

"No!" The answer was quick and sharp and automatic.

"Well," Julia said, "it's one way not to notice the time
crawling by. It's here"—she held up a hand—"and then it's
there, and you don't care what happened in between."

"No," Nicole said again, remembering her father coming

home plastered night after night. For the first time, she thought to wonder *why* he'd got drunk. Was he trying to blot out the time he spent in the factory every day? It wasn't enough reason, but it was *a* reason. She'd never looked for a reason before; it had just been part of her life. She scratched her head, then wished she hadn't—what was crawling through her hair?

"You feel pretty good, too," Julia went on, not really arguing with Nicole so much as reminding herself. "Oh, you may not feel so good the next morning, but who cares about the next morning? That's then. This is now." She looked longingly toward the long stone bar, as if to say she wouldn't mind at all if she got drunk.

"No," Nicole said once more, but she heard something in her voice she'd never expected to find there: hesitation. She'd smoked marijuana a few times, at Indiana and afterwards. She would have enjoyed it more, she thought, if it hadn't felt as if she were lighting smudge pots in her lungs. What could be so different about alcohol? She'd been drinking wine—watered wine, but wine—with meals, and she hadn't turned into a lush.

But your father did, said the stern voice in her mind. For the first time it sounded less authoritative than merely prim. Miss Priss, Frank had called her sometimes. At first it was affectionate, but later it gained an edge. Then he started adding, "You know, Nicole, people who preach like that usually do it because they're afraid they'll be tempted—and they'll like it." Not long after that, he was gone. Lady number two hadn't ever been prim in her life, or sensible either.

Nicole couldn't help it if she was congenitally sensible. Maybe that good sense was what she needed now, instead of blind abhorrence. *Dad drank boilermakers, for heaven's sake. A few cups of wine don't even come close.*

Do they?

"Can't do it all the time," Julia said, "but everybody needs to get drunk once in a while."

Moderation in everything, including moderation. Nicole couldn't remember where she'd heard that. She'd always thought it made good sense, but she'd never applied it to alcohol before. She'd been too busy running in the opposite direction—running away from the father figure, a therapist would say. So did it make sense now? God—gods—knew this wasn't Los Angeles. Life here in Carnuntum was profoundly, sometimes unbearably, different.

Gods, yes. Liber and Libera had, somehow, granted her wish, her whine, her prayer. They'd brought her to Carnuntum. They were, as she had discovered to her dismay, god and goddess of wine. What would they think, what would they do, if they realized how she felt about their very own and most protected substance? Or had they known all along, and set her up for just this dilemma?

Hadn't Christianity turned a lot of the old gods into devils? Right now, Nicole could see why. But she hadn't felt anything bad in Liber or Libera, not in their faces on the plaque and not in the way they'd granted her prayer. So maybe it was a creeping evil—or maybe it was simple godlike benevolence. *Be careful what you wish for,* she'd heard said: *you might get it.*

She was, she knew, talking herself into something she would have rejected in horror a few days—or, heavens, was it weeks?—before. She *had* rejected wine, and what had that got her? A case of the runs that almost turned her inside out, and derision from everybody who heard about her drinking water.

"Well, maybe," she heard herself say. "Maybe it'll get the taste of that cursed clerk out of my mouth." An excuse, an alibi—she knew as much. She also knew life was a bore, and an unpleasant bore at that.

Julia must have had a much more solid understanding of that than she did. The slave went over to the bar and filled two cups with wine, brought them back, and plunked one on the table in front of Nicole. Nicole stared at it. It was one of the cups she filled and washed and filled again all day long, brimful of the middle-grade wine. That was boldness on Julia's part, mixed with prudence: not the cheap stuff if they were going to drink it neat, but not the expensive stuff either, since they were going to drink a lot.

Nicole reached out a hand that was gratifyingly steady and lifted the cup. With the same deep breath she'd have drawn just before she jumped into a lake of cold water, she touched it to her lips and sipped.

The wine wasn't watered; they wanted it full strength, to get drunk the faster. It was almost as thick as syrup, and almost as sweet, too. But under that sweetness lay the half-medicinal, half-terrifying taste of alcohol.

Julia sighed and set down her own, emptied cup. "That's so good," she said. Her voice was low, throaty, sensuous. She might have been talking about something quite other than wine.

"Yes," Nicole said, although she didn't think it was particularly grand. Warmth filled her belly and spread slowly outward.

Julia tilted back her cup to catch the last of the wine, then rose to refill it. Politely, she picked up Nicole's, too, only to set it down and give Nicole a look the dim lamplight only made more reproachful. "You haven't finished yet, Mistress?" Beneath the words lay others: *what are you waiting for?*

What was Nicole waiting for? If she was going to do this, she wasn't going to do it halfway. She gulped down the wine—dizzied, half staggered, nearly ready to gag on the fumes and the sweetness, but by damn she did it. She thrust the cup at Julia. Julia nodded approval, filled it up again, brought it back.

That one Nicole drained as fast as she could. "You haven't finished yet, Julia?" she said, and laughed. It sounded too loud, as if she'd turned up the volume by mistake.

Julia laughed, too. Was she laughing because she thought it was funny, or because her owner had made a joke? *Damn,* Nicole thought. Her thoughts were turned up high, too. *I don't care. Tomorrow I'll care. Not tonight. No. Not tonight.*

A swallow or two later, or maybe it was three, Nicole touched the tip of her nose. It seemed to have gone numb.

That was funny—not big-laugh funny, not giggle funny. *Funny* funny. *I am getting drunk,* she thought. It was wonderful. Marvelous. Fascinating.

And it was her turn to fill the cups. Getting up wasn't bad, though the floor tilted underfoot. Walking straight was harder. *Yes, Officer,* she thought, *I'm walking under the influence.* She giggled.

So did Julia. If she found anything out of the ordinary in sitting down with her mistress and getting plastered, she didn't let on. Nicole wondered how often she'd done it with Umma. As Nicole carried the wine back to the table, walking with great care so as not to spill it, she almost came right out and asked. She caught herself in the nick of time. *Alcohol,* she thought clearly and—all right, primly—*makes you want to talk before you think.* Such a clear thought, and so wise. She was proud of it.

If she hadn't learned about talking jags from experience— if she hadn't already had a good notion of them from memories of her father and from what she'd seen in the tavern— Julia would have taught her. The slave's mouth ran and ran and ran.

Nicole had learned a long time ago that nodding every once in a while was enough to keep a drunk—in this case, Julia—going. Some of what the slave said was interesting in a lurid sort of way; Nicole found out more than she wanted to know about the intimate preferences of several of her regular customers. The one who liked his boys sweet and young, for example—the younger the better; and the one who'd buried or divorced three wives, not one of whom had ever given him an heir, because he couldn't bring himself to enter them through the proper orifice; and . . .

And then Julia said, "Mistress, if Titus is even half as good as Gaius, you won't find much finer anywhere you look. He's probably better, too—I bet he wouldn't be in such a hurry all the time." She sighed gustily. "And besides, Mistress, he's crazy about you. And you're angry at him. What did he do to get you in such an uproar? I never have been able to figure it out."

Her calling the two Calidii Severi by their praenomens left Nicole confused for a moment, but not for any longer than that. One thing was interesting: If Julia wondered what Titus Calidius Severus was like in bed, he'd never put down a couple of *sesterces* and gone upstairs with her when Umma was out shopping and the kids had gone off to play somewhere. A point of sorts for the fuller and dyer. Though a point for what, in what game, Nicole wasn't inclined to say.

Julia still waited expectantly for her answer. She chose her words with care. With all the wine she had in her, she, unlike Julia, couldn't have spoken quickly if she'd wanted to. "It's not any one thing," she said. "It's not any big thing, even. We just haven't been getting along as well as we did before, that's all."

"It's too bad," Julia said. In the dim lamplight, Nicole was surprised to see tears in her eyes. "The children really like him, too."

"Children or no children, if you think I'll have anything to do with a man who smells like sour piss all the time, you can think again," Nicole snapped—or rather, the wine did it, before she could stop herself.

That wasn't the whole story. It wasn't even most of the story. But the wine could have done much worse. It was a part of the story that would make sense to Julia, and apparently did. She nodded thoughtfully. "You've been fussy about things like that lately, haven't you, Mistress? I've seen you throw out a couple of pieces of meat we could have served without having anybody complain, or not much, anyhow."

"If it smells bad to me, it'll smell bad to the cush—*cus*-tomers," Nicole said. How wonderful: she'd got Julia to stop talking about Titus Calidius Severus. She laughed with the wonder of it.

When she looked at the lamp, she saw two side by side unless she screwed up her eyes and tilted her head just so. Getting up required a distinct effort of will. "I'm going to bed," she announced with a grand flourish that nearly sent her over onto her backside—and did send her into a fit of the giggles. Two blurry Juliases nodded vigorously and gulped down all the wine in their cups before they trotted along after her like obedient puppies.

Nicole had danced to the music of the wine—had she ever. And come morning, she paid the piper.

She'd felt worse her first night in Carnuntum, when her day of water-drinking caught up with her, but not by much. That had been concentrated misery, too: bowels in an uproar, but the rest of her not so bad. Now she hurt all over.

She sat up with excruciating slowness. If she moved one bit faster, her head would fall off. Just as she achieved a wobbly vertical, an oxcart with an ungreased axle squeaked and groaned down the street in front of the tavern. She held her head on her shoulders with both hands, and suppressed a groan that would have made it ache even worse. No wonder her father used to complain that her mother was scrambling the breakfast eggs too loudly. If she'd known then what she knew now, she'd never have laughed.

Her mouth tasted as if she'd been drinking from the chamber pot instead of a wine cup. What she wouldn't have given for a bottle of Scope or a tube of Crest with toothbrush to match—and a dentist on call while she was at it. Her bad tooth ached worse than it ever had before.

So that's what a hangover is, she thought. Every nerve ending turned up high. Every sensation more intense than usual. A lot more intense. A hell of a lot more intense.

Sunlight streamed in through the open window. She would have been willing to swear it was the same watery sunshine she'd always seen in Carnuntum, but her eyes blinked and watered and ached as if it had been the fierce glare of the Sahara. She yearned for sunglasses—one more lifesaving idea no one in Carnuntum had ever had.

When she first came to Carnuntum, she'd told herself—and believed—that the loss of material things didn't matter. She'd traded them for genuine equality: a good enough bargain, all things considered. Since then, she'd learned just how far off the mark she'd been. She'd lost all the little things that made life easier, and got in return less equality than she'd ever imagined possible, and almost as much sheer aggravation as she'd seen in the twentieth century. *That's not a bargain,* she thought nastily. *That's a consumer complaint.*

So where did she go to file? Was there a consumer protection bureau for victims of unscrupulous gods?

Her guts rumbled. They were happier than they'd been that first night, but they weren't dancing in the daisies, either. She was glad, once she'd used the chamber pot, to fling its reeking contents out the window.

An irate shout rose from the alley. A laugh shook itself out of her—and half killed her head, too. *Damn,* she thought, half in horrified embarrassment; but only half. Now there was a hazard of urban life no one in Los Angeles had to worry about.

On mornings when he was feeling the worse for wear, her father had dosed himself with aspirin and black coffee. No coffee here; she'd found that out the hard way. Would that willow-bark decoction make the rock drummer in her head stop his demented solo? What did the Romans do about hangovers—besides suffer, that is?

She got up; slowly, because her whole body ached, as if from a low-grade flu. When she looked in the polished bronze mirror in her makeup kit, she winced. *Eyes like two pissholes in the snow,* her mother had said of her father on mornings after he'd come reeling back late from another foray against the bottle. She'd been too young then to understand what that meant. Now here they were, staring back at her: two reddish-yellow holes in a flat white face.

She couldn't just sit here wishing she were dead. There was money to earn: bread to bake, food to cook and serve, wine to ladle out into waiting cups. It didn't, at the moment, seem any more appealing than sucking up to fat assholes of law partners. A couple of weeks in the tavern business had shown her all too clearly that, while a woman could make a living at it, she wasn't going to retire to the Riviera any time soon.

The loss of a day's proceeds would hurt.

Inspiration struck. She winced. Julia! Julia could run the tavern. She usually did anyway, more than Nicole hoped she knew.

No. Nicole winced again. That wouldn't do, not for more than a few hours. Some things—the cash box, for example—had to stay under Nicole's supervision. And it really took two to run the tavern properly; actually they could have used a third pair of hands, even with the kids' intermittent help.

No real help for it. Running a tavern in any era was no easy nine-to-five. Sunup to sundown, seven days a week, fifty-two weeks a year, no paid vacations—and no sick leave. She had to get herself out there and get to work. If she looked like grim death . . . she did, that was all. She'd had plenty of customers who looked the same way, and for the same reasons, too.

Julia was already downstairs, getting things ready for a new day. To Nicole's guilty relief, Julia, who was normally resilient to the point of perkiness, looked as if she'd been ridden hard and put away wet, too.

"Hello, Mistress." Julia managed a smile, but it was wan. "Now we remember why getting drunk all the time isn't such a good idea."

"What, you needed reminding?" Nicole said—not too loud; her own voice hurt her ears. Julia, she noticed, hadn't opened the shutters. Nicole didn't blame her one bit. The light creeping between the wooden slats already seemed bright enough to blind a person.

Another cart banged and rattled along the street outside. Nicole and Julia winced in unison. *Aspirin*, Nicole wished with all her heart. *Coffee*. Of course they didn't materialize. She'd run fresh out of wishes when she wished herself back in time to Carnuntum. "What do we do about this?" she moaned . . . quietly.

"I ate some raw cabbage," Julia said, "and I drank a little wine—not too much, by the gods!" Her sigh was mournful. "Hasn't done much good yet."

"Raw cabbage?" Nicole sighed just as Julia had, gustily.

"I'll try some, too—and a *tiny* bit of wine." She held thumb and forefinger close together.

She wasn't fond of raw cabbage to begin with. She was even less fond of it after she'd choked down a handful of leaves. Her stomach asked, loudly and pointedly, what the hell she thought she was doing to it. Maybe the idea behind this particular hangover cure was to make you feel miserable somewhere else, so you wouldn't worry about your head falling off. If that was the case—she'd rather carry her head around under her arm than deal with a stomach in open revolt.

She also discovered that, if there was any one thing in the world wine didn't go with, raw cabbage was it.

"Time to bite the bullet," she muttered. There was no toilet to run to, and no sink either, just the open front door. She couldn't even say the words in Latin; she had to resort to English. Latin knew nothing about bullets. *Bite the ballista bolt* didn't cut it, somehow.

Life in the second century was nothing like what she'd expected. One by one, every idea she'd had, had turned out to be wrong. Still, she thought with a kind of desperate optimism, this was a world without bullets, without guns. It had to be safer, didn't it? It had to be more secure than the world she'd left behind.

A few minutes after Nicole opened the door, the sun went behind a cloud—a nice, thick, rainy-looking cloud. Clouds like that had been a cause for universal groans in Indiana, but in California they were wonderfully welcome.

Here, too, after so long a drought—and after a hangover. She beamed at Julia. Julia beamed back.

That relief—and whatever she got from the cabbage and wine, which wasn't much—didn't last long. Lucius and Aurelia came downstairs and started raising hell. Probably they weren't any noisier than usual, but no way was Nicole up for kid-noise on that scale.

Nicole told them several times to be quiet, which did as much good as she'd figured it would: zilch, zero, zip. Her head hurt. Her tooth throbbed in sledgehammer rhythm.

Aurelia stampeded past with Lucius in roaring pursuit. Nicole snagged first one and then the other, and laid a solid smack on each backside. "Shut up!" she yelled at them both. "Just—shut—*up!*"

She stopped cold. *Oh, God.* Her father had done the same thing—the exact same thing—on his mornings after. She looked at her hand, appalled. "I'm sorry," she started to say. "Oh, God, I'm sorry."

She never said it, because even while the words took shape on her tongue, she noticed something. It was quiet in the tavern. The kids had slunk off to do something useful: Lucius chopping nuts, Aurelia helping Julia grind flour for the next batch of bread. They weren't sniveling or acting abused. They were simply . . . quiet. And they stayed quiet for a good while. Not forever, but long enough.

Nicole never did voice her apology. She didn't like herself much for it, either.

Were peace and quiet worth an occasional whack? The people of Carnuntum certainly thought so. Nicole never had. She'd sworn when she was a little girl, after her father had left another set of bruises on her mother's face—and her mother told people she'd walked into a door—that she'd never raise her hand in anger to anyone, adult or child. And here she'd broken that vow.

When in Rome . . .

She was breaking down, belief by belief, conviction by conviction. If the parents of Carnuntum had been transported as suddenly to Los Angeles as Nicole had to Carnuntum, every last one of them would have faced losing custody of their children. Most would have done jail time for child abuse. But here no one looked twice, even when a father was caught beating his son till the boy screamed for mercy.

From everything she'd read, that should have made the adults of Carnuntum—the grown-up survivors of abuse—a hateful pack of social misfits. And yet they weren't. They were just people. Maybe they were cruder than people in Los Angeles, but there was no denying the resemblance. Human nature, whatever that was, hadn't changed. People fell in and out of love, they quarreled and made up, they did business, they gossiped, they got drunk—as Nicole's aching head too well knew—all as they might have done eighteen hundred years later on the other side of the Atlantic.

So what did that say about all the books she'd read and the television talk shows she'd watched, and all the theory she'd taken as gospel? The Romans had a theory that it was perfectly acceptable for one human being to buy and sell another. That theory, as far as she was concerned, was dead wrong, no matter how elaborately they justified it.

The next thought, the corollary, was amazingly hard to face. What if her own theories—her own assumptions— weren't exactly right, either? What if they were all skewed somehow? So where did right end and wrong begin? Who could know, and how?

She clutched her head in her hands. It was pounding worse than ever, but not with the hangover, not any longer. Tough questions of law and ethics had done that to her, too, when she was in law school. She'd been glad to get out of those courses with a passing grade.

There wasn't anybody standing over her now, demanding that she think about things that she plain didn't want to think about. It didn't make any difference. The thoughts were there. She could make them go away, but they kept coming back, mutating and changing, till they changed *her,* and made her into something different from what she'd been. Something, maybe, she didn't want to be.

"Hurry up with my order there," a customer said. He hadn't given it much more than a minute or two before. Julia was scrambling as fast as she could to fill it.

And Nicole had had it up to here. If she wasn't going to take any guff from Lucius and Aurelia, she sure as hell wasn't about to let an obstreperous customer push her around, either. "Keep your drawers on," she snapped. "You'll get it when it's ready."

She held her breath. If he got up and stomped off the way

Ofanius Valens had when she wouldn't let him play doctor with Julia, then let him.

Instead, and to her amazement, he wilted. "I'm sorry, Umma," he mumbled into his greasy beard. "As soon as you can, please."

"That's better," Nicole said briskly. She couldn't help a last stab of guilt. Without the hangover, she probably wouldn't have barked so loud. But, she told herself, let's face it: in Carnuntum as in Los Angeles, a healthy dose of asser-tiveness was not at all a bad thing.

Rain pattered down on the roof of the tavern. Every so often, raindrops slipped in through the smokeholes in the roof and hissed angrily as they dove into the cookfires. Some of them missed the fires and hit the floor. That would have been a raving nuisance on carpet or linoleum. On rammed earth, it was a little too interesting for words. Rammed earth was fine when it was dry. When it was wet, it was mud.

Nicole had never understood mud before, not really. She picked her way past the muddy spots and the damp and odor-ous customers to peer outside. It had been raining for three or four days now, a mild, steady summer rain of a sort In-dianapolis knew well. She'd lost the habit of it in Los An-geles, had forgotten the look and smell and feel of it, the long gray damp days, the dripping nights, the mildew that grew everywhere. In Los Angeles, there were only two kinds of rain: not enough and too much.

As far as Nicole was concerned, a mild, steady summer rain was too much in Carnuntum. Raindrops plashed down on puddles in the street. Or so they had done that first lovely wet day. By now, day three or four—God, she'd lost count—the whole street was a vast, muddy puddle. Something that had been alive once upon a time, but not too recently, bobbed in the water. She had no desire to find out what it was.

An oxcart came trundling along, a little quieter than the usual run of them: the axle, though bare of oil, had plenty of water for lubricant. The cart wasn't going very fast. Every time the weary-looking ox lifted a foot, it lifted a clinging ball of mud. A mucky wake trailed the cart's thick wooden wheels. Mud clung to them as to the ox's hooves, clogging them till they seemed likely to stick solid.

Mud, in fact, clung to everything. Keeping it out of the tavern was shoveling against the tide. Whenever a customer walked in and set a dripping cloak on the edge of a table, a muddy puddle formed beneath it. Julia pulled dry rushes from a sack behind the bar to sop up a little bit of the worst puddles.

Concrete house pads weren't likely to happen for another eighteen hundred years, but carpets might have been of at least some help. It seemed the Romans had never thought of them. They were easy enough to describe, and easy enough to make, too.

Maybe Nicole should invent them—or would *discover* be the right word? Though not right away. For the time being, she was only thinking about it. Rammed earth was not the ideal surface on which to lay carpets. She might have to invent the hardwood floor first, or do something with tiles. Saltillo wasn't all that different from Roman brick, come to think of it.

As Nicole stood in her doorway with the rain misting on her cheeks, Fabia Ursa's husband, Sextus Longinius Iulus, poked his head out next door, evidently to get a look at the rain, too. The tinker was a cheerful little man, as garrulous as his wife, but where she was thin and frail and delicately built, he had the quick-moving round body, full cheeks, and buck teeth of a chipmunk. He smiled at her. She reflexively smiled back. It was hard not to. *Chip or Dale?* she caught herself wondering.

His voice, at least, was a normal voice, not the high gabble of an animated chipmunk. "Lovely day," he said, "if you're a goose."

"I'm sick of rain," she said. Heavens, she sounded like a Californian—and after all these years of being hopelessly Midwestern, too.

He shook his head, but his smile didn't fade. She was glad. She didn't want him to think she was annoyed at him. He was a good-natured sort, and, from everything she'd seen and heard, was devoted to his wife. "We do need the rain," he said, "but it could go away now and even the farmers wouldn't complain."

"*I* certainly wouldn't," Nicole said with deep feeling. She paused. Well: so say it. Soonest started, soonest over. "Can you and Fabia come over for a little while?"

He seemed delighted at the invitation, though he couldn't possibly know what it was for. "Why, of course! We'll be right there."

Nicole nodded with a faint and she hoped inaudible sigh of relief. "Good. Good, then. I'm going to fetch the Calidii, too."

"Are you?" Longinius Iulus laid a finger on the side of his nose. Probably he imagined that he looked sly. "Ah! *I* know what's going on. Fabia doesn't count for that, you know. She's only a woman."

Nicole wanted to wither him with a glare, but restrained herself. He might only be reminding her of how the law worked. She liked him; she'd give him the benefit of the doubt. This time.

"Fabia will come anyhow," he said. "Liven up the day, and all that. She's been a bit crabby lately, with the baby."

Nicole could imagine. Late pregnancy, as she knew too well, was hell. She nodded and waved to Sextus Longinius, who popped back into his house to fetch his wife. Nicole walked down the narrow, muddy stone sidewalk, thankful, and not for the first time, that the street boasted a sidewalk at all; some didn't. Like a mountain goat jumping from crag to crag, she crossed the street on the stepping stones. The sidewalk on the other side was even narrower. A patch of mud had oozed onto it from the overloaded street. She slipped and slid and almost fell into the morass; flailed wildly and caught herself up against the damp wall. She clung there for a moment, breathing hard, more with stress than with exertion. An involuntary swim in the odorous, ordurous mud of Carnuntum was not her idea of a good time.

Titus Calidius Severus hadn't set the amphorae in front of

his shop today. Maybe he thought the product he'd get would be too diluted to do him any good; probably he feared the jars would float away. A nice little river ran just about where he liked to thrust the pointy ends of the jars.

Nicole opened the door a little too quickly for her stomach's peace of mind. A monumental stink assaulted her and almost knocked her off her feet.

Through streaming eyes and gagging coughs, she managed to discern Titus and Gaius Calidius Severus near the end of a row of wooden tubs, doing the double-double routine with something thick, dark, and cottony-looking. It was, she realized, some kind of wool, and the substance they were sloshing it around in was stale piss. When they straightened up to greet her, the stuff ran down their hands and arms and dripped from their fingertips onto the floor. They didn't bother with rushes; they let the piss make its own noxious mud.

"Good morning, Umma," Titus Calidius Severus said. If the stench bothered him—if he even noticed it—he didn't show it. "Haven't seen you in here for a couple of weeks. What can I do for you today?"

Did he sound hopeful? Maybe he did. Nicole ignored his tone just as he ignored the smell. *Business,* she thought. *Stick to business.* "Can you and your son come over to the tavern for a little while?" she asked.

Titus looked at Gaius. They knew what was going on, too. This wasn't like Los Angeles, where people could live next door to each other for years without bothering to learn each other's names. Here, everyone knew what everyone else was thinking.

"Who else have you got?" the fuller and dyer asked.

"Sextus Longinius Iulus and his wife," Nicole answered.

"Fabia Ursa doesn't count," Calidius Severus said, just as Sextus Longinius had. But maybe Calidius Severus had learned something from the past week or two of dealing with the stranger in Umma's body. He held up his hand before she could snap at him, and said hastily, "Don't blame me, Umma! It's how the law works. You'll still have three men as witnesses, which ought to do you well enough. Of course it would be even better if Brigomarus were acting for you, but—"

"No," Nicole said sharply. "This is *my* business, and he's too stubborn to see it. *I'll* take care of it. She's my slave, not his."

"Now who's the stubborn one?" Titus Calidius Severus chuckled. So did his son. Nicole didn't see the joke, herself. She waited till they finished their male bonding or whatever it was. It happened soon enough, and the fuller and dyer sobered. He said slowly, "I'm not sure this is the wisest thing, and I'm not easy about it in my mind, either, if you want the honest truth. But you're clearly set on it, and you're the one I've got to live with day to day. You'll settle it with your family, or you won't—that's between you and them. Personally, I hope you do. Meanwhile," he said with an air of decision, "we'll do what you ask. Gaius, run upstairs and get our cloaks, would you? It's still coming down out there."

Gaius wasted no time in obeying. He had to be as hungry for entertainment as Sextus Longinius was.

He and his father threw the cloaks on over their tunics and pulled up the hoods. Nicole hadn't seen any umbrellas in Carnuntum. A parasol, yes, shielding the face of an obviously wealthy woman from the sun in the market square one day, but no umbrellas. *Maybe I could discover those, too,* she thought. She was developing a whole list of potentially profitable "inventions," any one of which would make life a fair bit easier.

Picture it now, she thought: a nice little operation, eight or ten or a dozen employees—all free men and women, of course—chatting happily as they made umbrellas. It was a bit too much like a Worker's Paradise ad, but then again, why not? They'd make a good living, collect benefits— another thing to invent, right there—and she . . . she'd get rich. Or well-to-do, at least. Latin might even come up with a new word, a word for *yuppie. Iuppa?*

What were Roman patent laws like? *Were* there any? Could somebody who owned slaves set them to making umbrellas eighteen hours a day, seven days a week, undercut her, and drive her out of business? What were Roman bankruptcy laws like?

She shook her head and suppressed a wry smile. From rich to down and out in five seconds flat. The Calidii Severi hadn't even noticed. She turned on her heel with a touch more dispatch than strictly necessary. "Let's go," she said.

Gaius slipped on the same stretch of muddy sidewalk that had almost sent her into the much muddier street. His father caught him, whirled him around and wrestled him up against the wall, so convincingly that Nicole was briefly alarmed. But they were both laughing, pushing each other like rowdy boys, all the way down the wall and over the stepping stones. Why neither of them splashed into the muck, Nicole couldn't imagine.

Pointedly, Nicole said, "If the law needs grown men and not little boys, maybe you two should go back home. I'll look for someone else."

"By Jupiter!" Titus Calidius Severus cried in mock dudgeon. "Methinks I've been offended." He lunged at Nicole, as if to knock her off the stone block on which she stood. She leaped by pure instinct to the next one, and from there to the safety of the sidewalk. The fuller and dyer followed, grinning like a blasted idiot.

Nicole planted fists on hips and glared. "That wasn't funny!"

"Oh yes it was," said Calidius Severus. Not even Nicole's deadliest scowl could wipe the grin off his face.

The tavern was a welcome refuge, stuffy air, odor of mildew, and all. Sextus Longinius Iulus and Fabia Ursa were there already, drinking wine and eating bread and salted onions. Nicole flinched to see a pregnant woman swilling down wine—just as she flinched at so many other things in Carnuntum. As with all the rest of them, there wasn't a thing she could reasonably expect to do about it.

Unreasonably, of course, she could tell Fabia Ursa she ought to be drinking milk instead. And Fabia Ursa would stick out her tongue and look revolted, just as Lucius and Aurelia and Julia had done on the first morning after Nicole found herself in Carnuntum. Life was too short.

For that matter, who could guess what diseases lurked in the milk here? Pasteurization was as unheard of as aspirin or carpets.

Titus and Gaius Calidius Severus pushed past her, not exactly rudely, and settled themselves at the table with the others, calling for wine. "The Falernian," Calidius Severus senior said. "Why not? This is an occasion." When Julia brought it, they lifted their cups in salute.

Her eyes went wide. Odds were, nobody had ever done that for her before—who would, for a slave? Her fair skin showed a blush as bright as a sunset, rising from the neckline of the tunic all the way to her hairline.

Gaius Calidius Severus watched as Nicole did, most attentively. If he'd been any more attentive, he would have thrown her down on the floor then and there.

Nicole coughed, rather more sharply than she'd intended, and said, "I think we all know why I asked you to come here. I wanted to set Julia free the formal way, but my brother has made it plain he won't sign the document, and my signature by itself isn't good enough." *And to one damned warm climate with that clerk in the town hall, too,* she thought. "So I'll set her free the informal way, among friends." She held out her hand. "Come here, Julia."

Julia came, walking slowly, as if in a formal procession— or as if she didn't quite believe it all was real. Nicole set a hand on her shoulder. It was stiff, held still by a clear effort of will. "Friends," Nicole said, "it is my wish that this woman should no longer be a slave, but should now and forever after be a freedwoman. You are witnesses to the fact that I am manumitting her in this way, and that I no longer claim her as a slave."

"I've heard lawyers in togas who didn't talk that fancy," Titus Calidius Severus said admiringly. Nicole looked at him in surprise and sudden, completely unaffected delight. He could have searched for a long time before he found a compliment that suited her better.

She was, she discovered, smiling widely and more warmly than she could remember doing, ever, in Carnuntum. She had to reel herself in, to remember the rest of what she'd planned. She went around behind the bar and rummaged in the box she'd found there. "I've written the manumission right here on papyrus: one copy for Julia and one for myself. If you please, you two Calidii and you, Longinius Iulus, should sign them as witnesses."

Julia's eyes and mouth were wide open. "Mistress! I didn't know you'd done that."

"Well, I did," Nicole said robustly, "and you don't have to call me Mistress anymore, either. You're free now, just as I said you would be."

She'd printed out the manumissions in block capitals, that being the universal style in Carnuntum. The reed pen she'd bought with the papyrus sheets worked about as well as a fountain pen, except she had to re-ink it every line or two. She'd spelled the Latin by ear and by guess, but she'd seen from signs and graffiti that she wasn't alone in her uncertainty.

Titus Calidius Severus mumbled to himself as he read one copy. "Not bad. Not bad at all. Nice and clear, nothing too pretty, no flowers of rhetoric, but it gets the job done. I've seen lots worse." He seemed to be surprised, too—probably because no one expected a woman to show even basic literacy, let alone a decent writing style.

Gaius Calidius Severus agreed with Nicole's impatience. "Come on, Father, leave off. This is no time for literary criticism."

Titus Calidius Severus shot his son a narrow glance, but he didn't seem inclined to pull rank. "No, it's not, is it? Umma, where's the pen and ink?" Nicole brought them to him. He signed his name on each sheet of papyrus, and his son followed suit. Both of them wrote with great labor and effort, tongues stuck out, as if they were a pair of second-graders. Nicole couldn't have proved they weren't, either, not by their handwriting. Which of them had the more painful scrawl was hard to judge, but neither would be entering a calligraphy contest any time soon.

Sextus Longinius Iulus couldn't write at all. He made his mark instead, a sprawling Roman numeral six—VI—for Sextus. The Calidii Severi witnessed it. There didn't appear to be any stigma attached to his illiteracy, no patronizing looks or one-syllable explanations. Some people wrote. Most didn't. That was the way the world was.

Once the documents were signed, witnessed, and duly executed, Nicole handed one copy of the manumission to Julia. "Here you are," she said. "I don't think we can get much more official than this, not without Brigomarus. Head up, now, and eyes front. You're a free woman."

Everybody clapped and cheered as if at a play. Julia clutched her sheet of papyrus in stiff fingers. She looked glad—oh yes, very glad indeed. But apprehensive, too, if not outright terrified.

Maybe she had a point, at that. She'd been dubious about the idea from the beginning; had done her best to impress on Nicole that freedom wasn't a purely abstract thing. It meant changes, profound ones, in her status, in her position, in her mode of living. Suddenly, she wasn't property anymore. She was her own person, with rights and privileges, but with responsibilities too. Slaves had none of those things, nor anything else but what their masters gave them.

Nicole might have been tempted to drop the whole thing, to let Julia go on as before, bound but safe. But she couldn't bear the thought of owning another human being. She knew—she'd known for a while now—she was going through the manumission at least as much for herself as for Julia.

"Now we celebrate!" Gaius Calidius Severus declared. "Wine all around, on me!"

Everyone cheered again. Through the last of the noise, Titus Calidius Severus said with a degree of indulgence, "Look at the kid spending my money. I'll have to buy the next round, I suppose."

"No," Nicole said firmly, squelching them both. "The first round is on me." She filled six cups from the amphora of Falernian—yes, even for herself. She might drink the cheap stuff for meals and the middle grade the one time she set out to get seriously drunk, but this called for the heavy artillery. *To hell with the unleaded,* she thought. *One cup of premium in the tank won't hurt.*

It was definitely sweeter and stronger than the wine she was used to. Everybody sipped slowly, with suitably appreciative noises, just like a wine tasting at Spago.

Because she'd served the good stuff on the house, Gaius Calidius Severus bought a round of Falernian, too. Left to himself, Nicole suspected, he would have been more likely to order the two-*as* wine.

Just as Julia fetched the cups for Gaius Calidius Severus' round, Ofanius Valens squelched in from the rainy outdoors. He hadn't shown his face in the tavern since Nicole had pried Julia off his lap.

Well, Nicole thought, if he did have to show up, now was a good time for it. Teach him a lesson, and a good one, too.

Sure enough, he looked at the gathering by the bar, with a particularly keen glance at Julia, and asked, "What's going on?"

"We're celebrating," said Julia. "I'm free." She sounded more cheerful about the idea, now she had a cup of Falernian in her.

Ofanius Valens smiled with apparently unfeigned pleasure. "Now that's worth celebrating," he said. Nicole smiled back at him, a little smugly, until he added, "You cost me the same old two *sesterces* the last time."

Nicole waited for Julia to throw something at him or pick up a stool and brain him with it, supposing he had any brains north of his crotch. But Julia's laugh was loud and obviously genuine. The men in the tavern laughed, too, but they were men. What else could you expect from them? Only when Nicole heard Fabia Ursa giggling did she realize the joke wasn't out of line here. *Local community standards.*

No matter what the local community thought, she didn't like it.

"Next round is mine," Ofanius Valens said, fitting himself into the party as if he had every right to do it.

"You're going to be a couple of cups short, Ofanius," Titus Calidius Severus said. They straightened out who owed how much wine to whom, with resigned amusement that showed they'd done such things many times before. Drunks, Nicole supposed, had plenty of practice in getting drunk.

She wasn't as scornful as she had been, not with that drunken night with Julia under her own belt. In its own way, it had been fun—while it lasted. The next morning . . . The less she thought about the next morning, the better.

Sextus Longinius was not to be left out of the party. He bought the next round. Nicole wished he hadn't, not with a baby on the way and him as far from rich as she was. But there wasn't any way to tell him so without bruising his pride. A person had to be able to hold his head up in front of his friends and neighbors—as much here as in Los Angeles, or Indianapolis for that matter.

All the rounds included Nicole—they wouldn't have been rounds if they hadn't. She had to empty her cup each time, too, or people would wonder what was the matter with her. Their conversation, which hadn't been particularly genteel to begin with, turned loud and silly. *She* turned loud and silly.

She wasn't drunk. She was sure she wasn't. She'd been drunk before. Drunk was when she couldn't stand up without wanting to fall over. Now, although her feet didn't quite want to do as she told them, she walked well enough. She said clever things, witty things: people laughed, didn't they? She couldn't remember the last time she'd been the life of the party. Had she ever been? Her memory was fogged a bit—time travel did that to a person, even without a few cups of Falernian—but as far as she could recall, mostly at parties she'd either circulated rapidly and got out as fast as possible, or found a corner to hide in while too many other guests got sloshed or stoned.

None of them had been as witty as she was being. She

didn't remember laughing this hard or feeling so much like someone who belonged, either. Now there was irony: she had to go back eighteen hundred years and halfway around the world to find people who accepted her as one of them.

Hardly anybody came in to distract from the celebration. She understood perfectly. She was amazed at how well she understood. Who would want to go wandering around on a wet, sloppy day? You couldn't stay dry in a car, not here, not now. You couldn't stay dry anywhere, unless you stayed indoors.

"You look happy, Umma," Titus Calidius Severus said to her in the warm haze of the wine, "happier than you have in a while. I'm glad."

Of course you are—you want to go to bed with me. But the thought lacked the sour edge it had had before. If she looked at him through the lens of better acquaintance—and several cups of wine—the fuller and dyer didn't seem so bad. No—he wouldn't have seemed so bad at all if he hadn't smelled like a public toilet, and not a well-maintained one, either.

Gaius Calidius Severus pulled his hood up over his head and headed for the door. The rain hissed down outside. He ducked a runnel of water off the roof, sloshed to the edge of the sidewalk, and lifted his tunic. Through the sound of the rain, the sound of piss hitting flooded street was tiny but distinct.

When he came back in, he was grinning. "Running water, as good as the baths," he said. Everybody laughed.

Or was it everybody? Nicole had missed a couple of voices. "Where's Julia?" she asked. She couldn't have mislaid her, now, could she?

Fabia Ursa giggled in between sips of wine. *Fetal alcohol syndrome,* Nicole thought fuzzily. The thought, for a mercy, blurred and faded before it touched her tongue. "Didn't you see her go upstairs with Ofanius?" Fabia Ursa asked. She seemed to think it wonderfully funny. "I wonder if that really is for free. The first time, maybe, but not many after that, I'll bet. Julia will be minding her *asses* now."

A pun lurked in there somewhere, but it needed to be in English to work. Nicole's warm, happy mood went suddenly cold. Lucius and Aurelia were upstairs playing—and shame on Nicole for not thinking about them till just now. Were Julia and Ofanius Valens going at it right next door to them?

Someone pushed a cup into her hand. It was full and all but slopping over. She gripped it like a lifeline, raised it to her lips and drank deep. The wine flowed through her in the now familiar sensation, warm as an open fire. *Central heat-ing,* she thought with a return of her antic mood. That was the wine, oh yes: making her forget cold things and sad things, grim things and bad things. So the kids were having a primal experience up there. It couldn't be anything they hadn't heard before—not the way Umma had been pimping Julia. They must have grown up to the sounds of flesh on flesh, thumps and moans and whatever other sound effects were in vogue in this age of the world.

She had to have another talk with Julia, yes. It might be normal behavior here, but it wasn't *nice* behavior. Julia was a free woman now. She had to learn about nice.

But not right now. Tomorrow. If Nicole remembered.

A little while later, Julia came trotting lightly down the stairs with Ofanius Valens right behind her. They weren't blushing in the least, or hiding anything either. He looked as if he should have been puffing smugly on a cigarette—if the Romans had had tobacco, Nicole was sure, they'd all have smoked like the chimneys they also didn't have. Julia's face had a loose, sated look. Her eyes were smoky; her tunic was awry. She straightened it absently, with fingers that paused to stroke the curve of a breast, then wandered on down past the rounded belly. Nicole held her breath, wondering in shocked fascination if she would start stroking her crotch right then and there, but her hand slipped sidewise over a hip and away. She smiled at them all with impartial benevolence.

"So," said Gaius Calidius Severus, "how do you like being a free woman?" That wasn't what he was asking. It was as clear as if he'd come with subtitles: *How would you like to do me for free, too?*

Julia's smile widened and blurred. "If it's this good all the time," she said equally blurrily, "I'm going to like it just fine."

Everybody gave that a round of applause. Everybody, that is, but Nicole. Even tiddly, she wasn't about to approve of Julia's notion of the proper way to celebrate her manumission.

But, said the voice that had been speaking up in Nicole's mind the past few days, if Julia was going to celebrate, what else could she do? There wasn't a whole lot *to* do except get drunk and screw the customers.

Time was, and not so long ago either, when Nicole would have felt obligated to say something censorious—for everyone's own good, of course. But there were just too many things to be censorious about. She'd hit overload. She couldn't raise the proper degree of indignation, or the right amount of crusading zeal, either.

She put on a smile. *Wet blanket,* that was the term for what she'd been tempted to be. Today was simply not the day for that. Things were more than wet enough as it was.

"Seems it's going to rain for forty days and forty nights," she said. Only after the words were out of her mouth did she recall that that was a Biblical allusion. These people—her friends and neighbors and freedwoman—were pagans. It would mean nothing to them. And if it did—might it not tell them that she was a Christian? Christians were fair game here. She'd seen that much already.

Well, as to that, wasn't she at least nominally pagan herself? She certainly hadn't come here by invoking any Christian deity.

They wouldn't know what she'd said. Of course they wouldn't. She was being ridiculous.

Then Sextus Longinius Iulus said, "That's a Jewish myth, isn't it? I've heard it from Jews, I think."

"Where have you known Jews?" Nicole asked in surprise;

Carnuntum was about as far removed from cosmopolitan Los Angeles as she could imagine.

It could have been a stupid question, or even a dangerous one, but he answered quite matter-of-factly: "A lot of coppersmiths are Jews. They'll drink wine with you, sometimes, and talk shop, even if their silly religion doesn't let 'em eat your food. They don't bother anybody, far as I can see."

"Not like those crazy Christians," Fabia Ursa said. She shivered a little. "You never know when those people are going to do something outrageous, when it's not outright dangerous. If you ask me, they *want* to be killed."

"They think they'll go straight to their afterworld," her husband said, as if reminding her of something that everyone knew. "Me, as long as this life's all right, I won't worry too much about the next one."

"I'll drink to that," said Gaius Calidius Severus, and did, draining his cup in a long gulp. When he came up for air he said, "You know what they do? They take babies, girl babies that they're going to expose anyway, and sacrifice them and eat them."

"I didn't hear that," his father said. "They bake bread in the shape of a baby, and call it their god, and eat *that*."

"Crazy," the others said, nodding and passing the winejar round. "Listen, didn't you hear tell . . . ?"

Nicole listened in a kind of stunned amazement. After a while, it dawned on her what their conversation reminded her of. In her own time, in her own country, people had talked the same way about Muslim suicide bombers in the Holy Land.

To the Calidii Severi, to Julia, to Ofanius Valens, and to Sextus Longinius Iulus and Fabia Ursa, whatever Christians Carnuntum had—all the Christians in the Roman Empire, for that matter—were wild-eyed fanatics. Their whole purpose in life was to cause trouble, to make martyrs for their faith. They were, in a word, terrorists.

So—was it true? Nobody had said any such thing in Sunday school. That was all holy Christian martyrs and wicked Romans and bloody-minded lions. Of course the Christians were right—they'd won in the end, hadn't they? Nobody ever showed the other side of it. Just the Christians defending their one and true and only faith.

Nicole had been awfully young then, young enough that the world *could* seem so simple. The older she'd grown, the less things seemed to fit the pattern of her Sunday-school lessons. She shouldn't be surprised to find this new truth, too: Christians as terrorists, Romans as solid citizens appalled at their extremism.

Or maybe that wasn't the way it really was, either. Maybe these people here were ignorant, and blindly prejudiced. If they were, and if everyone had a side and no one was all right or all wrong, what did that say about the way the people Nicole had called friends and colleagues in Los Angeles thought about Muslims? Was there any real difference between an early Christian martyr and a car bomber?

Somehow, the fact that there were Jews here bemused her even more than the presence of Christians. This was, after all, the second century of the Christian era. There would have been Christians around here somewhere. Wouldn't there? But Jews back then had had the Holy Land, or so she'd heard. What would they be doing in a remote backwater like Carnuntum?

Titus Calidius Severus spread a fistful of *sesterces* on the table. "Another round of Falernian," he declared grandly; like everybody else in the tavern, he was flying high. Nicole scooped up the money, pausing to savor the feel of the coins: cool and round, sliding over one another with a soft clink. They were heavy compared to twentieth-century small change, solid and unmistakably *there*. When you had a sackful of Roman money, you knew it. No losing a fifty-dollar bill in your pocket here.

She made her way back to the bar to fill more cups. She had to use the dipper slowly and carefully, to keep from dribbling wine on the stone countertop. As long as she didn't move too fast, she was just fine.

When she carried the cups back to the table, she had a couple of extras. She squinted at them, counted them, counted them again to be sure. Seven—that was the right number, wasn't it? She looked up from the cups to count noses. Fabia Ursa, Sextus Longinius Iulus, Ofanius Valens, Titus Calidius Severus—lord, these names were a mouthful. Didn't anybody do names like Joe and Bob and Sue here?

Probably just as well they didn't. She was letting her mind wander again, too. Four people. Five, counting herself. (Umma. Now that was a nice short name. Everybody should have a name like Umma.) Who was missing?

Julia, of course. And Gaius Calidius Severus.

Where they were, and what they were doing up there, required only one guess, especially since Ofanius Valens was staring at the stairway with a discontented expression. What was he thinking? Was he jealous? Or was he wondering if he'd left Julia dissatisfied?

Maybe he had, at that. Maybe, on the other hand, Julia was just setting out to get as much as she could today.

Fabia Ursa spoke Nicole's thought aloud, as if she'd caught it floating in the rain- and wine-soaked air. "She'll sleep sound tonight, I'm sure," she said with a small giggle that ended in a hiccup. Under the tight-stretched fabric of her tunic, the baby kicked as if in protest. She laughed with a catch in it, as if the baby had caught a rib, and rubbed her belly. "It will be a while before I can sleep that way again— what with the baby between us now, and, if Mother Isis is kind, it will wake me up in the night, and keep me running from sunup to sunup."

Nicole had heard Fabia Ursa mention Isis before; but she'd known the name even before that. She'd read a book once with the goddess' name in the title. Isis, the book had said, was a goddess in Egypt. Carnuntum and Egypt were a long way apart. The Romans might have had only those hideous, squeaking carts to haul goods and people, but ideas seemed to travel on wings.

Fabia Ursa and Sextus Longinius Iulus had retreated into a private and connubial world. She was simpering, he was smiling sappily. They gazed fondly into each other's eyes. He had taken her hand; she rested the other on the swell of her belly. He didn't seem too dismayed to be denied his wife's embraces. *Probably getting it from one of their slaves,* Nicole thought sourly.

While the tinker and his wife shared their little moment and the other two men engrossed themselves in the latest round of Falernian, Julia and Gaius Calidius Severus came bounding down the stairs. They looked indecently pleased with themselves.

Yes, that was the word. Indecent. Nicole fixed Julia with a jaundiced stare. No matter how much wine she'd taken on board, she could not bring herself to approve of Julia's conduct. Julia wasn't a slave any longer. She wasn't property— and she wasn't a sex object. Women weren't supposed to think of themselves as nothing but receptacles for men to fill. They certainly weren't supposed to have as good a time doing it as Julia was. It was not dignified.

Julia aimed in a straight line for her cup of wine, drained it in one long gulp, dropped to a stool and laid her head on the table and fell sound asleep.

They all regarded her in varying degrees of amusement— Nicole's the least, the men's the most, and Fabia Ursa's somewhere in the middle. "I take it back," said the tinker's wife. "She'll sleep sound right now."

Everyone laughed but Nicole. Julia never even stirred.

Sextus Longinius Iulus and Fabia Ursa took their leave not long after. Nicole couldn't tell which was holding which up. If she'd had to guess, she'd have said the tinker's wife was propping up her husband.

As if their departure had been a signal, Ofanius Valens wandered off as well. Nicole caught the glance he shot at Julia as he passed her: a strange expression, almost but not quite unreadable, composed of lust and affection, amusement and resentment. She could imagine what he was thinking. *I wasn't enough for you, was I? Well, next time we'll see what you think!*

Not, thought Nicole with sodden determination, that he was going to get a next time. She'd have that talk with Julia. Tomorrow. After the hangover that was coming. Yes.

Gaius Calidius Severus had been sipping his wine slowly, as if waiting for Ofanius Valens to leave first. It was a kind of possessiveness, Nicole supposed. *This is my territory,* it said. If he'd been a dog, he'd probably have lifted his leg at a spot between Ofanius Valens and Julia.

Once his rival was gone, he seemed to decide that Julia didn't need further staking out. He finished off his wine, pulled his cloak up over his head, and headed for the door. Just as he passed it, his father called out, "Don't fall into a vat of piss till I get back! I won't be but a minute." Gaius laughed and ducked out into the rain.

Which left Julia, sound asleep, and Nicole, too wide awake, and Titus Calidius Severus. As if to punctuate the moment, Julia let out a snore that was almost a bleat. Nicole wished she would wake up. Upstairs she heard the voices, not too loud, of Lucius and Aurelia playing. The children were being very good, extraordinarily good. Nicole wished they would have a fight and come down to tattle on each other. She didn't want to be alone, or as close to alone as made no difference, with Titus Calidius Severus.

He wanted to be alone with her. He'd made sure he would be, staying behind after everyone else had left. It was just as much a statement as the timing of his son's departure.

Nicole looked around for a blunt instrument in case he got out of hand. She didn't have to look far. The Romans didn't have soft plastics. Everything they made was pottery or metal or wood. She had only to choose her weapon.

But the fuller and dyer didn't look as if he planned to do anything too reprehensible. He sat on the stool, peering from his empty cup to Nicole and back again. "I miss you, Umma," he said. "I still haven't figured out what I did to get you upset with me, but I miss you. I want you to know that."

"I do know," she said. She wasn't just saying it to fill the silence. His approach, if it was an approach, was honestly civilized—more civilized than anything she'd got in Los Angeles after Frank dumped her. Frank hadn't exactly been the soul of gentility, either, come to that. She hadn't known a man *could* be.

This man was civilized enough to make her feel downright guilty. Till Nicole muscled herself, thanks to Liber and Libera, into Umma's body, Calidius Severus and Umma had had what they probably thought was a good solid relationship. So what did that make her? A homewrecker?

She couldn't help it. She couldn't help being Nicole and not Umma; being a twentieth-century lawyer and not a second-century tavernkeeper.

He was waiting for her to go on. That was civilized, too: a kind of instinctive politeness, a courtesy so well trained as to be automatic. She sighed. "I don't know what to tell you," she said. "The past few weeks . . . everything's been so confused. Half the time I don't know whether I'm coming or going."

"You haven't been yourself," Calidius Severus agreed. It wasn't the first time Nicole had heard that in Carnuntum. The people who said it didn't know how right they were— and Lord, was she glad of that. The fuller and dyer shrugged and got to his feet. "Well, I won't trouble you anymore about it now. I thought there might be something you wanted to say that you didn't want to say in front of people, if you know what I mean."

"It's nothing like that," she said in dull embarrassment. "I told you it was nothing like that when we were walking back from the market square."

In three quick steps, and before she quite realized it, he was standing beside her. She suppressed the flinch, she hoped, before he could have seen it. She hadn't known he could move so fast, or with such unexpected strength.

But he didn't touch her. He didn't do that. "What *is* it, then?" he demanded. His voice was as firmly under control as his body was, and as rigid with tension.

He must have realized that he wasn't going to get an answer. He shrugged again—he had a whole repertoire of shrugs, a shrug for every occasion—and leaned forward. Before she could pull away, before she was even sure of what he was going to do, he kissed her. It was gentle, no force;

just the brush of his lips, with a faint tickle of beard and mustache. "Take care of yourself, Umma," he said. "I do love you, you know." Before she could find words to reply, he was gone.

9

NICOLE STARED AT THE place where Titus Calidius Severus had been. "Now why did he have to go and say something like that?" she muttered in English. His kiss hadn't been revolting—on the contrary. That worried her more than if she'd wanted to gag at it. He'd been in the tavern, he and his son, long enough that she'd stopped noticing the reek of stale piss that followed them wherever they went. The rest . . .

She hadn't been the least bit interested in sex, with Titus Calidius Severus or anyone else, since she came to Carnuntum. She'd felt anything but sexy herself. She was grubby all the time. She was lousy. She had a yeast infection that didn't want to go away, which left her generally unenthusiastic about her private parts. She never got anywhere near enough sleep. It was hard enough to live in this body every hour of every day, without trying to warm up right good and proper, too.

And yet . . . It wasn't that she wanted Calidius Severus. It was that she might have wanted him. Her mind and self might not remember him, but her body too clearly did. It had memories, it seemed, small yearnings, tinglings that woke when he looked at her or touched her or, as he had just now, kissed her.

With thoughts as disturbing as these, and leading in even more disturbing directions, she was almost pathetically glad to greet the dripping customer who blew in out of the rain and loudly demanded bread and honey and wine—so loudly, in fact, that he woke Julia.

She started bolt upright, eyes enormous with terror, a deer-in-the-headlights look if Nicole had ever seen one. Nicole could read her face as if it had been yesterday's newspaper. Oh, gods—sleeping on the job. What would her mistress do to her? How would she talk her way out of it?

Then, as Nicole tried to watch and serve the customer at the same time, the truth dawned on her. Nicole—Umma—wasn't her mistress anymore. Her relief was as strong as her fear had been, swept over it and drowned it, and let her stand reasonably straight and make her way over to the bar, where she dipped a cup of the two-*as* wine and brought it to the still dripping, faintly steaming customer.

After the man had paid and left, Nicole said, "Julia, if you doze off on me tomorrow, you *will* be in trouble."

Julia grinned at her. "Oh, yes, I know that," she said. She carefully did not include the title that she'd always put in before. No *Mistress*, not any longer. "Today was special, though. With the wine and the loving and all." She stretched with a sinuous, sinful wriggle. Then she hiccuped, which made her laugh. She was full of herself, bubbling over with freedom—and, Nicole caught herself thinking, license. Nicole had known women like that. Girls, too, in high school. There, they were called sluts—even called themselves that, like a badge of pride.

Julia's straightforward sluttiness—all right, earthiness—had always irked Nicole. Now it made her jealous. And that made her angry at herself, because she was jealous.

She covered both jealousy and anger with work. Of that there was always plenty and then some. She washed cups and washed cups and washed cups; she'd almost run out of clean ones. Julia ground flour to bake bread. She and Nicole took turns at the oven, keeping the fire even and gauging when the baking would be done. Time was when Nicole had thought the labor-saving devices in her kitchen in West Hills didn't really save labor—that it was just hype. She knew much better now.

And today was a slow day. Because of the rain, it looked as if the tavern would get by with one baking, two at the outside, instead of the usual four. It didn't help the cash box much, but it made life easier for the staff—all two of them.

Maybe that was why, when Nicole went upstairs as gray day turned into black night, she was only tired, not exhausted. She lay down, but did not fall asleep as fast as she usually did—as fast as if someone had whacked her over the head with a club. The wine had worn off long ago. If she'd had a hangover, it had dissipated somewhere in between customers. So that was how to do it: get drunk in broad daylight and work it off. She'd have to remember that.

Except for the chirping of crickets, the buzzing of mosquitoes, and, somewhere far off, a dog that would not stop barking, it was eerily quiet behind her barred door. No distant racket of TVs and radios, no hiss of cars going past as was commonplace in L.A. even at three in the morning. Nothing. People were snug in their warm buggy beds, and would be till sunrise.

She was snug, too, snug but restive. She tossed and turned. Side to belly to back. Back to belly to side. Of itself—or so she thought till it got there—her hand slid between her legs and crept under her loincloth. It was the first time since she came to Carnuntum, the first interest she'd had in anything but falling flat on her face in bed and waking up however many hours later in some new state of misery or other: itching, griping, cursing dirt and vermin and discomfort.

It had been a long while. It was still strange to find herself smooth down there, except for the small itching scab where she'd cut herself shaving at the baths a day or two before. The difference aroused her. On the fantasy screen behind her eyes, where Mel Gibson and Adrian Paul had used to play out their little dramas, a completely new and different face took shape. It wasn't, God forbid, Titus Calidius Severus, but it wasn't *not*, either. He had a beard; bearded men had never fed her fantasies. He had warm dark eyes and a smile that had never known orthodontia. His shoulders were broad, the skin of his chest warm and shaved smooth: she could feel the faint catch of the stubble. He shaved below, too, around the noble loft of his organ—not huge, not as a man might imagine a woman would want, but a good size, a comfortable size, like the ones she'd seen on the gaudy statues in the market. She felt the shape and hardness of it, the heat that mounted as he smiled at her, smiled and smiled, and— wise man—said nothing at all.

Her hand quickened. Her breathing matched pace with it. Caught; paused. A little moan escaped her.

She relaxed all at once, let her body go limp. Oh, that was good; that was what she'd needed. And yet she shrugged as she often did afterwards, alone in the dark. It was good, but she knew better. The real thing could be as lonely as this, if he did what he wanted to do and then rolled off her, snoring before he hit the pillow. But when it was good, there was nothing like it. No, nothing in the world.

This would do. It had eased the worst of the tightness out of her, which was what she had wanted. She could sleep now.

As she drifted off, she felt one last, small stab of jealousy. Lucky Julia, who didn't bother her head—or her body—with such frettings.

Nicole woke to total strangeness. For a terrible instant, she knew she'd been yanked out of time again, to who knew where. Then she recognized the familiar bed underneath her, the familiar itch and skitter of her personal vermin, and the familiar septic stink of Carnuntum. The strangeness was in the light. It was just sunup—and there was a sun to light the sky. The clouds that had lain so heavy on the town for so long had tattered and torn. When she got up and stumbled to the window to look out, she saw patches of pale blue amid the scudding gray. The air that washed her cheeks was damp still, and cool, but no rain fell. The rain had gone away.

She yawned and stretched, arching her back like a cat. A good hot shower and a thorough delousing would have done her a great deal of good, but even without them she felt as good as she'd felt since she came to Carnuntum.

She was smiling as she went downstairs, a smile Julia returned—up before Nicole as usual, baking the morning bread. Freedom didn't seem to have done much damage—yet—to her work ethic. She might even work harder, now she worked for wages: now she had a stake in working well.

They did their morning chores as they'd come to do, moving through and around each other like partners in a dance. There was a kind of pleasure in it, the pleasure of a pattern well executed. The first customers—a handful of morning regulars—came in with their usual greetings: a smile and a cheery wave, a rheumy scowl, a hungover wince, depending on the individual. They settled in their usual places with their usual breakfasts, wine and fresh bread for the most part. Some liked to banter with Nicole or Julia.

Nicole had just finished a long and lively exchange with a muleteer whose name she could never remember but whose face she couldn't forget—he had a quite imposing wen at the corner of his left eye—when a half-dozen new customers came trooping in. All but one were strangers. That one, coming in behind but clearly a part of the group, as if he were herding it onward, was Umma's brother Brigomarus. His expression mirrored the rest. The best word Nicole could find for it was *thunderous*.

Her bright mood darkened, and not slowly either. From the way Brigomarus acted toward the others, and the resemblance the women bore to him and to each other—and, for that matter, to Umma—she couldn't exactly miss who they were. The two younger women had to be Umma's sisters, and the older one, she of the steel-gray bun and steely stare, their mother. The men, in turn, had to be the sisters' husbands. One was a great deal older than the woman whose elbow he supported. The other was thirty-five or so, and probably a few years older than his apparent wife.

Nicole had learned in her time in Carnuntum that clothes very definitely made the man here—or the woman. The rich never affected the local equivalent of torn jeans and ratty T-shirts, and the poor never tried to dress up like the rich, even if they could have afforded it. There were no designer knock-

offs in discount outlets here. One could, quite easily, determine a person's status by the type and quality of clothes he
or she wore, and by the kind and quantity of jewelry, as well
as by the intricacy of a woman's hairstyle.

These women, these sisters of Umma the tavernkeeper,
were a good cut above her with her combed-out-anyhow hair
and her two good tunics. They wore soft wool dyed in amazingly off-key colors, and linen that might have made a decent
summer power suit in Los Angeles; and they were hung
everywhere, it seemed, with necklaces and armlets, rings and
earrings. Not all or even most of it was gold, but enough of
it was, particularly on the sister with the older man, that
Nicole was left in no doubt as to their economic status. These
were the local equivalent of prosperous businessmen and
their wives. The older man was even tricked out in a toga—
about as formal as a dinner jacket, and overwhelmingly so
in the humble surroundings of a tavern.

Even the mother's simplicity of hair and dress—a couple
of layers of black tunic and a black cloak—was deceptive.
Her one ornament was a ring on her finger where Nicole's
twentieth-century eye looked for a wedding ring, and it was
gold.

Nicole was more than glad she'd drunk well-watered wine
with breakfast, and eaten a good half-loaf of bread and a
chunk of cheese. If she'd been as full of Falernian as she
was at Julia's manumission party, she'd have said exactly
what she thought: "Good morning, ladies and gentlemen.
Slumming, I suppose?"

They did have the look, and no mistake. The younger man,
a tall reedy fellow with the scars of old acne on his sparsely
bearded cheeks, dusted off a bench with an air of great fas-
tidiousness, and helped his mother-in-law to a seat thereon.
She allowed him to assist her, but not without paying for it:
"Not so solicitous, Pacatus, if you please. It makes you look
like a legacy-hunter. Not, I suspect, that you aren't eager to
see me die and leave you my holdings, but it's more polite
to act as if it doesn't matter."

She had a voice like poisoned honey, which was probably

what had brought her this far up in the world—widow of a
well-to-do man, Nicole guessed, but that man hadn't been
Umma's father, not by a long leap up the social ladder.

The old lady got herself settled with much clucking and
fussing from all concerned; all but Nicole, who stayed right
where she was, safe behind the bar. In the process she picked
up names to attach to faces: Pacatus the younger son-in-law,
Tabica his wife, Ila the older—and probably oldest—sister;
she looked older than Umma. And, most overweeningly
pompous of that whole pompous crew, Ila's togaed husband,
Marcus Flavius Probus. No one, not even his wife, called
him by his praenomen. Nicole doubted Ila ever did, even in
bed. He bore the full triune burden of his name, wherever
and whenever he was.

While the in-laws catered to the old lady, whom Marcus
Flavius Probus addressed as *my dearest Atpomara,* but everyone else called simply *Mother,* Brigomarus stood a little apart
with arms folded, quietly but conspicuously removed from
the fray. Nicole didn't know that she liked him any better
for it. He was the light of his mother's eye, she could see
that without half trying. Atpomara sneered at her sons-in-law
and tyrannized over her daughters, but when she looked at
her son her terrible old eyes almost went soft.

Queen bee, Nicole thought, and disliked the woman on
sight.

One way and another, the tavern managed to empty of
customers while Atpomara got herself settled. Either they
knew something was up and were too polite to hang around
and witness it, or people knew this family too well to want
to be anywhere near it once it assembled in force. Even Julia,
who wasn't usually any kind of coward, muttered something
about seeing if the kids were up to something upstairs, and
left Nicole to face the music alone.

She had no doubt at all that that was what was coming.
Six pairs of eyes followed Julia out of the room. If the men
had been dogs, their tongues would have been hanging out.
The women would have been bristling and snarling, of
course, like bitches everywhere.

Oh, dear, Nicole thought. She really had taken a dislike to these relatives of Umma's. There didn't seem to be a great deal of close affection among them, either, not even enough to put up a pretense of squealing and cheek-kissing and oh-it's-been-so-long. From the sisters' expressions, they didn't want to touch their poor relation for fear of catching a disease.

True, they were notably cleaner and better kempt than Nicole managed to be. By twentieth-century American standards they were still fairly ripe, and those elaborate hairstyles reminded Nicole rather forcibly of stories she'd heard her mother tell about the ratted and lacquered constructions of the Sixties, complete with urban legends of spiders and literal rats' nests. She let herself dwell on that for a while, as she stood behind the bar and waited for someone to speak.

It took a long uncomfortable while, but Brigomarus didn't disappoint her after all. "Good morning, Umma," he said.

"Good morning," she said civilly. "May I serve you anything? Wine? The bread's fresh, and we have a nice raisin compote today."

He glanced at the others. They were all affecting interest in matters far removed from this low and none too sanitary place. "No," he said after a pause. "No, thank you. We won't be staying long."

"Really?" Nicole raised her eyebrows. "You've come for the company, then? That's the only other reason to come to a tavern, isn't it?"

"In . . . a manner of speaking," he said. He was nicely uncomfortable. Or maybe his tunic was new and inclined to itch.

Nicole wasn't going to give him any help at all. She folded her arms and waited him out. It had been a useful tactic in court. It did the job here. He blurted out what he maybe had been instructed to frame more tactfully, from the way Atpomara's face clouded over. "Umma, what *were* you thinking? You know I forbade you to manumit that slave!"

"Julia," Nicole said with great care and attention to the

woman's name, "was my property. It was my decision, and my right, to set her free."

"It was not," Brigomarus said heatedly. She'd got him on the defensive, and he didn't like it one bit. "You, in case you've forgotten, are a woman. A woman should not act without the approval of her male relatives. That's the law."

"It is also the law that a person of either sex may manumit a slave informally in the presence of a suitable number of witnesses. *Male* witnesses," Nicole said pointedly. She reached under the bar where she'd stowed the box with the document in it, brought it out and laid it on the bar.

He made no move to pick it up, still less to read it. "You can't do that," he said.

"On the contrary," said Nicole, "I already did."

Evidently Atpomara decided that her son might be the light of her eye, but when it came to pitched battles, he needed stronger reinforcements. She shot a glare at the elder son-in-law that made him jerk forward as if stung. "What is done can be undone," he said with blustering confidence. "Come, dear Umma, consider the path of reason, the light of good sense, the beauty of obedience to one's blood and kin and kind. Was it not Homer who said, 'Happy the man who loves his homeland'? Is not one's family even more sacred? Should one not—"

Nicole had had plenty of practice in listening to pompous asses both on and off the judge's bench, but her time in Carnuntum had worn her patience a little thinner than perhaps it should have been. She let him rattle on a while longer, till he came to something approximating a full stop. His words and theme were remarkably similar to twentieth-century political bombast, right down to the stump-thumping about Family Values.

When he paused for air, she said, "No."

He gaped at her. He looked like a fish. "What—"

"No," she repeated. "I doubt very much that Homer said any such thing."

"Of course he did," said Marcus Flavius Probus. And

stood flat-footed, with all his fancy oratorical effects gone clean out of his head.

Good: she'd derailed him. Before he could scramble back on track, the other brother-in-law, Pacatus, opened his mouth to say something. Nicole ran right over him. "Does any of you have anything useful to say? I have a business to run, in case you haven't noticed, and you're keeping the customers out."

The collective intake of breath was clearly audible. The sisters looked as if she'd grown three heads and started to bark. Umma apparently hadn't been this outspoken, though from what Nicole knew of her, she'd had her share of problems with tact.

Atpomara confirmed it. She sniffed through her elegant nose and glared down it at the woman she thought was her daughter. Her severely déclassé, increasingly embarrassing daughter. "Umma, my dear," she said, "you were always headstrong and never particularly sensible, but this is remarkable even for you. Whatever possessed you to toss away four hundred *denarii* worth of highly useful slave? Whom, I may point out, your late lamented husband selected and purchased. Or is that why you did it? Have you found it so difficult to forgive a man the exercise of his natural impulses?"

"The man is dead," Nicole said in a conspicuously reasonable tone. "He has nothing to do with why I chose to set Julia free."

"Obviously," the elder sister—Ila, yes—said, "*nothing* has anything to do with why you did it. It's not as if you could afford to throw away that much money. Are you having an attack of remorse, the way the Christians are said to be prone to? Sometimes they give away everything before they believe they're due to die."

"She doesn't look anywhere near dying yet," the younger sister said with a sniff that tried and signally failed to be as haughty as her mother's. "Mother, Ila, this is such a bore. Pacatus, take me home, do. I've a new perfume I'm dying to try, and I've been promised my necklace today, and my dressmaker will be waiting. You know how I hate to keep her waiting!"

Everybody ignored her, including her husband. Tabica, Nicole deduced, was a chronic whiner. She seemed the sort of person who would flaunt all her successes in her sister's face, till it became habit so ingrained that she didn't even know she did it.

Ila had more backbone, though her air of discontent was just as strong. She reminded Nicole of certain of the partners' wives at her old law firm, in particular the ones who'd had ambitions—toward Hollywood, toward a profession, toward anything but being a trophy wife for a partner in a mediocre law firm. In Los Angeles there'd been a little scope for such women, jobs they could take, committees to lord it over, charities and benefits and the not-so-infrequent celebrity bash. Carnuntum had nothing to compare with that.

Ila didn't whine. Ila exercised herself in rancor: "It's not as if you were born to better things, Umma, though some of us have aspired to and even achieved them." She slanted a glance at her mother, who sat in regal silence, letting her daughters make idiots of themselves. "Even so, a person of your status in the world should know better than to do a thing as ill-advised as this—and against the family's wishes, too. Any foolish thing that you do, *we* bear the brunt of it."

"Oh, do you?" Nicole inquired. "And how are you materially impaired by the freeing of my slave?"

Pacatus surprised her by rolling his eyes and whistling softly. "Oho! Been talking to some of your educated customers, have you? Which of them taught you *those* words?"

"Maybe I found them for myself," Nicole said acidly. She folded her arms and tapped her foot. "Well? Do I get an answer? How does Julia's manumission hurt you—aside from the blow to your pride?" *To your little power trip,* she wanted to say, but no words in Latin quite matched the idiom.

Nobody did answer, so she did it for them. "It doesn't hurt you a bit, does it? It's my financial loss, and my choice to take it."

"And our burden when you fall into penury," Atpomara said, "as you will do if you make any more such choices. What will you do next? Give this tavern to some passerby off the street, and go off to be a wandering philosopher?"

"If I do that," said Nicole, "I suppose I'll live off the charity of others. Not you. Believe me, I won't come to you for one single *as*."

"What an ungrateful little chit you are!" said Ila. "Is this how you address your mother?"

She's not my *mother, lady,* Nicole wanted to say, but that would have been a very bad idea. She settled for a lift of the chin and a curl of the lip. "I'll make it on my own. Just you wait and see."

"But you can't do that," said Brigomarus. "Unless . . ." A look of wild speculation came over his face. "Don't tell me. You're going to marry old Pisspot across the way." He thumped his fist down on the table, too loud and sudden for Nicole to get a word in edgewise. "That's it. That is emphatically it. I will not have it. I forbid it!"

"You may go right ahead and forbid it," Nicole said with rising heat, "and I may go right ahead and do as I see fit. I am not your property, and I am not your child. I will not duck my head and do what you want, simply because it is you who wants it." She turned on the sisters. "Or you." And, last and fiercest, on Atpomara: "*Or* you. I am my own woman. I have my own life here, I make my own living, I decide for myself what I will do and not do. You have no say in it."

Pacatus and Marcus Flavius Probus exchanged glances. "Poor woman," said Pacatus.

"Hellebore," said Marcus Flavius Probus, nodding ponderously.

Pacatus blinked but seemed to get the point, which was more than Nicole could claim. "Oh, yes, she's off her head—or else she's up to something with that dyer. What if he encouraged her to free the slave for some purpose of his own? Is he clever enough for that? He'll have dyed his brains bright blue by now, I should think, with all the fumes from his work."

Marcus Flavius Probus had no sense of humor, that was evident. He seized on the one thing that must have made sense to him, and worried at it like a dog on a bone. "She can't marry that person. It's beneath us all."

"*She* is beneath us all," Ila said.

Nicole stepped in before they could go on. She was quite coldly angry by now, the same anger she'd honed so well in dealing with Frank and his late-model bimbo. "You had better leave," she said.

No one seemed to hear her. The brothers-in-law and Ila were too busy dissecting her mental state. Tabica was elaborately and tearfully bored. Brigomarus frothed and steamed. Atpomara sat in state, waiting for someone to notice her lofty silence.

Nicole hefted one of the heavy iron skillets near at hand, and let it fall with a ringing crash. That got their attention, one and all. She braced her hands on the bar and leaned across it, glaring at the lot of them. "Did you hear me? I asked you to leave."

"You can't do that," Brigomarus said. It seemed to be a favorite refrain.

"This is my house," Nicole said, shaping each word with care. "This is my business. This is my life. If you can do nothing better with or for it than play the petty tyrant, then I don't want or need you. I've been getting by on my own so far. I'll keep right on doing it, too."

"How can you get by on your own?" Brigomarus demanded. "You're a woman. You can't do a single legal thing without my approval."

"Would you like to bet on it?" Nicole asked him. She thumped a fist on the papyrus that still lay, unregarded, on the bar. "If there's anything I know about the way the law works, it's that there's a way around everything. Sometimes it's hard, often it's twisted, but it is there. No law was ever written that didn't have a loophole somewhere. And I," she said, "will be sure to find it."

"My, my," murmured Ila. "Aren't we cocky today? What's got you going, sister dear? Your so-fragrant beloved?"

"I don't need a man to get going, as you put it," Nicole shot back, "least of all that one—though he's worth ten of you. Now get out. I have work to do."

She thought she'd have to eject them bodily—and wasn't it ironic that she'd never needed a bouncer in all her time in the tavern, but now, with her putative family, she would dearly have loved to have one. Ila and Brigomarus seemed inclined to camp there till she broke down and let them run all over her.

They'd wait a good long time if so, and she wasn't lying. She did have work to do. Lots of it. Which she would go ahead and do, starting with cleaning the area behind the bar, till they got fed up and left.

It wasn't too hard to ignore them. They couldn't or wouldn't get at her with the bar between. Their bluster fell on deaf ears. Nobody was inclined to get physical—the one thing she'd been afraid of, because when it came right down to it, a woman was at a major disadvantage against three men.

Nobody came to her rescue, either. Julia was hiding upstairs with the kids. The Calidii Severi were safe in their shop, oblivious to the trouble she was in—and, she had no doubt, to the family's interpretation of her relationship with Titus Calidius Severus. Her regular morning customers seemed to have conspired to stay away.

Well, and so be it. She'd been alone when Frank deserted her, and she'd handled that just fine. She could deal with a frustrated and clearly dysfunctional family—after all, it wasn't *her* family.

As she'd expected, after a while they ran out of things to shout at her and started shouting at one another. When that palled without her taking notice, they gave up at last and left her, as Marcus Flavius Probus said, to her self-inflicted fate. The peace and quiet then were heavenly, and barely disrupted even by the stream of customers that came flooding in. Nicole greeted them with a wide and welcoming smile, and the first few got their orders at half price, just for being there and not being Umma's relatives. By that time Julia had come out of hiding and gone to work, so quietly Nicole couldn't find it in herself to ream the woman out with proper ferocity. She settled for a frown and a hard glance, which made Julia flinch rather more than was strictly necessary— slave reflexes, consciously suppressed as she remembered, yet again, that she was free.

Even after the rain stopped, the street in front of the tavern remained a wallow for several days. Lucius thought that was wonderful, and went out and coated himself in mud from head to foot. Nicole had been more affected by the relatives' visit than she knew at the time; she had no patience left for small muddy boys. The first time he came in black to the eyes and slopping odorous bits on her freshly swept floor, she yelled at him. When that didn't take the self-satisfied gleam out of his eye, she spanked him. She didn't feel nearly so guilty about that now as she had the first time. It was, she told herself, like a rolled-up newspaper for a puppy: a non-threatening but necessary form of discipline.

She poured a bucket of water over him, and then another one, and then felt like giving him another spanking, because that water didn't flow at the turn of a tap. She or Julia had to lug it from a fountain. Two buckets' worth of water didn't make him anything close to clean, either.

It was, fortunately, a men's day at the baths. In lieu of running Lucius through a car wash, that would have to do. She went next door to see if Sextus Longinius Iulus would take him. The thought of sending Lucius out by himself didn't appeal to her in the least. City upbringing, city para-noia: maybe it wasn't necessary here, but then again maybe it was.

When she came in and paused to let her eyes adjust to the dimmer light, the tinker was tapping a dented pot back into shape on a form. He smiled at her. She smiled back. But when she explained what she'd come for, he shook his head. "No, Umma, sorry. Not today. I'm backed up for a week as it is." She could see it, too: heaps and piles of broken or dented utensils, enough to fill the tiny space and spill out into the room behind. He wasn't insensitive to her disappointment: he said, "I really am sorry. I wish I could, mind, a bath would be nice. But I can't. Why don't you try Calidius Severus across the street?"

"I guess I'll do that," she said with something less than enthusiasm. It was embarrassing to keep asking favors of the fuller and dyer. Still, she thought, they were friends even if they weren't lovers—they were that, weren't they? If a friend wouldn't do you a favor, then who would?

She picked her way down the muddy sidewalk back to the tavern. Lucius, for a wonder, hadn't gone anywhere. He was in the public room seeing how many stools he could pile on top of one another, while Julia rather irresponsibly ignored him. Nicole rescued number four just before it toppled onto a customer's head, snagged Lucius, and dragged him out into the street.

Lucius didn't look at all disconcerted by her speed or her vehemence. Adventures were all to the good, he seemed to think, and it *was* an adventure to get magnificently muddy and throw his mother into fits. Her dire threats about what would happen to him if he "accidentally" fell off the stepping stones into the mud would have got a restraining order slapped on her by any judge in the United States. That meant they were—barely—strong enough to make him notice them.

Titus Calidius Severus was pulling a soggy bolt of linen from a wooden tub when Nicole and Lucius walked into the shop. His arms were blue to the elbow. "Well, well," he said, laughing as he took in Lucius' grimy hide. "Have you decided to turn Nubian on us, you young rascal?"

"Maybe." Lucius sounded as if he liked the idea. He pointed to the dye on Calidius' forearms. "So what are you? A mighty warrior Celt?"

That didn't mean anything to Nicole, but it made the fuller and dyer laugh louder. "Maybe I am," he said. "Maybe I'll chop off your head and hang it over my door there. What do you think of that?"

"Yes!" Lucius agreed with enthusiasm.

Violence. Nicole's lip started to curl, until she remembered some of the dire threats she'd laid on Lucius before she trusted him on the stepping stones. That made her blush faintly, which didn't help her mood a bit. "If you're going to the baths today," she said to Titus Calidius Severus, "would you be so kind as to take him with you and get him back to the color he's supposed to be?" She didn't call Calidius by his praenomen; that would have felt like using it to unfair advantage.

He nodded at once, with every appearance of goodwill. "It's been a while since I took him, after all, hasn't it? We could both use a good scrubbing." He grinned at Lucius. Lucius grinned back. Calidius Severus' expression changed slightly. "My, and aren't you getting to be a handsome boy? Just as well your mother sends you with a chaperon. A good-looking boy in the baths by himself—that's asking for trouble."

Lucius shrugged and looked bored. Calidius Severus sighed a little. "Well. You're young yet. That's to the good, maybe." To Nicole he said, "Don't you worry, Umma. I'll keep a steady eye on him and keep him safe, and bring him back as good as new."

Nicole shivered deep down inside. She'd only been worried about Lucius alone in the streets. She hadn't thought about what might happen in the baths. She should have, too. She'd seen what kind of place they were. If prostitutes came and went there on men's days, if women gossiped about masseurs who provided extra services on the side, why wouldn't men who went after boys—*chickenhawks,* a gay friend of hers had called them—also prowl there? She looked at Titus Calidius Severus with a new respect. "Thank you very much, Titus," she said, deliberately and carefully calling him by his praenomen.

He noticed. He smiled, nodded. He didn't press his advantage. Was he really as sensible as that?

Yes, she thought. He was. Which put him several steps

ahead of most of the men she'd known in Indiana and California, let alone Carnuntum.

"Come on, Lucius, let's get you cleaned up," he said. Lucius came without hesitation or backtalk. Calidius Severus' tone was familiar to Nicole, though she needed a moment to place it. When she did, she snorted. In 1950s war movies that even sleazy cable stations didn't show till three in the morning, the tough sergeant used precisely that tone with the green kid. It worked like a charm in the movies. Nicole had never imagined that it could work so well in reality.

Titus Calidius Severus called upstairs to Gaius to explain where he was going and why. His son came down yawning and chewing on a hunk of bread. He shoved the last of it into his mouth and settled without complaint to the work that his father had left—because the work, of course, would not go away.

Titus and Lucius and Nicole left him to it. After the reeking dimness of the shop, the open air was blinding bright and dizzyingly clean.

Lucius, whose young eyes adjusted fastest, tugged at Nicole's arm and pointed across the street. "Look, Mother! Someone's written something on our front wall."

Sure enough, there was a large scrawl by the door. With both eyes on Lucius to keep him from diving back into the mud, Nicole had walked right by without noticing. Now that he'd pointed it out, she read it aloud, sounding out the spikily printed words: "Big beast show in the amphitheater on the thirteenth day before the Kalends of August." She needed a moment to work out that that was July 20, and another to realize it was only a couple of days away.

"Ah, Caesar's victory games," Calidius Severus said, nodding. "They always put on a good show for those. They bring in beasts people don't see every day, not just the same old boring bulls and bears." Absurdly, Nicole thought of Wall Street, and wondered if Rome had, after all, had a stock market. The fuller and dyer went on, "Why, a few years ago, they even had a tiger. Do you remember what a mean-looking bastard he was?"

"Now that you remind me of it, yes," Nicole said, to be safe. No way she was letting him know that her memory of Carnuntum stopped cold less than two months before.

"They may not be able to manage anything that fancy this time, not with that pestilence down in the south and the war tearing up everything off to the west, but it still should be one of the best shows of the year." Titus Calidius Severus hesitated, then took the plunge: "Would you like to see it with me?"

A date, Nicole thought. *I've just been asked out on a date. Who says this place hasn't got any culture?* The fuller and dyer's voice didn't have anything of *and then you'll put out for me* in it, either. She'd heard more than enough of that since Frank walked out. She'd given up on men as a species then, after so many of them had proved that all a man wanted was one thing.

But Calidius Severus didn't seem to want *just* that. There was no way to tell for sure, not yet, and she'd been burned so badly that she wasn't going to believe it till she saw it— but she got the distinct feeling nonetheless that even if she kept on saying no to him, he wouldn't stop being her friend.

That was the most refreshing discovery she'd made in years. She nodded in his expectant silence, and said, "Yes, I would like that. I'll even pay Julia a little something extra to keep the kids from killing each other."

"If you hadn't set her free, you wouldn't have to worry about that," he said. But he shrugged, and let go a sudden and amazingly charming smile. When he smiled, snaggle teeth and all, he was almost handsome. No, Nicole thought; clean up his teeth, wash and deodorize him, and he'd cut a nice swath through the bored wives' set in West Hills. Those Latin looks of his weren't bad—weren't bad at all.

Fortunately, he couldn't read her mind, or she'd have been well and truly embarrassed. "Well," he said, "she's a freedwoman and that's that. You make your arrangements with her, and I'll be by sometime in the morning, to make sure we get good seats."

Nicole nodded, but he didn't give her time to say anything

more before he turned to Lucius. "Meanwhile, you, let's go get that mud off, and I'll have a bath, too, while we're at it. Won't do me a bit of harm."

"I should say not," Lucius said with rudeness that would have won him a swat from Nicole if he'd been close enough. "I might be muddy, but *you* stink."

Titus Calidius Severus didn't seem offended. He certainly didn't clobber the little brat. "Oh, I don't know," he said with a judicious air. "There's enough shit mixed in with the mud to give stale piss a run for its money, don't you think?" He ruffled the boy's hair, though Lucius ducked and spluttered and protested. "And I don't get piss up here, either."

Nicole swallowed bile. She'd watched her fair share of animals dropping dung in the middle of the street—and pissing in it, too. Somehow, that hadn't quite impressed itself on her in connection with Lucius. Mud, so far as she'd ever known it, was nothing but wet dirt. In Carnuntum, it was a lot more than that. It was wet, shitty dirt, full of tetanus and lockjaw—or were they the same thing?—and who knew what else. Christ, what was Lucius liable to come down with, now he'd had his wallow?

No doubt she'd find out, and quickly enough, too. For the time being, she focused on the thing that Calidius Severus' gesture reminded her of, the most urgent thing. "Please, make sure you get rid of as many lice and nits as you can. Will you do that for me?"

"I'll do my best," Calidius said, scratching his own head vigorously, as if she'd put him in mind of the colonies thriving there. "Not that you can ever get rid of all of them, but it never hurts to put them down as much as you can."

Nicole nodded tightly. Her jaw had set, grinding her teeth together—nothing she intended, and not much she could do about it, either. The broken tooth in back twinged worse than usual. She ignored it. Once or twice, after a trip to the baths and washing lots of bedding—to the dismay of Julia, who'd done most of the work—she'd thought she *was* rid of her lice, once even for three whole days. But they came back. They always came back. It didn't matter how—whether she'd missed a few, whether a customer had brought a new batch into the tavern, whatever. There just was no getting rid of them.

Titus Calidius Severus and Lucius headed off for the baths. The boy walked easily beside the man, chattering at a great rate, more than he ever did with Nicole or Julia. They looked, she thought, like son and father.

That thought brought her up short for a moment, stopping her on a stepping stone before she recovered herself and went on across the street. *Were* they father and son? Calidius and Umma had not exactly had a platonic friendship before Nicole arrived to disrupt it.

She shook her head. No. In all the gossip she'd overheard or been regaled with, she'd never heard the slightest suggestion that Umma had been getting it on the side with her neighbor while her husband was still alive. And he hadn't died that long ago, from things that Fabia Ursa had said: three or four years at most. Both Lucius and Aurelia were older than that.

Damn, what had the man's name been? The clerk in the town hall had told her, but it had slipped right out of her head. So far she hadn't needed it, but the way her luck ran, eventually she was going to. She just had to pray that the rest of her luck held, and someone said his name before she had to come up with it.

She glowered at the graffito on the tavern's wall. If she took a brush to it, she'd probably get rid of the whitewash, too. She'd have to buy more whitewash, then, and paint over it. She glowered more darkly. Another couple of *sesterces* thrown away. Maybe she'd leave it up, at least until the beast shows were done. It might, she told herself, even draw a couple of customers into the tavern.

Aurelia erupted through the front door, spotted Nicole, and said, "Eep!" She ducked back in even faster than she'd come out. Nicole laughed. She knew what *that* meant. Aurelia had been all set to play in the mud, like her brother before her. *Foiled,* Nicole thought wickedly.

She went inside with more decorum. The warm rich smell

of baking bread fought and almost overwhelmed the city stink. Julia was over at the counter, grinding flour for the next batch.

As Nicole went to spell her at the mill, a man's voice spoke behind her. "Mistress Umma?"

Nicole turned, trying not to seem too startled. The newcomer was a dapper little man, and a total stranger. He knew her, however, or thought he did. Little by little, she was getting used to that. It didn't drive her to panic much anymore, not the way it had at first.

Then again, maybe Umma *hadn't* known him. He blinked and peered at her as if he might be a bit nearsighted. "My name is Julius Rufus," he said. He was carrying a small wooden keg, which he set on one of the tables. "I hear you've been in the mood to try new things lately."

Her heart leaped from a standstill into a pounding gallop. "What? What about it?" Damn—were people all over Carnuntum gossiping about the new and highly eccentric Umma? *Old Umma used to be sharp, you bet, but lately she's gone soft in the head.* God—that could get dangerous. Somebody might even—

But Julius Rufus said, "I'll tell you what about it," and her heartbeat slowed to a fast canter. Safe, she was safe. This was a salesman, or she wasn't a Hoosier of Hoosier born. As if to reassure her even further, he went on in a fast patter that had to be as old as the hills, "I know this tavern has always served nothing but wine—good wine, too, everybody agrees on that. Still and all, if you've taken it into your head to try things you haven't tried before, how about this delicious barley brew here? It's my very own, brewed up of the finest ingredients, according to an ancient recipe that's come down through my family since the first Pyramid was a pup."

Julia looked up from the quern. "The Marcomanni and Quadi drink beer because they don't know any better," she said flatly. "When they get smart, they buy wine from us Romans."

Julius Rufus showed teeth as irregular as Calidius Severus' in an insouciant grin. "Beer has been good enough for the

Egyptians since time out of mind, and *my* beer has been good enough for a nice lot of people in Carnuntum for a good ten years now. There's some very fine taverns go through a whole barrel of it before they've emptied their amphorae of wine."

"Barrels," Nicole murmured. Beer had alcohol in it, of course. But, if it came in barrels, it wouldn't be full of lead. She fetched a clean cup and a dipper, and bore down on Julius Rufus and his sample cask. "Let me try some."

Julia looked astonished. Julius Rufus looked delighted. He lifted the lid of his keg with a flourish. "Help yourself, Mistress Umma—and see for yourself that you'll have no reason whatsoever to look down your nose at this fine product."

When Nicole and Frank toured Austria on their honeymoon, Frank had drunk Austrian beer with conspicuous pleasure. Nicole, despite his urging, had stuck to mineral water. What she wouldn't give to do that now . . .

She shook herself and focused on the task at hand. No help for it, and no escape, either. She dipped up a cupful, raised the cup to her lips, and sipped.

She had to work hard to hold her face straight. Wine, at least, was sweet. Frank had always said beer was an acquired taste. Nicole wondered why on earth anyone would want to acquire it. The stuff was bitter. It was sour. She could taste the alcohol in it. The only thing she could say for it was that it might make drunkenness more trouble than it was worth. If everyone reacted to beer the way she did, she might actually make some inroads against alcoholism in Carnuntum.

She made herself take another sip. It tasted no better than the first. "It'll never take the place of wine," she said.

"Told you so," Julia said from behind the counter.

But Julius Rufus was undeterred. "I don't intend it to take the place of wine," he said. "I drink wine myself—in fact, if you'll serve me a cup of your two-*as* there, I'll be grateful." He set a *dupondius* on the table by the keg. Nicole nodded to Julia, who poured out the wine for him. He tossed it down, smacked his lips with stagey relish, and said, "Sure, wine's good, and plenty of it. But the more choices you give your customers, the more customers you're likely to get. Don't you think so, Mistress Umma?"

He was good. If he'd lived in Los Angeles in the 1990s, he would have sold a hell of a lot of encyclopedias or aluminum siding or whatever he was peddling, because sure as hell he would have been peddling something.

Even so, if Nicole had intended to say no, he would have been out the door before he got well warmed up to his pitch. Her mother had been death on door-to-door salesmen, and Nicole had continued the family tradition with telemarketers.

But she wasn't going to turn this salesman down. If she could get in more choices that didn't involve ingesting lead in toxic quantities—not to mention a choice that might not involve ingesting quite so much alcohol—then she might not be totally happy, but she'd be happier than she was now. She looked him in the eye and said, "How much do you want for each barrel, and how many cups can I get per barrel?"

Julius Rufus beamed at her. "You think of your profit margin, I see. Good for you! If your arithmetic is weak, I'll be happy to help you with your figuring, so that you—"

"My arithmetic is fine, thank you," Nicole snapped. Her arithmetic, from what she'd seen, was a damn sight better than that of any local without a counting board in front of him. The Romans, naturally enough, used and thought in terms of Roman numerals, and Roman numerals were to arithmetic what cruel and unusual punishment was to jurisprudence.

The dicker that followed left Julius Rufus sweating. "Mistress Umma, do you want my children to starve?" he wailed at the midpoint.

"They won't starve," she retorted. "They can drink the beer you don't sell me. This isn't something I have to have. It's something I might want to have—if the price is right. This tavern's done fine without beer for a long time. We can go right on doing fine without it, as long as it's going to cost six times as much as it's worth."

"What a terrifying woman you are," Julius Rufus muttered.

Nicole smiled a smile that Frank had likened to a shark's. "You say the sweetest things," she said. He flinched as if she'd slapped him.

She ended up buying the beer at something less than half the price he'd quoted. She still had a scrap left of the papyrus on which she'd written out Julia's letters of manumission; she got out the pen and ink and set down on the scrap the terms to which she and Julius Rufus had agreed. When it was written up as it should be, she shoved the papyrus across the bar at him. "Just sign this, if you would."

"Sweet Isis the merciful!" he cried. He mumbled his slow way through the three-line contract, then scrawled something that might have said *Julius Rufus* below it. "There! Are you happy now?"

"I'm fine, thank you," Nicole said, and seized the papyrus and stowed it away in the box before he could think of grabbing it for himself. She turned to Julia. "Pour this nice man a cup of Falernian, if you please." She was the soul of politeness now, even if she'd been a barracuda only moments before. Why not? Nothing wrong with being friendly *after* she'd got her way.

10

WE'LL HAVE GOOD WEATHER for the beast show," Titus Calidius Severus said, as smug as if he'd ordered it especially for the occasion. "This sort of thing is a lot less fun in the rain and mud."

"Yes," Nicole said, barely remembering to answer him at all. She was excited out of all proportion to the occasion, almost quivering with eagerness at the chance to do something out of the ordinary. She'd even fixed herself up with a sitter: she'd promised Julia a couple of extra *sesterces* above her usual wages, to ride herd on things. Julia had agreed so readily, Nicole suspected she was plotting to earn a few more *sesterces* on the side—or on her back.

Nicole almost didn't care. Or, no: she cared. But there wasn't anything she could do about Julia once Julia was out of her sight. And she wanted—God, how she wanted—to get away for the day.

"This will be—" she began, but stopped abruptly, before she said something she might regret.

Titus Calidius Severus wasn't about to let her off that particular hook. "Be what?" he asked in all apparent innocence.

"Fun," Nicole said after a pause. It wasn't what she'd intended to say. But, while this would be the first time she'd gone outside the walls of Carnuntum, it certainly wouldn't be the first time Umma had done so. Nicole wasn't about to blow her cover now. Not after all this time.

A clamoring throng of people streamed toward the southwestern gate of the city, all heading, as she was, for the amphitheater. They chattered as they went, sounding at least as excited as she felt. "Lions, I heard," one said. "*I* heard tigers," somebody else declared. People scoffed at that, to disgust: he folded his arms and set his jaw and retreated into injured silence. "Bears," a woman said behind him. "There are always bears."

"Lions and tigers and bears! Oh, my!" Nicole was wearing sandals, not ruby slippers, and the road was neither yellow nor brick, but she kicked up her heels regardless.

Calidius Severus didn't seem to find anything too strange about her behavior, though his glance was more than a little amused. "I'm with everybody else except that one idiot," he said: "I won't believe they've got tigers till I see 'em with my own eyes."

Nicole blinked at the absolute literality of his comment. For an instant—a very brief instant—she felt a little of the old, sinking sensation, the awareness that went all the way to the bone, that no, indeed, she wasn't in Kansas anymore; nor in West Hills, either. She felt more as if she'd fallen into a sword-and-sandal epic from late-night TV.

They jostled through the gate. In the sudden coolness beneath it, as people crowded together to pass the bottleneck, Nicole found herself pressed against Calidius Severus. She had to clutch at his shoulder or trip and fall. He caught her easily, as if he'd done it often before, and held her in a calm familiar grip.

She stiffened. He let go. Neither exchanged a glance. Nicole was still breathing hard as she emerged into the sunlight. It was painfully bright after the dimness of the gate. That was why she blinked so hard, she told herself; and she'd been pushed to go a fair bit faster than she wanted to, to keep up with the crowd. That was why her breath came so quick. Of course it was. She wasn't feeling anything toward the man who walked decorously beside her.

The amphitheater stood not far outside the city's walls, a couple of hundred yards, she reckoned, surrounded by a meadow of knee-high grass.

At the sight of it, Nicole stopped cold. She'd come this way before, and seen almost exactly the same view, on her honeymoon. Frank had stood beside her then, a good deal cleaner and a good deal sweeter-smelling than the man who was with her now.

The impact, the sense of *déjà vu,* was much stronger than it had been inside the baths. She'd seen only the floor plan, so to speak, in a twentieth-century landscape of ruins and modern town. Here and now . . .

Even in the late twentieth century, the amphitheater had been clearly recognizable for what it was, with banks of earth leading down toward a central stage dug out well below ground level. Eighteen-hundred-odd years had changed remarkably little. In this much older time, retaining walls supported the banked earth, but they had a look of surprising age: well-seasoned timbers and stone much worn and overgrown with moss. Nicole on her honeymoon had been bored, jetlagged, and only vaguely interested in old dead things. In this old dead world that felt all too distinctly here-and-now, she knew a moment's vertigo, a confusion of places and times. That was then—nearly two thousand years in the future. This was now, eighteen hundred years in her own past.

She must have looked alarming. "You all right, Umma?" Titus Calidius Severus asked in evident concern.

"Yes," she said quickly, and as firmly as she could. She pulled herself together and made herself walk on. "Maybe a touch of the sun."

He eyed her sidelong, but he didn't call her on the lie. "Don't worry about it," he said. "You won't end up all brown like a farm woman."

In the twentieth century, leaving skin cancer out of the equation, tan was in—it showed you weren't confined to a factory or an office all day long. Here, it was just the opposite: a pale face was a face that hadn't been out sweating in the sun all day. But both meant the same thing: leisure to do whatever you liked, whenever you wanted to do it.

Nicole's head had begun to ache, as it usually did when she'd had enough of *here-and-there, now-and-then*. She distracted herself as she had before, with the details of her surroundings. The countryside, like the amphitheater, hadn't changed much—wouldn't change much—in eighteen centuries. It was still meadows and grainfields and patches of woods, with an apple orchard or two for variety. One of the meadows, off to the east, was planted thickly with—stones?

Gravestones. It wasn't a meadow; it was a cemetery.

She shivered slightly. To the Nicole who had stood here—would stand here—eighteen centuries from now, all this country, and all these people, were dead. Long dead and gone to dust.

Her gaze swept south, toward what on her honeymoon had been Carnuntum's largest and most imposing Roman monument. The locals called it the *Heidentor*, the Heathen Gate, a huge stone archway more than fifty feet tall. It had been partly ruined when she saw it. She wondered, as her eye searched for it, what it would look like intact.

It wasn't there.

She stopped once more, gaping. The first emotion she felt was an absurd sense of outrage, as if she'd been cheated.

Where in hell had the stupid thing gone? You couldn't just pick up that much stone and drop it in your purse.

The answer came belatedly and with somewhat of a shock. The *Heidentor* hadn't been built yet. When, in the United States, she'd thought about the Roman Empire at all—which hadn't been any too bloody often—she'd envisioned its history as a single, compact entity. *The Roman Empire.* It was there, and then it was gone. There wasn't any depth to it, or any development. It just was.

But that wasn't actually the way things worked. There were lifetimes upon lifetimes' worth of Roman Empire—and the lifetime in which the *Heidentor* went up hadn't happened yet. She wondered how far in the future it lay. Would she live to see it built, or even begun? How long *did* something like that take to build?

"Come on," Titus Calidius Severus said, loud in her ear, still determinedly amiable. "You keep stopping. Shall I dangle a parsnip in front of your face, the way the farmers do when their donkeys won't go?"

Yet again, Nicole shook herself back into what passed for reality. "It's a lot better than laying into me with a stick," she said. "I've seen too much of that lately. I think it's cruel."

The fuller and dyer shrugged. "One way or another, you've got to get the work out of them. If they won't go by themselves, you make 'em. They're just animals. It's not like they feel things the way people do."

Nicole was as certain animals did feel things the way people did as Calidius Severus evidently was that they didn't. She opened her mouth to argue the point, but something else more urgent pushed itself to the front of her mind. "People beat slaves, too, and they haven't got any excuse at all for that."

While they talked—she wouldn't quite call it argued—they'd reached the entrance to the amphitheater. Titus Calidius Severus handed a *sestertius* to an attendant—a slave? He got no change back; admission was a *dupondius* apiece.

Only when that was done and they'd been waved through the gate did he respond to Nicole. As he had before, he said,

"One way or another, you've got to get the work out of them."

Nicole swallowed a sigh. She should have known what he'd say. How could she expect anything different? "I'd rather use the parsnip of freedom than the stick," she said.

"The parsnip of freedom?" Calidius Severus grinned his crooked grin. "Now *there's* a phrase to send men marching into battle!" His grin faded. "Some masters do that. For some slaves, it works. But one man's not the same as another, same as one donkey's not the same as another. Some are too stubborn to go forward unless you make 'em do it."

That held a hard core of common sense—if you believed there was nothing wrong with slavery. "If a free man won't work, you can fire him and replace him with someone else who will," Nicole said.

"Or more likely with someone else who won't, either." The fuller and dyer held up a hand before she could counter that. "Like I said before, it's a nice day. We're here at the beast show. Is this worth arguing about right now?"

That also was hard common sense, but Nicole didn't like it any better for that. Her years in law school had left her convinced that anything was worth arguing about, any time she was in the mood to argue. But she *was* at the beast show, and she was curious about it; and she was also on a date. It was, in an odd way, both a first date and not. For her, yes; for Calidius Severus, no. "I guess it'll keep," she said, a little grudgingly.

"Good," he answered with apparent relief. "For a while there, I figured they'd put us down on the floor, and the crowd could watch us go at it instead of the beasts." He took a deep breath, shook his head, and held out his hand, offering it as if it had been a gift. His voice was brisk. "Come on."

Nicole was getting just a small bit tired of take-charge masculinity; but not enough, yet, to kick at it. She let him take her hand—if nothing else, it made sure they weren't separated in the jostle of the crowd—and lead her into the amphitheater.

It was larger than she remembered, or maybe it only

seemed so because there were so many people in it. When there'd been no more than a handful of tired tourists and a guide droning on in three different languages, it hadn't looked big enough to hold more than a few hundred. In fact, it held several thousand—maybe five, maybe ten; Nicole had never been much good at that kind of estimate. The seats on which they crowded together were backless wooden benches. Vendors ran up and down the aisles, singing out their wares: sweet rolls and sausages and wine. It wasn't all that different, in looks and atmosphere, from a college football game.

Titus Calidius Severus pointed up along a row of benches. "Hurry up, Umma! There's a couple of good ones, right on the aisle. Quick now, before someone else gets in ahead of us." He suited action to words, flinging his backside down just ahead of another man who'd spotted the same seats at the same time. Nicole sat beside him with, she hoped, a little more decorum but no less dispatch. The man who'd been aiming for the seats, and his wife or lady friend, glowered at them but didn't offer to fight over it.

Nicole took a deep breath of air that was, for a change, not particularly redolent, and made herself as comfortable as she could. She'd have been glad of a cushion like the one she'd carried to football games.

Some people nearby actually had cushions, or had thought ahead and brought a cloak or extra tunic to soften the seat. *Next time,* she thought. "How long before the show starts?" she asked.

"Shouldn't be too much longer." The fuller and dyer looked over his shoulder. She did the same, to see what he saw: rows of benches still open, and people shuffling into them, picking spots, calling to escorts and friends as they found good ones. "They'll let it get fuller than this before they turn the first critters loose. Slowpokes always grumble when they miss the opening rounds."

While Calidius Severus spoke, a vendor had been working his way toward them. Calidius Severus raised a brow at Nicole. "Want some wine?"

Nicole nodded with barely an instant's hesitation. She was

hesitating less and less over it now, and worrying less about it, too—which worried her in itself.

Calidius Severus ordered wine for them both, and paid for it, too, playing by rules as old, it seemed, as recorded time. The wine wasn't even as good as her one-*as* special in the tavern, and the cup she had to drink it from was indifferently clean. The vendor stood hovering expectantly till she and Calidius Severus finished, then took back the cups—no disposable paper or styrofoam here. He filled them again for a pair of young men down the row, and handed them over without bothering even to wipe the rims. Nicole ducked her head and wiped surreptitiously at her mouth with the sleeve of her tunic. It wouldn't even begin to do any good, but it did make her feel a little better.

Calidius Severus saw her do it, but he misunderstood why. "I know it's not very good stuff," he said, "but you can't expect much at a place like this."

Nicole nodded. God knew, she'd had food and drink as bad as this wine or worse at games and concerts, and probably not much more sanitary, either.

As she opened her mouth to respond to him, a stir, a change in the crowd, drew her eye downward. A plump little man strutted out into the middle of the sand-strewn floor of the amphitheater. He turned this way and that, arms spread wide, inviting people to notice him. The crowd's noise sank to a dull roar. He lifted his head and sent a surprisingly deep and resonant voice ringing up through the levels. "Welcome to the beast show for today."

Applause was his answer: shouting, cheering, clapping of hands. He turned all the way about, arms spread even wider than before, till the applause died to a few fugitive finger-snappings and a catcall or two. Then he went on, "As one half of our first event, we have a . . . *lion!*" The crowd roared at that, louder than any lion Nicole had ever heard of. The emcee—Nicole couldn't think of him any other way—went on, "Yes, ladies and gentlemen, captured with incredible courage and risk in the jungles of distant Cilicia and brought to Carnuntum across land and sea for your entertainment and delight, the fiercest killer in all the world—the king of beasts!"

Nicole was glad she wasn't drinking wine just then. If she had been, she would have snarfed it right out her nose. The tubby little Roman sounded exactly like every fast-talking pitchman she'd ever loathed on late-night TV. She couldn't help it; she started to giggle.

Titus Calidius Severus didn't giggle. It would have been unmanly. But he chuckled. "Faustinianus does lay it on with a trowel, doesn't he?" he said.

It wasn't particularly witty, but between wine and sun and the absurd little man with his oversized voice, Nicole laughed out loud.

From somewhere under the amphitheater, the lion let out a short, coughing roar. Nicole shut her mouth with a snap. God only knew how many millions of years of evolution were screaming at her, *That noise means danger!*

Calidius had fallen silent, too. His right hand snatched at something across his body, caught at air and stopped. "Mithras!" he said with a note of surprise. "I'll be cursed if I wasn't reaching for my sword."

"There you hear him, folks—the king of beasts indeed," the emcee—Faustinianus—said. His voice echoed up through sudden silence. "And with him today you'll be seeing a creature you know well. Yes, ladies and gentlemen: with him we have one of our very own Pannonian bears!"

He didn't get much in the way of applause this time: a scattering of handclaps from here and there around the arena. "Cheapskates," Calidius Severus muttered, speaking for them all. "Probably be the only lion in the whole show, too."

Nicole didn't say anything. *She* had never seen a Pannonian bear, whatever that was.

Faustinianus, it seemed, had finished his spiel.

The wall around the floor of the amphitheater was perhaps ten feet high. Faustinianus scurried toward it, not taking much time for dignity. Someone on the rim let down a ladder. He swarmed up it with speed commendable for one of his bulk.

No sooner had the ladder gone back up behind him than a rattle of chains drew Nicole's eyes to the rear wall of the pit, stage, whatever one wanted to call it. Two gates rose at once, one on either side. The crowd hushed, expectant.

For a moment, nothing happened. Then the lion roared again. Its first roar had been in the order of inquiry. This was raw fury.

A tawny shape bounded out of the darkness of the right-hand gate, sudden as if someone had stabbed it in the backside with the point of a spear. Cheers went up, whooping and whistling, like a football crowd when the star of the team comes loping onto the field.

A football player in full armor looked a whole lot more imposing than the beast that halted in the center of the arena and crouched with lashing tail. The lions Nicole had seen in zoos were fat, lazy, contented-looking things. They had nothing much to do but eat, sleep, and stroll around their enclosures.

This lion was anything but fat. She could count its every rib. Old scars, and others not so old, seamed its hide. Nor was contentment anything it knew the meaning of. It was more than furious. It was in a red rage. Maybe someone *had* goaded it out of its cage. Its mane stood on end. Its yellow eyes blazed. It snarled hatred at the people who watched it so avidly. The sound was like ripping canvas.

Nicole half rose from the bench. Her body shook. Her voice was no steadier. "They've been tormenting that poor animal!"

Calidius Severus shrugged, unimpressed at her outrage. "Can't be helped. They've got to get the beasts ready to fight."

"Fight?" Nicole said. So it was going to be that kind of beast show, was it? She gulped. She'd feared as much, though she hadn't wanted to believe it. "Oh, Christ."

But the fuller and dyer, fortunately, didn't hear her. His attention was fixed on the other gate, the gate to the left. The bear was shambling out of it, less precipitous than the lion, but no happier with its lot. It was skin and bone; its fur was eaten away with mange. Pus seeped from a sore on its muzzle, dripping to the sand. When it opened its mouth to snarl, a broad swath of teeth was gone. But those that were left looked long and sharp, though not so formidable as the lion's.

Still, the bear was larger, and even in this condition it had to be heavier. Which meant—

Nicole gasped and cut off that train of thought. She was— good God, she was figuring the odds.

Nor was she the only one. A man in the row behind her leaned forward and tapped Calidius on the shoulder. "Five *sesterces* on the bear," he said.

"I'll take you up on that," Calidius answered promptly. "If the lion's even close to healthy, he'll rip old bruin there to shreds."

Nicole might have caught herself reckoning the beasts' relative chances, but she still had trouble believing what she was hearing. "I wish they weren't fighting," she said mournfully. "I wish we could just . . . admire them."

Titus Calidius Severus looked at her as if she'd started speaking in tongues—or, more to the point, in English. "You can look at beasts for a little while, I suppose," he said with the air of a man making a sizable concession. "But then you fall asleep. If the beasts are fighting, it keeps you awake. It's interesting."

Nicole sucked in a breath. She was damned close to blowing her cover, if she hadn't blown it already. But she couldn't make herself care. It was the wine in her, she knew that. And the shock, and yes, the disappointment. Calidius Severus, whom she'd been thinking of as a kind man, could think this horror was *interesting*.

"*Interesting!*" she said. "It's not interesting. It's cruel."

His brows climbed up, then dropped down in a scowl. "Life's cruel," he said with callousness that had to be deliberate. "The faster people figure that out, the better they understand it, the easier they can bear it when the world flies up and hits them in the face."

That was as cold-blooded a way of looking at things as

she'd ever heard. She opened her mouth to protest, but even if she'd managed a word, the lion's roar would have drowned it out. It echoed in that deep hollow space, set deep in her bones and shook them into stillness.

The bear too seemed caught off guard by the power of that sound. The lion sprang. Its body was a tawny blur. She'd never imagined anything so big could move so fast.

The bear reared up to meet the challenge, and it roared, too, a deep, grunting sound. As the lion fell upon the bear, the crowd went wild. Nicole, reeling, deafened by the noise, had a dizzy memory of a college football game, when the home team sacked the visiting quarterback. He'd even looked a bit like the bear.

For an instant, she was *there,* in that crisp autumn afternoon, with the cheerleaders flaunting their assets and the band sending a razzberry across the field. Then the heat and the human stink of Carnuntum fell around her again. Someone was pounding on the bench close by her, shrieking, "Eat him! Eat him for lunch!" Whether the woman meant the bear or the lion, Nicole couldn't tell. But that she meant it literally, Nicole hadn't the slightest doubt.

That was the point, wasn't it? Starve the poor things till they were mad with hunger, then offer them fresh meat—if they fought for it. It was an endgame. Winner take all, and devil take the hindmost.

The lion and the bear tumbled together to the ground, rolling and kicking. Sand flew from their flailing feet. The bear's jaws clamped on the lion's shoulder, just below the neck. The bear's paws raked the lion's tawny flanks; its claws ripped blood-red gashes.

But the lion's hind claws ripped at the bear's belly, as if the great cat were a kitten playfully disemboweling a ball of yarn. Yet this was no game, no kitten-silliness. It was as real as death. The lion's teeth were sunk in the bear's throat.

If the lion growled, even if the sound had not been muffled in thick fur, Nicole couldn't possibly have heard it. The crowd was roaring louder than the lion ever had. Titus Calidius Severus, beside her, was yelling his head off. That calm, contained man with his easy affability and his air of quiet competence was as lost to the world as the most rabid twentieth-century football fan. And not just because he had money on the line, either. This was *sports*. You could sit him down on a couch in front of a TV in Los Angeles, shove a Miller Lite into his hand, and leave him there, rooting for the Lions against the Bears. Some things never changed.

She wanted to clap hands over her ears, and over her eyes, too, and why not her mouth while she was at it? It was all or nothing; so nothing it was.

Calidius Severus bounced right up off the bench. Her eye leaped to the arena, to see what had got him going.

The bear's paws had stopped flailing at the lion. Its jaws had slackened and fallen away from the tawny throat. And yet it wasn't, quite, still. It wasn't dead.

The lion drew away a little and began to lick its wounds. The bear lay stirring feebly, but made no move to attack the lion. When its wounds were as clean as they could be, the lion lifted itself, stretched stiffly, yawned. Then it bent its ragged-maned head and began to feed.

The amphitheater was a perfect bedlam of noise. Nicole's head was pounding. There was a sour taste in her mouth, a burn of acid in her throat. She was going to be sick, she knew it. Right there. Right in front of everybody. And especially Calidius Severus.

He beamed at her, as oblivious to her state of mind as any man whose team ever won a game. "That was a *good* fight, wasn't it, Umma? That lion could serve in my legion any day." He turned to the man behind him and held out his hand. "All right. Pay up."

The man shrugged and reached into his purse. Brass clinked as *sesterces* changed hands. "My turn next time," he said. Calidius Severus grinned as he stowed his winnings away. He wasn't gloating—much.

Down on the floor of the amphitheater, a group of men advanced warily on the lion. They carried spears and wore armor that looked amazingly like movie-Roman armor. Except that movie armor was always clean and shiny and impressive. This was battered and dented and dull. It wasn't a prop. It was real; everyday gear that had seen hard use.

The lion's tail twitched. In the silence that had fallen, as if the crowd had sated itself for a moment, Nicole heard it growl as it ate, a rumble of warning. Even in armor, even with a spear in her hand, Nicole wouldn't have wanted to go near it.

The men moved quickly enough. A bomb squad might move like that: fast, efficient, aware of the danger but not stopping to dwell on it. Stopping would get them killed.

Along with their spears, they carried a weighted net. One of them, the one nearest the lion, snapped a command: "Now!"

They would only have one chance. The lion tore at the bear's soft underbelly, but with each rending stroke, his head came up higher and his tail lashed harder. If the net missed, or failed to fall cleanly over him, there would be hell to pay.

They flung the net. It seemed to hang forever in the air. Nicole held her breath. So, she thought, did everyone else in the amphitheater. The net dropped—fell clean, enveloping the lion.

He roared his fury, and tried to spring. The net tangled him all the tighter. The more he struggled, the more thoroughly he was caught.

The handlers dragged the snarling, slashing bundle across the bloody sand. They were as matter-of-fact about it as if they'd been hauling a sackful of rocks.

They were still dragging the lion toward one of the gates as another group of men, these in ordinary tunics, trotted out of that same gate toward the carcass of the bear. They worked altogether without ceremony, lashing ropes around its hind legs and hauling it away. To the victor, obviously, went what passed for spoils: a few mouthfuls of stringy meat, a weighted net, and a chance to fight another day. At least, thought Nicole, the bear was out of his misery. The lion wouldn't win any such reprieve till something else killed him.

She looked down at the sand. It was empty now, if briefly.

Only drag marks and bloodstains showed what had passed there.

Then, like groundskeepers manicuring an infield, two more men emerged from the lion's gate. They carried rakes and sacks of fresh sand. In a few moments, the arena was smooth again, unmarked. Ready for the next battle.

Nicole didn't even dare to hope that the first fight would be the only one. She got as far as tensing her body to stand, but she was hemmed in. There were people on all sides of her, and a vendor blocking the aisle. The smell of his sausages made her knees go weak with revulsion.

Inert and trapped, she watched the emcee make his pompous way back down the ladder. His feet left a ragged line of prints in the freshly raked sand. "Ladies and gentlemen," he proclaimed in his deep fruity voice, "a northern fight next! From the trackless forests of Germany, fierce wolves will challenge the brute strength of the terrible aurochs. Enjoy the show!"

Again he climbed back to his front-row seat, where he sat mopping his brow while the ladder went up once more. A person in a tunic rather better than Nicole's best one—but a slave nevertheless, she was pretty sure—handed him a cup. He drank from it with evident pleasure. He wasn't getting the rotgut the rest of them were, she'd have been willing to bet.

How long does this go on? she wondered miserably. She couldn't ask; it was surely something Umma already knew. It was also something Umma surely enjoyed. Titus Calidius Severus, sitting there beside her, hadn't asked her to come as if to something exotic. He'd taken it for granted that she knew what would happen—and taken it for granted that she liked it, too. There was no way, knowing that, that Nicole could get up and bolt. No matter how much she wanted to— if she did, there was no way she could explain and still keep up the pretense.

To let go, to fall off the tightrope she'd walked for— Christ, how long? She had to stop and think before she could even remember. To stop pretending. To burst out with the truth, the whole truth—to just give up. Nicole almost wept with wanting it. But she wasn't as brave as that, or as crazy, either. Not yet. What did they do to the mentally ill here? Feed them to the lions? She wouldn't have put it past them.

That first morning here, she'd wanted to call the SPCA because a man had beaten his donkey. The only SPCA the Romans would have recognized was a Society for the Promotion of Cruelty to Animals.

She sat where she'd been sitting since Calidius Severus brought her here, sunk in on herself. Her eyes fixed on the arena with a kind of fascinated horror.

One of the gates opened. The one, she recalled, that had disgorged the lion. It was wolves this time, ten or twelve of them. They trotted around the arena in rapid, businesslike fashion, too fast for Nicole to count them exactly. They looked something like huskies, but they were bigger and meaner and scrawnier than any dogs she'd ever seen. A phrase she'd read somewhere—*a lean and hungry look*—niggled in her mind. It hadn't been written about wolves, she didn't think, but it fit tighter than O. J. Simpson's glove.

Nicole was as perfectly horrified as the emcee would have wanted her to be. But it seemed she was alone in that. "What's so much of a much about wolves?" Titus Calidius Severus said discontentedly. "Anybody wants to see wolves, all he has to do is go a couple of miles outside of town in the wintertime. He probably won't be very happy about it afterwards, but that's something else."

The other gate yawned open. The aurochs loomed in it, stamping its feet and tossing horns that seemed as wide as the whole of Carnuntum.

Nicole gaped, even sickness forgotten. Wolves she knew about. Didn't everybody? The aurochs—if she'd expected anything, she'd thought maybe it was a kind of deer, or another bear. She'd never imagined it would be a bull. A Texas longhorn bigger than the biggest buffalo she'd ever heard of.

Nothing like it walked the earth she'd come from. Of that she was almost sure. She would have heard about it, seen it in a documentary, found it in a zoo. It must have gone extinct sometime between this era, whenever exactly it was, and her own. For all she knew, it was an endangered species right now. And the Romans were killing it for their amusement. Didn't they have any idea what they were doing?

Calidius Severus turned to her with a bemused lift of the brow. "This should be interesting," he said over the rising roar of the crowd. "You never can tell what an aurochs will do. Remember the one that caught a wolf on its horns and pitched it up into the seats? Wasn't that a wild day?"

"Yes," Nicole lied. She cast about for ways to put some of what she was feeling into terms Umma might have used. "It seems a shame to see such a splendid beast fighting for its life."

"Wouldn't be very exciting, watching lapdogs and sheep," the fuller and dyer answered. "Besides, you know the aurochs is as mean a bastard as the Germans he shares the forest with. One less of them is one less mankiller roaming the woods." He leaned forward with sudden intensity. "Here we go."

To the wolves, obviously, the aurochs was not a splendid beast. It was lunch on the hoof, and they looked to have missed a lot of lunches. They circled it in a slow and surprisingly graceful dance, tongues lolling, golden eyes intent. Those eyes surprised Nicole, a little. She hadn't been thinking; she'd been expecting plain doggy brown, not yellow.

The aurochs knew what they were after. It would have met wolves before, away in the forest. It pawed the earth and bellowed. The noise was more like the bottom register of a bassoon with a bad reed than any sound Nicole could have conceived of as coming from the mouth of a cow. And yet, if the aurochs was a cow, it was the biggest damned cow she'd ever seen or heard of.

It lowered its head and charged. Sand flew beneath its hooves. The wolf in its path flung itself aside. Two more sprang at the aurochs from behind. The aurochs spun, impossibly agile. The wolves braced forelegs and skidded, scrambling out of reach of those arena-wide horns.

One escaped. The other had stopped a fraction too late.

The broad curving sweep of the left horn caught it broadside, hooked underneath, pierced and thrust and ripped. The aurochs shook its head as if in irritation. The wolf flew through the air and landed rolling. Its yelp of agony rang over the shouting and hooting and catcalls that filled the amphitheater.

Nicole pounded her fists on her thighs. "*Yes!* Give it to him!"

She clapped a hand over her mouth. God. She'd got into it. For a few seconds, she'd *become* one of these people. She'd understood why they came to these shows, what went through their heads as they watched poor innocent animals slaughter one other for humans' sport.

The worst of it was, the wolf didn't die right away. Blood poured from the terrible wound in its belly, soaking into the sand. A loop of glistening pink gut slipped out and trailed the ground. The wolf tripped over it, shook its hind foot as if in annoyance, and went on with the hunt, as if pain and mortal wound were, after all, nothing to it. It wanted its prey. It fully expected its share of the kill when the fight was over. It didn't know it was dead.

Even as the great bull gored the one wolf, others snapped at its legs, at its belly, and at its privates. "A eunuch for Cybele!" someone shouted near Nicole in a screechy falsetto. That drew a laugh from the crowd.

Cruel, thought Nicole. But the edge of censure was gone for a while. She'd been inside these people's heads. She'd seen the fight as they saw it. She didn't want to go back there, but neither could she maintain her position of moral superiority.

Wolves were everywhere now, swarming over the aurochs. They launched themselves at its side and shoulders. They clung, teeth sunk in flesh, eating the aurochs alive. Blood streamed and spattered. Who would have thought there could be so much blood in the world?

The aurochs bellowed in torment. It scraped off one of the wolves against the wall, as it might have used a treetrunk in the forest. Nicole gave up on trying to control herself. She cheered. The aurochs stamped with an enormous hind hoof, full on the wolf's panting middle. She heard bones crunch even through the roar of the crowd.

Titus Calidius Severus nudged her in the ribs with his elbow. She started and suppressed a shriek. "You're for the bull, are you?" he said. "Me, I always cheer for the wolves. They fight as a team, like legionaries."

It was, Nicole realized, a perfectly rational way of looking at the fight, if you wanted to look at it at all. Regardless of his taste in amusement—a taste plenty of people in Carnuntum obviously shared—the fuller and dyer was a long way from a fool. Could she blame him for having the same tastes as his neighbors? How far did cultural relativism stretch? Not to slavery. She'd be damned if it stretched that far. To actively enjoying animals in torment?

That she could come up with the idea in the first place didn't worry her. That she didn't dismiss it out of hand did worry her, a lot.

Calidius couldn't have imagined what she was thinking, or even known such a way of thinking could exist. It wasn't in his worldview.

"Mithras slew the great bull, you know," he said. She nodded, though she didn't know what he was talking about except that it must have something to do with his religion. She'd have to learn more about that one day. One day . . .

The aurochs gored another wolf in the side, not quite so terrible a wound as the first, and trampled another to death under its hooves. But while it slaughtered its enemies, the rest of the pack was literally eating it alive. It kicked and stamped and gored and swept its great horns in wild arcs, but its strength was failing. Its bellows grew weaker. At last, it sank to its knees. It struggled to lift itself, got one foot under its body, heaved. But its life had poured out of it with its blood. With a deep, shuddering moan, it rolled onto its side.

Like the bear, it didn't die completely, not then, and not for a long while afterwards. It was still kicking feebly when the wolves were shoulder-deep in its carcass.

Calidius Severus folded his arms and nodded, pleased.

"They got it down and lost only four," he said. "That's good work from the wolves' side. I've seen an aurochs clean out a whole pack of them—not often, but I've seen it."

How many beast shows had he seen, to speak with such casual expertise? How many had Umma seen? How many had been staged in Carnuntum that they hadn't seen? How many other towns were there in the Roman Empire, and how often did they stage beast shows? How many animals died bloody deaths for no better reason than to amuse a theaterful of Romans with time on their hands?

Her thoughts must have run away with her: she spoke that last question aloud. Titus Calidius Severus frowned for a moment. Then he asked, "What sort of deaths do you think they'd die if we left them where they were?"

Nicole started to answer, but stopped herself abruptly. She didn't think about death if she could possibly help it, no matter what form it came in. Death was bad. Death was unmentionable. It was—indecent.

Here, they took it as much for granted as they did any number of other indecencies. Head lice. Halitosis. Pissing in jars on a public street.

If she absolutely had to think about how a wild animal died, she supposed it went off somewhere quiet and died with dignity. But if wolves would eat an aurochs in an amphitheater before it was properly dead, what was to keep them from doing the same thing in the forest? They were starved, granted. But if they were hungry enough to take on something that big, they'd eat it alive wherever they were, in a desperate and completely instinctive bid for survival. That was the law of the jungle.

The year Nicole turned thirteen, the family dog had gotten sick. It was cancer, the vet said. Squamous-cell sarcoma: she'd looked it up, because something in her wanted to know exactly what it was that was killing fat old Gaylord. He stopped being able to eat his kibble. He left spots of blood on the carpet, which amazed her because her mother hadn't seemed to mind. Then one day Nicole came home from school to find the carpets all freshly cleaned and Gaylord gone. Her mother had had him put to sleep. It was for the best, she'd said. He was in pain. It was only going to get worse. There wasn't anything anyone could do to make it better.

If a wolf got squamous-cell sarcoma, there was nothing and no one to put it out of its misery. It would suffer till it died, which might take a long time.

There'd been little enough dignity for Gaylord, near the end. His muzzle had swollen with the tumors. Blood and saliva had dripped from his mouth, and mucus from his nose. He'd whimpered when he slept, from the pain. If he'd died quietly, it had been because he'd been given a lethal dose of whatever it was vets gave dogs to put them to sleep.

Out of all that, the only reply Nicole could find for Calidius Severus' question was a second, much lamer question: "We ought to be better than nature, don't you think, instead of as bad or worse?"

"Hmm." Calidius Severus gave her another look, an appraising one this time. "While you were teaching yourself to read and write, you made yourself into a philosopher, too, didn't you?"

Nicole laughed shortly. "Why, of course not," she said with bitterness that surprised even herself. "I'm a woman. I can't possibly be anything as elevated as a philosopher."

"Socrates' teacher was a woman," Calidius Severus said, and that startled her, too. Then he shook his head. His expression was odd, half a smile, half a scowl. "You're sticking pins in me to make me jump. I don't much feel like jumping today, if it's all the same to you."

"Not even a little?" she asked with a touch of archness—God, she was flirting. She couldn't seem to stop herself. It had to be the atmosphere in this place. It warped her out of her usual, enlightened self.

He didn't mind it a bit. His scowl faded; his smile grew just a little. He shook his head and turned his attention back to the arena.

The aurochs' death and the arrival of the beast-handlers hadn't put an end to the show. The lion had been an easy capture: there was only one of him, and he was weak with starvation and loss of blood. There were still half a dozen wolves, which weren't in any mood to be herded back to their cages. They had the taste of fresh blood, and a glimpse of freedom.

The first one or two were taken by surprise, netted and hauled away. The rest had time to fight back. They circled the handlers as they had the aurochs, snarling fit to curdle the blood.

The handlers seemed impervious. Their shields were long and tall, and looked heavy. They were as much weapons as defense. The handlers crouched behind them, and the wolves leaped futilely, snapping at the portable walls. One that moved quicker, or was luckier than the rest, almost got around a shield. Its edge caught him and sent him flying, to fall limp, with a split skull.

The wolf the aurochs had disemboweled was still alive, still feeding on the carcass. It hadn't joined the pack against the handlers. Maybe it was confused, or maybe just intent on finishing its last meal.

It looked up as one of the handlers advanced on it, and lifted its lip in a snarl. Coldly, calmly, the handler smashed its skull with a club.

Nicole swallowed bile. It was hideous, disgusting. It was also merciful. The man had put the wolf out of its misery. No lethal injections here. No peaceful slipping into sleep.

She wasn't any happier for knowing that. Whose fault was it, after all, that the beast had been in pain?

When the last of the wolves had been caught or killed, and taken away dead or alive into the bowels of the amphitheater, a team of mules hauled off the aurochs' carcass. They made a great deal of noise and some little fuss, braying and kicking against the drover's whip.

Titus Calidius Severus was not amused. "Takes too long between fights," he muttered in Nicole's ear. Other people had taken advantage of the intermission to call for wine or sausages, or to slip away to—the privies? There must be public privies somewhere in this man-made hill.

Nicole thought about it, but she wasn't inclined to fight the crowds. There'd probably be a line for the ladies' here as there always was in the twentieth century. Potty parity wasn't any more likely here than it would be in eighteen centuries.

The man beside her wasn't showing signs of going anywhere, either. He yawned and stretched and cracked his neck, and grimaced as Nicole winced. "Not getting any younger," he said, "and the day isn't getting any shorter, either." He shrugged. "Ah, well, the gods will have fat-wrapped thighbones for their altars, and the butchers will have fresh meat for their stalls." He paused. His eyes sharpened. "Are you all right, Umma? You look a little green."

"I'm fine," Nicole lied. Here was a beast killed by wolves, and they were going to sell the meat? If that wasn't the most unsanitary thing she'd ever heard of . . . She caught herself again. If that wasn't, then any of several other unfortunate practices was. The Romans' notions of hygiene, however proud of them they were, left damn near everything to be desired.

The day dragged on. There was no discernible end to the slaughter, and precious little variety, either. Bears and wolves and another aurochs—smaller than the first, but more agile, and almost fast enough to kill all of its attackers before the survivors pulled it down. And once, to frantic applause, a leopard. "Don't see *that* every day," Calidius Severus declared, clapping and stamping his feet along with everybody else.

Nicole would sooner not have seen any of it. Whenever a vendor came by with wine or food, she bought a cupful or a handful. By the time the leopard sprang snarling into the arena, she was full to the gills and halfway down the road from tiddly to snockered. Knowing she was abusing alcohol to keep from watching animals being abused didn't make her feel any better.

The leopard's adversary was a black bear. It was, Nicole gathered from the commentary around her, quite a large specimen of its kind. It made short work of the leopard.

People hissed and whistled in anger—not, she thought, out of sympathy for the cat. Because it hadn't fought well enough to amuse them.

A pair of handlers dragged the beautiful spotted body toward one of the gates. Nicole's eyes fixed on the bloody trail that it left behind. She swallowed hard against tears.

Somewhere down in Africa, the leopard had been living its own life, minding its own business. The Romans had expended heaven only knew how much effort (*and courage,* she admitted to herself with no small reluctance) to capture it and bring it up here alongside the Danube. And for what? To have it torn to bloody rags between one eyeblink and the next. Where was the justice in that? What was fair about it at all?

Life isn't fair, Titus Calidius Severus had said to her earlier. All of this was as graphic an illustration of that fact as she could have imagined.

Yet again, Faustinianus puffed and strutted his way down to the arena and raised his grand trumpet of a voice. "And now, ladies and gentlemen, something you've been waiting for for longer than most of us like to remember: the criminal Padusius, who murdered Gaius Domitius Zmaragdus the spice merchant and Optatus the physician even as he robbed them, having been duly and properly convicted of his crimes, now faces the maximum penalty." He paused as if waiting for a round of applause. The silence was thick enough to cut with a sword. Somewhat feebly, if not more faintly than before, he called out, "Enjoy the show!"

He left the arena, still in that thick-bodied silence. Nicole could hear clearly the puffing of his breath and the creaking of the ladder as he climbed back to his seat. When he had settled in it and the ladder been pulled up, scraping and rattling against the stones of the wall, a low growl ran through the crowd. There was nothing human in it. They sounded like wolves themselves, closing in for the kill.

Beside Nicole, Calidius Severus struck his fist on his thigh. "About time that bastard got what's coming to him. I thought they'd crucify him, but this will do as well."

"Cru—" Nicole began. He couldn't have meant it literally. Could he?

She'd never thought of crucifixion in connection with anyone but Jesus, even though she knew the Romans had crucified two thieves with him. Yet again, the phrase *cruel and unusual punishment* ran through her head. Crucifixion was cruel, no doubt about that. What if it wasn't unusual?

Two thieves and a revolutionary had died on that hill in Jerusalem. What were they going to do to the murderer Padusius, if they weren't going to crucify him?

Calidius assumed she knew. It was something everyone knew, just as everyone in twentieth-century Los Angeles knew the death penalty was hardly ever used in California. She didn't think Carnuntum was any more like California in this than in anything else. Whatever was going to happen to Padusius, she was sure it would be both bloody and painful.

She'd come to the conclusion some time since that the underdog in any fight came out of the left-hand gate. It opened now. There was a pause, a long holding of breath in the amphitheater. Then a shape wavered in it. A filthy man in a filthier tunic stumbled, or was pushed, into the arena.

He stood swaying, blinking in the dazzle of sunlight. A shield hung on one arm, a flimsy thing Lucius would have scorned to play with. In his free hand he clutched a club no bigger and apparently not much heavier than a child's baseball bat. It might have been adequate for killing mice. A rat would have laughed at it.

Nicole had deliberately stayed away from criminal law in her practice, but it wasn't from lack of experience. She'd done an internship one term in the county prosecutor's office, and had spent time and enough in the courthouse, watching plaintiffs and defendants come and go. Black, white, Asian, or Hispanic, the faces had all had a certain sameness, a common expression. She'd never quite taken the time to define it.

Now she knew. It was guilt. Even when they didn't care, even when they defied the system, something deep down in them told the truth. If they hadn't done what they were brought in for, they'd done other things perhaps even worse. Or else, if they were innocent, the sheer weight of their surroundings pulled them down till they looked as guilty as the rest.

Innocent until proven guilty, Nicole thought. Did Roman law even acknowledge the principle?

Whether it did or it didn't, this man had been tried, convicted, and sentenced—to death, she could assume, though the law made a pretense of giving him a fighting chance. It didn't stop him from standing in the middle of the arena with his flimsy shield and his ridiculous little club, and shrieking up at them all, "I'm innocent! By all the gods, I didn't do it!"

Jeers and catcalls answered him, and a rain of more solid insults: eggs and rotten fruit that people must have brought for the purpose, half-eaten sausages, even stones and bits of brick. Padusius lifted his shield against the barrage. He was still shouting: Nicole saw his lips move. But the crowd drowned him out.

Nicole had no idea of the rights and wrongs of the case. She wondered if anyone else did, either. Nobody around her looked to give two whoops in hell for rights, wrongs, or anything in between. They wanted blood.

And they got it. A pair of lionesses bounded from the right-hand gate. Nicole didn't know what she'd expected. A man, probably, or men. An execution squad, or another criminal pitted against this one, with the winner to be granted his life. She'd seen something like that in one of Frank's old movies.

As she looked at the lionesses, and as the truth dawned on her, she wished she hadn't eaten and drunk so much. She was going to lose it, right here between her grubby sandaled feet.

She'd heard in catechism class of Christians thrown to the lions. It was a cliché. She'd assumed—Sister Agatha had made her assume—that that was the punishment reserved for Christians. What if that wasn't it at all? What if they were sent to the lions simply because they were criminals, or because they were reckoned criminals?

She should have been used by now to the shock of her preconceptions crumbling. It wasn't going to let up—but it never seemed to get easier.

She closed her eyes and breathed as deep as she dared, which wasn't very; the people around her, and for that matter she herself, were getting fairly ripe in the heat of the sun. She counted carefully to a hundred. She scraped together all the calm she had, and made herself open her eyes.

At sight of the lionesses, the crowd had gone crazy. Padusius' scream of terror pierced even that pandemonium like a hot needle piercing butter.

If he'd wanted to live a little longer, a cold small part of Nicole observed, he should have kept his mouth shut. The lionesses had come out more baffled than furious; in fact, they seemed a little better fed than the animals that had fought earlier. They stood together just outside their gate, sniffing the air, crouching down under the force of the crowd's roar. One looked ready to bolt back into her den, if the gate hadn't slammed shut behind her.

Padusius' shriek brought both of them to abrupt and complete attention. There was their dinner bell, loud and clear. They shook off the daze of sudden sunlight and the crowd's roar, and loped toward the condemned man. They weren't even bothering with stealth. Something in their manner told Nicole they'd hunted criminals before, and killed, too. They had no fear at all of his humanity, and took not the slightest notice of his flimsy excuse for a weapon.

Nor, for that matter, did he. He dropped the useless shield and club and bolted for the wall. Nicole had never seen a human being move so fast or jump so high. His fingers actually caught the topmost edge, a good ten feet up, and hooked over it. His feet scrabbled at the wall below, inching the rest of his body upward.

There were people sitting in the first row above the wall, men and women better dressed than most, some with parasols to protect them from the sun. One such, a creature so epicene Nicole took it for a woman till it turned slightly and she saw the curled beard, stamped down hard on the straining fingers. The crowd cheered. The dandy turned grandly about, bowing and throwing kisses.

Padusius dropped wailing to the sand. The lionesses sprang.

He was unarmed, his toy weapons flung aside and far out of reach, not much more useless there than they would have been in his hands. His fists beat against one great cat's side. He kicked at the other. The lionesses took no more notice of his struggles than of the death-throes of a gazelle. He was nothing more to them than meat.

Nicole watched Padusius' writhing ebb. She couldn't shut her eyes, or turn her face away. She was caught in a sick, and sickened, fascination.

She'd never watched a man die before. Not for real, not right in front of her. People in California, in that world so far away in space and time, had spoken in favor of televising executions. Let the public see what capital punishment was really like, they had said. They'd abolish it then, in a fit of righteous horror.

Nicole had been rather inclined toward that view herself. Now she was sitting in a place where public executions were, from the looks of it, a common thing. The faces around her were avid, the eyes greedy, drinking in the sight of a human being dying hideously under the teeth and claws of lions. They'd made it a sport, like the slaughter of animals. It was a spectacle for their amusement.

Padusius' struggles had all but stopped. The lionesses paused to lick red and dripping jaws, then bent their heads and began to feed. They wouldn't wait for him to finish dying, any more than the male of their species had waited for the bear, or the wolves for the aurochs.

Calidius Severus spoke beside Nicole, startling her half out of her skin. The crowd's roar had sunk to background noise. His voice was surprisingly distinct, and rather loud. "Well, that's that. Pretty cursed quick, too—quicker than the son of a whore deserved." He paused as if to ponder that, then sighed and shrugged. "Still and all, he won't be breaking in the heads of honest people again, or doing worse, for that matter. I hear he outraged Domitius Zmaragdus' wife after he'd murdered her husband in front of her."

"Did he?" Nicole said faintly. It seemed her overloaded stomach would stay where it belonged. A few minutes before, she wouldn't have bet on it. Calidius Severus had just given her the most powerful argument of all in favor of capital punishment: *Now we know he won't do it again.*

Did hearing that Padusius was a rapist as well as a murderer make her feel easier about watching him die? Almost with his dying breath, he'd sworn he hadn't committed the crime for which he'd been condemned. Was he telling the truth?

There was no way, now, to know. All the witnesses were dead. The suspect was dying, was maybe already gone. His foot jerked beneath a lioness' paw, startling Nicole. The lioness snapped at it and began to gnaw, as a dog will gnaw on a favorite bone.

Whatever the truth was, whether the man was guilty or innocent, it didn't matter now. One way or the other, he was just as dead.

They—the authorities, Faustinianus, whoever was in charge—let the lionesses eat their fill of Padusius' body. People started getting up, stretching and belching, jostling one another as they headed for the exits.

Calidius Severus touched Nicole's arm, a light brush of the fingers, quickly taken away. Nicole shivered. She wasn't repulsed, not at all, but neither was she in a mood to be touched.

"Shall we go?" he asked. "No gladiators this afternoon; it's too early on in the games. The last couple of days, I expect they'll put on a healthy show."

"Gladiators?" Nicole knew what the word meant: she could hardly help it. She hadn't thought she would need the knowledge. Carnuntum kept surprising her, as usual in ways dismaying rather than delightful.

If you looked at them the right—no, the wrong—way,

gladiatorial shows made a horrid kind of sense. Beasts killed beasts for the Romans' amusement. Beasts killed men for the Romans' amusement, too; the lionesses were still gnawing meat from the bones of the man who had insisted he wasn't a murderer. If you took those two for granted, why not have men kill men for the Romans' amusement?

Nicole thrust herself to her feet and turned her back on the bloody spectacle below. "I have no interest in watching gladiators," she said firmly.

"All right," Calidius Severus said equably. "If I have time to go, I'll go with Gaius. He's always been more interested in the finer points of the fighting than you have, anyway."

He didn't sound annoyed at all, or even particularly disappointed. It was like a father taking his grown son to a football game and leaving his girlfriend at home.

And what did they show of football on the news? Half the time, it seemed to Nicole, they showed players getting spectacularly, if not usually bloodily, hurt. Maybe the gap between Carnuntum and West Hills was narrower than she'd supposed.

No. She shook her head. Football injuries were incidental to the game. They weren't the point of the exercise. Boxing? That was legalized mugging, pure and simple. But people didn't usually die in a boxing match.

But that wasn't all Calidius Severus had meant. He was a veteran, an ex-legionary. He'd really used sword and spear and shield. (And . . . killed people with them? Nicole didn't want to think about that. Not just this moment.) Fine points in his line of work weren't just about winning a game. They were about staying alive.

When in Rome . . . Nicole shook her head again, and shivered slightly as she always did when she caught herself understanding how the Romans saw the world. Things made sense if you looked at them in that particular way. It didn't make them any more right.

The crowd by now had thinned quite a bit. Calidius Severus led her back down the rows of benches, sidestepping the debris of a long day's entertainment. Instead of paper cups and cigarette butts and hotdog wrappers, Nicole made her way past empty sausage casings and half-eaten buns and spilled wine. It seemed an unconscionably long time before they reached the exit, and longer still before the bottleneck of people let go and disgorged them into the sunlit field. The green of its grass was cool and restful after the hard glare of sand in the arena.

Nicole let out a long sigh of relief. Her eyes slid back to the place where the *Heidentor* didn't stand. In much the same way, her tongue ran over the broken teeth in her mouth more often than it sought out the whole ones. What was missing and should have been there was more interesting than what was where it belonged.

"I hope you had a good time." Titus Calidius Severus sounded more like a nervous teenager coming home from his first date with a girl than a middle-aged man out with a longtime lover. He'd been eyeing her the same way she'd eyed the *Heidentor:* wondering where the familiar had gone.

She didn't let him see her smile. *He's not taking me for granted,* she thought. *Good.* Aloud, she said, "I enjoyed the time with you, but I've lost my taste for beast shows."

He started to speak. She would have bet a fistful of *denarii* it was something about womanish weakness. If that was so, he visibly and prudently decided against it, and cleared his throat instead. He walked on for a bit, toward the city gate. Then he said, with some care, "I always enjoy the time I spend with you, Umma."

Nicole regarded him with widened eyes. "Why, Titus! That's sweet." Did he blush? Hard to tell. She found she was smiling. He might smell like ancient piss, but he had more style than most of the California yuppies she'd known.

The moment she stepped through the gate of Carnuntum, Titus Calidius Severus' familiar stench blew right out of her head. She'd been away from the city stink for a few hours; it was gone from her nose. Now it struck her full force, every bit as strong as the day she found herself in Umma's body. It was like being slammed in the face with a long-dead salmon.

She must have grimaced. Calidius Severus slanted one of his lopsided grins at her. It warmed her in ways she hadn't expected, and didn't, at the moment, particularly want. "Always something in the air that lets you know when you've come to a town," he said dryly. "You do stop noticing after a while, the gods be praised."

"A good thing you do, too." Nicole tried her damnedest not to breathe. Yes, dammit, she'd lost the immunity she'd taken so long to acquire.

At least it cooled her down, and let her look at her companion through something other than a hormonal haze.

She let him lead her back through Carnuntum. She was reasonably sure she could have found her way back to the tavern without him; she'd come to understand that the main streets of the city were laid out in a grid, a sequence of large squares. But in between these wider avenues, lesser streets and alleys twisted in a bewildering maze.

Those were, at the moment, dry. For that, Nicole was deeply grateful. None was paved, and few had sidewalks.

Calidius Severus walked her back to the tavern. Outside the door, he hesitated. Nicole hadn't seen a man hesitate like that since her dates worried more about acne than about five o'clock shadow. *Working up the nerve to kiss me,* she thought with a glimmer of amusement. If he hadn't hesitated, if he'd tried to take a kiss as if he were entitled to it, she would have sent him on his way, with a clout on the ear to remember her by.

Because he was so diffident about it, so obviously unsure she'd allow it, she let the kiss happen. He tasted of wine. For all his shyness going in, he knew how to kiss. He was eager, but he didn't try to swallow her alive.

Something quivered, deep down inside. It wasn't desire, not quite, but a shadow of it: an awareness that if she wanted to, if she let it happen as she'd let the kiss happen, she could feel desire.

She didn't know which of them broke the kiss first. If it was Calidius Severus, he was in no hurry to let her go. As close as he held her, she couldn't be in any doubt as to how he felt about it.

Before things could get awkward, she slipped out of his arms.

He stood flatfooted, still reaching for her, though she'd moved just out of reach. "Umma—" he began.

She tilted her head. "Yes?" she asked. She didn't mean to be unfriendly, but neither did she want him to think she wanted to hop into bed with him then and there.

One thing she'd seen before this, and for which she gave him credit, was that he did actually listen to her. He paid attention not only to what she said but also to how she said it.

His frown, right now, said he understood perfectly well that that *yes* didn't mean, *Yes, let's do it.* "You've been funny lately," he said.

Nicole laughed. Once she'd started, she found she couldn't stop. Part of it was the wine. Part was the sheer magnitude of Calidius' understatement, and how little he knew, or could know, how great it was.

He waited with commendable patience for her laughter to run down. When at last it did, he said, "I didn't think I was that funny." His tone might have been wry, or it might have been bewildered. With a shrug that matched it, he turned away from her and headed across the street toward his own shop.

She watched him go. She didn't know what she was feeling. Regret. Relief. A little guilt—and that made her angry, because she'd wished herself into this place to get away from just this kind of emotional bullying. She hadn't wanted him. Why should she feel as if she'd done something wrong?

She turned abruptly, pivoting on her heel, and stalked into the tavern.

It was empty except for Julia, but, from the looks of the cups and bowls that the freedwoman was scrubbing, business had been brisk just a little earlier. Bread was baking, fresh and fragrant. The aroma of garlic and herbs wafted from the pot over the hearth. Julia had made one of her pot-dishes for the evening trade.

Julia didn't seem to notice anything odd in Nicole's face or gait. She was grinning, in fact, and clapping her hands. Nicole wondered dourly what Julia had been up to while she was away.

"Well?" the freedwoman pressed when Nicole didn't say anything. "Did you have a good time at the beast show?"

Watching animals fighting and killing one another, watching the lionesses pull down and feed on the condemned criminal—no, Nicole had not enjoyed the show. But that wasn't quite what Julia had asked.

In Indiana and later in California, Nicole had gone to plenty of lousy movies and still come home happy. She didn't know that happy was the word she'd have used of herself at the moment, and yet . . . "Do you know," she said, surprised and not altogether displeased, "after all, I think I did."

11

SEXTUS LONGINIUS IULUS CAME into the tavern one day not long after the beast show. He waited politely while Nicole took her latest batch of bread out of the oven. She nodded to him, not particularly surprised. He wasn't what she would call a regular, but he came in now and then, bought a cup of the middle-grade wine, and drank it slowly as if he actually savored the stuff. Sometimes she thought he came as much for the excuse to get out of the house as for the wine.

Today, however, he seemed oddly tense. He set a shiny brass *sestertius* in front of her and said, "Let me have a cup of Falernian, Umma. I'm going to be here for a while. Might as well start off with the best. I'll go back to the cheap stuff later, when I've stopped caring what it tastes like."

Nicole lifted her brows as she drew him a cup of Falernian. She'd never heard him sound so determined about anything.

It dawned on her slowly. Too slowly, if she wanted to be honest about it. She thrust a finger at him. "Don't tell me. Fabia Ursa's in labor."

"She is that," Longinius Iulus said. "Chased me out of the house, too. 'No place for a man,' she said—you know how women do. 'None of your business. Go get the midwife, go get my sister, go get my friends, and go away.' I knew I'd end up here, and you're right next door anyway, so I saved you for last."

Frank had been at the hospital with Nicole when Kimberley and Justin were born. She'd been glad to have him there, holding her hand and coaching her through labor and birth. She hadn't known he'd fall for a blond bimbo before his son took his first step.

Carnuntum had no hospitals, as far as she could tell. Babies were born at home. And fathers were not welcome in what was obviously women's work. Female friends and relatives of the mother joined her instead to celebrate the new life. Nicole rather liked that, even if it left the father out of his own child's first hours. Being there at his children's births hadn't kept Frank from running off with the first big-busted babe who came along.

Another *sestertius* clanked down on the bar, startling Nicole back into the here-and-now. "More of the same," Longinius Iulus said. "Then you'd better go on over. Julia can get me the rest of the way drunk."

Nicole nodded. "All right. But why—?" she stopped. *Why* wasn't that hard, not when she let her brain run for once ahead of her mouth. Fabia Ursa had had two babies already, and lost them both. Her husband wouldn't have been worth much if he weren't worried.

Nicole thrust the coin back toward him. "This one's on me," she said firmly. "Everything will be all right. You'll have yourself a fine daughter or son to be proud of."

Longinius left the coin where it was, and gulped down the wine without seeming to taste it. He'd been keeping up a good front, but his face was paler than it might have been, and his hand shook as he set down the cup. "Fabia's been praying to Mother Isis. Pray the rest of the gods it helps."

"It can't hurt," Nicole said, which was true enough, if a little on the lame side.

Sextus Longinius Iulus nodded solemnly; the Falernian was hitting him hard. "Egyptians are the oldest people in the world. If their great goddess can't keep a mother safe, no god can. She's had practice, she has."

"I hope it all goes well," Nicole replied. That was also true. Whether Isis existed at all, let alone had any power to help Fabia Ursa . . . well, who knew? Liber and Libera had brought Nicole here, hadn't they? Maybe Isis would answer the woman's prayer.

She left Longinius deep in his third cup of wine—the cheaper stuff this time—with Julia to keep an eye on him and the children to help her, and went out across the alley to Fabia Ursa's house. Just as she reached the door, someone else came up beside her: a lean, determined-looking woman loaded down with a heavy leather sack and what looked more like an adult-sized potty chair without the pot than anything else Nicole could think of. After a moment, Nicole realized it had to be a birthing chair. She'd heard of such a thing somewhere, but she'd never seen one. Compared to the way she'd had to deliver her two, flat on her back with her feet in metal stirrups, the chair looked a hell of a lot more comfortable.

The woman noticed her glance, but misinterpreted it. "Good day to you, Umma," she said, her voice civil but brisk. "Yes, this is the same chair you had for yours. It was made to last."

"It certainly looks that way," Nicole said. The midwife nodded with the barest hint of a smile. She wouldn't let Nicole take the bag or the chair, but did submit to having the door held open for her. Nicole had resigned herself to picking up the woman's name from context. She'd done that so often by now, it no longer threatened to pitch her into a panic attack.

In all the time Nicole had been in Carnuntum, she hadn't ever gone into the living quarters of the tinker's house. Fabia Ursa had always come to the tavern with her store of gossip, or Nicole had stopped by the shop without going the rest of the way.

Today was no different. Nicole could see why it might make sense for Fabia Ursa to have her baby down below, in the much larger, lighter, and probably cleaner room. The shop had been cleared of much of its debris, the heaped pots pushed against the walls and the tools put away, probably in the box in the corner. In the cleared space, Fabia Ursa was walking with grim determination that Nicole well remembered from her own labor. It was supposed to help move things along. Whether it did or it didn't, it gave the pregnant woman something to do. When the contractions grew too strong, she'd settle into the birthing chair and get to work in earnest.

Fabia Ursa greeted Nicole with the quick flash of a smile, and said to the midwife, "Aemilia! I'm so glad you've come."

Nicole sighed faintly. Ah, good. This wasn't as hard as usual.

Four or five other women were crowded into the shop, doing their best not to get in Fabia Ursa's way. Nicole recognized all but one as neighbors from houses along the street. Some were regulars in the tavern, one or two she'd seen coming and going about their daily business. The last, whom Nicole didn't know but Umma probably did, had Fabia Ursa's narrow, pointy face and her quick, birdlike mannerisms. That, then, would be the sister whom Longinius Iulus had said he was sent to fetch.

On the work counter, leaning against a dented copper kettle, stood a small painting of a smiling mother suckling a baby. At first glance, Nicole took it for an image of the Madonna and Child. But when she looked again, she saw that the artist had thoughtfully labeled his work: ISIS ET OSIRIS.

Fury roared up in Nicole, startling her with its intensity. How dared these pagans steal this of all images that they might have stolen? There was nothing more sacred; and nothing, except the crucifix, more distinctively Christian.

As quickly as it had risen, the fury died. Hadn't Fabia Ursa's husband said something about how ancient the Egyptians were? They had to go back even further from this time than this time did from her own. And if that was so, who had borrowed the symbol from whom?

Well, she thought with a flicker of amusement, and a slightly stronger flicker of annoyance. There she went, thinking pagans stole, but Christians borrowed. The part of her mind that found and marked fine details in legal documents wouldn't let go of the slip, or let her forget it, either.

Perspective was everything. *I am persistent. You are stubborn. He is a pigheaded fool.*

She blinked out of her musings to find Fabia Ursa talking to her. "We've got plenty of wine here, Umma," the tinker's wife said. "We—" She paused; her face tightened. Nicole watched a contraction ripple across her belly beneath the tight-stretched tunic. When it was gone, she went on calmly enough, "We shouldn't need to go back to the tavern for more."

"That depends on how bad the pains get," one of the neighbors said. "When I delivered Cornelius—my firstborn, if you'll remember; he died when he was six, a fever took him off suddenly, but before that he was a fine strong boy—I was in labor two whole days and two nights, and come the third day—"

Nicole tuned her out, and hoped Fabia Ursa did, too. The horror stories were as familiar as the sight of the hugely pregnant woman pacing the floor. Eighteen hundred years and halfway around the world, and misery loved company just as much as it ever would.

But Aemilia wasn't having any of it. Her voice was sharp, cutting across the woman's babble. "Stop that, Antonina.

This is not Fabia's first delivery. She's done it twice before; she knows what to expect. Don't go upsetting her with your foolish chatter when she needs to keep her spirits up."

Antonina glowered at the midwife, but she shut up. Nicole felt like applauding. The last thing Fabia Ursa needed to do at the moment was panic over her safety or the safety of her baby. Antonina didn't appear to care a bit about that, but she wasn't going to argue with Aemilia, either. The midwife looked as if she'd be bad news in a fight.

After an uncomfortable pause, Fabia Ursa's sister said, "May the gods grant good health to my new nephew or niece. It's hard, you know. Loving the little ones, knowing they'll be lucky to live past weaning. It's so easy to lose them— and so hard to help loving them regardless."

The rest of the women in the room nodded, and echoed her sigh. From the looks of it, they'd all lost babies or young children. Some more than one—Fabia Ursa herself had lost two, hadn't she?

Nicole felt that sinking sensation again, the hollow in the pit of her stomach that went with culture shock. Back in Indiana, she'd known a woman whose son had had some sort of congenital heart trouble. He'd died before he was big enough, or strong enough, for the surgery that might have cured him. More than grief, she remembered anger, and a sense of betrayal. Babies weren't supposed to die. Doctors were supposed to be able to fix them. Death was for the old—and even they were kept from it as long as humanly or medically possible.

Nicole shivered in the odorous warmth of the shop. No wonder they made a spectacle of death here. Death was a commonplace thing, and death of children most common of all.

"Fabia Honorata," Aemilia said, more gently than she'd spoken to Antonina, "we shouldn't talk about anything unfortunate here today. A birth is no place for words of ill omen."

Fabia Ursa's sister blushed faintly. "Yes," she said. "Yes, of course. What was I thinking?" She tugged at the neck of

her tunic as Nicole had seen Julia do now and then, bent her
head and spat onto her breast. She was turning away the
omen. No one grimaced or upbraided her for silly superstition. All the women looked on with deadly seriousness. Antonina and Fabia Ursa even imitated her.

Bad omens were as real and appalling here as hard-drive
crashes or power failures were to Nicole. But she'd never
have been so foolish as to think that snapping her fingers or
spitting down her shirt would keep the gremlins away.

Somehow, she didn't think it would be too wise to say as
much.

Nicole sighed. So many things she couldn't say. People
here had very different notions from hers about what was
self-evidently true. She didn't know exactly what they did to
people whose ideas were too far from the norm, and she
wasn't eager to find out. There hadn't been any place to run
or hide, down on the floor of the amphitheater.

Fabia Ursa had paused in her pacing only long enough to
avert the omen. She went back to it grimly, but not for long.
Suddenly she staggered. Nicole, who happened to be closest
to her, caught her arm. She was surprisingly heavy for a
woman so slight.

She smiled at Nicole, a thin, tight smile. "Thank you,
Umma," she said a little faintly. And then, more clearly, she
said, "I've done all the walking I'm going to do this time.
So if you don't mind . . ." Still clinging to Nicole, leaning
heavily on her, Fabia Ursa waddled over to the birthing chair
and lowered herself into it. She sat for a moment, just
breathing; Nicole, relieved of her weight, did much the same.

Fabia Ursa seemed to recover first. "Bring me some wine,
somebody," she said with imperiousness that Nicole had
never heard from her before. "I'm not getting up from here
until I do it with my baby in my arms." She swept the room
with a glare, as if challenging them all to argue with that.

Nobody even tried. "That's what we're here for, after all,"
Aemilia said mildly. She shifted her leather sack till it lay in
front of the birthing chair, just out of reach of Fabia Ursa's
foot, and scanned the room. Her eye fell on a stool not far

from Nicole. She pointed with her chin. "Umma. Bring that over here, would you?"

Nicole nodded, and fetched the stool. Its legs were short. They set Aemilia's head considerably below Fabia Ursa's— just about at the level of her waist, in fact. The midwife measured the height and the distance, and nodded, satisfied. She bent slightly and burrowed in the sack, pulling out a jar of oil, strips of cloth rolled into a tidy bundle, several sponges, and a cushion. When she had arranged them around her within easy reach, she said, "Get me a bowl of water, someone, please."

Fabia Honorata moved quickly to obey her. She knew where the bowls were, and where the water-jar was, too, which was more than Nicole could have managed.

Aemilia received the bowl with a brisk nod. She washed her hands and dried them on a bandage from the roll she had laid on the floor. That was, Nicole supposed, better than not washing at all, and the bandages were at least visibly clean. But it was a long way from keeping things surgically sterile. No rubber gloves here: no rubber at all, that Nicole had seen. No antiseptics, either, and not much by way of genuine cleanliness. She tried not to look at or think about the dirt under the midwife's fingernails.

Fabia Ursa hiked her tunic up over her swollen belly, no more shy about public nudity than anybody else Nicole had seen in this world and time. Her navel protruded as Nicole's own had done in late pregnancy. Nicole had been startled, the first time, and disproportionately upset. She hadn't been as bothered by the way her breasts and belly swelled out of all recognition as by that one apparently minor thing. Her whole body image seemed tied up in it, twisted and distorted and pushed out of shape.

Fabia Ursa inhaled sharply. Her face set; her eyes fixed inward, intent. Her belly went rock-hard as a contraction took hold.

Aemilia set her hand just below the everted navel. Fabia Ursa seemed oblivious. Nevertheless the midwife spoke to her. "Very good," she said. "That's a nice, firm pang. Are they coming closer together than they were before?"

"I ... think so," Fabia Ursa answered as the contraction eased.

Nicole glanced at her left wrist, checking a watch that wasn't there. She started a little as she realized what she'd done. She hadn't done it in a while.

No watch. No way to tell time but by the beating of her heart and the motion of breath in her lungs. *Closer together* would have to do. No sure way of telling whether the contractions came seven minutes apart, or five, or three, not here, not now. No monitor around Fabia Ursa's belly to chart how strong they were, either, nor a monitor to check the fetal heartbeat. All they had was Aemilia, with her none-too-clean hands.

The midwife rubbed sweet-scented olive oil from the jar onto those hands, then, quite without ceremony and without even asking the woman's leave, slipped her oiled hand up inside Fabia Ursa's vulva. Fabia Ursa's breath caught, but she didn't protest. Nicole didn't know how competent Aemilia was, but she was certainly confident; Nicole's own gynecologist back in California hadn't been any more matter-of-fact about what she was doing.

Fabia Ursa's voice came quick and a little breathless. "Here comes another one." Aemilia's hand slipped quickly out. Nicole nodded rather grudging approval. Good thinking, there, and smart midwifery. She hadn't wanted anyone messing with her in the middle of a contraction, either.

"Your womb is widening nicely at the mouth," the midwife said to Fabia Ursa. "Everything is the way it's supposed to be. I don't think this labor will last very long. Neither of your first two did, did they?"

"I don't think so," Fabia Ursa said. "They didn't last all day and all night, the way some women's do, I know that." She sighed. "Maybe, if this one lasts longer, the baby will, too."

When, at nine in the morning, a nurse had told Nicole she'd probably have Kimberley by noon, Frank had said blithely, "Oh, that's not very long." The nurse had been right, and it really wasn't long at all as labor went, but it had seemed plenty long to Nicole. Pregnant women didn't need Einstein to understand how time could bend and crumple in peculiar ways.

She suppressed a snort. Time didn't just bend, it folded in on itself, and spiraled down and down into another time altogether. Wasn't that how she'd got here, after all?

Fabia Ursa's contractions continued. The other women had each got comfortable in her own way: some sitting on stools or on the tinker's bench, some on the floor, and one leaning on the worktable with her arms folded under her ample breasts. The wine went round. It had stopped including Fabia Ursa. She was too busy, laboring in earnest. The contractions came closer and closer together.

Nicole had never thought of having a baby as a spectator sport. But here they all were, standing or sitting, drinking and chatting, chewing over gossip as Fabia Ursa so loved to do. She joined in when she could, distracted and clearly glad of it; but those intervals grew shorter as her labor pains grew stronger and closer together.

After what seemed like forever but was, from the angle of the light through the opened shutters, maybe three or four hours, Fabia Ursa began to curse her husband with concentrated viciousness. Nicole would have been horrified if she hadn't done just the same to Frank when she was in labor with Justin. She had a vivid memory, just then, of how much it had bloody-bedamned hurt, and it was his fault. He had put that baby in her. He had stuck her in this place and made her go through this for his petty little ego. "Next time," she'd snarled at him, "*you* have the damn baby."

Frank had been shocked, too shocked to talk back. "It's normal," the nurse had told him. "They all do it sooner or later."

"Ah," he'd said in the knowing way he had, which she'd found more charming than not while she was dating him, but which made her hate him with rare passion in the middle of delivering his son. "Projection. Perfectly understandable."

No one here knew anything about twentieth-century psychobabble. But from the looks they exchanged, this was nothing abnormal here and now, either.

Indeed, Aemilia seemed to recognize it as a sign of progress. She oiled her hand again, palpated Fabia Ursa once more, and nodded approval. "The mouth of the womb is open wide enough," she said. "See if you can't push the baby out."

Fabia Ursa grunted and strained—and gave birth to a startling, and redolent, quantity of excrement. Nicole gasped and nearly choked on the stink. She'd had an enema in the hospital, a refinement that obviously had not occurred to the Romans.

Everyone else was taking this latest development perfectly for granted. With reflexes honed by now to a fine edge, Nicole did her best to do the same. Antonina scooped up the evidence with a scrap of board, and flung it out into the street.

Nicole's eye was caught by that motion, and by a moment's reflexive revulsion at the thought of walking in the street after this was over. Fabia Ursa's shriek brought her back with a snap to the shop and the birthing chair.

"There," the midwife was saying with rough gentleness as she drew her hands from Fabia Ursa's body. "The baby was turned about a little. I straightened it. It should come out more easily now."

"*Straightened* it?" Fabia Ursa gasped. "Was that all you did? I thought you were sawing me to pieces."

Aemilia's face didn't change, either with annoyance or amusement. "The head is down, and it's straight, as it should be. It's all ready to go. You just have to push it out."

"Push—" Fabia Ursa looked suddenly exhausted. "I've *been* pushing."

"Push harder," Aemilia said.

Fabia Ursa pushed. She pushed till her face darkened to purple. Gravity helped, Nicole saw, almost in envy. The birthing chair was a better idea by far than delivering horizontally in a bed. The only advantage to the latter that she could see was that doctors and nurses had better access if something went wrong.

If anything went wrong here, Nicole didn't know what Aemilia could do about it. Probably not much. That being so, the birthing chair had everything going for it.

"Come on," Aemilia urged. "The baby's head is right there. I can feel it. One more good push and you'll be all done."

She'd just given Fabia Ursa the best incentive in the world. Nicole remembered how it had felt. One last push. One last screaming pain. And then—*done*. Fabia Ursa put every ounce of effort into it. A groan wrenched itself out of her, as if she'd tried to lift a loaded cart—and had the front wheels off the ground.

And suddenly the baby's head was out, wet and covered with cheesy-looking membrane and a little blood. The rest was almost too fast to take note of. Aemilia reached inside and guided the shoulders out. The rest of the baby almost squirted into the world. The head was the big part and the hard part, literally and figuratively.

"A boy!" Aemilia, Fabia Honorata, and Antonina said it in chorus, like characters in a play. Fabia Ursa let out a long sigh—more exhaustion, Nicole judged, than joy.

But Aemilia wasn't about to let her rest. "Don't quit quite yet," she said. "See if you can push out the afterbirth. Believe me, it'll be easier for you if I don't have to go in and get it."

Fabia Ursa's eyes closed. Nicole had cursed the doctor roundly, almost as roundly as she'd cursed her husband before the baby came. Fabia Ursa seemed resigned to this last effort. She had, after all, been through it twice before.

Aemilia left her to it, wiped the vernix from the baby and dug mucus from his mouth and nose with a finger that hadn't been washed since the labor began. He struggled feebly and started to wail, a thin, furious sound. The cry brought air into his lungs at last. His face and body brightened from dusky bluish-red to healthy pink, then from pink to raging red as Aemilia dug an oiled little finger into his anus—which Nicole had never seen any nurse do to her own babies—and dabbed at his eyes with a scrap of cloth soaked in olive oil.

From the volume and longevity of his howls, nothing whatever was wrong with his lungs.

Fabia Ursa gasped, almost inaudible underneath the baby's
cries, and grunted in a mingling of pain and relief. The afterbirth slipped from her to the rammed-earth floor. It looked
like nothing so much as a large, bloody chunk of raw liver.

Aemilia nodded at the sight of it. She bound the umbilical
cord and cut it, and sprinkled the baby with salt. Nicole wondered a little wildly if she was going to put him in a pan and
pop him in the oven like a Christmas goose.

"Good," Fabia Ursa said. Her words dragged; her eyelids
drooped. "Yes, that's good. Toughen up his skin. Keep the
rashes away." She shook herself out of her exhaustion and
the lassitude that went with it. "Umma, will you go? Tell my
husband he has a son."

"I'd be glad to," Nicole said. She hoped she didn't sound
too glad to be out of that cramped and airless room with its
stink of blood and birth.

Sextus Longinius was still in the tavern, and feeling no
pain. When she gave him the news, he fell on her in a reek
of wine and tried to kiss her. "Now, now," she said with
mock severity. "Save that for your wife."

Sextus Longinius laughed as if she'd just made the best
joke in the world. He got to his feet somehow—she doubted
even he knew how—and reeled across the alley to his shop.

Nicole followed more sedately, but quickly enough to
evade the customers, and Julia, who wanted to know every
detail. "Later," she flung at them. No one chased her down,
at least. As she left the tavern, she heard someone call for a
round in the new father's name. And probably, she thought
uncharitably, on his tab, too.

No one in the tinker's shop seemed to find his condition
in any way remarkable. They took little enough notice of
him, even Fabia Ursa, though he half fell on her and depos-
ited the sloppy kiss he'd tried to bestow on Nicole. She
fended him off with an indulgent smile and sent him veering
toward the cradle and the baby.

While he wavered over it, struck mercifully mute, Aemilia

and Fabia Ursa went on with their conversation. They were discussing wet nurses. "No, not the one I had last time," Fabia Ursa said. "I don't see any way what happened could have been her fault, but—"

"But," Fabia Honorata said. "There's always that but, isn't there? No, you don't want her. Let me think—I didn't much like the one I used for my youngest, though Lucina knows she had plenty of milk. How about the one you used, Antonina? Was she reliable?"

The others chimed in on that, batting names back and forth. Women in Rome didn't nurse their own babies, Nicole realized, even those who were far from rich. Everybody hired wet nurses. There must be a whole industry devoted to it—the Roman equivalent of bottles and baby formula.

At least the baby would have real milk from a woman's breast, though it wouldn't be his mother's. That had to be better than the twentieth-century alternative.

The party broke up not long after. Sextus Longinius snored on the floor beside the baby's cradle. Fabia Ursa had fallen asleep rather abruptly, and almost in midsentence. Her sister went to see if the wet nurse they'd decided on was available. The other women had children to tend and work to do. Only Aemilia showed signs of staying, which assuaged Nicole's conscience. She didn't particularly want to babysit for exhausted mother and blotto father, though if she'd had to she would have done it. Fabia Ursa and Sextus Longinius had looked after Lucius and Aurelia often enough.

Nicole was free to go home, and glad to do it, too. It was still daylight, rather to her surprise. The tavern was in between the noon crowd and the sundown rush, an interlude of quiet, with one or two dedicated drinkers in the corners, but no demands on Julia's time.

Julia wanted to know all about the birthing. "Not that I know anything about birthing babies," she said. "But maybe someday."

Nicole widened her eyes. "What do you mean, you don't know anything about birthing babies?" Then, because she'd had a great deal of wine next door, she came out and said it. "Gods know you've had plenty of opportunity to make one."

Julia wasn't visibly offended. "Not if I can help it," she said. "I don't need a fatherless brat dragging at my hem. I smear a twist of wool with pine resin and stuff it up there before I start." The angle of her eyebrows said that Nicole should know about this rough-and-ready form of birth control, but if Nicole wanted to play at ignorance again, Julia wasn't of a mind to stop her.

Nicole wondered what the FDA would say about pine resin as a spermicide. *Better than nothing,* was her guess. She didn't think a twist of wool would be as effective as a proper diaphragm, either, but it was also likely to be better than nothing. Put them together and they probably made a halfway decent—or perhaps a halfway indecent—contraceptive.

Several times that night, the baby's crying across the alley woke her from a sound sleep. The first time or two, she lay with all her nerves jangling, ready to leap up and look after her baby. But slowly it sank in even on her sleep-drugged senses that this wasn't her baby. She didn't have to do anything about it except listen to it. Fabia Ursa, on the other hand . . .

Aemilia had left her to it just before dark. Nicole had served the midwife a cup of the two-*as* wine for the road, as it were, and seen her on her way to a well-deserved rest. "And that's if nobody takes it into her head to pop tonight," Aemilia had said as she headed for the door.

Nicole recalled only too vividly how frazzled she'd been after Kimberley and Justin were born. She hoped Longinius Iulus and Fabia Honorata and the wet nurse were giving the poor woman some help. Nicole would look in on her, she thought fuzzily. In the morning.

She woke with the memory clear in her head, and no sound coming from next door. As soon as she'd got the tavern going and set Julia in charge of it again, she went next door to see how Fabia Ursa was doing. She found Fabia Honorata there already, and Longinius Iulus fixing the dented pot against which the image of Isis had leaned. With each stroke of the hammer, he winced. He must have the headache from hell, and well earned, too.

The baby lay asleep in his cradle, swaddled like a mummy. Fabia Ursa sat on a stool nearby. Nicole was shocked at the sight of her. She knew what a woman was supposed to look like just after she'd given birth: as if a truck had run over her. Fabia Ursa looked worse than that. Her eyes had a hectic glow that raised Nicole's hackles. "Are you all right?" she asked sharply.

Fabia Ursa didn't respond. It was her sister who said, "You see it, too, don't you, Umma? I'm afraid she's got the fever."

Nicole couldn't see that either Fabia Ursa or her husband had heard a word that either of them said. She crossed the room and laid her hand on Fabia Ursa's forehead. If the woman wasn't running a temp close to 102, Nicole would have been astonished. Aloud and in some frustration she said, "She's awfully warm."

"She's burning up," Fabia Honorata said. Worry made her tactless, or else she didn't think her sister could hear.

Nicole recalled how often Aemilia had slid her hands inside Fabia Ursa, how much pushing and prodding the midwife had done, and how few pains she'd taken to keep her hands clean. If Fabia Ursa had an infection, what could anybody in Carnuntum do about it? There were no antibiotics here. Aspirin? The willow-bark decoction was the closest thing to it, but it wouldn't do anything about the actual cause of the fever. *Bed rest and hope for the best,* Nicole thought. The thought made her uneasy. She hadn't ever known anybody who'd died in childbirth, but she'd heard enough about the mortality rate before the advent of antisepsis. Puerperal fever was nothing to take lightly.

"Is there something we can—" Nicole began, without much hope, but she had to ask.

Fabia Ursa interrupted her. "I'll be all right," she said.

She didn't sound all right. She didn't merely sound exhausted, either. She sounded sick, with the same whining, dragging quality to her voice that Nicole's kids had when they were coming down with something. It reminded her so vividly of Kimberley that last day in West Hills, her heart contracted. If she could be back there, right now—if she could be right there, with all the troubles she'd had, and the stink of vomit, and every other delight of that awful day— oh, God, what she wouldn't give to have it all back again.

She'd never wanted it so much. At first she'd been too elated. Later she'd been too busy surviving. Now . . .

Now she couldn't indulge herself. "I have some willow bark," she said with a tinge of desperation. "Wait here; I'll go get it." As if they could do anything but wait. They didn't say so. Both Sextus Longinius Iulus and Fabia Honorata nodded gratefully. Fabia Ursa sat mute, sunk again in that frightening lethargy.

Julia frowned when Nicole asked for the decoction. "Fabia Ursa?" she asked. Nicole nodded. "That's not good," Julia said. "Fever after you have a baby—that can kill you."

"I know," Nicole said irritably. She didn't, not down in her bones where real belief was, but she'd seen Fabia Ursa. That was a very sick woman. Sick, she thought, as a dog.

Julia fetched the willow-bark decoction from its storage place, moving quickly, but not nearly quickly enough for Nicole's peace of mind. She snatched the jar with scant thanks and hurried back to the tinker's shop.

Fabia Ursa had gone upstairs—a good sign, maybe, if she could travel that far: now wasn't it? Sextus Longinius Iulus took the painfully inadequate jar with gratitude that made Nicole want to burst into tears. "Thank you, Umma," he said. "You're a good neighbor."

Nicole started to brush him off, but caught herself. He needed to be grateful more than she needed to be comfortable about it. "I'll bring you a loaf of bread every day," she said, "and food your wife might like. All you'll have to worry about is getting her well."

She'd done it now: he looked ready to fall at her feet. "You are the best of neighbors," he said. "The gods blessed me and my family when they set us next to you."

Nicole mumbled something and fled. It was cowardly, and she really should have gone upstairs with him to make sure Fabia Ursa took the medicine, but she'd had all she could stand.

It wasn't cowardice, she told herself, not really, that kept her away all the rest of that day and all the next. There was the marketing, there was the laundry, there was a flood of customers that ran her flat out from dawn to dusk. It was two days before she could scrape out enough time to get away. She had managed to send food over, once by Lucius and a time or two by Julia. She'd kept her promise in that much.

She found the tinker's shop deserted. The same pot he'd been mending before, or another just like it, lay forgotten on the workbench. As she stood hesitating in the doorway, a man's voice floated down the stairs: "—warm fomentations on the belly, an enema of warm olive oil, and gruel for nourishment. If she should show improvement, thin, sour wine would be best."

A doctor, Nicole realized. A few moments later he trod briskly down the stairs. He looked like his voice: thin, intense, and profoundly preoccupied. He was younger than she would have guessed. His brows were drawn together. He did not look either pleased or hopeful. With a curt nod in her general direction, he left in a quite unmistakable hurry. *To his next patient?* Nicole wondered.

None of what he'd told Longinius Iulus sounded unreasonable, though Nicole wouldn't have wanted an enema if she felt like hell. But they were all things she would have done for the flu in L.A. They weren't much good for anything more serious.

He was trying to make Fabia Ursa as comfortable as he could, because he couldn't make her well. Nobody could do that, except Fabia Ursa herself. And that included Nicole.

She wavered, debating the good sense of going up to see if there was anything after all that she could do. But in the end she didn't go. She left the loaf of Julia's fresh-made bread and a bowl of stewed pears on the counter, and re-treated to the tavern.

The rest of the day passed in a blur. The night again was broken by the baby's crying, quickly suppressed: the wet nurse was doing her job, Nicole had to suppose.

Fabia Honorata was downstairs in the shop when Nicole went over the next morning, sitting on the tinker's bench, looking as if she hadn't sat down or rested in days. She looked up as Nicole came in, and managed a greeting, but not a smile.

Nicole asked the question she had to ask. "Fabia Ursa?"

"Not good," Fabia Honorata said, too exhausted for anything resembling dramatics. "She doesn't recognize any of us. She thrashes in the bed. The fever burns her like fire. Pray to whoever you think will hear you. I'd even pray to the Christians' blustering fool of a god if I thought it would do any good."

Nicole felt as if she'd been hit in the stomach. It didn't matter that she'd been expecting such news. She'd hoped—against hope, she'd known from the start—that she'd find Fabia Ursa sleeping, the fever broken, and everything as well as it could be.

She should have known that this world didn't have much to do with hope. Again she left the food she'd brought, again she fled to the sanctuary of the tavern. There in the comforting smells of bread and wine and humanity, she prayed as Fabia Honorata had asked her to. She did it halfheartedly, self-consciously. Somewhere on the road out of childhood, she'd lost the knack. But she tried. She hoped that would count for something.

That evening, as she was closing the tavern, she discovered what it had counted for. A storm of weeping and wailing broke from the shop next door. Fabia Honorata ran out in its wake, hair awry, tunic torn. "She's dead!" she cried. "My sister's dead!"

12

THE NEXT DAY DAWNED bright and warm, by no means as common a thing in that part of the world as it was in California. Nicole had come to welcome sun through the newly opened shutters of a morning, instead of taking it for granted. But today, as she squinted in the bright light after the stuffy dimness of her bedroom, the smile died as soon as it was born. There was an empty place in the world, a vacancy where Fabia Ursa had been. She'd been a constant, almost daily presence in Nicole's life, not drinking much, but eating like a teenager, packing it away somewhere in that bird-boned frame. Her voice had washed over Nicole while she went about the business of the tavern, a half-annoying, half-comforting rattle of gossip, opinions, hearsay, and cheerful nonsense. She'd always had something to say to the kids, and had looked after them when Nicole needed an extra hand, without complaint and without asking to be paid. Nicole had found ways: a bowl of stew or a chunk of bread with olive oil on the house, or a cup of wine for her husband if he happened by.

Now she was gone. The funeral was this morning, just late enough to let her open the tavern and yet again leave Julia to look after it while she went elsewhere. Julia didn't object. She liked the sensation of being the owner of the place, Nicole thought; and if she was turning tricks for spending money, she could do it a whole lot more easily when Nicole was away.

Nicole didn't want to think about that today. She didn't want to think about death, either, but death wasn't so easily evaded.

Most of the neighbors had turned out for the funeral procession. They seemed like a decent crowd as they gathered in the alley, waiting for the body to be carried out of the house, but there couldn't have been more than a couple of dozen in all. Two women whom Nicole couldn't immediately place by name or face took their places at the head of what would be a small, sad procession. They were hired mourners, she realized, in garments artistically rent and with hair almost too dramatically disarrayed. As two strapping undertaker's assistants carried the body out of the house, wrapped in a linen shroud and laid on a wooden bier, the mourners began to keen. A pair of flute-players, one with a large instrument, one with a small, joined in just out of synch. The combined racket put Nicole in mind of scalded cats.

The procession wound its slow way out of the alley and into the broader street beyond. Nicole happened to be close to the front, not far in back of Sextus Longinius Iulus, who walked behind the bier. He carried his son in his arms, the son for whose life his wife had given her own. He looked eerily calm. *Shock,* Nicole thought. It wasn't real to him yet. Later, when it hit, he'd fall hard, but for now he was well in control of himself.

She debated disturbing him now or waiting till later. Later might not come; now was here. She said it, then, and hoped for the best: "Is there anything I can do?"

He shook his head. "Oh, no. The funeral club is paying for everything. I've put in my *sesterces* for years; now it's my turn to get the use of them."

"Oh," Nicole said, feeling oddly foolish. "How—forethoughtful." The funeral club sounded like the closest thing to life insurance she'd heard of since coming to Carnuntum. Not that she could imagine genuine life insurance in a world like this one. The premiums would have been murderous. If somebody as young and healthy as Fabia Ursa could die from a simple infection . . . If Fabia Ursa could die like that, nobody was safe. Nicole shivered, though the day was warm as days went in Carnuntum.

"We have the babies buried under the stairs," Longinius Iulus said in conversational tones. "If it weren't for the pollution, I'd have put Fabia beside 'em, but adults have to go outside the city wall."

For a moment Nicole wondered how, except by its size, an adult's body would produce pollution but a baby's wouldn't. Decay was decay, regardless of the scale.

It dawned on her belatedly that he had to mean religious, not environmental, pollution. As far as she could tell, all the Romans wanted to do with the environment was exploit it.

The funeral procession made its way through the city to the gate that led to the amphitheater. Once outside, however, it swung southeast toward the graveyard Nicole had seen on the day she went to the beast show. A woman stood waiting there, in a tunic that shone blinding white in the sun. A priestess, Nicole thought. Sexists or no, the Romans had female priests. The Catholic Church rather emphatically didn't, nor did most of the other conservative Christian denominations. *And what does* that *say?* she thought.

"Isis," a man said off to the side, dismissively. "Isis is a women's god."

"Well, and what do you expect?" said the man beside him. "It's a woman we're burying. If it had been a man, now, we'd be saying our prayers to a proper god."

"Mithras," the first man said. "Yes, there's a god for men." The way he said it, men were so far above women in the food chain that there just was no comparison.

"And no women allowed, either," his friend said. "That's a proper god for a soldier, that is."

They sounded so smug, and so perfectly certain of their god's superiority, that Nicole would have loved to tell both of them where to go, with detailed instructions on how to get there. But this was a funeral procession. All she could do was shoot a glare at the men, who took no notice whatsoever, and steam in silence.

Rather belatedly, she recalled that Titus Calidius Severus followed Mithras. And what did that say about him? He was in the procession: not too far behind her, in fact, though he hadn't intruded on what must have looked like a fiercely private grief. That was a degree of sensitivity she wouldn't have granted most sensitive Nineties guys in L.A., let alone a Roman of the second century.

As her eye caught his, his own lit up, but he didn't go so far as to smile. She couldn't tell if he'd heard the two men talking. He must have. If so, he wasn't passing judgment, or at least, not that she could see.

Maybe he didn't want to. He was a veteran, she knew that. Should she give him the benefit of the doubt? She shrugged. Maybe.

The procession made its way into the cemetery. It had spread out along the road; now, as it passed among the stones, it formed into a straggling line.

The priestess waited for them. She hadn't moved at all except for the wind tugging at her robes. Nicole wondered how, in a world bereft of bleach or detergent, she managed to keep them so blindingly white.

Nicole needed a little while before she could see past that white and shining shape to the darkness beside it. The priestess stood near the edge of a newly dug grave. The men who must have dug the grave sprawled on the grass not far away, passing a jar back and forth. *Slaves or free?* Nicole wondered.

No folding chairs here, and nowhere to sit but on a gravestone—which no one went so far as to try. The mourners stood around the grave, each seeming somehow to stand a little apart from the others. They'd seemed pathetically few in the city and on the road. Here they closed in and made a sizable crowd. Nicole had to slip between two taller neighbors to keep her eyes on the priestess.

The mourners had fallen silent. Nicole hadn't realized how intensely irritating their shrieking and keening was until it stopped, and she luxuriated in silence. The undertaker's assistants brought the bier down from their shoulders with a little too much evident relief. One's bones cracked as he bent to lower body and bier into the grave. The body rocked slightly, shifting sideways. Nicole caught her breath. But the bier steadied; it sank down into the dark earth.

It hadn't been real before, not really. Somehow that one

bobble, that almost-fall, brought it home to Nicole. Fabia Ursa was dead.

The priestess hadn't moved at all, or spoken a word, or seemed aware that any of them was there. Just as the body sank below the level of the ground, she raised her hands to the heavens. The voice that came out of her was strong, a little harsh, with a flatness in it that was vaguely familiar. So too were the words she spoke. "Queen Isis is she that is the mother of the nature of things, the mistress of all the elements, the initial progeny of the ages, highest of the divine powers, queen of departed spirits, first of the gods in heaven, the single manifestation of all the gods and goddesses."

It was no prayer Nicole had ever heard before, but it had that odd, familiar feel. "The luminous summits of the sky, the wholesome breezes of the sea, and the lamented silences of the dead below, Isis controls at her will. Her sole divine power is adored throughout the world in many guises, with differing rites, and with differing names, but the Egyptians, preeminent in ancient lore and worshipping her with their special rites, give Mother Isis her truest name."

Fabia Ursa's baby began to cry. Sextus Longinius Iulus passed him to the woman next to him, a nondescript woman of indeterminate age. She slid her arm out of one sleeve of her tunic and exposed a breast, thereby informing Nicole, and anyone else with eyes to see, who she was and what she was doing here. The baby's cries subsided into gurgles.

Nicole, distracted by the baby and his nurse, had missed a few words of the priestess' prayer, declamation, whatever she wanted to call it: "—take the spirit of this woman who worshipped her and cherish it. May Isis take the spirit of this woman who worshipped her and comfort it. May Isis take the spirit of this woman who worshipped her and give it peace and rest and tranquility forever."

"So may it be," several of the people gathered around the grave said in unison. The hired mourners took up their racket again, wailing and beating their breasts. The musicians kept them company with a racket that certainly made Nicole sad— sad that she had to listen to such a ghastly imitation of music.

Fabia Honorata had carried a covered jar to the graveside. Now that Longinius Iulus' arms were free of the baby, she handed the jar to him. He took it as if he didn't know quite what to do with it; then with a start he seemed to remember where he was. He was still in shock. He bent stiffly, and set the jar in the grave beside his wife's shrouded body. "My dear wife," he said with the same flatness Nicole had heard in the priestess, the flatness of rote, "I offer you food and drink to take with you on your journey from this world to the next."

His voice was steady. But as he knelt beside the grave, looking down at the shape that lay within it, something in him crumpled. For a moment Nicole thought he would faint, or fling himself into the grave with Fabia Ursa's body.

Of course he did no such thing. He straightened painfully, as if he were a very old man. As he turned his face again to the sun, Nicole saw tears streaming down his cheeks.

That, it seemed, was all there was to the funeral. As Longinius Iulus stepped away from the grave, the two gravediggers woke from what had looked like a fairly complete stupor, picked up their spades, and ambled toward the grave. They didn't pay attention to the rapidly dispersing group of people, nor did they show any notable concern for the solemnity of the occasion. Without a word, they dug spades into the pile of earth beside the grave and began to fill it in. Dirt thudded down onto the shrouded body of the woman who had been Umma's friend, and whom Nicole had liked well enough.

Nicole suppressed a stab of guilt. *Well enough* was a cold thing when she stopped to think about it, but the fact was, Fabia Ursa had been a neighbor and an acquaintance. She had not, in Nicole's mind, been a friend.

Whatever she had been, one thing was certain. "It's not fair," Nicole said to no one in particular. The others had turned away from the grave and headed toward the gate. They weren't a procession anymore; they were a scattering of individuals and couples, who happened to be in the same place at the same time. Some even seemed to have forgotten what they'd come for: they were laughing and talking. Nicole wanted to grab the lot of them and shake them. "It's *not* fair! She had too much to live for, to die like that."

Somewhat to her surprise and rather to her dismay, the priestess of Isis heard her. "The gods do as they please," she said with the hint of a frown. "Who are we to question their will?"

Shut up, don't ask questions, and do as you're told. That was what that meant, in the second century as in the twentieth. Nicole couldn't buy it, not here. With any real concern for cleanliness, Fabia Ursa never would have contracted that infection in the first place. With a doctor who knew his ass from his elbow, she wouldn't have died of it. This funeral wasn't the will of the gods; it was no more and no less than ignorance.

She said so, injudiciously, but she was past caring for that. The priestess' expression of shock was almost gratifying— it proved just how ignorant and downright criminally negligent people were in this world and time. "Aemilia is one of the best midwives in the city," she said, "and as for Dexter, he studied medicine in Athens. Anything mortal men could have done to save your friend, they did. It was no human creature's fault that she died."

Nicole shut her mouth with a snap. *If I'd had a shot of penicillin to give her, you'd be singing a different tune,* she thought fiercely; but some remnant of common sense kept her from saying it aloud. She'd done enough damage as it was.

And still—how many people here in Carnuntum, here in the Roman Empire, here all over the world, died young, died in anguish, of injuries and illnesses from which they would easily have recovered in Los Angeles? How many babies died of childhood diseases against which they couldn't be immunized, because no one knew how?

She didn't know the exact answer, but she knew the general one: *lots.* She shivered. If you were in your thirties in Carnuntum, you couldn't count on another thirty or forty or fifty years of healthy, active, productive life, as you could in

L.A. or Indianapolis. You could wake up dead, for any reason at all. Then, the day after tomorrow, some wine-sodden lout of a gravedigger would be shoveling dirt over your corpse.

Maybe Julia had the right idea after all. In a world in which you didn't know if you'd be alive next week, let alone next year, you really would want to grab hold of whatever pleasure came your way. *Eat, drink, be merry. Tomorrow you may die.* It had been a greeting-card joke in Indianapolis. Here, it was real. It was the truth.

Everybody else was gone from the cemetery. Even the priestess had disappeared, Nicole had no idea where. For all she knew, the woman had sunk back into the ground, to emerge again when a devotee of Isis came to be buried. The gravediggers had made substantial inroads on the pile of dirt. One of them belched; the other farted. They grinned at each other as if it had been a grand joke.

Nicole had some vague idea that there was a funeral feast—or a collation of some sort, if not quite on the scale of a banquet—at Longinius Iulus' house. Hadn't Fabia Honorata said as much? Nicole should probably make an effort to go, put in an appearance, as she'd done at Frank's faculty parties. She wasn't any happier about this than about those uncomfortable and ultimately unprofitable gatherings.

In the end, she didn't take the extra steps across the alley from the tavern. She went home instead, and took refuge in the smell of wine and beer and bread, the sight of people eating and drinking and being—yes—merry, and the sound of Julia's voice calling out a greeting that actually sounded glad. Nicole didn't flatter herself that it was joy to see her; now Julia would be wanting a break from running the place by herself. Not that she wasn't competent to do it. She was, and highly so. But it was a lot of work for one pair of hands.

She was laughing as Nicole came in, exchanging banter with one of the regulars. At sight of her former mistress, however, she put on a somber expression, and even managed the gleam of a tear. "How sad," she said. "Poor Fabia Ursa. Remember how she cried after her babies died? First one and then the other—that must have been so hard for her to bear."

Nicole nodded without speaking. Hard wasn't the word for it. How could any woman lose two babies in a row and stay sane, and still want to try again? And yet how could anyone lose two babies in a row and *not* want to keep trying? Fabia Ursa must have been torn in two, not wanting to lose another, but wanting desperately to have one, just one, that lived.

"And now she finally had one that seems healthy, pray the gods it stays so," Julia said, unconsciously echoing Nicole's thoughts, "and she dies herself. Where's the sense in that?"

"I don't know," Nicole answered wearily. "I just don't know. Maybe things happen for no reason at all. I don't know that, either."

"Then what's the point of believing in gods?" Julia demanded. Nicole shrugged. Julia's eyes had gone wide as they always did when she was thinking hard and not particularly conventionally, as if she needed to let more light into her brain.

Her eyes narrowed again, shutting off the ray of reason. She shook her head. "You have to believe in the gods. If you don't, what's the point to *anything?*"

Nicole shrugged again, heavily. At the moment, she wasn't convinced anything *had* a point. "Pour me a cup of one-*as* wine, would you, please?" she said. Maybe it would take the edge off her gloom.

Only after Julia had filled the cup and handed it over, and Nicole had drunk it half down, did it strike her. She was using the wine as a drug again, as she had at the beast show. She was drinking to dull her senses. To forget her grief and the anger that went with it. In short, to take the edge off reality.

She had been on the way toward feeling better. Now she felt worse. She set the cup down with an effort that dismayed her. She steeled herself to do something, anything. Wait on one of the customers who'd begun to drum on the tables. Take the bread out of the oven. Check the seasoning in the stewpot.

She'd do all those things. But first, she picked up the cup again, and drained it.

"A good evening to you, Mistress Umma." The last of the day's customers ate a salted olive, spat the pit on the floor, and took the last swig from his cup of beer. He set a *sestertius* on the table and got to his feet. "I'd better head on home, before my wife sets the dog on me when I come through the door. She's bound and determined that anybody who comes in after sundown must be a thief in the night."

"Not quite so dark as that," Nicole said. The sun was setting, and twilight lingered, though for a shorter time than it had at the height of summer. The man had an *as* coming in change, but he didn't wait for it. He hurried out the door. Maybe he hadn't been joking about his wife and the dog.

"I'll light some lamps," Julia said behind her.

"Why bother?" Nicole said. She was still tired, and her mood was still black in spite of liberal applications of wine. She'd have closed the tavern after the funeral that morning if she hadn't needed the money. To Julia, she said, "We might as well shut down. We're not going to bring in many more people at this hour of the day."

"More like the first hour of the night," Julia said. The Romans gave every day twelve hours and every night twelve, too. Daylight hours were long in summer, short in winter, nighttime the reverse. It wasn't the system Nicole was used to, but it worked well enough, especially in the absence of clocks. The only problem came in the in-between hours, when nobody quite agreed on what time of day or night it was.

As Nicole was turning toward the stairs, someone called from the doorway: "Am I too late for a cup of wine?"

Had it been someone Nicole had never seen before, she would have said yes and sent him on his way. But it was Titus Calidius Severus. She almost frightened herself with how glad she was to see him. "Of course not," she answered him. "Come in, come in. Julia, light a lamp after all."

Julia nodded just a shade too eagerly. She lit a lamp and

set it on the table at which Calidius Severus had chosen to sit. Then she yawned—theatrically? Nicole couldn't tell. Julia said, "You're right, I think. We're not going to get many more tonight. By your leave, I'll go on up to bed."

That was more transparent than any of the glass Nicole had seen in Carnuntum. But ordering her freedwoman to stay down here with her would have been pretty transparent, too, to say nothing of insulting to Calidius Severus. Nicole had seen often enough that he wasn't the sort who couldn't hear *no*. She nodded to Julia without visible hesitation.

Calidius set a couple of *sesterces* on the table. "Let me have a cup of Falernian," he said, "and get one for yourself, too. Fellow came in this afternoon, paid me a debt he's owed me most of a year. I've got a little money." His chuckle was wry. "Who says the gods don't work miracles every now and again?"

Nicole didn't feel like having any more wine, but she didn't see how she could turn down her friend, either—for friend he was, just as surely as Fabia Ursa had been no more than a cordial acquaintance. As she plied the dipper, the baby next door started to cry. She jerked her head toward the noise. "Sometimes the gods choose not to work miracles."

"That's so." In the lamplight, the fuller and dyer's frown was full of shadows. The baby kept on crying. Calidius Severus sighed. "Poor Longinius. He's going to have a tough time now. He thought the sun rose and set on Fabia Ursa."

"They were happy together." Nicole carried the two cups of wine to the table, hooked a stool with her ankle, and sat opposite Calidius. She was peripherally aware of tables that still needed wiping, floor that could use a sweeping, and the last of the day's stew baking onto the bottom of a pot. None of them mattered much right at the moment.

Calidius Severus took the cup she pushed toward him and sipped. Cheap wine you chugged down as fast as you could, to get past the taste. Falernian you sipped if you could, savoring the rich sweetness. "Ah," he said. "That's the stuff." He frowned. "You're not drinking."

She made herself raise the cup to her lips. The wine was

sweet. If she didn't think about lead, if she didn't think about alcohol, she might even have said it was good. "It was hard losing Fabia Ursa," she said at last. "That should never have happened."

"Dexter's a pretty fair doctor," Titus Calidius Severus said. "He did everything he knew how to do."

"But he didn't know enough!" Nicole blazed at him as she hadn't quite had the temerity to blaze at Isis' priestess.

Still, she thought unwillingly, it wasn't Dexter's fault, not really. In an odd way, it was Nicole's, for knowing what would be possible eighteen hundred years from now, and blaming the doctor because he didn't. The fuller and dyer was right; Dexter had done everything he knew how to do.

"Talk to any honest doctor and he'll tell you he doesn't know as much as he'd like to." Calidius Severus reached across the table and set his hand on Nicole's. In a different tone of voice, he went on, "Who does?"

The lamp sputtered and flared, bringing out the dark stains that would never leave the fuller and dyer's skin. Nicole smelled the hot olive oil inside the lamp. After a moment, she realized that was all she smelled. Calidius Severus had lost his usual summer-privy reek. "You've been to the baths!" she said.

"What if I have?" He shrugged with elaborate casualness. "If I pay a call on a lady, I don't want her to think less of me because my work makes me smell like a pissoir."

"Oh," Nicole said. It was more of a gasp than a word. She didn't know if she dared laugh. It wasn't funny, not at all. And yet she hadn't thought, not really, that he understood how bad he smelled. His nose must have accustomed itself to the reek, just as hers had got used to the stink of Carnuntum.

He was watching, waiting for her to speak. "That was very . . . thoughtful of you," she said a little desperately— and with dawning awareness. She knew what he had in mind. She wasn't surprised. What else, after all, did a man usually have on his mind?

What was surprising, and not exactly thrilling either, was

the realization that she had it on her mind, too. She glowered down at the wine cup, as if the Falernian in there had betrayed her. But alcohol had very little to do with it. She was sober as a judge—more sober than a couple of judges she'd known. Some of it was fear of extinction hammered home by Fabia Ursa's untimely death. More, she admitted, had to do with Calidius Severus' patient pursuit of her. He hadn't taken no for an answer, but he hadn't made a nuisance of himself, either. But most of it was the loneliness and isolation she felt here. This, she'd thought, would be her ideal world, her best escape from the twentieth century: simple, idyllic, egalitarian, worth even abandoning her kids; after all, didn't men do it all the time? It was none of those things—not even close. And now, to her deep dismay, she needed an escape from the escape.

If she could go back—

No. Not even for Kimberley and Justin. She loved them, a fierce, visceral love that had nothing to do with anything she'd done or not done. It hadn't kept her from leaving them, and it wouldn't bring her back. Not as long as she found life in that world unlivable. Even Dawn-the-bimbo was better for them than Nicole in the state she'd been in when she made her prayer to Liber and Libera. Nicole now, worn thin with the simple effort of survival in a world she'd never been prepared for and certainly never fit into, was even less able to be the kind of mother they needed. She couldn't even make this world a better place, and she was living in it. All her grand plans, her ambitions to "invent" everything from the chimney to the cotton swab, had lost themselves somewhere, so completely she couldn't even regret that they were gone. Every scrap of energy she had was devoted to staying alive, fed, and more or less sane.

All of that came together into a decision of sorts. "Let's wait a little longer," she said, "to make sure Julia's gone to sleep."

"Well, well," Titus said in unguarded surprise. Then he laughed quietly. "Well, well." He laughed again, more freely, with a brightness of joy in it that she found contagious.

"However you like. I've been saying that all along."

She sipped at the wine without answering. She'd made a choice, and it wasn't easily revocable. She should have relaxed into it; been glad for the release, at long last, of tension. Instead, she was twitchier than ever. She was, in a manner of speaking, about to lose her virginity again—her first time in this body. First times were always strange. How much stranger this was, when her lover didn't even know it was the first time. As far as he knew, this was the same woman he'd made love to—how many times before? Many, if Nicole was any judge.

After a while, her cup was empty. So was Calidius Severus'. It probably had been for a bit. He raised an eyebrow and smiled that lopsided smile of his. It had always appealed to her. Now it made her belly quiver.

She took a deep breath, and nodded. They rose from the table together. She took the lamp to light their way upstairs. No flicking switches here.

At the top of the stairs, she paused to listen. All she heard was a triple chorus of deep, regular breathing. She nodded to Calidius. He slanted her an approving look and headed down the hall toward her bedroom. His strides were long and confident. Why not? He knew the way.

The door shut with a slightly disturbing thud. Nicole resisted the urge to run back and fling it open. She set the lamp on the chest of drawers. By its dim, flickering light, she barred the door as quietly as she could. When she turned back to face the room, she saw two things. The first was what lay beside the lamp on the chest, that Nicole had certainly never put there: a twist of wool and a small wooden box. Nicole could well guess what it contained. Wool and pine resin, Julia had told her. Julia, it seemed, had decided to help Nicole in the best way she could.

The second thing Nicole saw was Calidius Severus standing by the bed. The light made him look younger, and really, not bad at all in his Latin way. Better than Frank Perrin had ever been, that much she could be sure of.

She bent abruptly and blew out the lamp. The room

plunged into darkness. "Ahh, why did you go and do that?" Titus Calidius Severus said in a grumpy whisper. "I wanted to see you. Not to mention," he added pragmatically, "I'm liable to break my fool neck going downstairs without a light."

"Don't worry," Nicole said, with a bit of a snap in it. "We'll manage. We'll manage everything just fine." She couldn't see her hand in front of her face. Groping along the top of the chest of drawers, she found the wool and the little box. She couldn't retreat to a bathroom, and didn't want Calidius Severus watching while she put the twist in place. Maybe that was twentieth-century modesty, but she didn't care. It was hers.

She squatted and did what was needful, working by feel. It wasn't any worse than putting in a diaphragm in a hurry while Frank cooled his heels, and certain other parts of his anatomy, in the marital bed.

When she'd done as well as she could, she rose and groped across the room. She heard him breathing and shuffling around—undressing? Probably. Just short of where her skin told her he was, and the bed just past him, she yanked the tunic off over her head and let it fall to the floor. It was a defiant thing to do, even if he couldn't see it. She slid down her drawers and stepped out of them, and shifted till she felt the bed's edge against her knees. She lay back on that solid, invisible surface.

She felt Titus Calidius Severus lie beside her: a creak of the bedframe, a weight tugging at the mattress. His bare flesh was warm against hers. They'd have to be careful in what they did; the bed was narrow for two. Nicole, who slept, as Frank used to say, all over the place, sometimes thought the bed was narrow for one.

He slid an arm under her back. "It's good to be here with you again," he breathed in her ear. "I've missed you. I've missed you a lot."

She couldn't say the same; it would be a lie. She settled for something that maybe was better. "Titus," she said, clasping her arms around his neck.

"I love you, Umma," he said as she drew him down.

*   *   *

It wasn't as awkward as she'd feared it would be. The body remembered, and the mind wasn't inexperienced, either. She let him lead, and followed as she could. It was much like living in this world. After a while, the dry tightness went out of it. She relaxed and flowed with it, took the release when it came, and was profoundly glad to have been given the gift.

Afterwards, they lay side by side on the narrow bed, body to body as they couldn't help but be: one of them would fall out otherwise. Nicole looked up at the ceiling. She could make it out by now, by the starlight filtering in through the unshuttered window.

Titus Calidius Severus rested a hand on her hip. It was an easy touch, undemanding, and strikingly intimate. "Happy?" he asked.

"Yes," she answered, on the whole sincerely. Given the way the Romans took male domination as an article of faith, she'd wondered—too little too late—if he would climb on, get his jollies, and climb off again, wham-bam-thank-you-ma'am. If he had, she would never have let him see the inside of her bedroom again.

But he hadn't. He'd taken the time and effort to make sure she enjoyed herself. He hadn't made it seem like effort, either; he'd plainly been enjoying himself as he pleased her. *Entertainment,* she thought. If your options for pleasure were as limited as they were here, wasn't it sensible to string out the ones you did have, to make them last as long as you could?

"Yes," she said again, more firmly this time. "I'm happy." In a way, taking Calidius Severus to bed *had* been like making love for the first time. He knew better than she did how her body—no, *Umma's* body—responded; what it wanted, what made its synapses sing. That wouldn't last, not with her living inside it, changing it, but this time at least it had been true.

Umma's body was different from her own, sensitive in a place or two—the web of flesh between thumb and forefinger, the fold at the crook of the elbow—where she hadn't been; less so in the earlobes, which was a pity. The shaving of the pubic hair, the naked skin where she'd been used to something quite different, changed the way she felt. She'd had to swallow giggles once, which she could never have explained without getting into trouble. Razor burn down *there?*

As for how it felt, scratchy bits aside—she couldn't exactly tell. Better? Worse? She frowned. More precise, perhaps.

She moved a fraction closer to him, a conscious decision and one she didn't intend to regret. "And you?" she asked. "Are you happy?"

She'd intended it for a rhetorical question. She had no doubt he'd liked what was going on while it was going on. And he answered, "Oh, yes," but his voice held a trace of uncertainty that surprised her. After a moment, he went on, "Some of the things you did . . . you've never done before."

If he hadn't been lying there next to her, she would have kicked herself for stupidity. She hadn't made love like Umma. She couldn't make love like Umma; she didn't know how Umma did it. She'd made love like Nicole, and Calidius Severus had noticed the difference. He could hardly have helped it. Anyone who thought all cats gray in the dark was a fool, and a blind fool to boot.

As soon as she'd worked her way through that, she felt like kicking herself again. Why would he think she was different now from the way she had been? What likelier explanation than that she'd learned the new ways from somebody else?

She didn't want him thinking that. Now that she'd decided this relationship was worth having, she didn't want it poisoned at what was, for her, the very beginning. As lightly as she could, she said, "You know how Julia likes to talk. Some of the things she was talking about sounded like fun. I thought I'd try them."

He weighed that. Nicole could all but watch the pans of the balance wavering, swinging in his mind, now up, now down, now trembling in the middle. At last, he let out a short bark of laughter. "Julia likes to do more than talk. Never a dull moment there, if half of what Gaius says is true."

Nicole was so glad he'd accepted the explanation, she almost forgave Julia for being—no bones about it—a slut. Almost. "One of the reasons I freed her was so she wouldn't feel as if she had to prostitute herself to get a little spare cash, but I'm sure she still does it when I'm away."

Beside her, the fuller and dyer shrugged. "What can you do? You're not her mother. You're not her owner anymore. A patron can do just so much with a client, and then it's the client's own lookout. Some people just like going to bed with somebody new every time. I never thought that was so great myself, but maybe I'm the odd one."

"Yes, you are odd," she said, sharp enough to surprise herself. "If you ask me, most men are like Julia. It's women who are like you."

"Yes, that's probably so." And he wasn't even upset about being told he was like a woman. That took the edge off her temper, and made her feel more than a little foolish. He grunted, the noise he made when he was thinking. After a few breaths, he said, "Ah . . . Umma."

"What is it?" Nicole said. Something in his tone told her he was changing the subject. And why did he sound hesitant again?

"Mm . . ." Yes, he was hesitant, but once he'd got into it, he went on in a rush: "No matter what Julia says, if you pull my foreskin back *quite* that hard, you're liable to make a Jew out of me."

She opened her mouth, then closed it again. She'd expected something philosophical, or something personal, but— she'd hurt him? "Oh." Her voice came out much smaller than usual. "I'm sorry." She was blushing, blessedly hidden in the darkness. In the time she came from, she'd never made love to an uncircumcised man. She'd been a little startled to find something extra down there, until she realized that no one here went through circumcision, except, as she'd supposed and he'd just confirmed, the Jews.

He set a kiss on her lips, light, almost too quick to catch.

"It's all right. No damage done. Everything still worked, didn't it?" Just for a moment, he sounded disgustingly, smugly male. Before she could call him on it, he sat up, jostling her just a little. "I'd better get back across the street. Before I do, though—where's that chamber pot?"

She fished around under the bed till her hand stumbled against it, pulled it out and handed it to him. He held it in one hand while he pissed standing up. Nicole sighed, not too loud. That was a hell of a lot more convenient than squatting over the damn thing, as she had to do.

For all his grumbles about breaking his neck in the dark, he went down the stairs as sure and quiet as a cat. Nicole followed more slowly. She didn't fall there, but she kicked a stool near the front door and hopped the rest of the way, hissing till the pain lost its red edge. Still standing half on one foot and all on the other, she unbarred the door. "Good night," she said. Somehow that didn't feel quite right. Something more was called for. "It *was* a good night, Titus."

"I thought so," he said—not so smug, this time, that she wanted to smack him. "I'm glad you did, too." He gave her one more kiss, a light one, with no heat in it, but as much warmth as she could ever have wished for. "Good night, Umma."

"Good night," she repeated. She stayed in the doorway till he opened the door to his own house and went inside. Above his roof, the sky was full of stars.

"Well?" Julia asked the next morning. *"Well?"* She was practically hopping up and down with curiosity.

"Very well, thank you, Julia—and you?" Nicole said blandly. Unlike the freedwoman, she subscribed to the belief—or possibly labored under the delusion—that one of the things that made a private life private was not talking about it.

Julia stamped her foot in indignation. "Oh, come *on,* Mistress." She still slipped and called Nicole that every so often; the habits of years didn't disappear in a few weeks. She planted her hands on her hips. "You don't think that wool got there in your room by itself, do you? Or the resin?"

"Maybe they walked," Nicole answered, deadpan. Julia stared at her. Nicole stared levelly back. Julia began to laugh; she laughed and laughed, till she had to hug herself to stop. Some of the stale jokes of the twentieth century passed for fresh wit here.

Seeing her freedwoman break up made Nicole relent . . . a little. "Everything is just fine, Julia."

"Well, that's good," Julia said after a pause in which she plainly perceived that she wasn't going to find out any more. "It's about time, if you ask me."

Nicole had gathered some while since what Julia thought of her relations—or lack thereof—with Titus Calidius Severus. While Julia set about building up the fires for another day's cooking and baking, Nicole went to the front door, unbarred it, and threw it open to show the tavern was ready for business.

Across the street, Titus Calidius Severus was just opening up, too, and setting out the amphorae that gave him the urine he needed for his work. "Good morning, Umma," he called with a smile and a wave.

Nicole caught herself stiffening, searching for hidden meanings. *Stupid,* she cursed herself. She waved back— lightly, good; not too strained. "Good morning, Titus," she said.

Behind her, Julia made a small, interested noise. Nicole realized she hadn't greeted the fuller and dyer like that of a morning since she'd come to inhabit Umma's body. This had the look and feel of a custom returned to after a hiatus.

Calidius Severus noticed, too. His smile broadened. He blew her a kiss. Julia made that interested noise again. Absurdly, Nicole felt herself blushing as if she'd been caught *in flagrante delicto*—a fine Latin phrase—rather than simply receiving a friendly greeting from the neighbor across the street.

She fought down the heat of memory, and blew the kiss back toward him. He grinned and bowed and went inside.

Nicole rounded on Julia. Julia had the sense to get very busy very fast.

Lucius and Aurelia put a merciful end to what was becoming an uncomfortable stretch of silence. Their noise and clatter drove the shadows out of the tavern. Their voices rang in it, demanding breakfast *this instant.* Julia was quick to shut them up. She ate with them, and Nicole after a short pause. She was hungrier than she'd expected. She realized, in the middle somewhere, that she'd used her bread to sop up all the olive oil in the little bowl Julia gave her. She didn't remember having started to do that, but it seemed a habit these days. It wasn't making her fat. Some days, in fact, that oil was the only fat she got in her diet. Maybe her body had quietly told her she needed it.

Ofanius Valens was her first customer. He wasn't a regular anymore, but he had started coming back now and then since Julia's manumission party. Nicole brought him his bread and scallions and walnuts and a cup of the two-*as* wine. *His usual,* she thought, and remembered how terrified she'd been the first time she saw him. Now she knew what two or three dozen people liked to order, maybe more. It felt as easy, as natural, as keeping track of the files in her computer.

Titus Calidius Severus came in at midmorning for a loaf of bread and a cup of wine. *And thou,* she thought facetiously, till she caught a whiff of him. His ammoniacal reek was back in force. Nicole let out a small, silent sigh. If he ever tried to get her to take him to bed when he smelled like that . . .

Surely he had better sense. If he didn't, she'd teach him some, and fast. Not that she really thought he needed any education. He'd never even tried to kiss her when he smelled bad.

She realized she was standing over him, staring blindly at him. As she moved to busy herself somewhere else, he said between bites of Julia's fresh and still-warm bread, "Fellow who came into the shop to pick up some wool I'd dyed for him told me there's a troupe of actors coming in from Vindobona in a few days. Do you want to take in one of the mimes they put on? He said they were supposed to be pretty good—and if they're not, we can always throw cabbages at them."

Vindobona, Nicole had learned, was the name by which Vienna went these days. Although Vienna would go on to put Petronell in the shade, here-and-now Carnuntum was at least as important a city.

"Yes, I'd like that," she said. Then the apprehension struck. She'd thought she'd like the beast show, too. Who knew what surprises might lurk in a seemingly innocent mime? "They're not going to kill anybody, are they?"

Calidius Severus arched a brow, but he answered seriously enough. "I wouldn't think so. Too expensive for a troupe outside of Rome or maybe Alexandria to butcher a slave when the show calls for somebody to die. The gore'll just be pig's blood in bladders, same as usual. But it'll look real."

She stood flat-footed. She was always taken aback when a cultural difference flew up and hit her in the face, but this time was worse, somehow. This man was her lover, and she was glad of it, too. He was genuinely thoughtful and considerate, out of bed and in it. Her kids—Umma's kids, but one way and another she'd come to think of them as her own—thought the sun rose and set on him; there stood Lucius now, hanging on his every word. And the only thing he saw wrong with killing slaves in a show was that it was too expensive to be practical.

His attitude was standard here. Witness the beast show. Witness the execution that was its climax. Witness the gladiatorial shows—which she hadn't, and for which she thanked God. In Carnuntum, life was cheap.

It shouldn't have been surprising. She could still feel Fabia Ursa's absence like the healed socket of a tooth; and Fabia Ursa had lost two babies before she died delivering a third. Maybe, since life was so easy to lose, it was that much easier to take. People lived surrounded by death, till death was commonplace.

Resolutely, she pushed such thoughts to the back of her mind. She couldn't afford to linger over every incidence of culture shock. She had to live in this world, regardless of what she thought of certain parts of it. And that meant recording the datum as Calidius had given it, a thing she needed to know to survive. She would deal with that. Later, if she had time—if she ever had time—she'd worry about other things.

All of which added up to the simple answer she gave him. "I'll come to the mime," she said.

He'd taken time to sip from his winecup while she woolgathered. Once he had her answer, he set down the cup. "Well, good," he said. "I don't quite know when they're getting into town, but they should be worth an afternoon's diversion when they do. Anything to make one day different from another."

"Oh, yes," Nicole said, this time without hesitation. Most people in Carnuntum didn't come close to agreeing with her on the importance of life, but when it came to making life interesting, she agreed wholeheartedly with the rest of the population. Life might be precious, but it was also, without TV, the VCR, or even electric lights, rather massively tedious.

The players arrived none too soon, in Nicole's estimation. Schedules weren't set months in advance as they would have been in L.A. Entertainers came and went as weather and the roads allowed. In this case, a spell of good weather gave way to several days of pouring rain. When the clouds cleared away and the sun came boldly out, the players appeared in Carnuntum. Graffiti on the walls proclaimed their arrival, and one morning, as Nicole headed to market, she saw an outlandishly dressed person standing in front of a market stall, haggling with the vendor over the price of white lead. Nicole bit her tongue before she pointed out that the stuff was poisonous. She was learning, though it was taking her a while.

She did her marketing and went home with suitable dignity, but once she was there, she couldn't resist telling Julia about the actor she'd seen. Julia clapped her hands and did a little dance. One of the regulars half-choked on his bit of sausage. Julia in her almost-new but still somewhat too tight tunic, dancing with glee, was a sight for hungry eyes.

Nicole suppressed the frown that thought engendered. "You like the mime shows?" she asked.

"Oh, *yes*," Julia said, and transparently remembered not to add the habitual *Mistress*.

"Well," said Nicole. "Then we'll have to see that you get a day off, won't we?"

She'd made Julia a happy woman—but not so happy she forgot to be diligent in her duties. Quite the opposite. Julia with a break in sight was determined to be the best freed servant anyone ever had. She was a little *too* eager, if truth be told; but she didn't ask Nicole to let her go to the show first. That wouldn't have been proper. She conceded Nicole the right to opening day, and stayed behind uncomplaining. It would be her turn tomorrow. She'd made sure everybody in the tavern knew it, and cared about it, too.

The mime show was in the same place as the beast show had been, the amphitheater outside the city's southern wall. There wasn't really anywhere else in Carnuntum that could hold a crowd in comfort.

Nicole wasn't exactly comfortable. The memory of the beast show was still too fresh. But she was determined to enjoy the day, and particularly the person she was sharing the day with.

"Nice of you to give Julia time off tomorrow to come see a show," Titus Calidius Severus remarked to Nicole.

"It's only fair," she answered. "Besides, we'll get along better this way."

Calidius Severus misunderstood her deliberately, and with a spark in his eye, too. "I like the way we get along just fine." He'd been over the night before, fresh from the baths and smelling as sweet as anyone ever smelled here. Nicole, remembering one or two things they'd done together between dusk and dawn, stretched almost as Julia liked to, like a huge and sensuous cat. She liked it fine, too—and she was glad of it. Finally, she'd found something in Carnuntum that wasn't painful, barbaric, or shocking.

Even if nobody got killed or maimed, she hadn't expected to like the mime show. And yet she liked it very much indeed. It was called *The Judgment of Paris,* which at first meant nothing to her but seemed perfectly familiar to the crowd. Paris, who came from Troy, not France, was trapped into judging a beauty contest among goddesses: Juno, Minerva, and Venus.

If it had been on TV, she would have called it a comedy-drama. The audience laughed at the machinations of their deities, a level of irreverence that brought her up short. It was as if one of the networks had made a sitcom out of the Bible.

After a little while, however, she stopped fretting. Obviously no one expected to be struck by lightning, or found this levity anything but right and proper. She settled back with a gusty sigh, and determined to enjoy the show.

The plot was thin, like the plot of a TV sitcom. As with a sitcom, she let it wash over her instead of analyzing it like a legal brief. The music—flutes and drums and horns—was loud and insistent. The costumes were gaudy: yellows and reds and greens of an intensity that no one ever saw in everyday clothes. If Rome had known day-glo colors, these actors would have used them. They had a distinct, almost fluorescent glow as they strutted and danced in the arena where, not so long ago, so many beasts and a single man had died. The women who played the goddesses and Helen of Troy took every opportunity to wear as little as possible. Whenever those opportunities arose, as they frequently did, the men in the audience roared their approval. *Sex sells,* Nicole thought. It was as true for ancient Rome as for modern Hollywood.

Titus Calidius Severus didn't shout, but he was most attentive to the actresses jiggling and strutting across the ground where lions and wolves and bears had prowled not so long before.

Watching him watch the pretty women, Nicole decided she didn't mind the way he did it. She could hardly have asked him not to pay attention to them; that was what they were there for, and he was a healthy male with all his hormones in working order . . . as she had good reason to know. What mattered was that he didn't give the impression that he would sooner have been with one of them than with his real companion, as so many men would have done. Frank had stared up at an awful lot of movie screens as if he'd forgotten she was there beside him, and not just toward the end, either. And what had he gone for when he was ready to dump Nicole? Ms. Blond Hollywood Bimbo, what else?

She surprised herself, not with the virulence of the thought, but with the coolness of it. Frank Perrin was centuries unborn and half the world away. The edge was off her bitterness. She was too busy surviving in this world to waste energy on a marriage that had been dead long before Frank walked out the door.

Calidius Severus for sure was better-looking than Frank, though Frank smelled a whole lot better. He was also just as attentive to the swordfights as to the women in their skimpy draperies. He leaned forward on the bench, muttering under his breath at this bobble or that wobble. "If I'd used a sword like that," he told Nicole in a pause between acts, "I'd be twenty-five years dead."

The swordplay was as obviously choreographed as a bar fight in a Western. Like a Western, it wasn't meant to be realistic. But she could hardly explain that to Calidius Severus. She settled for the glaringly obvious instead. "It's only make-believe," she said.

He muttered and scowled and shifted on the bench, but little by little he subsided. He was almost too reasonable a man to be real. Nicole tried to imagine him in a Stetson and carrying a six-shooter, sauntering into a saloon in time-honored movie-cowboy fashion. It was amazingly easy, though his looks tended more toward the Mexican sidekick than the tall lanky cowhand.

Not very many movie Westerns were as extravagantly gory as this Roman equivalent. Still, despite the copious blood, the killings were obviously faked. She'd believed Calidius Severus when he said there wouldn't be any excessive realism in the mime, but she couldn't help the small sigh of relief that, after all, the actors would get up to strut the stage another day.

When Paris and Helen leaped gleefully between the sheets—in this case, a blanket as gaudy as their costumes—that looked choreographed, too. But, as enthusiastic as it was, Nicole wondered if, after all, it was faked. The audience didn't seem to think it was, or else was delighted to buy into that particular illusion. Men and women both cheered on the performers. The imagination could do a lot with a pair of heads, a strategically arranged blanket, and a set of highly suggestive gyrations.

There was a collective groan when the gyrations ended, and with it the scene. In the next, with neither sex nor sword-play to engross them, the audience indulged in a spate of restlessness. Paris struggled nobly against it, crying over-written defiance at the Greeks who threatened to come and take Helen back from Troy. But even his trained voice couldn't overwhelm the shout from a few rows behind Nicole that pretty obviously wasn't in the script: "Is there a physician in the amphitheater?"

Along with most of the other people right around her, she turned to stare. A man with a seriously worried expression held up a woman who seemed to have fainted. Her eyes were closed and her body limp; her head lolled on the man's shoulder. Even if she'd been awake, she would have looked sick: her face was flushed, and a distinctive, spotty rash mottled one cheek. It looked to Nicole like measles. She was just old enough to have had them herself before her parents got around to getting her vaccinated—she still felt the sting of the unfairness, and the magnitude of her luck that she'd had no worse than a face and body covered with blotches, and a week in bed being fed whatever she asked for. She'd only learned later how many dangerous side effects measles could have.

She didn't ever remember being so sick she passed out; mostly she'd been covered with spots and distressingly itchy. This woman had it a lot worse.

Someone was edging and sidling his way down from higher up. "Move aside, if you please. I'm a physician. Excuse me, sir. Madam. If you don't mind." She recognized the voice as much as the face and the walk, with its brisk politeness and its underlying air of impatience with the bulk of the human race. Dexter the physician had taken a day off; but, like doctors in every place and time, he wasn't going to get that much of a break.

The man on the other side of the woman moved over to give Dexter room to sit beside her. It didn't look like altruism. It looked like getting out of range of contagion.

Dexter ignored the man's cowardice. He took the woman's pulse, felt her forehead, and bent close to examine the rash. Nicole turned back to the show, which had indulged itself in another swordfight, but she kept being drawn to the sick woman and the physician. Each time she looked, Dexter looked unhappier.

He murmured something to the sick woman's companion, too low for Nicole to hear. She didn't have long to be frustrated. As soon as Dexter had bent over the woman again, the man cried, "The pestilence! What kind of quack are you, anyway? Can't you even tell when someone's had too much sun?"

Any doctor Nicole had known in Indiana or California would have blown sky-high if he'd been screamed at like that—either blown sky-high or called in a slander lawyer. Dexter only bowed his head in humility—which Nicole found incredible—or else in the kind of arrogance that didn't care what the world thought. "May you be right," he said. "May I be wrong. Take her home. Make her comfortable. Her fate is now in the hands of the gods."

The woman's companion glowered at the doctor, but didn't fling any further abuse. He hefted her up with a grunt, staggering under the dead weight, and maneuvered between the benches to the aisle. People scrambled back out of the way. Nicole was just about to think of offering something, a hand, Calidius Severus' hand, whatever could help, when a man a row or two down did it for her.

Maybe he was a relative. The woman's companion seemed to know him, at least. Between them, they supported her in a kind of fireman's carry and carried her down and apparently out of the amphitheater. She went like a gust of wind through dry California scrub, fanning a spark into wildfire. "Pestilence," people whispered. Then louder: "Pestilence!"

The show ended not long after the woman's departure. Applause was sparse, abstracted. The actors tried to drum it up, strutting and gesticulating on the stage. One, who'd played a comic villain, favored the ampitheater with an obscene gesture and a flash of his bony behind.

Nobody but Nicole seemed to take any notice. Some of the audience kept glancing toward the place where the woman had been sitting, uneasily, as if something dark might be lurking there still. Others craned their necks, peering at anyone who might be inclined to keel over.

Titus Calidius Severus' sigh had a wintry sound to it, though it was still only August. "So," he said. "It's come here after all. I was hoping it wouldn't. From everything I've heard, it's been bad—very bad—in Italy and Greece."

"It looked like the—" Nicole broke off. The Latin she'd been gifted with when Liber and Libera sent her to Carnuntum had no word for *measles*. No word, she'd learned, meant no thing. But measles, even before there was a shot for it, had been a common childhood disease. You were sick, and maybe there were side effects, but you didn't usually die of them. That had been true, her mother had said, for as long as anyone remembered. How could there be no word for the disease in Rome?

No. That was the wrong question. If the Romans didn't have a word for it, what did that mean? That it wasn't a common childhood disease here and now? If that was the case . . . For the first time, Nicole felt a stab of fear. Sometime not too long before she left TV behind for good, she'd watched a show—on the Discovery Channel? A&E? PBS?—about the European expansion. It might have been much less easy for the sun never to set on the British Empire if the Native Americans and the Polynesians had had any resistance to smallpox or measles. The British, the French, the Spanish, the Dutch, brought their diseases as well as their trade goods and their guns. As often as not, the bacteria and viruses did the conquering, and the Europeans took over what was left. Native populations had, the documentary said, died like flies.

And here she was in a world that had no name for measles, and Calidius Severus was staring at her, obviously waiting for her to go on. "It looked like the what?" he asked. "I didn't think anybody'd ever seen anything like this before. Do you know something I don't?"

Sudden tears stung her eyes. The world blurred about her. *I know so many things you don't, Titus,* she thought in a kind of grief. And what good did knowing them do? Knowing that there could be such a thing as a measles vaccine was a hell of a long way from knowing how to make one. She wasn't like the hero in a time-travel movie. She didn't come equipped with every scientific advance and the means to manufacture it. All she had was day-to-day, more or less random cultural knowledge, which could flip a light switch but couldn't begin to explain what made it work.

What had Dexter told the sick woman's companion? Take her home and make her comfortable? Nicole couldn't have given better advice, not here. That was all anybody in second-century Carnuntum could do. It was all the physician had been able to do for Fabia Ursa. And Fabia Ursa was dead.

Calidius Severus was waiting, again, for her to answer. He always did that. She still wasn't used to it—to having a man listen to her. God knew Frank never had. She hadn't always listened to Frank, either, but then Frank was a bore.

She gave Calidius Severus an answer, though maybe not the answer he was looking for. "No, I don't know anything special," she said. All at once, to her own amazement, she hugged him fiercely. "I just want us to come through all right."

"So do I," he said. He didn't sound overly convinced. "That's as the gods will—one way or the other. Nothing much we can do. Maybe Dexter *was* wrong. Physicians don't know everything, even if they like to pretend they do. Or maybe he was right, but there'll be only the one case. It won't be an epidemic."

"Maybe," Nicole said. She grasped at the straw as eagerly as he had, and with as little conviction. Maybe saying it would make it true.

Or maybe not.

They left the amphitheater in silence that extended well beyond the two of them, and walked back toward the city. On the way in, everyone had been lively, cheerful, chatting and calling back and forth. Now only a few people spoke, and that in low voices. The rest slid sidewise glances at them, peering to see if they looked sick.

For the first time, Nicole wished Liber and Libera had brought her body here as well as her soul, spirit, self, whatever it was. Her body was a pasty, doughy, only moderately attractive thing, but it had had measles. Umma's hadn't. As long as Nicole lived in this body, she was as susceptible as anyone else in Carnuntum.

When she'd wished herself here, she'd given up more than she'd ever imagined. Would she have to give up her life, too?

Until now she'd been coasting, living a long, generally not very pleasant dream. She'd been too busy just surviving, and too tired out from it, to think much past the moment. And, to be honest, she'd been too stubborn to admit that she'd made a mistake; that she'd been dead bone ignorant about the past. Maybe not any past—but this one certainly wasn't anything like what she'd expected.

She didn't want out. Not yet. She was stubborn enough for that. But she was beginning to think that she might be healthier, if not happier, back in West Hills.

"Maybe it won't be so bad," she whispered, more to herself than to Titus Calidius Severus.

He nodded, a little too vigorously. "Maybe it won't," he said. He reached to take her hand just as she reached to take his. They clung to each other as they made their way through the clamor and stinks, the flies and smoke of Carnuntum.

"Maybe it won't be so bad," she said again, in the street in front of the tavern. But she knew what crouched there in the dark, however loud she whistled. She gave it a name: "I'm scared."

"So am I," Titus Calidius Severus said.

13

FOR A DAY OR two, nothing much happened. Nobody fell over dead in front of the tavern. None of Nicole's customers brought in rumors that people were dropping dead anywhere else in Carnuntum. She began to hope Dexter was wrong after all. As Titus Calidius Severus had said, doctors didn't know everything. That was true in the twentieth century, and a hell of a lot truer here in the second.

When she went to the market, it seemed she heard an awful lot of people coughing and sneezing. More people than usual? She wasn't sure. Her nerves were on edge. She was hypersensitive, jumping on every hack and sniffle.

The next day, when she took Aurelia to the baths, she told herself the same thing. Nobody was looking any more or less healthy than she ever had. Sometimes she even believed it, and held onto the belief for an hour or two—until someone else started sneezing and started a chain reaction, or a walk down the street sounded like a percussion section.

The night after that—the night after a men's day at the baths—Titus Calidius Severus came across the street at sunset and stayed on after the children and Julia had gone off to their beds. Julia sauntered upstairs with elaborate casualness. Nicole had to work hard not to notice it.

She and Calidius Severus didn't linger long over the last of the wine. There was so much to say, they ended up not saying much of anything. In a little while they went upstairs, she leading, he following—for the view, she supposed, such

as it was. Next time she'd insist on following him. He had
a nice ass, as she had good reason to know.

At the top of the stairs, she paused for an instant. The
children were snoring in two high, unmusical tones. No
sound came from Julia's room.

Nicole shrugged. Silence would do. "Come on," she said,
as she had on every night after a men's day at the baths since
the mime show. Her bedroom was waiting, and Calidius Severus was in it. She slipped in behind him, and barred the
door.

She was easy enough with Calidius now to leave the lamp
burning on the chest of drawers while they made love. Her
body wasn't a whole lot in this culture, but in her own it
was enough to be proud of. She put some of that pride in
the way she held herself. If she could have been really clean,
if she'd had access to shampoo, makeup, moisturizers, even
plain old soap, she'd have been really something, but as it
was, she wasn't bad. She liked the tautness of her stomach,
and thighs that had never heard of cellulite. Her breasts were
small and pointed but rather nice, and not too soft in spite
of two children—not nursing one's own did make a difference.

He was enjoying the view, as he must have done on the
stairs. She took time to return the favor. He had a good body,
better than her own by current standards, and not bad at all
for an old man, as he liked to say. The dyes he worked in
had stained his hands and arms indelibly, and there were
spatters on his feet. They made him interesting. She liked to
follow the patterns with her finger, to stroke upward to the
clean olive flesh of his upper arm, and across his shoulders
where a soft furze of black hair grew, then down his back
and around to the rampant thing in front, that Romans liked
to call the "little man." He was ticklish down the line of his
spine, would wriggle and fuss if she ran a nail along it, but
he loved to be massaged deep and painful-hard in the broad
muscles of his shoulders.

There were scars. Sometimes he'd tell her where he'd got
them: the arrow in the arm, the sword-thrust that grazed his

ribs, the deep pitted hollow in his thigh where the spear had struck. Each one recalled pain that people in her world seldom knew, not just the pain of the wound but the pain of treatment, and no drugs but wine and, once in a while, poppy juice—crude opium, nowhere near as effective as the modern arsenal of painkillers. Wine was the only antiseptic, too, and no antibiotics to back it up. It was a miracle he'd survived, and not only that, that he walked without a limp. "Except in the dead of winter," he'd told her a time or two back. "Then everything stiffens up. Price of old age, and being an old soldier."

He wasn't so old in bed, as she liked to reassure him. "Boys are always in a hurry," she said. "Men take their time."

"That's good," he'd say then, "because it takes me a little more time to warm up and a little more to cool down, these days."

When Nicole made love, the world went away. The yammering of thoughts went quiet, and she was spared, for a little while, the constant strain of living somebody else's life.

Tonight they joined with an urgency that had as much to do with holding fear at bay as with any kind of bodily passion. They clasped each other tight, he driving hard and deep, she urging him on, legs locked about his middle, holding him even after she'd come to climax and felt the hot rush of him inside her.

Only then did it strike her. The twist of wool and the box of resin lay on the chest, untouched, forgotten.

At the moment she couldn't find it in her to care. Next to the fear she'd lived with since the day in the amphitheater, this was nothing. If she had caught something, so to speak, she didn't doubt that Julia would know how to take care of it. Unlike the pestilence. The pestilence—it put her in mind of the plague, the great plague of long ago (or a long time coming, from this end of time)—no one could stop.

She was holding him so tight, he gasped for breath. Reluctantly, she let him go. They lay nested in the narrow bed, and he managed a shallow gust of laughter. He groped for her hand and pressed it to his chest. His heart was still drumming hard. "You see, woman? You wear me out."

Bless him for knowing just what to say, and how to say it, to shake her out of her megrims. She seized on the mood, and let it take her over. It was amazingly easy. She snorted. "Oh, nonsense. If the baths took women every morning and men every afternoon, you'd be over here bothering me every night."

He poked her in the ribs. She squeaked, then clapped a hand to her mouth. Damn—she'd have bet an amphora of Falernian that Julia was lying in her bed across the hall, laughing her head off.

"Can't think of a better reason to want to go to the baths," Calidius Severus said. Nicole snorted again. He went on, "Likely just as well they do things this way. Any man past forty who says every other day's not easier is lying through his teeth."

She liked him very much, just then. Loved him? Maybe. But love was easy; it was mostly hormones. Liking was harder to come by. As far as she'd ever known, the handful of men who weren't convinced they were permanently nineteen would sooner have faced cross-examination by Johnnie Cochran than said as much out loud, especially to a woman. Honesty was novel, and highly refreshing.

Without warning, and without a word, she kissed him. He widened his eyes at her. "What was that for?" he asked.

"Just because," she said.

He laughed. "Good enough reason for me."

His laughter didn't last. Little by little, it leached from his face. She'd been holding onto her bright mood by sheer force of will, but he'd run out of stamina. Slowly, he said, "The attendants had to carry somebody out of the cold plunge today. He had a rash on his face and neck, and on his chest, too. He looked like the woman at the show."

Nicole went still. If her heart could have stopped, it would have. "Are you sure?" she asked.

"No, I'm not sure," he answered, but he didn't sound any more reassured than she felt. "I didn't see either one of them for very long, and I didn't get a very good look at them. But the rash is hard to miss—and they both had it."

"It probably was, then." Nicole spoke the words like a judge passing sentence. Maybe she was passing sentence—on Carnuntum. She shivered. She'd been shivering a lot lately, though it was summer, and warm enough by Carnuntum's standards.

When he clasped her to him, she felt the cold in him, too, the chill that had nothing to do with the air's temperature. He warmed quickly enough, all the way to burning. Over forty or no, he had it in him to go a second round.

"It's the company I keep," he said when they'd slipped apart again, each a little more winded than the last time.

"You're just being sweet," she said. She could have flattered herself into thinking her own allure made him so randy. So maybe that did have something to do with it. But she knew the sick man in the baths was as much in his mind as in hers.

He yawned. "Now look at me. I'll want to sleep till noon, and Gaius will have to drag me out of bed to get the day's work done." Gaius would tease his father too, probably, about old men and young ambitions.

The lamp guttered abruptly and went out. Nicole cursed: she'd forgotten to fill it before she went to bed. Going to bed with company could do that, distract her from life's smaller concerns.

Titus Calidius Severus cursed more pungently than she, as he groped for his sandals in the dark. Nicole found her own tunic conveniently near to hand and slipped it over her head, smoothing it down her body. Her hands paused of their own accord. She was all warm still from making love.

Her eyes had adapted to the tiny amount of light that slipped through the shuttered window. She had no trouble seeing her way to the door, or unbarring it and peering out. She listened, head cocked, then nodded. Julia was snoring, a deeper counterpoint to the children's diatonic scale.

She padded barefoot down the stairs. Calidius Severus followed so close he almost trod on her heels. She plotted a path through the tables and stools between the stairs and the door, and cheered herself under her breath when they both reached the door unscathed. She saw his crooked grin in the light of a wan moon. He hugged her tight. "I'll get through tomorrow, and the day after that, and the day after that," he said. "I'll just go on and on. Just the way we all do."

She sighed, and nodded. She, too. There was no other way to get through life in Carnuntum and still keep herself within shouting distance of sanity. "You have good sense," she said.

"Do I?" He shrugged. "What am I doing here in the middle of the night, then?" He started to chuck her under the chin, but caught himself, and kissed her instead. "Kissing's better," he said, "after all."

She could hardly argue with that. It was hard to let him go; hard, maybe, for him to let her go. But they were practical people. They parted briskly enough. He went to his own place and his son and his work. She went to hers. Day after tomorrow, when it was again a men's day at the baths, he'd be back. She could count on that, as sure and as regular as the clockwork that Rome had never known.

The next morning, when Nicole opened her door for business, the amphorae were out in front of Calidius Severus' shop. Maybe Gaius had put them there, she thought, until she saw movement inside, and recognized the bristle of Titus' beard. She felt logey and slow. He must feel much the same. For the first time in a while, she'd have given a great deal for a pot of coffee and a pair of mugs, and a jump-start for both of them.

As she scooped salted olives from their amphora into a wooden bowl, Dexter the doctor trudged past. He had his leather satchel in his hand: not quite a little black bag, but close. On impulse she left the bar, went quickly to the door and called to him: "Dexter! How is the woman who took sick in the amphitheater?"

He paused in his stride. He didn't seem as annoyed to be stopped as he might. He looked tired, she thought, and pale. Up all night, probably, practicing his trade.

"The woman in the amphitheater?" he asked. "They buried her yesterday."

Nicole stood flatfooted. She'd expected it. She'd dreaded it. And yet . . .

He didn't wait for her to get her wits back. "I'm off to another case now," he said. "Aesculapius grant me better fortune." As he turned to go, a storm of sneezing overtook him, and a rattle of coughing in its wake.

Oh Lord. He had it, too. Nicole caught herself wiping her hands frantically on her tunic, though she hadn't touched him at all. How many people had that woman infected at the show? How many of them were sneezing and coughing, but hadn't yet broken out with the rash that signaled full onset of the disease? How many people were going to catch the disease in the baths? Just about everyone in Carnuntum went to the baths; they were always crowded. A plague couldn't ask for a better breeding ground.

Nicole's last bastion of optimism crumbled. She shook her head and turned back to the tavern. There was a cold feeling in her stomach, and an ache that wasn't hunger. She was familiar with it from this and that: an accident on the freeway, the California bar exam. It was fear.

Julia was up at last, a little late—and was that a sign she was getting sick? Nicole quashed that stab of worry. Julia was cleaner than she'd been when Nicole first arrived in Carnuntum, now she had money and a little time for the baths, but she still had a fondness for tight tunics and a disgusting tendency to wake up cheerful and stay that way till the rest of the world caught up with her. Or not; Julia didn't care.

Her curiosity was as sharp as ever, too. "What were you talking to Dexter about?" she asked as she worked flour into the first batch of the day's bread.

Nicole started chopping nuts and raisins for sweet cakes. She took her time in answering. "We were talking about the woman who got sick when Titus and I were at the mime show," she said. She didn't really have to, or particularly want to, but Julia was the closest thing she had to a female friend in this world. She had a pressing need, suddenly, to share the worry with someone else.

Julia didn't appear to know or care that there was something to worry about. She smiled at Nicole's use of Titus Calidius Severus' praenomen. She'd made it clear long since that she thought the two of them were a good match. If she could see them married off, Nicole was sure, she'd be the happiest freedwoman in Carnuntum. "How is the woman?" she asked.

"Dead," Nicole answered baldly.

Julia didn't go pale, or reel, or seem at all shocked. "Oh," she said without much evident emotion. "That's too bad."

People in Carnuntum were on very much more intimate— and much more casual—terms with death than people were in the United States of the late twentieth century. Julia's off-hand observation was one more signpost on a well-marked road. She took for granted the possibility that a person could get sick and drop dead, just like that. From what Nicole had seen of the state of the medical art, that wasn't the least bit surprising.

They worked in silence, in the well-worn groove of two people who'd been coworkers for so long, they no longer needed to think about how they shared this task or that. Just as the bread came out of the oven, the first of the morning's regulars showed up at the door. He hawked and spat before he came in, and coughed.

Nicole had let down her guard a little. Her stomach had even begun to unclench. Now it went as tight as a fist. Julia, oblivious, served the man his regular cup of one-*as* wine and his half-loaf of bread with olive oil to dip it in.

As he thanked and paid her, a confusion of distant sound resolved itself into sense. A funeral procession made its sorrowful way toward and then past the tavern. Professional mourners wailed and keened. Musicians thumped and tootled their dirges. Friends and relatives of the deceased straggled behind the bier. They'd gone for an older extravagance than Fabia Ursa's funeral party had: faces streaked with ashes, tunics ceremonially rent. Under the marks of formal grief, their expressions were set, stunned. Just outside the doorway, one of them said, "But he was so young!"

So, Nicole thought numbly. People could think like that here, too. She resisted an urge to run out and ask what the boy had died of. People did die of things other than pestilence. Young people especially, and children most of all.

She was not reassured. When the procession had passed and faded into the background hum of the city, someone in the street sneezed. She jumped like a startled cat.

Right behind her, Lucius sneezed explosively. Her heart leaped into her throat. She whirled. "Are you all right?" she practically shrieked at him.

When she'd first come to Carnuntum, that concern would have been partly feigned. Not now. Little by little, by almost imperceptible stages, Lucius and Aurelia had become hers. And if one of hers was sneezing—

But he looked at her as if she'd gone demented, and laughed at her expression. "Oh, Mother! I'm fine."

Julia glared at him, and shook her finger under his nose. Which, Nicole happened to notice, had a somewhat dusty look to it. "He was trying to breathe flour," she said. "I saw him grab a pinch."

"Oh, he was, was he?" Nicole said in a dangerous purr. "You did, did you?"

Lucius might be silly, but he wasn't stupid. He recognized the sort of question that meant he should make himself scarce.

He didn't recognize it quite soon enough. Nicole caught him by the arm as he scooted past. Her free hand applied a fundamental lesson to his seat of knowledge. His squawk had more surprise in it than pain. Her second whack remedied the imbalance.

She let him go. He scampered off, not much the worse for wear. He didn't indulge in the tears and histrionics that an American child would have gone in for. Less than a minute later, he was laughing again.

Children were tough little creatures: tougher than Nicole had realized. She was the one who stood as if poleaxed, staring at her own hand. Why in the world had she just done *that?* She never had before. She would have been appalled if she'd thought before she did it. She was worried, that was it. Worried half to death. That worry had magnified her anger at what was, at worst, mild misbehavior.

It didn't seem reason enough. It probably wasn't. But it also probably hadn't been child abuse. Nicole wouldn't have said that before she came to Carnuntum. It was happening again: the Romans she lived among had infected her with their own attitudes.

It was better than being infected with measles, or whatever this new and deadly disease was.

She was still thinking about that when Sextus Longinius Iulus came in and sat at one of the tables near the door. "Let me have a cup of your one-*as* wine, would you, Umma," he said, "and some olives, too, if you please."

When she'd given him what he asked for and he'd paid her, she paused. He looked all right—not wonderful, not happy, but not broken down with grief, either. People who couldn't deal with death wouldn't last long in this world. "How's your son?" she asked.

He spat out an olive pit and drank a swallow of wine. "He seems healthy enough, the gods be praised. Fabia Honorata's looking after him right now."

Nicole suppressed a stab of guilt. She should have gone over there days ago and seen if she could help. But she'd been busy, the tavern took up most of her time, she had her own kids to raise—

No, she thought. Face it. She hadn't gone over because she hadn't known what to say, and she couldn't be bothered with a baby on top of everything else.

She raised an eyebrow at the baby's father. "Fabia Honorata? Not the wet nurse?"

"No, not the wet nurse," Longinius Iulus answered. He did look a little haggard after all. "That's the other reason I came in here. She's sick. It's the new sickness that's been going around, the one that really hits you hard. Gods only know if she'll pull through. I wanted to ask you who nursed Aurelia.

That wasn't so long ago—she might still be in business."

Nicole's first thought was pity. What a life for a woman, going from baby to baby, no more valued for herself than a milk cow, and not too different from one either. Perpetually full and aching breasts, no relief from baby howls and babyshit, and no time off unless she wanted her livelihood to dry up.

Hard on the heels of that came fear. If the wet nurse was down with the pestilence, that meant she'd brought it into the tinker's shop. Even now it might be fighting a still-silent war against his body's defenses. And if that was so, then he was breathing it right into her face.

She didn't want to feel what she felt—it wasn't noble at all. She wanted him to go away. She gave what answer she could, as patiently as she could, considering. "I don't really remember the name of the woman who nursed Aurelia," she said. "It's been a bit of a while, after all. Julia, do you recall?"

Julia came to the rescue as she so often had before, with the ingrained habit of obedience, and a nature that accepted whatever people chose to throw at her. "Wasn't that Velina, the wet nurse who used to live on the other side of the place where the town council meets?" she said. "Didn't she and her husband move back to Vindobona last year, to be with his kin?"

"Yes, she did. I remember that," Longinius Iulus said. Nicole nodded and hoped her face didn't look too blankly foolish. She'd had to do that again and again when pretending to recall things Umma certainly would have remembered. Sooner or later, someone was going to trip her up over it.

Not today. Please God, not tomorrow either, or the day after.

"What will you do now?" she asked Longinius Iulus.

He sighed. "Have to look for somebody else, I suppose," he answered. "I can't feed him myself, though I wish to heaven I could. It'd be a lot easier and cheaper. If Fabia Ursa had lived—" He broke off, took a deep breath, blinked rapidly but held in the tears. "It's the gods' will. Isis' priestess said it, so it must be true."

But it *wasn't* the gods' will. It was plain old ignorance and lack of sanitation. Fabia Ursa needn't have died.

If Nicole had told anyone how antibiotics could cure childbed fever, they'd have thought she was mad. And she couldn't prove that it worked. She knew *that* it worked, but not *why* it worked or *how* to make it work. It had been just the same with the measles vaccine, and with the concept of antisepsis, of touching a woman in labor with absolutely clean hands so that she wouldn't pick up the germs that caused childbed fever. Nobody here believed that such a thing could exist. And she had no way to show them.

If she'd stopped to think at all, before she lived this life, she'd have thought that she could save the world with all the things she knew. But she didn't know anything that really mattered—anything that could *help,* or that anyone would let her use to help.

"I'm sorry," she said, meaning all of it, more than he could ever know.

"I'm sorry, too," Longinius Iulus said. "I miss Fabia."

And yet, even as he said it, and seemed to mean it, his eyes slid toward Julia, who stood at the hand mill grinding grain into flour. Julia couldn't even be conscious of the way the tunic clung to her body as she worked, or how her breasts bounced, big double handfuls that had never been softened or slackened by the bearing or nursing of a baby.

All Nicole's sympathy for him evaporated. Was that why he missed Fabia Ursa: because she was available whenever he wanted a stroke? Did he think he could go upstairs with Julia, someday when Nicole wasn't around to say no?

Nicole scowled. She was angry at him, but at herself too. He'd loved his wife—he'd worn it on his face when he looked at her, and in his voice when he spoke of her. If he was still a normal man, if he still could want what a woman gave, who was she to fault him for it? Nicole hadn't exactly shut herself down when Frank walked out, either.

I didn't go looking for a prostitute, she thought starchily.

But there'd been that fast-talking son of a bitch who'd made all that noise about being the youngest man in his firm to make senior partner, except of course he hadn't made it *yet,* but everybody knew it was just a matter of time. She couldn't even remember his name. She'd let him talk her into bed just to prove that she could still get a man; that a man could still want her, even if Frank had traded her in on a younger model. Compared to that, a straightforward transaction with a whore didn't look quite so bad.

At long last Longinius Iulus finished his wine. "Thanks, Umma," he said, wiping his mouth on the sleeve of his tunic. "I'll head over to the market square, I guess. Either I'll find a wet nurse there who can take on another baby, or else I'll find somebody who knows one."

"Ask at Sextus Viridius' stall," Julia said. "I heard one of his daughters might be setting up as a wet nurse, since her husband walked out on her and left her with a newborn baby."

Longinius Iulus looked ready to kiss her, but either he was too shy or he had more self-control than Nicole might have credited him with. "I'll try that," he said. "Thank you, Julia."

She smiled. He waved impartially at them both, but mostly at Julia, and left in rather better spirits than Nicole might have expected.

She let out a long sigh. Part of it was sympathy for the tinker's plight. The rest was a desire to rid her lungs of as much of the air he'd breathed at her as she could.

Julia echoed her sigh. "He's having a hard time," she said. "First his wife, now his baby's nurse—you'd think he'd done some god a bad turn. And yet he's such a nice man. If I had any luck to spare, I'd give it to him."

"Would you?" Nicole said slowly.

Julia nodded. Her eyes were wide and earnest. What was she thinking of, taking Longinius Iulus upstairs as a personal act of charity?

Nicole actually caught herself thinking, *Maybe, the next time he comes and the place isn't busy, I'll find myself an errand to run. Just once. As a gift to him.* She wasn't even particularly shocked to catch herself at it. Julia wasn't being coerced. She honestly wanted to do something for him, and that something was all the gift she had to give. He'd be happy. She'd be happy. Nicole could live with it, if she had to.

On the day when Julius Rufus was due for his regular beer delivery, he showed up as he always did, leading a small and tottery donkey with four large barrels of sour beer strapped to its back. Nicole caught sight of them outside the tavern, in between one customer going out and another coming in, and reached the door in time to see him unfasten one of the barrels from its cat's cradle of leather lashings and ease it to the ground. He tipped it on its side and rolled it into the tavern. She had to jump aside or it would have rolled over her toe.

"Good day, Mistress Umma," he said as he always did. "Good thing my next stop is close by, or poor old Midas here would get all lopsided." He laughed, but he wasn't his usual hearty self. He looked as worn as his joke, and his cheeks were flushed. He heaved the barrel up on its end beside the bar, and leaned there for a moment to get his breath back. "Let me have a cup of your two-*as* wine, would you? Gods, it's hot today."

Nicole hadn't particularly noticed. After Indianapolis and especially after L.A., none of the summer weather she'd seen in Carnuntum struck her as anything more than warm. A lot of it, today included, didn't even measure up to that.

She slipped past him behind the bar and dipped up his cup of wine. When she turned to bring it to him, he'd sunk down onto a stool. He was scratching the side of his neck between the edge of his beard and the neck opening for his tunic, and frowning. "Has something bitten me there?" he asked her. "It itches."

Nicole peered at the reddened skin. It wasn't just the scratching that had turned it that angry shade. "It doesn't look like a bite," she said. "It looks more like some kind of a . . . rash." She swallowed. She felt as if she'd just done a one-and-a-half gainer into a dry pool. Yes, it looked like a rash. The kind of rash that went with the measles. She'd seen it at several rows' distance in the amphitheater, and marked the resemblance. Now, from close up, there was no mistaking it.

Her thoughts must have shown in her face. Or maybe Julius Rufus had been coughing and sneezing for the past three or four days, and all the while done his best to tell himself he was fine, he was just coming down with a cold. As his eyes met hers, they went wide. He knew what a rash could mean. His voice lowered to a whisper. "Is it the pestilence?"

"I don't know," she lied—a white lie, she told herself. She debated the next thing, but really, if she was going to get it, she would; she couldn't be any more exposed than she had been by now. And wasn't measles one of the diseases that was contagious before the symptoms showed? Whether it was or it wasn't, the damage was done by now. As if he were a sick child, she said, "Here. Let me feel your forehead."

Obediently, he raised his head and tilted it back. Nicole laid her palm on his forehead. Even before she touched him, she felt the heat radiating from his skin. She had to will herself not to jerk away in alarm. God, he was hot. 104 degrees? 105? 106? She couldn't tell, not exactly. She hadn't felt that kind of fever often enough to gauge the temperature. She didn't ever want to again, either. He was burning up.

"Have I got a fever?" he asked.

She felt the hysterical laughter rising, but she had a little control left. She didn't let it out. Why on earth hadn't he passed out right there in front of her, as the woman in the amphitheater had done?

She answered him, because she had to say something, and he was waiting. "Yes," she said. "You are pretty warm." *And the Danube is damp, and the sun is bright, and . . .* As surreptitiously as she could, she wiped her hand on the coarse wool of her tunic. Too late, of course. Much too late. But she couldn't stop herself. "Maybe you shouldn't deliver the rest of your beer this morning," she said as tactfully as she could. "Maybe you should go home and lie down."

He shook his head, and wobbled when he did it, so that he almost fell off the stool. "Oh, no; Mistress Umma. Even if it is the pestilence, I can't do that. Too much work to do. Besides, I hear it kills you if you're lying down, same as if you're standing up. Got to keep going." He shook his head again, this time vaguely, as if he didn't know where he was going even if he was going there.

Nicole wanted to shake him, but if she did, she'd knock him clean over. There wasn't anybody around to pick him up, either. One way and another, anybody who'd been in the tavern had managed to make himself scarce. Julia was nowhere in evidence, nor the kids either. She was alone with a very, and perhaps deathly, ill man.

She did what she could, which was damned little. "If you rest, you'll be more able to fight off the disease," she said.

"I can't help it," he said with the kind of mulishness she'd seen before in people too ill to think straight. "I've got to go on." It took him two tries before he could stand up. "Thank you for the wine." He'd had only the one cup, but he staggered like a man far gone. Which he was—but not in wine.

Nicole stayed where she was as he made his listing, swaying way to the door. She couldn't make herself move, still less lend him a hand. A kind of horror held her rooted, a sick fascination. *This is what death looks like,* a small voice said in the corner of her mind.

The donkey waited patiently under its somewhat lightened burden. Julius Rufus took its leadrope with something that, at a distance and in bad light, might have been taken for his usual briskness. The donkey, well habituated to its rounds, took a step forward. Julius Rufus crumpled to the ground, right there in the middle of the street. The donkey stopped and stood, head low, ears drooping. Very well, its stance said. If one step was all it needed to take, then one step it would be.

Nicole couldn't seem to take her eyes off the fallen man till a shadow fell across his body. Gaius Calidius Severus stood there, staring down. He must have been watching from inside the dyer's shop.

Something about him, maybe just his presence, freed Nicole. She could move, could make her way out of the tavern and stand on the doorstep while an oxcart rattled and creaked its way down the street. The man in it caught her eye as he came closer. His expression was blankly hostile, the expression of a driver on a California freeway, going where he was going and God help anyone who got in his way. But oxcarts being what they were, wide open and dead slow, he had time to bellow at her as he came on: "Get that cursed drunk out of the road, lady, or I'll roll right over him."

"He's not drunk, he's sick, and you'll be a lot sicker if you try running over him," Nicole snapped—with no little satisfaction. On the freeway, you never got to answer back, or if you tried, you got shot.

She was threatening the drover in fine L.A. fashion: Don't Tread On Me, and I'll clobber you if you try. But he didn't get the nuances. His ox had brought him within peering distance of the fallen man. "Gods and goddesses," he said, "he's got the pestilence!" He plied his stick on the ox with ferocious vigor. The ox bent its head and pressed on at half a mile an hour instead of a quarter, steering as wide around the crumpled body as it could. Nicole didn't see it slacken, but the drover redoubled his efforts once he'd passed the obstacle. The ox lowed in protest. The cart's axle squeaked and groaned. The man in it looked over his shoulder till the street bent and took him out of sight, as if the death in the street could follow him, and be beaten off if it came too close.

Gaius Calidius Severus stood watching him go, just as Nicole had done. When he was gone, the young dyer turned back to Nicole. "*Has* he got the pestilence, Umma?" he asked.

"Yes," Nicole answered. She didn't try to soften it for him. Maybe she should have. He was her lover's son, after all. But right at the moment, she had no softness in her. She rolled Julius Rufus onto his back, got a grip on his armpits, and set about dragging him back toward the tavern.

"Here," Gaius Calidius Severus said, "you don't need to do that all by yourself." He got hold of Julius Rufus' ankles and lifted while she dragged. Between the two of them, they carried the sick man into the tavern.

Nicole was more than glad of the help, but she wished Gaius Calidius Severus hadn't exposed himself to the disease. She also wished she hadn't exposed herself, but it had been too late to worry about that since Julius Rufus rolled her barrel of beer into the tavern.

She eased the unconscious brewer down next to the wall by the door, where no one would step on him, and thanked her helper with honest gratitude. He blushed a bit and shuffled his feet. "Any time," he said. "There was too much of him for you to haul by yourself, I could see that. Mithras teaches that a man shouldn't just think what's right: he should *do* what's right."

Nicole liked that. Yet Mithraism, from all she'd heard, had no place for women.

She shrugged. This was hardly the time to worry about the finer points of religious doctrine.

Julia was back in the tavern from wherever she'd been: women's day at the baths, from the look and smell of her. The place was empty of customers, a stroke of good luck for which Nicole was deeply grateful.

Julia's eyes were a little too wide, her stare a little too fixed. But she had wits enough not to burst out in hysteria. Nicole brought her to order with a sharp word. "Julia—do you know where Julius Rufus has his brewery?"

"I—think so," Julia answered hesitantly.

"I do," Gaius Calidius Severus said. "I know just where it is. Do you want me to take the donkey back and let his family know he's—indisposed?"

"Would you?" Nicole said. And had to add: "Will your father mind if you take so much time off from work?"

"Not if I'm doing a favor for you," he answered. That flustered her more than she might have expected. Of course he knew what was going on. There couldn't be much of anybody who didn't.

Her nod was sharper than his comment deserved. He bobbed his own head by way of reply, with no irony that she could discern, and went to take charge of the donkey.

"He's very nice," Julia said. "A little too young, but very nice."

She hadn't thought he was too young when she went upstairs with him on the day of her manumission. Nicole found she'd come to forgive him that, or most of it. You really couldn't expect a man that young not to think with his crotch. It was like expecting a cock not to crow at sunrise: you could hope for it, even pray for it, but it wasn't bloody likely.

Lucius and Aurelia came tearing in from some game out back, and stopped short to stare at Julius Rufus. They didn't know or care enough to be scared, as Julia was. "What's wrong with him?" Aurelia wanted to know. But, tavernkeeper's daughter that she was, she found a logical answer to her own question: "Is he too drunk to go home?"

"No," Nicole said flatly. "I'm afraid he's got the pestilence."

The rash was coming out on his cheeks and forehead, developing almost like Polaroid film. Aurelia and Lucius had seen plenty of drunks at the tavern, but a man with the pestilence was new and therefore interesting. They edged closer for a better look.

Nicole caught them both with a braced arm. Lucius stopped, but Aurelia pushed against her, scowling. Aurelia never liked to be thwarted.

Nicole didn't, right now, give a damn what Aurelia liked or didn't like. "You stay back," she said to the two of them, sternly enough that she hoped they'd listen. "This is a bad sickness. You can get it if he just breathes on you. Stay away from him."

"But you brought him inside," Lucius pointed out. "You and Calidius carried him. Does that mean you'll get the pestilence, too?"

"I hope not," Nicole answered, three of the most sincere words she'd ever spoken.

While she was distracted with the kids, a customer came briskly in. He glanced at Julius Rufus, there on the floor, and raised his eyebrows. "He's got it, has he?" He passed the sick man without evident qualm and sat at a table near the middle of the tavern. "A cup of your two-*as* wine," he said, "and some bread and oil."

Julia served him with a kind of numbed efficiency. While she did that, the kids slipped free of Nicole's tiring grasp, but didn't try to get any closer to the sick man. They did hover, big-eyed, clearly waiting for him to do something— bleed, maybe, or vomit spectacularly, or die.

The customer ate, drank. He paid for his order in exact change, and walked out. Either he was as phlegmatic a man as Nicole had met, or he was just plain callous. Or maybe he was both at once.

Nicole had just scrambled herself together and taken thought for spelling Julia at the bar, when Julius Rufus let out a small sigh. A second or two later, Lucius wrinkled his nose. "I think he's gone and shit himself," he said matter-of-factly.

The odor that wafted toward Nicole was unmistakable. She felt her own nose wrinkle, and her gorge start to rise. *Damn,* she thought as she watched a wet spot spread on the front of Julius Rufus' tunic. "He's wet himself, too," she said.

Lucius snickered. "Just like a baby."

If he'd been within Nicole's reach, she might have slapped him silly. The impulse was so strong it scared her. "It's not funny," she said when she could trust her voice. "He's not doing it on purpose." She turned to Julia, who was hanging about as if she couldn't tear herself away. "Fetch me some damp rags, will you? I can't leave him lying here in his own filth." Cleaning him was the last thing she wanted to do, but what choice did she have? Unlike Julia, she'd already touched him, already had his breath in her face. She knew she was exposed to the pestilence; she didn't know whether the freedwoman was. Best not to make it a sure thing.

She swallowed the sour taste of bile, and breathed shallowly so as not to take in more of the combined reek of ammonia and ripe shit. His mouth had fallen open. His eyes were open, too, wide and staring. A moment after she realized she didn't see him blinking, she noticed she didn't hear him breathing.

She dropped the dripping rags and snatched his wrist. It was hot, as hot as his forehead had been—maybe hotter. Her finger found the spot outside the tendons, below the fleshy swell at the base of the thumb.

Nothing.

She bore down on the spot, the pulse-spot, where she should feel the beating of his heart. The only pulse she felt was her own. She pressed her palm to the left side of his chest. Nothing there, either. Nothing at all.

"He's dead," she said in dull wonder.

"I was afraid of that," Julia said. "When his bowels let go . . . that happens, you know. Every time."

Lucius and Aurelia stared more avidly than ever. A sick man was interesting. A dead one was absolutely riveting.

Gaius Calidius Severus came back while Nicole was still trying to figure out what to do, bringing with him a woman about Julius Rufus' age and two young men who strongly resembled the brewer. They also had the donkey, from which they'd removed the barrels. Obviously, they'd intended to pack the unconscious man on the donkey's back, and get him home more easily than if they'd had to carry him.

Nicole had been dreading the moment when she had to tell them the man was dead. It was just as bad as she'd imagined. The men began to bellow, the woman to shriek and wail. "What will we do without him?" she shrilled, over and over. "What are we supposed to *do?*"

Nicole could think of just one thing. She retreated to the bar and pulled out a toppling pile of cups, and filled them pretty much anyhow. Alcohol was the only tranquilizer the Romans knew. She administered it liberally.

They didn't thank her for it, or pay her either, but they drank it down. It quieted them somewhat, though the woman couldn't stop asking what she was supposed to do. *Cope,* Nicole wanted to snap at her, but refrained.

Still sniveling and weeping, Julius Rufus' two sons took up his body and draped it over the donkey's back. It slipped and slid bonelessly; they had to tie it in place. Still without a word of thanks, they set off on their sad journey home, or more likely to the undertaker's.

People stared as they made their slow way down the street. The cries of Julius Rufus' widow faded with distance, and sank into silence.

"Times will be hard for them now," Gaius Calidius Severus said as he paused in the doorway on his way back to work. "I remember how things were when Mother died. They weren't much different for you, were they, when you lost your husband?"

How would I know? Nicole almost asked, but caught herself in time. Instead, she said, "Times will be hard for the whole city now, if this pestilence is as bad as they say."

"I'm afraid it's worse," Gaius Calidius Severus murmured, but he managed a smile at Nicole.

To her amazement, she found a smile in return. "Thank you for your help, Gaius," she said. "It was very, very kind of you."

She'd been a bit daring in calling her lover's grown son by his praenomen, but he didn't protest. He dipped his head to her, that was all, and went quickly across the street.

Nicole stayed by the door, staring at the space where he had been. It was better than what she wanted to stare at, which was the place where the brewer had collapsed.

She hadn't known how long she stood there, until Julia asked, "Are you all right, Mistress?"

"No, I'm not all right," Nicole said, "but I'm not sick, either, if that's what you mean."

Julia didn't look too greatly reassured. Nicole didn't have any reassurance to give her. All she had had drained away when she looked into Julius Rufus' face, and saw that he was dead.

If anyone had asked her afterwards, she couldn't have said

how she got through the day. When sunset came at long last, and business slowed and then mercifully stopped, she did something that she'd have been horrified to contemplate, back in West Hills. But in this place and time, it was the only reasonable or rational thing to do. She got quietly and systematically drunk.

14

HARD TIMES THROUGH THE *whole city*. When Nicole had said that to Gaius Calidius Severus, she'd had only an intellectual understanding of what it meant. Over the next month or two, as summer passed into autumn, as sunlight softened and morning mists from the Danube began filling the streets of Carnuntum with fog, she felt the meaning of *hard times* in her belly as well as her head.

In the early days of the pestilence, hardly an hour seemed to go by without the shrieking and moaning of professional mourners, as funeral processions made their somber way out of the city and toward the burial ground. After a while, however, the sounds of formal lamentation, almost as formal as the Mass, began to diminish.

Ofanius Valens explained that to Nicole when he stopped by for breakfast one morning. "From what I hear," he said, "so many of the mourners are dead, the rest can't come close to keeping up with all the funerals."

"That's horrible," Nicole said.

"It's not good," he conceded, taking an unenthusiastic mouthful of bread and oil. "My family's been lucky so far, the gods be praised. I've only got one cousin down with it, and she doesn't look like dying. If you make it through the rash, they say, you're likely to get better, and she's done that. Half her hair fell out, and she's peeling like the worst case of sunburn you ever saw, but she's still with us. How about your kin, Umma?"

"I don't know," she said. "I haven't heard a word." And she wouldn't have much cared if she had, she thought but didn't add. Whatever Umma thought of her relatives, Nicole had no earthly use for any of them.

Ofanius Valens looked shocked. Everyone in Carnuntum was shocked when someone failed to keep minutest track of anything that had to do with family. But, after a moment, his face cleared. "That's right." He nodded as he reminded himself. "You had that squabble with them after you man-umitted Julia. Still haven't made it up, eh?"

Nicole shook her head. "I'm the bad apple in the barrel, as far as they're concerned." She straightened. "They can think whatever they please, for all of me. I'll get along just fine."

"You certainly seem to be getting along." Ofanius Valens spoke with no small wonder. "I've known other people who fought with their families. Most of them act like fish hauled out of the Ister"—by which he meant the Danube. He imitated a fish out of water with such pop-eyed aplomb, Nicole couldn't help laughing.

Julia laughed, too. So did Lucius, who'd come downstairs while Ofanius Valens was eating. Nicole said, "It's good to hear people laughing. Not much of that sound in the city these days."

"Not much reason for it these days," Ofanius Valens said. "Let's see what we can do about it." He aimed his dead-fish stare at Lucius, who broke up in giggles.

Julia started to laugh again. It was like a yawn: contagious. Nicole caught herself just as Julia's eye caught hers. Their laughter died. They'd been startled into it the first time. They couldn't invoke it with conscious effort. Lucky Lucius, to be so young and so untroubled.

"Off I go," Ofanius Valens said. "The gods grant you all good health." He made one more fish-face at Lucius, who crowed with delight, nodded to Nicole, and blew Julia a kiss.

She blew one back. Whistling a jaunty tune, he went on his way.

"He's a nice man," Lucius said.

"He *is* nice," Julia said with the hint of a sigh. She meant something—several different somethings—other than what Lucius did. Nicole gave her a sharp look, which she ignored. Julia thought with her body first and her mind definitely second.

Business that morning was brisk. *Asses, dupondii, sesterces,* even a couple of silver *denarii* clanked into the cash box. Nicole was pleased, but not so pleased as she might have been. Every time somebody coughed, every time somebody sneezed, she jumped. People had been coughing and sneezing in the tavern ever since she'd come to Carnuntum, and no doubt for many years before that. Now she wondered if each cough and sneeze meant a case of pestilence brewing—and if viruses were flying her way, or toward her children, or toward Julia.

A little before noon, Brigomarus came into the tavern. "Uncle Brigo!" Lucius and Aurelia cried out in delight. Nicole, on the other hand, was somewhat less than delighted to see Umma's brother. By the way he stood, as if he was only there under duress, and by his cold nod, he wasn't delighted to see her, either.

"How are you?" he asked politely enough, and then the question that seemed more important in Carnuntum than any other: "Have you been well?"

Nicole could answer that, if only to meet politeness with politeness. "Yes, all of us here have been fine, thank heaven," she said. "And you?"

"I'm as you see. If I'd caught this horror of a disease, I wouldn't be up and about." Brigomarus took a deep breath, nerving himself for what he had to say next. "Mother is down with it. I don't know what her chances are. If I had to guess, I'd say they weren't good. She still has her wits about her, and she wants to see you. Ila didn't even want to let you know, but I said I would do it. Just because you wronged the family doesn't mean we have any business wronging you."

"I had every right to do what I did, and I was right to do it," Nicole said stiffly.

"You're—" Umma's brother checked himself. "Never mind. I didn't come here to start the quarrel over again. Will you come see Mother or not?" *To hell with you if you don't,* his tone and posture plainly said.

A deathbed visit to Atpomara, Umma's disagreeable mother, was about the last thing Nicole wanted. Visiting any-body who was likely to give her the pestilence didn't rank high on her list, either. But, things being as they were, she didn't see that she had a choice. She was wearing Umma's body. She had to take on at least the bare minimum of Umma's obligations. "I'll come," she said.

"Well, good." Brigomarus sounded pleasantly surprised, as if he'd made the call expecting to be turned down flat. "Let's go, then."

"Aren't you going to stay and play, Uncle Brigo?" Aurelia asked plaintively.

"I can't," he told her with more gentleness than Nicole might have expected. "Your grandmother is sick, and she wants to see your mother."

"Is she going to die?" Lucius asked. In California, a child would have asked the question in tones of disbelief. Lucius merely sounded curious. He knew people died. In Carnuntum, nobody could help knowing it.

"That's in the hands of the gods," Brigomarus said. "She wants to see your mother. We have to go."

The children didn't beg to go with them, which Nicole found somewhat odd. She'd thought Lucius might, at least. But he stood with his sister and watched them go. They were both unusually quiet, unusually wide-eyed. They'd seen too much death, she thought. They didn't need to see any more.

Nicole followed Umma's brother out of the tavern. He strode along for a while with his head down, until they both had to wait as a funeral procession went past. Whoever the deceased was, he'd been important; most of the mourners wore togas, not tunics. Instead of lying on a bier, the corpse was carried in a sedan chair, so that he surveyed the city with his unseeing eyes. A dozen musicians brought up the rear of the procession, making a tremendous racket.

Nicole resisted the urge to clap her hands over her ears. When the procession had passed, while her ears were still ringing with the noise, Brigomarus sighed. "In times like this, I don't want to quarrel with anyone in my family. Who knows what will happen tomorrow?"

"Nobody," Nicole answered. That was true in California, too, but seemed truer in Carnuntum. It was, also, she realized a little more slowly than she should have, an offer of truce. "All right, Brigomarus," she said. "I won't argue with anyone if no one argues with me."

He pursed his lips. He might have been expecting more, though what else he could want, she couldn't imagine. Then he nodded. "That will have to do."

Damn him, she thought in a rise of temper. She was being generous, and he made her generosity seem a paltry thing.

She made herself relax. However grudging his acceptance, nevertheless, he had accepted the gift. It would, as he'd said, have to do.

Two streets farther on, another funeral procession went past. This one delayed Nicole and Brigomarus less than a minute. Two shrouded corpses, one large, one small, lay side by side on the bier. A woman and a youth on whose cheeks the down was just beginning to darken paced behind it. Both of them wore the blank, car-wreck look of sudden disaster. A few friends and relatives followed them. They had no musicians. Maybe they couldn't afford any; they looked poor. Maybe the rich man's family had hired all the musicians in town for his send-off. And maybe, too, there weren't so many healthy musicians left to hire.

The bereaved woman sneezed several times, violently, and wiped her nose on the sleeve of her tunic. Her son coughed rackingly and continuously, as if he had no power to stop.

"They're coming down with it, too," Brigomarus said

bleakly. People in the city hadn't needed long to recognize the early signs of the pestilence.

"Not everyone who gets it dies from it," Nicole said. "I've heard of people getting better." A couple of heartbeats after she should have, she added, "I hope Mother will be one of them."

Brigomarus noticed the lapse. He opened his mouth as if to call her on it, then sighed instead. She glared at him. He glared back. They walked side by side, each obviously wishing the other were a hundred miles away.

He led her down a street not too much different from the one Nicole herself lived on, to a combination house and shop that differed from her own only in having a narrow porch supported by half a dozen undistinguished columns. They weren't even well made; in fact, they looked as if they'd been hacked out of limestone with a blunt chisel. They reminded her irresistibly of the sort of house one found in tackier parts of L.A., cheap pop-up housing designed for people with large pretensions and relatively small bank accounts: plastic marble and gold-painted faucets, and indications of cut corners in closets and under sinks. The plastic cracked inside of a year, and the paint flaked off the faucets, but they got their point across.

Brigomarus sounded just like the owner of one of those as he declared, "Ila and Marcus Flavius Probus, now—*they* have a proper Roman façade."

It was a sore temptation, but she didn't laugh in his face. She might as well have been living in a trailer park for all the status she could claim, and he was making sure she knew it. She didn't say what she was thinking, either, which was that after meeting the inhabitants, she'd expected a noble villa, and not this cheap excuse for a house. At least Umma's tavern was honestly downscale.

She looked him in the eye, and was gratified when he looked away. "Take me in to Mother," she said with something that might, just possibly, have been taken for gentleness.

He obeyed her, somewhat to her surprise, and without

quibbling, either. Had she shocked him with her display of backbone? She hoped so.

The nobly named Marcus Flavius Probus, she saw as Brigomarus led her past the ill-made pillars, was nothing more or less than a woodworker. In West Hills he'd have been much admired: handcrafted this, that, and the other was all the rage. In Carnuntum he was an artisan, which set him considerably below the patrician he liked to pretend to be.

She didn't like him any better for it, at all, but it was an honest pleasure to walk into a room that smelled of clean new wood, fresh lumber and sawdust, and the sweet subtle odor of wax that was rubbed into the finished article. She took the first voluntary deep breath she'd taken in Carnuntum, and let it out again.

Umma's brother-in-law crouched in a patch of sunlight, dressed in a tunic like anybody else, no toga in sight. He was pounding a peg into the end of a table leg. The table itself waited for the leg, leaning against a wall nearby.

She watched him with some interest. Roman carpentry, she'd noticed, used lots of pegs and very few nails. Nails here were made one by one, by hand, and were ridiculously expensive.

As she stood watching and breathing the scent of sawdust, another odor crept in under it. It wasn't just the reek of the city. It was closer, and subtly fouler: a sickroom odor that had raised her hackles even before she was conscious of its existence. She defined it even as she once more breathed shallowly to avoid it—a mixture of full chamber pot and sour sweat.

Brigomarus asked the question that Nicole probably should have: "How is she?"

"About the same," Flavius Probus answered. He didn't quite look at Nicole, or acknowledge her, but he said, "So she decided to come, did she?"

Brigomarus nodded. Nicole rode over anything he would have said. "Yes, I'm here, and I'm quite capable of speaking for myself."

Umma's brother-in-law snapped erect, as if he'd been

slapped. Then Nicole saw the pompous ass who'd acted as
if the tavern wasn't good enough for him, and heard him,
too. "I am not accustomed to being addressed in that particular tone, least of all by a woman."

Nicole didn't laugh, though she was sorely tempted.
"Aren't you?" she said. "Then maybe it's time you learned.
There's this thing called politeness. Have you ever heard of
it?"

Even after his earlier encounter with her, he obviously
hadn't expected quite that degree of independence. Brigomarus, who'd seen rather more of her, sighed and shrugged.
"She's like that these days," he said. "Short of hauling her
out and horsewhipping her, there's not a whole lot we can
do about it." He paused, shook his head, went on in a slightly
different tone. "Still. Mother asked to see her, and she's not
likely to get another chance."

Flavius Probus nodded curtly, again without acknowledg-
ing Nicole, and bent again to his table leg. His work was
meticulous, his hands deft and skilled, as if the pretentious
idiot who lived in his head bore no relation to the craftsman
in his hands.

They'd been dismissed. Nicole might have made an issue
of it, but Brigomarus was headed toward the stairs. She almost didn't follow. Even needling Flavius Probus was preferable to paying a last visit to someone else's mother. But
the sooner she got it over with, the sooner she was out of
there and back in the tavern that, for better or worse, she'd
come to think of as home.

The stairway was less rickety than the one she used every
day. Marcus Flavius Probus kept it in good repair. The hallway at the top, however, was just like the one in her house,
narrow and malodorous and nearly pitch-dark. Aside from
its porch and its wretched columns, this building was no
fancier than her own.

Brigomarus turned into the first door on the right-hand side
of the hall, the one that corresponded with Nicole's in the
tavern. The master bedroom, then? Interesting, she thought,
that the old woman had it. Though not at all surprising.

While she paused in the hallway, letting her eyes adjust to the brighter light within, she heard Brigomarus say, "Here she is, Mother. She came after all, as you asked." His voice had the odd, uncomfortable gentleness that people often put on in front of the sick.

The sickroom reek was stronger here. Nicole nearly gagged on it as she stepped into the bedroom. Umma's sister was perched on a stool by the bed on which her mother lay. Ila favored Nicole with a venomous look and a sarcastic, "So good of you to join us."

It was going to be a united front, Nicole could see. Some part of her knew she should make some effort to smooth things over—but to do that, she'd have to undo Julia's manumission. And that wasn't possible.

She settled for a long, cold glare at Ila, and a silence that, she hoped, said more than words. Then she forgot Umma's sister. The woman huddled in the bed, the woman who'd given birth to Umma, the woman who Nicole thought was an ancestor of her own, looked more nearly dead than alive. Atpomara's skin clung like parchment to her bones; the fever had boiled most of the water from her flesh. Along her forehead and cheek, the rash that marked the pestilence was red as a burn.

But, whereas Julius Rufus had died almost at once when the fever exploded in him, Umma's mother still clung to life, still had some part of her wits about her. She stretched a clawlike finger toward Nicole. Her eyes bored into—bored through—the woman who inhabited her daughter's body. "You are the cuckoo's egg." Her voice was a dry rasp. "Cuckoo's egg," she repeated.

"Ungrateful daughter, ungrateful sister," Ila hissed from beside her.

Nicole hardly heard. She stared at the woman who had given birth to the body she now inhabited. What did Atpomara mean? Just that Nicole was ungrateful, as Ila said? Or could she somehow sense that a stranger's spirit now dwelt in Umma's body? Were the fever and perhaps the approach of death letting her own spirit roam wider than it might have otherwise?

"Have a care, cuckoo's egg," Atpomara said. "If you and your own eggs fall, if the shells break before you hatch—" She had to stop; a paroxysm of coughing wracked her.

"Her wits are wandering," Brigomarus murmured to Ila, who nodded. Neither of them spoke to Nicole.

She didn't mind. She didn't want to speak to them, either. She didn't want to be here at all. She hoped Brigomarus was right: she hoped Atpomara's wits were wandering. If they weren't, the dying woman's words made sense—disturbing sense.

Almost since the day she'd come to Carnuntum, Nicole had believed Umma was a distant ancestor of hers. If Umma died of the pestilence, and if Lucius and Aurelia—one of them, at least, also an ancestor, difficult as it was to believe of so young a child—also died of the pestilence . . . where did that leave Nicole Gunther of Indianapolis, who would marry Frank Perrin and live to regret it?

Nowhere?

Umma's mother seemed to gather herself. Her hand rose again, finger stabbing at Nicole. "Go back," she rasped. "I am done. Go back." Did she mean, *Go back to the tavern?* Did she mean, *Go back to Los Angeles and the end of the second millennium?*

It was like a blow in the solar plexus. Nicole actually gasped. Go *back?* Back to Los Angeles? God; if only she knew the way. The past she'd dreamt of, wished for so desperately, prayed for till she found herself in it, was nothing like what she had imagined. It was crammed full of ignorance and drudgery, filth, superstition, disease and brutality and more sheer blatant sexism than she'd ever thought possible. In California, she'd been oh so sure that her glass was half empty. Now she saw, with painful clarity, that it had been more, much more, than half full.

But she was not in California. She was in Carnuntum, with only a tiny splash of water—and polluted water, at that—in the bottom of her glass.

"Why are you still standing there?" Ila snapped at her. "Didn't you hear Mother? She doesn't want you here anymore. I never wanted you here."

Nicole looked at this woman, this stranger who was her own, if distant, kin. She saw nothing there that she could relate to. And from the look and sound of it, this wasn't new hostility. It was much older than Nicole's presence here, and than Nicole's freeing of a slave. Umma hadn't received any better treatment than Nicole was getting, nor ever had.

"Sweetheart," Nicole said for both of them, "the sooner I leave your sour face behind, the happier I'll be."

She'd guessed right about Ila: the woman could dish it out wholesale, but she couldn't take it. The splutters were utterly gratifying. They followed her all the way out of the room and down the stairs.

And there stood the other half of the act, even less witty than his wife. "Good riddance," he growled to the table leg that he was fitting to its table. Nicole started to flip him off, but she hadn't ever seen the one-fingered peace sign here. She replaced it with the two-fingered gesture a muleteer had given an oxcart driver in front of the tavern a day or two before.

Flavius Probus staggered back as if she'd struck him a physical blow. "Don't you put the evil eye on me," he gasped. "Don't you dare!"

He was white as a sheet. He really did believe she could do it. It wasn't nice of her at all, and it might blow up in her face later as family quarrels had a way of doing, but she didn't care. It felt *good* to scare the spit out of that pompous ass and his bitch of a wife.

She was smiling as she turned back toward the tavern. Brigomarus hadn't followed. None of them had. Were they all that superstitious? Or were they just as glad to be shut of her as she was of them?

She walked slowly, with frequent glances about her. Ila and her husband lived in one of the mazes that made Carnuntum a warren between the main streets of its grid. Nicole had

paid close attention to the route Brigomarus took once he
left the grid, or thought she had. But when she should have
been turning back onto one of those main streets for an easy
walk home, she found herself in a twisting alley instead.

The alley was deserted except for a skinny young man in
a threadbare tunic of no color in particular. He had a lump
of charcoal in his hand, and was scribbling on a wall with
it. At the sound of her step, he whipped about. His face was
as thin as the rest of him, set with a pair of enormous eyes.
They fixed on her, and held her rooted.

In Los Angeles, a meeting with a tagger could be dangerous. In Carnuntum . . .

The young man flung down the charcoal and bolted as if
the whole nation of barbarians were on his tail. She'd never
seen anybody run so fast.

He was scared right out of his wits. Nicole couldn't imagine why. If the penalties for writing graffiti were that severe,
surely there wouldn't be any graffiti—and the walls of Carnuntum were covered with scribbles and scrawls and amateur
art.

She moved closer to see what he'd written that was so
dangerous. *I am the resurrection and the life,* she read. *He
who believes in me, even if he should die, will live. Everyone
who lives and believes in me shall not die, not ever.* The
simple Latin lacked the flavor of the English Bible she knew,
but that text was unmistakable. Even if it hadn't been, the
young man had drawn a cross on one side of the passage
and on the other a two-stroke fish—◁—like those she'd
seen in gold plastic mounted on car bumpers.

Nicole frowned. The message seemed perfectly harmless—
until she remembered what people in Carnuntum thought of
Christians. That young man had taken his life in his hands
to scribble the graffito. If she'd recognized him, if she'd
raised a hue and cry here, or given his name to the town
council . . .

If she'd done that, maybe fat Faustinianus, at some future
beast show, would have announced the just and proper execution of So-and-So, convicted of the heinous crime of

Christianity. Lions? It was always lions in the Sunday-school stories. From what she'd seen with Calidius Severus, bears or wolves would do as well.

She left the alleyway a little too quickly, as if someone could guess that she too, in the spirit, was born and raised a Christian. Foolish fear; a Christian in the world she came from was as solid a citizen as a pagan here.

Still, she was glad to leave that wall behind, and gladder yet to find that the alley opened onto a street, which opened onto one of the long, straight main avenues. That one, she recognized. She was deeply relieved to see no sign of the young Christian with the extraordinary turn of speed.

Titus Calidius Severus was in the tavern, eating walnuts, and now and then tossing bits of shell at Lucius, who thought it was great sport. He had a cup of wine in front of him, from which he'd clearly been sipping. "How's your mother?" he and Julia asked in the same breath.

She's not my mother! Nicole knew better than to say. She mustered a sigh, and an expression that, if not devastated, was at least grave. "She's got it, no question. Maybe she'll get better. Maybe—" She shrugged.

Calidius Severus nodded in evident sympathy. "Don't say it. That way you won't have words of evil omen on your conscience if—" He didn't say it, either.

"Get me a cup of the one-*as*, would you, Julia?" Nicole sat at the table with the fuller and dyer. He set a hand on her shoulder, reassuringly, just for a moment, then let it drop. She was more comforted than she might have expected, and surprised, because she hadn't expected to need comfort. When Julia brought the wine, she emptied half the cup in a long, dizzying swallow.

Her trouble wasn't what they had to be thinking. She felt nothing for the loss of a mother she'd never known, who'd never been hers. Atpomara was a horrible old woman, rude and high-handed, with not a jot of compassion in her. Nicole hated her guts.

The wine didn't dim the thing that bothered her. She couldn't forget what Atpomara had said. She couldn't make herself believe the woman had been out of her head from fever, either, however much she wanted to believe just that.

And there wasn't a single person she could talk to, whom she trusted enough to share even part of her secret. Titus Calidius Severus would reckon her mad. Or, worse—he might believe her. He'd think her possessed by a demon. Who knew what he might do then? He was a reasonable man, as men went here. But in a situation that went beyond reason, he'd turn on her. He wouldn't be human if he didn't.

In part to break the silence, in part to turn her mind aside from fretting to no useful purpose, she mentioned the Christian she'd surprised. It was stupid, maybe, but it did turn the conversation onto a new track.

"I've seen those scrawls," Julia said. "I didn't know what the words say, but I've seen the fish and the cross. There've been more of them lately than there used to be."

"There have, haven't there?" Titus Calidius Severus said. "I can read the words. Bunch of cursed nonsense, if you ask me. The Jews go on and on about only having one god, so how can that god have a son, especially a son who's a crucified rebel? If you ask me, too many people don't think these things through. Even the Jews can't buy this one."

Nicole had never considered herself religious; if anything, she'd been an agnostic. But this was not just the faith but the culture she'd been raised in, and here was this urine-reeking man with his hands dyed blue to the elbows, dissecting it as if it were just another crazy cult. The nerve he'd struck was almost as painful as the one in her sore tooth.

"If it's all nonsense," she asked him tightly, "why are there more Christian slogans on the walls these days? Doesn't that sound as if more and more people are believing what the Christians say?" She knew it; she had eighteen hundred years of hindsight. Not one of which she could safely claim—but that, for the moment, was beside the point.

"Maybe more people are believing in it," the fuller and dyer answered, "but maybe they aren't. Times are hard, with the pestilence and with the war against the Germans off to the west of here. The world's not a very nice place right

now. When things go bad in this world, it's only natural for
people to worry more about the next one. And if that Christian nonsense were true, it'd be easier to have a happy afterlife as a Christian than any other way I can think of. No
wonder light-minded folks drift that way."

So there, Nicole thought. The annoying thing was that, as
he had a way of doing, Calidius Severus made a lot of sense.
His own Mithraism, for instance, seemed to be for men only,
and especially for soldiers. From what the men at Fabia
Ursa's funeral had said, Isis-worship was a women's cult.
Would Christianity triumph for no better reason than that it
was the religion of the lowest common denominator, the network television of its day?

Whatever the reason, she knew Christianity had triumphed—would triumph. Did Calidius' argument mean it
had triumphed in part because more hard times were ahead
for the Roman Empire? If they were, how soon? Not for the
first time, she caught herself wishing she'd paid a lot more
attention to history. If she had, she might know more about
the world and times in which she was living.

She hadn't answered Calidius Severus, and she didn't have
an easy answer handy. Julia grinned at her. "He's got you,
Mistress Umma."

"And glad of it, too," Calidius Severus said with a grin
just as wide and rather more wicked.

Nicole bit her lip and tried not to look as if she were
fretting. If she had any more good to say of Christianity,
both of them would start to wonder why.

She chose a safer way out. "Titus told me once I sounded
like a philosopher. Now I get to tell him the same thing."

"What? Me? An old soldier up to his elbows in piss? I get
to tell you that's nonsense." He sounded gruff, almost angry.
Underneath that, he sounded very pleased. He threw another
piece of walnut shell at Lucius. Lucius, greatly daring, threw
it back. Titus Calidius Severus laughed. Nobody talked anymore about religion, Christian or otherwise.

*   *   *

Two days later, Brigomarus came into the tavern again. The look in his eyes, blank and shellshocked, told her what he was going to say before he said it. She didn't like him, let alone love him, but he was a creature in pain. "Here." She dipped a cup of wine. "Drink this."

"You're sure you can spare such largess for your family?" The sarcasm didn't keep him from taking the wine or from draining it in a gulp. It seemed to steady him. He let out a long, shuddering sigh, then gave her the news she expected: "She's gone. It was peaceful, at the end. She breathed, then she stopped for a bit, and then, when I thought it was over, she breathed one more time, and that was the last."

Nicole didn't imagine that he told her this for her own sake. It was something he needed to remember, and to repeat to himself. "I'm glad she didn't suffer," she said truthfully. Then, remembering what Calidius Severus had said, she added, "I hope she's happy in the next world."

"The gods grant it be so," Brigomarus said, and fell silent, staring down into his empty cup. Nicole didn't choose to take the hint, if hint it was. Maybe he was simply preoccupied.

At length he said the other thing that weighed on his mind. "I'm afraid Flavius Probus is coming down with it."

"I'm sorry," Nicole said. She had very little use for Ila's husband, but this wasn't a disease she'd wish on anyone. "I hope he gets better. Some people do."

"Yes, some people do." Brigomarus looked at Nicole as if he was trying hard not to hate her. And what did he think she'd done now? With the air of a man who has run out of patience, he flung words at her. "This is our *mother*, Umma."

So. She wasn't acting mournful enough to suit him. And acting was what it would have to be. She hadn't known Atpomara well, and certainly hadn't liked her. But that didn't remove the essential fact. As long as she wore Umma's body, she had to act as Umma would be expected to act. She tried to imagine how she'd feel if her own mother died. The parallel wasn't too far off: even in West Hills, she'd been distant in space and time and interests, and, since the divorce, the distance had grown worse. Sometimes she thought her mother regarded divorce as a fundamental moral failure— her own as much as Nicole's.

Still, if her mother had died, she'd grieve. It was as Brigo had said: that was her *mother*.

Out of all that, she drew a sigh that shook a little, and rubbed her eyes that ached with tiredness and stress. "I'm sorry," she said. "It's just . . . it doesn't feel real. So many people are dying, so much death, till everybody's numb. And to have her gone, of all people—didn't we used to think she'd outlive us all?"

That was a gamble, a stab in the dark, but it found a target. Brigomarus nodded. Even so, he studied her. So many people in Carnuntum had measured her with that steady stare, she was about ready to rise up in revolt. At last he said, "We haven't been happy with you, so I don't suppose you've been happy with us, either." There he went, making her explanations for her, just as everyone else did who'd weighed her and found her wanting. "We'll have to pull together, that's all, however many of us are left alive after this pestilence goes back wherever it came from."

"Yes," Nicole said. That was safe enough, but she couldn't bring herself to add to it.

However many of us are left alive. There was a phrase that did not belong to the twentieth century. People must have said it in the Black Death, and that was later than this, though she couldn't remember offhand just how much later it was. This wasn't the bubonic plague, either. California and the other southwestern states got occasional cases, much publicized on the TV news, so she had an idea of the symptoms, and these weren't it. But this other plague, whatever it was, was hitting the whole Roman Empire just as the Black Death had hit medieval Europe.

Brigomarus was clouding up again. For a wonder, she managed to figure out why before the clouds turned to thunder and lightning. "When will the funeral be?" she asked.

"Tomorrow noon," he answered, easing—yes, that had been the right question. "We'll start the procession at the

shop of Fuficius Cornutus the undertaker—down the street
from the town-council building."

"We'll be there," she said. Lucius and Aurelia, too. From
old Indiana memories, she knew the children would be expected to say good-bye to their grandmother. She wouldn't
have asked it of Kimberley and Justin, but these were older
children, and, tougher, and much more familiar with death.
They'd lost their father, after all, and who knew whom else?

Brigomarus nodded, and startled her somewhat by thanking her for the wine. "Stay healthy," he said as he went on
his way. Just after he'd reached the door, he sneezed. Nicole
hoped devoutly that he was only coming down with a cold.

Five funerals went on at the same time, here and there across
the graveyard outside Carnuntum. Nicole wondered how
many more there had been earlier in the day, and how many
would follow in the afternoon. Too many—no doubt of that.
The gravediggers lay limply on the grass, looking like men
in the last stages of exhaustion. They must have taken the
job as a sinecure: lie around, drink wine, dig a grave now
and then. Now they were earning their keep a hundred times
over. Did they get hazard pay? Or did the Romans have any
such concept?

The priest who waited at the gravesite was male and not,
it was clear, a devotee of Isis. Somehow it wasn't surprising
that Atpomara hadn't entrusted herself to the women's goddess. The prayer he gabbled out, in fact, was to Dis Pater
and Herecura, deities whom Nicole had never heard of. From
the wording of the prayer, she gathered they were consorts,
rulers of the underworld. Parts of the prayer to Herecura
weren't even in Latin; the words came to her as mere noise.
Did that mean Herecura was a local goddess? Then how had
she acquired a Roman husband? Nicole couldn't even ask:
she'd have been expected to know the answer.

The prayer was short and rather perfunctory. Brigomarus
laid a loaf of bread and a cheese and a bowl of dried nuts
and dried fruit in the grave—an ostentatious gift compared
to the one that Longinius Iulus had given Fabia Ursa. Nicole

suspected Atpomara's shade would reckon it barely adequate.

Marcus Flavius Probus stood at the graveside, leaning on Ila's arm, coughing and sneezing like a man with a nasty cold. His eyes were red and watery and blinked constantly, as if the murky daylight troubled them.

Nicole's mouth twisted. Brigomarus had been right. Flavius Probus had the pestilence.

When Brigomarus straightened from offering tribute to the shade of Umma's mother, the gravediggers struggled wearily to their feet and began spading earth onto the mortal remains. Nicole turned away. As with Fabia Ursa, the sound of earth thudding onto a shrouded corpse was too final to face with equanimity, too blunt a reminder. *Dust we are, and unto dust we shall return.* By ones and twos, the mourners straggled back toward Carnuntum. If not for Lucius and Aurelia, who had been soberly quiet through the brief service, Nicole would have been a *one*. Although she might have gained a point by coming and bringing the children, the rest of Umma's family still didn't want to have much to do with her. They hadn't spoken to her in the procession, nor invited her to walk beside them in front of the bier. She'd taken a place just behind it, ignored if not forgotten.

She didn't reach out to them, either. If they cared more for what a slave's manumission might do to their financial and social status than for what was morally and ethically right, so be it. Let them stay estranged. They weren't *her* family. She didn't need them or want them, and she certainly didn't like them.

As she neared the city gate, another funeral procession, a larger one, emerged from beneath its archway. She wouldn't have paid any particular attention if one of the mourners hadn't turned to stare at her. She was . . . no, not resigned to having men in Carnuntum give her the slow once-over, but she'd given up on trying to avoid it.

This stare was different. It hit her after the procession had passed, so that she stopped and turned to stare back at the young fellow who'd written the Christian graffito on the wall.

She should have known better than to think any of this would go unnoticed by her—that is, by Umma's—offspring. "Who's that, Mother?" Lucius asked.

Brigomarus had also noticed—she hadn't even known he was behind her. "Who's that, Umma?" he asked, echoing Lucius.

She wished he hadn't spoken her name. The Christian might have heard it. After a moment, she realized how peculiar it was that she'd thought such a thing. This young man didn't worship one or several of these implausible pagan gods. He worshipped the God she'd been brought up to worship; whether she did or not was beside the point. They should be companions in the spirit. Instead, she didn't want him to know who she was, where she lived, anything about her. It was a visceral objection, and made no sense at all, but there was no getting around it.

"Who is he?" Lucius and Brigomarus asked again. Aurelia chimed in too, for the evident pleasure of ganging up on her mother.

Nicole grabbed at the first lie that came into her head. "I don't know his name," Nicole answered. "He's come to the tavern a time or two, and had a cup of wine."

"I never saw him," Lucius said.

"Me, either," Aurelia said.

Nicole drew a steadying breath—and pulled rank: a thing she'd sworn she'd never do, every time her own mother did it. "You haven't seen everything that goes on in the world, even when you think you have," she said.

The kids shut up, which was exactly what she'd wanted, and Brigomarus said, "Oh. Well then. I guess there's nothing to worry about, though he looks a little crazy to me. Staring at you like that—you'd think he had designs on you."

Damn him, just when she'd thought he'd leave well enough alone, he had to turn into the overprotective brother. He was supposed to be at odds with her; not butting into her life as if he had every right to do it.

She couldn't even speak in the young Christian's defense. It was too dangerous—for him and for her. And, she had to admit, he did look a little crazy. "He hasn't given me any trouble," she said rather lamely.

"Good." Brigomarus started to turn away, then hesitated. "Stay well. If you don't, send your slave— "

"My freedwoman," Nicole said sharply.

He made a sour face. "Your freedwoman. Send your *freedwoman* to me or to Ila or Tabica. We'll do what we can for you, in spite of everything."

They would, too, though they'd make her pay in guilt for every minute. Still—after all, and however reluctantly, he meant well. She thanked him, which he took as no less than his due, and gathered up Lucius and Aurelia. "Come on, chicks. We've got a tavern to run."

Julia had things well in hand. She also had a mark on the side of her neck, which Nicole knew hadn't been there when she took the children to the funeral. Nicole couldn't decide whether to ream the woman out or to burst into laughter. In the end, she didn't quite do either. She *was* disappointed to discover that she couldn't find a precise Latin equivalent for *hickey*.

Business—hers, if not Julia's—was slow. People were staying away from taverns for fear of catching the pestilence, or else were too sick to leave their beds. Whichever it was, the place wasn't bringing in much in the way of cash.

"We're not using so much, either," Julia said when Nicole commented on it—complained, really, if she wanted to be honest. "A lot of what we sell won't go stale. It will keep till things pick up again."

Nicole nodded. That was true—if things ever did decide to improve again.

She spent much of the afternoon grinding flour, until her shoulder started grinding, too. She was stockpiling, figuring to get ahead of the game; then she could have a few relatively easy days later on. The prospect of a break of any kind, relatively easy days, made her work all the harder. She hadn't had much time off since she came to Carnuntum.

Deafened by the gritty rumble of the quern, she didn't notice the man who came into the tavern until he rapped the table at which he was sitting. She put on her company face, the one she reserved for customers, with a smile still bright after the long slow day—until she recognized the eyes that lifted to meet hers. Her smile evaporated. "Oh," she said. "It's you."

"Yes, Mistress Umma." The young Christian smiled. "It is I." The smile was a little wider than it might have been; his eyes glittered even in the gloom of the tavern. Nicole had seen smiles like that on Hare Krishnas at airports, on Jehovah's Witnesses who came to the door. The people behind the smiles were usually harmless, but . . .

She did her best to hide her unease. "What can I get you?" she asked him.

"Bread and wine," he answered. He was watching her closely—too closely. He noticed how she hesitated on hearing those words. His smile widened. There was triumph in it. "You know the meaning of bread and wine?"

"What if I do?" she said roughly.

"Then you are one of us," he answered. "You are one of those who know the name of Jesus Christ. You are one of those who know about his Passion, through which we too are resurrected. You are one of those who know judgment is coming for everyone, for even the heavenly hosts, the cherubim and seraphim, if they have no faith in the blood of Christ."

"What if I do?" Nicole repeated. The young man wasn't saying anything she hadn't heard in church and in Sunday school. And yet, there, the world to come had been mentioned, but it hadn't been at the heart of all her lessons. This world, and living one's life in clean and godly fashion, had counted for more.

Living in the material world had been easy in the United States. Nicole hadn't thought so at the time, but now she had a basis of comparison. Titus Calidius Severus had had a point, after all. When times were good, this world was easier to live in, and the next seemed distant, irrelevant.

Times weren't good now, and they were getting worse. And if the young Christian eating bread and drinking wine in her tavern wasn't a wild-eyed fanatic, Nicole didn't know what he could possibly be. "Do not cleave to those who believe not, Umma, even if they be of your own flesh and blood," he said with quivering urgency. "Do not, I beg you in the name of the risen God. They go to torment eternal. This pestilence is the sword of God. When you are close to the sword, you are close to God. When you are surrounded by lions, you are close to God. Soon you will meet him face to face."

"How about when you're writing things on the wall?" Nicole inquired acidly. "Did you want to be surrounded by lions then? You should have stayed and let someone catch you."

His head drooped. When it came up again, to her astonishment there were tears on his cheeks. "My body was weak," he whispered. "My spirit was weak. Here and now, as I speak in life, I should yearn for death with a lover's passion. I want to eat the bread of God, the flesh of Jesus Christ, and to drink his blood, which is love undying. I pray to be found worthy of martyrdom. And so," he said, leaning toward her, trembling again with the zeal of the proselyte, "should you."

His voice, his manner, were compelling. He believed with his whole heart and soul that every word was the absolute truth. *Gospel truth,* she thought in a kind of dim alarm. And he was determined that Nicole should believe as he did, should take as little notice of this life as she could, the sooner and the better to get on with the next one.

He scared the hell out of her. If somebody gave him the keys to a truck full of fertilizer and fuel oil, maybe he wouldn't push the button when the time came—he had, after all, run from her. But maybe he *would,* too, if he nerved himself first. Even the possibility was terrifying.

Carefully, she said, "You owe me three *asses.*"

He looked so astonished, she almost laughed in his face. It took him several tries, and a fair bit of spluttering, before he could say, "You would put the coin of Caesar ahead of the salvation of your soul?"

"Don't you fret about my soul," she said. "That's no one's business but my own."

The Christian's astonishment changed in tone and intensity. Twentieth-century individualism hit people here hard . . . *the way wine hits people who aren't used to drinking,* Nicole thought with experience she hadn't had, or wanted, before she came to Carnuntum. She took a deep breath and drove the point home. "And, since my soul is still in my body, I need those three *asses.*"

Maybe the look in his eyes was pity and love. It seemed a lot more like outrage. He got up, dug in the leather pouch he wore on his belt, found three copper coins, and slammed them down on the tabletop. The tavern's earthen floor didn't help him much when it came to stamping noisily out, but he gave it his best shot. His back was as straight—and as stiff— as a redwood.

Julia came in from the market just after he'd flung himself out the door, carrying a jarful of raisins and a bunch of green onions. "What was bothering *him?*" she wanted to know.

Nicole shrugged as casually as she could manage. "Oh," she said, "just another dissatisfied customer."

Julia raised an eyebrow, but mercifully didn't ask questions. Sometimes, Nicole reflected with a twinge of residual guilt, it wasn't too inconvenient that Julia had been a slave. Slaves learned, better and faster than most, when it didn't pay to be curious.

Lazy in the afterglow, Nicole sprawled next to and on Titus Calidius Severus. Her head lay on his chest, one arm stretched across his belly, one thigh draped over him so the rest of her leg lay between his. She was, emphatically, a satisfied customer.

"It's good with you," she said, and raised her hand to stroke his cheek. In the light of the one lamp on the chest of drawers, the arm's shadow leaped and swooped.

His own free arm slid slowly along her flank, tracing the smooth, economical curves of Umma's body. One corner of Nicole's mouth twisted. In Los Angeles, this body would have been sleek. Here, it was skinny. Just one more example of *you can't win no matter how hard you try* syndrome.

"You make me a happy man," he said, and, as if to prove it, tilted her face up and kissed her. He wasn't after a second round. He was just . . . enjoying himself. So, for that matter, was she. He was good in bed, and she didn't think she was too bad there either; but more than that, they liked one another. They took pleasure in each other's company.

Idly, she wondered why she'd been lucky enough to find a good lover when so little in the rest of Carnuntum had turned out to be any good at all. Polluted water, lead everywhere, slavery, brutality, sexism, appalling notions of medicine—and, in the middle of all that, as good a lover as any she'd ever known in the United States. She pondered Calidius' shadowed face the way a D.A. pondered a piece of evidence that didn't fit a pattern.

And then, after a moment, it did, or she thought it did. In their waterworks, in their pottery glazes, in their political and legal institutions, in what their doctors knew—in all those things and more, the Romans lacked eighteen hundred years of collective experience she'd taken for granted. She'd had no idea how much she'd taken it for granted, either, till she'd had her face rubbed in it.

But sex wasn't something that tended to improve through collective experience. It was something everybody learned for herself or himself over the course of a lifetime. It might get more athletic, it might get more esoteric—she remembered some rather interesting nights when she was in law school, when she and a certain young man had worked their way through the greatest hits of the *Kama Sutra*—but when it came down to it, it could be just as good in plain vanilla as in the fanciest flavor you could imagine. Maybe that meant Alley Oop the caveman had been able to keep Mrs. Oop happy, too. For Mrs. Oop's sake, Nicole hoped so.

She laughed a little. The exhalation stirred the hair on Calidius Severus' chest. He raised an eyebrow. "What's funny?"

"I think I've figured out why you're so good," she answered.

"And that's funny?" He snorted. "You didn't need to go and do any figuring for that. I could have told you: it's the company I keep."

Nobody had ever said anything remotely like that to her. Frank certainly hadn't. Most of the men she'd dated since Frank had been too busy thinking about either themselves or their chances of getting laid to imagine saying such a thing. For a stretching instant, she wanted to cry. Then she wanted something else. She was amazed to discover how much she wanted it. *Well,* she thought, *aphrodisiacs are where you find them.*

Getting what else she wanted took considerable effort, but, in the end, it turned out to be effort well spent. She was, she thought, pretty well spent herself. So was Titus Calidius Severus. He peered up at her while she still sat astride him. "You can be my jockey any day," he said.

She reached down to stroke his cheek again. Her hand lingered, savoring the crispness of his beard and the smoothness of the cheek above it, then paused. Almost of itself, it went to his forehead. "You're warm," she said in sudden sharp suspicion. No afterglow this time; alarm killed it even though he still nestled, shrinking, inside her.

He laughed and made light of it: "After what we've been doing? You'd best believe I'm warm." Without warning, he pinched her. She jerked and squeaked. He flopped out of her.

She let him jolly and cajole her as he got into his tunic and sandals. But she knew the sweaty feel of skin after love; that was how her own skin felt now. He hadn't felt like that. He'd been warm and dry, the way Kimberley and Justin sometimes were before they came down with something. If you came down with something in Carnuntum now . . .

"I'm fine," he said downstairs in the doorway, as they embraced. They'd taken to doing that, safe enough in the shadow of the entrance, but this night or very early morning, it lasted a little longer, and held a little tighter. He sounded as if he was trying to convince himself as much as her. "Fine.

See? Fit as can be, and ready to whip my weight in lions."

He still felt warm, or Nicole thought he did. She wasn't quite sure. Maybe she was a little warm herself. Or maybe she was letting her imagination and her fear run away with her. She hoped so.

Titus Calidius Severus coughed sharply, several times, as he crossed the street. When he got back to his own door, he looked over his shoulder. Nicole stared at the dim white smudge of his face in the dawn. His eyes were almost preternaturally dark. He shook his head and went inside. His step had a jaunty bounce to it, as if to prove to her that there was nothing wrong with him. No, nothing at all.

Nicole fled upstairs. Behind the barred door of her bedroom, she gave way to the brief luxury of tears. They were more tears of rage, rage that the pestilence might come between her and most of the good she'd found in Carnuntum, than tears of fear.

She sneezed. A moment later, she sneezed again. And again. It didn't feel like a cold coming on. It felt like the flu. It felt like a killer flu.

She wished she hadn't thought of it that way. The tears that came next *were* tears of fear.

She slept for a little while, maybe, a heavy sleep, full of formless dreams. When she got up, she still felt fluish, fluish and a little hung over, too; though she hadn't drunk that much the night before, the light hurt her eyes as it had when she'd deliberately got plastered with Julia. The tavern seemed too bright, though it must have been almost totally dark. When she opened the front door, she had to blink several times against the glare.

While she was blinking, Titus Calidius Severus emerged from his shop with his amphorae. They waved to each other. "How are you?" they said, each an echo of the other. It was not a simple morning pleasantry. They both really wanted—needed—to know.

"Fine," they answered, both at the same time. Nicole knew she was lying. And so was Titus Calidius Severus. If he didn't know that, she would have been astonished.

She went back inside, welcoming the dimness after the blaze of the morning. Julia was just coming downstairs, heavy-eyed and yawning. She swallowed her yawn, nearly choked on it, in embarrassment at finding Nicole there ahead of her. "I'm sorry, Mistress," she said, sounding genuinely apologetic but not terrified, the way she had before Nicole manumitted her: one small step at a time, she was learning to be free. "How are you this morning?"

"Fine," Nicole answered, as she had for Titus Calidius Severus. If she said it often enough, if she made other people believe it, maybe it would turn out to be true.

She failed before she'd begun. Julia stiffened at the sound of her voice, and peered at her. "Fine? Are you, Mistress Umma?" She strode to a window and set hand to the shutters. "Come over here," she said sharply, "and let me take a look at you." She might have been talking to Lucius or Aurelia.

That was irritating, but Nicole lacked the energy to rise to it. Julia flung the shutters wide. Daylight streamed in, dazzling her. Tears of pain ran down her cheeks. She started to flinch away from it, but forced herself to hold still. Even so, she raised a hand to shield against the worst of the glare.

Julia clicked her tongue. "Oh, Mistress," she said. She laid her hand on Nicole's forehead. When she lowered it, her face was tight with worry. "Oh, Mistress," she said again. "I'm afraid you've got—" She didn't say it. Instead, she tugged at the neckline of her tunic and spat onto her bosom.

"I'm afraid I've got it, too," Nicole said. She didn't say the word, the one whose ill omen Julia had tried to cast aside: *pestilence*. She let out a sigh that, she realized too late, had probably sent a few million viruses into Julia's face. She sighed again, this time averting her face. "Whether I do or I don't, I've got to keep going as long as I can."

It wasn't bravery, not really. It was denial. Julius Rufus had said it while he stood in front of her with a fever hot enough to bake bread. Bare minutes later, he'd collapsed in the street. Within the hour, he was dead, slipped away quietly while he lay just inside the doorway of the tavern.

That was a nice, cheerful note on which to start the morning.

Nicole was sicker than a dog, but she wasn't close to collapse. Yet. She didn't think. When Lucius and Aurelia came down for breakfast, Nicole examined them like a hawk—from a distance, to minimize the chance of breathing disease onto them. They both seemed fine: hungry and rowdy. She didn't know how much that proved. She'd been rowdy herself the night before. She coughed. Wet snot tickled her nose and made her sneeze. The love she'd enjoyed—and how she had enjoyed it!—with Titus Calidius Severus seemed a million miles away.

Customers came in: not too many. That helped Nicole, who was moving slower than she should have, to deal with them. Some of them were moving slower than they should have, too, as if they'd been recorded at 45 rpm and were playing back at 33⅓.

That phrase wouldn't mean anything to Kimberley and Justin. All they'd know would be CDs and tapes. Records would be primitive, outmoded. She laughed. She'd learned more about primitive and outmoded than she'd ever dreamt possible. Was a record primitive in an oxcart?

She was aware enough to realize her wits were starting to wander. When she thought about it, she could force them back into—or close to—their proper path. When she didn't think about it, they started drifting again.

Brigomarus came in that afternoon. He was still healthy, but he looked grim. "Flavius Probus just died," he said. He didn't sound astonished, as an American would have been to announce the death of someone in the prime of life. He sounded weary; this was but one more death piled on many. "He—Umma, are you listening to me?"

"Yes," Nicole answered. It wasn't easy to make herself pay attention, but she managed. "Too bad about him."

"Too bad? Is that all you can say?" Brigomarus started to cloud up, but checked himself. He took a long look at her. "Oh, by the gods, you've got it, too."

"I think so," Nicole said vaguely. Again, she forced herself to focus. "You'd better go home, Brigo. It's catching from person to person, you know. I don't suppose I want to make you sick." She wouldn't have put it that way if she'd been well, but she wouldn't have had to warn him then, either.

He didn't take offense. Maybe he didn't notice the way she phrased it; maybe he made allowances for the pestilence. He said, "As long as I'm well, I'll come back and see how you're doing. I'll do what I can for you—you are my sister, no matter how—" He broke off. "You *are* my sister."

"That's true. I am your sister." It was nice to know they could agree on something.

Brigomarus didn't linger after that. Nicole was interested to see how he got up and drifted out the door, moving as if he were underwater. After a while—Nicole wasn't sure how long—Julia said, "Mistress, you ought to go upstairs and go to bed."

"No, that's what you do," Nicole said: the first thing that popped into her head. She laughed. She thought it was funny. But she didn't have a sense of humor. Nothing was funny to her. Frank had said it often enough. "Dawn makes me laugh," he'd said after he split. Damned blasted cliché.

Damn: she was sicker than she'd thought.

Julia didn't seem to think the joke was very funny, and Julia did have a sense of humor. "I don't mean go to bed *with* anyone," she said. Maybe she, like Brigomarus, was making allowances. Maybe she was just feeling literal. "I mean by yourself, to rest."

"But I can't rest." Even through the haze of illness, Nicole knew that. "If I rest, the work won't get done." Yes, she sounded like Julius Rufus. She pressed her hand to her own forehead. She was hot. She didn't think she was as hot as the brewer had been, but her palm was hot, too, so she couldn't be sure. "I've got to go on."

"What if you fall over?" Julia asked reasonably.

"If I fall over, I probably would have fallen over in bed, too," Nicole replied. "You can drag me upstairs then." *Maybe I'll die on the way up. Maybe I'll take two aspirins and feel better in the morning.* No. No aspirins. She remembered—no aspirins. But something . . . something. "The willow-bark decoction!" she exclaimed, inordinately proud that she'd remembered.

But Julia said, "We haven't got any more. Poor Fabia Ursa used what we had—and how much good did it do her?"

Nicole hadn't remembered that. "Go out and buy a new jar." It had done a little good when she'd been down with the galloping trots. Maybe it would do a little good now. Would that be enough? What could Nicole do but hope?

Julia seemed eager to snatch whatever hope she could find. She scooped coins out of the cash box and left at a lope. After she was gone—quite a while after—Nicole realized she had no idea how much money Julia had scooped up. Well, if her freedwoman had ripped her off, she damn well had, and that was that.

Julia came back fairly quickly with a little jar clutched in her hand. She dumped a handful of money back in the cash box. Either she'd been honest or she was covering her tracks. Nicole rebuked herself as soon as she'd thought that, poured the potion into a cup of wine and honey, and drank it down. It still tasted hideously bitter—yes, like aspirin in the back of her throat. She chopped onions, trying not to chop off any fingers while she was doing it, and waited to see if the medicine would help.

It did—a little. Instead of feeling very hot and disconnected from the world around her, after an hour or so she felt hot and distantly connected to the world around her. She still didn't feel good, or anything close to it. She snapped and railed at Julia and the children. Every little thing set her off; it was all she could do not to take it out on the customers. Of course she knew why she was so irritable, but she couldn't help it. The words came out all by themselves, with nothing conscious in them at all.

Toward evening of what had seemed an endless day, Titus Calidius Severus crossed the street and swayed into the tavern. Maybe it was her fever, but he seemed to weave where he stood, like waterweeds in a current. He ordered bread and wine, but before Nicole could reach for the loaf, he grimaced and shook his head. "No, just wine," he said, setting a *du-pondius* on the bar. "The two-*as*. I haven't had any appetite today."

Nicole realized she'd hardly eaten anything, either. The thought of food, even food as bland as bread, made her stomach cringe. "How are you?" she asked as she brought the fuller and dyer his wine.

He studied her. It took a while; he seemed to have to pause and remember why he was doing it. Finally, he said, "About the same as you are, I expect." He sighed and shook his head. "Not much point to pretending anymore, is there? We've got it, sure as sure."

"Yes, I think we do," Nicole said with a kind of relief. She hadn't known how much effort it took to deny the truth. It was like a load off her back—even with the fear that replaced it, the bone-deep dread of death.

Calidius Severus frowned and stuck a finger in his ear, as if he didn't think he'd heard right. "What was that?"

"Yes, I think we do," Nicole repeated. Listening to the words, she realized they were in English. She said them again, this time in Latin.

"Ah." Calidius' face cleared. "I wondered if you couldn't talk right, or if the fever was doing funny things to my ears. What were those noises you were making? Sounded almost like the grunts the Quadi use for a language."

"I don't know—I suppose it must be the fever." Nicole had never made that kind of slip before. She hoped she never made it again. This time, at least, she had an excuse for it. Next time . . .

There couldn't be a next time. There *mustn't* be.

"The fever," Titus Calidius Severus agreed. "And the eyes—I'm like an owl in the daylight." Nicole nodded. He went on, "Then the rash comes—and then we find out if we live or die." He tossed back the rest of his wine. "One way or the other, it won't be too long."

"No." Back in Los Angeles, Nicole hadn't worried about dying young, except for a few brief, dreadful moments on the freeway. She thought she should have been more upset.

If she'd felt better, if she'd been more fully a part of the world, she would have been terrified. On the other hand, she wouldn't have had so much to worry about if she'd felt better.

"Everyone else here well?" the fuller and dyer asked.

"So far," Nicole said. "And your son?"

"Gaius is fine—so far, as you say," Calidius Severus answered.

Wearily, blearily, Nicole shook her head. "My brother-in-law died today—Brigomarus brought me the news. By the time it's over, half the people in town will be dead."

"It's not quite that bad," Calidius Severus said, but before Nicole could feel even a little bit hopeful, he went on, "By what I've heard, down in Italy and Greece it's killing one in four, maybe one in three."

A fourth to a third of the people in Italy and Greece— dead? From a disease? A pestilence? Nicole thought again of the Black Plague, and of that TV documentary about the horrible things disease had done to the Native Americans. Again, the sickness already in her kept her from knowing the full weight of horror. Even through the fog, it was bad enough.

Titus Calidius Severus finished his wine, got up, and kissed Nicole on the cheek. His lips were warm, but not in a way she liked. "See you tomorrow," he said. When he spoke again, she thought he was talking more to himself than to her: "I hope I'll see you tomorrow."

The night was bad. Nicole alternately burned with fever and shook with chills. Coughing fits racked her. It was like the worst flu she'd ever had. But no antibiotics here, no pain-killers, nothing but willow bark and tincture of time.

Morning came none too soon, and somewhat to her surprise. She was alive. She didn't feel any worse when she staggered out of bed than she had when she fell into it, which was maybe good, and maybe just delusion.

Titus Calidius Severus was standing in his doorway when she opened up. He seemed as proud as she was, to be on his feet and moving.

The day was gray and nasty and chilly. She was almost glad of the fever that burned inside her. When the chills hit, they'd be all the worse, but meanwhile she didn't need more than the tunic she'd put on when she got up.

Toward midmorning, the rain came, hard and cold. The wind—a wind with teeth in it—drove it lashing sideways. No mild summer downpour, that. It had a taste of winter. In Indianapolis, the next storm would have brought ice with it. Nicole thought that might be the case here as well.

Even the fever wasn't enough to keep her warm in that. She put on the thick wool cloak that had lain in the drawer since she'd come to Carnuntum. She put on socks, too. Even with them, she shivered. She would have been cold had she been healthy. Sick as she was, she felt as if she were walking naked through a meat locker in a supermarket.

No supermarkets. No meat lockers. No way to get warm, either.

From somewhere, Julia dug out a couple of square brass contraptions. They looked like hibachis. "Time to light the braziers," she said. She filled them with charcoal and got them going. When Nicole stood right next to one, she almost started to thaw. When she moved more than two feet away, she froze solid again. She remembered Indianapolis, and getting the furnace going, and staying warm no matter how cold the winter got.

But she seemed to remember—hadn't the Romans had central heating?

Not here. Not for the poor, at least. Braziers—the space heaters of this world—were all anyone had.

The next day was more of the same, only worse: maybe because the bad weather lingered, maybe because Nicole couldn't escape the truth. She was sicker. Two funeral parties squelched through the noisome mud outside. If the pestilence didn't get the mourners, pneumonia would finish them off just as conclusively.

That night, Nicole didn't bother to bar her bedroom door. Some of the last bits of rationality left in her warned that,

come morning, she might be in no shape to get up and unbar
it.

Her sleep was uneasy, broken with fragments of dreams,
stray bits of nightmare, memories so real that she sat up with
a gasp. She'd been reaching for a coffee cup in the office,
or nuking a hotdog for Justin, or throwing a load of laundry
in the dryer. There was nothing romantic about these moments at all. They were relentlessly, blissfully mundane.

Then she'd wake and the manifold stink of Carnuntum
would hit her like a blow to the face. No coffeemakers, no
microwave ovens, no clothes dryers. No drugs, either, to fight
this disease that was eating her from the inside out. Once
she actually stared at her hand in the nightlamp's flicker,
looking for the lines of flame that must mark the muscles
and the bones. But it was only Umma's thin long-fingered
hand, with its olive skin and its work-worn palms.

She drifted for a long time between sleep and waking, not
sure at all that she wanted to wake, but unable to cling to
sleep. At last, sleep shrank and vanished. The waking it left
her with was a cold and pallid thing. She was shivering so
hard she couldn't even sit up. All she could do was lie there
and scrabble feebly, pulling the blankets around her as tightly
as she could. Her teeth chattered as if she'd been standing
naked in an icy wind.

After what seemed like a very long time, someone tapped
on the door. Nicole tried to tell whoever it was to come in,
but the sound that came out bore little resemblance to intel-
ligible words.

It didn't matter. The door opened somewhat tentatively.
Julia's round Germanic face and big blue eyes peered around
it. The eyes went as round as the face. "Oh, no, Mistress,"
she said.

Oh, yes, Julia, Nicole thought. She tried to say it, too,
because it was surely the wittiest thing she'd come up with
in—why, forever. All she got for her trouble, again, was an
unintelligible croak.

Julia ventured fully into the room, chattering as she came,
as if words could hold the horrors at bay. "When you didn't

come down to open up or to eat breakfast, I was afraid you were too sick to get out of bed. As soon as I get the fires built up, I'll bring you some warmed wine and some soup."

Nicole had owned this woman. No, dammit, *Umma* had owned her. Sick as she was, Nicole insisted on the distinction. Julia could have done nothing, or next to it, and let her former mistress die in bed. No one would have said a word. Not with the harvest the pestilence was reaping. But, in spite of having been another human being's property, Julia was doing what she could to keep Nicole going. Maybe she was a genuinely nice person. Maybe Nicole didn't understand exactly how slavery worked. Maybe both of those things were true at once.

Warm wine slid down Nicole's throat with surprising ease. The soup tasted strongly of leeks, rather less so of salt pork. It was warm, which counted for more than its flavor.

"I'll look in on you every so often, Mistress," Julia promised.

Nicole nodded. The soup and wine made her feel a little more alive. But when Julia pressed a hand to her forehead, the freedwoman looked grave, as Nicole had herself when she'd felt the heat that radiated from Julius Rufus.

The touch didn't hurt, but it felt strange, as if there should be pain somewhere: an odd, twitchy, uncomfortable feeling. When Julia left the room, through the fog that blurred Nicole's sight these days, she saw the slow headshake, and the slight slump of the wide meaty shoulders.

On the way downstairs, Julia sneezed and then coughed, twice in a row.

Julia, too. Nicole didn't know why she should be surprised. Part of her tried to grieve, or at least to be scared, but she was too weak for either. She'd begun to shiver again under the blankets and the heavy cloaks. Her wits drifted away. This time, she lacked the strength of will or the strength of body to call them back. They were going. She wasn't. Her eyes slid closed.

Some time later—she had no idea how long—she found herself floating weightlessly above the body she'd been inhabiting. Its face was reddened and roughened with the tell-tale rash of the pestilence. Its chest still rose and fell, rose and fell, shallow but steady. She could feel the heat coming off the body, and yet, every now and again, it shivered.

From her vantage above it all, she wondered how Titus Calidius Severus was doing. As quickly, as easily as that, she was no longer hovering above her body, but above his. He writhed and tossed in a bed not too different from her own—and why, she asked herself, hadn't she ever seen it before? Now and then, a hoarse cry escaped him. Anger, it might have been, or alarm, or remembered battle. His face and neck bore the same scarlet marks as Umma's cheeks and chin and forehead.

Sextus Longinius Iulus' baby, she thought. She didn't know why it mattered, but she wanted to see him, to see how he was. No sooner had the thought crossed her mind, than she was in the tinker's house. And there was the baby, nursing at the fat pale breast of a woman who looked more nearly Irish than Roman. Baby and nurse both seemed healthy: no coughing or sneezing, and no rash on face or breast.

That sight comforted Nicole more than she'd thought possible. Even knowing the sickness could strike those two within the day, even within the hour, she still was glad to see them safe. The next thing, the thing she should have done, to look in on her own—Umma's own—children, she couldn't bring herself to do. If they were well, then that was well. If they weren't, she didn't want to know. She couldn't do anything to help them. And she'd drive herself wild, like a bird against a window, beating and beating herself for no purpose at all.

She was drifting while she maundered, floating as if in water. One way and another, she found herself once more above Umma's body. As unattractive as the prospect was, she knew she should find her way back into it. Spirit belonged in body. Spirit alone was air and nothingness. Was—dead.

But when she tried to slip back as she'd slipped out, it was like pressing one pole of a magnet into the same pole of another. Some force thrust her softly but irresistibly back, as if to tell her, *This place is not safe for you.*

Had Umma's mother journeyed like this? Was that how she'd known a stranger looked out at her from her daughter's eyes? If Atpomara had done that, she had managed to rejoin her body. And then, almost at once, she had died.

Nicole's mind in its disembodied state was more distract-able even than it had been through the haze of fever. It fled the thought of Atpomara, and Atpomara's death, toward the much wider world. If Carnuntum was in such straits, all the way out by the Danube, what was it like in Rome itself?

Somewhat to her dismay, she didn't shift to the imperial capital. She'd left the tavern behind, but escaped only as far as the amphitheater, to the seat from which she'd watched the mime show with Titus Calidius Severus. From there she looked south, across the fields to the darkness of a forest that, some part of her knew, went on for miles. That was as close as she'd come to Rome. It was as far in that direction as her spirit could go.

And where else could she go? Her mind stretched across alternatives, and seized on the wildest one, the one she'd have thought craziest of all if she'd heard this story from the comfort of West Hills. God—gods, how she wished Liber and Libera had never brought her to Carnuntum.

And there they were, floating before her in a vast expanse of nothingness. They looked just as they had on the memorial plaque beside her soft, clean, blessedly vermin-free Califor-nia bed: rather plump, naked, and pleased with themselves. Their eyes were fixed on some rosy distance, far away from Nicole and her inescapably mortal self.

She didn't even think before the words poured out of her. *Let me go home. Let me go back. I don't belong here. I belong there. This*—and God, it hurt to say so, to admit she'd failed at anything—*this was a mistake. I should never have come here. I want to go home!*

When she'd shaped a wish into a prayer back in West Hills, not even knowing she'd done it, Liber and Libera had responded in an instant. Why not? They'd had nothing better to do—probably hadn't for centuries. Who believed in them enough to pray to them? Nicole hadn't, either, but she'd wanted out so badly, and been so absolutely desperate, that it hadn't mattered who or what answered her prayer.

Now she was in their world, a world full of believers, and therefore of prayers. Nicole could dimly sense others winging their way to the god and goddess, as she sometimes heard the ghosts of other conversations on the phone when she waited for a long-distance connection to go through. She might as well have been calling Ticketmaster, trying to land seats for a hot show. Sometimes your call went through right away. But if everyone decided to jam the lines at once, you'd get a busy signal . . . again and again and again.

Just as she rang—dialed—prayed again, driving the force of her need at the unheeding gods, her spirit made its own, completely unwanted connection. As suddenly as it had left, it was in Umma's body again, trapped in the reddish dark behind her eyelids. Someone had taken the covers off her. She was freezing cold. Hands groped under her tunic, tugging at her drawers.

Her eyes flew open. Gaius Calidius Severus loomed over her, the face so like his father's, the pitting of adolescent acne on the cheeks, the beard that was still coming in in patches. She gasped, coughed, choked. *Gaius* violating her? Was he out of his mind? Was she? No way in the world she could fight him off. But—Gaius—

He raised his eyes from what he was doing with her drawers, and caught her stare. "Oh, good," he murmured in profound relief. And then, louder: "Can you understand me, Mistress Umma?"

It took several tries—her head was as heavy as one of the gaudy statues in the baths—but at last she managed a nod. His expression lightened immeasurably. "My father made me promise to look after you," he said. "Everyone else is too sick to help. You've—fouled yourself." He blushed while he said that, like the boy he was, but he went on gamely: "I'm going to clean you off and get you a fresh pair of drawers. I'm doing the same thing for him. By the gods, that's all I'm going to do. Do you understand? Is that all right?"

She sighed faintly, relaxing a tension she hadn't known she had, and nodded, a little more easily this time. He pulled the soiled drawers off her, strode to the window, undid the shutters, and pitched the drawers out. They landed with a wet splat. He turned back into the room, leaving the shutters open to let in a pale gray light, and rummaged through the chest. He emerged with a rag, which he wet in the washbasin, and wiped Nicole clean. She got the strong impression he would have averted his eyes if he hadn't needed to see what he was doing. The water on the rag felt icy cold on her burning skin.

He found another pair of drawers, and awkwardly, with much shifting and fumbling, got them onto her. She was as weak as a baby; she couldn't even lift her hips to help him. When he was done, she was as glad as he must have been. "There you go," he said. "Wine?" She nodded; words were still a long way beyond her.

He held the cup to her lips. She drank, a few swallows' worth. Even that little exhausted her.

He didn't try to force more wine into her, but let her lie back. He slipped his arm free of her, laid the blanket and the cloak over her, and stood for a while, as if he couldn't think what to do next. Then it came to him. He turned without a word and all but fled.

She lay where he'd left her, clean, drowsy, and almost warm. He'd been real, then. Her spirit was secure in Umma's body again, or as secure as it could be with the disease eating away at it. She tried to slip free once more, but the anchor was sunk, the chains secured. She sighed. No more out-of-body experiences—or more likely, no more being out of her head from fever. She'd tried to telephone Liber and Libera, hadn't she? She could remember something. Lines busy. *All our representatives are currently assisting customers. Your call is important to us. Please stay on the line. A representative will take your call as soon as . . .*

If she wasn't out of her body any longer, she was still just a little bit out of her head. What had Gaius Calidius Severus said? Everyone here was too sick to take care of her? Julia? Lucius? Aurelia? All sick? All—dying? Flying? Traveling around Carnuntum, seeing the astral sights?

She slapped herself back into something resembling coherence. They were sick. They couldn't take care of her. She had to take care of them. She had to get—up—

With every ounce of strength she had, she rolled halfway over. The effort overwhelmed her. Unconsciousness hit her like a blow to the head.

When she woke, it was dark. *Night,* she realized after a terribly long while. That same night, or the one after, or the one after that? She had no way of knowing. Her hand moved leadenly, but it moved. She touched her drawers. They were dry. Gaius might have come in again and changed her without her waking.

She felt terrible: thirsty, hungry, feverish. Steamrollered. It was the best she'd felt since she woke up and realized that there was no way she was getting up to face the world. "I think I'm going to live," she whispered, mostly because she could. Her lips and mouth were desert-dry, her tongue a sand-coated bolt of flannel. Even so, she heard the wonder in the ruins of her voice.

Her eyes closed again, and she slept—really slept this time, as opposed to passing out. She woke some time in the morning: light was leaking through the shutters. She sat up. The room spun around her, but she didn't keel over. After a while, it steadied. Could she stand? The first time she tried, she sat down again in a hurry. But she tried again. Darkness came and went; spots swam in front of her eyes. She stayed on her feet. When the world stayed more or less steady, she ventured a step. Once she'd done that, she had to finish, or fall. She fetched up against the chest of drawers, and leaned against it, panting as if she'd finished a marathon.

She had to look in on the others. She couldn't stay here. For one thing, there was water in the *terra sigillata* pitcher by the bed, but no wine to kill the germs in it, and no food. She had to eat. She had to make sure the others were— weren't—

She couldn't go any farther for a while, not till she gathered what rags of strength she had. While she did that, she could see how *she* was. She fumbled in the drawer for the makeup kit, and pawed it open. The mirror nearly slipped from her shaking fingers, but she caught it somehow and propped it on the chest.

Her eyes widened in horror. The eyes of the concentration-camp survivor in the bronze mirror widened, too.

She'd been fashionably slim for a West Hills matron. Now she was skeletal. Skin stretched drumhead-tight over cheekbones and jaw. The rash lingered on her neck and in the hollows of her cheeks. Some of it was peeling, as if she'd had a dreadful sunburn. Someone—Ofanius Valens?—had told her that could happen. She was almost proud that she remembered.

Her hair was like sweat-matted straw. When she raised her free hand to brush it back from her forehead, clumps of it came away between her fingers. He'd told her about that, too. "My God," she muttered in English. That so much of her hair was dead told her more clearly than anything else, how close she'd come to dying.

The water in the *terra sigillata* pitcher tempted her— Christ, she was thirsty!—but not enough to make her drink. Another bout of the runs would kill her.

She lurched to the doorway. She had to rest there, leaning against the wall. When she could breathe again, more or less, she opened the door. It was as heavy as the city gate, and about as tractable. Another lurch propelled her across the hall to Julia's room. No sound came through the curtain. She set her weight to it and pulled it aside.

Julia sprawled across the bed. Light poured across her from a shutter that she hadn't fastened, or that had come unfastened while she was too ill to tend to it. In her fever, she'd kicked off the covers. Her tunic was hiked up almost to her hips, but a man would have had to be a necrophiliac to want her then.

Still—she was alive; her breast rose and fell in the rapid, shallow breathing that Nicole remembered all too well. She didn't look ready to stop at just that moment. Nicole went on, fighting to keep her breathing quiet, to concentrate on setting one foot in front of the other.

Lucius and Aurelia lay in their beds. Lucius moaned and thrashed in delirium. Aurelia lay very still. At first, Nicole was relieved. Sleeping, then, and maybe on the way to recovery.

But Umma's daughter lay too still. Julia, even unconscious, had looked alive somehow, and her breathing had been visible from the doorway. Aurelia lay like a doll that some enormous child had discarded.

Step by step, Nicole made her way to the bed. Her hand shook uncontrollably as she reached to set it on Aurelia's forehead.

Aurelia did not have a fever, not any longer. Her flesh was cool, almost cold. It would never be warm again.

Nicole wouldn't believe it. She couldn't. She groped for the bird-frail wrist, searching for a pulse. She found what she'd found with Julius Rufus: nothing.

She wanted, very much, to cry. Crying would loosen the knot in the middle of her, the hard, cold, hurting thing that had swelled in her when she saw Aurelia's stillness. But the tears wouldn't come. Her body was too ravaged. There was no water in it to spare.

If she was truly descended from Umma, then it must be through Lucius. If Lucius died of this pestilence . . . what then? Atpomara had warned her. No ancestor, no descendant. Not just death but nonexistence. Nothingness. Complete oblivion.

She would have been afraid for Lucius' life even if he'd been nothing to her, but for the dozens, maybe hundreds of lives that would come after him, her fear mounted to terror. She bent over him, breathing hard, and struggling for composure. His drawers were wet and stinking. She changed them and cleaned him, as Gaius Calidius Severus had done for her. He tried to fight her off, but his body wasn't paying much attention to what his brain told it.

At least, she thought, he had enough strength in him to fight.

Julia didn't, when Nicole did the same for her. But she was still breathing, and her body was still fever-warm. As long as she had breath and heat in her, there was hope. Genuine unselfish hope, unconnected with Nicole's very existence. It felt almost virtuous.

One slow step at a time, Nicole made her way downstairs. The tavern was dark and quiet. There were half a dozen loaves of bread by the oven. All were stale, at least three days old, maybe more. Nicole didn't care. She tore a chunk off a loaf and ate it with a cup of wine, soaking bits of the hard, dry stuff in the sweet heavenly liquid. The bread sat in her stomach like a stone. The wine, though, the wine was rain in a desert. Her body absorbed the moisture with joyous gratitude, and began to bloom.

She dipped up a second cup. When she'd got about halfway through it, the front door swung open. Gaius Calidius Severus strode in in a gust of wind and a scent of rain. The hood of his tunic was up, darkened with wet. Mud caked his booted feet.

He was well into the tavern before he saw Nicole standing by the bar, holding onto it to keep from tilting over. "Mistress Umma!" he cried in glad surprise. "Mithras be praised— you're on the mend. And the others?"

"Lucius and Julia are very sick, but they're still alive. Aurelia is . . . Aurelia is . . ." Nicole couldn't make herself say it. *Wouldn't* make herself say it. Instead, she asked, "How is your father? How's Titus?"

"He died yesterday," Gaius Calidius Severus said. Just like that, baldly, without any effort to soften the blow. Once Nicole would have thought he didn't care, but she knew better now. He was numb; running on autopilot. Saying what he had to say, and getting it over with. "In the end, it was a mercy. I was going to find an undertaker after I came here. It'll take some looking, from what I hear. A lot of them are dead."

Black humor, Nicole thought. It was even slightly funny,

and yet she wanted to laugh. *A lot of them are dead.* A lot
of everybody was dead. Butchers, bakers, candlestick-mak-
ers. Except they didn't have candles here. They had lamps.
Lamp-oil vendors. Tavernkeepers. Fullers and dyers. Fine
and gentle men. Lovers.

She called herself to order. She couldn't crack up. She
didn't have time. "If you find an undertaker," she said, "let
me know his name. I'll need him, too. Because—because—"

With the wine inside her, at last, she could cry. For Aurelia, who had become her daughter. For Titus Calidius Severus, whom she had—loved? Yes, loved. For the world in
which she was trapped, the world from which she couldn't
escape, the world that was falling to pieces all around her.

Gaius Calidius Severus wept with her. He'd been carrying
the same leaden burden, the same crushing weight of grief.
Tears didn't wash any of it away, but they lightened it a
little. A very little.

When they'd both run out of tears, they stood in the gloom
of the shuttered tavern, in the drumming of the rain, and
stared bleakly at one another. "It can't get worse than this,"
she said. "It can't."

15

THE NEXT DAY, TITUS Calidius Severus was laid in the
cemetery outside the city's walls. Nicole was still too
weak to leave the tavern, let alone walk so far. Just crossing
the street that morning to sit with Gaius Calidius Severus left
her exhausted. But that much she could do, and that much
she did. She was glad she had: the young dyer was all alone
in the shop, sitting in the reek of ancient piss and the muddle
of colors on the floor and walls and on the sides of the vats.
He wasn't doing anything, hadn't tried to ease his sorrows
with work. He was simply sitting there, on a bench by the

wall, as she'd seen people wait in bus stations, with a kind of blank and bovine patience.

He brightened at the sight of her, jumped up with something of his old energy, took her arm as if she'd been an ancient grandmother, and helped her to the bench he'd just vacated. She breathed shallowly to keep from gagging; her stomach was delicate enough without adding the dyer's effluvium to it. But he was so glad to see her, she couldn't bring herself to turn and bolt back out into the relatively fresh air of the street.

When she'd caught what breath she could manage, she said, "I wanted—I should go to the cemetery with you. But—"

Gaius Calidius Severus patted her arm awkwardly. "No. No, don't fret about it. You've got your boy and your freedwoman to take care of. And Father wouldn't want you to put yourself in any more danger, not after you've come through this far. We'd need another funeral if you did. He'd hate that."

Nicole swallowed. Her throat hurt. "Thank you," she said when she could trust her voice. She felt as if she'd received absolution. But it needed a little more. After a moment she said, "You're a lot like him, you know."

Gaius Calidius Severus blushed and ducked his head. Was he remembering the times he'd gone upstairs with Julia? Maybe, maybe not. And, Nicole thought, his father would probably have done the exact same thing at his age. There wasn't anything wrong with him that a decade and a few cold showers wouldn't fix. "Now I thank you," he said. "It's better than I deserve, but thank you for saying it." He paused, as if to nerve himself for what he meant to say next. "How are Julia and Lucius doing?"

Titus Calidius Severus would have put Umma's son ahead of the freedwoman, but he hadn't gone to bed with her, either. Again Nicole noted the difference without rising to it. The question was kindly meant. That was real concern—real friendship.

She answered him warmly then, and fully. "They'll pull

through, I think. Both of them. They're almost to the point I was at yesterday when you found me. But Aurelia—" She stopped to pull herself together. That ordeal would come the day after tomorrow. Even in the fall chill, it wouldn't wait any longer. "They should be there, and I have to be there. Somehow."

"They won't be able to come." Gaius Calidius Severus spoke with some of his father's authority. He was right, too; Nicole knew it. She wasn't any more pleased by that than she'd been when Titus was too damnably right for his own good. "I'll look after them, don't worry about that. And as for you," he said, shaking a finger under her nose, "hire a sedan chair to take you to the graveyard and back. You should be strong enough by then to manage that. No one will think it's ostentatious, not when you've just got over the pestilence, and not for your own daughter's funeral."

Nicole didn't want to argue with him. She was too tired. She got out of there somehow, not too discourteously she hoped, and crawled back to the tavern and her two charges.

Titus Calidius Severus' funeral procession rocked and wailed its way down the street that afternoon. Nicole watched it from her doorway, standing very still, holding to the doorpost when her knees started to buckle. There were a few people in the procession after all, and a whole quartet of hired mourners, and two fluteplayers who vied with one another to see how far off key they could go and still be somewhere within shouting distance of a tune. Titus would have had something wry to say about that, and a smile to go with it, warm and a little crooked.

That wasn't Titus on the bier, that still and shrouded shape. No. It wasn't anyone she knew. Titus was still alive somewhere. Her skin could still remember the touch of his hands, the way his beard tickled when he kissed her, the sound of his voice in her ear, murmuring words that made her giggle even while they made love. Had she loved him with a grand passion? Hardly. But she'd *liked* him. She missed him, his dry wit, his comforting presence, even his habit of always being right, rather more than she missed taking him up to her bed on nights after men's day at the baths.

She still didn't have any tears. She gave him memory instead, and the strength she could spare to stand in the doorway till the last of the procession had rounded the corner and vanished. Then she turned, and walking slowly, making her way from table to bench to stool to bar, she made her way back up to the two of hers who were still alive, and the one who waited, wrapped in a blanket, for the undertaker's assistants to come and take her away.

Nicole ended up taking Gaius Calidius Severus' advice. The sedan chair was like a four-man stretcher with a seat. Riding in it was beastly uncomfortable, but it was far easier than walking—particularly as half the way was sloppy with mud. The sky was ugly as unwashed wool, heavy and gray and full of rain, but none was falling just then. If they were lucky, they'd get there and back again before the threat of rain became reality.

Gaius Calidius Severus had been right about what people would say, or not say, of Nicole's resorting to a sedan chair. Ila said not a word as she walked along beside the litter. If Umma's sister didn't complain about something Nicole did, it wasn't worth complaining about.

Ila probably had other things on her mind, at that. She was sneezing and coughing in a way that made Nicole's stomach clench. Brigomarus wasn't there; he was down with it, which explained why he hadn't come to help Nicole as he'd promised. She'd been fool enough to hope he was just being censorious again, or that he'd found some new reason to be aggravated with her. His absence mattered more than she would have expected. He'd been a sort of constant in this world, as close to family as she could get, arguments and all. She didn't want him hanging about playing Big Brother, but she didn't want him dead, either.

Along with Ila came Sextus Longinius Iulus, who hadn't caught the pestilence in spite of everything; Ofanius Valens, who'd survived a milder bout than Nicole's; and sharp-tongued Antonina and her husband, a mousy little man whose name Nicole never had learned. As funeral processions went in these days, it was a largish gathering, and kindhearted. None of these people needed to be here; they all must be worn out with attending funerals. And still they'd come to see Aurelia to her rest.

Nicole had refused to hire mourners—another thing that Ila had declined to comment on; really, she had to be ill, if she kept quiet about that—but she had asked the undertaker to arrange for a priest. The one provided was a type that must be universal: thickset, florid, with a well-padded middle and an even more well-padded vocabulary. He mouthed platitudes about innocence plucked too soon, and flowers cut down before their prime, and the golden hope of a better world. She'd heard just about the same words, in just about the same plummy tone, on a Sunday-morning Gospel hour. All this man lacked was the shiny suit and the pompadour.

Nicole tuned him out as best she could. She'd asked for a priest, after all. She should have expected what she got. It wouldn't have been any different in the twentieth century; it hadn't been when her grandfather died. He'd been a determined nonchurchgoer, but the family had been just as determined to give him a Christian sendoff. The priest they found hadn't known the man at all, had given a eulogy so generic as to be ludicrous, and had referred throughout to the deceased, whose name was Richard Uphoff, as "our dearly departed Bob Upton."

At least this man got Aurelia's name right, if nothing else about her. Nicole fixed her eyes on the bier, on the small shrouded figure, seeming so much smaller in death. No larger, really, than Kimberley had been, the night before Nicole vanished out of that world and into this one. This dream turned nightmare, this life suddenly so full of death.

Nicole's throat was aching-tight. She couldn't cry. She wanted to scream. Someone else was, away across the cemetery: shrieking and wailing. It wasn't the voice of a hired mourner; those had their own style, almost like a religious chant. This was too wild, too unrestrained.

That wasn't the American way of death. Even in a world

that had never heard of America, Nicole couldn't bring herself to indulge in it. She sat in the sedan chair in silence while the undertaker's assistants laid the body in the small, muddy hole that was all the grave Aurelia would get. Then she had to get out of the chair, and, though she tottered like an old woman, lay one of Julia's good loaves and a jar of raisins and a jug of heavily watered wine in the grave. She'd wanted to bring Aurelia's favorite honeyed cake, but she'd thought of it too late. There'd been no time to make one.

It was ridiculous to think the dead child could notice what was missing, or care; and yet it mattered very much. Too much, maybe. The wine was Falernian—that much Nicole could give her. Poor little Aurelia, who'd never had the chance to have much, at least had that to take into the grave with her.

As Nicole knelt by the grave, unable to muster the strength to rise, the skies at last gave up their burden of rain. "Even the heavens are weeping," Ila said, proving the Romans were no more immune to sentiment than to the pestilence.

The gravediggers hadn't been lazing on the grass on this of all days. Even before Nicole was ready to stand up, they were standing over the grave, spades shouldered like rifles. *So shoot me,* Nicole thought bitterly. Somehow, she got to her feet, slipping a little on the muddy grass, and wrapped her cloak about herself. Stiffly, unsteadily, she half climbed, half fell back into the covered chair. "Take me home," she said to the bearers. They hardly grunted as they lifted her. She'd never been other than lean, and now, with the sickness, she was skeletal. And they must be eager to get in out of the rain.

Gaius Calidius Severus was sitting in the tavern, holding the fort as he'd promised. He'd acquired reinforcements since she left: a vaguely familiar man of about his father's age. They'd been drinking wine: there were cups in front of them. Maybe they'd put brass in the cash box, maybe not. Nicole wasn't going to worry about it. Calidius Severus was doing her a favor by being here at all. Two cups of wine, or however many it turned out to be, was small enough price to pay.

He greeted Nicole with a smile that seemed just a little bit too glad. He was just a boy, after all, and she'd left him with a heavy responsibility. "Julia and Lucius are asleep, Mistress Umma," he said. "They woke up for a while, and I gave them some gruel and a little bit of bread sopped in wine, and they even ate a bite each. But they're still pretty weak. The least little thing flattens them."

Nicole drew a faint sigh. She hadn't known till she heard him, that she'd been expecting him to tell her they were worse; they were sinking, they'd soon be dead. But they were better. Notably so, if they were eating and drinking, however little they might be keeping down. "The least little thing flattens *me*," she said, "and I was getting better days before they did."

Gaius Calidius Severus nodded. His relief was still palpable. It made him seem to take refuge in a change of subject. "Mistress Umma, you know Gaius Attius Exoratus, don't you? He came to call on me, and I asked him over here."

Nicole remembered the face: he'd eaten and drunk in the tavern a few times, though he wasn't a regular. She hadn't remembered his name, if she'd ever heard it. But she could say "Of course I do," and even sound as if she meant it.

Attius Exoratus nodded. "Aye, we know each other, lad." His voice was a bass rumble, like falling rocks. "I'd have come anyhow, whether you chanced to be here or not." He pinned Nicole with a hard stare under a bristle of brows. "It's a cursed shame he's gone, Umma. That's all I've got to say. He was one of the good ones."

Titus Calidius Severus, he meant; he had to mean. "That he was." Nicole got herself some wine—dipping up a cup seemed so natural now, she didn't even notice herself doing it half the time—and stood next to the two men. "That he was," she repeated quietly.

"And young Calidius tells me you just put your daughter

in the ground." Gaius Attius Exoratus let out a long sigh. "Life's hard. I'm sorry for that, too."

"Thank you," Nicole said. There seemed to be more that she should say, but she couldn't imagine what.

He didn't seem to find her response inadequate, at least. "We've all done too much mourning lately," he said. Nicole nodded, unable to find words to respond to that. He went on, "I only came by to tell you, it did my heart good to see how happy you made my old mate. We fought side by side, you know, and mustered out within a couple of weeks of each other, then moved here from the legionary camp down the river." He pointed east. "He was as happy a man as I ever saw, when this lad's mother was alive. I was afraid he'd never be happy again after he lost her. But you took care of that. He's not here anymore to thank you for it, so I reckoned somebody ought to."

"He did let me know," Nicole said. That was true for her, and had surely been true for Umma. Still, there was more that needed saying, and this time she managed to say it. "It's very good of you to make sure it's taken care of."

"I know how these things should go," Attius said.

Nicole nodded again. They sat, she stood leaning lightly against a table. She thought about sitting, but she wasn't in the mood just yet.

Attius was looking at her. Staring, really. Giving her the eye, she thought. So: was he going to try hitting on her, now his old war buddy wasn't in the way? She took a deep breath, to laugh in his face. She had no interest in anyone right now, new or old, and less than no interest in sex. The only thing even vaguely related to it that she cared for at the moment was lying down. Alone.

Gaius Attius Exoratus lowered his eyes, grunted, and got to his feet. "I'd better get on home," he said. "My wife will be waiting for me."

Nicole almost choked on the breath she'd been holding. Was he sending her a message? Or had he just been trying to remember her face, to keep his memory clearer? Maybe he did have the hots for her.

If he did, he wasn't going to act on it. Wife, was it? "I hope she stays well," Nicole said. "And you, too, Attius."

"Thank you kindly," he answered. He drained the cup of wine that Gaius Calidius Severus must have dipped for him, and set it down, and belched. Then, wrapping his cloak around him and pulling a fold of it over his graying hair, he went out into the rain.

"He's a good fellow, Attius is," Gaius Calidius Severus said after a judicious few moments. "My father liked him a lot."

"I understand why," Nicole said; and she did. "He was very nice." She hesitated. Then she said, "And I want to thank you, too, for taking care of me and for taking care of all of us. For everything."

She didn't feel like going into any more detail than that. He understood what she meant; like his father, he wasn't stupid. He coughed a time or two, maybe in embarrassment, maybe in something worse. "I didn't mean to scare you," he said. "It was easier when you didn't wake up, but when you did—I guess that meant you were starting to get over it."

"I think so," Nicole said. "I wasn't out of my head anymore after that." She still felt as if the least puff of breeze would blow her away; she wouldn't be all the way better for a long time yet. The tears that filled her eyes were partly tears of weakness, but only partly. "I wish your father had made it, too. I wish Aurelia had. I wish—"

"Everybody," Gaius Calidius Severus said somberly. Nicole nodded. When he spoke again, he almost seemed surprised at himself, as if such large concerns were new to him: "I wonder what Carnuntum will be like after this."

"Your father told me it was killing one in four, sometimes one in three, down in Italy," Nicole said. "It's not over yet, not here."

"I know it's not," young Calidius Severus answered with a touch of impatience, and a touch—just a touch—of fear. "He told me the same thing."

One in four, sometimes one in three. That wasn't simply a disease. It was more like a nuclear war. Nicole tried to imagine a disaster on the same scale in the United States. Seventy-five or eighty million people dead in a few months— the country would fall apart. No doubt about it. The different parts of the Roman Empire weren't so tightly connected as those of the U.S.A., but even so, this had to be a staggering blow.

As if to underline the thought, a funeral procession went by outside, not much bigger than Aurelia's and even more miserable: the rain was coming down in sheets.

"Harvest wasn't very good this year," Gaius Calidius Severus mused, "even before the farmers started getting sick. That's going to make things even harder."

"I've heard people talking about that," Nicole said. It hadn't seemed particularly real at the time, but for some reason, now she understood. No farmers meant no one to bring in the harvest. No one to bring in the harvest meant no food in the market. And no food in the market meant . . .

Young Calidius Severus laughed. It sounded like a man whistling in the dark. "I hope there's enough in the granaries to keep us fed till spring."

"If there's not," Nicole said with a renewal of hope, "they'll bring it in from somewhere else." But as soon as she'd said it, she saw the hole in it. "If farmers elsewhere aren't too badly hit by the pestilence, and they have any grain left over."

Young Calidius Severus nodded. As if it were some kind of game, he found yet another hole, one that Nicole hadn't thought of: "And if they can get the grain to us."

No trucks, she reminded herself. *No trains.* Transportation by land was hideously expensive and even more hideously slow when everything went by muleback or oxcart; she saw that every time she bought a new amphora of Falernian. Mules and oxcarts couldn't carry that much, either, not when you were talking about feeding thousands of people.

But Carnuntum lay by the Danube, and dumped raw sewage into the river every day—downstream, she admitted; she was always amazed when the Romans paid even the most basic attention to sanitary matters. Barges and boats plied it.

If the pestilence hadn't touched anybody farther west . . .

Before she made a fool of herself by speaking of it, her clouded memory brought her up short. The west wasn't safe, either. Even if the pestilence hadn't reached it, war had. What were the names of the people the Romans were fighting? "The Quadi and the Marcomanni," she said, half to herself.

Gaius Calidius Severus looked as grim as his father had when he watched the German tribesmen swagger through the market square. "And the Lombards, too," he said. He peered north past his own shop, toward the Danube, and looked grimmer yet. "I only hope they don't come over the river here, too, once they've had word of all our losses. They're like vultures, those barbarians. They love to flock around a carcass."

Nicole shuddered at the image, and tugged at the neck of her tunic. Before she quite realized what she was doing, she'd spat onto her bosom.

He followed suit, turning aside the ill omen. "The pestilence has to be going through the legions in the camp east of here and at Vindobona, the same way it's going through this city. The barbarians will know it, too. Curse them."

"Maybe it's going through them, too." It was neither compassionate nor politically correct to wish an epidemic on people she didn't know. But if it came to a choice between pestilence and war . . .

Not in my backyard, people in Los Angeles shouted when they didn't want a jail or a housing project or a nuclear-power plant or anything else necessary but unpleasant built anywhere near them. Mean-spirited, Nicole had thought them. Selfish. Deficient in humane impulses.

To hell with humane impulses. Carnuntum was just barely making its way through a pestilence. Death was walking through the streets. Famine stared it in the face. There was only one horseman of the Apocalypse missing, and she'd be damned if she'd wish a war on the city as well. As trivial as they suddenly seemed, she shaped the words in her mind regardless. *Not in my backyard. Please, God, not in* my *back-yard.*

"Maybe the barbarians are as bad off as we are," Gaius Calidius Severus said. "Let's hope they are. Let's pray for it." He levered himself to his feet, moving like a much older man. He had to be as worn out as she was. "Here, I'd better do some work. You take care of yourself, Mistress Umma, and don't push yourself too hard. If you need help, call. I'll come." He pulled his hood up over his head, hunched his shoulders, and ducked out into the rain.

She watched him go. He detoured a bit, down the sidewalk to the stepping stones, to cross as dry as he could. He paused when he reached the narrow walk on the other side, as if to gather his forces, then strode on up it and into the shop. He and his father had lived above it in all apparent amity; no squabbles that Nicole had ever seen or heard. And now he was alone.

No wonder he'd paused. It was hard enough for her to go up those back stairs, knowing there'd be one fewer sleeper above, and praying that neither Julia nor—please God—Lucius had taken a sudden turn for the worse and died while she was fuddling about below. What it must be like to walk into those rooms, to know there was no one else there—she didn't want to imagine it, and yet she couldn't help herself.

She wanted to leap up, run, make sure Lucius and Julia were alive and recovering. The best she could do was a slow crawl, creeping like an old woman, taking each step with trembling care, and resting every few steps. She couldn't even spare the energy for frustration. Patience, she willed herself. *Patience.* That should be her watchword for this whole, primitive, maddeningly slow-moving world.

All through the fall and winter, the pestilence lashed Carnuntum. Both Lucius and Julia recovered—ever so slowly, as Nicole did herself. Losing one in four in her household left her statistically average, as best she could tell. She would have given anything to escape that tyranny of numbers. Aurelia's absence was an ache behind her breastbone.

She'd taken little enough direct notice of the child while she was alive; life had been too busy, her head too strained with the effort of living in a world so totally foreign. But Aurelia had been a part of the world in ways that Nicole hadn't even noticed until she was gone. Waking up in the morning, beginning the day, marking its completion by the kids' tramping down the stairs and demanding their breakfast—without coffee, it had become a waking ritual of its own. She'd become accustomed to Aurelia's presence. She'd grown fond of the little dark-haired girl with the gap where one front tooth had been, who loved to go with Nicole to women's day at the baths. Who'd got into Nicole's makeup box once, and painted herself to look a perfect horror, and been so proud of her achievement that Nicole didn't dare laugh at her. Who had fought with Lucius as only siblings could, and not always been the one to make up—she'd been the tougher-minded of the two, Nicole had often thought.

And now she was gone, and Nicole ached with the loss. Would she have ached any more for Kimberley or Justin? *Had* she, ever, since she came to Carnuntum?

Ah, but they were alive, somewhere in time—alive and, if there were gods, and if those gods had any mercy, well. She missed them still, in unexpected moments, or in the dark before dawn. But neither of them was dead. She missed them. She didn't grieve for them, for the lives they'd never have, or the death that had taken them so ungodly soon.

Their safety on the other side of time was her anchor, the thing that made it possible for her to live in this world without them. She hadn't known till too late that Lucius and Aurelia had been the counterweight. While she had those two in her care, she could tell herself she had a clear purpose here. With one of them gone . . . how could she hold? She had to; Lucius needed her, and Julia needed her, and even Gaius Calidius Severus seemed to rely on her presence across the street. And yet she could feel herself slipping. She had to hold on, but it grew harder rather than easier, the longer it went on.

Brigomarus pulled through, though so narrowly that he

looked like a ghost of himself. Ila died—which Nicole had a great deal of difficulty pretending to be sorry for. Tabica and Pacatus never took sick at all.

Nicole heard that with almost resentful envy. She was glad they didn't come to the tavern to flaunt the accident of their good health. Brigomarus came, more than once, never very cordially, but as he said, family was family. And maybe he wasn't terribly fond of his sister and her stick of a husband, either. Umma, or Nicole in Umma's body, might actually be preferable, day for day and scowl for scowl.

Some of her neighbors and customers came through the sickness better than Umma's family had. The wet nurse had brought the pestilence into Sextus Longinius Iulus' house, but both he and his son escaped it. Sometimes he would bring the baby with him when he came over for a cup of wine or a bowl of whatever Nicole or Julia had on the menu. Longinius Iulus the younger was a happy baby. He was always smiling or gurgling with laughter. He knew nothing of pestilence, or of death. For that, Nicole envied him.

Ofanius Valens, that cheerful little man, bounced back fast from his dose of the sickness. He came in nearly every day, bringing this dainty or that for Julia: figs candied in honey, cuts of ham that were more fat than meat. He was perfectly open as to his motive. "Got to put some flesh on you, sweetheart," he said to Julia in Nicole's hearing. "You're nothing but skin and bones. I'm not too terribly fond of lying on a ladder."

He was fattening her like a goose. Nicole wanted to get angry at him, and at Julia, too. She did manage a small flare of temper, but it died down as soon as it rose. It was the sickness, she told herself. It left behind a lassitude that was terribly slow to pass.

That was even true—to a degree. She had neither the energy nor the inclination for a truly towering outrage. And if she had—what could she do? Short of throwing Julia into her room and walling up the entrance, she didn't see how she could keep the freedwoman from doing what she obviously wanted to do.

Lassitude or no, Nicole kept a weather eye on Lucius. If he so much as headed for the door, she pounced. "Have you got your heavy cloak on? Put the hood up, you'll freeze. Go back and put on your socks!"

He put up with it better than she would ever have expected from a boy his age: for the first day or two he suffered without complaint, but on the third day, as she came swooping out of the upper reaches with an extra pair of socks in hand, he planted his feet and put on a ferocious scowl. "*Mother!* I'm not made of glass. I won't break."

"Maybe you won't," she fired back, "but you're all I've got in this world. I'm going to look out for you, and that's that."

He rolled his eyes and shook his shoulders—less a shrug than a shedding of her suffocating concern—and ran off to play with the remnants of the old noisy gang of neighborhood boys. As children will, he was recovering much faster than an adult. He came in from playing earlier than he used to, and fell into bed without even token protest, but his appetite was voracious and he was gaining strength by the day.

"Mind you don't get wet!" she called after him, "or I'll give you something to remember it by."

He didn't even acknowledge the threat. Brat. He knew she wasn't up to chasing after him and giving him the swat he deserved, either.

Nicole stood with the socks still in her hand, turning and twisting them in her fingers. The rough burn of knitted wool kept part of her mind in the world where it belonged, but the rest was wandering afield.

All I've got in this world. If Nicole was in fact descended from Umma, that was true in more ways than she could explain to Lucius. If something happened to him, if the chain broke, what would become of her? Would she disappear? Would it be as if she had never been? There was no way to tell, and no way she wanted to test it. She'd keep Lucius safe whether he wanted it or no, for her sake as well as his own.

The price of grain rose. It never got above a level she

could afford, but it did rise enough that she had to charge more for bread. Customers grumbled. She lost a few, but they came back when they discovered that bread wasn't any cheaper elsewhere. "It's criminal," one of them said, "but you still make the best loaf in Carnuntum."

"You get what you pay for," Nicole said—and was a little startled by the pause, the stare as he worked it out, and then the burst of laughter. Another twentieth-century cliché that people here had never heard before.

Even with people coming back for the best bread in Carnuntum, business was not what it had been in the summer. Part of that was the fault of the pestilence, but part, she realized, was the season. When she'd come into this world, spring was gliding into summer; the sun rose very early and set very late. Now that was reversing itself. Without the aid of watch or clock, she couldn't be sure of the days' length as winter drew near, but they seemed far shorter than in Los Angeles, and in Indianapolis, too. Eight hours of daylight? Nine at the most? Damned little, in a world lit only by fire.

But even that was deceptive, because it assumed the sun shed much light when it did deign to scurry above the horizon. What with rain and sleet and occasional snow and endless masses of dirty-gray clouds and fogs off the Danube that sometimes didn't break up till nearly noon and sometimes didn't break up at all, Carnuntum was shrouded in gloom.

The outer weather mirrored Nicole's inner climate. With the coming of winter, she felt, as she hadn't since the first days after she arrived, how very much she missed artificial light. No torch or oil-burning lamp could compare to a plain old forty-watt bulb. They barely lifted the skirts of the dark. They couldn't ever drive it away.

She wanted it driven away. She *needed* it driven away. It pressed on her, weighing her down. She was always gloomy, always depressed. She couldn't get herself moving in the morning; she went to bed as soon as the light was out of the sky. She snapped at people for no reason. Her mood was filthy, and filthier as the winter went on.

Sometime in December, a phrase came back to her from the part of herself that she'd shut away in the dark, her lightbulb-lit, daylight-bright twentieth-century self: *seasonal affective disorder.* If she didn't have it, she sure as hell had its first cousin. Had Umma been the same way—was it her physiology responding to the lack of light? Or was it Nicole herself reacting more strongly because she wasn't used to it?

Either way, she amazed herself with how much she could sleep. She might almost have been a hibernating animal. When slate-gray gloom turned black, she would wrap herself in her blankets, and not know another thing till black lightened again toward gloom. After a while even a bursting bladder couldn't wake her; she slept straight through, woke and half-fell on the pot, and staggered downstairs to scrape out another day's living.

As December advanced, Julia and Lucius started to get excited about something called the Saturnalia. With all that they said about it, Nicole understood how and why the English word came to be associated with revelry. It was a whole week's festival, centered on the winter solstice; it celebrated the sun's turn back toward the north. Sunreturn—inch by inch, day by day, creeping once again toward the long brilliant days and brief starlit nights of summer.

No wonder they made a festival out of it. Even the dim vague dream of honest daylight was enough to perk Nicole up, though the dirty-gray reality of the days dragged her down soon enough.

Then Lucius started dropping hints. "Did you see the game board old Furius Picatus has in his shop around the corner? It's hollow, and it's got a set of dice in the middle. Jupiter! The games I could play, if I had that."

Why, Nicole thought, Saturnalia was like Christmas. People gave presents—and kids dropped hints. A game board and dice were preferable to the latest media tie-in, hands down, no questions asked. So—had Christmas presents begun in the tradition of the Saturnalia? Did they really go that far back?

She'd always loved Christmas, even when it was trendy

to emulate Ebenezer Scrooge. Choosing and buying presents, hiding them, waiting to see the faces when they were unwrapped at last—she was like a little kid. "About the only time you ever were," Frank had said to her after the divorce. At this distance, she could grant that maybe he was right. But better to be a kid once a year than never to be a kid at all.

Yes, even in a year that had brought so much shock, and so much death. This was a time for warmth, and for such light as there could be. She wouldn't forget grief, or put the dead out of her mind completely, but she could give herself, at least for this season, entirely to the living.

She bought the board and dice for Lucius, bargaining Furius Picatus down to a price that was almost reasonable. Then she found a little greenish glass jar of rosewater for Julia, packaging that would have been the height of trendiness in Neiman-Marcus, and a pair of sandals for Brigomarus. She measured his feet from prints he left on the muddied tavern floor—pretty damn clever, if she thought so herself. For Gaius Calidius Severus she bought a belt of woven leather, very fine and fancy, with a gleaming brass buckle. She was vastly pleased with that, and with the price she'd got the leatherworker down to—her bargaining skills were honed by now to a wicked edge.

Two days before the first day of the festival, Gaius Calidius Severus came over for a cup of wine. He hadn't been by for a day or two: busy, she'd supposed, with orders for gifts. He greeted her less brightly than usual, and stumbled as he sat down. Then, as she brought him his cup of two-*as* wine, he doubled up in a fit of sneezing and coughing. It looked—oh, God, it looked like the pestilence.

He straightened, wiping his eyes. Something in his face told her not to say anything. He drank his wine, made small talk that she forgot as soon as the words had gone through her head, and went back home, mumbling something about a dye lot that had to come out right then, and he hoped it was the right shade, too; it was for one of his pickier customers.

Nicole stood by the bar, watching him go. There was no one else in the tavern just then, only Julia kneading a batch of the best bread in Carnuntum. "It's not fair," Nicole said to her, bursting out with it before she even had time to think. "It's not right. He took care of his father. He took care of us. The sickness passed him by. Now it's been gone for months—and he's got it. *Why?*"

Julia shrugged. She knew as well as Nicole did, there wasn't any answer to that. After a bit, she said, "He didn't seem too bad yet, did he?"

"No," Nicole said, "not yet. But we know it gets worse. Don't we?"

"Oh, yes." Julia didn't say anything more than that. She didn't need to. Her cheekbones still showed sharp as wind-carved rock under her skin, with no padding of flesh to smooth their outline. She'd have been a knockout in certain parts of Beverly Hills, where you could never be too rich or too thin, but in Carnuntum Ofanius Valens was right: she was a creature in sore need of feeding up.

She finished kneading the lump of dough on the countertop, washed her hands in a bowl of water, and dried them on her tunic. Then, in a tone that said she'd made her decision and that was that, she said, "He took care of me when I was sick. I'm going over there to take care of him. I'll be back in a bit."

Nicole blinked, startled. Julia had never asserted herself this way before. Nicole should be welcoming it as a declaration of freedom. Instead, she found herself—annoyed? No, of course not. She was being practical, that was all. There was work to do here. "If he's not that bad, he won't need to be taken care of yet," she said.

Julia looked at her. They were both speaking Latin, but they were not speaking the same language. As if to make that clear, the freedwoman said, "He'll still enjoy it now. Later . . . who knows? He may never have another chance." While Nicole was still groping for a reply, Julia walked calmly out of the tavern and down the sidewalk, toward the stepping stones.

Nicole opened her mouth to call out, but closed it again. Julia was a free woman, and an adult. Even if she was Nicole's employee, her mind and her decisions were her own. As Nicole watched, she came up the walk on the far side of the muddy street and opened the door to the shop where Gaius Calidius Severus now worked alone. She closed the door after her. Nicole couldn't see any more than that, but she didn't need to. Her imagination worked perfectly well.

She'd never used sex to say *thank you* even to Frank, let alone to a neighbor who'd been nice to her. Most of the time, Julia's freewheeling approach to such things made her want to pound her head against the top of the bar. This once, she resolved to say not a word.

Frank would have been amazed. She was the epitome of the Midwestern prude, he'd told her often enough. "Judge plenty, and be damned sure nobody judges you," he'd said. She didn't even remember what she'd replied. Something lame, she was sure.

Julia came back not too long after—an hour, maybe; maybe less. She wasn't any more or less kempt than ever, but there was a flush on her cheeks that hadn't been there before. It almost made her look like her old robust self.

Nicole didn't ask, but Julia answered regardless. "Tomorrow might have been too late," she said, "but today—it was fine."

That practically forced Nicole to say a word. She found one: "Good." Julia shot her a quizzical glance. Nicole wondered why. Umma, surely, would have said the same thing. But Nicole had been in Umma's body for more than six months now. Julia had got used to her odd, squeamish reactions to perfectly normal and acceptable things.

Good grief, thought Nicole. She'd done it. She'd surprised the by now unsurprisable Julia.

She nodded slowly, letting the moment stretch. "Good," she said again. No one ought to be too predictable.

Saturnalia felt amazingly like Christmas. No one had ever heard of a Christmas tree, which was too bad; Nicole loved the glitter of the tree, and one would have looked—well, interesting over by the bar. But everything else was remarkably similar.

The resemblance extended all the way to getting a present from someone for whom she hadn't bought one in return. Skinny, short-tempered Antonina presented her with a glazed pottery dog that was one of the ugliest things she'd ever seen—and that included her mother's set of Staffordshire dogs. Even those were more appealing than this thing was.

"Thank you so much," she said as warmly as she could. For all she knew, the damn critter was the height of swank in these parts. "Wait just one moment, would you? I have your present upstairs."

She hurried up the stairs in a haze of desperation, with the rags of her smile still clinging to her face. Her bedroom offered little enough sanctuary. But—for a wonder, her eyes lit on just the thing. She snatched the *terra sigillata* bowl from the set on her chest of drawers, dusted it off hastily, and trotted back down the stairs. She was getting stronger at last: she didn't even think about passing out from so much exertion. With as much of a flourish as she could muster, she presented the bowl to her neighbor.

Antonina made gratified noises much like the ones she'd used herself. She and Nicole drank wine together. Good cheer reigned, as much as it ever did around Antonina. After a suitable interval, she said as cordial a good-bye as Nicole had ever heard from her, and went on out the door, bowl in hand.

As soon as she was gone, Julia picked up the dog and made a ghastly face—almost as ghastly as the dog's own. "By the gods, that's a hideous little thing, isn't it?"

"You think so, too?" said Nicole. "Well; one has to be polite. Maybe she thinks it's the height of fashion."

"Hardly!" said Julia, in a tone so like a Valley Girl that Nicole almost burst out laughing. But there would have been no explaining the distinctive intonations of "As *if!*" to a second-century Roman freedwoman in the valley of the Danube.

It was a relief, actually, to know that she might get rid of the ceramic tumor without offending local standards of good taste.

"I'll bet somebody gave it to her, and she's just getting rid of it to keep from spending any money on a decent present," Julia said.

"Then we're even," Nicole said, "because I pulled that bowl off the dresser and dusted it off, and there it was."

"It wasn't a bad bowl," Julia said. "But this . . ." She juggled the dog from hand to hand. It slipped; Nicole held her breath. But it didn't fall. Julia plunked it down on the bar, right by the bowl of nuts.

"It doesn't look half bad there," Nicole observed.

"Maybe a customer will have a few too many and knock it on the floor," said Julia.

"Maybe there's treasure hidden inside it."

Julia's eyes gleamed. Then she laughed in disbelief. "No! Not if *Antonina* gave it to you. You can bet, if there'd been anything in there, she'd have winkled it out."

"Dear old Antonina," Nicole said with a theatrical sigh.

One way and another, the two of them spent a very pleasant half-hour dragging Antonina's name through the mud. There was plenty of that outside, and not a little inside, either. No point in letting it go to waste.

When the dishfest wound down, Nicole filled a bowl of soup and a jar of wine, and took them across the street to Gaius Calidius Severus. He was in no condition to romp on the sheets with Julia now. The pestilence had him fully in its grip. If she could get a little nourishment into him, he might be able to fight the disease. There wasn't much more she, or anyone else in Carnuntum, could do.

It was almost as chilly inside the shop as on the street. That was true in the tavern, too. Fires and braziers were all very well—when you stood right by them. If you didn't, you froze your backside off. That probably had a lot to do with the death rate. People who might have recovered if they could have got warm, shivered and sank and died. *Please, God*, Nicole thought, *don't let that happen to Calidius Severus.*

Even in winter, the fuller and dyer's shop stank to high heaven. Nicole held her breath as she strode quickly through it and climbed the stairs to Gaius Calidius Severus' bedroom. There she had to breathe or turn blue, drawing in a whiff of a completely different stink: the sickroom reek of slops and sour sweat that Nicole had first smelled in the room where Umma's mother died, and then soon after in her own house.

Gaius Calidius Severus had kicked off most of the covers she'd tucked over him the last time she visited. He hadn't, fortunately, kicked over the chamber pot by the bed. Nicole scooped it up and dumped it out the window. "There," she muttered. "That'll be better."

The sound of her voice made him look in her direction. He wasn't altogether out of his head with fever, as she had been. But he wasn't quite connected to the real world, either. He proved it by asking, "What are you doing, Mother?"

"I'm just getting rid of what's in the chamber pot," Nicole answered. She didn't say she was his mother, but neither did she say she wasn't. If thinking his mother was taking care of him made him feel a tiny bit better, that was good; let him think it.

It didn't seem to help a lot, if it helped at all. His expression changed; he began to wriggle, and then to thrash. She braced to leap, in case his fever had turned to convulsions, but as suddenly as he'd begun, he lay still. In a small voice full of shame, he said, "Mother, I'm afraid I've had an accident."

Nicole's nose would have told her as much: the stink in the room had worsened, even though the chamber pot was empty. "Don't worry about it," she said soothingly. "I'll take care of it." Did he think he was a little boy just learning to use the pot? Or did he know how old he was, but not who she was? It didn't really matter. Either way, she had to clean him off, just as, last summer, he'd done for her.

In a way, it wasn't too awfully different from changing Justin's diaper after an especially messy load. In another, it was completely different. Gaius Calidius Severus was emphatically and rather impressively made like a man, not a boy. *No wonder Julia likes him,* Nicole thought through the slight vertigo of trying not to breathe. "I'm sorry," he kept saying. "I'm sorry."

"It's all right," she reassured him. "Everything will be all right."

When he was as clean as he was going to be, and the remains tossed out the window with the rest, she let her hand rest for a moment against his cheek. As soon as she'd done it, she wished she hadn't. She didn't really want to know how high his fever was. But he let out a sigh and leaned very lightly against her palm. Maybe it was cool; maybe it comforted him. Either way, he seemed a little better, a little less troubled.

She spooned soup into him. When he'd taken all he was going to take, which was about a third of the bowl, she poured a cup of wine and held it to his lips. He coughed and spluttered. With a faint sigh, she dipped the spoon into that, too, and got it into him more successfully. One small swallow at a time, he did pretty well, all things considered: he took more than he had the last time, and much more than the time before that. It was progress. She'd take it.

Just as she was about to leave, when she thought he'd fallen asleep, he roused enough to speak. "Thank you, Mistress Umma."

She turned in surprise. He still sounded like hell, but he knew who she was.

"How are you feeling?" she asked, more to be saying something than for any other reason. She knew how he felt: as if he had one whole foot and three toes of the other in the grave. She'd felt the same way herself not so long before.

"Terrible," he answered, right on cue. He sounded it. He looked it. But he had recognized her, and that was a big step forward. He yawned. "Do you mind if I sleep?"

"Not even a little bit," Nicole said warmly. That was good; oh, that was very good indeed. She'd slept, too, slept and slept, after she came out of her delirium. She'd awakened feeling lousy, but she'd been on the mend. Maybe he was, too.

She hated to leave him, but she had the tavern to run, and Julia was waiting. She broke the news as soon as she'd passed the door. Julia clapped her hands in delight. "Maybe we've turned the corner," she said. "Maybe we've turned the corner at last."

"Please," Nicole said, not knowing Whom she was entreating, and not much caring, either, "let it be so."

Gaius Calidius Severus lived. The first time he came across the street on his own, he looked like a tattered shadow of his usually vigorous self. But he was up and moving, and that was all that really mattered. Nicole gave him a plate of fried snails and a cup of Falernian, and wouldn't take an *as* for any of it. "Your father knew how far he'd get, arguing with me," she said when he tried to protest. "Are you going to give me trouble now?"

"No, Mistress Umma," he said meekly. He ate obediently, and drank, with the little widening of the eyes everyone got at the first wonderful taste of Falernian.

Julia sauntered past his table, putting everything she had into it, which was quite a lot. He didn't look up from the wine. *Well*, Nicole thought, *he isn't quite back to normal yet*. A little while longer, and a little way to go. But he was well on track, and that was good enough.

New Year's was celebrated not with horns and paper hats but with clay lamps stamped with the two-faced image of Janus. On the morning of the festival, Julia pulled a couple of them from the back of a shelf, dusted them, filled them with oil, and lit them.

"This year," Nicole said, studying one of the images in the flicker of its flame, "I want to look ahead, not behind. Things will be better. They won't get worse."

"May it be so," Julia said fervently. And after a moment: "The gods know, it would be hard for things to get much worse."

Half an hour couldn't have gone by before a funeral procession made its slow way down the muddy street toward Carnuntum's southwestern gate, the gate that led to the graveyard. Nicole watched it for a moment, then deliberately turned her head. She'd already seen more death in half a year in Carnuntum than in her whole life in the United States. She didn't want or need to be reminded of it again. Not today. Not when there was a future to look forward to, and a life to live.

Since the day he got up from his bed to savor snails and Falernian, Gaius Calidius Severus had come over every day at about the same time. He was back to paying for his own food and drink, which dropped him down to bread and oil and onions and two-*as* wine, but he professed himself happy with it.

Today Nicole served him with a flourish, and gave him a smile to go with it. *Death doesn't win every time*, she thought.

Better and better: he took longer to eat than he might have, because his eye kept turning toward Julia. Nicole felt the smile stretch—not the least bit lessened by the small shock of realization. She was *glad* to see his tongue hanging out over her freedwoman again. It was another sign of his recovery—another sign of life, as it were.

That evening, she was presented with a different sign of life, and not a pleasant one, either. The tooth that had been hurting in a low-grade, steady way ever since she found herself in Umma's body decided it had had enough. Between one heartbeat and the next, a demon picked up a hammer and started trying to drive a tenpenny nail into her lower jaw. It didn't succeed on the first blow, or yet on the tenth. It was going to keep hammering away, it was clear, for as long as it took.

She'd been eating supper with Lucius and Julia. Julia was still in a daze, smiling dreamily—no doubt remembering her hour upstairs with Gaius Calidius Severus. Lucius, however, was alert, a little too much so. He left off babbling about his latest triumph with the game board, fixed her with a penetrating stare, and asked, "What's the matter, Mother? You look awful."

"Toothache," Nicole said thickly. "Bad toothache." She

twisted her tongue back toward the throbbing tooth and prodded it as hard as she dared. The flesh there was hotter than it should have been, and felt puffy and loose. She nearly gagged at the taste. Without even thinking, she thrust fingers into her mouth and tried to twist the tooth a little, to make it more comfortable. That was a mistake. The demon gave up on hammering nails and resorted to railroad spikes. The tavern went dark for a moment—a darkness that had nothing to do with bad weather, three-o'clock sunset, or miserable excuses for lamps.

She sank down onto a stool. If one hadn't been close by, she would have settled for the floor. She would have sunk down through that, if it made the pain go away. But of course the pain had no intention of doing any such thing. It had moved in, lock, stock, and railroad spike.

Her fingers had snapped back as soon as the pain hit the red zone. She stared down at them. The tip of her index finger was smeared with something thick, semiliquid, and grayish yellow. After a moment of pure blankness, she recognized it. "Pus," she said, which could have been either Latin or English. Whichever language it was in, it was not good news. She had to struggle to go on in Latin: "I've got an abscess back there."

Julia shuddered. "Oh, Mistress! That's not good. No, not good at all. I'm afraid you'll have to have it pulled. If you don't, it will keep on festering, and as it festers it will spread. You'll lose a whole lot of teeth. You could even die."

"Right!" said Lucius with altogether too much relish. "All your teeth fall out, and it festers and festers, and you fall over dead."

Nicole narrowly resisted the urge to smack him. "Thank you so much, both of you," she said frostily—but not through clenched teeth. That would have hurt like hell.

The worst of it was, she knew Julia was right. She shuddered just as Julia had. Even in Los Angeles, an abscessed molar wouldn't have been fun. But a dentist in Los Angeles would have had novocaine or a general anesthetic for the pulling, and pain pills for the aftermath. She would have had antibiotics to shrink the abscess, and sterile instruments and rubber gloves and a surgical mask to keep infection away.

A Roman dentist wouldn't be a she. A Roman dentist wouldn't have any of those things, either antisepsis or analgesics.

And it didn't matter. Whatever a dentist could do to her, it couldn't possibly be worse than what her own tooth was putting her through. She shuddered again at the thought of what she faced tomorrow, but living with this hammering pain would be far, far worse.

She even thought, for a longish while, of finding someone to do the job tonight. But it was dark already, and rain was dripping off the eaves. From the sound of it, it was turning to sleet. No way she could venture out in that, nor was any dentist likely to want to try it, even if she'd had a way to get him over here without sending herself or one of her family out into the dark and the wet.

She had to get drunk before she could sleep that night. The wine didn't make the pain go away, but it did shove it off to one side. As long as she didn't have to stare it in the face, she could cope. Mostly. If she had another cup of the one-*as* wine. And another to chase that one down, because it tasted so godawful. Then a third, just because. And . . .

She woke long before sunrise. Her body was a perfect symmetry: a pounding headache exactly matched the toothache. She stumbled downstairs, lit a lamp with shaking hands, and drank another cup of wine. It tasted just as horrible as she'd expected. She poured another cup, but couldn't bring herself to drink it. She nursed it instead, hunched miserably on a stool, until at long last a gray and leaden light filtered through the slats of the shutters.

Julia's robust footfalls on the stairs beat a counterpoint to the pounding in her head and the throbbing in her mouth. She glowered at the freedwoman.

"Oh my," Julia said. "It's too bad the pestilence got Dexter. He was supposed to be very good at pulling teeth."

Nicole wanted to knock Julia's head off, and her bright, healthy voice with it, but she chose to focus instead on the words, and on the thoughts behind them. Focusing helped. "There's that physician named Terentianus," she said, "not far from the market square. I've gone by his place often enough."

Julia shrugged. "I haven't heard much about him, good or bad," she said. "If he's still alive, you might as well try him. They're all pretty much the same."

That wasn't true in L.A. It was sure to be an even greater lie in Carnuntum, which had no licensing arrangements of any sort. Here, if you hung out a sign and said you were a doctor, you were. Even the good doctors here were pathetically bad. The bad doctors were right out of the ballpark.

But Nicole didn't have an awful lot of choice. Her tooth had grown worse as the morning went on. Her whole body ached in sympathy. "If he's still breathing," she said, "I'll try him."

He was in the shop—*office* didn't quite seem to fit—that she'd seen so often: a skinny little man with a nose that looked even larger than it was, because the rest of him was so small. He greeted Nicole with a nearsighted scowl and an audible sigh as she told him her trouble. "Step out into the light and let me see," he said.

Passersby veered off course and paused to gape while Terentianus positioned her in a convenient patch of sunlight— imagine; sunlight, and she was in too much pain to enjoy it—and peered into her mouth. "Yes," he said, more to himself than to her. "Yes, yes. Bad, very bad. I'm afraid— yes, it will have to come out."

"Why should *you* be afraid?" she snapped. "It's not your tooth."

He looked startled, but then he laughed. He had a remarkably pleasant and infectious laugh. "Oh!" he said. "Good, that's very good. I'll have to remember it." Which meant, no doubt, that he'd be boring people with it for the next twenty years. After a brief pause, he added, "My fee is one *denarius*. Payable in advance."

Nicole had had the forethought to bring a purse with her— no health insurance here. She laid four *sesterces* in his waiting hand. As they disappeared into the depths of his belt pouch, she said, "I don't suppose anybody ever wants to pay you afterwards."

"Not likely," he agreed dolefully. Then he gave her a prescription that no twentieth-century dentist would have resorted to: "You see Resatus' tavern there, across the street? Go on over. Drink three cups of wine, neat, as fast as you can. Then come back. I'll give you a draught of poppy juice. As soon as that takes effect, I'll pull the tooth."

He wanted her as numb as she could get. She gave him credit for that.

The tavern was a somewhat larger place than her own, and somewhat more upscale: she paid two *asses* for her own one-*as* wine, and it was served in Samian ware. Resatus himself took her order, and gave her a good dose of sympathy with it. "Another one of Terentianus' patients, are you?" he said. "Good luck to you, then."

She thanked him with somewhat less than complete sincerity, and drank the wine down doggedly, cup after overpriced cup.

When she made her way to Terentianus' shop, her feet wanted to go off in a different direction altogether. She'd never been drunk in the morning before. It was a peculiar sensation. All the shadows were pointing the wrong way. But then, being drunk itself was peculiar. Till she came to Carnuntum, she'd never known what it was like. She wished to the innumerable Roman gods that she didn't have to do it at all.

Terentianus regarded her wobbly stance and bleary eyes with somber approval. He rummaged in a box under a table, and produced a small jar of murky blue glass. "Here. Drink this down. It won't be long now till it's over."

Nicole didn't know if she liked the sound of that. She took a deep breath, to steady herself, and nearly heaved up the wine she'd drunk; but it stayed put. She pulled out the stopper and saluted Terentianus: *Bottoms up*.

The stuff was thick and syrupy. It tasted of wine and, overpoweringly, of the poppyseeds on the egg bread her mother would buy every once in a while, when she could scrape up the extra cash for something tastier than Wonder or Langendorf. The memory kept her, somehow, from gagging on it. Terentianus waved her to a stool by the window. She drifted rather than walked to it, and sat when he told her to, because she couldn't think of anything better to do. The poppy juice—opium, yes—struck her a stronger yet softer blow than the wine had. She felt sleepy and stupid and floaty. The pain backed away, never quite absent, but not quite present, either. The effect was a little like CoTylenol, and a little like being drunk out of her skull. Somewhere far away and yet very near, there was still pain, a great deal of it. But it didn't touch her.

She yawned. The poppy juice, so full of sleep, reminded her that she'd slept hardly at all the night before.

She didn't notice when Terentianus left the shop. She did notice when he came back with a pair of burly strangers. She stared at them in dreamy confusion. "Who are they?" she asked. Her tongue felt thick; the words sounded slurred. "Why are they here? Do they have toothaches, too?"

"They're to hold you down, of course," Terentianus said calmly. He gestured. One of the men got behind Nicole in one long stride. Before she could move, he seized her arms. The other squatted beside her and got a grip on her legs. She struggled feebly, but they were immovable. Altogether, the preparations seemed more conducive to rape than to dentistry.

If she'd been even slightly less gone in wine and the drug, she would have tried to fight her way out of there. But she was helpless. If the doctor was into raping his patients, there was not one thing she could do about it.

Terentianus loomed over her. He was fully and warmly clothed, and no sign of any erection, either. What he held was far worse. It looked like nothing so much as a large pair of needle-nosed pliers. "Open up," he said. "The sooner it's begun, the sooner it's over."

Nicole took a deep, steadying breath, and opened her mouth as wide as it would go. The dental forceps advanced inexorably, till her eyes crossed in trying to follow it. It wasn't chrome-plated or shiny. It was plain gray-black iron, unrusted at least. She didn't even want to know how unsanitary it was.

She clamped her eyes shut as it disappeared into her mouth. She could taste it, the cold, metallic taste of iron. It closed on the bad tooth: pressure, and the beginning of a twinge. Before she could jerk away, Terentianus' left hand braced on her forehead, holding her steady. He grunted, gathering himself. He pulled.

Pain. No, *pain*. No—*PAIN!*

No wonder he'd brought in hired muscle, she'd think later, when she had any room in her for thought. At that moment, all she wanted was to rip out his balls and stuff them down his throat. Or if that wasn't enough, beat him to a bloody pulp. Then maybe—maybe—he'd feel a tenth of the pain he inflicted on her.

She tried to lunge to her feet and run like hell. Hands like iron bars held her down. One of the thugs grunted: she was fighting good and hard. Maybe she'd caught *him* somewhere that mattered.

Wine or no wine, poppy juice or no poppy juice, the pain drove her right out of her mind. She heard, far away, a bubbling, half-choked scream. That was her own voice. She didn't even get the gift of unconsciousness. She was awake, aware, and hideously alert.

After an eternity of white-hot agony, she heard and felt a snap. Her eyes snapped open. Terentianus staggered back with something clenched in the forceps: the cartoon-simple shape of a tooth, with a horror-comic smear of pus and blood. Blood flooded Nicole's mouth, thick and foul. She spat scarlet, barely missing the grinning bastard who held her legs.

Terentianus stood back, safely out of reach, and examined his prize. "Very nice," he said. "Very neat job, if I say so myself." He fished around in a basket and handed Nicole a square of wool that must have been part of a tunic once, long ago. "Here you are. Keep it pressed to the wound until the bleeding stops. Rinse your mouth out with wine two or three times a day—it will heal better if you do. You might say a prayer or two to Aesculapius, see if it helps. It certainly couldn't hurt."

Nicole spat again, another bright splash of blood on the rammed-earth floor. The ape who'd held her arms not only let her go, he gave her a sympathetic pat on the back. "It's not easy," he said. "Terentianus did one of mine a couple of years ago, and it hurt like a red-hot poker."

She stared blankly at him. Sympathy was the last thing she'd expected, and just about the last thing she wanted. She couldn't bring herself to thank him. She nodded, which was the best she could do, and spat once more, and took the cloth from Terentianus. Her hand trembled uncontrollably. The pain had diminished a little, but it still lapped at every corner of her world. Wine and poppy juice had taken the edge off her toothache. Against the pain of this minor surgery, they were no better than a child's sand-dike against a tidal wave.

Terentianus patted her shoulder lightly. "Sit there as long as you need to," he said. "There's no hurry."

Good thing he didn't charge by the hour, she thought. She was vaguely aware of him thanking his helpers, paying them an *as* apiece, and sending them on their way. The cloth turned more nearly red than gray. Little by little, the bleeding slowed. She should go, she thought. She should get back to the tavern. She stood up. Her head reeled. She sat down again, in a hurry.

A fat man stalked through the door, backed Terentianus up against a table, and let go with a litany of complaint about his hemorrhoids. "That cream you gave me didn't do a bit of good," he said indignantly.

Terentianus might be cornered, but he wasn't cowed. "It's the best I have, Pupianus," he said. "The only other choice is the scalpel."

"No, thank you!" the fat man said with the air of a man who knew what he wanted and, more to the point, what he didn't. "I'm not letting anybody near me with a knife, and that's flat."

Terentianus shrugged. Pupianus balled up his fists and

looked ready to challenge him to a round, but clearly thought better of it. With a loud snort and a stamp of his foot, he turned and stalked out.

Nicole knew exactly how he felt. If she hadn't been ready to fall over with pain, she wouldn't have let Terentianus near her with his forceps, either.

She wasn't in pain any longer. She was in agony. The pain wouldn't have gone away if she hadn't had the tooth pulled. She could only pray that the agony would fade.

After a while, the length of which she was never exactly sure of, she found she could get to her feet and stay there. Terentianus had been watching her between patients: he had a damp cloth waiting, to wipe her face. It came away stained rusty red. "You were brave," he told her.

"You bet I was," she said thickly. The wine and the opium were still in her, making it very hard to care what she said. She pressed a hand to her throbbing jaw—which didn't make it feel better, but kept it from feeling worse as she moved— and headed for the door. Terentianus didn't try to stop her. He was probably glad to see the last of her.

As she made her slow, painful way back to the tavern, with every step sending a fresh twinge through the empty socket, she found some degree of distraction in the graffiti on the walls. There seemed to be a lot of them, and many of that lot seemed to be Christian. At first she thought her bleared eyes were playing tricks, but it was hard to mistake the two curved strokes of the fish, or a row of crosses with something biblical scrawled beneath. She found herself standing with her nose almost pressed to a wall full of such scribblings. The letters writhed and wriggled, but even so, they made a disturbing lot of sense. They were all about the Last Judgment, and they were downright ferocious. Their tone might have given even a Pentecostal preacher pause.

This wasn't her Christianity. Hers, insofar as she had any- thing to do with it, was a lukewarm thing: Christmas, Easter, and a few rote prayers muttered out of habit. The one Chris- tian she'd met here gave her the creeps, and these graffiti were worse. They didn't make her think of Sunday quiet.

They made her think of terrorists. Just like some of the more extreme Arab sects, these Christians wanted the next world so badly, they didn't care what they did to this one.

She stood by the wall, hand pressed to her jaw, and stared blankly at a drawing of a man on a cross, with blood gushing from his numerous wounds. Some wag had added an enormous, equally effusive phallus. It was blasphemy, part of her said; but in this world, in this context, she couldn't be as appalled as she should have been.

Particularly with reality staring her in the face. She hadn't been one bit better than the wild-eyed fanatics who scrawled this graffito. Like them, she'd paid too little attention to this world and the things of this world. Just as with everything else in the country and the century she was born in, she'd taken decent medical care for granted. Then Fabia Ursa died; then the pestilence came; and now, on a far smaller but much more immediate scale, this cursed tooth had shown her, in detail, just how far medical science still had to go. Terentianus was perfectly competent by local standards, she was sure. He'd done what needed doing, done it as well and as fast as he could, and caused her as little pain as possible. He couldn't help it that he knew nothing of antisepsis, next to nothing of analgesics, and nothing whatsoever of antibiotics.

Enough.

She had, at last, hit a wall. She'd been living from day to day, moment to moment, surviving, coping, even—sometimes—managing to enjoy this world she'd wished herself into. She'd been remarkably passive, when she stopped to think about it. A few doubts, some midnight regrets, a lot of culture shock and plain old all-American squeamishness—she'd had all of that. But she hadn't ever really got up enough sheer force of feeling to wish herself away. It was all, however marginally, preferable to the life she'd left behind—even if she didn't quite, ever, find the time or energy to change the things about the world she'd thought she'd change, back when she first arrived in Carnuntum. She could make herself think so, at any rate, if she tried hard enough.

It hadn't really been real to her. That was the trouble. Even the deaths she'd seen—those people had been dead for eighteen centuries before she was even born. She'd felt them as she might have felt deaths in a book, with grief, yes, and real pain, but at a slight remove.

But one by one, blow by blow, they'd cracked through the shell that protected her. A good part of that was selfishness; she admitted it. Frank had said that of her before he walked out on her—one of his many pointed little gems of wisdom: "You don't really care about anybody else. You say you do, you recite all the words, put on all the expressions. But when it comes right down to it, there's nobody in your world but you."

It was justice of a sort, then, that the last straw had been something that affected only her: an encounter with real, personal, private pain.

No matter where it came from, or how. She'd had enough. She'd learned her lesson. She was finished. With all her heart and soul, and with all her aching and abused flesh, she wished herself away. Back. Home to that other world, long and far removed from Carnuntum.

She squeezed her eyes tight and wished till her head pounded and her jaw screamed for mercy. Nothing.

Somewhere in delirium, while she was ill with the pestilence, she'd begged Liber and Libera to send her back to Los Angeles. She'd got a busy signal then, and then forgotten, till now. Till she knew beyond any doubt that she wanted out.

Well, she thought. When the line was busy, you hit the redial button, or put the phone on autodial, and kept on trying. And since this wasn't exactly a line, and what she wanted was as close to magic as made no matter—what made this kind of magic work? Magic ring, phantom tollbooth, ruby slippers . . .

The plaque. She'd clean forgotten. The plaque she'd bought on her honeymoon and kept by her bed in West Hills. She'd focused on it, hadn't she? She'd prayed to the gods whom she'd never have known if they hadn't been depicted on that one piece of faux antiquity.

Or was it false? What if it was real? It seemed preposterous, but what if, somehow, the maker of the reproductions had made a mistake, and shipped the original with the copies? What if she'd been sold, not a reproduction, but an actual late-Roman votive plaque? What if that was the key?

In the fever of discovery, she almost forgot how much pain she was in. She pushed herself away from the wall she'd been leaning against all this time, and looked around with eyes that saw almost clearly. Somewhere along here, she seemed to remember, was a stonecutter's shop.

Yes, there it was, right in the next block—as if it had been placed there specifically for her need. Samples of the stonecutter's work were laid out along the front of the shop, propped against the wall. Some were headstones; he'd probably done a land-office business in those while the pestilence raged in Carnuntum. The sample stones were distinguished by gender: a soldier, a woman in a tunic. There were even partial inscriptions, stock phrases awaiting the insertion of a name.

And yes, he had a selection of votive plaques, dedicated to a wide variety of gods and goddesses. None of those on display was inscribed to Liber and Libera.

She quelled the sinking in her stomach. Maybe he had one inside. If not, he could make one. She didn't have to drift passively through this life. She could take matters into her own hands: manufacture, or have manufactured, her own way home. If she couldn't change this world, she might still escape it.

She went boldly into the dim space with its odors of stone dust and old sweat, and asked her question in a voice that wasn't too mushy, she didn't think. He'd been picking away at a bit of garland on a tombstone, but when she spoke he looked up a little sharply; saw what had to be a heroically swollen face; and blinked once before resorting to a bland expression. "What, Riper and—oh; Liber. Yes, Liber and Libera. There's one right here—two, actually, now I stop to think. People are right fond of Liber and Libera, likely 'cause they're right fond of what they're god and goddess of." He winked at her as if he expected her to share the joke, and pulled a pair of plaques from among the many on the wall behind him. "Here you are. Take your pick."

Neither one was *the* plaque, the one she'd bought on her honeymoon. One was larger, one was smaller, both were rather cruder work. She eyed them in disappointment. Didn't magic need a solid link between her now and her then? Preferably the *same* link?

Still, she thought with robust twentieth-century skepticism, would it be necessary? If she was making her own future, then all that mattered should be that the plaque was like the one she'd used to bring herself here.

Or she could have one made. But, from the look of the shop, he was backed up for weeks; and she couldn't wait. She wanted out *now*. "I like the smaller one better," she said firmly. "What do you want for it?"

"That one?" The stonecutter considered. "Ten *sesterces* ought to do it."

Distracted by pain and fogged by wine and poppy juice as she was, Nicole remained astonished. The limestone from which he'd carved the plaque was surely cheap, but he couldn't set much value on his own labor—either that, or he'd turned out the piece much faster than she would have thought possible. On the other hand, he wasn't inclined to haggle, and she'd been too badly battered to bargain as hard as she would have otherwise. She paid him eight *sesterces* and a couple of *asses* in lieu of a *dupondius,* got him to throw in a piece of sacking to wrap her purchase in, and carried it home with as much care as if it had been made of glass.

Julia greeted her with a cry of dismay. "Mistress! You've got blood all over your tunic."

Nicole looked down at herself. She hadn't even noticed. No wonder the stonecutter had looked at her so oddly. He must have thought her husband had belted her a good one—and she was buying off the gods of wine to soften him up the next time he polished off a jar or two or three.

At least she knew a cure for blood on wool. "Cold water," she said, "that's what it needs. And wine."

"Wine?" Julia frowned. "Wine doesn't do a thing for bloodstains."

"The wine is for me," Nicole said. She sat at a table near the bar—nearly falling the last inch or two onto the bench—and uncovered the plaque so that Julia could see it. "I'll give Liber and Libera a little, too."

Julia seemed excited all out of proportion to the occasion. It must have been a slow day for Julia, upstairs as well as down. "Let me see!" she said eagerly. She didn't wait for Nicole to finish making her way through the stools and benches and tables. She negotiated the course with more agility than Nicole could have managed just then, and peered at the low relief. "That's good," she said. "That's very good. We could use a god or two to watch over us."

If they watch over me as well as I'd like, Nicole thought, *I won't be here.*

The thought was both delicious and—to her amazement—sad. Julia had been to the baths today, and found a clean tunic somewhere, too. She smelled as good as anyone in Carnuntum could. She was warm, standing next to Nicole, and solid, and somehow comforting. Julia, however unwitting, had been absolutely invaluable in showing Nicole how to cope with this world she'd found herself in. They weren't friends, not exactly; friends were equals. Employer and employee? Somewhat more than that. Allies. Comrades in arms.

Nicole was going to miss Julia. The thought was so astonishing that she almost forgot to keep it to herself. The thudding ache in her jaw saved her. She must have clenched her teeth; she was struck with a sudden, piercing stab of pain. "Wine," she said again, tightly. Julia gasped a little, as if she'd clean forgotten, and ran to fetch a cup.

Terentianus had told Nicole to rinse her mouth with it. He hadn't told her it would feel as if she'd drunk gasoline and then thrown in a lighted match. She whimpered. Her eyes filled with tears of pain. Nevertheless, she gulped the stuff down. The second swallow wasn't quite so bad. The damage was done; pain had gone into overload.

When the cup was almost empty, Nicole wet her forefinger with the dregs and smeared a little on Liber's mouth, and a little on Libera's.

Julia shook her head and smiled. "I never saw anybody give them a drink quite that way, Mistress. But I'll bet they like it."

"I hope they do," Nicole said. She hadn't been thinking before she did it, she'd just done what seemed appropriate. She was lucky. If she'd crossed herself backward, everyone in church would have known she was no Catholic. Here, what she'd done wasn't wrong, just different. The cult of Liber and Libera, it seemed, didn't have as many rules as the Christianity in which she'd grown up.

The Christianity they had here—did it have rules, aside from terrorist graffiti and apocalyptic mania? She wasn't sure she wanted to know. And if she did happen to learn the answer, she had every intention of doing it from the twentieth century.

She drank a lot of wine that day. With each cup, she gave the stone god and goddess their share. If the wound got infected after all that, then the germs that did the job would be cutting through the alcohol bath in wetsuit and swim fins.

She drank a double cup, one of the cups she kept for her thirstiest customers, before she went upstairs to bed. Maybe, just maybe, it would dull the pain enough to let her sleep. She was in a fog as it was, drifting as if underwater, bouncing gently off walls and furniture. But the heart of the fog was a red and throbbing pain.

Sleep was as elusive as she'd feared. She couldn't even toss and turn: it hurt too much. She lay as still as she could on the thin, lumpy mattress, and did her best to ignore the tiny stabs and stings of the vermin that inhabited it. She'd brought the plaque up with her, and propped it on the chest of drawers where she could see it from the bed. *Liber and Libera,* she prayed, *take me back to my own time. Take me back to my own world. I don't belong here. I was wrong to*

*pray as I prayed. Please, make it right. You granted one
prayer of mine. Only grant this one, and I'll never trouble
you again.*

She couldn't tell if she was getting through. The wine
couldn't do what the fever had done, blur the boundaries
between the waking world and the world the gods inhabited.
All it did was dull her reflexes and slow her mind, and drop
her at last into a sodden sleep.

She drifted off in a dream of electric lights and chlorinated
water, automobiles and stereos, antibiotics and, oh God, an-
esthetics, telephones and television, supermarkets and refrig-
erators, soap and insecticides and inner-spring mattresses.
And—yes, yes indeed—equality under the law, whatever it
might be in actual practice. If the gods were kind, if she'd
worked the—magic?—rightly, she'd wake in a deliciously
soft, heavenly clean bed in the century that was, after all
she'd done to escape it, the one and only century for her.

She woke, yes. On a rough and scratchy, redolent and
verminous mattress, in a century long before the one in
which she was born, in the Roman city of Carnuntum.

16

IT WAS A BITTER waking, but Nicole had no intention of
giving up. She'd storm heaven if she had to. Every night,
with wine and impassioned prayer, she called on the god and
goddess. She smeared their lips with wine, she left a cup of
wine in front of their plaque, she drank more wine than she
rightly should have. She was sincere. She was devoted. She
wanted, above anything in this world, to go home.

And every morning, as surely as the sun rose over the
eastward wall of Carnuntum, she woke in Umma's bed, in
Umma's body. The gods were ignoring her, or else, as she
began to fear, actively refusing to grant her prayer.

They'd brought her here. They could damned well send her home again.

Julia approved of this sudden access of piety. "We're sure to have better luck around here now," she said. Julia had two mottoes: *Never ask questions* and *Always look on the bright side.* Manumission hadn't done a thing to change either of them.

That much Nicole had given her: her freedom. Umma, when she came back to this body, if she came back to it— small dark difficult thought, there, quickly suppressed— couldn't legally undo what Nicole had done. It was a good thing, a decent gift to leave behind.

Nicole wasn't ever tempted to stay. The one real friend she'd had here, Titus Calidius Severus, was dead. Lucius was Umma's child, not her own, though yes, she'd miss him. Julia, too, and young Gaius, and one or two others. She was fond of them as she might have been of people she met on a long vacation, but with the sense, always, that this was their world and not hers; that whatever happened here, it was temporary. She wasn't going to live out her days here.

Liber and Libera were silent, though their plaque was smeared with wine and the cup in front of it had been filled and refilled and filled again. Nicole, in the beginning of despair, prayed to the God she'd grown up with, the God whose followers in second-century Carnuntum seemed so much like twentieth-century extremists. He gave her no more answer than the Roman deities had. He was angry at her, she was sure, for having other gods before Him. Or maybe the Christians here and now were shouting so loud, they drowned her out.

She hadn't wanted anything or wished for anything so strongly or with such concentrated determination since— when? Since she passed the bar, at the very least. Even the prayer that had brought her here was a dim and halfhearted thing beside this.

I made it one way, she thought on waking up yet again on the hard narrow bed in the upstairs bedroom behind the tavern. *There has to be a way for me to go back.*

The legally trained part of her mind pointed out that there didn't *have to be* any such thing: hadn't she ever heard of a one-way ticket? The rest of her was damned if that was the case. Really, truly, literally damned.

Slowly, reluctantly, and almost unregarded, the hole in the back of her mouth healed. When it was finally gone, she found herself free of pain for the first time since she'd come to Carnuntum.

The difference it made was amazing. "I should have had that tooth pulled a long time ago," she said one day in the dead of winter, a long way still from spring.

"I've heard a lot of people say that," Julia responded, looking up from the dough she was kneading. "They say it afterwards, yes, but before? You couldn't get a one of them near the nice man with the forceps in his hand."

Remembering the burly man holding her arms and the other one grabbing her legs, remembering the forceps in her mouth and the roots of the molar tearing out of her jawbone, Nicole shuddered. "You are right," she conceded. "You are too right."

That afternoon—a fine one, as winter days went, with the temperature probably in the high forties and the sun peering out between spatters of rain—some very unusual customers swaggered into the tavern. The room that had always seemed, if not spacious, then large enough to swing a cat in, was suddenly not much larger than a closet.

There were only three of them, though at first there seemed to be more: big men, burly, and ripe even by the standards of this age. They were Germans, no doubt about it, Marcomanni or Quadi, she couldn't tell which. They ordered wine in Latin with a distinct accent, guttural but understandable.

"One-*as,* two-*as,* or Falernian for four *asses?*" she asked, warily but crisply. As had the tribesmen in the market square, they surveyed the place as if they owned it. If they drew their swords and demanded the cash box, she couldn't do much but hand it over. Really, when she stopped to think, it was a wonder she hadn't ever been robbed or mugged— crime here was low, though not nonexistent.

Nor was she about to become a statistic now. One of the Germans set a shiny silver *denarius* on the bar. "Falernian," he said. The others nodded, tripling the order. "And you will give us bread and raisins and smoked pork to eat with it." That was an order, and in more ways than one.

Nicole kept her temper. She nodded curtly, bringing to bear the skills she'd acquired perforce, for dealing with obnoxious customers. They'd given her money instead of simply taking what they wanted—that went a long way toward easing her temper.

She looked around for Julia, but the freedwoman had made herself scarce. If these bruisers from beyond the Danube wanted a little ripe woman with their smoked pork, they weren't going to get it. Nicole was somewhat annoyed: she'd have welcomed backup, and some help filling plates and cups and bowls. But Julia had made it clear when she was manumitted that while she'd cheerfully sell her body, she wasn't about to sell it to just anyone.

And if they took a fancy to a skinny black-haired piece with a missing tooth?

Not likely, Nicole thought grimly. Nor were they eyeing her in that particular way. They emptied their bowls and licked them clean, and ordered another round of Falernian, with another *denarius* to pay for it.

"Wine," one of them said in reverent tones. "Wine is . . . good." The others nodded as if he'd said something profound.

Nicole set a *sestertius* on the bar as change. The man pushed it back. "No. Give us more bread and meat and raisins. Tell us when we need to give you more money for it."

Nicole nodded again, more warmth in the gesture now—the professional warmth any businessperson offered to big spenders. "Would you like some olive oil to go with your bread?"

They all made faces at her, the same sort of faces Lucius and poor Aurelia had made when she suggested they drink milk. "Olive oil is not good," said the one who'd declared that wine was. "Have you butter?"

If only, Nicole thought, with a fleeting memory of cold, sweet butter on fresh crusty bread from the bakery near the law offices. She overrode it with the reality she was condemned to. "No, I have no butter. People here like olive oil better."

She resisted the temptation to tell them to rub the bread in their hair if it was butter they wanted—they were downright rancid with it; she had to hold her breath when she came close. It might offend them. Even worse, they might do it.

The three Germans sighed in unison. "We will eat the bread bare, then," said the spokesman, whose Latin seemed to be best.

Before long, they laid down another *denarius* for still more wine and bread and meat. All three coins, unquestionably, were Roman. Nicole held up the third one. "If you don't mind my asking, how did you get so much of my country's money?"

They smiled. They looked, just then, like the beasts in the amphitheater when they had spotted prey. The one who did most of the talking said, "We have been in the Roman Empire before." He turned and spoke to his friends in their own language. Nicole caught the word *Roman* again. He had to be translating the remark. They all laughed.

She didn't like that laughter. Like the smiles, it seemed . . . carnivorous. Had these Germans been part of the war farther west? Had they come into the Roman Empire as invaders, robbers, looters? Was that how they'd got their hands on Roman coins?

They were behaving themselves now. Whatever might be happening farther west, things were peaceful in Carnuntum. Nicole couldn't turn on the evening news and watch the latest videotape of Romans and Germans fighting . . . wherever they were fighting. Wolf Blitzer was eighteen hundred years away. Without daily reminders, the war felt unreal.

Best change the subject. "Has the pestilence been very bad on your side of the river?"

They talked among themselves for a while, low and somehow urgent, though they were smiling and acting casual. Then the spokesman said, "No, the sickness has not among us been too bad. We have had some among us take ill and die, but not many."

"I wonder why that is," Nicole said. At first, it was just another polite phrase. Once it was out of her mouth, however, she really did wonder. She asked, "You don't live in cities on the other side of the river, do you?"

The two who hadn't said much—at least one of whom, she suspected, had little or no Latin—conferred with the spokesman again, and shook their heads. He did the talking, as before: "Oh, no. So many people all in one place? Who could imagine that on our side of the river?"

Nicole had all she could do not to laugh in his face. Carnuntum was a real city, no doubt of that. It might have held fifty thousand people, maybe even seventy-five, before the pestilence cut the population by at least a third. What would this solemn German have made of Los Angeles, with three and a half million people in the city, nine million in the county, fourteen or fifteen million in the metropolitan area? For that matter, what would a Roman have made of Los Angeles?

Los Angeles had been horrifying enough for somebody from Indianapolis, which was no small city itself. You could drop Carnuntum into Eagle Creek Park and still have room to run your dog.

"So many people all in one place is not good," the German said. His friends nodded. So did Nicole, though perhaps not for the same reason. With people more thinly scattered on the northern bank of the Danube, the pestilence wouldn't have had such a large reservoir in which to flourish. But then the German said, "So many good things all in one place is very fine and wonderful."

His friends nodded again, in a way Nicole didn't like. It wasn't so much admiring as covetous.

At long last, they seemed to have filled up on wine and bread and meat—she'd begun to wonder if each of them had a black hole where his stomach should be. They got up from their stools, belched in an ascending chorus, and swaggered out as they'd swaggered in.

Nicole breathed a sigh of relief. She'd made a good day's living from them, but she'd been braced for them to start breaking up the place if they had much more to drink. They'd had a look she knew too well: elevated, but not actually drunk. Her father had come home from the bar that way sometimes. If he stayed away from the kitchen cabinet, he wasn't too bad; he'd go into the den and sit in front of the TV till he fell asleep. But if he went to pull a bottle out of the cabinet, that meant trouble.

The Germans hadn't been gone five minutes when Julia trotted downstairs and applied herself to making a new batch of bread. "Nice of you to join me," Nicole said with a sardonic edge.

Julia bent over the bread-bowl, her hair falling forward, hiding her face. Her voice was subdued, as it had been when she was still a slave, and very seldom since. "I'm sorry, Mistress. I couldn't be in the same room with those—those barbarians. They're nothing but trouble. If you remember— that pack of Quadi, last year . . ."

She didn't go on. Nicole wondered if she was being challenged, if Julia was testing her memory.

Of course not. That was trauma, that set to Julia's shoulders, and that tension in her fingers. Nicole could easily imagine what kind. "It's all right," she said. "I remember." Which of course was a lie, but not if she'd been Umma.

Julia lifted her head. Her face was as tight as her shoulders, but it eased a little as she looked at Nicole. "I'm glad they didn't bother you," she said.

"So am I," Nicole said. "I could have grabbed a knife, I suppose, and fought them off, or tried to. They might have been too surprised to go for their swords. Or I could have yelled, and all the neighbors would have come running."

"Like last time?" Julia shook herself hard, and went back to working flour and water and yeast together. "Maybe they'd have got to you before—" She stopped. She bent over the dough, attacking it as if it had been a broad and greasy German face. In a very little while, she'd pounded it to a pulp.

Nicole stood where Julia's words had left her. Rape was too familiar a thing in Los Angeles, too; but no neighbors would have come running to the rescue. People didn't get involved. The most they did, if they did anything at all, was call 911. Or grab a camcorder and go for the media gold.

Nevertheless, that was a world she understood. She wanted it back. That night before she went to bed, she prayed to Liber and Libera as she had done for the past however many nights, till the prayer was worn to habit, and the words were turned to ritual. *Please, god and goddess. Take me home.*

Slowly and reluctantly, winter gave way to spring. After the last snow fell, a hard and driving rain moved in like insult on top of injury. Snow over mud was bearable; the mud froze, and you could cross the street without choking on dust or sinking in muck. To be sure, if it rained, or if there was a thaw and then a freeze, the snow froze into ice, and you slipped and slid and cursed and tried not to fall down and break an elbow or your tailbone. But then snow had a way of falling and making the ice passable again.

Spring rain melted the snow and with it the mud beneath. Every unpaved road in Carnuntum turned into black bean soup. Cold, glutinous, congealed black bean soup, ankle-deep and as apt to suck your boot off as to turn suddenly treacherous and send you skidding into a knot of passersby.

The tag end of winter was a lean time. The storerooms were nearly empty of grain. There were no fresh vegetables to be had, and not much meat on the market that wasn't salted, smoked, or cured. Nicole didn't even want to think how much sodium was in each portion that she served out to customers or to her family. There was fish, at least, fresh as well as salt. Fresh fish kept better in this weather, and she bought more of it. Her basic fish fry—olive oil, with crumbs from yesterday's bread—was rather a popular item. She only wished she'd had some tartar sauce to put on it, or some chips to go with it. Nobody here had ever heard of the potato,

though an experiment with onion rings didn't turn out too
badly.

Every time she went to the market, she saw more Germans: big fair men with, now and then, a big fair woman
striding robustly alongside. They seemed on their best behavior, but everyone watched them warily. Some of the vet-
erans of the legion that had its encampment a few miles
downstream took to wearing swords, which they hadn't done
before.

One men's day at the baths, Nicole was amazed to see
several Marcomanni or Quadi—she still couldn't tell one
tribe from another—coming down the stairs. They looked
mightily contented. She wondered how they bathed on their
side of the Danube. To her way of thinking, the baths left
something to be desired, but her basis of comparison was a
hot shower and soap. Compared to a plunge into an icy
stream or a half-frozen lake, the Roman baths had to seem
like heaven.

A detachment of Roman soldiers in their fancy armor
came over from the legionary camp and began patrolling the
walls and streets of Carnuntum. Every so often, one or two
of them would drop into the tavern.

One day when spring was well advanced, a pair of legionaries came rattling and jangling in just as Nicole finished
pouring a round of wine for a tableful of Germans. The air
was always vaguely tense when the Germans were in the
tavern, but Nicole had learned to ignore the tension.

She couldn't ignore this. The legionaries didn't say a word
except to order the one-*as* wine. The Germans, drinking Falernian and paying for it in silver as they always did, went
on with their low growl of conversation. Neither side acknowledged the other.

Nobody else spoke, or moved much either. Julia, who
hadn't been able to make herself scarce this time, took refuge
in scouring plates and cups and bowls. Lucius helped her, or
tried; he kept dropping things. The two or three ordinary
customers, trapped in the back and unable to escape without
running the gauntlet between the soldiers and the barbarians,

nursed whatever they were eating and drinking, and did their best to seem inconspicuous.

The Germans finished their wine, belched—a little louder than usual, maybe—and left. A few minutes later, the legionaries did the same.

As soon as the soldiers were out the door, a long sigh ran through the room. Nicole hadn't known she was holding her breath till she let it out.

"Phew!" Ofanius Valens said for them all. "Another cup of the two-*as* for me, Umma. That could have been ugly."

"It *was* ugly," Nicole said.

"It could have been uglier," he said. He took the cup Nicole had filled for him, thanked her, and drank deep.

Nicole was tempted to keep him company. She'd had precious few brawls in the tavern, and nothing worse than a pair of young idiots going at each other with fists and getting pitched into the street. The Calidii Severi, father and son, had played bouncers that day, she remembered. It still hurt to think of Titus, how he was dead and would never walk through that door again.

She remembered, too, how surprised she'd been, not by the fight, but by the fact that it was the first that had escalated that far. She'd come to Carnuntum convinced that drinking equaled drunkenness and that was that. And drunkenness, she'd been just as sure, had meant a fight—her father sending her mother to the ER yet again, where she'd lie as always, claiming she'd run into a door or fallen down the stairs.

In fact, neither of those assumptions had turned out to be universally or even generally true. Most of her customers drank without getting drunk. Of the ones who did go over the edge, more got friendly or talky or sleepy than got belligerent. She'd made a point of sending the nasty drunks on their way, and making it clear that they weren't to come back. They'd mostly stayed away, too. "Plenty of other places to get a load of wine," as one of them had informed her before she booted him out.

She'd been running a tavern in small-town Indiana. And the L.A. gang scene had come to town. "If those barbarians had gone at it with those legionaries," she said, "it wouldn't have been a tavern brawl. It would have been a war."

Ofanius Valens finished off his cup of wine and held it up for another. When Nicole had brought it, and scooped up the *dupondius* he set on the table, he said, "Yes, it would have been a war. It might have started a fire here to match the one that's been burning farther west."

Nicole needed a moment to realize that, whereas she'd been using a figure of speech, Ofanius Valens had meant his words literally. "You don't really think so, do you?" she said. "We've stayed at peace all this time. Why should it all blow up in our faces now?"

"We've been at peace, and the gods know I'm glad of it, too," Ofanius Valens said. "But the gods also know I've never seen so many Quadi and Marcomanni in town as I have the past month or so. We'd always get a few: they'd cross the river to buy things in the market or drink in the taverns or just to stare at our fancy buildings. The barbarians couldn't build a bathhouse like ours in a thousand years."

"Now, though," Julia said, "now they look like dogs in front of a butcher's stall."

A lean and hungry look, Nicole thought. She'd thought it before, about the Romans in this city, with their thin dark faces—and hadn't Shakespeare written it about a Roman, now that she stopped to think? But it fit these Germans just as well, in a different way.

She'd thought—she'd been sure—she was getting away from war when she fell back through time. She'd thought—she'd been sure of—all sorts of things when she came to Carnuntum. Very few of them had turned out to be true, or anything close to it. She'd hated the late twentieth century while she was living in it. From the perspective of the second century, it looked like the earthly paradise.

Perspective, she thought, *is a wonderful thing.*

"We have the wall," she said. And had she ever stopped to think *why* Carnuntum had a wall? Very basic principle of legal theory: laws existed to prevent people from doing things to harm other people. A wall wasn't just there to look pretty and provide a nice high place for lovers to walk on fine summer evenings. It was there for a reason: to keep out nasty neighbors.

Everybody here knew that. They knew something else, too—even the children. "We have the wall," Lucius agreed, "*and* the legion." He slapped the hilt of his toy sword. It was thrust in his belt at the precise angle at which the Roman soldiers wore their real ones.

"That's not a whole legion," Ofanius Valens said gloomily, "and what there is of it won't be enough. They'll defend their camp first and worry about us afterwards. I'd do the same in their sandals."

"What I want to know," Julia said with unaccustomed sharpness, "is why the barbarians won't leave us alone. We haven't done them any harm."

My God, Nicole thought, even here and now, the small and the weak came out with the same cry of protest as they had all through the blood-spattered twentieth century. And yet this was the Roman Empire. It was by no means small, and she'd never heard it was weak. "Don't the Germans know they're like a dog fighting an elephant?" she demanded.

Ofanius Valens laughed, but the sound was bitter. "They know they've had a fine time plundering Roman provinces and then scurrying back across the river into their forest. Now we're weak from the pestilence—easy pickings, they'll be thinking."

"We drove them out of Aquileia." Nicole remembered that from her very first, panicky trip to the market square. She still didn't know exactly where Aquileia was, but what did that matter?

Ofanius nodded. "So we did. And I'd be happier if they'd never got down that far."

"Maybe everything will come out all right here," Julia said, reaching for Nicole's optimism—which Nicole was almost ready to call naïveté. "Maybe it will, if the gods stay kind."

"Here's hoping it does." Ofanius Valens lifted his cup,

peered into it, and seemed astonished to find it empty. "Have to do something about that," he said, and fumbled a couple of *asses* out of the pouch he wore on his belt. Nicole took the cup and filled it yet again.

"Thank you, Umma," he said when she set it on the table in front of him. He lifted it once more, wobbling a tiny bit—he'd had three cups, after all. "Here's to peace, prosperity, and the Germans staying on their side of the river."

Back in California, Nicole had had an earthquake emergency kit, with blankets and food that would keep, and bottled water and a frying pan and matches and charcoal for the barbecue and a first-aid kit all stored in a plastic trash can and waiting for a disaster she hoped would never come. She wondered if she ought to start a war emergency kit here. And if she did, what would she put in it? So many things she'd taken for granted in California didn't exist here. She could get together wine and salt fish and olive oil. That would be better than nothing—and if the war held off, she could always sell what was in the kit.

She shook her head. She was as twitchy as a cat on a freeway. The Germans and the legionaries had set everyone's nerves on edge. Still—there were soldiers in the city where there hadn't been any before. Someone else, someone who might have reason to know, was twitchy too. Maybe she'd get together that emergency kit after all.

The Marcomanni and the Quadi broke into Carnuntum on a misty spring morning. They used the mist to their advantage, for it kept anyone on the southern bank of the Danube from spying their boats till they were almost ashore.

Nicole was just putting the first loaves of the morning into the oven when the sound of horns throughout the city brought her bolt upright. The fierce brass bray put her in mind of the civil-defense sirens that had wailed on the last Friday of each month when she was a girl in Indiana. If this was a drill, it was awfully realistic. A commotion outside brought her running to the door. People were running up and down the street, shouting and screaming. She picked words out of the tumult: "Marcomanni! Quadi! Germans!" Then even those were lost in the general roar of alarm and dismay and fear.

A squad of legionaries streamed past, running east toward the nearest wall. The iron scales of their armor clattered against one another. They would have sounded much the same if they'd been wearing suits made of tin cans. Nicole wondered if any of them was carrying one of Brigomarus' shields.

Julia tugged at Nicole's tunic, urgent as a frightened child. "What can we do, Mistress? Where shall we go? How can we hide?"

Nicole took a deep breath. She'd have loved to cling to someone bigger and stronger, too, but there wasn't anybody here to take on the job. "I can't think of a thing to do that we aren't doing already," she said. "Let's just sit tight."

Julia was white around the edges, and her eyes were wild. She was coping better, at that, than anyone outside.

If you can keep your head when all about you are losing theirs, ran a fragment of what couldn't have been a real poem, *odds are you don't understand the situation.*

Julia, unfortunately, understood all too well. "If they get into the city, Mistress—"

She didn't go on. Nor did she have to. Nicole had seen enough televised horror to have some idea of what could happen. She'd never in her wildest nightmares imagined that it might happen to her.

Suddenly, she began to laugh. Julia's eyes opened even wider. Nicole took the freedwoman by the arm. "Come on," she said. "Let's go across the street." Julia plainly thought she was crazy, but equally plainly was not going to let Nicole out of her sight.

Gaius Calidius Severus was stropping a sword that must have belonged to his father. The edge had already taken on a sheen, striking against the dull gray-black of the blade. He looked up from his work in surprise. "Mistress Umma! Julia! What are you doing here?"

Julia didn't have any answer for that. Nicole took a deep

breath. As always, the fuller and dyer's shop stank. This once, the ammoniacal reek was not only welcome, it was a blessed inspiration. "If the Germans get into Carnuntum, who knows what they'll do?" she said. "Whatever it is, I don't want them doing it to Julia and me." She beckoned briskly. "Come here, Julia."

Obedient as if she were still a slave, Julia followed Nicole to a wooden tub in which wool was soaking in stale piss. "Here, dip your arms in it up to the elbow. Splash yourself with it, too," she said, matching action to words. "If any German wants something from us that we don't feel like giving, he'll need a strong stomach."

Julia gaped. The laughter that burst out of her was half hysterical, but it was laughter. She kissed Nicole on the cheek; the corner of her mouth barely brushed the corner of Nicole's. "Mistress, how did you ever think of anything so clever?" She plunged her arms into the vat with a good will, and with much less revulsion than Nicole had felt.

"That *is* clever," Gaius Calidius Severus said, running a fingertip down the edge of the blade. He frowned, and went back to his stropping.

"Do you know what to do with that thing?" Nicole asked him.

"As much as my father and his friends taught me," he replied calmly. "Better to use it on the Quadi and Marcomanni than to sit around here till they use their swords on me, don't you think?" He left off stropping, tested it this time on his arm. It shaved a neat patch of soft black hair. He nodded, satisfied. Before Nicole realized what he was up to, he sprang to his feet and loped out of the shop. "Shut the door behind you when you leave, will you?" he called back over his shoulder.

By the time Nicole pulled the door closed, Gaius Calidius Severus was around the corner and out of sight. "How much chance do you think he has?" she asked Julia.

It wasn't quite a rhetorical question, and Julia didn't treat it as such. She shrugged. "Who knows? It's in the gods' hands." Nicole looked down at her own hands, which still

stank of sour piss. Julia went on, "If we can keep the barbarians outside the wall, we'll be all right. If we can't—"
She shrugged again.

That about summed it up, Nicole thought. She led Julia
back across the street.

Lucius was sitting on the stoop, playing with the dice from
his Saturnalia gift. As they came within smelling distance,
he wrinkled his nose and made as if to push them back into
the street. "What have you been doing, swimming in Gaius'
amphorae? You stink!"

"That's the idea," Julia said.

"You bet it is," Nicole agreed. "Nobody messes with a—"
She wanted to say *skunk,* but Latin lacked the requisite word.
She did the best she could: "—with a polecat."

"You smell *worse* than a polecat," Lucius declared. He got
up and ran off—fortunately inside and up the stairs, not out
in the panicky streets. Nicole shrugged, sighed, and almost
gagged. God, she smelled bad. "We'd better wash our
hands," she said to Julia, "or we'll make our customers sick."

"Sick of the way our food tastes, that's for sure," Julia
said. That wasn't quite what Nicole had meant, but it wasn't
wrong, either.

As it happened, they had only a handful of customers. The
people who weren't trying to hold the Marcomanni and the
Quadi out of Carnuntum were staying close to home.

Nicole couldn't blame them. She was doing the same
thing, and trying to figure out how long the supplies in the
tavern would last for her and Lucius and Julia if they
couldn't get any more. She hadn't stored away the emergency kit—she'd kept putting it off. She swore at herself for
not doing it as soon as she thought of it.

It was a tense, watchful day, punctuated by shouts and
screams from the direction of the wall, which was only a
couple of hundred yards away. Every so often, she or Julia
or Lucius or sometimes all of them together would go out
into the street and listen to the fighting.

Sometimes a cry would ring clearly through the general
din: "Ladders!" or "Look out!" or "There they are!"

Once, a rattling crash startled Nicole half out of her skin. "What in the gods' name was that?"

"Ladder full of Germans in armor going over, I hope," Lucius answered.

Nicole hoped so, too. She was astonished to discover how much. She'd been a politically correct, enlightened woman, with a properly modern attitude toward war: *A plague on both their houses.* But now she was inside one of the houses. Amazing, how much difference that made.

A little before noon, the quality of the noise from the wall changed: it grew both louder and more frantic. A moment later, a man in a torn and filthy tunic came running down the street, shrieking, "The Germans! The Germans are in Carnuntum!"

Nicole was very calm. Calmer than she'd ever thought she'd be. She stayed by the bar where she usually was when business was slow and the chores were done. It happened to be within easy reach of the shelf on which she kept the knives.

Not that she was sure she could use a knife on another human being, or, if she could, whether it would do anything much more than make an attacker angry, but she wanted the option. It made her feel better; and that, in the circumstances, mattered a great deal.

The shouting died down for a while. Then, rather abruptly, it came back in force. The tavern was empty; the last customer had gulped his wine, left half a loaf behind, and headed on home.

Nicole went to the door, shut it and barred it. She turned in the sudden gloom. "Julia, Lucius, shut the side windows," she said. "We'll leave the front ones halfway open." Neither Julia nor Lucius argued with the order. As Julia closed the shutters on one side, she said, "There—now we can see out, but nobody can see in; it's too dark. That's clever—as clever as slathering piss on us to keep the barbarians away. You're lucky, Mistress; you can be clever even when you're scared to death."

Not lucky, Nicole thought. *Combat-trained in the streets of Los Angeles. And by an awful lot of war movies.* Still, she felt a small quiver of pride, one of the very few she'd felt since she came to Carnuntum. Nothing she did might make the least difference, she knew that, but it felt good to do something—and to be admired for it, besides.

Would Umma have been as clever? It was hard to tell, from Julia's reaction. And Lucius was too scared to notice much, and too busy hiding it to care if his mother was acting out of character again.

Iron clanged on iron, too close for comfort and getting closer fast. It sounded like kids at a construction site, playing let's-make-the-biggest-racket with lengths of steel reinforcing rod. Which meant—she found that she was breathing too shallowly; she made herself draw a deeper breath—those were swords clashing on swords. And it wasn't a game. It was real.

Caution would have kept her deep inside the tavern, even upstairs if she'd been truly sensible, but she found herself beside one of the front windows, peering cautiously around the shutter. Julia had done the same, and Lucius crept in under Nicole's arm like a dog in need of a pat.

A Roman legionary turned at bay in front of the tavern. His helmet was gone, his curly dark hair a wild tangle. He was panting and cursing, both at once. Sweat cut channels of clean olive skin through the dust caked on his face. A big redheaded German hammered at him with a sword that looked twice the size of his short, thick-bladed *gladius.*

Even so, he was holding his own, even driving the German back with thrusts and stabs of his weapon. Then a second German, loping down the street, took in the situation with the blue flash of a glance, grinned, and hacked him down.

That's not fair, Nicole thought. As if there were anything fair about the game these men were playing. *All's fair in love and war.* Love she'd thought she knew. And this was war.

The big redhead's sword swung up. It came down with a sound like a cleaver smacking a side of beef. Just like that.

The legionary screamed, a shrill wail like a woman's,

breaking into a wet gurgle. The German's sword rose and fell, rose and fell.

The second German, who'd stood back to rest and watch, waded in after a while and joined in the butchery. The gray iron of their blades was red with blood. With every stroke, scarlet drops flew wide, spattering the walls and the street.

The redhead stopped first, looked down at the red glistening thing that just a few moments ago had been a man, and said clearly, *"Dauths is ist."*

He's dead, Nicole thought. *That's what it means.*

The second German threw in a last, contemptuous blow, laughed—a weird, wild sound—and loped off down the street. The other followed at a trot.

Nicole didn't want to look down. But she had to. She had to know. The Roman lay in a scarlet pool of blood. His head was almost severed from his body. His arms were hacked almost out of recognition; his armor was split and torn. His bare legs beneath the pleated military kilt were intact and almost unbloodied. And they twitched, grotesquely, as if he were still in some way alive.

No. Not with his head at that angle. He was dead, as the German had said. Very, very dead.

The contents of Nicole's stomach stayed where they belonged. That surprised her a little. She was keeping it at a distance; closing it off in a small, tight compartment, and sitting firmly on the lid. Eventually she'd blow. But not now and, if she was lucky, not soon.

She could think clearly, therefore, and think through what this meant. Last year in the market square, she'd seen the Marcomanni and Quadi as gangbangers strutting around on enemy turf. If gangbangers killed a cop, the force hunted them down. But what if gangbangers killed off the whole force? That question wasn't rhetorical, not here. And she was going to learn the answer to it.

After the first two Germans disappeared, others trotted down the street, swords in hand, moving like wolves on the hunt. Some of the blades were bloodied, some not. A few of the

barbarians wore the same kind of armor as the legionaries—
captured, maybe—and some wore chainmail. Not a few wore
simple tunics and trousers, no armor at all except for the
dubious protection of a leather vest. They all wore the same
expression: fixed, intent, as if they were casing the place.
But it was more immediate than that. They were looking for
more Roman soldiers to kill.

Julia looked ready to climb into Nicole's arms, if Lucius
hadn't already been there. "They have the city," she whispered. Her face was white with fear. "If they have the soldiers' camp down the river, too, the gods only know when
we'll be rescued. If we ever will. If—we don't—" Her voice
trailed away.

Lucius hadn't said a word since before the legionary fell.
He slipped out from under Nicole's arm and ran upstairs.
Nicole started after him, but held herself back. If he needed
to be alone, she'd let him. She'd go up in a little while and
see if he was all right.

But he came down almost as soon as he'd gone up, clutching his wooden sword. Nicole had never liked or approved
of it, but she'd never quite got round to taking it away from
him. She held herself back now, with an effort that made her
body shake. If he needed that comfort, she wouldn't take it
away from him.

He sat on a stool near the back of the tavern, with the
sword in his lap. He sat there for a while, stroking the
wooden blade.

Suddenly, violently, he flung it away. "It's just a toy," he
said bitterly. "It can't hurt a thing, except maybe a fly."

Nicole walked over and put her arm around him. At first,
he tried to shrug her away. Then he clung as he had at the
window, and started to cry. The tears were as bitter as his
words. She held him close and rocked him as she would have
rocked Justin.

People were shouting in the distance, with a new note in
it, a new urgency. It was a word, one single word. "Fire!"

For a heartbeat or two, idiotically, she listened for sirens.
No fire engines here. God knew what they had; maybe noth-

ing, though more open flames burned here than she'd ever seen in one place. And even if there was something, what could anybody do about it while the city was being sacked?

She glanced at Julia. The freedwoman had looked frightened before. Now she was stiff with terror. "Mistress," she said in a small, tight voice, "if that gets any closer, we've got to run. I'd rather take my chances with the Germans than stay here and burn to death."

"If the city's burning," Nicole said, "the Germans will be running, too." Nicole took a deep breath, to steady herself, and nodded. "We'll run if we have to. The shouting's coming—yes, from the north, and the west, past the market square. The fire may not be able to go around an open space that big."

"Maybe." Julia cocked her head, listening. "Yes, north and west—I can hear it, too. I think you're right. Please the gods, I hope you're right!"

They sat in the gloom and waited. Nobody spoke. Lucius fidgeted for a while, then pulled his dice out of the pouch at his belt and squatted on the floor, playing a game of one hand against the other. The rattle of dice in the cup and the dull clatter as they rolled out on the floor struck counterpoint to the distant sounds of fighting and of terror.

Nicole sniffed. Did she smell smoke? Of course she smelled smoke. She always did in Carnuntum. No one ran screaming down the street, pursued by the lick of flames. What had Nicole heard once? Fire was *fast,* yes. Faster than anyone could imagine who hadn't seen it.

More than once she tensed to jump up, grab whatever she could grab, and take her chances with the Germans. But some remnant of sense kept her where she was. As long as there was no sign of fire nearby, she was infinitely safer behind the barred door of the tavern than running in panic through the streets.

Julia had been sitting still in what might have passed for bovine calm except for the darting of her eyes. "I hope Gaius is all right," she said suddenly. She spoke young Calidius Severus' praenomen without self-consciousness. Why not?

She'd gone upstairs with him both here and over the dyer's shop. If that didn't entitle her to call him by his first name, what did?

Once upon a time, Gaius' father had complained that Nicole didn't call him by his praenomen. She'd learned that courtesy, and a great deal more.

God, she missed that quiet, practical man with the infuriating habit of being right. His son was going to grow up just like him; she could see the signs.

If, she thought, he lived through the war. If any of them did.

There'd been a long lull, a quiet space in which no one ran past, enemy or friend. Then a new wave of Germans poured in from what had to be a breach in the wall or a gate forced open. Most still carried swords, but they weren't so wary now. They moved at walking pace, traveling in pairs and threes, gawking at the sights. If they'd had cameras, they would have been taking snapshots. They looked like tourists, not like men who expected to have to fight their way through the city.

It took Nicole a distressingly long time to understand what that meant. It was over. The Germans had won.

And to the victors went the spoils. One of the Germans pounded on a door a little way down the street from the tavern. A moment later, Nicole heard the barbarian let out a happy grunt, like a pig in a corncrib. A moment after that, a woman shrieked.

"That's Antonina," Julia said, her voice the barest thread of whisper.

"Let me go!" Antonina cried, fear and anger warring in her voice. "Let me—" The sharp sound of flesh slapping against flesh cut off her words. She shrieked again, high and shrill. The German laughed. He didn't seem to mind the noise at all.

He wasn't alone, either. From the sound of it, there was a whole pack of them out there, yipping with glee and calling back and forth in their own language. The words weren't comprehensible, but the tone was all too plain. So was the tone of Antonina's scream.

Nicole didn't move from her seat well back in the tavern. Her head shook of itself. *They couldn't,* she thought in disbelief. *They wouldn't.*

Stupid. Of course they could. And if they wouldn't, why had she and Julia doused themselves with stale piss?

From where she sat, she could see through the front windows, at least to the middle of the street. As if he had known that, a great hulking brute of a German dragged Antonina into the frame of the windows and threw her down. Nicole watched in sick fascination, unable to move to her neighbor's rescue, and unable to look away. The rest of the gang crowded in, overwhelming Antonina. She got in one good kick before they had her spread-eagled on her back.

The Germans were shouting and singing, convivial as a gang of frat boys in a campus bar. But, as could happen in a bar, their good cheer turned abruptly to anger. Antonina's husband, that weedy little man whose name Nicole had never got around to learning, appeared from somewhere—the back of his house, maybe, or down the street—and sprang on them, flailing about him with a length of firewood. The barbarian who'd seized Antonina stepped back leisurely from a wild swing, lifted his sword with the same air of unhurried ease, and swept it around in a deadly blur. It slammed the side of the little man's head with a noise like a Nolan Ryan fastball slamming into a watermelon. Blood sprayed, the same explosion of scarlet as Nicole had seen a while ago, when the legionary fell. As the legionary had done, Antonina's husband dropped bonelessly to the ground. The only mercy, as far as Nicole could see, was that he never knew what hit him. Not like the legionary, who had seen his death coming at him in a sweep of bloodied steel.

Antonina screamed on a new note. The Germans holding her down laughed and cheered, not even slightly discommoded by her renewed struggles. The man who'd slain her husband strutted and preened. He was *proud* of himself. And the rest were proud of him. The one who held Antonina's left arm set his knee on it for a moment and beckoned with his freed hand, as if to say, *Here, you go first.*

The killer grinned. He swaggered back toward the huddle of men and the lone, suddenly very quiet woman. He squatted between her legs and ripped off her drawers. The others laughed with a note of incredulity, and let out a spatter of exclamations. The way they pointed and stared, Nicole knew all too well what had set them off. Their women didn't shave down there—and if they hadn't known that women here did, then this was their first rape in Carnuntum. Right here, in front of Nicole. Who couldn't move a muscle to intervene.

The German yanked down his breeches with a grunt, as if to say, *Enough of that.* Without further ado, he thrust his great red club between Antonina's legs, and ground deep.

Nicole turned her face away. Even with her fingers in her ears, she couldn't banish Antonina's cries. They went on and on, as if she'd lost all control over her voice.

Even through that shrill keening, Nicole heard the second, deeper grunt as the barbarian hammered himself to climax and pulled free. He sounded like a pig, a big, self-satisfied boar.

That wasn't the end of it. Not by a long, ugly shot. They took turns, every one, and a handful of others who happened by and stopped to join the fun. After a while, Antonina stopped screaming. Her mouth was open; her voice was gone. Several of the Germans took advantage of that, too, roaring with laughter as they spent themselves down her throat. *Bite him,* Nicole thought fiercely when the first one started. *Bite it right off him.* But Antonina didn't. Maybe she was too far gone. For her sake, Nicole hoped so.

After Frank walked out, Nicole had taken self-defense classes. She'd learned all about what to do if a rapist accosted her.

Or so she'd thought. Knee him in the nuts and scream for the police, and he'd stagger off groaning and clutching at himself. Wouldn't he?

Sure, and if he came back with a dozen burly bastards just

like him, each one toting a sword, and they *were* the police—what then?

In California, liberated or not, she'd felt insecure without a man in the house. Even as miserable a specimen as Frank was still male, and therefore, somehow, a deterrent.

There wasn't anyone here but Lucius. The fuller and dyer's shop across the way was empty; Gaius Calidius Severus was God knew where. Julia was worse than useless. Her ripe body was incentive to rape even at the best of times. Now . . .

One of the Germans who'd just finished his round with Antonina came ambling toward the tavern, adjusting himself inside his trousers. He took his time about that. *Go away,* Nicole willed him. *God damn you, go away!*

If God heard, He wasn't paying attention. The barbarian cupped his hands to shield his eyes from the sun, and peered into the gloom of the tavern. Nicole tried to shrink into invisibility. Lucius had already managed it so well she couldn't see him unless she actively looked for him.

But Julia couldn't bear to sit still any longer. She backed away from the window, pressing against the wall.

The German caught the movement. His eyes gleamed under his heavy brows. He drew back, only to turn and pound on the door.

17

NICOLE WASN'T TERRIFIED. SHE'D gone past that, into an eerie, brittle calm. Julia was shivering so hard, her teeth rattled. She was completely out of her mind with fear. Lucius had crawled under a table, which seemed a good idea to Nicole.

The pounding came again, loud, peremptory. Nicole

stayed where she was. If she didn't do anything, if nobody moved, maybe—maybe—

He didn't go away. Not hardly. "You open in there!" he bellowed in atrocious Latin. "You open, or we burn. With fire, we burn."

Was that what had happened beyond the market square? She didn't doubt for an instant that he'd do it. The place would go up like a torch, and the whole block with it— maybe this whole part of the city.

Whatever these barbarians did to her, it couldn't be worse than burning alive. *If rape is inevitable,* her self-defense instructor had said—not reluctantly enough, she'd thought at the time—*lie as still as you can, and don't resist. You're less likely to get hurt.* Some of the students had argued with him, she remembered. But not the ones who had been raped or mugged. They'd nodded, if bitterly. That was the way it was, they said. And wishing wouldn't make it any different.

Her feet moved of themselves, carrying her blindly toward the pounding. She drew the bar and opened the door.

He was huge, this German. Her head was level with his great barrel of a chest, just about where a bloodstain spattered across his breastplate. It *was* Roman armor, legionary issue, though that must have been one big legionary.

She raised her eyes from the stain, which she doubted very much was his own blood, to a face that took her every fear, and studied it, and assured her solemnly: it was true. It was pure, unadulterated male, male in the worst sense, male as predator. Lust, ferocity, arrogance—he would do whatever he damn well pleased with her and to her. It didn't matter the least bit in the world, what she thought or felt. He wanted. He took. That was the way of his world.

He sucked in a deep breath, drinking in the rich scent of his own power. And something a lot more pungent than that.

His nose wrinkled. His first expression was of incredulity. His second, disgust. He made a guttural sound deep in his throat, half a gag, half a snarl.

One of the other Germans called out to the man in front of Nicole. She couldn't understand a word, but she could well deduce what he was saying: *What the devil are you waiting for? Grab her and let's get on with it!*

The German turned his head to answer. Whatever he said, it sounded furious. When he turned back to Nicole, his expression was even uglier than before.

That part, she hadn't thought through. If he was too revolted to rape her, he could perfectly well kill her instead, and have nearly as good a time doing it. Quick—she had to think quickly.

She beckoned, and spoke slowly and carefully, in case he could understand Latin. "Here, sir. Come in. Would you and your friends like some wine?"

"Wine?" the German repeated. As the word sank in, he grinned, displaying a mouthful of strong yellow teeth. He shouted it out with a roar of glee. *"Wine!"*

Maybe the word was the same in their language as in Latin; maybe it was simply a Latin word they all knew. Either way, they all came running. They hadn't bothered—or, more likely, hadn't got round to—slaughtering Antonina as the climax to their sport. Even as Nicole shrank back to let the Germans crowd into the tavern, she saw how it ended. Slowly, like a dog whipped and then forgotten, Antonina crawled past the pool of blood around her husband's corpse, and into her house.

Julia, thank God, had kept her wits about her, though the place was bursting at the seams with Germans. Maybe she reckoned the bar was defense enough to her peace of mind. She stood behind it, dipping up cups as fast as she could. Her face was pale and set; despite the evidence of Nicole's safety, she didn't fully trust the stink to protect her. And yet it did—all the more since she was giving the Germans something else they wanted.

Giving? Once they got drunk (or, in some cases, drunker), what would they do? Shopkeepers got killed all too often in Los Angeles robberies; Nicole wasn't fool enough to think things were any different here.

A thought struck her. It was wild. It was probably crazy. It might get her killed. And yet—maybe, if this wasn't a robbery . . . "My friends," she said, which was a vagrant assumption without means of support if she'd ever seen one, "my friends, the wine is two *asses* a cup."

She'd got their attention, and then some. They all stared at her. Julia's eyes were wider than any of the Germans'. Those who had understood translated for the few who hadn't. Then they all started to laugh. Some of the laughter was amused. Some—more—was nasty.

One of them, who wore his hair in a topknot that reminded Nicole forcibly of one of the sillier beach-bunny fashions in Malibu, proved to speak rather decent Latin: "Why should we pay for what we can take?"

"If you take without paying, how will anyone in Carnuntum be able to get more for you to have later?" Nicole countered.

If she'd made him angry enough, she was dead. She was also dead if he realized that, with Marcomanni and Quadi and even Lombards—or so Gaius Calidius Severus had said, wherever he was now, and please God let him be all right— rampaging over the landscape, no one in Carnuntum would be able to get much more of anything regardless.

The German reached out and chucked her under the chin, the same gesture Titus Calidius Severus had used—once. She slapped his hand away, as she had Calidius Severus'. She did it altogether without thinking. Only after she'd done it did she realize she'd found another way to get herself in deep, deep trouble.

He stared at her. Some of the other Germans stared at her, too. Rather more of them stared at him, to see what he'd do. Slowly, he said, "You are a woman who thinks like a man." He reached out again and patted her on the head, as he might have done with a toddler who amused him.

She didn't bite the hand that patted her, as she would have dearly loved to do. *Overbearing, sexist oaf.* But, in his overbearing, sexist way, he'd admired her for her boldness. He wouldn't go on admiring her if she backed down. Whereas, if she kept it up, he might just admire her enough to let her alone. She thrust out her own hand. "Pay up, then," she said.

Silence stretched. If he decided the joke had gone too far, the next few minutes would be among the most urgently unpleasant she'd ever known, and very likely the last she ever knew. His right hand slid down to his belt. She held her breath. His hand bypassed his sword, and paused at the pouch behind it. He pulled out a coin and slapped it into the palm of Nicole's hand. "Here. This pays for all, yes?"

It was a little coin, smaller than an *as,* about the size of a nickel. It was surprisingly heavy, and gleamed brighter than even the shiny brass *sesterces* that looked like gold . . . till you had the real thing with which to compare them.

Julia spoke in an awed whisper: "That's an *aureus.*"

Nicole had never seen a goldpiece, not in all the time she'd been in Carnuntum. Even silver wasn't in common circulation, not at the low rung of the economy where the tavern dwelt. She thought—she wasn't sure, she'd never needed to be sure—an *aureus* was worth twenty-five *denarii.* A hundred *sesterces.* Four hundred *asses.* A hell of a lot of money.

"Yes," she said dizzily. "This pays for everything." Her wits started working again: "Everything to eat and drink, that is."

The German's nod was impatient. "Yes, yes," he said, and then, to put her in her place once more after he'd deigned to yield, "You flatter yourself if you think we want you or your servant here. You stink."

She hung her head, as if chastened. Down where the German couldn't see her do it, she grinned. She made herself wipe the expression from her face. But oh, how fine it had felt while she wore it!

The Marcomanni and Quadi—and perhaps even Lombards—drank all the wine she had, and ate most of the food. A few of them left. A few newcomers joined the crowd. Nobody touched Nicole or Julia or Lucius, or offered harm. They'd won a kind of immunity, between Calidius Severus' stale piss and Nicole's food and drink.

She knew how lucky she was. She'd seen horror. She'd heard it. She kept hearing it, too. Every so often, close by or far away, a woman would start screaming. She knew what that meant. The first time or two or three, she told herself she should rush out, find a weapon, do something about it. But no matter how brave she might be, she'd end up killed or thrown down beside the other woman and served up as the second course. It made her sick, but there was no getting away from it. Not one person in Carnuntum, male, female, it didn't matter, could do a thing. They were conquered. And this was what conquest was. She'd built a tiny raft of what might be safety. In the fallen city, that was—that would have to be—miracle enough.

The gathering was becoming rather rowdy. The frat-party ambience had thickened, till Nicole could almost see these murdering bastards as a gang of Sig-Eps and Tri-Delts celebrating a hard day's beer-bashing with a nightlong carouse.

One of them sprang up, egged on by his friends, and put on such a long, jut-jawed face that there was no mistaking what he was trying to be: a Roman citizen in the full draped weight of the toga, thirty pounds of chalk-whitened wool, throwing up his hands and squealing like a woman as a big bluff German cleaned out his cash box.

It was terrible, reprehensible, and ultimately very sad, and yet it was screamingly funny. The Germans were rolling on the floor, howling with laughter. And it *was* funny. Eddie Murphy could have used it without changing a thing—thirty pounds of toga, forty pounds of gold chains, what difference did it make? Nicole couldn't help herself. She burst out laughing.

The sound of it brought her up short. These men had just murdered one of her neighbors and gang-raped another in the middle of the street, and she was *laughing* with them? God, for a vial of poison to drop in their wine. And a dose for herself, for succumbing to the oldest disease in the world: falling into sympathy with the oppressor.

As had been happening once in a while as the afternoon wore on, somebody new swaggered through the door. He was a horrible sight, his tunic and trousers splashed with blood. None of it was his. He took a place at a table in the middle of the room, roared for wine—Nicole spitefully gave

him the last of the one-*as* rotgut; he swilled it down without
seeming to notice. Everybody wanted to know, by gestures
and grunted words, how he'd come to be covered with gore.
His answer was graphic, with much thrusting and slashing
of the air. They laughed and pounded the tables. He stabbed
a finger at his crotch and mimed the thrust and grind of a
good fast rape.

They clapped and cheered. They gathered round him and
pounded him on the back. Amid the gluey vowels and guttural consonants of their incomprehensible speech, Nicole
understood clearly what they thought of him. He'd scored in
their reckoning, and scored big.

And would anything change, really, in eighteen hundred
years? Never mind the small scale of fraternity hazings and
barroom gang rapes. The twentieth century had institution-
alized slaughter, and turned rape into a science. Serbs mas-
sacred Croats in Bosnia-Herzegovina, and drove women into
rape camps. She'd be willing to bet they boasted of the horrors they'd committed, and sat around in bars and cheered
one another on.

But, in one respect, things had changed. Once the Serbs
had had their fun, they'd done their best to hide it from the
world. They buried in mass graves the people they'd slaughtered, and denied that the rape camps had ever existed.

These Germans didn't think like that. Not in the least.
They saw nothing shameful in what they did; felt no need
to hide it from the world. They had every right, they seemed
to believe, to rob and rape, murder and pillage.

They were terrible people. And they were proud of it.
They were completely, unreachably alien.

All too soon and all too completely, the wine ran out.
Nicole poured the last dregs into a cup, served it to a German
who wouldn't have cared if she'd given him vinegar, and
stood empty-handed and beginning, all over again, to be
afraid.

But the German with the topknot, the one who'd given
her the *aureus,* patted her on the head again as if she'd been
a favorite dog, and said, "No one hurts you here today. I say

this—I, Swemblas." He struck a pose, with a lift of his head that told her the topknot and the Roman armor meant something. He was a man of substance, a chieftain maybe, or someone who had ambitions to be.

"I'm glad," she said to him. Then, after a pause and a moment's thought: "I'd be even gladder if you granted the same immunity to everyone in Carnuntum."

Swemblas laughed. "Ho! Ho, little woman, you make good jokes! Carnuntum is ours now. We will enjoy it. You Romans are too weak to stop us. If you were not, we would not be here."

He was honest, she granted him that. *You have what we want, and we're strong enough to take it away from you. So we damn well will.*

The twentieth century had spilled more blood than this small-time butcher ever dreamt of, working toward proving that greed and violence were not to be tolerated in an enlightened world. Here in the second century, greed and violence were the virtues of the hour. And who was she to tell them otherwise?

One of the Germans sat where he could see at an angle out the door. He pointed, laughed, and said something in his own language that made his friends echo his laughter.

"What's funny?" Nicole asked Swemblas, emboldened by the knowledge of his name and by the promise he'd made her.

He actually condescended to explain. "We are many drunken Germans, and here is also a drunken Roman."

And there he came, staggering along the street. Nicole saw the stagger first, before anything else. Her lip curled in anger and contempt. Carnuntum had fallen, and this idiot could think of nothing better to do about it than soak himself in wine.

Then he lifted his head, and she gasped in recognition. It was Gaius Calidius Severus. He'd never get drunk at such a time. He'd gone off to fight; there was no way he'd come back sloshed, even to drown his sorrow at defeat.

"He's not drunk," she said suddenly. "He's hurt." She ran

out past the staring Germans, caring only that none of them tried to stop her.

Her lover's son had lost his sword. When he turned his head to stare blankly at her, the left side of his face and his beard were crusted with dried blood. Her eye followed the track of it to an enormous lump above and in front of his ear.

He stopped, swaying, and blinked at her. "Mistress Umma?" he said doubtfully, as if he wasn't sure he knew her.

One of his eyes had a large pupil, the other a small. Concussion. "Gaius," Nicole said sharply, hoping the sound of his name would help him focus. "What hit you?"

"I don't know." His voice was vague. He winced. "I have an awful headache." He peered down at his right hand, and opened his eyes wide in surprise. "Where did my sword go?"

"I don't know," Nicole said. Maybe he'd dropped it when he got hurt. If he had, he was probably lucky. The Germans would have been sure to set upon an armed man, where an unarmed one might be—appeared to have been—a figure of fun. "Where have you been all this time?"

"Wandering, I suppose," he said, still in that dreamy, foggy tone. "I only remembered where I live a little while ago."

Nicole nodded. Concussion indeed. She didn't want to bring him into the tavern; no telling what her unwelcome guests might decide to do. She pointed him toward the door of his own shop. "Go in there. Go upstairs. Lie down, but *don't* go to sleep. You might not wake up. I'll come and check in on you as soon as I can."

He started to nod, then stopped with another wince. A small hiss of pain escaped him. "I'll do that." He hesitated, then added, "We lost, didn't we?"

The legionary's corpse still lay in the street, though Germans had stolen his sword and armor. The body of Antonina's husband sprawled not far from it. There were no dead Germans. All of those were alive, well, and roaring their way through a drinking song behind her.

"Yes," Nicole said dryly in a lull between verses. "We lost."

"I thought so," he said. He looked around a little more alertly than before. "What happens now?"

"I don't know." Nicole took a deep breath. If it struck him as normal to stand in the middle of the street talking about the fall of Carnuntum, and with no fear of the enemy either—maybe, after all, it wasn't invariably fatal to be an adult male in a conquered city—then he was still sufficiently fuddled to be in need of a keeper. She turned him bodily and pointed him toward his own door. "Don't worry about it now. Just go in, go upstairs, but remember: try to stay awake. Julia or I will check on you as soon as we can."

He didn't argue with her, which was also an indication that he wasn't quite right. He went where she directed him, into his shop. She heard the slide of the bar in the door, and drew a sigh of relief. Some of his wits were scrambled, but some still worked. If he could keep from falling asleep in the next few—minutes, she decided; she'd send Julia over right away, and make her stay there. Julia's methods of keeping him from falling into a coma might not be exactly family fare, but if they worked, Nicole didn't care.

But first, as long as Nicole was out, there was one more thing that needed doing. Her stomach crunched at the thought of it. But who else was there?

She slipped back into the tavern. Nobody appeared to notice her. They were all either drowning in the beer that was holding out now the wine was gone, or snoring on the tables or between the stools.

Julia was still standing behind the bar. She greeted Nicole with a look of joy that stabbed Nicole with guilt, but the guilt would be worse if Nicole didn't do this second errand. Nicole spoke as softly as she could and still be heard: "Will you be all right here by yourself for a little while? I have to check on poor Antonina."

Julia's face fell, but she kept her chin up regardless. "I suppose it will be all right," she said. "If they were going to throw us down and do what they did to her, they'd have done it by now."

Lucius had gone upstairs not long before Gaius Calidius Severus found his way home. None of the Germans had given him any trouble. One of them had picked up his wooden sword from the floor, thwacked him on the bottom with it, not very hard, then handed it to him. The German had laughed, even when he glared, and called him something in German that got Lucius a round of salutes. He'd kept Lucius by him for a while, plying him with walnuts and coaxing him until finally, unwillingly, he smiled. Then the German let him go. The man was still there, still eating walnuts, swapping war stories with a tableful of his fellows. There was no scarlet brand on his forehead, nothing to mark him as rapist or murderer. He was rather ordinary, really. Shave him, cut his hair, dress him in jeans and a shirt, and he'd be just another big blond guy in a bar.

Nicole knew better. She slipped out of the tavern again and walked warily down the street to Antonina's house. When she was out in front taking care of Calidius Severus, it had been one thing; she'd been in sight of the tavern, and under Swemblas' protection. Antonina lived just far enough to be out of reach if another barbarian happened by, and happened to be hungry for blood or a woman or both.

But no one accosted her. The street was deserted. She made it safely to the door, and knocked.

No one answered. She knocked again. Still no reply. A chill ran down her back. Antonina might have hanged herself, or slit her wrists, or thrust a knife into a vein. After what the Germans had done to her, she might not want to live. Nicole knew enough of rape trauma to know that, and to be seriously afraid.

This was Nicole's worst twentieth-century nightmare come to life. Men with unlimited license to do as they pleased, with and to women. Next to this, Tony Gallagher's crude come-on in the office had been the height of Old World courtesy.

She braced to knock yet again, but hesitated. Hadn't the

German pounded on the door before he dragged Antonina out? She must think there was another barbarian out here, looking for more sport.

"Antonina?" she called. "It's Umma."

Something stirred inside, a rustle, a muted scrape. Nicole sagged in relief. It might not be Antonina—for all she knew, it was a rat scuttling across the floor—but there was something, someone, alive in there. She knocked again, less peremptorily.

"Go away!" Antonina snapped at her from within, as sharp as ever, and deeply exasperated. "Leave me alone."

Nicole almost laughed. Yes, that was Antonina, all charm and sweetness. "I want to help, if I can," Nicole said.

The door opened abruptly. Antonina glared out at Nicole. "Help what? Help spread news of my shame through the whole city?"

"No!" Nicole protested. Damn, if only she'd found a spare hour a day to serve on a crisis hotline. She knew what those operators were supposed to do, but not how they were supposed to do it. She'd been too busy divorcing Frank, raising two kids, making partner . . .

She breathed deep and let it out slowly. Patience. That much she knew. You had to be patient. "Look. What happened wasn't your fault. No one should think any less of you because of it."

Antonina stared at her as if she'd never seen her before. After a stretching pause, she said, "You'd better come in." Nicole gathered her wits and did as she was told. Antonina shut the door behind her and barred it tightly. "Don't want those murdering demons coming by and seeing us," she said.

"I should think not," Nicole said. Voice soft, movements slow. It worked with animals; why not with a severely traumatized human? They stood in a darkened room, darker than the tavern had been, with all the shutters closed tight, and one stingy lamp burning. The room was full of shadows: shadows draped over furniture, hung on the walls, piled on the floor.

Antonina's late husband had been a tailor. These weren't

shadows. These were cloaks and tunics and hoods, some cut, some half-sewn, some all but finished and waiting for the final touches. Bolts of cloth stood against the far wall, some with pieces cut and hanging, others bound up tightly. The air was full of the odor of new wool.

"I'm sorry about your husband," Nicole said. "He was a brave man."

"Castinus?" Antonina snorted. "Sure he was brave. He was stupid." Nicole couldn't think what to say. Antonina sounded as if she'd barely known the man at all, still less loved and married him. "Stupid," she repeated. "He never in his life did anything so—so—" Then, to Nicole's lasting astonishment and considerable dismay, she gasped. Her eyes opened wide. And she cried out, a great, raw wail of pain and loss. Tears spilled down her cheeks. She flung herself into Nicole's arms and wept as if her heart would break.

Nicole unlocked the joints that had gone rigid when Antonina sprang at her, and stroked Antonina's filthy hair as she had Lucius' earlier. "Yes. Grieve. It's all right. It's good. Let it all out. You'll feel better."

"I'll never feel better!" Antonina cried. Then she stiffened. She pulled away from Nicole and looked about wildly. "I have to be quiet. They'll hear me if I'm not quiet." And yet, as she looked around, as she saw the evidence of her husband's labors wherever her eyes fell, a new, long wail escaped her, and she dove again for what security she might find in Nicole's arms.

"It's all right," Nicole said somewhat lamely. "I'm sure it's all right." And then, bitterly: "They like hearing women mourn. It reminds them how bold and brave and downright manly they are, to give us cause to weep."

"Barbarians," Antonina spat, in between spasms of tears. She clung to Nicole for a very long time. When she pulled away, it was sudden, as if she'd brought herself forcibly under control. Tears still dripped from her eyes; her nose was running. She wiped it on her sleeve. No handkerchiefs here. No Kleenex. She looked at Nicole through those red and streaming eyes, and sniffed loudly. "Thank you," she said with what for Antonina was considerable graciousness. "The way things usually are between us, I hadn't expected this from you." She paused to draw a long breath. "Sometimes it's not so bad to be wrong."

"No," Nicole said. "It's not."

Antonina sniffed again, almost her old scornful sound. "I can tell why the barbarians didn't bother you. What did you do, take a bath in the chamber pot? I wish I'd thought of that." This was good, Nicole thought. Antonina was herself again, more or less.

Nicole answered the question with some pride: "I took Julia across the street to Gaius Calidius Severus' and splashed us both with the really ripe stuff."

"That *was* clever," Antonina said, "though I'd have thought Julia would have enjoyed taking on a dozen or so stalwart Marcomanni." Yes, she was definitely on the mend: she was up to being bitchy again.

Nicole sighed. "If Julia wants to sleep with the Germans, she probably will, and there isn't much anybody can do about it. But if she doesn't want to, they have no right to force her."

"They have a right," Antonina said bleakly: "the right of the strong over the weak." She held up a hand before Nicole could speak. "Yes, my dear, I do understand you, but when has the world ever paid attention to a woman's rights?"

"Not often enough," Nicole had to concede.

Antonina nodded. She had no idea how long that would continue, but neither did she have any idea how much better things would get. Los Angeles of the Nineties, warts and all, was an infinitely better time and place for a woman than second-century Carnuntum.

Nicole knew that now. She also knew, or feared, that like most such wisdom, it came too late to do her any good.

Antonina's storm of weeping had passed, and she seemed much the better for it. She wouldn't be a danger to herself now, Nicole thought. Later, if she had a relapse, she might try something, but somehow Nicole suspected that Antonina was too tough for that.

"Listen," Nicole said. "I have to go back—poor Julia's all alone with a tavern full of drunken Germans. You come by if you need me, or call. One of us will come."

"I'll be all right," Antonina said. "You go. Slit a German throat or two for me, will you?"

"I wish," Nicole sighed.

Antonina didn't laugh, or even smile, but her expression as she saw Nicole off was brighter than it had been since before Carnuntum fell. Nicole knew a moment's apprehension: what if Antonina found a kitchen knife and came hunting Germans?

Not likely. People here might be unsanitary and they might be inclined toward sexism, but they weren't casual killers. Not like the people who had conquered them. Which was probably why the Germans had won and the Romans had lost, but that was not a thought Nicole wanted to dwell on. Not if she had to face a tavern packed with drunken, snoring Germans.

Julia had drawn a stool up behind the bar and perched on it, elbows on the bar, chin in hands. She acknowledged Nicole with a lift of the brows: for Julia, a strikingly undemonstrative greeting. Her words revealed the cause of her preoccupation: "If we had anywhere to hide the bodies, I'd cut all their throats."

"You and Antonina both," Nicole said.

"Really? She's alive?" Julia's lack of enthusiasm wasn't laudable, but Nicole could more or less understand it. Antonina wasn't the most popular person in the neighborhood.

"Alive and well enough," Nicole answered.

"That's good," said Julia, deliberately, as if she'd thought over all sides of it, and made a considered decision.

That was more than Nicole could do, but somehow she had to try. She surveyed the human wreckage, and noted the chorus of snores, which was a bit more melodious than what the Romans called music. "Let's leave them here and go up to bed. With that *aureus,* we're ahead of the game no matter how much more they eat." Then, as a new thought occurred to her: "If you want to bring your blanket and sleep behind a door that locks, I don't mind at all."

"That's kind of you, Mistress, but I'll be fine where I am," Julia replied. "If they're in that kind of mood, a barred door won't stop them. Breaking it down might even get them more excited."

Nicole hadn't thought of that. "You're probably right," she said.

Julia didn't dwell on it. She yawned hugely and stretched. "I'll look in on Gaius Calidius Severus before I go to bed," she said.

"Good," Nicole said. "I was going to ask if you'd do that. Make sure his pupils are the same size. If they are, it's probably all right to let him sleep."

"I do hope they are," said Julia. "He's not happy about having to stay awake and listen to the city fall." She paused. "If he needs to be kept awake . . . I'll stay with him."

Nicole opened her mouth, thought better of it, nodded. "Go on," she said. "I won't be closing up, with this many men on the floor. You can come in when you're ready, and not worry about disturbing me."

Julia didn't linger. When she was gone, Nicole sighed faintly and looked around her. The wine was all gone, but there were dregs enough in the cups that Julia had collected and set aside for cleaning. Nicole found the one with the most in it, and poured the contents in front of the image of Liber and Libera. She didn't say her prayer just then. But the wish was stronger than it had ever been.

When she'd barred the door of her room and lain down in bed, then she prayed. She prayed as she'd never prayed before. Not just to be free of a world and time that weren't and had never been her own. To be safe. To be where war like this never came, and cities weren't sacked, or women raped in the street in broad daylight, except in backward parts of the world where she need never go.

For all the potency of her wishing, and for all the strength of her prayer, when she woke, she woke to Carnuntum. Down below, men were groaning and swearing in guttural

German, cursing the wine they'd drunk and the hangover it had given them.

She shook her head. They'd be wanting breakfast, and she'd better see what she could find. No matter who was in charge here, she had to stay alive until she could find a way to escape. There was a way. There had to be one. Didn't there?

The sack of Carnuntum went on for five days. As long as chaos was the order of the day, Nicole and Julia made daily trips across the street to keep themselves stinking and unattractive to would-be rapists. Gaius Calidius Severus had needed to be watched for much of that first night, according to Julia, but by morning he was groggy, headachy, but on the mend. He didn't need much looking after, once he was back on his feet, except what Julia was minded to give him.

One morning, just as Nicole was coming out of the shop with Julia, pungent with a new application of what Nicole was thinking of as rape repellent, they met Antonina on her way in. She wrinkled her nose, nodded, and went on by. Nicole swallowed a smile. So: Antonina had decided to join the anti-rape league. Good for Antonina.

Young Calidius Severus endured several days of dreadful, pounding headaches before the pain gradually began to recede. He never did recall how he'd got that lump on the side of his head. "It must have been a rock," he said, over at the tavern, in an hour when it was blessedly empty of Germans. "It must have been. If a German had caught me with the flat of his blade, he wouldn't have stopped there. He'd have slit my throat or cut off my head."

Nicole nodded. "I think you're right. It had to be something like that, something that made you drop your sword."

"I suppose so," he said, "but I don't know. I expect I never will."

He dipped his bread in olive oil and ate. Nicole still had plenty of grain and, if anything, an oversupply of oil for the tiny amount of business she was doing. She was out of wine: the Germans had made sure of that.

Being out of wine meant drinking water. She didn't dare go over to the market square to find out if more wine was to be had, not yet. She didn't think any would be, anyhow, not judging by all the drunken barbarians she'd seen. At her insistence, Julia boiled water in the biggest pots they had. "This is a silly business, Mistress," the freedwoman insisted.

"Do it anyhow," Nicole said. Being the boss gave her the privilege of being arbitrary. She'd long since seen that arguments and explanations based on what the twentieth century knew and the second century didn't were worse than useless. "It can't hurt anything, can it?"

"I suppose not." Julia was still dubious, but did as she was told. When, after a day or two, nobody came down with the runs, she allowed as how it might not have been such a bad idea. That was the biggest concession Nicole had ever wrung from her.

More and more Germans came into Carnuntum. Some were celebrating the destruction of the legionary camp down the river. Some came to plunder and steal, though the pickings by now were thin. A lot simply passed through, on their way south toward other Roman towns and more Roman loot.

"All the Roman Empire will be ours," Swemblas boasted one day. "Every bit of it."

Nicole didn't argue with him. She thought there'd been Roman Emperors after Marcus Aurelius, but she wasn't sure enough of it to say so. Not to mention that disagreeing with one of the new German masters of Carnuntum was likely to prove hazardous to her health.

He didn't stay long, in any case. A tavern without wine had far less appeal to him than one with it. "If you have no wine, what good are you?" he demanded.

"You and your friends drank all I had," Nicole answered, not too sharply, she hoped. "How am I supposed to get more?"

"In the market, of course," Swemblas said in a tone she knew all too well. Male arrogance and superiority, patronizing the silly little woman, and letting her know just what an idiot she was.

His astonishment was all the stronger for that, when Nicole laughed in his face. "Suppose I can go to the market without having a dozen of your friends pull me down and rape me, the way they did to my neighbor," she said. Swemblas' expression went from astonished to shocked, likely because she dared talk so directly about what he did for fun. "Suppose I can do that," she said. "I'm not sure I can, but suppose. You people have drunk or stolen all the wine the merchants had on hand. Where are they going to get more?"

"It is not my problem," Swemblas said. "It is for the merchants to do."

"Good luck," Nicole said serenely. "Now the war is here, and south of here, not off somewhere farther west." Being vague let her conceal how ignorant she was of local geography. But then, a lot of people who'd been born and raised in Carnuntum knew little of Vindobona, twenty miles up the Danube, and less about any place farther away. "If you were a Roman wine merchant, would you want to come up to Carnuntum from Italy, knowing there were Germans in the way?"

"I am not a merchant. I am not a Roman. I do not want to be either," Swemblas said with dignity. And without a further word, he strode out.

He'd entirely missed the point. Nicole sighed. She shouldn't have expected anything different. Had the Germans been able to see anything from anyone else's point of view, they wouldn't have reckoned robbery and rape and murder to be fine sport, or applauded one another for them.

The next day, whether she wanted to or not, Nicole had to go to market. She was out of everything but grain and oil, and those were starting to run low.

Julia tried to talk her out of it. "Mistress," she said, "the less you show yourself, the safer you'll be."

"Yes, but if I get to the market square now, I have a better chance of finding things before it's picked clean," Nicole answered. She wasn't as bold as she sounded, but Julia didn't call her on it. Julia was still shaking her head as Nicole went out the door.

There were Germans in the streets, swaggering about with a lordly air. In front of the shop where Nicole had bought her image of Liber and Libera, one of the conquerors picked up a votive plaque with an image of the naked Venus. He ran a hand over the limestone curves as if fondling a real woman. *"Gut!"* he grunted, or close enough. The shopkeeper stood motionless. The German laughed, tucked the plaque under his arm, and sauntered off. The stonecarver stared after him, but knew better than to demand payment.

Something about the incident stopped Nicole cold. It wasn't the theft—that was common enough these days. It wasn't the shopkeeper's powerlessness, not really. And yet . . .

I don't have the right plaque, Nicole thought. The thought was very clear. She'd had it before, and more than once, but never so distinctly. *The god and goddess aren't listening, because the plaque I have—it's not the one I bought in Petronell. It's not just the image, or the intent. It's the connection to me, to my past and future. I need that one, and no other.*

She couldn't prove it. Nor was there any way to do so, unless she found the actual plaque, the one that had brought her here. Did it even exist yet? Would she have to wait another twenty or thirty years before it was made?

No, she thought with a shiver. She had to believe, for her own sanity, that the plaque had brought her back to the time when it was carved. Otherwise, what would be the point of it at all?

She put the thought away for now; because she had an errand, and it was urgent. It wasn't too terribly hard to distract herself: the city had changed since she last went out to market. Shops that had once been open were closed and shuttered, Germans came and went from houses that had belonged to solid Roman citizens, the few women who were out and about went warily as Nicole herself did, and probably with some kind of weapon concealed in their clothing. Nicole, whose chief weapon was her stink of ancient piss, was just as glad not to be armed. Her self-defense instructor had been blunt about it. "A knife or a gun may make you feel better when you carry it, but you're just giving a mugger another weapon to use against you. Unless you can shoot or stab to kill or disable, and do it instantly, he'll get hold of it and he'll use it. And you'll be worse off than you were before."

Armed with a stink that kept even the locals from crowding in too close, Nicole passed the baths and came in sight of the open space of the market square. She stopped, and gasped.

The space was larger, much larger, than it had ever been before. It opened to the north and west, openness in shades of black, the charred ruins of the fire that she'd heard but not seen on the first day of the sack. Houses and shops and a handful of four- and five-story apartment buildings were flattened, burned to the ground.

Romans and Germans, their clothes and hides black with soot, sifted through the wreckage. Some of the Romans were probably trying to salvage what they could from the disaster. Many must have been thieves—as were all of the Germans.

When a Roman found something he was looking for, he slipped it into a pouch or hid it somewhere on his person, as quickly and unobtrusively as possible. When a German found a coin or a ring or anything of value, he held it up and crowed over it. *He* didn't care who saw him, or worry that someone else might take his prize away from him.

Nicole shook her head at the fortunes of war, and ventured into the market. Most of the largest stalls were empty, their keepers dead or robbed or simply lying low. The Germans helped themselves to whatever struck their fancy. She watched a barbarian walk away from a sausage-seller gnawing on a length of garlicky stuff he hadn't paid for. Like the stonecutter, the merchant could only look unhappy. There wouldn't be a revolt here, not while the Germans were large and strong and trained to fight, and the locals were smaller, weaker, and inclined to leave the fighting to professionals.

Nicole bought a length of sausage for herself. She didn't have to haggle much to get a good price, rather to her surprise. "You're only the third person today with money to spend," the sausage-seller told her. "I'm happy to see any brass at all."

With the sausage stowed away in her bag, she bought a sack of beans and a sack of peas, and filled another sack with lettuce and onions and cucumbers. That was as much as she could carry. There wasn't any wine, as she'd fully expected.

Loaded down with her purchases but still trusting to her rape repellent, she left the market with relief. While she'd been busy shopping, she hadn't taken time to notice the way the Germans eyed the women who'd ventured out to market. Once she was done, as she turned toward home, she grew all too well aware of it: long raking glances, and looks that stripped a woman bare and had their will of her. They didn't actually drag anybody down and line up for the fun, but that didn't mean they couldn't do it, or wouldn't. The sooner she was out of their sight, the better. Her ears burned. She couldn't move nearly fast enough, burdened as she was; she had to keep to a slower pace.

It felt like a crawl. To these bastards she was meat, nothing more, as free for the taking as a sausage or a sack of barley. If one of them decided to have fun with her, and never mind the stink that surrounded her, she couldn't stop him. Not if she wanted to stay alive.

As it happened, no one touched her or accosted her. She made it home without undue trouble, and set down her burden of sacks and bags with a sigh of relief.

Julia wasn't any less relieved than Nicole was. "Mistress!" she said. "You got away with it."

That was pretty much how Nicole felt, but she wasn't about to let Julia know it. "We have to eat," she said. "We can go without a lot of things, but not food." And if Julia knew exactly how much Nicole was going without, she'd never believe it.

"I just hope there's food to be had," Julia said. "The gods only know what the barbarians have done to the farmers outside the city—the ones who didn't die of the pestilence, that is."

"If they want money, they'll have to bring crops into town," Nicole said. Julia nodded, but she still looked worried. She wasn't the only one. In all the hard times Nicole had back in the United States, she'd never missed a meal, or even come close. Going hungry because there was no food was something she'd seen on the news, flashed into her living room by satellite from somewhere else. That it could happen to her . . . With all the horrors she'd seen since she came to Carnuntum, she was a fool if she thought she'd be immune to any of them. She had to plan ahead. If she could lay in a supply, she'd better do it soon. And not just for herself, either. For Lucius—because if he starved to death, all his future died with him, and Nicole with it.

Later that afternoon, Brigomarus came by: his first visit since the city fell. Nicole couldn't really fault him for taking this long to do his brotherly duty. She hadn't exactly taken pains to make sure he was all right, either. When he was well past the door and within smelling distance of the bar, he sniffed and nearly gagged. "Phew! Smells like somebody dumped a pisspot in here."

"That's how it's supposed to smell," Nicole answered tartly. "It keeps the Germans away."

"Keeps the customers away, too, I shouldn't wonder," Umma's brother said.

"Customers are the least of my worries right now," Nicole shot back.

"Really?" Brigomarus raised an eyebrow. "I would have thought your family was the least of your worries. Didn't you even stop to wonder if Tabica and I were alive?"

Nicole had a perfectly good excuse, and she didn't hesitate to use it: "Today was the first time I'd even gone to the market square. I don't go out if I can help it. If Tabica is doing anything different, she's a fool."

He chewed on that for a while, frowning. Then he nodded. She was supposed to be grateful, obviously, that he, the mighty male, had come round to her way of thinking. He wasn't any different from a German, when you got down to it.

At least he wouldn't hack her head off for talking back to him, though he might try to bite it off. "All right," he said ungraciously. "Tabica's staying in, yes. Now let it go. I didn't come over to start the fight again."

"No?" Nicole inquired. "It sure seemed that way."

"I said I didn't." He scowled. After all this time, he still wasn't used to backtalk from someone he recognized as his sister. "What do you want from me?"

"An apology would be nice," Nicole said.

Now he stared. So did Julia. Nicole knew she was pushing it, but she didn't care. If Brigomarus didn't want to play by her rules, she was perfectly willing and able to have nothing more to do with him. It had taken her a while, but she'd come to realize just how much leverage that gave her. She really didn't care—and he did. Desperately. As far as he knew, she was family. As she very well knew, she wasn't. What mattered greatly to him meant nothing to her.

She held all the power. He might not understand it, but he knew it. Therefore, with bad grace, he yielded. "I'm sorry," he said, doing a better job of it than Lucius might have, but not much. "I'm glad you're safe here." That sounded a little more as if he meant it.

"Safe?" Nicole's laugh had a raw edge. She saw in her mind Antonina turned into a toy, a thing, for the amusement of any barbarian who happened to wander down the street. She knew how easily that could have happened to Julia, or to her. She saw Antonina's husband, too, with the side of his head smashed in and blood puddled in the street, soaking into the dirt. "We're not safe. It's just that nothing horrible has happened to us yet."

Brigomarus didn't like that any more than anything else she'd said, but he was an honest man, on the whole. He nodded. "I see. Anything can happen to any of us, any time. And there's nothing we can do about it." He paused. "I suppose . . . it must be worse for a woman."

Nicole and Julia exchanged glances. *Amazing,* Nicole thought. *He sees it. He actually sees it.*

It *was* amazing. Women here really were the weaker sex.

On the whole, they were smaller than men, and not so strong. Without the machines that made brute strength largely irrelevant, that mattered. Nicole had never realized how much women had benefited from the Industrial Revolution. She'd either taken machines for granted or sneered at them. If she ever got back to California, she promised whatever gods might be listening, she would never sneer again.

And, beyond even that, women had babies. That still complicated their lives in the twentieth century, but by that time the risk of dying in childbed had grown very small. It was alive and well in Carnuntum. So was the risk of getting pregnant whenever a woman lay down with a man. She knew how unreliable the plug of wool she'd used had been, and how lucky she was not to have been caught.

Engineering. Science. Medicine. She'd never realized how important they were till she had to do without them. Without them, could women in the modern West have come as close to equality as they had? She doubted it.

Resolutely, she dragged her mind back to the here-and-now. This was no time to be mulling over the extent of her education, still less to be yearning for her own place and time. Brigo, unlike Julia or the Calidii Severi, wasn't likely to cut her slack while she lost herself in a reverie. She put on an expression of polite interest and inquired, "What are you doing these days?"

He seemed relieved to take refuge in small talk. "Same as always," he answered: "making shields. Only difference is, the Germans take them now, not the legion. My work is good enough to keep them happy, so mostly they leave me alone."

"You make shields . . . for the Germans?" Nicole asked in disbelief. What was the old word for a collaborator? *Quisling,* that was it. Umma's brother was a quisling.

Or was he? "Yes, I make shields for them," he said. "If I say no, they'll kill me—either that or I'll starve, which amounts to the same thing. When they come in here, do you say, 'No, I won't give you any bread. Get out!'?"

She lowered her eyes. No. She didn't. She never had, not even when they'd come straight in from gang-banging An-

tonina. She'd been afraid, and she'd wanted to live. So—
was that what a quisling was? Someone who went right on
doing what he would have been doing if the Germans hadn't
come, but doing it, now, for the Germans?

But he was making an implement of war. She was simply
feeding them. An army ran on its stomach. Where had she
heard that? It didn't matter. Collaboration was collaboration,
whatever the extent of it.

She held up a hand. "No, I didn't turn them down when
they ordered me to feed them. Let it go, Brigo. You're doing
what you need to get by. So am I." He opened his mouth to
say something. She thought she knew what he had in mind.
She forestalled him. "I am sorry for the way it sounded."

"Well!" For the first time in a long while, she saw Umma's
brother grin. "I was wondering if you could only take apol-
ogies; you had no idea how to give them back. I'm glad to
see it isn't so."

"Fair is fair," Nicole answered.

"I suppose so," Brigomarus said, by which he no doubt
meant he was perfectly content to hang onto the privileges
that went with being male. He half-turned as if to leave, but
turned back with a snap of the fingers. "When I was coming
through the market square, I saw that one of the farmers had
brought in a cartload of wine. It's just the cheap local stuff,
of course, but if you can't get anything else, it starts to look
pretty good."

"I'll say it does!" Nicole wasn't about to hug him, but she
was as tempted as she'd ever been. She headed straight for
the cash box instead. "I was in the market just this morning,
but he hadn't come in then. If I can get a jar or two before
he sells out—"

"Or before the Germans steal everything he has," Julia put
in.

"Or that, too," Nicole agreed. She turned to Brigomarus.
"Will you come with me and help carry some of it back? I'll
give you a jar to take home." She hesitated. Then she said
it, hating it but knowing it was the truth: "It would be nice
to have a man along."

She wasn't trying to do or say anything to feed his ego, but she'd succeeded in doing precisely that. He could hardly look eager—that would give away too much—but he didn't turn his back on her, either. "I'll come," he said. "I don't know how much good I'll be if the Germans decide to get nasty, but I'll do what I can."

Nicole thanked him honestly enough. He wasn't really a bad man, as men went in this century. She'd seen better, in the Calidii Severi, but she'd also seen much worse.

It was a men's day at the baths. When Nicole and Brigomarus came round the corner, Romans and Germans came and went interchangeably, though neither fraternized with the other.

Then out through the entranceway strolled a pair of courtesans in nearly transparent linen tunics. Maybe they were the same pair Nicole had seen when she first went up the stairs to the baths herself. Every German within sight whipped his head about and stood transfixed.

Ye gods, Nicole thought. Prostitutes could be raped, too, and these women were flaunting everything they had. No civilized jurisdiction accepted revealing clothing as an excuse for rape, but this was no civilized jurisdiction. If the Germans dragged an ordinary and none too attractive woman from her own home and gang-raped her in the street, what would they do to women on display like this?

They fawned on them. If they'd had chocolates and vast bouquets of flowers, they would have showered them on the hookers. As it was, they stared and gaped and stammered like awed teenagers suddenly confronted by Claudia Schiffer. Nicole suppressed a strong impulse to retch.

Brigomarus, on the other hand, was highly amused. "They don't have anything like *that* in the forests of Germany, I'll bet you."

Nicole started to snap at him, but checked herself. What was his comment but the second-century version of her reflection on teenagers and supermodels? In the end, she simply said, "When you think how they treated so many women here, seeing this hurts."

"Ah." Brigomarus nodded. "Yes, I can see how it might. The world must look different out of a woman's eyes."

She leaned over and kissed him on the cheek. He looked astonished. It wasn't that family didn't kiss here; they did. But she had been on anything but kissing terms with Umma's family. Here, for once, Brigomarus had found exactly the right thing to say.

She felt like kissing him again when she was able to buy two jars of wine from the fellow in the market square. The farmer demanded Falernian prices for it, though it was the local rotgut in the local yellow-brown earthenware. Nicole took her best shot at getting him to come down: "Suppose I walk away and let the barbarians steal it from you? How much will you get then?"

He didn't blink. "The chance I take of that is part of the reason I have to charge so cursed much for what I do sell."

When he wouldn't budge, Nicole paid up. As she and Brigomarus were carrying the wine back toward the tavern, he said, "You'll have to charge Falernian prices, too, or you'll lose money."

"Then I will," she said robustly. "Not many places will have any wine at all. People will pay." She was sure of that. Half the people who came into the tavern complained about having to drink water; a good many complained about coming down sick afterwards. Whenever she suggested boiling the water before drinking it, people looked at her as if she were nuts.

She and Brigomarus were almost home safe, and unmolested, when two big red-faced Germans planted themselves in their paths. One rested a meaty hand on the hilt of his sword. The other proved to speak some Latin. "What have you in those jars?" he demanded. "Is wine, yes?"

Nicole's mind raced. "Is wine, no," she answered. "Is piss for my dyeworks. Want to drink some?" She thrust her jar at the German.

The outhouse reek that still came off her lent force to her words. The barbarian recoiled, spitting out dismayed gutturals. His friend asked a question. The answer he got left him revolted, too. They both took off in a hurry.

Brigomarus looked ready to burst with suppressed laughter. He kissed her instead, quick but firm, as a brother should. "Even if you do smell bad," he said.

"That's all right," she said. "That's better than all right."

They were still laughing when they walked into the tavern. Julia looked up at them in surprise. "I haven't heard the two of you laugh like that in a long time," she said.

"Since the pestilence," Nicole said. Her laughter had died.

"Longer than that," Julia said. "It's probably been since— hmm." She paused. "Since last spring, I guess."

Since Umma moved out and Nicole moved in. I ruined the neighborhood—and the neighborhood has been doing its best to ruin me.

She actually enjoyed telling Julia why she and Brigo had been laughing. God, she had changed.

Not for the worse, she hoped. Julia laughed at the joke. So did Lucius, when he came running in from outside. He laughed harder than anyone else. At his age, gross-out humor was the best kind.

Nicole set her jar of wine behind the bar. Brigo followed suit. She grinned at him suddenly. "Let's have some wine," she said. And if she'd known a year ago that she'd say such a thing, let alone say it with such relish, she'd have been flatly appalled. Carnuntum had changed her in ways she never could have imagined. It had also, and forcibly, changed her attitude toward life in Los Angeles. She longed for that life, even while she laughed and bantered and poured out cups of horrible wine. But she was trapped here, in this life she'd thought she wanted. She might never escape; never be free of it, unless or until she died.

18

LITTLE BY LITTLE, THE folk of Carnuntum learned to live with the occupation of their city. They drank water, though sometimes it made them sick, or beer or bad local wine in place of the better vintages that could not come up from the south. When the olive oil ran out—which took a while, because, in contrast to the wine, the Germans had no interest in helping to consume it—they made do with butter. They complained about it, too, loud, long, and rarely with any inventiveness. Nicole liked butter quite a bit, as long as it was fresh. But without refrigeration, it went rancid much faster than oil.

Gaius Calidius Severus despised the stuff. "The smell stays in my mustache," he complained, "and I have to live with it all day long."

Compared to rancid piss, rancid butter didn't seem that bad to Nicole, but she didn't tax him with it. She was too fond of him. He'd done a great deal for her, and he was a hell of a good kid. Very soon now, he was going to be a very nice young man.

Little by little, she and Julia left off splashing themselves with *eau de pissoir*. The Marcomanni and Quadi still sometimes casually walked off with things without bothering to pay for them, but the excesses of the sack didn't go on for long. It gradually dawned on the Germans that, having overrun Carnuntum, they would get the most out of it if it ran as near normally as possible.

One day, a man who happened to be selling apples in the market square said to Nicole, "Umma, have you heard? My cousin Avitianus, the one with the farm out past the amphitheater—you know, the one who's got the six girls and just the one boy and that one's addled in the head? Well, the

Germans took two of his sheep and wouldn't pay him, which is nothing at all new, you know, but you know what he did?"

Nicole hadn't the faintest. She opened her eyes wide and looked expectant.

"He complained to the chiefs, that's what!" the man said. "Imagine that."

Nicole could imagine. She didn't like the picture she was getting. "That was brave, but it can't have been very smart."

"Well, that's Avitianus, you know?" The apple-seller sighed. "They gave him a kick in the arse and sent him on his way. That Avitianus, he's got bigger balls than a he-goat, but he's got to use his thumbs to count them."

"And so much for justice, too," Nicole said.

"Only justice a poor man ever knows is what he gets hit over the head with," the man replied. "The Germans'll hit you over the head with a sword. Before they came, the rich bastards would hit you over the head with a lawyer. The sword hurts more, but the lawyers took more."

She stared at him. Even in ancient Rome, people made snide jokes about attorneys? "If it weren't for lawyers, we'd all be after each other with swords all the time," she said with a touch of asperity.

"Well, maybe," the apple-seller said. "But maybe we'd leave each other alone more, too, if we had swords instead of lawyers."

"Tell it to the Germans," Nicole said, bending his own words back against him. He grunted, shrugged, and finally, grudgingly, nodded.

"Those are nice ones," Julia said when Nicole brought the apples back. "You must have bought them before they were picked over."

"I suppose I did," Nicole answered. The apples didn't look that nice to her. They were on the smallish side compared with what she'd been able to buy in the supermarket. Produce here was wildly inconsistent; some apples would have a firm texture and a delicious, complex sweetness as good as anything she could have hoped for back in L.A., while others from the same orchard wouldn't be worth eating.

While she stared at them, inspiration struck. She rummaged through the spices in back of the bar till she found a quill of cinnamon. Spices, she'd discovered, traveled more than most things: they were valuable, didn't take up much room, and didn't spoil. She ground up part of the quill in a mortar and pestle. The sweet pungent fragrance made her nostrils twitch. It smelled of autumn in Indiana, and a bakery on a rainy day, and apple pie on the table at Thanksgiving. It was wonderful, and it made her throat go tight and her eyes sting. Julia saved her from bawling into the mortar. "What are you going to do with that, Mistress?" she asked.

"I'm going to make some baked apples," Nicole answered.

Julia's eyes went wide. "I've never heard of anyone eating apples any way but raw."

"Well, you'll learn something, then," Nicole said.

They weren't perfect. Had they been, they would have been sweetened with sugar instead of honey, and they would have been swimming in cream. But Julia and Lucius didn't have to know there was anything missing. They devoured theirs in what seemed like two bites apiece, and loudly demanded more. Nicole savored hers, the taste on her tongue and the aroma in her nose. It filled the whole tavern, and for a little while drove away the stink of Carnuntum. "You could make a fortune with those," Julia said, wiping her mouth on her sleeve.

"No," Nicole said. "Too easy to figure out what I did. Besides, where can I get more cinnamon once this is gone?"

Julia made a face. "You're right about that—it won't be easy. There's probably not any left in the city, and no merchants in their right minds are going to come this way, not with the Germans running wild through Pannonia. By the gods, no merchants who are out of their minds would come this way, either."

Nicole and Lucius laughed, Nicole with a little incredulity; serious, literal-minded Julia almost never said anything witty. Still, Nicole sobered quickly: the joke cut too close to the truth. She said, "Nobody much will come this way, except for the farmers close to town. The market square is half empty."

"We didn't have a famine in spite of the pestilence," Julia said. "If we don't have a famine in spite of the pestilence and the Germans, the gods will truly be looking out for us."

Lucius said, "If the gods are truly looking out for us, why did they let the pestilence happen? Why did they let the Marcomanni and Quadi conquer Carnuntum in the first place?"

"Why? Why, because . . . because . . ." Julia floundered. She scratched her head. In scratching, she found something, which she squashed between two fingernails. That still gave Nicole the horrors. She kept on fighting the battle against lice, though now she knew it was a losing battle. Julia turned to her. "Mistress, why do you suppose the gods did let those terrible things happen, if they are looking out for us?"

Nicole swallowed a sigh. Such was the lot of mothers everywhere: to be expected to answer the unanswerable. "I don't know why the gods do anything," she said. "I don't think anyone does. You can *believe,* but how can you *know?* No one has ever questioned a god, that I know of." Maybe no one ever had, but Nicole certainly wanted to. She'd have given a lot to ask some good, hard questions of Liber and Libera—and better yet, to actually get answers. *Why on earth did you send me back here? Why on earth won't you send me home to California?* She'd done everything she knew how to do to get the attention of the god and goddess. She'd prayed, and nobody could doubt her prayer was sincere. She'd given enough wine to swim in if they'd been so inclined. But they weren't listening to her.

She hadn't given up her search for the actual plaque, the one that had brought her back here. Once it was safe to go out again, and while she had errands to run—trips to market, women's day at the baths—she took time to hunt. She hadn't seen anything closer to it than the one she'd bought from the stonecutter near the market, but she hadn't given up. Nor did she intend to, not till she'd scoured every street and poked into every shop.

Looking for something in Carnuntum, she'd discovered, was nothing like shopping in L.A. or Indianapolis, not if you wanted to be thorough, as she emphatically did. She couldn't let her fingers do the walking; she had to do it with her feet. It wasn't just that there were no phones here. There were no phone books, nowhere she could check under STONECUTTERS to see if she'd found them all. There wasn't a Chamber of Commerce from which she might have got a list of such artisans, either. If she wanted to hunt them down, she had to do it herself.

"In all my spare time," she muttered, which would have been funny if only it were funny. She'd thought she was busy in Los Angeles. Work here in Carnuntum never seemed to get done. If she couldn't find the plaque, if she couldn't escape the second century . . . Had she seen her own gravestone when she came to Petronell on her honeymoon? She didn't remember seeing any inscribed to a woman named Umma, but that proved nothing. She could as easily say it proved Umma had never existed, and all this was a dream.

In which case, Nicole had taken to dreaming historical epics.

A week or two after Nicole invented baked apples, the tavern ran low on grain. When Nicole went to the market square in search of more, she found none for sale: no wheat, no barley. She'd never seen rye or oats. "What am I supposed to do?" she asked a man who was selling plums at a preposterous price.

"Tighten your belt," he answered.

She hissed at his total lack of sympathy, and went searching elsewhere. As she'd recalled, a miller or two had shops between the market and her tavern. One of them sold her a little barley flour at five times what it should have cost. The other shook his head and said, "Sorry, but I haven't a kernel to spare. I'm hanging on to every grain in every jar to keep myself and my kin alive. Hard word to give you, I know, but that's how it is." Nor would he give way, even when Nicole pleaded for something, anything, a handful would do.

"My wife's having a baby," he said. "I've got to keep her strength up."

Nicole left the miller's shop in a state of considerable aggravation. Before she could make it out into the street, a gang of Germans swaggered down the sidewalk, arm in arm and giving way to no one. She had to flatten herself against the wall to keep them from walking right through her. They laughed to see her cringe. They were big and ruddy-cheeked and healthy. They hadn't missed any meals lately, and didn't look likely to, either. Whatever grain there was or had been in Carnuntum, it was in their hands now. And the Romans? They plainly didn't give a damn about the Romans.

She waited till they were well past before going on her own way. As she walked, she found her eyes following a flock of pigeons in the street. Their brainless strut wasn't a whole lot different from that of the mighty conquerors. If this lot learned to carry swords, the rest of the birds would be in trouble. And how, she wondered, would they taste roasted, or stewed, maybe, with the few herbs she had left, and some of that awful local wine? They hadn't changed a bit, to be sure. Their habits were just as disgusting as they'd ever been. Even as she watched, one of them pecked at an ox turd in the street. Her stomach turned over. But as it did that, it growled. Pigeons were meat. Her stomach knew it, regardless of what her brain might have to say.

Julia exclaimed in dismay when she brought home so little in the way of grain. "Mistress, what will we do?"

"Tighten our belts," Nicole replied, as the man with the plums had done with her. It was no answer, and yet the only one possible.

No, not quite the only one possible. "I think we'll close down for a while," she said, "just worry about feeding ourselves, till more food comes into the city. And . . . I think I'll send Lucius out tomorrow, to bring us back as many snails as he can catch."

How many calories in a snail? How many other people, children and adults alike, had gone out hunting snails? How long before Carnuntum had not a snail left in it, and people still hungry? Those were all good, relevant questions. She had answers for none of them—yet. What she did have was the bad feeling she would not only get answers, they wouldn't be anything either easy or comfortable to deal with.

For a while, at least, they'd manage. The next day, Lucius went out hunting and returned with a good-sized basket full of snails. The tavern smelled of garlic and fried molluscs the rest of the day. Nicole, Lucius, and Julia all ate till they were full, and there were still live snails left in the basket for tomorrow.

A German came in while they were eating. He grimaced at what was to Nicole the wonderful odor of garlic, and turned the color of a bream's belly when he found out what she and the others were eating. He literally fled the tavern, a hand clapped to his mouth.

Nicole laughed for a long while after he was gone. The others followed suit, but they were a little puzzled. She had to stop, wipe away the tears of mirth, and try to explain. "Isn't it strange? Murdering people for fun doesn't bother these bastards. Violating women doesn't faze them. Robbing people doesn't trouble them in the slightest. But snails with garlic? That makes them turn up their toes."

"If we'd known it, we could have splashed ourselves with garlic juice instead of sour piss," Julia said seriously—she still wasn't quite inclined to laugh at a German. "We would have liked it better, and the Germans still would have left us alone."

"They *might* have left us alone," Nicole said. "What we did worked. That's good enough." She patted her belly, which felt wonderfully full. "And a big mess of snails is good enough—or better than good enough—too, no matter what a cursed barbarian thinks."

Julia nodded. So did Lucius. It took Nicole a moment to realize what she'd just said. *Cursed barbarian?* If that wasn't the precise local equivalent of *damn nigger* or *stinking wetback,* what was it? She looked up at the soot-smeared ceiling. She was horrified, but she was also a little amused—that wasn't like the old Nicole at all, at all. Of all the things the second century had done to her, slinging casual ethnic slurs was one of the last she'd expected.

Neither of the others saw anything at all unusual or reprehensible in it. Lucius packed away the last snail from the bowl, sat back, and belched luxuriously. Nicole frowned, but she held her tongue—still more evidence of the new, far from improved version. "I'll catch more snails tomorrow, Mother," Lucius said.

"Good." Nicole ruffled his hair. He ducked his head, but not too much, and put up with it better than she might have expected. She patted her belly again. It came down to a simple choice, she thought. She could worry about whether her belly was full, or she could worry that she was improperly denigrating the magnificent achievements of the Quadi and Marcomanni and, as far as she could tell, the Lombards.

It took leisure to be politically correct, and to see all sides of the question. Leisure—and a well-stocked larder. And no good and sufficient and very immediate reason to blame the ethnic group of choice for the gnawing in her middle.

Snails grew scarce, as she'd known they would. Pigeons proved tasty, though she cooked the meat right off the bones to make sure it was safe to eat. After a while, they got harder to catch: the survivors turned streetwise. The sight of a human within a stone's throw sent them skyward in a whirring racket of wings.

There was always fish in the market, no matter how hard the times were. The Germans didn't mind if the locals went out in their little boats with nets or hooks and lines. But, when it was almost the only food available, fish became expensive. Nicole regretted every frivolous *as* she'd spent since she entered Umma's body—to say nothing of the coins Umma had spent before Nicole came to Carnuntum.

That *aureus* Swemblas gave her had seemed a huge sum of money, like a thousand-dollar bill. And, like a thousand-dollar bill when no other cash was coming in, it melted away, an *as* here, a *dupondius* there, a couple of *sesterces* somewhere else.

Nicole found herself in a cruel dilemma: if she sold the food she managed to find, she earned money with which to buy more food, but she couldn't eat what she sold. If, on the other hand, she ate the little food she managed to lay hold of, she stopped being hungry for a while, but money flowed out of the cash box as inexorably as sand running through an hourglass.

The uneasy compromise that she settled on left the three of them both hungrier and closer to broke than she wanted them to be. Her drawers fit more loosely than they had when she first woke in Umma's body, even more loosely than they had when she was recovering from the pestilence. Her belly growled at her all the time.

She'd known hunger before. In Indiana and California, she'd spent enough time on diets that hadn't done much but fray her temper, nibbling carrot sticks when her stomach was yelling for a banana split. But all the hunger she'd endured had been voluntary. Whenever she'd wanted to, or whenever she couldn't stand it anymore, relief had been no farther away than the nearest bacon double cheeseburger or package of Twinkies or Milky Way bar—anything guaranteed to leap six weeks of Lean Cuisine at a single bound.

Not here. Not now. That mournful litany played yet again in her mind, as it had—how many times?—since she'd come to Carnuntum. This hunger was not consensual. It was forced on her, as much as the Germans had forced themselves on poor Antonina. She'd never thought there could be a connection between hunger and rape, but there it was.

That wasn't the only unpleasant connection she found. One day, after she came back to the tavern with a couple of trout and a little cheese for which she'd paid more than she could really afford, she put the money she hadn't spent back in the cash box. By then, she knew to the *as* how much was supposed to be in there; as hard as times were, she paid much closer attention than she had when they were easier.

She frowned. The box held a few *sesterces* more than it should have. Till she came back, there hadn't been any food to eat, let alone to sell to anybody else. Her eye fell on Julia.

Julia was scrubbing tables, mostly for something to do; business was too bad to keep her occupied with much else, and there was no flour for bread. She looked the same as she always did, thinner of course, but she was still what yahoos in Indiana would have called a nice piece of ass. Nicole sucked in a breath, and let it out in a spate of words: "Julia! I've told you not to—"

Julia wasn't to be cowed this time, even by Nicole at the start of a rampage. "No, Mistress. We need the money. If we can't find some way to pay for food, pretty soon I'll be too skinny for anyone to want me at all. And," she added after a brief pause, "one of them even knew what he was doing. It wasn't too bad. He's the one who paid me double— because, he said, I was worth it."

She didn't blush while she said it, or apologize for having a mind of her own. Julia had changed, too. She wasn't the childlike creature Nicole had first met, who had ducked her head and lowered her eyes and done as she was told.

Nicole found that her fists were clenched. They ached. Carefully, with some effort, she unclenched them. She made herself think, and see what Julia had already seen before her. The big brass coins would help—a great deal. There was no way Nicole could deny it. If it came to a choice between selling oneself and starving . . . there was another set of choices she'd never imagined herself having to make.

"We should be glad," Julia said, "that some people still have money to spend on something besides food."

Disposable income, Nicole thought. She bit down hard on laughter she might not have been able to quell, and said the thing she had to say: "Thanks for sharing what you made instead of keeping it for yourself."

Julia did look down then, and shrugged as if in embarrassment. "You weren't bad to me when you owned me. You never kept me hungry, the way some people do with their slaves. Then you went and set me free. That hasn't been as scary as I thought, especially since you've let me stay on here, and earn my keep honestly. I could have had to go out and sell my body just to stay alive. Instead I got to do it when *I* wanted to do it. I wanted to do it now. I wanted to help."

That hasn't been as scary as I thought. Nicole had never heard freedom more faintly praised. And yet, the rest of it was just as honestly put, and it was, in its way, the most genuine expression of gratitude Nicole could ever have asked for. She couldn't find anything more eloquent to say than, "All right, Julia. Thank you. Just—thank you."

Julia shrugged and went back to scouring tables. Nicole groped for something more to say, but there wasn't anything that would work. She went back to the cash box instead, and paused before she shut and locked it, staring down at the brassy gleam of the coins. Her mind was running of itself through everything those extra *sesterces* would buy, and all the ways she could make them stretch.

Pragmatism. It wasn't a pretty word, or a laudable trait, but here, in this time and place, it meant survival.

As a lean and hungry spring swung into a parched summer, Nicole had time, once in a while, to wonder about the war between the Romans and the Germans—Marcomanni, Quadi, she never had learned how to tell the two apart. There was no easy way to get an answer. Even before the invasion, events at a town as close as Vindobona reached Carnuntum slowly and often in garbled fashion, if they arrived at all. When the war had been fought farther west, it was like noise in a distant room of the house—there, but difficult to understand.

Now the war had rolled right over Carnuntum—and it was still hard to interpret. Every so often, Germans would come through town with loot obviously gathered somewhere farther south in Pannonia. Other Germans passed through on the way south, heading toward the fighting—or maybe just toward chances to murder and rape and plunder.

Were they winning the war? If they were, did that mean they'd go down into Italy and sack Rome the way they'd sacked Carnuntum? Was *this* the fall of the Roman Empire? Was *now* the time when everything went to hell? For far from the first time, Nicole wished she knew more ancient history. Had Liber and Libera thought they were doing her a favor, dropping her right in the middle of the great collapse?

She spent a few anxious days worrying about that in the odd moments when she wasn't worrying about being hungry. Then, to her own surprise, she found an answer. No news had come in, and she still knew next to nothing of the history of the Roman Empire—but there was one thing she did know.

The *Heidentor* wasn't there. That was the key. When she'd done the budget tour of Petronell on her honeymoon, the guide had droned on and on, nearly putting her to sleep; but one part of his spiel she did remember. He'd said, quite distinctly, that the gate was Roman work. Therefore, the Roman Empire couldn't be gone from Carnuntum for good. Sooner or later, Roman power would return here. The *Heidentor* would go up to mark it.

Was it sooner? Or was it later? Would the Romans take Carnuntum back from the Quadi and Marcomanni next month, next year, or ten years from now? That might not make any difference in the building of the *Heidentor,* but it would make a hell of a lot of difference in Nicole's life. If the Germans were still in Carnuntum ten years from now, she was damned sure she wouldn't be.

About the middle of August, she began to feel something that might have been hope. More Germans began coming back through Carnuntum, and fewer of them were carrying booty. Some were wounded: they were bandaged, or they limped, or they were missing a limb. They didn't volunteer information, and nobody seemed inclined to ask.

For a little while, life in Carnuntum had been—*acceptable* was too strong a word. It had been somewhere within shouting distance of bearable. People had been hungry, but they hadn't been—too—afraid to go through the city to see what they might find. The Marcomanni and Quadi remained arrogant, but, while they might steal, they seldom committed worse outrages.

Now, when things didn't seem to be going so well for the Germans farther south, the situation in Carnuntum turned nasty again. People whispered of robbery and rape. They hinted of even worse.

And one morning, as Nicole made her way to market, she turned a corner and stumbled over a corpse. There wasn't much doubt the man was dead. Drunks didn't lie in that boneless stillness, in a clotted pool of blood. Nor would a drunk have worn a ragged tunic rent with crisp, new, two-inch slashes. Those weren't knife wounds. Those had been made by a sword. Blood had darkened the tunic almost to black; its original color, as near as she could see, had been blue.

Until she came to Carnuntum, Nicole hadn't realized how much blood a man's body held: one more lesson she would sooner not have learned. Flies congregated in a buzzing cloud. One walked leisurely along a gash that laid open the corpse's cheek, exposing the teeth in a ghastly grin.

Nicole shuddered convulsively and gulped hard. She would not—she would *not*—vomit all over the street. She wheeled blindly and ran, not caring what anyone thought, wanting only to be back in the safety of her own four walls.

When she'd shut herself inside them and barred the door, and never mind that it was broad daylight, Nicole dropped down to the nearest stool and hugged herself till she stopped shivering and trying to gag. She ignored Julia's wide-eyed stare and Lucius' startled, "Mother! What happened? What—?" She made herself think, and think clearly.

The man couldn't have been dead for long. If she'd turned that corner a few minutes earlier, would someone else have gasped in horror at discovering her dead body there? *Wrong place at the wrong time,* she thought. That could have been the epitaph for most of the senseless slayings in Los Angeles.

It might be her own epitaph, for the matter of that. No one had ever been in a wronger place, or in a wronger time.

But wherever and whenever she was, and however right or wrong that was, she had to live. She had to leave the tavern in search of food, but that wasn't all she had to go out for. If it had been, she would have stayed at home and sent Julia in her place. No; she had to go out to look for the plaque of Liber and Libera, the one and only plaque that had brought her to Carnuntum. That was no errand she could pass on to Julia. No matter what it cost her to set foot outside that door each day, for the plaque, she did it.

For all her hunting, she never found it. She still gave Liber and Libera their daily libation of wine, when she had any, on the principle that it couldn't hurt and might help.

And one day, when she'd come home with a bag of mealy apples and a string of little bony fish, and no votive image, she found the plaque on the bar, broken in half and shedding bits on the scrubbed surface. Julia stood over it with exactly the same look of guilt and horror and welling tears as Kimberley might have had if she'd spilled her milk all over the living-room carpet.

This wasn't just spilled milk. Nicole sucked in a breath. She had no idea what she was going to say. She wasn't going to scream. She promised herself that.

Julia spoke before Nicole could begin, a rapid rush of words. "Mistress, I'm sorry, so sorry, I picked it up to dust it, and it slipped out of my hand, and it broke. I'll pay you for it, get you a new one. Just take it out of my wages."

While she babbled on, Nicole had calmed down considerably. She picked up the two largest pieces and weighed them in her hands. Liber stared blandly at her out of one, Libera out of the other. If they were dismayed to be so abruptly separated, they weren't about to show it.

"Don't worry about it," she said to Julia, and she meant it. "It's not as if it were any great relic. It wasn't even working very well—the god and goddess weren't doing much for us, were they?"

"I don't know," Julia said. She'd calmed down, too, with the quickness of a child or a slave, now she knew she wasn't in trouble for breaking her mistress' plaque. "Things could be better for us, but they could be a lot worse, too. Remember Antonina."

"I'm not likely to forget Antonina," Nicole said, a little

coldly. She held onto the coldness. It kept her calm. "Things have been getting uglier lately. I think it's time to splash ourselves again with Calidius Severus' perfume."

Julia made a face. "Oh, do we have to? I'll never get any extra *sesterces* for the cash box if we do."

"Would you rather the Germans took it without paying for it?"

"No!" Julia said, as if by reflex. Then, as thought caught up with instinct: "I don't want to give the Germans anything."

"Of course you don't," Nicole said. "If you don't want to give it to them, they have no business taking it."

Julia thought about that, long and visibly hard. Then she nodded. "*Nobody* has any business taking it, if I say no."

Nicole's smile was so wide and so rusty, it actually hurt. Maybe after all, in spite of everything, she was managing to do a little consciousness-raising.

Brigomarus came to visit a day or two later, as he made a habit of doing. He stopped inside the door, sniffed and grimaced. "You're visiting the dyer's shop again," he said. Nicole wondered if he meant to sound quite so accusatory.

"The time seemed ripe," she answered calmly.

Umma's brother spat in disgust. "Ripe's the word, and no mistake."

"That's bad," Nicole said. "Very bad."

He grinned at her. "You started it."

"I did, didn't I?"

They smiled at one another. Somehow, over the weeks and months, they'd become, maybe not friends, but definitely not adversaries. They got along. They could laugh together. It wasn't bad, as sibling relationships went.

Nicole's smile died first. "So," Brigomarus said, "tell me what got you going this time."

She told him bluntly about the murdered man in the street. Brigomarus nodded, all laughter gone. "From what I'm hearing, he wasn't the only one. In fact, I came here to warn you to stay inside as much as you can for a while. But you seem to be a step ahead of me."

"Maybe not," Nicole said. "What have you heard?"

"Not a whole lot," he answered somberly, "but none of it's good. The Germans are screaming at me—they're screaming at everybody. More shields, more arrowheads, more blades, more spearpoints, more everything."

"And I bet they want it all by yesterday, too," Nicole said.

"By yest—" Brigomarus had to pause and work that one out. However tired a joke it was in English, it must have been new in Latin. He regarded her in dawning admiration. "That's just when they want it, by the gods. You've had a way of coming out with things lately, haven't you?"

"I don't know," Nicole said with a shrug that wasn't nearly as innocent as it looked. "Have I?" Before Umma's brother could dig her in any deeper, she hurried them both back to the subject at hand: "What else do you know? How badly *is* the war going for them? Do they talk about it?"

"Not in any language a civilized man can understand. They grunt and bark like a herd of hungry pigs. But even when they're babbling among themselves, the names of towns don't change that much. The past few days, they've been talking about Savaria and Scarabantia—and those aren't that far down the road from Carnuntum. If the Emperor is coming this way, he'll be here before too long."

The Emperor. Nicole had hardly given a thought to him since she came to Carnuntum. His words didn't dominate TV, radio, the papers, and the newsmagazines, as an American President's did. There were no media for the Roman Emperor to dominate. If it hadn't been for his coins, she wouldn't even have known what he looked like, or what his name was. Marcus, Marcus Aurelius. According to the coins, he was a middle-aged man with a beaky nose, a receding chin a beard couldn't quite hide, and curly hair that looked as if it needed brushing.

All of which told her exactly nothing. People didn't talk about him at all, or seem to think about him much, either. Brigo certainly didn't sound awed at the prospect of an imperial visit. "Is he coming himself," she asked, "or is it just some general leading the army in his name?"

"From what I've heard, he's leading his own army," Brigomarus said. "He took the field himself farther west, I know that. Whether he'll beat the cursed Marcomanni and Quadi and come this far—there's no way anyone can know that."

"I hope he does," Nicole said fervently.

Brigomarus rolled his eyes. "Oh, by the gods, don't we all," he said. "I can't think of anybody in Carnuntum who's done well under the Germans. Except . . ."

When he didn't go on, Nicole thumped him on the arm. "Come on—who?"

"The undertakers," he answered promptly—and hastily threw up a hand. "Don't throw that cup at me! They got more work than they deserved during the pestilence. The Germans gave them even more. They're getting cursed rich."

"Maybe they are," Nicole said, "but I don't expect they'll cry too hard when the Germans go."

She wouldn't be sorry to see them go, either—preferably out on their ears. She wouldn't be sorry, if she was perfectly honest with herself, to see the lot of them killed. She'd been pretty young when Saigon fell to the North Vietnamese. When she thought about it, she realized how much the Vietnam War had colored her attitude toward war in general. She'd thought the Gulf War a waste of money and men, fought mostly over oil—never mind the rhetoric about democracy and freedom. But now, from the middle of a war, she didn't just remember how rapturously the people of Kuwait had welcomed the soldiers who drove out the Iraqis. She understood right down to the bone why the Kuwaitis had been so overjoyed. She was ready—more than ready—to plant a big fat kiss on the first Roman legionary who came tramping up the street. And if there was blood on his sword, all the better.

Brigomarus slapped the bar in front of her, startling her back into herself. "You seem to have things here pretty much in hand. How are you fixed for food?"

"Not too bad," she said, which was only a slight exaggeration. "We're hungry, but we aren't—quite—starving. And you, Brigo? If you need help, we can spare a little." She couldn't, not really, but neither was she—quite—on the edge.

Umma's brother shook his head. "No, thank you, we don't need anything. I'm hungrier than I ever wanted to be, but I'm not dying of it."

She drew a breath and nodded. She was relieved, there was no point in denying it. Every scrap she didn't share was that much more for Lucius and Julia and herself. "We'll just keep our heads down and hang on, and wait till the Emperor comes."

Till the Emperor comes. It sounded like a fairy tale she might have read to Kimberley, not one of the real, old, grim ones, but one of the sugar-coated, saccharine-overloaded, sweetness-and-light fables that were deemed safe for impressionable young children. But there was nothing either sweet or harmless about Carnuntum. The little blue birds would have gone into somebody's pot, and the pretty butterflies been trampled underfoot by a horde of marching Germans. It would take more than a pastel prince to rescue Carnuntum. It would take an emperor.

Nicole hoped, a little crazily, that he didn't try to buy himself any new clothes. "I hope he comes soon," she said.

"So do I," Brigomarus answered. "So does everybody—except the Quadi and the Marcomanni. And they're the ones with the most to say about when he gets here, or if he gets here at all."

More and more Germans in filthy bandages prowled the streets of Carnuntum. Fewer and fewer peasants brought in produce from the villages and farms around the city. Carnuntum might have been the only place where they could get money for it, but Carnuntum was also the place where they were most likely to be robbed and killed. They didn't need any sort of cost/benefit analysis to draw the appropriate conclusion. They stayed away. And Carnuntum went hungry.

One who did dare the market square brought news of a

battle outside Scarabantia. "Who won?" Nicole demanded in the middle of trying to haggle down the price of his prunes.

He wasn't inclined to haggle. Intellectually, Nicole understood that: if she didn't feel like paying his price, some other hungry citizen would. It infuriated her even so. He had a lot of damn nerve, lining the pockets he didn't wear with profits made from hunger. He also wasn't inclined to answer her question in a hurry. He reminded her of a farmer from downstate Indiana, sparing of words and suspicious of everybody he hadn't known since he was four years old.

"Who won?" she repeated, wishing she could appeal to a judge to get an answer out of the reluctant witness.

"Cursed lot of dead on both sides," he answered at last, which made her want to feed him all his prunes at once—if she couldn't loosen up one end, she'd damned well loosen up the other. Then, grudgingly, he let drop a kernel of information: "Romans are still coming north."

Nicole let out a long sigh of relief. "Why don't you sound happier about it?" she asked. "There aren't any Germans around to hear you." Even as she spoke, she looked about to make sure she was right: the age-old glance of the occupied, checking to see that the occupiers were busy elsewhere.

The farmer shrugged. "I'm making good money these days. And the Marcomanni and Quadi haven't got the faintest notion what taxes are: haven't had to pay 'em an *as* on my land or my crop. You can bet it won't be like that when the usual pack of clerks is back in the saddle."

That he was surely right didn't make his attitude any more appealing. Nicole had to remind herself she wasn't likely to improve his outlook by tearing him limb from limb, strictly rhetorically of course. Nor was she inclined to call a German to do it for her. And she needed those prunes. Reluctantly, she shelled out ten times what she reckoned they were worth, raked them into her sack, and left him to his prosperity.

Hunger had long since taken Lucius past the point where he turned up his nose at anything even vaguely resembling food. He would have gobbled all the prunes if Nicole had given him even half a chance. She snatched the bag out of his greedy fingers and stowed it safe behind her. "Oh, no, you don't! Julia and I get to have some, too. Do you want to spend the whole night squatting over a pot because you made a pig of yourself?"

Lucius scowled and stamped his foot. "I don't care. I want to eat. I'm all empty inside!"

"We all are," Nicole said. Not that he cared: he was a child. To children, nothing mattered but the moment. She tried to console him, at least a little. "Maybe we won't be hungry much longer. The man who sold me the prunes said the Romans won a battle outside of Scarabantia."

"Outside Scarabantia?" Julia echoed. "That isn't very far away at all. The Emperor could be here in just a few days." Her face had been bright with hope, but all at once it fell. "I hope the Germans don't try to stand siege here. They might hold off the legions for weeks, maybe even months."

"Siege?" That hadn't occurred to Nicole. She wished it hadn't occurred to Julia, either: now they both had something to gnaw their empty bellies over. "God, I hope not, too." She tried to look on the bright side, if there was such a thing: "We didn't keep out the Marcomanni and Quadi for very long. Maybe they won't be able to hold off the legions, either."

"I hope you're right." But Julia didn't sound convinced. "We didn't have much of a garrison here, and the Germans took us half by surprise. The legions won't be so lucky. The Germans will be expecting them—and there are an awful lot of Germans in Carnuntum."

That made a depressing amount of sense. Nicole stared blankly at Lucius' outstretched hand, blinked, doled out a handful of prunes. He might be greedy about the whole bag, but he'd learned how to eat his prize once he won it: piece by piece, savoring it, making it last. When he'd got the last scrap of flavor out of the first one, he spat the pit on the floor and said, "If it is a siege, the barbarians will keep all the food for themselves. We'll starve."

"You aren't supposed to understand that much this young," Nicole said. He shrugged, already halfway through his second prune. She provided the answer he wasn't about to. In this world, yes, he had to understand that much. Otherwise he wouldn't survive. She was the one who was lacking here. Her capacity for estimating man's inhumanity to man had proved time and again that it wasn't up to, or down to, dealing with the second century. Of course the Germans would lay hold of all the food they could—hadn't they done it already? Of course they would treat the people of Carnuntum, the people who actually belonged in the city, as expendable. Yes, it made perfect sense. The Serbs in Bosnia wouldn't have needed it spelled out for them.

Nicole glanced at the spot behind the bar where, once, the plaque of Liber and Libera had stood. *Don't you see?* she said in her mind. *I'm too . . . civilized to live in this time.* Even if the plaque had still been there, she wouldn't have got any response. She was bitterly certain of that. She'd made her bed. It was hard and lumpy and uncomfortable, with scratchy blankets and vermin uncounted. She had to lie in it. The god and goddess weren't listening.

She took a prune out of the bag and popped it into her mouth. It was sweet and good. She had to make the best of things here. She chewed the flesh off the pit, and very carefully, too; and not only because she wanted to savor the taste. The last thing she wanted was to bite down too hard and break another tooth. That would mean, sooner or later, another visit to Terentianus. One of those was enough to last her two lifetimes, and then some.

Food was scarce, but at least, as people were inclined to remark, there was plenty of water. That wasn't always the case in a siege, Nicole had gathered.

She was just on her way out the door, amphora in hand, headed for the fountain two blocks over, when she nearly collided with Brigomarus. He was in a fair hurry, and he had something tucked under his arm. "What's that?" Nicole wanted to know, once they'd stopped laughing at the comedy of errors: each leaping back with a little shriek, then doing the "Which way do I go next?" dance till they both stopped and stared at each other.

"What's this?" Brigomarus brought the cloth-wrapped oblong out from under his arm, grunting a bit: it was heavy for its size. "It's a present for you."

"Really? For me?" Nicole couldn't clap her hands: they were full of amphora. "Show me!"

He obligingly let slip the wrapping and held it for her to see.

She felt the handles of the amphora slipping through her fingers. She felt them, but she couldn't do a thing about it. The amphora struck the rammed-earth floor and went instantly from pot to potsherds. She didn't care. She didn't care at all.

"By the gods, it's not such a big thing as that," Brigomarus said, more than a little taken aback. "I happened to notice you'd lost the other one you had up here, and so I thought I'd—"

Nicole hardly heard him. *"Where did you get that?"* she whispered.

"This?" Brigomarus shrugged. "Stonecutter named . . . what was his name? Celer, that was it. Pestilence got him, poor fellow. I bought it . . . oh, must have been toward the end of spring last year, I guess. So when I saw you didn't have yours up anymore, then Julia told me what happened to it, I thought I'd bring you this one to take its—"

He didn't get to finish the sentence. Nicole threw her arms around him, being very, very careful of the plaque, and kissed him soundly. There was nothing sisterly about it. When she let him go, he was red from the neck of his tunic all the way up to his hairline. She didn't care about that, either. With great delicacy, she took the plaque of Liber and Libera from him.

It was *the* plaque. She recognized it instantly. The carving was sharper and crisper than it had been when the limestone slab sat on her nightstand. Of course it would be. The plaque was much younger than it had been then.

When had Brigomarus bought it? Toward the end of

spring last year, he'd said. She didn't know—she didn't have any way to discover—exactly when he'd bought it, exactly when Celer had finished it, but she would have bet it was right about the time when she'd taken up residence in Umma's body. No wonder she hadn't been able to find it till now. Brigo had had it all along. Had the gods intended that? Had they cared enough to hide it, effectively, in plain sight?

"It's—perfect!" she said. "Absolutely perfect."

"I'm glad you think so." Brigomarus still sounded bewildered. Nicole didn't blame him. But there was no way she was going to enlighten him. She was only half crazy.

"I don't just think so. I know so." Nicole hoped she did. To be wrong now, to be disappointed again . . . She didn't want to think about that. If this plaque, the very same, the self-same one that had brought her here, couldn't get her back to West Hills, nothing could. If nothing could . . . No. She *wasn't* thinking about that.

Brigomarus coughed a time or two. Nicole's stomach clenched—legacy of the pestilence. But no, it was just a catch in his throat, or maybe a touch of a cold. "There's another reason I came, too," he said, "and look, I almost forgot. I heard it from a German who came in screaming for a shield. The Emperor and the army are on their way. They'll be here any day. The barbarians are yelling at the top of their lungs for something, anything to help them drive the Romans back."

"Are they?" Nicole was listening with only half an ear. Her eyes kept coming back to the stone faces of the god and goddess. Those carven lips had kissed her palm in promise. Those bland and heedless faces had turned on her, and smiled, and granted her prayer.

It was as if she couldn't keep two purposes in mind at once. Either she was surviving in this world, devoting every scrap of her attention to it, or she was concentrating totally on getting out of it. Now that she had the key—please, god and goddess, let it be the key—there was no room in her for anything else.

Those lips had kissed her palm well over a year ago, as

Umma's body reckoned time. What had happened to *her* body? How long had it been there? Had Umma been struggling to survive there as Nicole struggled to survive here? Ye gods, a Roman woman who couldn't even read, trying to cope with all the complexities of life in Los Angeles—two minutes of that and they'd lock her away. Nicole had survived because life *was* simpler here, if orders of magnitude harder. The things she needed to cope with, she'd at least dimly heard of. What could Umma have made of the automobile, the telephone, the microwave oven?

Or—and maybe worse—what if Umma hadn't been there at all? What if there was nobody home? Would Nicole leap forward in time, only to find that there was nothing there, no body to move into? What if she was—if she was—

She wasn't dead. She *wasn't*. She caressed the votive plaque with fingers that shook a little. She had to try. No matter what waited for her, it had to be better than what faced her here.

Brigomarus left, still baffled that his sister should be so delighted with his present and hardly seem interested at all in the news he'd brought. There was no way he could understand that the votive plaque was the best, the greatest news she'd ever wanted.

Nicole set it where the other one had been. She found a little wine—dregs, to be honest—in the bottom of one of the jars set into the bar, and offered it to the god and goddess. Then and only then did she get around to picking up the pieces of the broken amphora, finding another one, and going out and lugging back water.

Julia had been across the street in the fuller and dyer's shop when Brigomarus came by. She was back by the time Nicole brought in the jar of water. Nicole didn't ask what, if anything, Julia had been doing with Gaius Calidius Severus. It was none of her business.

The freedwoman was leaning on the bar, chin in hands, contemplating the plaque. When Nicole came in she rolled an eye at her and asked, "Where'd you get that, Mistress?"

"Brigo brought it," Nicole answered. "Didn't he tell you?

He said you told him how the other one got broken."

"Oh," Julia said with a hunch of the shoulders. "Well. I forgot about that." Had she? Nicole wondered. And wondered something else, too: something that was really rather reprehensible. Oh, surely not. Julia sold herself to strangers, but when it came to people she knew, she tended to either keep a roster of regulars or, as with young Calidius Severus, give it away for free. No, she was just remembering that she'd broken the first plaque, and indulging in a bit of guilt.

She came out of it soon enough. "That was nice of him," she said. She tilted her head and squinted. "If you don't mind me saying so, I think it's a nicer carving job than the one we had before."

"I think so, too," Nicole said. And if she didn't mean quite the same by that as Julia did, then Julia didn't need to know it.

That night before she went to sleep, she begged Liber and Libera to send her back to California, back to the twentieth century. She was reaching them—she was. The way seemed open, as it hadn't before. She drifted off with a smile on her face.

She woke . . . in Carnuntum.

19

GETTING UP WITH HER belly empty and her scalp itching and her skin dark with soot was harder than it had ever been before. She stared around the bare little bedroom, and dismay changed rapidly into unabashed loathing. For the first time in a very long while, she wondered if she'd lost her mind.

She'd been persisting in the conviction that Carnuntum was the hallucination. But—what if it wasn't? What if it was real, and West Hills a dream? Had she really known frozen food and printed books and automobiles and air conditioning and computers and airplanes and the United States Constitution? Or had she been Umma all along, gone round the bend for a while, and now at last begun to recover?

"I am Nicole Gunther-Perrin," she said in quiet but impassioned English, "and I *will* go back to California." She clenched her work-battered hand into a fist and slammed it down onto the thin mattress. "I *will*. But not today, God damn it."

She believed that. She had to believe it. If she didn't . . . she'd have to come to terms with staying in Carnuntum for Marcomanni and Quadi holding the city and the Roman legions likely to be knocking on the door any minute now, the rest of her life probably wouldn't be measured in decades. Days, more likely. Or hours.

"God be thanked for small mercies," she muttered.

She trudged downstairs to a meager breakfast of barley bread that sat like a brick in her stomach—but a small brick, oh, a very small brick. Julia was already up and gone, as far as she could tell. Lucius was nowhere to be seen. Out playing with the neighborhood kids, she had to hope. She raided the cash box and went out to see what she could find to keep herself and Lucius and Julia eating for another day or two, or maybe just for another meal.

Few Germans roamed the street so early. They didn't have to worry about making a living; they lived off everyone else's labor. They could sleep late—or later, anyhow, since no one here moved too far out of rhythm with the sun. For that reason, the early morning was a good time to hit the market square, if anyone happened to have anything out for sale.

Nicole felt like clapping her hands when she saw not one but two fishermen setting out a gleaming array of trout and carp. She wasn't the only one buying, but there weren't so many people there that they started frenziedly bidding against one another, as she'd seen happen once or twice. She paid an arm, but managed to keep the leg in reserve for a jar of wine a farmer had brought into Carnuntum. It was the last one he had left. "Glad to be rid of it," he said. "Now I'm going to get out of town while the getting's good."

That struck Nicole as eminently sensible; what hadn't made a lot of sense was his coming into town in the first place. She got out of the market while the getting was good, too, and the gods were kind. The streets were still all but deserted. She made it back to the tavern unmolested, without even the usual quota of whistles and catcalls from passing Germans.

Julia had been to the baths: she was clean and relatively fresh. Nicole made a mental note to go later, if the quiet continued. Julia regarded Nicole's purchases dubiously. "That's a lot of fish, Mistress," she said. Then she shrugged. "Well, we'll stuff ourselves like force-fed geese, because it won't keep long. And then we'll moan and groan about how full we are—and then we'll be empty again."

"So we will," Nicole agreed. "But being full for even a little while feels good."

"It certainly does," Julia said, in a tone and with an expression that made it plain she was not talking about food. Nicole snorted. Julia looked altogether unabashed. Nothing Nicole had ever done could make her feel that her way of dealing with men—and striking deals with them—was wrong.

It worked for her. In times like these, that meant something. *More power to her,* Nicole thought, with a little wrench of the gut. Paradigm shift. That was never either easy or painless.

Baked fish and a quarter of a small loaf of barley bread did not make for a balanced diet, but Nicole went to bed without the feeling that, if she had a tapeworm, it was about to sue for lack of proper maintenance. She'd had that feeling too often lately. Now that she was without it for a little while, she wasted very little time worrying about proper nutrition. Any nutrition at all was enough to carry on with.

When the sun rose the next morning, the Marcomanni and Quadi rose with it. So did the rest of Carnuntum; Nicole would not have been surprised to learn that the braying of the Germans' horns had roused the recently dead from the graveyard outside the walls. It sounded like an elephant being flayed with a dull pocketknife.

The street outside the tavern was hardly quieter. Germans ran in packs down the street, swords in hand, baggy trousers flapping against their legs, shouting back and forth in their guttural dialects. Nicole had picked up a few words—enough to be quite clear on what they were yelling about: "The Romans are coming! The Romans are coming!"

One if by land, two if by the Danube, she thought dizzily. She leaned on the window frame for a moment, letting the wan sun warm her face. It would cloud up later, she suspected. It almost always did.

She dressed with a little more than her usual care, and went downstairs to a breakfast of cold fish. Julia and Lucius were not far behind her. She was interested to note that Julia was also a bit cleaner than usual, though Lucius was his disheveled small-boy self.

They didn't open the tavern, or even unbar the door. "With any luck at all, this will be over soon," Nicole said. She glanced at the image—*the* image—of Liber and Libera. *If you won't send me home, will you at least let me live as good a life here as I can?*

A prayer wasn't supposed to be reproachful, but she didn't care. They'd brought her here. They could live with the consequences.

In the beginning, the second battle for Carnuntum sounded very much like the first. The shouts from the walls were in German now and not in Latin, but the tones of anger, desperation, rage, even wild glee, were much the same.

But after a while, as the morning went on and the sun began to play hide-and-seek with the gathering clouds, a new sound brought Nicole bolt upright. It sounded like the beating of an enormous heart, deep and ponderously slow.

Lucius looked up excitedly from the board game he was playing with Julia. "Battering ram! That'll do it for the gate. Then—in come the legions. March! March! March!"

He marched himself all the way upstairs to fetch his

sword, and all the way back down and around the room, leaping and spinning and stabbing with it, till Nicole ducked in and caught him and held him fast. He was hot and sweaty and breathing in gulps. And he'd forgotten completely how little use his wooden blade had been against the Germans.

Nicole's grip slackened. He wriggled free, still panting, but he'd calmed down enough to sit on a bench conveniently near the door.

He didn't go back to his game, which he'd been losing anyway. Quietly Julia stowed the pieces inside the board and put it away, and sat with folded hands, waiting with a slave's patience for whatever was going to come.

The Romans kept knocking on the door to Carnuntum. A second ram joined the first, striking a counterpoint from another gate. With each crashing thud, Nicole thought surely it would break through.

But the gates had been built strong, nor did they care who tried to break them. They held for the whole of that day, until the pounding became as monotonous as a migraine, as relentless as the pulse of Nicole's own heart in her ears.

Lucius alternated between playing legionary and waiting for the real legionaries to come marching down the street. At length, Nicole prevailed on him to go upstairs with Julia and, if not sleep, then at least get off her nerves.

She sat where she'd been for most of the day. If she'd had a stack of magazines to read, she'd have been too twitchy to bother with them. She contemplated a big job, a job that would keep her too busy to think, but even if she'd had tools to sand down and refinish the tables, she'd never get it done before dark. She'd have to ask Brigo next time he came by, whether she could borrow any—for that matter, whether he'd like to help. He'd might surprise her by agreeing to it.

Daylight faded, and the pounding went on. Nicole circled the room, coming to a halt in front of the votive plaque. Liber and Libera regarded her with serene complacency. "All right," Nicole said to them, rather defiantly, in English. "Maybe you wanted me to see the Romans take back Carnuntum. Maybe I was supposed to see that, sometimes, the good guys win." She glowered at them. "With all due respect, I'd sooner have taken that on faith, and gone home."

The god and goddess didn't move, or say a word. A little wear and tear aside, they looked just as they had when their plaque had stood on her nightstand in clean, quiet, safe West Hills. Nicole looked around at this filthy tavern in a barbarian-held town taken from an empire that reckoned itself civilized only because everything around it was so absolutely barbaric. She sighed deeply, turned her back on the heedless divinities, and trudged upstairs to bed.

She slept rather better than she'd expected, a deep, sodden sleep, though she'd drunk no wine the night before. She woke as she'd fallen asleep, to the sound of the rams battering away at the gates.

The last of the fish weren't fit for human consumption. Nicole tossed them out the window. Julia, who was just coming down the stairs, exclaimed in dismay and ran to the window beside Nicole, but Nicole had done the job a little too well: they'd landed in a steaming pile of ox manure.

"Mistress!" Julia said. "They might still have been all right to eat. Now when are we going to get any more?"

"If you want them so much, you can go out there and bring them back," Nicole said. Julia shot her a look—as close to defiance as she'd ever come—and startled Nicole by doing exactly as she was told.

Nicole watched her as she paused at the door, looking rapidly up and down the deserted street, and scuttled toward the fish. When she was within a few feet of them, her face screwed up in disgust. Nicole wasn't surprised. The reek of them still clung to the bowl they'd lain in.

Julia came back without the fish, and with a crestfallen expression. She'd gone out to make a point; but Nicole, for once, had won it instead. They scraped together a breakfast of stale barley bread and boiled water, punishment fare, and settled for another day of siege.

Toward midday, one of the gates went crashing down. Screams and shouting and something else—a deep, rhythmic, profoundly arrogant sound—proclaimed the legions' arrival in Carnuntum. They were singing, Nicole realized, in a strong, marching beat, to the braying of horns and the beating of drums.

Nicole looked at Julia and Lucius. Julia and Lucius looked back. Was her grin as wide and crazy as theirs were? They leaped up all at once and whooped. Julia grabbed Nicole's hand and Lucius'. His free hand grabbed Nicole's. They danced madly around the room, kicking into stools and tables, and not caring in the slightest.

When they'd danced themselves breathless, Nicole and Lucius flung themselves down to rest, but Julia had something else in mind. She dipped a rag in the dishwater barrel and scrubbed at her arms. "Now I don't smell like a chamber pot anymore," she said triumphantly.

Then, as if she'd gone completely out of her mind, she unbarred the door and ran out into the street, headed toward Gaius Calidius Severus'. She was damned lucky: the street was full of Germans running away from the wall. None of them stopped to grab a last taste of Roman flesh.

Nicole stared after her. Then, incredulously, she started to laugh. Julia always had been consistent about what constituted a celebration.

It wasn't all bad, either. Nicole was sick of smelling like *eau de pissoir* herself. She scrubbed her arms and neck, even added a little bit of vinegar from the stores. Better to smell like a salad than like a hot day in an outhouse.

When she looked up from what were still sadly inadequate ablutions—God, what she wouldn't have given for a bar of soap—Lucius had disappeared, and his toy sword with him. She cursed, first in Latin, then, more satisfyingly, in English. He'd gone to watch the fighting, the little lunatic. He'd never in his life imagine that he could get caught in it. She could— and it scared the hell out of her.

She ran to the door and shouted his name. Nothing. She called again, louder. No sign of him. Why should there be? He had what the twentieth century had learned to call plausible deniability. "Oh, no, Mother," he would say, eyes wide and sincere. "I didn't hear you. Everybody was yelling so loud."

"I'll warm his backside," Nicole muttered. The idea didn't give her the collywobbles, as it would have when she first came to Carnuntum. He'd proved himself immune to any lesser suggestion. He did not need to know just how vitally important his life was to her. He was, literally, her lifeline, the one assurance she had of her continued existence.

Without further pause for thought, Nicole ran out of the tavern. She barely remembered to shut the door behind her.

The street was even fuller of Germans than before. Some were headed at a gallop for the wall, swords drawn, faces set in masks of ferocity. Some were falling back, retreating deeper into the city. Their swords were notched or bloodied or broken, and their masks had cracked. Beneath lay fear— the first fear she'd seen in anyone but a Roman since this war began.

Serves you right, she thought viciously. Some of the Marcomanni and Quadi coming away from the wall were bleeding. That served them right, too. It was time they had a taste of their own medicine.

The barbarians yelled back and forth, comers to goers, incomprehensibly. None took the slightest notice of Nicole, any more than they had of Julia. Who was probably, right at that moment, screwing her brains out. Nicole didn't know whether to be jealous or annoyed. Annoyed, she decided: if Julia had waited a little longer before running over and hopping into bed with Gaius Calidius Severus, maybe Lucius wouldn't have had the chance to sneak out the door.

"Lucius!" Nicole called again, but her voice was lost in the chaos. Maybe he really couldn't hear her. And maybe, too, if she stayed out here on the sidewalk any longer, one of those Germans running past was going to take a swipe at her with his sword, just for the hell of it.

She ducked into the alley between her house and the house where Sextus Longinius Iulus lived and Fabia Ursa had died. As soon as she did it, she wished she hadn't; the stink of dumped chamber pots was appalling. Flies rose in buzzing clouds, furious to be disturbed in their feasting. She flailed her arms. Maybe one or two failed to land on her.

Just as she turned to try another route, a German loomed in the mouth of the alleyway. Nicole stopped cold.

The German looked at her in—surprise? With a sound like an ox lowing, he collapsed. Blood poured into the filthy dirt from a wound on the inside of his thigh. So much blood— how had he run all the way from the wall?

The flies didn't care what he'd done or how. They swarmed toward the spreading pool, milling around its edges, sampling it to see if they liked it as well as yesterday's slops. It would do, their manner said. It would definitely do.

Nicole couldn't bring herself to step over the dying German. She turned and went farther up the alley, picking her way past the piles of filth. At the back of her house, the alleyway jogged to the left instead of cutting straight through to the next street. The houses and shops facing that one weren't directly in back of hers and its neighbors, as they would have been in a Los Angeles subdivision. Nobody here had bothered to think that might be desirable.

Nicole couldn't see what was going on in the next street, but she could hear it loud and clear. People were screaming in several languages, and clashing iron against iron. Lucius would reckon it a great show, the bloody-minded little rascal. God, if he got embroiled in that . . .

Footsteps pounded toward her from the other street, heavy steps, much too heavy for a child's. Armor clanked. A shout rang out in Latin: "The Emperor!"

She sagged against the indifferently whitewashed stone of the wall—her own wall, the back wall of her house. Not a German bent on rapine and plunder. A Roman legionary, a soldier of civilization—such as it was—one of Carnuntum's rescuers from its barbarous conquerors.

"The Emperor!" he shouted again, just as he rounded the corner. He and Nicole saw each other at the same instant. Had he been carrying a gun, she might have died. By the gasp that escaped him when he spied her, his first thought when he saw anyone not a legionary was *enemy*. But instead of the twentieth-century soldier's rifle, he had a sword in his right hand and a great, clumsy-looking shield on his left arm. He was still two or three strides away from her when he realized she wasn't dangerous.

He skidded to a stop, heavy sandals scuffing up dust. His sword lowered. Nicole dared, at last, to breathe. She let it out as a word: "The Emperor!" And, as he stood still, staring at her, "Thank God you're finally here!"

A moment too late, she realized that it should have been, *Thank the gods you're here!* But the Roman soldier did not seem inclined toward literary criticism. He grinned. Between his black beard, the iron cheekpieces of his helmet, and the low rim that projected almost like a cap's visor, she couldn't see much of his face: that grin, a nose that looked like a nose, and dark eyes that stayed alert, wary, even while he grinned at her.

Then she did what she'd promised herself she would do with the first legionary she saw inside Carnuntum: she marched up to him and gave him a kiss. She'd had in mind a kiss on the cheek, but the soldier's beard and the cheekpieces made that impractical. She kissed him on the end of the nose instead.

He laughed out loud. "Hello to you, too, sweetheart," he said. "You can do better than that, I'll wager." He let the shield slip to the ground, wrapped his arms around her—sword still clenched in his right fist—and bent his mouth down to hers.

That kiss, crushed against scale mail and with a sword bumping her backside, was odds-on the most uncomfortable she'd ever had. She didn't care. It was—damn, it was fun. Just like the basketball game years ago before she ever met Frank, when Indiana clawed from behind to beat Notre Dame with a shot at the buzzer. She'd let out a squeal and kissed not only her date but the guy who sat on the other side of her. They'd all laughed. It had been that kind of moment: dizzy, crazy, and oh so sweet with victory.

The legionary's left hand closed, painfully hard, on her breast. She wasn't really alarmed, not yet. She stiffened and tried to pull her head away, with a protest all ready to burst out as soon as her mouth was free. But he followed her, prolonging the kiss, driving his tongue deep into her mouth, grinding against her teeth.

She bit down hard. He yelped and recoiled. She slapped his hand away. "That's enough!" she said sharply.

He laughed again, not pleasantly at all. There was blood on his lips. He licked it away, wincing: his tongue must have hurt like hell. His words were thicker than they'd been before, and his tone had a nasty edge. "Now, now. That's not nice. Not nice at all."

"Look," Nicole said, doing her best to ignore the stab of fear. "I didn't mean to tease you. But just because I was glad—I *am* glad—to see my city back in Roman hands, doesn't mean—"

She should have listened to her fear. She should have shut up, twisted loose, and run like hell. All that, she realized afterwards, when it was much too late.

The legionary listened to her just long enough to realize she wasn't going to give him what he wanted. She was still explaining, in logical, lawyerlike, twentieth-century fashion, how a kiss didn't necessarily imply anything more, when he shut her up for good and all: he kicked her feet out from under her and threw her to the ground.

She landed exactly as he wanted her to land. Afterwards—that word again—she decided that throwing people to the ground would be an important skill for a soldier to acquire in an age when fighting was face to face, up close and personal. In the middle of it, she had time for one startled squawk before he flung himself down on top of her.

By chance or by design—she strongly suspected the latter but could not have proved it in a court of law—one of his elbows caught her in the pit of her stomach. For the next minute or so, she had not a chance in the world of using the self-defense techniques she'd learned in another life. By the time she could think about anything but the agonizing struggle for air, he'd poised himself between her legs, yanked down her drawers, and driven deep into her.

It hurt. She hadn't wanted him, and she was dry. He didn't care. He didn't care in the slightest. That was the worst part, worse even than the pain—and yes, it hurt like hell. In and out, up and down, his weight on her, the scales of his cuirass digging into her belly and breasts, crushing her, making it even harder for her to breathe.

When at last she did manage to suck in a quarter of a breath, she thrashed and writhed, arching her back, twisting and struggling, anything to get him off her. He grunted. It was, to her horror, a grunt of pleasure. "That's more like it, sweetheart," he said. "Don't just lie there—do something."

She did something, all right. She hit him. Every part of him she could reach was covered in iron. Her fists throbbed with the pain of it, and he never even felt it. He pounded away on top of her, not caring that she didn't want him on her or in her, not caring that he hurt her. Not caring at all.

There above her was the nose she'd kissed only a couple of moments before. She snapped at it. He jerked his head back—he'd stayed alert, damn him. Something caressed the side of her neck: the edge of his sword. It felt cold and very sharp.

"You don't want to do that, sweetheart," he said between thrusts: a word, a thrust; another word or two; another thrust. "It's not friendly, you know what I mean?"

She knew. She hated him; she hated herself, for knowing it—and worse, for giving way to it. She lay still. It was small comfort that he wanted her active; that if she lay like one of the fish she'd thrown out the window this morning, he'd get less pleasure out of her. He didn't stop or even slow down. Another dozen breaths, and he grunted again, shuddered, rammed home. She felt the hot gush deep inside her, in her most secret place.

He lay on top of her for a stretching moment, stiff as the armor he was cased in. Then, as suddenly as he'd forced himself into her, he jerked out—one last, small stab of pain, like insult on top of injury—and got smoothly to his feet. He was an athlete, of course he was, with an athlete's grace and an athlete's arrogant strength.

He straightened his pleated military kilt—no inconvenience of underwear in that uniform—and looked down at Nicole. His face was as impenetrable as ever: black beard, iron cheekpieces, gleam of eyes under the visor. "So long, sweetheart," he said. "That was fun." And then, as if she'd never interrupted him, he ran on up the alley, lifting again his ringing shout: "The Emperor!"

She lay where he'd left her till he was long out of sight. She would have lain there till Rome fell, but the flies were buzzing, tickling her lips and her eyelids. She slapped at them, hard enough to sting, and lurched to her feet. Every part of her hurt: the back of her head, her haunches, her solar plexus, her chest and belly where his armor had crushed and pinched. And worst of all, she hurt where he'd violated her, a throbbing, burning ache, as if he'd scraped the skin raw. She stood as she'd stood the night she lost her virginity, as if she'd been riding a horse all day and half the night. But that had been an almost welcome pain, a pain she'd bargained for and wore like a badge of pride. There was no pride in this. And the pain—that had been an ache or two, some chafing, and a tendency to walk spraddle-legged. This was *pain*.

"He raped me," she said. She said it in English. Latin wasn't enough, not for this. "The bastard just—went ahead—and raped me." As if to mock her with incontrovertible proof, semen dribbled down the inside of her thigh, wet and sticky-slimy. Her drawers were tangled around one ankle. She yanked them up. She tried to think. Her thoughts kept scattering. Her memories kept fragmenting, coalescing in a single spot—the end of his nose, the grind of his pelvis against hers—then shattering again. And again. Think. She had to think.

All around her, battle was raging. She heard the sounds of it both nearby and farther away, like an iron foundry in a lower level of hell. Another stalwart defender of civilization was going to come charging down the alley, she could bet on it. Would he care that he was getting somebody else's sloppy seconds? Would he even take time to notice?

Walking was hard. She wasn't built bowlegged. But walking normally rubbed tissues outraged beyond endurance. She was probably bleeding. She didn't stop to investigate.

She made her way up the alley, back past the stinking piles of ordure, to the German who'd fallen in front of her. He was dead now, though his blood still soaked into the dirt. In the street beyond him, live Marcomanni and Quadi still fought the Romans.

Nicole shrank back against the wall. Romans, barbarians— God forbid anyone see her. Was one of them the son of a bitch who'd violated her? She couldn't tell. They were all crowded together in a knot. They all wore the same clothes, carried the same gear. *Uniform*—that was what it was, uniform dress, uniform looks and fighting style. Wasn't that the point? Look alike, fight alike, kill alike. Rape alike, too. And never mind if the victim was friend or enemy.

The Romans drove the Germans back, away from the city wall and toward the center of town. Nicole waited till they were some distance down the street, too far to grab her if she moved fast enough. She scuttled around the corner and dived through the door of the tavern.

"Hello, Mother!" a voice called, startling her near out of her skin. It was, of course, Lucius, safe, sound, and smiling, watching the fighting through the window as if it had been a TV screen. He'd probably been doing it, the little wretch, since about thirty seconds after Nicole went outside to look for him. If he'd come in half a minute earlier . . .

Spilled milk, Nicole thought. She slammed and barred the door. "When Julia comes back, let her in," she said. "Otherwise, leave the door barred. Don't you go outside again. Do you hear me?"

Maybe he did, maybe he didn't. But her black scowl made up for any deficiencies in his verbal comprehension. He gulped and nodded. He actually, for a moment, looked obedient.

That didn't last long, to be sure. "Why is the back of your tunic all dirty?" he asked as Nicole gritted her teeth to tackle the stairs. She didn't answer. He didn't pursue it, either, to her relief.

She made it to her room after what seemed an age. As soon as she was inside, with the door bolted behind her, she ripped off her drawers and hurled them away. She wet a rag in the *terra sigillata* pitcher, soaked it till it ran with water. Then she scrubbed and scrubbed and scrubbed at her thigh and between her legs. Evidence for forensics didn't matter, not here. No matter how many times she washed herself, she didn't feel clean. She doubted she'd ever feel clean again.

She was still scrubbing, whimpering with the pain, when the door opened below. It had better be Julia. Because if it wasn't, Lucius—and Nicole, too, to be honest about it—was in big trouble. She hurled the rag after the drawers and bolted downstairs.

It was Julia, of course, looking lazy and sated and altogether content with the world. "Hello, Mistress," she said brightly. "Have you seen? The legions are back! Now we'll all go back to . . ." Her voice ran down. Her eyes narrowed. For the first time she seemed actually to see Nicole. "By the gods, what *happened* to you?"

"The legions are back," Nicole said. Her voice was flat, dead. "You didn't need to tell me. I . . . met a legionary."

Julia had lived in this world a lot longer than Nicole had, and had seen a lot more of it, too. Her eyes went wide: that almost bovine expression of hers, one of the intractable relics of her slave days, which concealed a great deal of her intelligence. "He didn't," she said, but her tone belied the words.

"Yes, he did," Nicole said. "All this time, the Marcomanni and the Quadi didn't, and the first cursed Roman legionary I saw . . . did. Let's hear it for the defenders of civilization." Tears dripped down her cheeks. She hadn't even noticed that she'd started to cry.

"He did what, Mother?" Lucius asked, butting in between them, innocently curious.

"Never mind," Nicole and Julia said together.

Then there was a silence. Lucius looked from one to the other of them, obviously thought about asking again, equally obviously decided it wasn't the wisest thing to do. Nicole went on standing at the foot of the stairs, with her eyes leaking tears.

Julia crossed the tavern in a few swift strides, and folded her arms around Nicole. Nicole shrank inside them. She was comforted, she was supposed to be comforted.

She never wanted to be touched by another human being again.

Julia petted her as if she'd been a child or an animal. "There, Mistress," she said. "There. That's a terrible thing to happen to a woman."

"Isn't it?" Nicole said, still in a voice a thousand miles—a thousand lightyears—from her own. "I don't even know who he was. I couldn't pick him out from any other soldier. He was just—a man in a helmet. A son of a whore in a helmet."

"Even if you can't pick the wretch out of a crowd, you ought to complain to the Emperor," Julia said. "He's supposed to care that things like that don't happen."

"The Emperor?" Nicole would never have thought of that, not even close. She hadn't thought there was anything she could do, except be a victim—the universal lot of women in this time and place. But to go right up to the *Emperor* and tell him what had been done to her—She tried to imagine going up to the President of the United States, past his wall of press corps, White House staff, Secret Service . . .

Here she was, diehard product of a democratic nation, and she had a better chance, if Julia was right, of walking up to the Roman Emperor and getting him to listen to her, than she did with her own elected President.

Still. Julia knew this world. She hadn't been wrong about it yet. If she thought Marcus Aurelius himself might listen to a tavernkeeper from the fringe of his empire, then maybe, just maybe, he would.

With the coming of purpose, fear and shock ebbed. Anger and outrage were swift to take their place. "The Emperor," Nicole repeated, grimly now. "Yes, I'll take my case to the Emperor."

20

———※———

MARCUS AURELIUS ENTERED THE city the day the German hordes broke and fled. He took up residence in the town-council building near the market square. Nicole wondered just how complicated it would be to get an audience with him. Less complicated, probably, than it would have been to get in to see the President, or Julia wouldn't have suggested it, but even kings of minor countries had hordes of flunkies to keep the great unwashed away from their majesty. The more minor the country, in fact, the greater the hordes seemed to be.

By that token, since Rome was the greatest empire in the world, it should be a relatively simple matter to see its Emperor. Nicole approached the town hall with a bold face and a fluttering heart—and found that she was not the first nor yet the last to come in search of the imperial ear. People were going in and coming out, nearly all men, most in armor or in togas but a few in tunics. She worked her way into the stream, passing the armored guards who decorated the door just like guards in a Hollywood epic, and working her way inside.

There the stream divided, some going here, some going there. She had no idea where to begin.

She chose a direction more or less at random, and started down a hallway. A man stepped out of a door, so suddenly she started, and barred her way. He wasn't a guard, and he wasn't in armor. He wore a toga, a surprisingly white affair with a narrow and somehow pretentious crimson stripe. "And what may be your purpose here?" he inquired in Latin almost painful in its purity.

She'd prepared a speech for just such an eventuality: short, pithy, but comprehensive. The functionary heard her out with an arched brow and a supercilious expression. "And what evidence have you that the alleged assault in fact occurred?" he asked when she'd come to the end of it.

Nicole drew herself up to her full height, which wasn't all that inconsiderable. "Would you like to see the knot in my head? The bruises on my chest? The ones on my backside? Do you want to see what forcible sexual intercourse does to a woman's private parts?"

The aide's eyebrows leaped. "Thank you, no," he said with a flicker of disgust. Maybe he wouldn't care to view a woman's private parts under any circumstances. He went on with the same chilly precision as before: "If you would care to present me with a written statement of your claim, so it may be examined before being put to the Emperor, who is, after all, you will understand, a busy man . . ."

His voice trailed away. His smile was small and smug. His meaning was abundantly clear. *Just blow yourself off, lady.* What were the odds that a tavernkeeper would be able to give him a written statement, or have enough money to hire someone to do a proper job of it?

Nicole favored him with a sweetly carnivorous smile. No matter what the odds, he'd bet and lost. He just didn't know it yet. "May I borrow pen and ink and papyrus?" she asked in dulcet tones.

His eyebrows climbed again. "You wish to prepare this written statement *yourself?*"

Nicole nodded. He pursed his lips. *This I've got to see*—he didn't shout it, but he didn't need to.

He clapped his hands. A younger man in a toga without a stripe appeared as if conjured out of the air. He received the order without expression, and disappeared as abruptly as he'd appeared, to return a moment later with the articles Nicole had asked for.

Marcus Aurelius' aide nodded to Nicole. "Go ahead. Use that desk there, if you like. Take all the time you need." Sure as hell, there it was again—*This I've got to see.*

"Thank you," Nicole said pointedly. She went to stand behind the desk—it was small and high, almost like a lectern—and set to work. The aide watched her for a while, long enough to see that she really was writing. Then he shrugged a tiny shrug and turned away to obstruct the next foolish innocent who ventured into his lair.

She laid out her statement like any other legal brief she'd ever drafted: first the facts, then their implications. *What is civilization worth when the Marcomanni and Quadi held Carnuntum for months without molesting me in any way, but I was brutally raped by the first Roman legionary I saw during the reconquest of the city?* She said not a word about what the Germans had done to poor Antonina. That wasn't how the game was played.

Finally, she came to the important part: what she wanted the presiding authority—here a Roman Emperor, not a Superior Court judge—to do about the issue at hand. *Unfortunately, I cannot positively identify the soldier who violated me. If I could, I would ask for him to be punished to the limit of the law, and for me to receive compensation both from him and from the government of the Roman Empire, under whose agency he acted. I still deserve the latter compensation, for as an agent of the government of the empire he grossly abused the authority entrusted to him, and used it to commit this outrageous crime against me.*

Setting it down in writing made her angry all over again. "Bastard," she muttered under her breath. "Fucking bastard." She'd welcomed him as a rescuer, and what did she get for it? Thrown down in the dirt. God, if she could make him pay personally for every stroke he'd driven home, she'd do it. But if he didn't have to pay, *somebody* would. She'd make damned certain of that.

When she stepped away from the desk, the Emperor's aide waved her over to where he sat at a table piled with neatly labeled scrolls. "Let's see what you've done," he said, not quite as if he were talking to a six-year-old child, but close enough. Without a word, she passed him the closely written sheets.

Like every other literate Roman Nicole had seen, he mumbled the words to himself as he read. His eyes swept back and forth a couple of times before those expressive eyebrows of his made another leap, this one higher than either of the other two. After a bit, he paused and stared at Nicole. Then he went back to his mumbling.

"This is astonishing," he said when he was finally done. "If I had not seen you write it with my own eyes, Mistress, ah, Umma"—he had to check the papyrus for her name, though she'd given it to him; obviously he was one of those people for whom nothing was real till it was written down—"I would not have believed it. Why, this might almost be a brief prepared by a gentleman of the legal profession. Astonishing," he said again.

He'd intended his words as high praise. But it wasn't high enough to suit Nicole. "What do you mean, almost?" she demanded.

"Well," he replied, glad of a chance to get sniffy again, "of course you do not cite the relevant laws and imperial decrees, nor the opinions of the leading jurisconsults, but the reasoning is nonetheless very clear and forceful."

"Ah," Nicole said. *Damn.* She *wasn't* a trained lawyer here; she didn't have the citations at her fingertips, nor know where to find them.

She could learn. She was sure of that. She'd learned in the United States, and things were undoubtedly simpler here. But where would she find the time? Most days, at least before the Germans came, she'd had trouble finding time to use the chamber pot. Even if by a miracle she could squeeze a spare hour out of the day, where would she find someone to train her, or books from which to study? The next book of any sort she saw here would be the first.

She'd missed a few words of the aide's reply. He condescended, superciliously, to repeat himself: "I will be certain this comes to the Emperor's attention. It may intrigue him. Let me see." He glanced again at the statement. "Yes, you have described your place of residence most precisely. Should anything further be required of you, you will be summoned."

That sounded altogether too much like, *Don't call us;*

we'll call you. "What if I'm not summoned?" Nicole asked.

"The choice is the Emperor's," the aide replied. "As I say, I will bring this to his notice. Past that, the matter is in his hands. Who could be above the Emperor, to compel him to change his mind?"

"The law could. Justice could," Nicole said. That was certainly true in the U.S.A., where no one was above the law. Did it also hold in the Roman Empire? If it did, did it hold for Marcus Aurelius?

Maybe not, by the way his administrative assistant's jaw dropped. But the man didn't tell her she was crazy, either. "What a—sophisticated attitude for a tavernkeeper to hold." His nod had a certain finality to it, an air of dismissal.

Nicole didn't bother to argue. There was a limit to how far anyone could push a bureaucrat. She'd tested his limits and then some. It was the best she could do; the rest was in the hands of the gods.

Julia was waiting at the tavern, fairly dancing with eagerness. She barely let Nicole get in through the door before she started in. "Did you see him? Did you?" She might have been talking about a god, or a god's first cousin.

Nicole almost hated to disappoint her. "No, I didn't. I had to leave a petition with an aide. We'll see if anything comes of it." *It had better,* she thought. If Marcus Aurelius ignored her case, how much trouble would picketing the town-council building cause? Plenty, she would imagine. She almost smiled at the prospect.

"I hope something does come of it," Julia said. "I think it will, I really do. He *is* supposed to be a good man."

"We'll see," Nicole said. She wasn't as sure of Marcus Aurelius' goodness as Julia was. He was the Roman Emperor, after all. She'd taken time to find out what exactly that meant. He wasn't a king, not exactly, and it wasn't necessarily hereditary, though it could be. What Marcus Aurelius was, was the chief political figure in a vast, ancient, and sometimes terribly corrupt empire.

Nicole had precious little use for politicians—which, considering the state of politics in late-twentieth-century America, was hardly surprising. As far as she was concerned, the higher a politician rose, the more lies he had to tell to get there, and the more likely he'd tell even bigger lies once he got to the top.

Julia didn't share Nicole's worries, or her cynicism either. She was already off on another subject. "While you were out," she said, "a crier came by. There'll be grain in the city in a day or two."

That caught Nicole's attention. "Oh! That is good news." Bread, real bread. Cakes. Buns and rolls and . . . She stopped before she got carried away. "I hope the price isn't too outrageous. Though they probably wouldn't dare to try too much gouging, not with the Emperor right here to see it."

Before Julia could answer, an odd, rhythmic clanking brought them both to the windows and the open door. This wasn't the sharp clash and clang of swordplay. It was duller, steadier. Down the street toward the eastern gate marched a somber procession of Marcomanni and Quadi—Nicole never had learned to tell the tribes apart—chained together in gangs of ten. Many, many gangs of ten. Roman soldiers herded them onward, some with knotted whips, others with drawn swords.

"They're on their way to the slave markets," Julia said with vindictive satisfaction. "I hope they all get worked to death in the mines."

But Nicole was watching the legionaries, not the Germans. Was one of them the man who'd violated her with such callous—practiced?—efficiency? Of itself, her left hand rose to her neck. She'd felt a Roman blade there. Had she given the legionary any trouble, she had no doubt that blade would have drunk her life. In the capture of a city, what was one body more or less?

Her gaze might have gone fearfully from one Roman soldier to another, but more people were watching the Quadi and Marcomanni. Passersby on the sidewalk jeered the captured barbarians. One of the locals almost echoed Julia: "A short life and a merry one, boys, grubbing for iron or lead!" He laughed, loud and long.

The Germans ignored him. They must have heard a hundred such jeers as they marched through the city. Their heads were down, that had been carried with such casual arrogance. Their broad shoulders were bent, their feet shuffling, not even a hint of their old swagger.

A shriek of raw rage split the afternoon. Nicole jumped half out of her skin. "That's Antonina!" Julia exclaimed. She sprinted for the doorway, with Nicole in close pursuit.

Nicole got there just in time to watch Antonina burst from her own door, dodge a legionary with a move Michael Jordan would have envied, and smash an enormous pot over the head of one of the Germans. Shards flew like shrapnel. The German staggered. Blood poured down his face. Nicole marveled that he didn't fall over dead.

"Mithras, lady, what was that for?" bellowed the legionary Antonina had evaded.

"What do you think?" she shot back. "The day the town fell, he and a gang of his cousins raped me right here in the street." She tried to kick the prisoner in the crotch, but he twisted away; her foot caught him in the hipbone. She followed him down the street, kicking him and cursing as vilely as she knew how. The guards laughed and clapped and cheered her on.

Nicole was astonished at the bolt of jealousy that pierced her. Antonina had at least a measure of revenge for what had happened to her. She had closure. When she finally left off trying to maim the barbarian who'd raped her, she walked back toward her house with her shoulders straight and her head high. She had, at last, put the nightmare behind her.

And what have I got? Nicole's laughter had a bitter edge. *Closure?* She laughed again. How was she supposed to avenge herself on the Roman legionary who'd forced himself on her and into her? She couldn't identify him five minutes after he shot his seed into her. She'd never recognize him now. He was—a man. That had been an advantage in the United States. It wasn't just an advantage here. It was everything.

Her gaze flicked to Liber and Libera, sitting serenely in

their plaque behind the bar. They'd given her exactly what she'd thought she wanted. What a cruel gift it had turned out to be.

And now they would not send her home. Maybe they were busy. Maybe they just didn't care. Maybe they were laughing at her, just as Frank must have done when he started his affair with Dawn.

She looked back toward Antonina's house. Her sour-tempered neighbor was getting on with things—and she couldn't. That would take a miracle. She'd already had one; that must be her quota. It was more than most people ever got.

At last, the parade ended. Hundreds, maybe thousands, of Marcomanni and Quadi had shambled past her doorway. Nicole kept an eye out for Antonina, in case she emerged to smash more crockery over the head of an astonished German, but that door stayed shut, and Antonina stayed within.

As the last straggling prisoner shuffled out of sight, pricked on by a sword in his backside, Julia stretched and wriggled and sighed. "It's so *good* to be back inside the empire again."

"Why?" Nicole asked bleakly. "Do you feel so much safer with the heroic legionaries to protect you?"

Julia nodded automatically. Then memory struck: she bit her lip.

Nicole didn't tax her with it. Nicole's problem was Nicole's own. She did her best to get on with the rest of the day, to do what she would normally have done: look after the tavern, rustle up meals, make sure the three of them were fed. Once the grain came in, if the price was low enough, she could open the tavern again. That would be good. That would take her mind off—things.

Sometimes, for a few minutes at a stretch, she actually managed to forget. Then something—a shadow, a voice in the street, the clank of armor as a soldier strutted past— would bring back memory: reeling, falling, scale mail pressed to her body, hard hand ripping at her drawers. Then she would start to shake. Almost, she wished he'd cut her throat when he was done. Then she wouldn't have to relive it, over and over again.

The sun sank in the northwest, throwing a long shaft of sunlight into the tavern's doorway. The interior brightened then, as much as it ever could. But her gloom was pitch-black. No mere sunlight could begin to pierce it.

Shadows in the doorway made her look up; made her tense, too, involuntarily, braced for fight or flight. Even in silhouette, she could tell that the men she saw were strangers: they wore togas, as few of her customers ever had. "Mistress Umma, the tavernkeeper?" one of them asked in Latin more elegant than that commonly spoken in Carnuntum.

"Yes," she said after a pause. Then: "Who are you?"

He didn't deign to answer that. He stood just on the threshold, though it meant he had to raise his voice slightly to converse with Nicole by the bar. There was no way, his attitude said, he was going farther in. Even as far as he'd gone, he'd need a good, long stint in the baths to wash off the stink of commoner.

That rankled. And never mind that Nicole had felt remarkably much like it when she first came to Carnuntum. He wasn't too savory, either, by American standards. Not without soap or deodorant.

He sniffed loudly. In that Latin equivalent of an Oxford accent, he declaimed—*said* was too mild a word: "The Emperor has received your plea. I am instructed to invite you to supper with him, to discuss the matter."

He didn't ask if she'd come. That would have given her too much choice in the matter.

Just for that, she was tempted to be too busy. But the Emperor wasn't necessarily responsible for the rudeness of his staff—and he was the Emperor. If she tried to play power games with him, she would lose. She didn't have the faintest hope of winning.

"Yes, of course I'll come," Nicole said. Her own words sounded harsh and unlovely in her ears, like raw down-home Indiana next to the most mellifluous Oxbridge.

Julia was staring as if her eyes would fall out of her head.

Nicole wondered if there was a single thought behind them, or any emotion but awe.

She didn't have time for awe. "Wait here while I change my tunic," she said.

Marcus Aurelius' messengers looked, just then, as flummoxed as Julia. Nicole smiled at them, nodded, and went serenely upstairs. Not till she was out of their sight did she leap into a run, rip into the bedroom, tear off her ratty old tunic with the grease-stains on the front, and pull on her best one. If she could have showered and done her hair, she would have. She made what order she could with fingers and comb, which wasn't much, and stopped to breathe. No matter what she did, the Roman Emperor was going to know what kind of life she led. Her best tunic probably wouldn't be good enough for a slave in his household.

So let him see, and let him ponder it if he could. She was an honest businesswoman, a solid if by no means wealthy citizen. She had just as much right as anyone else, to justice under the law.

She firmed her chin and squared her shoulders and marched back downstairs. A sneaking niggle of doubt evaporated: the Emperor's messengers were still there, arms folded, feet tapping, all too obviously displeased by what they must regard as her insolence.

Too bad for them. "Let's go," she said briskly.

As they walked toward the town-council building, the aide who'd done the talking kept right on doing it. "The Emperor would have you know that he means no insult by supping with you seated rather than reclining. It is his own usual practice: one of his many austerities."

Nicole raised an eyebrow. "Really? Thank you, then. I'm glad to know what to expect."

She was, in fact, relieved. She'd never eaten while lying down, and she hadn't the faintest idea how to do it without slopping dinner all over herself. Certainly nobody in her social circle did any such thing. It must be the height of high fashion.

Stolid legionaries stood guard outside the town hall. They might have been the same who'd stood there this morning, or they might not. There was no way to tell. In the manner of sentries even in her own time, they kept their eyes fixed straight again as Nicole passed through the gate. Her gaze flicked from one side to the other. Was one of them the man who had assaulted her? How would she ever know?

She'd never look at a Roman legionary in armor again without wondering, *Is that it? Is he the one?*

For that matter, how many of them had done to other women in Carnuntum what that one had done to her? Had any other victims come forward? Would women in this time actually do any such thing?

All this time, Nicole had lived in this world, and still she didn't know the most basic things: how people thought, how they felt, how they reacted to trauma. She was in a country so foreign that she just barely began to understand a small part of it, and even of that she wasn't completely certain.

Her reflections brought her down one passage and then another, till she found herself in a largish room that faced west. The last of the sun, with the help of several lamps much larger and more ornate than her own, lit the chamber amazingly well, even without electricity. Even so, she couldn't see much of what was in it against the glare: only that there was a man standing by one of the windows, a black outline against the sunset light.

One of her guides had pushed in ahead of her—officiously, she thought. "Sir," he said, "here is the woman."

"Of course," said the shadow by the window. The aide backed out of the room, as smooth as if on wheels, and ushered Nicole in with a sharp flick of the hand.

She found her heart was beating hard and her palms were clammy. What in the world was she supposed to do or say in front of the Emperor of the Romans? What if she committed some hideous faux pas? What would he do then? Throw her out on her ear? Fling her into jail? Shout "Off with her head!"?

The shadow moved away from the window, coming

clearer little by little, till finally she had a good view of his face. That reassured her, a little. He looked both older and tireder than he did on his coins. And he looked more like a college professor—a philosopher, as Titus Calidius Severus would have said; she had to put down the stab of loss at the memory, as sharp now as it had ever been, and there was no time for it here, dammit—

Oh, damn, she thought, groping for the train of her reflection. More like a college professor than a politician. Yes. Maybe that was a good sign.

He peered at her—no eyeglasses or contacts here. "You would be the tavernkeeper Umma?"

"Yes, sir," Nicole answered, using the same form of address as the aide had. If that wasn't fancy enough to suit the Emperor, no doubt he'd let her know.

But he only said, "Come in, then, and we shall go from eggs to apples, as the proverb puts it." His Latin was even more astringently pure than that spoken by his servitors. When Nicole spoke, she often dropped a final *m* or *s*, as someone speaking casual English might say *workin'* for *working*. Everybody in Carnuntum talked that way. Marcus Aurelius didn't. In his mouth, every verb form, every noun ending, was perfectly distinct.

"Thank you, sir," she said to him in her rough country accent, and went where he beckoned, to a beautiful wooden table with an inlaid top, set near enough to the window to catch the light, but not so near as to dazzle the eyes. She took the chair that had been set on the far side. An army of guards didn't leap out of the walls to haul her off to the dungeon. Boldly, she ventured to add, "And thank you for hearing my petition."

Marcus Aurelius smiled as he took the chair across from her. "You are welcome," he replied. "That petition is one of the most intriguing documents to have come before me in some time. Had Alexander not seen you write it with his own eyes, he would have thought it the work of someone of much higher station in life. Most intriguing."

"All I did was set out what happened to me and what I'd

like you to do about it," Nicole said. There was no way she
wanted Marcus Aurelius to ask too many questions about
how she'd learned to write like that. She had no good answers for him, and nothing he was likely to believe.

He wasn't going to let it go. She should have known he
wouldn't. "The reasoning is as forceful and direct as if a
skilled advocate had composed it. I do not agree with all
your conclusions, not by any means, but you argue them
well."

"Thank you, sir." Nicole was saved by the dinner bell, in
a manner of speaking: just then a servant—or more likely a
slave—brought in a jar of wine and the first course. It did
include eggs, eggs hard-boiled and seasoned with olive oil
and pepper. They rested on lettuce also oiled and peppered—
and vinegared as well. It could have been a salad from a
trendy bistro in L.A., where the cuisine was nouvelle and the
decor minimalist.

"If you were expecting some sybaritic feast, I fear you
will be disappointed," Marcus Aurelius said, almost as if in
true apology. "My tastes are far from ornate."

"This is wonderful." Nicole had to work not to talk with
her mouth full. "We didn't have much of anything to eat
while the Marcomanni and Quadi held Carnuntum."

"A sufficiency of material needs is good. An excess is
bad," Marcus Aurelius said. His tone had changed, taken on
almost a singsong note, as if he were declaiming on a stage.
"These eggs come from the same orifice as a hen's droppings. Wine is but the juice of a bunch of grapes, my purple
toga dyed with the blood of a shellfish. None of these things
deserves any affection beyond the ordinary."

That sounded very noble—till Nicole looked down at her
own best tunic, of shabby linen streakily dyed with woad.
Marcus Aurelius might choose austerity, but he had a choice.
When Nicole went hungry, there'd been nothing voluntary
about it. She hadn't had any choice when the legionary raped
her, either.

She pointed out that last, not too sarcastically, she hoped.
Evidently not. Marcus Aurelius nodded. "I understand as

much," he said. "Your petition made it very plain. If you could identify the soldier who violated you, he would be liable to severe punishment. The legions exist to protect the Roman commonwealth, not to pain and distress those living under that commonwealth."

"I certainly hope so," Nicole said. "That's why the government should be liable for what he did to me."

Before Marcus Aurelius could answer, the servant brought in a new jar of wine and a heavy silver platter piled with pieces of chicken roasted with garlic and herbs. Not even the Roman Emperor had heard of a fork: Marcus Aurelius ate with his fingers, as Nicole did herself. He was neater than she was, and more obviously practiced. "The food pleases you?" he inquired.

"Very much, thank you," Nicole answered, "even if it is only dead flesh."

He started slightly, and stared. She wondered if she'd get into trouble for having the nerve to put a sardonic twist on what he said. *To hell with it,* she thought, and instructed herself to stop worrying. She never would have got an audience with the Emperor if she hadn't had a fat dose of chutzpah.

"Anything would taste good now," she added. "As I said, we haven't had much to eat since the Germans came."

To her astonishment, Marcus Aurelius lowered his eyes as if in shame. "You may justly reproach me for that," he said. "Had I been able to best the barbarians before they broke into Carnuntum, I would gladly have done so. But I had neither the strength nor the ability to prevent them."

That he felt he deserved blame for his failure was perfectly, even painfully, obvious. That he was also very, very able was just as obvious. In the late twentieth century, such a politician would have been a prodigy of nature—and very likely would have found it impossible to get elected to office.

But nobody had elected Marcus Aurelius to anything. He was Emperor of the Romans. He held that office for life. Rulers of that sort were out of fashion in her time, and with good reason. Without the need to keep the people happy enough to keep on voting for them, rulers could do whatever they pleased. Even if they bought votes and forced their election, in the end they fell, and often bloodily.

And yet, without the need to pander to the electorate, rulers might also be as good as they chose. They didn't have to slip and slither and slide around every issue, to make sure the voters kept on voting them back into office. Nor did they have to back off from unpopular positions, if those positions were right, for fear of being voted out. They could do whatever needed doing, and do it to the best of their ability.

As Nicole listened to the man across the table, she understood something altogether new about accountability. Not all freedom was license, and not all power was corrupt. This Emperor of the Romans, whose rank and office were as undemocratic as they could possibly be, made even the best American politician seem an unprincipled hack.

While they sat silent, each lost in reflection, the slave brought in bread and honey. Nicole took the first, fabulously sweet bite, and had all she could do to keep from wolfing down the rest. "This is wonderful honey!" she said.

Marcus Aurelius smiled. "I'm glad you enjoy it. It is from Mount Hymettus, in the Athenian land."

Nicole realized she was supposed to be impressed, though he was obviously trying to make little of it. She was certainly impressed with the flavor, whatever the origin. Of course the Emperor would have only the best.

After the bread came apples, just as he'd promised at the beginning of the meal: apples sliced and candied in more of that wonderful honey. When she'd licked her fingers clean, Nicole felt replete for the first time in longer than she liked to think. She savored it. She'd known so little bodily well-being lately; it was delicious just to sit there and feel that sense of fullness.

The servant cleared away the remains of the dinner. The sun had gone down, leaving only fading twilight beyond the windows. More lamps glowed in the chamber than Nicole had ever seen in one room. Even so, they did not, could not, banish darkness as electricity did. They pushed it back a bit, that was all. Every time Marcus Aurelius moved, fresh shadows stole out and sheltered themselves in the lines of his face. He looked older than he had in the daylight, a tired, fiftyish man who'd had too little sleep and too much stress for much too long.

He made a steeple of his fingertips and studied her over it, homing in at last on the purpose of the meeting. "I am curious as to the logic by which you reached the conclusion that the Roman government is in some way responsible for the vicious and lewd act of one soldier."

Now he got down to it. This wasn't a courtroom; it felt more like settling out of court. But she was working—playing—with the law again even so. Parts of her that had felt dead, closed off, since she'd come to Carnuntum awoke to sudden and vibrant life. Rain in the desert, she thought, awakening seeds in the dry earth, a bloom of flowers after years of drought.

Oh, she had missed it, if she was waxing rhapsodic about its return. She pursed her lips and folded her hands and got down to business. "It seems plain enough to me," she said. "If a soldier isn't the agent of the government that employs him, what is he?"

"A collection of the atoms that make up a man," Marcus Aurelius replied. "A product of the divine fire, living according to nature."

"That's philosophy," Nicole said. "I thought we were talking about law."

"There is a connection between the two, you must admit, for good law can spring only from a sound grounding in that which is ethically proper. Would you not agree?"

He sounded like a book, with his rounded sentences and his careful ordering of ideas. But they were fuzzy, muddy ideas compared to the crisp architecture of the law.

All theory and no practice, she thought. He wasn't the first such thinker she'd seen, or even the tenth. With a faint sigh of exasperation, she said, "Isn't that irrelevant for the moment? We're talking about what the law *is,* not what it should be."

Marcus Aurelius startled her with a disarmingly boyish grin. "Oh, indeed, Alexander did not err when he sent you to me," he said. "You have a great natural aptitude for a profession of which you must hitherto have been altogether ignorant."

Nicole drew breath to object to that, but a belated attack of sense kept her silent. There was no way she could explain how she really knew about the law. Let him think her a prodigy, if it got her what she wanted.

She hadn't diverted him from his line of thought, either. He veered right back to it with a quiet obstinacy that would have served him well on the tenure track at a university. "A soldier, like any other man," he said, "is obliged to live according to that which is ethically right."

Nicole pounced with a cry of glee. "Ha! How can you say that a soldier is doing what is ethically right, when he rapes a woman he's supposed to defend?"

"I do not. I never have," Marcus Aurelius replied. "I do, however, dispute your claim of agency applying to my government."

My government. Maybe he didn't even notice he was reminding Nicole of who he was. It was literally true. The government was his. He owned it. No one in the United States could say such a thing, not and be believed. That was not a phrase she would ever have heard in the United States. "You still haven't answered my question," she said. Marcus Aurelius smiled again, perhaps at her stubborn presumption. "If he's not an agent, what is he? What can he be? If a soldier doesn't belong to a government, what is he?"

Nothing, was the answer she expected. But Marcus Aurelius said, quite seriously, "A brigand." Once again she realized, as Dorothy had after the tornado, that she wasn't in Kansas—or Indiana, or California—anymore.

"I suppose that may be true," she said, "but it hasn't got anything to do with what we're talking about here."

"I should be hard pressed to disagree with you." The Emperor inclined his head with studied courtesy. "By all means continue your argument; perhaps you may persuade me."

He meant it. Nicole had long experience in the ways of judges and juries, and he was telling the truth. If she could persuade him, he'd give her what she wanted.

This was an honestly, incontestably good man. He wasn't pretending. He wasn't playing a part. He was a little on the imperial side for her democratic tastes, but of his goodness she had no doubts whatever. Nor was he doing it to gain himself a jump in the polls. He did it because of what he was; because, for him, there was no rational alternative.

Nicole had to stop to get her wits together. Genuine goodness in a politician was profoundly disconcerting.

She took refuge in the security of legal reasoning. "Your soldier was under orders to recapture Carnuntum from the Marcomanni and the Quadi, was he not? He was your agent—one of your agents—in that, am I correct?"

He nodded and smiled, as pleased as if she'd been his own protégée. "I believe I see the argument you're framing," he said. "Go on."

"If that soldier was your agent when he was doing the things he was supposed to do, how can he stop being your agent when he commits a crime against me?" Nicole demanded. "He wouldn't have been in Carnuntum in the first place if he hadn't been acting on your behalf."

"Yes, I thought this was the port toward which you would be sailing," Marcus Aurelius replied happily. "But let me ask a question in return. If I send a man from Rome to Carthage to buy grain, I am liable if he should cheat on the transaction, not so?"

"Of course you are," Nicole said.

"You take a broader view of the concept of agency than the jurisconsults are in the habit of doing, but never mind that," Marcus Aurelius said. "Let me ask you another—you do understand the concept of what is termed a hypothetical question?"

"Yes," Nicole said. Part of her, the quick, unthinking part, was irked that he needed to ask. But Umma the tavernkeeper by the banks of the Danube—would she have understood the concept?

Marcus Aurelius, in his turn, seemed surprised Nicole did understand. His eyebrows rose. He paused as if to marshal his thoughts—as if he needed to delete a whole section of argumentation she'd just rendered unnecessary. "Very well," he said at last. "Suppose, then, that my agent, while in Carthage to buy grain, violated a woman. Would I be liable then?"

"You certainly wouldn't be liable in a criminal sense," Nicole said, "but if he wouldn't have gone to Carthage except at your order, you might have some civil liability." That at least was the way of it where she came from, particularly in front of a sympathetic jury.

But Marcus Aurelius shook his head. "He is responsible for his own actions then, and solely responsible for them. No man learned in the law would dispute this for a moment; please believe me when I tell you as much."

She did believe him. She had to. He wouldn't lie; it wasn't in him.

So why was his concept of agency so much narrower than hers? It did fit a pattern she was seeing: that everything to do with government was much more limited here than in the United States.

What exactly did the government of the Roman Empire do? All she'd ever seen it do till the Marcomanni and Quadi took Carnuntum was feed one condemned criminal to the lions. Obviously, Marcus Aurelius commanded the legions. She supposed the imperial government kept up the roads; the guide had said something about that, all the way back on her honeymoon in Petronell. Past that . . .

Education? If you wanted any, you bought it yourself. Welfare? If you couldn't work, either your family took care of you or you starved. Health care? Health care here was a cruel joke to begin with. The environment? The Romans didn't care. They would have exploited it worse than they did, if only they'd known how.

The worst of it was, in context it made sense. Even in good times here, people walked one step from starvation. There was just barely enough to keep them going, let alone to give to the government in the form of taxes and service fees. She'd never thought of an active government as a luxury only a rich country could afford, but she'd never had her nose rubbed in poverty like this before, either.

Neither had she stopped to think about the effect the Roman government's inherent limits would have on the law. By the standards she was used to, the government didn't and couldn't do much. Moreover, if it was that limited, then so were its obligations to its citizens. *Quid pro quo* was good Latin, and perfectly logical. If you didn't have much to do with the government, the government wouldn't have much to do with you.

And that left her with precious little by way of a case. Roman law simply didn't see liability in the same way American law did. It couldn't. There wasn't the structure to support it.

Like a boxer sparring for time after taking one on the chin, she said, "But if you send your man to Carthage to buy grain, you don't give him the tools he needs to commit forcible rape." The edge of that sword against her neck had been sharper than any of the razors she'd used to shave herself.

"Possibly not," Marcus Aurelius said, "although I suppose he might use a stylus to threaten rather than to write on wax in a tablet."

"I beg your pardon, sir," Nicole said, "but that's reaching."

"Perhaps it is." The Emperor yielded the point without rancor. "But I did not give the miscreant legionary his tools to enable him to violate women. I gave them to him to drive the invaders from the Roman Empire. Having regained Pannonia, I aim to go on and conquer the Germans in their gloomy forests, that this menace may never again threaten us."

He sighed. If he was a born soldier, Nicole was a born Indy-car driver. But he was doing what he thought he had to do to make the world a better place, and doing it as best he knew how. Nicole couldn't help but admire him, even when he was ruling against her.

Would he succeed in his goal? She didn't know. All she

knew was that, sooner or later, the Roman Empire would fall. She didn't know when, or exactly how. She hoped, just then, that it didn't fall on this man's watch. If there was any fairness in the world, he deserved to win his war and hold back the darkness a while longer.

He said—and he said it with some regret, too, "I am going to deny your petition for damages from my government for the attack upon you."

Nicole drew breath to ask if she could appeal that, but stopped, feeling foolish. If the Emperor refused her, who could overrule him? There was no Supreme Court here, no check or balance to the Emperor's power. To her amazement, she wasn't angry at this man, this good and—yes—wise ruler. She didn't feel cheated. He was playing the game by the rules he understood, and playing it as fairly as he knew how.

"I still think you're wrong," she said, "but what can I do? I can't make you agree with me, any more than I could make your soldier"—she was too stubborn to stop calling him that—"stop doing what he did."

Marcus Aurelius held up a hand. "I have ruled that the Roman Empire owes you no compensation for what you suffered at this unknown legionary's wicked hands. That ruling shall stand. Whether you deserve compensation for the wrong you have suffered may perhaps be another question. Alexander!" For the first time that evening, the Emperor raised his voice. It made Nicole start a little. He was softspoken by nature and inclination, but she knew, just then, that he had taught himself to be heard across a battlefield.

The man who hurried into the room was none other than the secretary who had been so surprised at Nicole's petition that he'd actually accepted it. He ignored Nicole completely. Marcus Aurelius beckoned him close and murmured something to him, all but whispering in his ear. Nicole tried her best to eavesdrop, but they were both too skilled at keeping private conversations private.

Alexander glanced at Nicole. His mouth was thin with distaste. "Sir, are you sure?"

That, Nicole heard perfectly clearly. She obviously was meant to. Interesting, she thought: Marcus Aurelius' subordinates respected him, that was evident, but they also felt free to talk back to him.

"Yes, yes," said the Emperor of the Romans with the slightest well-bred hint of impatience. "I am most certainly sure." In Sheldon Rosenthal's fondest dreams, he was perhaps a quarter as suave as Marcus Aurelius.

With a sigh, Alexander left the chamber. While he was gone, Nicole didn't know what to say, so she settled for saying nothing. The Emperor seemed lost in thought—meditating on the cares of empire, she supposed.

In a little while, Alexander came back with a small leather sack, which he handed without ceremony to Marcus Aurelius. He left shaking his head. The Emperor, his every movement said, was doing something Alexander could not possibly approve of.

Marcus Aurelius knew it, too; his eyes glinted as he set the sack in front of Nicole. "The Empire cannot compensate you," he said. "I, however, as a citizen of the Empire, can offer you, privately and personally, some small recompense for your misfortune."

And you can do it without setting a precedent that you and your successors are bound to follow, Nicole thought. No, no flies on the Roman Emperor, not a one. But, having ruled against her, he could have sent her home with nothing. She'd fully expected that; been braced for it, even tried to formulate some kind of argument that wouldn't make her look either greedy or presumptuous.

She thanked him automatically, with her eyes on the sack. It was very small. Give her a few *denarii,* pack her off, rest content that she had no further recourse—how easy for him to do. Easy, and cheap.

It wasn't exactly fine etiquette, but she untied the string that closed the mouth of the sack. If Marcus Aurelius imagined he could shut her up with a handful of silver . . .

She shook the sack out on the table. It had hardly any heft

to it at all. If it was empty—if this was some kind of bitter joke—

It was a damned good thing she'd kept her mouth shut before she saw what the aide had brought her. These weren't a few token *denarii*. They were *aurei*—all gold, brilliant in the lamplight. Ten of them. She counted, very carefully; picked them up and tipped them into her palm. They gleamed there, more wealth than Umma had ever held in her hand at one time.

Marcus Aurelius didn't frown at her rudeness. Maybe he even understood it. "I understand that no money can punish your violator, or undo what he did to you. But what money can do, I hope this money will do. The gods grant it be so."

It was a great deal of money. Two hundred fifty *denarii*—more than half the price of a slave. A thousand *sesterces*. Four thousand *asses*. It was like an incantation, an invocation of prosperity. More than a month's business—not profit, business—at the tavern. The rough equivalent, in second-century purchasing power, of the price of a Lexus.

Nicole had expected less, and would have settled for it. But the lawyer in her frowned at the ten *aurei* and reflected that, in terms of pain and suffering, she should have got more. He probably had it, too. If the deep-pockets rule applied, whose pockets—or moneybags—were deeper than those of the Emperor of the Romans? The rest of her knew that wasn't realistic. Money went a whole lot further here than in West Hills. Nor, by the law of the Empire, had Marcus Aurelius been obligated to give her any compensation at all. It was the action of a good man, a man who gave not because he had to, but because he felt that it was right.

Carefully, she said, "What money can do, I think this money will do. Thank you, sir. You are very generous." She'd said things like that more times than she could count. Far more often than not, she was conscious of the hypocrisy even as the words passed her lips. This time, she meant it from the bottom of her heart. How strange, in a world not just conspicuously but dreadfully worse than the one she'd been born to, to find at the head of the Roman Empire a man head and shoulders and torso above any of the rulers or statesmen of the late twentieth century. Mediocrities in expensive suits, every last one of them.

"I shall give you torchbearers to escort you back to your house," Marcus Aurelius said. "Any town, even one so much smaller than Rome as this, may prove dangerous to an honest woman walking alone in darkness. Having suffered one calamity, you ought not to fear another."

"Thank you again for your thoughtfulness," Nicole said.

To her astonishment, she saw she'd embarrassed him. "Some take pride in claiming credit for service," he said. "Some will not claim it aloud, but still secretly regard those whom they help as being in their debt. I try, as I believe all should try, to do one right thing after another, as naturally as a vine passes from yielding one summer's grapes to those of the next."

If another man had said such a thing, he would have sounded like a pompous ass. Marcus Aurelius brought it out as if it were, or should be, simple truth.

Nicole smiled. Now, finally, she understood what he was. It was more than a word. It was a whole manner of being. "The Romans are lucky," she said, "to have a philosopher for an emperor."

He surprised her again, this time by shaking his head. "A general at the helm, a Trajan or a Vespasian, would serve us better now," he replied. "But I am what we have, and I can but do my best." He rose from the table, and called for servants. They came quickly, torches at the ready, crackling and trailing a stream of fire. He handed her into their care, with a grace and a courtesy that were in keeping with all the rest of him. The last she saw of him, he was standing by the table in the light of those many lamps, his shoulders bowed a little, borne down by the weight of his office. It was late by second-century standards, but he looked as if he had a long night ahead of him still.

Outside in the darkness, the torches seemed dismayingly feeble, casting only a dim, flickering light at the feet of their bearers. The moon, which hung in the southeast on this clear late-August night, gave more and better light, but anything at all might have lurked in the moonshadows. A bright red star—Mars?—glowed a little above the moon. Even brighter was Jupiter, splendid and yellow-white below the moon, not far above the eastern horizon. Was that Saturn between them? Nicole would have known once, when it was a family pastime to spot the planets and call out names of the constellations. She hadn't done it since—Indianapolis? A long time. Night skies in Los Angeles were drowned in light, and she was too busy, most of the time, to notice.

This was the first time that she'd had to navigate Carnuntum by night. It was a dangerous pastime if you were too poor to afford guards and torchbearers. In the dark, in the absence of either streetlights or signs, she almost lost herself in the twisting ways of the city. Nothing looked the same as it did in daylight. Her steps grew slower and slower. The torchbearers began to mutter behind their hands, rude remarks in Latin and in another, unfamiliar language. Greek? It was much too mellifluous to be German.

At last, to her relief, she found the fountain near the tavern. From there, she had no trouble finding her way home. At the door, though she was suddenly, desperately tired, she paused to thank the Emperor's servants. They were polite to her because Marcus Aurelius had been, but they plainly couldn't wait to get the hell out of there.

Dim lamplight flickered through the slats of the shutters on the front windows. How nice of Julia, Nicole thought, to leave a lamp burning, so that Nicole wouldn't have to fumble her way in the dark.

She opened the door and slipped through it into the familiar, slightly funky interior of the tavern. Julia was sitting on a stool beside the lamp. She looked ready to fall over.

"For heaven's sake," Nicole said, "what did you wait up for me for? Go to bed before you fall asleep where you sit."

Julia shook her head stubbornly, though a yawn caught her and held her hostage in the middle. "I wanted to make sure you were all right," she said. "I know Marcus Aurelius is supposed to be a good man, but he *is* the Emperor. He can do whatever he wants. I was afraid of what he might do when you had the nerve to ask him to pay you back for what that legionary did, as if it were *his* fault."

"He wouldn't admit to that," Nicole said. "We had quite an argument about it, as a matter of fact. He wouldn't admit it was his fault or his government's fault." Even though she thought she understood why Marcus Aurelius reasoned as he did, anything less than complete success irked her.

It impressed the hell out of Julia. "You . . . argued with the Roman Emperor, Mistress?" she said incredulously.

"I sure did," Nicole answered, "and even though he wouldn't admit that he and his government were at fault, he gave me this." She tossed the little leather sack down in front of the freedwoman. Julia stared at it dubiously, as Nicole must have done when the Emperor gave it to her. "Go ahead, open it."

Julia did as told. Her gasp was altogether satisfactory. She spilled the *aurei* out on the tabletop. Nicole watched her closely as she put them back into the sack one by one, and made sure all ten were in there when she returned it. That was a lot of money—temptation even for the most honest employee.

"By the gods," Julia said, softly and reverently, though Nicole thought she revered the cash more than the gods. "He wouldn't have given you this much if he'd gone to bed with you himself."

"I didn't go see him to go to bed with him," Nicole said with rather more sharpness than was strictly necessary.

"But if he'd wanted to—" Everything was very straightforward in Julia's mind. Nicole had seen that time and again. She'd also seen that trying to change Julia's mind was like pounding your head against a rock: your head would break long before the rock did. This time, she didn't even try. "Let's get some sleep," she said. "Everything turned out as well as it could."

"I'll say!" Julia exclaimed. "Almost makes me wish—"

Nicole's expression brought her up short. As clearly as if it were happening again, Nicole could feel the Roman soldier forcing himself onto her, ramming deep, driving home a lot more than simple physical pain. What it did to her spirit . . .

"You don't know what you're talking about," Nicole said harshly. "Be glad of that."

Somebody in the Bible—Jacob?—had seen God face to face, and his life was preserved. After that, he'd become a great man among the Hebrews. Nicole didn't remember all the details; she hadn't been to Sunday school in a long, long time. But she'd seen Marcus Aurelius face to face, and not only was her life preserved, she'd come away with ten *aurei*. That was enough to make her a celebrity in the neighborhood, if not in all of Carnuntum.

She would much rather not have been raped. But since she had been, she would much rather Julia hadn't said anything about the compensation Marcus Aurelius had given her. Asking Julia not to gossip, though, was like asking a rooster not to crow when the sun came up. You could ask, but it wasn't likely to do you much good.

As the word spread, she gained customers. Fortunately she had food and drink to sell them; local farmers, those the Marcomanni and Quadi hadn't killed or kidnapped, started coming back into Carnuntum. And the army had its own supply train with it, and some of the flour and sausage and wine went to the people in the city. Part of that was Marcus Aurelius' care for the people over whom he ruled. Part, Nicole suspected, would have happened anyhow. Where money and food came together, those with the one couldn't fail to get their hands on the other.

One consequence of her attack of chutzpah saddened Nicole: Antonina stopped speaking to her. She didn't know what had caused the estrangement, but she could make a fair guess. If Antonina too had asked for compensation, but been turned down, that would do it. Nicole would have been the first to admit that Antonina had suffered worse than she had herself—but, as a lawyer, she knew only too well that how you phrased your claim often mattered more than what had actually happened to you.

Before long, thanks to all the legionaries in town, the tavern was doing at least as much business as it had before the pestilence and the Germans. A lot of the customers, of course, were the Roman soldiers who had come up to Carnuntum with Marcus Aurelius.

They gave her the creeps. Every so often, one or another of them would ask either her or Julia, "What's the matter, sweetheart? Don't you feel like being friendly?" Sometimes Julia did. Though she did her best to stay discreet about it, she was probably doing more business than she ever had before.

But the mere words *sweetheart* and *friendly,* spoken together or separately, were enough to freeze Nicole where she stood. Every time she heard them from a legionary, she would stop cold. Her eyes would ache with the effort of peering at a face that was interchangeable with any number of other black-bearded, big-nosed, olive-skinned faces. Was this the man who'd flung her down on her back in the alley and violated her with such efficiency, even aplomb?

She didn't know. She couldn't tell. Maybe the Roman who'd raped her had died five minutes later, killed by a spear in the gut. Maybe, on the other hand, he was sitting on a stool in the tavern this very moment, drinking a cup of cheap wine, eating bread and oil, and watching her backside. Maybe he was laughing, knowing she couldn't have recognized him in his armor and helmet. And maybe he was thinking, *That's the piece of ass I had the day we took this little rathole of a city. Not bad, for provincial meat. Maybe I'll have me another taste.*

One night after closing time, as she and Julia were finishing the last of the cleanup, she couldn't stand it anymore. She told Julia what she went through with every legionary who talked the way they seemed to make a point of talking. Julia paused in scrubbing down the last of the tables. "I do understand why you're worried about it," she said, "but I wouldn't be, if I were you. What happens when an army takes a city isn't likely to happen again once the city's safe and settled."

That made sense, as did most of what Julia said. She'd seen it with the Germans here. And even in the twentieth-century United States, *act of war* went into a lot of contracts and insurance policies alongside *act of God* as a justification for nonperformance.

Nicole said, "The top part of my mind understands what you're saying. It even thinks you're right. But down underneath—" She shuddered. "Every time I see a legionary, I want to go somewhere and hide—or else I want to kill him. Sometimes both at once."

"I think I know what you mean," Julia answered. "But you can't do that, you know. You have to go on with your life as best you can."

"I suppose so," Nicole said with a sigh. Again, Julia's advice was brisk and rational. If Nicole followed it, she'd be better off than if she ignored it. But, as she'd said, what the Roman soldier had done to her went down far below the part of her mind where rationality lived. A man had treated her as if she were nothing but a piece of meat with a handy hole. There was nothing reasonable or logical about her reaction to it.

She glanced behind the counter, toward the plaque of Liber and Libera. There sat the god and goddess, just as they had for so long on her nightstand back in West Hills. They weren't any more active than they'd been then, either, or any more helpful. They just . . . sat there.

What more do you want from me? she demanded silently. *What more can you want from me? Do you want me to die here? Is that what you're waiting for?*

The god and goddess were as uncommunicative as ever. It wasn't, now, that they didn't hear her, as when she'd had that other, now broken plaque, or that all the lines were busy. It was subtly different. They heard her, but, for whatever reason, they were choosing not to listen.

She trudged up to bed, and lay there in the light of the lamp she kept lit, now, all night long. The shutters were closed and tightly barred. It wasn't likely any man would come creeping in through the window, but she just felt more comfortable knowing that he'd have to break down the shutters if he tried it.

She lay in bed, and she kept up her barrage of prayer, pleading, whatever one wanted to call it. Wasn't enough enough? She'd worked her fingers to the bone, she'd been hungry, she'd slowly poisoned herself every time she ate or drank, she'd been sick and almost died; she'd gone through anything but painless dentistry and almost wished she'd been dead. She'd seen the city sacked, she'd seen cruelty to animals and cruelty to slaves and cruelty to women that was so automatic, people didn't even know they were being cruel. She'd been raped. And still she was trapped here.

And what did she have to put on the good side of the ledger? Titus Calidius Severus—yes, certainly. But the pestilence had killed him. And Marcus Aurelius. She'd never regret that she'd been able to meet him. There'd never been a man like him before, nor ever would be again.

She would have done anything this side of being raped again, to escape Carnuntum for California. Even that . . . Would she? Could she go through that, if it brought her home?

Yes. She could. It was the worst thing that had ever happened to her, the worst thing she could imagine. But if that was the price of her escape from the second century—she would pay it.

Marcus Aurelius proved to be a rare politician in yet another way: he kept his promises. As soon as he had Carnuntum in some sort of order, he took his army across the Danube to bring the war home to the Quadi and Marcomanni. Nicole stood on the riverbank with most of the rest of the population of the city, and cheered as the Roman flotilla crossed over to enemy territory. People all around her marveled over and over at the great size and magnificence of the force. She held her tongue. Maybe she'd seen *The Longest Day* too many times on late-night TV. To her eyes, the flotilla was neither large nor imposing. It seemed no more than a collection of barges and rafts, and rowboats that reminded her of oversized racing shells.

And when they were gone, when fires began to burn on the northern bank of the Danube, she felt more alone than ever. Some of her—*a conservative is a liberal who's just been mugged*—rejoiced that the Germans were getting what was coming to them. But she wished Marcus Aurelius had stayed in Carnuntum. She wouldn't have found it easy to get another audience with him, but the lure of intelligent conversation, even in the second century, had a powerful appeal.

And she felt less safe with the Roman Emperor out of the city. Though he and his army were gone, Carnuntum remained full of legionaries: garrison troops, reinforcements passing through on their way to the northern bank of the Danube, wounded men coming back from the other side of the river to recuperate. Medical care here was better than it was with the army in the field. Nicole pitied the soldiers in the forests, stalked by Germans who knew the land far better than they did, and no help for them if they were wounded but the roughest of field surgery.

"Those whoresons'll go hungry, that they will," a veteran said as he eased himself down onto a stool in the tavern. He'd come in with the help of a walking stick, limping on a bandaged leg. "We hit 'em as their grain was starting to get ripe, and we've taken a lot of it, and burned whatever we didn't take."

"Serves 'em right," Lucius said. In his biased opinion, legionaries were splendid creatures. He wore the wooden sword on his belt all the time now, and marched everywhere. Nicole was hard put to keep him from talking like a legionary, too, complete with the appalling vocabulary. She'd never told him what one of them had done to her. What point? He wouldn't understand.

"It certainly does serve the Germans right," Julia said. All the Roman soldiers in the tavern nodded. Most of them had their eyes on Julia. She could have said the sun rose in the afternoon, and the legionaries' heads—among other things—

would have bobbed up and down. *Men,* Nicole thought scornfully.

Every so often, a soldier would pat Julia or Nicole on the bottom, or try to pull one of them down onto his lap. Sometimes Julia would let a legionary get away with it, sometimes she wouldn't. Nicole never did. She developed a whole range of ways to get the message across.

"Arr!" a legionary roared when she spilled a bowl full of stewed parsnips and salt fish into his lap. He sprang to his feet and did an impromptu war dance. "That's *hot!* You did that on purpose, you miserable bitch."

"You'd better believe I did, you stinking bastard," Nicole snapped. "If your hands don't stay where they belong, your supper won't go where it belongs."

He had a sword at his belt. If his hand dropped to the hilt, she didn't know what she'd do. Scream and duck, probably— what other choice did she have? Instead, he cocked a big, hard-knuckled fist. "I ought to beat the crap out of you for that, lady," he growled, glaring from her to his dripping tunic and back again.

But one of the soldiers at another table said, "Oh, take it easy, Corvus. You grope a broad and she doesn't like it, shit like that's going to happen to you."

"Shit is right," the legionary with the Roman hands said. "Look at the mess she made of me." He swiped at his tunic, but only managed to smear it worse.

He didn't get much sympathy from any of his cohorts. They laughed and jeered: "A little lower and to the left, Corvus! My, what a fine, *artistic* outfit you've got on!"

He spun on his heel and stamped out of the tavern. Nicole, freed of his attentions, made sure she didn't keep too close a watch on the wine bill for the soldier who'd told Corvus off. If he got a free cup, or two, or three, then so be it.

It's worth it, she thought. Only afterwards did it occur to her that she'd fallen into a way of thinking she'd always deplored. She'd needed a man to protect her from another man. There wasn't any getting away from it—but neither did she have to accept it.

It was the way things were, here in Carnuntum.

Still, nobody tried to take her or Julia by force, not now. There was a line, and the Roman legionaries did keep to the polite side of it. What they reckoned polite, however, would have turned Navy fliers at a Tailhook convention into outraged feminists. Nicole never was sure they would stay on the polite side, either. That one bastard had gone from friendly smile to criminal assault in a few dizzying seconds. Any of these other legionaries was capable of the same thing, with just as little warning.

How would she ever be able to trust a man again? After what Frank had done to her, she hadn't had much use for men. Now . . . In the long run, killing any hope for that trust might have been the cruelest thing the rape had inflicted on her.

"They're swine, a lot of them," Julia agreed—Julia was always happy to agree about the shortcomings of men, of a good many of which she was likely to have more intimate knowledge than did Nicole. "They're swine, sure as sure, but what can you do about it?"

"There ought to be laws," Nicole said. In her time, there would be. They wouldn't be perfect. She'd had to come back here to discover that they would be pretty damned effective, all things considered.

"Laws?" Julia tossed her head just as she did when she turned down a proposition from a horny soldier. "Fat lot of good laws would do. Laws are for the rich. Laws are for men. Who makes laws? Rich men, that's who. You think they'll ever make them to help anybody else? Not likely."

Nicole took a deep breath. She'd have liked, very much, to tell Julia of the change in attitude that would come when education spread widely among both men and women. But what was the use? How was education supposed to spread when every single book had to be laboriously copied out by hand?

Just another machine, she would have thought if somebody at a party in Los Angeles had started going on and on about the printing press. In an age of desktop publishing and home copy machines and the Internet, it seemed antiquated, obsolete.

But next to a reed pen, it was a stunning advance in technology. And with technology came advances in thinking. The more people had access to books, the fewer were ignorant, and the less superstition there could be. And women could start making laws, or finding ways to assure that laws were made.

A better day was coming. In the time from which Nicole had chosen to flee, you could see its dawn on the horizon, bright enough to read a newspaper by. It was midnight here, darkest midnight. And there weren't any newspapers to read, either. Nicole had never thought of *USA Today* as an instrument of liberation, but it was. In what it signified, in what it implied: a literate population that wanted, and expected, to be fed the news in bite-sized pieces.

And she was eighteen hundred years away from it, and she couldn't go home. She had no one to blame for it but herself. She'd wished herself into this. No one else could wish her out.

The first tears caught her by surprise. Ever since she'd realized Carnuntum in the second century wasn't what she thought it would be—wasn't anything even close—she'd done her best to stay strong, to grit her teeth: even the one that had troubled her in this body, the one that had had to be pulled at such a cost in pain. She'd tried to roll with the punches, to keep from giving way to despair. Her best hadn't been too bad, either. When she'd cried before, she'd always done it in the privacy of her bedchamber—her miserable, bare, stinking bedchamber.

Now, as if at last a dam had broken, more and more tears followed those first two, and she couldn't seem to stop them. What would Julia think, watching her employer, her former owner, go to pieces right in front of her?

Julia, as far as Nicole could tell through tear-blurred vision, was astonished. "Mistress!" she said. "What on earth is the matter?"

"Everything," Nicole answered, which was true, comprehensive, and absolutely useless.

Julia got up, came around the table, and laid a hand on Nicole's shoulder. "Everybody feels that way now and again. You just have to get through the bad times and hope they'll be better tomorrow."

Again, that was good, sensible advice. Nicole knew as much. But she was, for the moment, something less than sensible. "No, it won't!" she cried. "It'll be just the same as it is today." She could conceive of no stronger condemnation of Carnuntum than that.

"Well—" Julia hesitated. "When things change, they usually get worse."

"How *could* they get worse?" Nicole demanded. "What could be worse than—this?" The sweep of her hand took it all in: stinking tavern, stinking city, stinking world.

But Julia had a ready answer: "Things were just—the way they always had been, till last year. Then the pestilence came, and that was worse, and then the Marcomanni and Quadi, and that was worse yet, and then the legions drove them back across the river, and that was better for the city, yes, but it was worse for you, wasn't it, on account of that one cursed soldier?"

She had to stop there, to draw a breath. Nicole fired back before she could go on: "Yes, and how many other bastards like him are there in the army that we'll never, ever hear about, either because the women they raped are too ashamed to come forward, or because the legionaries killed them after they were done screwing them?"

"Bound to be some," Julia agreed with chilling calm. "But that isn't what you asked, is it, Mistress? You asked how things could be worse. I told you."

Nicole shook her head so violently that the tears veered wide of their accustomed tracks. "That's just how things have got worse already. Not how they could get worse than they already are."

Julia blinked, then stared, then started to laugh. For sure she was amused, and a little taken aback. Maybe she was trying to jolly Nicole out of her gloom. "No wonder Marcus Aurelius listened to you when you complained about that legionary. You can split hairs just like a lawyer."

But Nicole was not about to be jollied. "And a whole fat lot of good that does me, too," she said.

"It got you ten *aurei*," Julia pointed out.

"Getting raped got me ten *aurei*," Nicole said with bitter, legalistic precision. "Believe me, I'd rather not have them. Besides," she added even more bitterly, "who ever heard of a lady lawyer? Who ever heard of a lady *anything* in Carnuntum?"

Julia sighed. "Well, Mistress, it doesn't look as if anything I can say will cheer you up. Do you want a jar or two of wine? Would that help?"

"No!" Nicole stamped her foot. If she'd been Kimberley, that sort of behavior would have earned her a time-out. If she'd been Lucius, it would have got her a whack on the fanny. Because she was an adult, she could do as she pleased—but nothing she could do here pleased her. There was nothing *to* do, except get drunk or get screwed. She wasn't in the mood to invite a hangover. The other . . . her whole body tightened, and her stomach clenched. If she tried very hard, she could remember that last, tender night with Titus Calidius Severus. But no matter how hard she tried to cling to it, the Roman legionary's hard hands and mocking voice ran over it and drowned it.

Julia had given up on her. "I'm going to bed," she said. "Why don't you do that, too? And hope—or pray to Liber and Libera, since you've become so fond of them—that you'll feel better in the morning." She turned away from Nicole and headed for the stairs. "Good night," she said over her shoulder.

That was as blunt, and as close to outright rude, as the freedwoman had ever dared be. It demonstrated rather forcibly how far Nicole had strayed from anything resembling decent manners.

She didn't care. She had perfectly good reason for being unreasonable. If Julia couldn't see that, then too bad for Julia.

As soon as Nicole had shaped the thought, she knew a stab—small but distinct—of guilt. Julia had been her best friend and ally in this whole ugly world. She didn't deserve to be treated this way. "Then she should try harder to understand how I feel," Nicole said to the air.

Nicole knew she should go up after Julia, and if not apologize, then at least try to smooth things over. But Julia was long gone.

Tomorrow would be soon enough. She'd wake again in Carnuntum as she always had. She'd do something to make it up to her freedwoman—something small but telling. She didn't know what. She couldn't, once she'd made herself think like a civilized adult, think much past the moment, or past the burden of this whole awful age.

She sniffled loudly, and blew her nose on her fingers. No Kleenex, no handkerchief. She grimaced and wiped her fingers on the rammed-earth floor, which at least had the virtue of being newly swept. She rubbed her hand on her tunic. A smear of dirt stained the faded wool. She brushed ineffectually at it. It was a losing battle. Every bit of it was the same: futile and hopeless.

She thrust herself to her feet, went over to the bar, opened the lid of one of the winejars and stared down into it. Plenty of wine in Carnuntum these days, with so many legionaries in town. The rich, fruity scent filled her nostrils. Even through the heaviness of tears, she grew a little dizzy with the fumes.

When she first came to Carnuntum, the very smell of wine gave her the horrors. Now she saw in it only oblivion, and blessed numbness.

And in the morning she'd wake up with a headache, and the world would still be too much with her, and what would she do after that? Drink another jar of wine? Her father had taken that road; she knew where it led. But now she understood why he'd done it. She even came close to forgiving—a thing she'd never imagined she'd do.

She reached for the dipper. Instead of pouring the wine into a cup, she poured out a puddle in front of Liber and

Libera. She let the last dribble of wine spill down the faces of the god and goddess—side by side, coequal, and maddeningly indifferent.

If you don't bet, you can't win. Who had said that? She heard it in her father's voice, a voice she'd spent most of her life trying to forget. *Imagining things,* she thought. And if she saw, or imagined she saw, a sparkle in Liber's limestone eyes, and in Libera's, surely it was but lamplight catching the wetness of the wine. There was no hope. There was no winning this game of gods and shifting time. The die, as the Romans liked to say, was cast. She couldn't go back. What she did now in front of the votive plaque, she did by force of habit, nothing more.

She dropped the dipper back in the winejar and covered it with the wooden lid. She blew out all the lamps but one, which she carried with her up the narrow rickety stairs.

Julia was already snoring. She had a clear conscience, or else she had no conscience at all. Or maybe she was just dead-tired from having worked sunup to sundown.

Nicole wasn't much better off herself. She went on stumbling feet into the bedchamber, set the lamp on a stool by the bed, and closed the door behind her and barred it. It wouldn't stop an intruder who really wanted in, but it would slow him down a little. That was as much as she could hope for in this world.

She lay down on the hard, lumpy, uncomfortable bed and blew out the lamp. Her nightly prayer was worn thin with use, the same plea as always, word for ineffectual word. She should give up on it. But she was too stubborn.

If you don't bet, you can't win. Was that her father's voice? Or another? Or even . . . two others? Or was it nothing but her imagination? She'd prayed this prayer for so long, and been ignored so completely. The god and goddess couldn't be turning toward her at last. Of course not. She was bound here forever, condemned to this primitive hell, for her great sin, the sin of hating the world she was born to.

* * *

On the votive plaque, Libera's limestone eyes turned to meet Liber's. The goddess' naked stone shoulders lifted in a shrug. The god's hands rose in a gesture that meant much the same. If there had been anyone in the tavern, he would have heard a pair of small, exasperated sighs. *Mortals,* Libera's shrug said. And Liber's gesture agreed: *Give them what they want, and watch them discover they never wanted it in the first place.* They were really too busy in this age of the world, to trouble themselves with this refugee from that dull and sterile age still so far in the future. Why on earth was she so desperate to go back there? There, she'd merely existed. Here, she'd *lived.* She'd known love and pain, sickness and war, danger and excitement and all the other things that made life worth living. How could she abandon them for a world in which nothing ever really happened?

Still, there was no doubt about it. She honestly wanted to go back. Now that Liber and Libera had turned their attention on this petitioner, every prayer she'd sent, every plea she'd raised, ran itself through their awareness. She'd been storming heaven, crying out to them to let her go.

She hadn't framed her prayers in the proper form. Some gods were particular about such things. But if Liber and Libera had been of that disposition, they would never have granted Nicole's first petition. Neither were her offerings of precisely the right sort. Still, they were offerings, and sincerely meant. No divinity could fail to be aware of that.

Once more the limestone gazes met. Liber's expression was wry. Libera's was exasperated. *Well; if this foolish woman thinks she can change her mind yet again, she'll just have to live with it.*

They nodded in complete agreement. For a moment, they basked in its glow, well and divinely content to have solved this niggling problem. A house spider, weaving its disorderly web on the ceiling above the plaque, froze for a moment at the brief flare of light. A moth started toward it, but it faded too quickly. The moth fluttered off aimlessly, its tiny spark of awareness barely impinging on the god and goddess' own. The tavern was dark again, and utterly still.

* * *

When Nicole lay down, she had feared she'd never fall asleep. But once she was as comfortable in that bed as she could be, she spiraled irresistibly down into the deeps of sleep. Worry faded, hopelessness sank out of sight. Dreams rose up around her, strange and yet familiar. A stair going down, a stair going up, round and round and round and . . .

21

NICOLE WOUND SLOWLY BACK toward consciousness. She lay with her eyes closed. The mattress under her was hard and lumpy and uncomfortable. A sigh, her first willed breath of the morning, hissed out through her nostrils. Another day in Carnuntum. Another day to get through without too many disasters. Another day to pray with all her heart that she could somehow, someday, without dying first, get out of there.

She rolled over. The mattress wasn't any more comfortable on her side than on her back. It crinkled and rustled, shifting under her, jabbing into a rib. What the—?

Her own mattress, such as it was, was stuffed with wool. It didn't rustle when she rolled over on it. Was she sick again? Had Julia or someone moved her onto a straw pallet while she was delirious?

She opened her eyes. She was looking out an open doorway into a hall.

But she'd shut the bedroom door the night before, shut and barred it, as she always had, ever since she came to Carnuntum.

The doorway was taller, wider. Its edges weren't indifferently whitewashed wood. They were—painted metal? And that shimmer close to her eyes, so close she had to shorten focus, almost cross her eyes, to see it, was a railing, bright silver—aluminum.

She was dreaming. She drew in another deep breath. And smelled—nothing. No city stink. No reek of shit and garbage and smoke and unwashed humanity. In their place was . . . not quite nothing, after all. A faint, tingling, half-unpleasant smell. Floor wax and—disinfectant? Yes.

She rolled onto her back again. This was a wonderful dream, realistic to the point of pain. She didn't ever want to wake up.

She drank in every detail. The mattress under her, with its crinkly plastic cover. The sheets, white and faintly rough on her skin, but smoother than anything she'd known in Carnuntum. The ceiling: no hand-planed boards fitted together unevenly, but acoustic tiles, each one exactly like the one beside it, machine-made, perfect; and a frosted-glass panel over a pair of fluorescent tubes. Their pale, purplish-white glow was the brightest thing she'd seen, except for the sun itself, in well over a year.

Nicole shivered. Part was wonder. Part was chill. She'd got used to being chilly in Carnuntum, where fires and braziers didn't do nearly enough to fight the cold.

She *was* in Carnuntum, then. As vivid as the dream was, as real as it felt, the cold was unmistakable.

Or else . . . it was air-conditioned to a fare-thee-well. She looked down at herself, at her body lying in the bed. Crisp white sheet, industrial strength. On top of it, a baby-blue blanket better dyed than the one she'd had in Carnuntum, but only about half as thick, and not wool, either. On top of the blanket, her arm.

Her arm. She needed a moment to recognize it. She hadn't seen it in a year and a half. Pale, on the fleshy side, manicured fingers—no, this wasn't Umma's work-hardened arm. This one, without question, belonged to Nicole Gunther-Perrin. It had something—probably the lead for an IV— taped to it. There were other discomforts, wires, leads taped here and there, connected to monitors that beeped and whis- led when she moved. And one niggle that mounted to annoyance, which felt like the worst bladder infection she'd ever had, and was—had to be—a catheter.

All of which meant, which had to mean—

She lifted the sheet and let out a startled snort of laughter. The white cotton gown, or front of a gown, was even less prepossessing than the grimy wool tunic in which she'd first awakened in Carnuntum. But the body it so halfheartedly concealed was *hers,* slightly flabby tummy, heavy thighs, and all.

A tall black woman in a nurse's uniform strode into the room, alerted probably by the changes in the monitors. At sight of Nicole half sitting up, staring at her, she stopped. Her eyes went wide. "You're awake," she said.

Nicole swallowed against a sudden and completely involuntary surge of terror. The same terror with which she'd faced every morning in Carnuntum. Would today be the day? Would she finally, somehow, blow her cover, and let the whole world know that she wasn't anything like what she seemed?

She took refuge, and warmth, in a small flash of temper at the nurse's belaboring of the obvious. *"Scilicet vigilans sum. Sed ubi sum?"*

The woman's eyes widened even further. "Say what, honey?" Under her breath, she muttered something that sounded like, *Possible brain damage?*

Nicole opened her mouth to snap at her: *What are you, deaf? Didn't you hear me?* But she stopped. She'd been speaking Latin. It had come out that way automatically, as it had for the past year and more. But the nurse had spoken plain, ordinary, wonderful, familiar English.

Nicole had to kink her brain a bit to remember how the words went. When they came back, the vowels were flavored still, a little, with Latin. "I said, of course I'm awake. But where? I know this is a hospital. Which one?" The last of it came out in the harsh Midwestern accent she'd tried to soften since she moved to California, but it was better than the mock-Italian of the first few words.

"West Hills Regional Medical Center, ma'am," the nurse

answered her. That was the closest hospital to Nicole's house; she'd taken Kimberley and Justin to the ER there a time or two.

The nurse frowned, wondering, maybe, if she'd really heard gibberish from this patient after all. "Do you know your name, ma'am?" she asked.

"Nicole Gunther-Perrin," Nicole said—biting down hard on the temptation to answer, *Umma*. She rattled off her address for good measure, with satisfaction entirely out of proportion to the achievement. Street number. Street name. Zip code. All the lovely architecture of the modern identity.

The nurse glanced at the card at the foot of the bed, then nodded. Nicole had got it right. She hadn't known she was holding her breath till she let it out. She asked the question she'd been working her way up to, the one that truly mattered: "How long have I been here?"

She held her breath again, consciously this time. She'd been in Carnuntum a year and a half. If she'd been gone so long, Kimberley would hardly know her. Justin—Justin wouldn't remember her at all. And the bills she would have run up! The law firm's medical coverage was more than decent, but a year and a half in the hospital? She'd be as broke as if she'd stayed in Carnuntum.

Or— She froze. What if it was even worse? What if she'd been in a coma for five years? Ten? Twenty? What if—?

The nurse cut off her thoughts before they spiraled into hysteria. "Honey," she said in her warm Southern drawl, "you've been here six days."

Nicole nearly collapsed with relief. She stiffened herself as best she could, and looked down at her hands—*her* hands. Yes, that was the nail polish she'd put on last, badly grown out and somewhat chipped, but definitely her own.

Six days. Thank God. No—thank gods.

Now the next question, much less painful, but she had to know. "How did I get here?"

But the nurse held up a hand. "You just stay right there, Ms. Gunther-Perrin. I'm going to call Dr. Feldman. She'll tell you everything you need to know. She'll want to run some tests on you, too, I bet."

"Wait!" Nicole cried. "Just let me ask about my childr—"

But the nurse had already whipped about and gone. Fled, Nicole almost thought, except that nurses were often like that. They didn't want to get involved, and for sure they didn't want to assume the responsibility of treating the patient like a human being instead of a piece of furniture.

She stayed where she was, drinking in the sight of that bare and sterile room. The other bed in it, nearer the window, was empty. Beyond it, through glass, actual glass without bubble or waver or crack, she saw blue, faintly hazy sky and the sun-baked, brush-covered hills that said, distinctly, *California*. They had never looked so good in all the years she'd lived there.

A different nurse, Hispanic or maybe Filipina, appeared in the doorway. She stared at Nicole. "Could you bring me this morning's *Times*, please?" Nicole asked, taking care to speak English.

The nurse looked more startled than ever, turned and fled. What was wrong with them all? Hadn't they ever had a person in a coma wake up before?

Probably not sitting up, talking, and demanding the latest news. Nicole lay back on the crackly bed. She couldn't exactly luxuriate in it, but it was *clean*. That alone was well worth wallowing in.

She was still not entirely sure she wasn't dreaming. Pinching herself didn't help. She could dream that sharp little pain, couldn't she?

Even the little things were wonderful. The blank face of the TV hung from the ceiling: she couldn't find the remote, and wasn't inclined to hunt for it. Just knowing it was there, somewhere, was enough. The IV on its rack, and the different monitors. All that plastic and metal and glass, none of it even imaginable to a mind raised in the second century.

She lay for a long while staring at the clock on the wall. What a marvel it was. Time measured out in hours and minutes and seconds. No need to rely on the sun, or to remember whether it was summer or winter, whether the hours were longer or shorter depending on the length of the day.

Forty-five minutes and sixteen seconds after the black nurse fled, a woman strode briskly into the room. She was short and very thin, the sort of person who crackles with nervous energy. Her hair was brown and wavy and beginning to go gray. She didn't seem to take much notice of it; it was pulled back in a bun, out of sight and out of mind. She wore little makeup—next to none by Roman standards. Under the white coat, she wore a plain linen shirtdress in a shade of beige that didn't exactly suit her. No jewelry, no wedding ring. Stethoscope around neck, clipboard in hand: she was as little like a Roman physician as it was possible to be.

Her voice was as brisk as her gait, firm, no nonsense in it. "Good morning," she said. "My name is Marcia Feldman. I'm a neurologist here at West Hills Medical. I understand you're back with us again?"

"I think so, yes," Nicole answered a little dryly.

"So," Dr. Feldman said. Her quick eyes had settled, fixed on Nicole's face. "Suppose you tell us what happened."

"You don't know?"

That was almost insolent. Dr. Feldman didn't bridle at it, but maybe she stiffened very slightly. "No," she said, "we don't. Anything you can tell us will help."

Nicole lowered her eyes, shamed into politeness. "I don't know. I went to bed—six days ago, the nurse said. Next I knew, I was here." That was the official story, the one she'd stick to. Anything else would get her the rubber room. "How did I get here? The nurse wouldn't tell me."

"Your older child came in to wake you. When she couldn't, she dialed nine-one-one." Dr. Feldman frowned at a line on her clipboard, and tapped her pen on it. "Could you give me the child's name, please?"

"Kimberley," Nicole answered promptly. "She's four. Her brother L—*Justin*—is two." Lucius was gone, eighteen hundred years dead. But he'd fathered someone who'd fathered or borne someone who . . . Nicole shut the thought away. She missed him suddenly, fiercely, and altogether unexpectedly. She—yes, she mourned him.

No. Think of the living children—of her own continuance, and her own future. Whom she hadn't seen in a year and a half. Whom suddenly she missed with a sensation like pain. "Are they all right?"

The doctor made a note on the chart, and cast a flicker of a smile at Nicole. "Yes, they're fine. They're with your ex-husband and his—girlfriend?"

Of course they would be. Nicole couldn't rise to anger at Dawn now, or at Frank for falling for her. "That's right," she said. "Thank you." Above all, she must convince this doctor that she was sane. She had to convince herself, too, if in a different way. Had she, could she have, dreamed it all in six days of coma?

Not now. Convince the doctor, then worry about the rest. "Doctor, what happened to me?"

"We're still trying to determine that. You've been completely unresponsive from the time you were admitted till a few minutes ago." Dr. Feldman tapped the chart again. "I understand you suffered a disappointment at work the day before your daughter discovered you unconscious and unrousable."

"Oh. The partnership." To Nicole, it felt as if it had happened a year and a half before, not a week. She'd been through so much since, and so much worse since, that, while it still rankled, it didn't seem so very catastrophic anymore. Then, perhaps more slowly than she should have, she got Dr. Feldman's drift. "You think I tried to kill myself."

Dr. Feldman nodded. "That certainly crossed my mind, yes. But I must say the evidence supports your denial. No drugs, no alcohol, no excess carbon monoxide, no gas. No trauma, either, nor any brain tumor or injury or aneurysm or anything of that sort. But no responses, not above the reflex level." She grinned suddenly, wryly. Nicole liked her just then, liked her a great deal. "Layman's language lets me put it best, Ms. Gunther-Perrin: the lights were on, but nobody was home."

You have no idea how true that is. It was just as in Carnuntum: no one else understood the irony of the situation, and no one could know. It was too crazy. "Wherever I was," she said, "I'm back. Have you ever seen a case like mine before?"

"Complete loss of consciousness without apparent causation?" Rather to Nicole's surprise, Dr. Feldman nodded. "Once, years ago," she said. "I was just completing my residency. We ran every possible test. We never did find out why he . . . just stopped. I kept track of him after I began my own practice. Two years later, he simply died. We never knew why, or how. It happened, that was all."

She didn't like it, either, though she clearly tried to be objective. No scientist was fond of uncertainties.

Nicole shivered. If she'd been killed in Carnuntum, what would have happened to her here? Would she have gone on indefinitely in that vegetative state?

And where was Umma? Had she been here? Had she awakened and, finding herself in a different body, in a world so strange as to be incomprehensible, simply gone catatonic?

It wasn't likely Nicole would ever learn the answer to that. She couldn't afford to dwell on it. Not in front of this dangerously perceptive woman. She put on a brisk front. "Since I am here and conscious again, how do I go about getting out?" she asked.

Dr. Feldman frowned. "You'll stay for at least another day or two. We'll want to run more tests on you, to make sure there is no risk of a recurrence."

"How do you propose to do that, when you don't know what caused the trouble in the first place?" Nicole wanted to know.

The doctor looked stubborn. Nicole's teeth clicked together. The last thing she needed was for Dr. Feldman to think she was questioning anybody's competence. And—if Nicole hadn't known what had happened to her, she would have been demanding tests, not complaining about them.

"All right," she said. "I suppose you'd better. But could I

have some breakfast first? And I'll want to get on the phone, let people know I'm okay."

"I don't see either of those things being a problem," Dr. Feldman said. She looked pleased with herself, now that she'd got her own way, and subtly reassured, now that Nicole was acting like what she was: a brisk young lawyer and single mother. "I'm going to order you the soft breakfast, since you've been on intravenous fluids since your admission. If you handle it without upset, you can have a normal lunch. Let me phone Dietary, and it should be up in half an hour or so. It's very good to have you back with us."

"It's very good to be back," Nicole said, most sincerely.

The neurologist prodded her and poked her and listened to her heart and checked her reflexes and peered into her eyes and nose and mouth and ears. "Everything seems to check out," she said, sounding almost reluctant to admit it. "But if everything is as normal as it looks, what happened to you?"

"I haven't the faintest idea," Nicole said. Breakfast came up just then, right on the half-hour: oatmeal, a medium-boiled egg, and a square of blue hospital gelatin, industrial strength like the sheets, thicker and tougher than she would ever have made at home. Nicole had no idea what flavor it was supposed to be. She didn't care. She inhaled it. She inhaled every scrap on that white plastic plate, and would have inhaled the plate if she could have got away with it. There was only one bobble: forgetting, and trying to eat with her fingers. She covered for it quickly, picked up the spoon and dove into the oatmeal.

Dr. Feldman watched her with a good measure of bemusement. "How does that feel?" she asked.

"Wonderful!" she answered, wiping her mouth—on the napkin, at the last instant, and not on her arm. She felt like asking for another tray just like this one. But she didn't think Dr. Feldman would let her have it. She'd been this hungry in Carnuntum, and more. She kept quiet.

Dr. Feldman said, "I'm going to set up another CAT scan and MRI and some more diagnostic procedures for you, Ms.

Gunther-Perrin. While I'm doing that, you can go ahead and use the telephone."

In the way doctors have, she spoke as if she were granting a great boon. Which she was. She had no idea how great it was. She took it all, all the technology, the tests, the telephone, completely for granted. Nicole didn't, not anymore. How long would it be, she wondered, before the novelty palled?

Dr. Feldman went out as she'd come in, brisk, bright, and competent. With a sigh of pure pleasure, Nicole picked up the phone. Its smooth plastic was cool in her hand, its shape familiar, its weight, the buzz of the dial tone as she held it to her ear.

She sat for a long while with the receiver to her ear. Number—what was the number? She held down panic. It was somewhere in her mind, unused, filed away. But she hadn't forgotten it. Of course she hadn't.

There. There it was, right in her fingertips. She punched in the numbers, and held her breath. If she'd remembered it wrong, or forgotten it altogether, and had to ask—they'd start doubting her sanity again. She couldn't have that. She'd never slipped up enough to get in real trouble, back in Carnuntum. There was no way she was going to slip up here.

The first ring startled her half out of her skin. Her fingers clenched on the receiver before she dropped it.

The ringing went on. After the fourth ring, the answering machine would pick up. But just at the end of number four, the ring broke off. A breathless female voice said, "Hello?"

Nicole's mouth twisted. She'd been expecting Frank, if she didn't just get the machine. But of course it would be Dawn.

Well, no help for it. "Dawn?" she said. "Dawn, this is Nicole. I'm calling from the hospital."

"Nicole!" Of all the things Nicole had expected, she hadn't expected this rush of gratitude and relief. "I'm *so* glad to hear your voice. How *are* you?"

She really did sound glad, and not just, or not entirely,

because if Nicole was awake and making sense, it got her off the hook with the kids. A homewrecker without a mean bone in her body? A girlfriend who honestly cared that the first wife was all right? Nicole would have laughed at the thought, six days or a year and a half or eighteen centuries ago.

Actually, she sounded a great deal like Julia. The same kind of voice, breathy and light, the kind men went for and women tended to regard with disgust. A Marilyn Monroe sort of voice. The sound of it stabbed Nicole with guilt so sudden she almost gasped. She'd never apologize to Julia now for being so childishly unreasonable. She'd never make it up to Julia. Julia was lost at the other end of time.

That stab of guilt was like a shaft of sun in a dark place. She could see something she'd never have seen before, or wanted to see. Julia had been, not to put too fine a point on it, a slut, but she'd never been either stupid or mean. And neither, Nicole admitted to herself, was Dawn.

She'd think the rest of it through later, when she wasn't supposed to be holding up one end of a tense and rather awkward phone conversation. "I'm all right," she said. "At least I think I am. Nobody has a clue as to what happened to me." *Except me.* But she wouldn't say that. "How are the kids?"

"They're doing all right," Dawn answered. "They miss you. They keep asking when you'll be coming back. I haven't known what to tell them."

"If I check out all right, it'll be another day or two," Nicole said. An entirely different and even more powerful wave of guilt washed over her. She'd done far worse than let her last words to Julia be the end of a quarrel. She'd abandoned her life, her family, her kids—No time now. She had to be glad that she'd only been gone six days. Still, she said something she never would have said if she'd truly been gone for less than a week: "I'm sorry I messed up your trip."

Yes, she was having trouble working up a good head of loathing for Dawn. Perspective? Maybe just distance? It just didn't seem to matter as much as it used to. After war, plague, and famine, a little adultery seemed almost unremarkable.

"Don't worry about our trip," Dawn said cheerfully, as unperturbed by the ways of the world as ever. "We'll get away again soon." Maybe, Nicole reflected, that talent for letting things be explained how she put up with Frank. *Why* she did was another question, but Nicole wasn't likely to get an answer for that.

And speaking of Frank . . . She braced herself. "Let me talk to Frank, would you please?"

"Why, sure," Dawn said. Her voice faded as if she'd turned away from the phone. "Frank? It's your ex. She's awake."

And, fainter yet, a male voice, with sarcasm that came through loud and clear: "I never would have guessed."

Nicole's own thoughts were running on much too similar lines. *If I weren't awake, would I have called?* She caught herself with a snap. She *wasn't* that much like Frank. Was she?

Then his voice came on the line, with the sarcasm carefully screened out of it. "Nicole? How are you doing?" Was he actually diffident, or was he just playing at it?

She decided to play it calm, be polite, and see if that shocked him. "I think I'm all right," she said. "I woke up this morning, that's all, just as I always have." *At this end of time, that is.* "The doctor's still trying to figure out what happened."

"Yeah, I talked with the neurologist," Frank said in that faintly snotty tone that always pissed her off. If for any reason he'd been unsure of himself, he'd got his equilibrium back. "No, she has no idea what it was. When I got the call in Cancún, I thought you were so pissed at me, you'd OD'ed on pills just to screw up my vacation. But she says you didn't. So you didn't. I'm glad you're feeling better."

Good old Frank, just as charming as ever, and just as convinced the world revolved around him. It was like him to make sure she knew what he'd thought, but it was also like him to believe Dr. Feldman when she'd told him it wasn't so. Nicole had to give him that much.

Now, if he'd just give her what she had coming to her . . . But this was not the time. It would come, she promised herself, but not yet. First things first.

"Let me talk to the kids," she said. "I want them to know I'm all right."

"I'll get them," Frank said. "I haven't known what to tell them. I've said you're sick, that's all, and I hoped you'd be well soon."

That was adequate, Nicole thought. She started to say something more, it didn't matter what—*Good-bye* or *Thanks* or *Just put the kids on, will you?* But before she could begin, Kimberley's voice shrieked in her ear: *"Mommy!"* And, close enough behind it to make it a chorus: *"Mommy-mommy-mommy!"* Justin must have been swinging on the phone cord, from the way his voice came and went.

Telephone conversations with preschoolers range from incoherent to downright surreal, but Nicole managed to assure both Kimberley and Justin—fighting at top volume over who got the phone—that she loved them, that she was feeling better, and that she would see them soon. Her throat kept locking up, which was annoying. As fond as she'd become of Lucius and Aurelia, as much as she'd mourned Aurelia's death, these were *her* babies. *Her* children. If she'd had any chance at all of getting away with it, she'd have left the hospital right then and there, and gone straight home, and hugged them both so tight they squealed in protest. Even their shrieking, which she'd done her best to train out of them—God, she hated screaming kids—was a blessed thing, because it was theirs.

She hated to let them go, but they were getting overexcited. She heard Dawn round them up, a soft murmur that sounded more than ever like Julia taking Lucius and Aurelia in hand. Then Frank came on the line. "How soon are they letting you out?" he demanded.

Trust Frank not to miss the essentials. "Another day or two," she answered, "if everything looks good." Something tugged at her awareness. Something she should be remembering. Some crucial thing about the kids.

Yes. That awful day on top of too many awful days, when she'd prayed to Liber and Libera, and to her lasting amazement, been answered, there'd been one crisis that she couldn't let slip from her mind. "I'm going to have to look for a new daycare provider," she said.

"I know," he said. "I've heard all about Josefina—the good, the bad, and the ugly. I've been looking for someone to replace her."

"You have?" Nicole was flat astonished. Frank, exerting himself for anything of that relentlessly mundane sort?

Well. Frank was an asshole, but he wasn't stupid. If Nicole was going to be incapacitated for some unspecified time, he'd want to get on with his life. He'd been perfectly happy to kick back and let her handle the kids. If they were suddenly thrown into his lap—*cold-bloodedly efficient* was the term that came to mind. "Any luck finding a new provider?" she asked.

"There's this preschool over in Tarzana," he said. "I was going to take them over this morning, see how they liked it, see how Dawn and I like the setup," he said. "Woodcrest, that's its name."

"I've heard of it," Nicole said dryly. "It's supposed to be good. It's not cheap."

"So? What is, these days?"

Frank was perfectly willing to spend the money when it was his convenience that was at stake. But would he pay child support while the kids were in Nicole's custody?

Stupid question. Nicole would deal with it in due course. Los Angeles had ways and means that had never been dreamt of in Carnuntum, if she only had the will to use them. She'd let things slide too long. It was time to start cracking the whip.

But not just this minute. "Go ahead and take the kids over to Woodcrest," she said, not so warmly she'd alarm him into wondering what she was up to, but not as rudely as she could have, either. "Tell me what you think of the place. Can you bring the children by to see me tonight?"

"I'll take the kids to the school," he said, "but I can't bring them to you. Hospital rules. No one under six anywhere but in Maternity. That's hard and fast. We already tried it."

"Oh, did you?" Careful; don't sound too skeptical. Maybe he had. In which case, she had to give him credit.

Push on. Focus on realities, the daily details, the things she'd never needed to think about while she was a tavern-keeper in Carnuntum. "Look, if you get a chance, will you park my car in the hospital lot? Bring my purse, too, and some clothes. I'll drive myself home."

"I'll take care of that," he said. She'd expected he would. It saved him trouble, and saved him having to deal with her face to face. It was cold and rather inconsiderate on the face of it, but it was just as she preferred it. All in all, a decent way of arranging things.

"One last thing," she said. "Did you call any of the family?"

"I called your mother," he said. "She'd have come out here, but one of your sisters is pregnant again, and her oldest one needs new braces, and I forget what else—your mother does go on a bit. She didn't offer to take the kids."

Nicole suppressed a sigh. Her mother was preferable to Atpomara by a wide margin, but it had been clear ever since Nicole left Indiana for Los Angeles, and particularly since the divorce, that charity began closer to home. Nicole's sisters had stayed right in the city, married a nice Indiana boy and a nice Polish boy, and proceeded to populate the world with little Johnsons and Kursinskis. They needed a grandmother more, it had been implied, than Nicole's infant Angelenos.

Even a coma hadn't been enough to get her mother out of Indiana. If she'd died—would that have done it?

There was absolutely no point in dwelling on it. This was the life Nicole had made for herself. Some of it she'd chosen, some had been forced on her. Now more than ever, she appreciated both the cost and the rewards.

Frank would never understand. Nobody would. But that didn't matter, not really. She was home. *That* was what mattered.

"Thanks for everything," she said. *Keep it polite, keep him off balance, till you drop the hammer.* "I have to go now. Give the kids a kiss for me."

"I'll do that," Frank said. "Take care of yourself."

Why, she thought, Frank was trying, too. Not too hard, but harder than she remembered. Maybe it took a solid scare, and six days of unmitigated parenthood, to teach him a little basic civility.

Frank had hung up without giving her a chance to say good-bye—which was more his usual style. Nicole shrugged and cut the connection at her end. She sat with her finger on the button. The dial tone sang in her ear.

The only number from the firm of Rosenthal, Gallagher, Kaplan, Jeter, Gonzalez & Feng she could remember was her own, and she wasn't too sure about that. But when she dialed, hesitating on the third digit—was it four or five? Oh, hell, five—it was picked up on the second ring. And there was her secretary's voice, crisper on the phone than in person, but still unmistakable: "Ms. Gunther-Perrin's office."

"Cyndi," Nicole said, not taking much trouble to hide how glad she was to hear that voice.

"Nicole!" Cyndi's exclamation was more heartfelt than professional. It made Nicole feel wonderful.

There were other people in the background, too, a babble of questions, exclamations, even a muted cheer. That wasn't for Nicole, surely. Someone must have won the betting pool on whatever sport was in season this week.

Cyndi pressed on through the babble. "Nicole! How are you? What happened?" She hesitated slightly there. Was she wondering, as Frank had, if Nicole had attempted suicide?

Maybe Nicole had, in a way, not really knowing she was doing it. She gave Cyndi the edited, and official, version: "I don't know what happened. Neither do the doctors. I went to sleep, I woke up six days later in a hospital bed, and I feel fine. All the tests are negative. They'll do some more, now that I'm awake. If those are normal, they'll let me go home."

"They couldn't find *anything?*" Cyndi sounded as if she couldn't believe it. It wasn't meant for an insult, or to imply anything about Nicole's mental state. Not at all. People in this place and time trusted medical science. They expected it to work, and they were astonished when it didn't.

How different from Carnuntum. How very, very different.

Nicole found that she was running her tongue over her teeth. The whole mouthful, filled, capped, crowned, and not a single gap or twinge of pain. "They didn't find a thing," she said.

"That's terrific," Cyndi said, and relayed the news to the noisy crowd that, now Nicole stopped to listen, must be clumped around the desk. When she spoke again into the receiver, she didn't even bother to lower her voice. "I just want you to know, Ms. Gunther-Perrin, there's been a lot—I mean a *lot*—of rumbling in the undergrowth about the way you got passed over for partner."

"Has there?" Nicole said. At the time, it had felt like the end of the world—just like that, she remembered. That she'd still had a job as a salaried employee had given her no comfort at all.

After a year and a half as a tavernkeeper in Carnuntum, she didn't find the job, even the dead-end, no-future thing that it was, anywhere near so intolerable. Her basis of comparison had changed. And because it had been a year and a half in a world so alien it might as well have been another planet, rather than six days of oblivion, she could stand apart from the reality of it. The pain was gone, scabbed over long ago, and long since healed. She barely even felt the scar.

Just a second or two later than she should have, she said, "So people care what happened to me. I had no idea."

"They do care," Cyndi said. "A lot of people are upset about it."

They had to be, if she'd say so in front of a crowd of people. Nicole needed to think about that; to fit it into her view of the world. She'd been so alone the night before she woke up in Carnuntum. Or she thought she had been. No friends, no family but a couple of sick kids; no daycare for the kids, a bastard of an ex cavorting in Cancún with his late-model floozy. It seemed she had friends, maybe even a few she hadn't known she had.

She was sniffling again, as she had been when she talked to the kids. She managed to speak through it. "I'll be back as soon as the doctor says I can. I don't even want to think what my desk must look like."

"It's not really so bad," Cyndi said. "Everybody's been chipping in when they have the chance. There are things that need doing, but you'll be able to catch up. You just take it easy till you're all better."

A small jab of paranoia caught her by surprise. *Easing me out? Giving me the kiss-off? Is that what's happening?*

No. This was honest goodwill. "Thank you," Nicole said, and she meant it. "I'll be in as soon as I can. Say hello to everybody, will you?"

"Everybody says hello to you," Cyndi replied. "You take care of yourself, all right? We want you back."

Cyndi didn't want to hang up. Nicole was touched, but there were other calls she had to make while she still had the stamina, and before she got much hungrier. She eased Cyndi off the line with the same trained smoothness she'd use on a client, and hung up. She needed to pause, to get her breath a bit. Her mind was wide awake, but her body had lain in a coma for six days. It needed to rest.

She lay back, gazing out across the empty bed to the window, to the clear California sky and the dry brown hills. This was home. It wasn't perfect, but it wasn't terrible, either. She knew what terrible was, now.

She ran fingers through her hair. It felt oily, stringy, but it was as clean as Umma's had ever been. And no lice. Not one single itching, crawling creature. By God, she was *clean.*

The ring of the phone startled her, and sent the heart monitor jumping. She needed a moment to get herself together, and two more rings, before she reached for the receiver.

"Nicole?" a man's voice said. "It's Gary."

"Gary," she said, groping for a split second. "Gary, hello! It didn't take you long to get my number."

"I already had it," Gary Ogarkov said. "I've been calling every day, trying to get someone to tell me how you are. Do you know what they said? *Stable,* they said. Christ, when you're dead you're stable!"

Nicole couldn't help but laugh. "Gary, that was really nice of you. But—"

He kept right on, as if she hadn't spoken: "I want you to know, I thought Mr. Rosenthal was going to make us both partners. He ripped you off. I've been saying so, too, to everybody who'll listen."

But he hadn't resigned his own partnership, to open it to Nicole. She'd have been unbearably revolted about that, once. Now she understood. She wouldn't have given it up, either. She didn't know that she'd have had the guts to rock the boat that much, either, not that early in a partnership. "I appreciate that," she said. "Believe me."

"It was the least I could do," Ogarkov said. By Jupiter, Nicole thought: Gary had a conscience. Who'd have thought it?

When he'd hung up, she paused again, but only briefly. Then she called her mother in Indiana. She got the machine, as she'd expected. She left a message: "Mom, it's Nicole. I'm awake, I'm all right. Doctors don't know what happened. I'll be home in a couple of days." And, after a second's pause: "Love you."

By now it sounded pat, the words well worn with use, as if she'd been a well-coached witness in court. And yet, even as the words unrolled themselves, she wondered. What if it was all nonsense? What if she'd imagined the whole thing, Liber and Libera, Carnuntum, the people, the privations, the whole smelly, verminous world? It was crazy to think she'd traveled back in time down the helix of her own DNA, and climbed back up along it, to wake in this hospital bed.

And yet, she thought. There was a way to tell. If they ever got around to letting her go . . .

*   *   *

She roused herself with a start. A young man in a white coat—a lab tech, she guessed—stood smiling down at her. He had a syringe in his hand, with a needle that looked, from her perspective, as long as her arm. "Hello," he said cheerily. "My name is Roberto. I'm your vampire for this morning."

While she gaped at him, he got a grip on her arm, found the vein with practiced ease, slipped the needle in and took what he needed. He was good: she barely felt it. He slapped on a patch of gauze, secured it with adhesive tape—marvels of modern technology, both of them—and went on his way.

Dr. Feldman must have passed him in the hall: she came in as soon as he'd gone out. A nurse followed her, pushing a wheelchair. "Here you go," the doctor said. "We're going to take you downstairs and see if we can figure out what's going on with you."

Nicole gritted her teeth on any number of fierce rejoinders. The nurse unhooked her from her banks of monitors, and— thank God—removed the catheter, and eased her into the wheelchair. She didn't need that, but she put up with it. If they wanted to think her weak, let them. Hospital personnel had a way of reducing patients to dependent children in any case.

Dependent children didn't have to sign endless consent forms. Nicole did, dutifully; taking time to skim the wording, as a good lawyer should, before she signed her name to it. She wasn't averse to tests, not in the slightest. She was as eager as the doctor to know if somehow her brains had fried.

They ran an ultrasound. They took a series of ordinary X-rays. Dr. Feldman did a spinal tap—that hurt. It hurt rather badly, but never as badly as having her tooth pulled without anesthetic. She had to hold still, that was the hardest part. But she did it.

They ran a CAT scan, which was claustrophobic, and an MRI, which was both claustrophobic and noisy. It was much like going through a car wash, except for the water, and the hot wax afterwards.

Being silly helped. So did just being—being here, in this world and time, where pain was seldom worse than a brief discomfort, and where everything was so very clean.

It was the middle of the afternoon before she got back to her room. She was exhausted, and she was starving. It was well past the lunch hour, but Dr. Feldman was ready for that: she called Dietary, and the kitchen sent up a tuna-salad sandwich, a plate of orange heavy-duty Jell-O, and an oversized chocolate-chip cookie. The bread was soft and wonderfully free from grit, though it didn't have a tenth the flavor of her own baking in Carnuntum—but Umma's shoulder and elbow had ached endlessly from working the quern.

But even better than the bread was the cookie. Until she bit into what was, really, an indifferently good cookie grudgingly flecked with poor-quality chocolate, she'd forgotten just how much she missed that dark sweetness. No chocolate in Carnuntum. No food of the gods. Even knowing how much better it could be, she savored each bite. God, it was good.

When she'd eaten her lunch in blissful solitude, she hunted around for the remote and turned on the TV news. There was plenty of local crime, but there were also New York and Moscow and Angola and the Persian Gulf, right in the room with her. She could find out what was going on in any of those places more readily than she could have learned what was happening in Vindobona, twenty miles up the Danube from Carnuntum. What a wonder of a world this was!

She reined herself in before she got too giddy. She should calm down or she'd get into trouble, but it was rather wonderful to be so very much aware of all the things she'd taken for granted. It made her feel more alive; more *in* the world.

She was still thinking about half in Latin, till she ran into concepts that needed English. Or she thought it was Latin. If she'd hallucinated a year and a half in Carnuntum, she could just as easily have hallucinated a language to go with it. She'd been at a party once, one of Frank's academic mill-and-swills, in which she'd overheard one of the guests telling another about a colleague who'd apparently gone around the bend: "He claims he's been channeling one of Alexander the Great's historians—in Greek, no less."

"And is it real Greek?" the other had asked.

"Well," said the first with a touch of scorn, "it is Greek—but it's much too archaic for the place and the time."

At the time she'd laughed, thinking how very academic that conversation was. They weren't disturbed by the channeling, but channeling in too archaic a dialect—that was very bad form.

Now she wondered. What if . . . ?

No. It was preposterous. And yet . . .

Somewhere between the international scene and the financial report, a nurse brought in a plastic bag filled with clothes. Frank hadn't wasted any time sending them. Neither had he taken the time to come up and visit. He wasn't *that* considerate.

Then again, maybe he was. They couldn't stay in the same room without squabbling. It was a great deal easier on her nerves if he stayed in his place and she stayed in hers.

The day could have dragged, but she had the TV and the remote, and she entertained herself with relentless channel-surfing. Soap operas, game shows, movies old and almost new, kids' programming, women's programming, talk shows, reality shows, the entertainment report, the news, sports, Discover, PBS, the Learning Channel . . . She was as drunk on images as she'd once been on wine.

Dinner came on time: frozen fried chicken, frozen peas, mashed potatoes with the same gluey gravy she remembered from her high-school cafeteria, and in place of tough Jell-O in colors never seen in nature, a scoop of gelatinous tapioca pudding. The novelty *was* wearing off: she was starting to think that hospital cuisine left a bit to be desired. But the styrofoam cup held real coffee. How on earth had they let *that* through Dietary?

She didn't care how, just that it was there. She sighed with pleasure over every lukewarm sip.

Just about two sips from the bottom of the cup, Dr. Feldman strode into the room, not quite so springily as she had in the morning. Her face wore a distinctly sour expression.

She didn't linger long in small talk of the good-evening-how-are-you? variety. "I've been going over your new tests," she said.

Nicole's heart thudded. She was glad the monitor was disconnected: it would have brought a nurse at the run. "Yes?" she prompted when the doctor didn't go on.

"And," Dr. Feldman said, looking more sour still, "as far as they go, you seem to be a normal, healthy specimen. Except that normal, healthy specimens aren't in the habit of lapsing into six-day comas. Something went wrong in there. We just can't determine what it was."

"But I'm all right now?" Nicole asked.

"So far as we can determine, yes." Dr. Feldman didn't sound happy at all.

Nicole pounced on the important thing. "Then will you let me go home tomorrow?"

The doctor frowned. "If your insurance will cover it, I'd really like to keep you here for another day of observation. You wouldn't want to lose consciousness again as you were driving home, would you?"

"No," Nicole said. She wasn't enthusiastic about going to sleep, either. She'd gone up to her bedchamber in Carnuntum every night hoping, praying, she would wake up in L.A. If she fell asleep here, would she wake up in Carnuntum again? Had that journey been real, and was this the hallucination?

She was going to go crazy unless she could get an answer to that. But this neurologist all too obviously, and all too unhappily, didn't have one.

Best to do as she was told. If she didn't wake up in the second century, the hospital wasn't so bad a place. And if she didn't wake up at all . . .

"My insurance will cover an extra day," she said.

"Good," Dr. Feldman said. "That's wise. And while you're resting, I'll see if I can come up with more tests for you. I do want to get to the bottom of this if I possibly can."

"I understand," Nicole said.

The doctor left, still frowning, still obviously unhappy to have no answers. Nor was Nicole about to give her any, even if she'd had one that a modern medical scientist would accept.

The evening wound down between primetime television and the ringing of the telephone. Her mother called from Bloomington, with interpolations from the elder of her two sisters and the kids. Nicole gave them an expanded version of the official story, and got the expected hammering of questions for which she had no credible answers. She might still have been fending off "But *why? Why* were you out like that for a week? Don't tell me the doctor doesn't know! So get a new doctor!" right through the change of nursing shifts at eleven o'clock, and never mind what time it was in Indiana, if a nurse hadn't come in to take her pulse and temperature and meddle generally with her arrangements.

After the nurse went to harass the next patient, Nicole took refuge in television. That was what it was, a refuge. She'd fled to it every night when she came home from the office, used it as a pacifier to wind down from the stress of the day. And yet, if you'd asked her what she thought of television, she'd have come out with a whole canned rant against it, complete with assertion that she would never, no, never, use it as a babysitter for her children.

And all the while they'd be parked in front of it while she got her head together after a hard day at the firm, and when she'd put them to bed, she'd park there herself till she fell asleep. The Emperor, she had to admit, had no clothes.

And yet, she thought, she'd met an Emperor, and he most definitely was not blind to his own faults. Quite the opposite: he'd gone in search of them so that he could get rid of them.

Of all the things she'd found in the second century, Marcus Aurelius was the one the twentieth couldn't match. If he turned out to be a dream or a hallucination, she'd be more than sorry. The world was a better place, by a little, for that he'd been in it.

At eleven o'clock, a nurse marched in and turned off the television. "We do have to get some rest," he said primly.

What do you mean, we? Nicole refrained from saying. She was wide awake and in fine shape. And she did not want to sleep. She did not want to wake in that tavern in Carnuntum.

The nurse couldn't know that, nor would he have cared if he had. He turned out the light in the room and laid the bed down flat. His air of superior virtue made Nicole want to kick him.

She lay in the not-quite-dark, dim-lit by the lights in the hallway and the flicker of the heart monitor that the nurse had hooked up again—*Making sure I don't sit up and turn the TV back on,* she thought sourly. The mattress was not what she'd have called comfortable, and yet it was thicker and softer than the one she'd slept on above the tavern.

They'd told her she'd been asleep six days. It *was* sleep, the doctors had admitted grudgingly, though right on the edge of true coma. No dreams. She'd asked. She'd stayed in the deepest level of sleep throughout. "As if there was nobody home," one of the nurses had said between tests. Dr. Feldman had said the same thing.

So she didn't need more sleep now, did she? And she'd had coffee with dinner. She would stay awake. She would. Even if she yawned. Even if . . .

Nicole's dreams were muddy, confused. Sometimes she was in Carnuntum, but no one could see or hear her; she ran here and there, trying to get Julia to listen, then Gaius Calidius Severus, then—and by this she knew it was a dream—Titus Calidius Severus. He smiled at her and said, "Welcome back among the dead, Umma."

Then she was in West Hills, trying to get a much younger Justin to eat his prunes, but Kimberley kept tugging at her to go and feed the "other baby," except it wasn't a baby, it was Lucius in a blue bunny bib and a toga.

She woke with a start, suddenly and fully aware, and grimly determined not to open her eyes. There was light beyond her eyelids, she couldn't escape that. And—she breathed deep. Nothing. No complex reek of Roman city.

Her eyes opened. She was in West Hills Medical Center, in the bed in which she'd fallen asleep. Had anyone ever been so happy to wake up in a hospital?

Reality came crashing in as soon as she sat up and set the heart monitor off again. There was breakfast, sponge-bath—though she could perfectly well have bathed herself, they weren't letting her—and, when she was cleaner, even by this sketchy method, than she had been in a year and a half in Carnuntum, a nurse with the stack of paperwork. The deductibles were going to strain her to the limit, but just then she didn't care. She'd manage. And Frank, she thought with a slow smile, was going to help. It was time he paid up.

After paperwork came more tests, and more frustration for Dr. Feldman. There wasn't one anomalous thing anywhere, no matter how often she repeated her tests, or how many variations she tried. At last she flung up her hands and sent Nicole back to her room. "Ms. Gunther-Perrin," she said as the nurse settled Nicole in the obligatory and unnecessary wheelchair, "even now we have much less knowledge of the brain and its functions than I wish we did."

What about the functions of the brain under the influence of two Roman gods? Nicole thought. But she nodded, and held her tongue.

That afternoon, faced with a wasteland of TV soap operas, Nicole determined to give herself a gift she'd yearned for since the day she arrived in Carnuntum. After consulting with Dr. Feldman, the nurses let her get away with it.

She took a long, hot, wonderful shower. With soap. And shampoo. And towels that, while not exactly luxurious, were thick enough and soft enough to be a pleasure on her clean skin. It was an almost orgasmic delight to be so clean. Her body still felt strange, as if it didn't quite fit. Its skin was too pale, its middle too thick and soft. And yet there wasn't a louse or a fleabite on it. For that alone she loved it.

Then, when she'd showered, she rummaged in the bag Frank had sent and found the little blow dryer she'd bought a long time ago for traveling—and a small makeup kit that had to be Dawn's contribution; she couldn't imagine Frank thinking of such a thing.

It was a brand-new Nicole Gunther-Perrin who came out of the steamy bathroom and settled again in the bed. She was more than ready for her dinner. And when, after the tray had been taken away, Dr. Feldman appeared in the doorway, Nicole greeted her almost happily.

The doctor's expression was as sour as ever. She wasn't at all pleased to say, "I can't see any valid medical reason for keeping you here past tomorrow morning. You are, as far as any test can determine, perfectly normal and healthy. I wish I could tell you if your syndrome will recur, but I can't."

Nicole bit her tongue. She could guarantee a longer stay by telling the doctor exactly what, as far as she could tell, had happened to her during those six days. For that matter, she could talk herself right into a nice long stay in a padded cell.

No, thank you. "We'll just have to hope it was a one-time thing, won't we?" she said.

"Hope is just about as much as we've got," Dr. Feldman said. "I'd like to see you in my office next week—it's right across the street." She handed Nicole a business card. "Call and make an appointment, and I'll see you then."

"I'll do that," Nicole said. She meant it. If, as she was increasingly convinced, she really had traveled in time by the offices of a pair of antique gods, it wasn't bloody likely she'd ever do it again. But if it kept the doctor happy, and if it made her look like a normal, baffled, honestly concerned victim of an unknown syndrome, then she'd do it and welcome it.

"Please do come and see me," the doctor said. "Just because I can't find anything now doesn't mean nothing happened. People don't lose consciousness for six days for no reason at all."

"Yes," Nicole said. "I understand. It's like when the car is acting up, and you take it to the mechanic and it's working just fine."

"Just like that," Dr. Feldman said with the flicker of a smile.

They parted on good terms, all things considered. Nicole settled down in front of the TV feeling surprisingly unsettled.

She was sure—but she wasn't. Before she went home, she decided, she was going to make a stop. If she turned out to be wrong . . . If she turned out to be wrong, she'd need that appointment with the neurologist. And she'd be just as eager as Dr. Feldman to get to the bottom of whatever had happened.

NICOLE GOT HER WALKING papers with a breakfast of scrambled powdered eggs, rubbery toast, and canned fruit cocktail. She was allowed to take another shower, just as delicious as the first, and to put on the clothes that had come in the bag: bra, panties, white Reeboks, a pink top she seldom wore because she hated the color, and pink socks, both of which went well with faded jeans.

Dawn must have done the packing. The pink top gave it away. So did the coordinated colors. Frank paid as little attention to his own clothes as he could get away with, and even less to anyone else's. Unless it was a woman, and she wasn't wearing enough of them. That, he noticed.

Dressed, if casually, and ready to face the world, Nicole called Frank to let him know she was coming. She got the machine, which was fine with her. She wasn't in the mood to talk to him; when she got home would be more than soon enough.

The nurse who wheeled her downstairs and the staffer who signed her out both looked at her somewhat oddly. As she claimed her purse from the safe, she realized what it was. Sympathy. They thought she minded that she was checking out alone, with no family to help her, and no one to drive her home. It was a rather Roman attitude, when she stopped to think. But she was profoundly modern. She was glad she was alone. She needed time to sort things out—and she certainly wouldn't get that once she'd gone back to being Kimberley and Justin's mommy again.

Her purse came from the safe in its own good time. There was a note taped to it: *Car is in section D-4, over by the California Tumor building.* The words were scribbled in Frank's angular handwriting. No best wishes, no nothing—only what needed saying, and that handled with as much dispatch as possible. Very much in character for Frank.

They wheeled her out to the door, and no farther. Beyond that, she was on her own. She stood in front of the medical center, with its glass and steel and concrete behind her, and the expanse of asphalt in front of her. It was awash in sunlight, drenched with it. She blinked and squinted and, after a long, dazzled moment, remembered to rummage in her purse for her sunglasses. They cut the force of the light, made it bearable—but even with them it was brighter than it had ever been on the banks of the Danube.

When she could see again, and when her lungs had accustomed themselves to the sharp dusty smell of a California street, with its undertone of auto exhaust and its eye-stinging hint of smog, she made her way toward the building with the horrible name. The oncology group that inhabited it had obviously never heard of PR.

By the time she'd taken three steps into the lot, she was sweating. The day would be well up in the nineties, maybe triple digits. She hadn't felt—she didn't think she'd felt—weather like that for a long time.

She found section D-4, and her dusty, nondescript Honda. It felt strange to do all the usual things, unlock the door, get in, fasten the seatbelt, hold her breath till it finally, reluctantly, agreed to start. She drove out slowly. Her reflexes were coming back, and rapidly, but she didn't trust them, not yet. Five minutes from the hospital—two or three miles, give or take, farther than she'd ever gone from Carnuntum—at the corner of Victory and Canoga was a Bookstar that opened at nine in the morning.

It was just opening when she got there. She parked the car and hurried in past the employee who was still straightening displays. In Carnuntum she'd have received a greeting, and been expected to stop and talk. But this was L.A. She was ignored completely, and she ignored the staff in return. She paused to get her bearings, reeling a little in the presence of so many books—so much information, and so many assumptions about it: that the population was universally literate, or nearly so; and that the technology existed to make the printed word available everywhere, to everyone who wanted it.

, The children's section was its usual determinedly cheerful self. Nicole approached it quickly, but with a kind of reluctance. Yes, there was the book she'd noticed a week or two before—or a year and a half, depending on how she wanted to look at it. She pulled it off the shelf, taking a moment to enjoy the heft and feel of it, before she let her eyes focus on the cover. There was the bear in ceremonial armor, and the small pig beside him bearing a legionary standard. Both were accurate as to details. She remembered that pleated skirt, oh too well. And that standard as it had gone by in parade.

So maybe that was what she'd spun the whole of the dream out of, from this and from any number of movie epics. Maybe—

With trembling fingers, Nicole opened *Winnie Ille Pu* and began to read. And she could. She could read the Latin translation of the book she'd read to Kimberley so often in English. She read it just as easily as she'd read *Winnie the Pooh*.

"I was," she whispered. *"I was there."* Nothing could have happened to her in six days of unconsciousness at West Hills Regional Medical Center to make her read Latin as easily as she read the daily paper. Liber and Libera had given it to her as a gift, a sort of bonus for traveling in time. Obviously they'd let her keep it when they sent her back. *Forgot I had it, probably,* she thought, not uncharitably. Gods were busy beings. Why shouldn't they leave her with a gift she couldn't use, and a proof she needed?

She almost took *Winnie Ille Pu* up to the register, but she stopped. She'd found the proof she needed. If she took the book home with her, someone would ask questions she didn't want to answer. She could do without the book—and if she could, she would. There was a lesson of Carnuntum in action.

She had to get herself home. Yes, that came next. She was desperately eager to see Kimberley and Justin, and yet she was almost afraid. What if they saw something in her, some change? Frank would never notice, and Dawn was too conscientiously nice to say anything, but kids were kids. If Justin started to scream at the sight of her, and Kimberley wanted to know, loudly, why Mommy was different—what would Nicole say? What could she say?

That she'd been sick and now was better, that was what. And that she was really, really glad to be home with her kids again.

Frank's Acura was in the driveway, filling it. That was Frank all over. Nicole sighed and parked on the curb. Her heart thudded as she extricated herself from the car, shouldered her purse, and walked—not so briskly as usual—toward the front door.

It had been only a week for the kids, but so much longer for her. There were going to be things about them she'd forgotten, things that might arouse questions. But—she shrugged. She'd got by with Lucius and Aurelia. She'd manage here. Here, at least, she knew what she was doing. Even with all the strangeness, the sense of belonging, of *fit,* was unmistakable. This was her world. She knew its rules. She could improvise without getting into trouble.

Just for a moment, she wondered how Umma was faring, back on the other side of time. Had her own spirit returned, to be confused by all the changes? Or was her body lying in her bedchamber as Nicole's had lain in the hospital: empty, untenanted? In that world, that was a death sentence. There were no facilities for maintaining people in comas. She'd die, or her body would, if her spirit was already long gone.

No. Nicole wouldn't think that way. Gods didn't have to be fair, but she persisted in thinking that they might choose to be. They'd have brought Umma back. And she'd have found a way to cope with the sudden shift in time. Lucius would do well, and Julia, who'd been both friend and ally to Nicole for so long. She even paused to mourn Aurelia, and Titus Calidius Severus who'd been her lover and her friend.

Then she stood in front of the door. Before she could fumble for her keys, it opened. Dawn stood there: blond hair pulled back in a ponytail, cheekbones, and ripe figure on display in tight T-shirt and short cutoffs—Barbie come to life. She was smiling. She actually looked—and sounded—pleased to see Nicole. "Nicole! I'm so glad you're feeling better."

"Thanks," Nicole said, returning civility for civility. Then, out of the year and a half she'd been away, she said as she wouldn't have done before, "And thanks for looking after the kids."

"Hey, no problem," Dawn said, as if she meant it.

Then Nicole didn't have to bother about being civil. Two small figures erupted past Frank's girlfriend, in a hot contest to see who could run the fastest and scream "Mommy!" the loudest. Kimberley probably won on points, but Justin took the prize for enthusiasm. They launched themselves at her like a pair of rockets. She had just enough time to brace herself before they knocked her down.

She let her knees give way, and sank down on the front step, hugging the warm wriggling bodies, kissing whichever was handiest, babbling at them—she never did know what, nor care. They were so small. And so *clean.* Her fingers combed through their hair, automatically—affection, no doubt of it, but habit also, checking for lice as she'd done with Lucius and Aurelia whenever she could get them to stand still for more than a few seconds.

These two were even more wiggly and even more bois- terous than Umma's older, larger children. They calmed down eventually, enough to each take half of her lap and cling there. Just as Kimberley sucked in breath, probably to start regaling Nicole with a rapid-fire account of every event of the past six days, Frank's voice said, "Nicole. Hi."

Nicole had got so wrapped up with the kids—literally and figuratively—that she hadn't even noticed his taking Dawn's place in the doorway. "Hello," she said coolly from the bottom of the pile of kids. Frank was exactly the same as ever, early-middle-aged, his dark hair thinning, and his sturdy body—so much like Justin's—beginning to get paunchy, with that supercilious expression Nicole had mistaken, very early on, for an indication of superior intellect. She couldn't imagine what Dawn Soderstrom saw in him. A year and a half in Carnuntum hadn't made it any clearer.

But Dawn plainly adored him. The way she stood, deferring to him, the way she looked at him, her whole attitude and posture, must have struck him as profoundly satisfying and perfectly right. Nicole had been awed enough by him when she first knew him, and she'd bought into it enough to marry him. But she didn't think she'd ever worshipped the ground he deigned to walk on.

He frowned down at her. No doubt he didn't think it was dignified of her to be sitting on the step of her own house, half drowned in kids. *Too bad,* she thought as he said, "So they think you're all right. Do they have any idea what happened to you?"

"Not a one," Nicole answered. "All the tests came back negative. The neurologist wants to see me again next week."

"Dr. Feldman," Frank said, precise as usual. "Yeah, I talked with her. She does seem to know what she's doing, but people don't just go to sleep for six days. Did she say whether you'd be likely to do it again?"

"She didn't know," Nicole said, not without malice. Frank looked sour. He liked definite answers, and he very much disliked disruptions. It must have been a dire inconvenience to have to give up Cancún in favor of a week of looking after his own kids.

Nicole bit her tongue. Time was when she would have said all that to his face, and taken active pleasure in the fight that followed. But she'd come too far and seen too much to indulge herself now, and the kids were starting to wriggle. Kimberley spoke up in her clear, precise voice—just like Frank, but by as many gods as it took, Nicole wasn't going to let her grow up to be just like her father. "I called nine-one-one, Mommy, just like you told me to," she said.

Nicole hugged her so hard she squeaked in protest, then hugged Justin, who was demanding equal time. "I know you did, sweetie. They told me in the hospital. You did just what you were supposed to."

Kimberley looked thoroughly pleased with herself. She got to her feet, and watched as Nicole unknotted herself and stood, still holding Justin.

"We're going to Woodcrest now, Mommy," Kimberley said.

"Woodcrest," Justin agreed.

"My teacher is Miss Irma," Kimberley went on, "and Justin's teacher is Miss Dolores, and—"

She'd have gone on, and probably at great length, if Frank hadn't interrupted. "I signed them both up to start Monday, and paid the first month up front."

Nicole's eyes widened slightly. "All right," she said. "Good. How much is that going to cost?"

He told her. She winced. It didn't take long to do the mental calculations. "If I'm going to be paying that every month, you'll have to keep up with the child support."

"I know, I know," he said, as he always did. That was his way of taking the easy way out. Promises, promises. Well, Nicole thought: words were cheap, but court-ordered support payments were a whole lot more concrete than that.

She was going to have to work to get what was legally due her. She resented like hell having to struggle for it, but the fact remained that if she pressed her case, she could get what was coming to her. No need to put up and shut up. She was entitled to that money, and she would get it.

She didn't push him, not yet. But she smiled a little. She would. Oh, yes. She would.

With Justin still in her arms and Kimberley clinging to her leg, she stared Frank down till he gave way and let her into the house—her own house, she made a point of noting. Even after a week of being run by somebody else, it had its familiar smell, the smell of home. There was a clear component of baby lotion and slightly sour milk, microwaved dinners and fruit juice. Next to spilled wine, burning charcoal, and the sweat-dung-dirt stink of a Roman city, it was heavenly.

The place was clean. Cleaner than it had been when she left it—Frank was an astringent neatnik. The microwave in the kitchen was brand-new. She smiled; trust Frank, yet again, to suit his own convenience. She smiled at the faucet, at the coffeemaker, at the stove, at the refrigerator. She wanted to hug the refrigerator. And the washer, and the dryer. All the things she'd taken for granted, that she'd been forced to live without.

"We've got our suitcases all ready to go," Dawn said as she left the kitchen to make the rounds of the rest of the house. "Unless you'd rather we stayed for a little while? Will you be all right by yourself?"

Nicole glanced automatically at Frank. His expression was distinctly sour, but he nodded. They were both trying very hard to be decent about things.

"I appreciate that," Nicole said. She surprised herself: she meant it. "I'll be okay, I think. If I start to feel rocky, do you mind if I call you?"

"No, not at all," Dawn said. "Not in the slightest. Here, let me put our number up by the phone, why don't I? Kimberley, you see this number? If your mommy starts to feel sick and can't dial the phone, you call it, all right?"

Kimberley looked as if she wanted to burst out crying, but was too big a girl now to succumb to the urge. She held her head up high and nodded.

Nicole hugged her again—any excuse for a hug—and said, "I don't think you'll need to do that, honeybunch. I feel fine." And she did. She felt wonderful. That wasn't the whole of it, or even a tenth part, but it was as true as that she stood, at last, in her house in West Hills.

Frank eyed her a little oddly—hoping she was right, afraid she was wrong, she supposed—but then he said, "Okay. We'll finish packing up, then. It won't take long."

Frank was efficient—efficient to a fault sometimes, as in the way he'd dumped her. She wasn't at all sorry to see him and Dawn out of her bedroom, her house, and, for that matter and however temporarily, her life.

The children hugged and kissed them both good-bye. Frank was their father; Nicole could hardly mind that they seemed sorry to see him go. But it was as much as she could do to keep a smile on her face while they did the same to Dawn. For all her good intentions, she couldn't help wondering which of those two would be the first to trade the other in for a new model.

Meow, she thought. But it felt good. It felt—cathartic. Yes.

Then, at long last and yet also a bit soon, they were done. Nicole was alone in the house with her kids. She caught herself looking around for Julia, to ask her to lend a hand.

It amazed her how much she missed Julia. Not just the helping hand. The company; the alliance against the world; even, to an extent, the friendship.

"This is funny, Mommy," Kimberley said from waist level, where she'd been since Nicole came into the house. "We're not home with you in the daytime very much."

"You aren't, are you?" Nicole said. They were at daycare during the week and at Frank's on the weekends. She'd had to stop and remember that, after so much time inhabiting the body of a widow who worked out of her own home. She was going to miss some of that. Having the kids so close, day and night, weekdays and weekends. Not having to commute.

She hugged Kimberley yet again, and Justin for good measure. Kimberley grinned at her, with Justin half a beat behind, as he always was. "Monday we go to Woodcrest," Kimberley said. "I can't wait. It's *way* cool, Mommy!"

So much for Josefina, Nicole thought.

"Tomorrow!" Justin said emphatically.

Kimberley rolled her eyes and put on an elaborate give-me-strength expression. "No, Justin. Not tomorrow. Monday."

She knew the days of the week; Justin didn't. Anything that was going to happen in the future would happen tomorrow, as far as he was concerned.

Wouldn't it be nice if the world really worked that way?

But then, from the perspective of eighteen centuries ago, everything in this century really *was* tomorrow. Somewhat bemused by the thought, Nicole wandered into the bedroom, with the children tagging after her. There was a lingering strangeness in the place: a hint of Dawn's perfume and Frank's aftershave. She'd crank the air conditioning in a minute, and blow it all away.

But first, there was a thing she had to do. She looked toward the nightstand. Yes, there it was: the plaque dedicated to Liber and Libera. It *was* the one Brigomarus had given her in Carnuntum. She recognized the ding in the upper right corner, and the tilt of Libera's head toward her consort. Even worn and stained by all the centuries, it was unmistakably the same.

That same wearing and staining made her shiver a bit. So much time had passed. Every human being she'd known in that other world was centuries dead. Their city was a ruin or an archeological dig, their lives the concern of scholars. Regular people, people like Nicole herself, never gave them a moment's thought.

She brushed a finger across the carven faces. She was almost afraid to feel the brush of tiny lips, the shock of electricity as they woke, but they remained cool, stony, still. She'd get a bottle of wine later, so she could properly thank them for sending her home again. *I may even taste some,* she thought. *I really may.*

Frank and Dawn had put fresh sheets on the bed, for which Nicole was duly grateful. They were the beige ones that had been a wedding present—from one of Frank's cousins, who was a beige-sheet person if Nicole had ever seen one. She stripped them off and dumped them over Kimberley and Justin. The kids giggled madly. "I'm a ghost!" Kimberley declared.

"Ghost!" Justin agreed heartily.

While they ran around flapping and booing at one another, Nicole remade the bed with a vivid ocean print. The kids liked it. They abandoned their game to help put on the new bedclothes. Between the two of them, they were about as much help as a cat.

While the sheets Frank and Dawn had used were in the dryer, and while the kids were occupied with a stack of coloring books, Nicole put in a call to the office. Cyndi was almost as glad to hear from her as she'd been the day before. "I've got your check here, Ms. Gunther-Perrin," she said. "I didn't know what to do with it while you were, uh, out."

" 'Out' is right," Nicole said. "Save it for me, why don't you? I'm calling from home; I expect to be back Monday, to start getting out from under whatever's waiting for me. Doctor wants to see me next week, but nobody's going to keep me from doing what needs doing."

"That's all good news," Cyndi said, and she sounded as if she meant it. "I'll be glad to see you then, Ms. Gunther-Perrin." She hadn't had to say that. It made Nicole feel good that she had. It was nice, no, more than nice, to be appreciated.

The day went smoothly, no fights, no annoying phone calls, just the quiet pleasure of a day at home with her own—her very own—two kids. They didn't mind being grabbed and hugged at random intervals, and they certainly didn't mind that she had the time or the stamina to sit and play with them by the hour.

In the late afternoon, after Justin's nap, Kimberley cracked. She'd been too good for too long. She started teasing him, teasing and teasing, determined to keep at it till she had him in a screaming tantrum.

"Knock it off," Nicole said sharply. Kimberley obeyed for a minute, but most of the way through the second minute, she was at it again.

"I said," Nicole said more pointedly, "knock. It. Off."

Kimberley kept right on going—with a glance at Nicole that invited Nicole to do something about it. Nicole was delighted to oblige. She was beside her in two long strides. Before Kimberley knew what was happening, Nicole had swatted her on the fanny.

It wasn't anywhere near as hard a whack as she'd often

had to administer to Lucius—he'd required a wallop just to get his attention. It wasn't even hard enough to make Kimberley cry. She stared, open-mouthed, too astonished to say a word.

"When I tell you to stop something," Nicole said evenly, "I expect you to stop it. Do you understand me?"

"Yes, Mommy," Kimberley said in a subdued voice. Nicole knew an instant's guilt, but she hardened herself against it. If there was one thing she'd learned in Carnuntum, it was that kids needed understanding—but they also, occasionally, needed the application of palm of hand to seat of pants.

Kimberley wasn't cured of her habit of teasing Justin. That would take a miracle. Fifteen minutes, an hour at most, and she'd be back at it. Still, she was a good kid. She wouldn't need too many lessons. Justin, now—Well, Justin was only two. Maybe, when he got to Lucius' age, she wouldn't have to correct him with a two-by-four. Maybe.

Life settled to a routine that was wonderful in its very dullness. Get up, shower (oh, that delicious hot water!), get kids up, get kids dressed, feed breakfast, and so on through the day. Sometimes she went to the supermarket—which was an experience in itself. So many things to buy. So much to take home in her car, as much as she could use. And no haggling over prices; though the price of lettuce was downright near gouging, and chicken had gone through the roof. She'd have haggled over that if she could.

Frank called every day to ask if she was all right. He had little to say when he did call, but that didn't matter. She had little to say to him, either. If they'd had more to say to each other, they might have stayed married.

She wondered what he talked about with Dawn. Then, even more to the point, she wondered how long they would go on talking about it.

It was not, thank God, her problem. She didn't waste much time feeling sorry for Dawn. Dawn was likable, after all, but she was one of those women who always landed on their feet, and always with a man in the bag.

The strangest thing of all, stranger than being as clean a

she wanted to be, and even stranger than driving to the supermarket and buying as much as she needed and being able to pack it all home, was sleeping in her own bed at night. Not that it wasn't comfortable—after the tavern and the hospital, it was wonderful—but because whenever she lay there in the dark, listening to the hum of the air conditioning and the whoosh of cars on the street outside, she kept feeling that Liber and Libera were watching her. She'd turn on the lamp—marveling as she did it that she could produce light, and such light, clear and bright as day, with the simple flick of a switch—and stare at the god and goddess on the plaque.

They'd stare straight ahead with empty limestone eyes.

Sometimes she turned off the lamp, then turned it on again very quickly, hoping to catch Liber and Libera at whatever they were up to. But they hadn't moved. They weren't up to anything—or, if they were, they weren't about to let her catch them at it.

She kept the kids through the weekend this time, by agreement with Frank. He'd had enough of them while she was in Carnuntum, and she couldn't get her fill of them. It was a nicely mutual arrangement.

On Monday morning, the alarm blasted her awake. She woke as she had so many times before, face to face with the god and goddess. She got up, she got moving, she got the kids up. That, for once, wasn't even hard. She had the magic words: "Today's the day you go to your new preschool."

Woodcrest was on Tampa, a few blocks south of Victory—east of her office, yes, but not even half as far as Josefina's house. The parking lot the preschool shared with several small businesses and, she was most interested to note, an attached elementary school, was cramped and awkward, but for once she had good parking karma: there was a spot right near the entrance.

Kimberley and Justin, full of themselves because they'd been there before and their mother hadn't, were delighted to serve as guides. "It's this building, Mommy—right through this door," Kimberley said, tugging at her arm. "Come on!

You don't want us to be late, do you?" She sounded so much like Nicole in a hurry that Nicole could hardly rebuke her, even when she started off at a run across the lot. Nicole got a solid grip on her hand and let her tow the rest of them along.

The building was standard California stucco. It already hummed with activity. There were more kids outside than in, running through the yard and climbing on apparatus and playing in sandboxes filled with bark chips instead of sand. A plumpish woman of about forty stood amid the chaos like an island of calm. Kimberley dragged Nicole right up to her and announced, "Mommy, this is Miss Irma: *my* teacher."

Miss Irma smiled at Kimberley, but her warm brown eyes rested on Nicole's face. "Oh, yes," she said. "I showed your—ex-husband, is it?—around last week. I'm very glad you're feeling better." She didn't sound dismayed by the fact of divorce, or because Nicole had been ill. Nothing would ever dismay her, Nicole suspected. That had to serve her very well in the middle of this horde of preschoolers—anyone with a nerve in her body would have had a coronary inside of a week.

Nicole thanked her for her sentiments. She'd done that more often since she came back to herself than in the year before that, she was sure. Somehow, in Carnuntum, she'd learned the art of gratitude. "Frank's my ex, yes," she said.

"Ah," said Miss Irma. She smiled again, and took Nicole in hand. "Here, now, I walked him through it all, but I'm sure you'll want your own tour, yes?"

Nicole nodded—good; she didn't have to ask. Under Miss Irma's capable tutelage, she met Miss Dolores, who would be Justin's teacher: another comfortable, early-middle-aged woman, Hispanic this time, who also had that nothing-fazes-me look in her eye. She nodded approval at the kits Nicole had made up with changes of clothes, instruction sheets, medical releases, and everything else that the children were likely to need—Frank, ever efficient, had left the school's literature with the bills on the kitchen counter, for Nicole to find and read. Evidently not every parent did: she won points for having the full kit. It was a small thing, but it made her feel good. In *this* world, by damn, she knew how to cope.

Miss Dolores, good preschool teacher that she was, asked The Question: "And how well are they trained?"

"Very well, I think," Nicole answered. "Kimberley hasn't had an accident in months." She preened at that, too, and stood tall, as a big girl should. "Justin's still learning."

"That's about right," Miss Irma said. "He's just a little fellow—aren't you, Justin?"

"*Big!*" Justin countered, as contrary as any two-year-old worth his training pants.

Miss Irma laughed. "Big, then. But you're still learning about going potty, aren't you?"

"Go potty!" Justin replied.

"Now?" Miss Dolores asked.

"Now," he said firmly.

She held out her hand. He took it. Nicole felt a tug as he trotted away, but she didn't try to call him back.

Kimberley stayed with Nicole and Miss Irma through the rest of the daily procedure: the sheet on the door of each class on which each child was signed in and out, and the cubbyholes, each labeled, for the child's work and for communications from the school. It was all very clear, very ordered, very—yes—efficient. Nothing like Josefina's casual arrangements. Maybe that was as well. It wouldn't remind the kids too forcibly of what they'd lost.

Just as Miss Irma finished showing Nicole where everything went, Justin came hurtling down the hallway. "Kiss, Mommy! *Kiss!*" Nicole caught him on the ricochet, whirled him around, and planted a loud, smacking kiss on his cheek. His answering kiss was sloppy enough to smear the powder on her cheek; she'd repair the damage when she got to the car. For now, it didn't matter.

He was already wriggling to get down. She let him go, and scooped up the waiting Kimberley, whose kiss was a fraction more demure. Then Kimberley too was ready to make the break. For Nicole it was like ripping Velcro, but they seemed quite unfazed.

At the entrance to the yard, Nicole looked back. Kimberley was already playing with another girl about her age. Justin had found a ball and was chasing after it, yelling at the top of his lungs. They both seemed to have forgotten she existed.

She should have been pleased that they were so independent. She felt like crying.

The turn back onto Tampa from that miserable parking lot was a challenge, to put it mildly, but when she finally did get out to the street, she was only ten minutes' drive from her office. *This, I could get used to,* she thought as she turned into the lot and found her space vacant as it should be. She'd almost wondered if it would be given away—as if she really had been away a year and a half.

Even before she got to the elevators, the wave of welcome had started. She gave up trying to find variations on *Thank you, I never felt better,* and settled for that one, canned line.

She'd more than half expected to feel depressed about returning to the place that had relegated her to a dead-end job, but the familiar spaces, the people she'd known for the whole of her working life in L.A., even the sight of her own cubby of an office and her secretary sitting in front of it, gave her a sense of being home again—just as she'd been in her house. This was her life, too, no matter how badly it had treated her.

Cyndi bounced up from her desk to give Nicole a giant hug. "It's great to have you back," she said.

"It's good to be back," Nicole answered. "You have no idea how good it is." *And isn't that the truth?* "Now let's see if I remember anything about the law."

Cyndi laughed, as anyone would who'd welcomed a lawyer back to work after a little over a week off. But Nicole meant it. She'd been away a lot longer than anyone knew.

Still, if her memory had gaps in it, she had her books and she had a computer. She might not be so quick with an answer as she'd been before, at least not at first, but the answers she gave would be the right ones. If law school had taught her nothing else, it had given her a solid grasp of combat research skills.

There was a small silence, which Nicole became aware of
somewhat after Cyndi did. Cyndi broke it a little abruptly.
"Everyone was upset about the way things happened," she
said. "Very upset." She hesitated. Then she went on, "I'm
really glad you didn't . . ." She paused again, looking for a
safe way to say it. At length, she found one: ". . . you didn't
do anything foolish."

*You have no idea what a foolish thing I did. I had no idea
what a foolish thing I was doing.* "Not making partner isn't
the end of the world," Nicole said from the perspective of a
year and a half in another world and time. God knew, she
hadn't felt that way when Sheldon Rosenthal pulled the rug
out from under her.

Cyndi nodded vigorously. Her curls were elaborately
styled and piled, but by no means as elaborately as the styles
the wealthy Roman matrons had affected. Those had looked
as immovable as marble curlicues on a monument. These
bounced as she moved, in a way that was pure modern America, and pure Cyndi. "I should say it's not the end of the
world," she said, "especially compared to losing your
health."

Like people in Carnuntum, she was putting her own spin
on Nicole's words, making them fit into patterns she found
familiar. It was the human way of doing things. Nicole was
glad of it, too: it made life easier for those who didn't fit
those patterns. If she even approximated one of them, the
people around her filled in the rest.

Not that Cyndi was wrong in this particular instance. Nicole said, "I was never so surprised in my life as when I
woke up in that hospital bed." That wasn't exactly wrong,
either, though it was only about an *as'* worth of an *aureus*
of truth: certainly less than a cent on the dollar.

Nicole didn't linger too long, and Cyndi didn't try to keep
her, though Nicole could tell she'd have been glad to babble
on indefinitely about everything and nothing. The office was
waiting. Nicole had to face it now or not face it at all.

It didn't look anything like the cluttered cubicle she'd left.
It was jammed full of flowers and get-well cards, arranged

by Cyndi, she could suppose. There was just barely room in the middle for the desk and chair, and for the IN basket with its stack of papers waiting to be dealt with.

She'd deal with it. It would take a while, but she'd dig out from under. For sure it was better than grinding flour for hours at a stretch, than keeping fires fed a few sticks at a time, than breathing smoke all day long because nobody had heard of chimneys.

Her voice-mail tape was close to maxed out. She'd have to ask Cyndi to fill her in—she even had a good pretext: some of her business had been taken over by other people in the firm.

Why, she thought in a pause between messages, Cyndi was her Julia in this world. She hoped, at least, that Cyndi didn't feel like a slave, or feel she needed manumission.

It took her a moment to remember how to use her computer, but her password came right back to her: JUSTKIM, the first syllables of her children's names. It wasn't secure, it was much too easy to guess, but if she'd been more paranoid she might never have remembered it. Once the system came up, she found herself as inundated with e-mail as with voice calls and paperwork. Most of the e-mail was intraoffice, and most of it was personal: sympathy notes at first, some from surprising people, and then get-well wishes. She had more friends here than she'd thought. It touched her, made her eyes prickle and her throat go tight.

So many cards, so many flowers, so many good wishes. She took a deep breath and set them aside to savor later, and turned to the IN box. She'd pick up where she left off, she resolved. Right . . . *here.* She reached for the top folder in the stack.

But she'd reckoned without the rest of the world. Once word had spread that she was back, everybody and his third cousin from Muncie came by to say *Hello* and *Glad you're feeling better.* Hardly any of them stayed more than a minute or two, but a minute here and two minutes there added up to a good many minutes altogether.

She wasn't the slightest bit startled when, toward midmorning, Gary Ogarkov poked his head into her office. He looked as if he expected her to throw something at him, and probably something sharp.

His expression was so nervous, she started to laugh. "Come on in," she said. "I won't bite, I promise."

"No?" He didn't sound convinced. "I wouldn't blame you if you did." But he slid in and sat on the edge of the chair she kept for clients.

Nicole looked at him and sighed. "Gary, it's over. It happened the way it happened. This isn't the end of the world. I'm not starving"—*I've done that*—"or sleeping in my car." *Even if it might be more comfortable than that bed over Umma's tavern.*

Gary eyed her a little dubiously. "You're taking it really well," he said. "I guess when you set a partnership against your health, it's not such a big thing after all. But even so . . ." His voice trailed away.

"That is part of it," Nicole agreed. Part of the rest, she realized, was the emotional distance her time in Carnuntum had given her. And part was an insight she'd also gained on the other side of time: the distance between bad and worse was a lot greater than the distance between good and better. Winning the partnership would have been better. What she had was still pretty decent.

Fortunately, Gary Ogarkov didn't ask her to elaborate. Like everybody else in the world, he worried about himself and his own concerns first. And a good thing for her, too, all things considered. "I felt terrible about the way things turned out, and then I was afraid . . ." He stopped again.

Afraid you tried to kill yourself because I got the partnership and you didn't. Nicole had no trouble filling in the blanks. Such things happened. Sometimes they made the news. More often, they spread along the attorneys' grapevine. After all, lawyers made their living by writing and talking. What else would they do for entertainment but gossip?

"I didn't try to kill myself," Nicole said firmly. "If my doctor doesn't understand what went wrong, don't expect me to"—*even if I do, don't expect me to say so*—"but it wasn't that, believe me."

He spread his hands in a gesture of surrender. "All right, all right. I believe you. I'm glad. And I'm glad you're back, and I'm glad you don't hate me. I wouldn't have blamed you if you did."

He looked very boyish when he worried—and he *was* worried. She wasn't altogether sure she'd reassured him, either. She soothed him a bit more, reflecting as she did it that it was a good thing he didn't spend a lot of time in court. His opponents would have read altogether too much from his face.

Finally he seemed to realize that she was busy, or trying to be. He pushed himself to his feet, dipped his head—it was almost a bow—and fled back to his own desk. It was still the same one, she couldn't help but notice. She'd have thought he'd have moved into the rarefied expanses of partner country by now.

So maybe, she thought, her absence had disrupted the firm just a little bit. Then she shook her head. No, of course not. The mills of the firm ground exceedingly fine, and ground exceedingly slow. Gary would get his new office in the firm's good time, and not a moment sooner.

She shook herself and wrenched her mind back to the work she'd been trying to do all morning. Just about four memos down the stack, yet another visitor tapped lightly on the doorframe. She let out a grunt of annoyance. Best wishes were all very well, but so was getting some work done. That was what she was here for, wasn't it?

But when she looked up, she wiped the frown off her face in a hurry. Sheldon Rosenthal stood in the doorway of her plain, plebeian office, attaché case in hand, looking the very model of the modern founding partner.

"It's very good to see you back, Ms. Gunther-Perrin," he said, cool and precise as always. "We were concerned about you, especially in light of the circumstances." So: he'd been wondering if she'd popped a handful of pills, too.

She kept her voice civil, but annoyance gave it an edge it

might not otherwise have had. "Circumstances don't have anything to do with it," she said. That was a lie, but it wasn't a provable lie. "Life would be a lot more convenient if you could pick and choose when you were going to get sick."

"So it would," Rosenthal said dryly. He didn't wait to be invited, but stepped right into the office and swung the attaché case up onto Nicole's desk. It landed with a solid thump. Obviously, he hadn't brought it along as a dignified prop. He snapped open the solid brass locks and lifted out a thick sheaf of papers. "Now here is something you may find interesting."

Nicole stared at it. She didn't find it interesting. She found it formidable. Saying as much to the head of the firm didn't strike her as the best thing she could do. "What is it?" she asked, hoping she sounded interested rather than wary.

"Among other things, the environmental impact statement on a parcel of land somewhat north of here," Rosenthal answered. "I want you to analyze that statement and the other documents you will find here, and to give me an opinion as to whether development is likely to be allowed to go forward if a litigant seeks to block it in the courts."

"Sounds a lot like what I was doing with the Butler Ranch project," Nicole said.

"There are similarities, yes," Rosenthal said imperturbably. "The expertise you acquired through working on that project is one of the reasons I'm assigning this one to you."

"I see," Nicole said, in lieu of screaming, *You son of a bitch!* Had she truly been lying unconscious for six days, she would have screamed at him, she had no doubt of that at all. A year and a half in Carnuntum had taught her a new degree of patience, and a degree of self-preservation, too.

It hadn't taught her not to keep her thoughts in check. If he'd liked her work on Butler Ranch so well, why hadn't he made her a partner on account of it? But she'd been away long enough to cool the outrage she'd felt right after Rosenthal shafted her—and to show her there were a hell of a lot worse things than working in a law office.

On the strength of that, and after a few seconds' pause to

get her voice under control, she asked, "Are we representing the developer here, or someone who is thinking about trying to stop him?"

"An extremely professional question." Did Sheldon Rosenthal sound the least bit surprised? Maybe he did. Maybe he'd dropped this project on her desk to see if she would lose her temper, or to try to make her lose it. That would have given him the perfect excuse to let her go.

But she'd refused to give it to him. He scratched his chin along the edge of his neat little beard. "Perhaps it would be best if you did not know the answer to that. I want the analysis to be as nearly disinterested as possible."

Nicole took time to think about that—time in which he stood there, waiting in apparent patience. "All right," Nicole said at last. Rosenthal made a certain amount of sense. Lawyers were by trade advocates, hired guns. If she knew which way he wanted the analysis to come out, she'd slant it that way. As it was, he could go to the client, whoever the client was, and say, *Here's exactly why you can,* or maybe, *why you can't do what you want to do with this land.*

"Do you think you can have this on my desk a week from today?" he asked.

Nicole nearly let go regardless of all her combat training in circumspection. But her resolve held. She was able to say with a reasonable degree of aplomb, "I'll try. If I weren't coming back from being sick, I'd be sure of it. But with everything else backed up a week and more—"

Rosenthal cut her off with a chopping gesture. "This has priority. If everything else has waited for you to return, it can wait a little longer."

Nicole drew a deep breath. If the founding partner said *Hop!* the wise frog didn't ask *How high?* till she was already on the way up. "All right," she said. "In that case, I'll have it done on time." Or die trying.

"Good," Sheldon Rosenthal said. "I'll look forward to seeing what you do with it." His nod was as carefully wrought as everything else about him. "And let me say once more, I am very glad to see you back in good health." Without even waiting to hear her dutiful thanks, he nodded one last time, turned and headed back to the eminence of the seventh floor.

He'd left the attaché case, brass fittings and all. Nicole refused to run after him like a flunky. She'd send somebody up with it later. For now she closed it and set it aside, pausing to stroke the fine leather. Then she turned back to her desk, took another deep breath, and started skimming through the documents the case had carried. The sooner she knew how brutal this job was going to be, the better.

As she read through the papers, she felt how long she'd been away, even more than she had with her kids. Time after time, she remembered the outline of the legal points she'd made in the Butler Ranch report, but not the details. And the details were what mattered, because the outline fell to pieces without them.

She pulled up the old report on her computer and scribbled notes for the citations she'd need to check to write this new one. She'd have to hit the books, too, because she couldn't recall what went into some of those citations.

She stifled a sigh. She'd known it would be this way. Even if she wasn't quick, she'd be right. Here, she needed to be right and quick both—either that or take a lot of work home.

Well, if she had to, she had to: part of the price she paid for going away. It was cheap enough, she reckoned. She could have had to stay in Carnuntum till the day she died.

Another part of the price was the continued stream of attorneys and secretaries, all of whom professed themselves glad to see her back. She started to wonder just how important to the firm she was, if so many people were making a point of welcoming her. Or were they just being careful? She could sue, after all. You could sue for just about anything— and she *had* been passed over in favor of a male employee. Sheldon Rosenthal had warned her that any attempt to sue would get her nowhere, but that was before she landed in the hospital for just under a week.

Or maybe she was too cynical. They really did seem happy to see her. Several teased her for working so hard so soon. Her answering smile was decidedly wan. She wished they would go away and let her do the work instead of commiserating with her about it.

There was one notable exception to the procession of well-wishers. Tony Gallagher did not come down from the seventh floor to see how she was. She didn't miss him a bit—and not only because he spared her yet another interruption.

A little past eleven, the telephone rang. She jumped; she'd finally had fifteen minutes free of interruptions, and had managed to immerse herself in what she was doing. "Nicole Gunther-Perrin," she said. It was still a deep pleasure to say that name instead of the one she'd lived under for so long. She *wasn't* Umma. If the gods were kind—and that was a literal truth—she'd never be Umma again. *No offense,* she said to the spirit of her ancestress, wherever by now it might be, *but you are you and I'm myself, and I'm most pleased to keep it that way.*

Cyndi's voice sounded in her ear. "It's Mr. Ogarkov," she said.

Nicole rolled her eyes. What, another round of guilt? This time, she really would tell him to find himself a mommy. Her calendar was full, thank you very much.

Still, he was a partner, and she was being the good and faithful servant. "Put him through," she said.

As soon as the line clicked over, he said, "Nicole? I was wondering if you'd let me take you to lunch to celebrate coming back. How about that Mexican place next to the Bookstar?"

She was just about to make an excuse—God knew, she had enough to do here—but something made her stop and think. This wasn't an unusual invitation. They'd gone out to lunch a good many times while they worked on the Butler Ranch report. Sometimes he'd bought, sometimes she had. He'd never given her any trouble—at least, not that kind. Maybe she wasn't his type. The other kind, the new kind, the guilt-edged one . . . well, if that was what he was up to, she'd set him straight, that was all. As with the work in front of her, the sooner it was done, the sooner it was over.

"All right," she said. "Fine. Twelve-thirty okay? I'm pretty busy here."

"So am I," he said. "I'll see you then."

When the phone was back in its cradle, Nicole frowned again at the environmental impact study. It wasn't as thorough as the one for Butler Ranch. Everyone had gone into that game sure the proposed development would end up in court. Both sides had had their ducks in a row right from the start. Here, the ducks were swimming all over the pond.

She'd almost forgotten the lunch date by the time Gary Ogarkov rapped on the door. She scrawled a note to herself, marked the place where she'd left off, and blinked up at him for a moment, slowly putting the world back together outside of the work she'd been doing. He waited with a decent amount of patience, and let her walk ahead of him out of the office and down to the parking lot. She didn't even pause by the Honda, but went down the line to his Buick. If that bemused him, he didn't show it. It was his invitation, after all. Inviter drove; invitee rode along. That was the unwritten protocol.

"You'd better buy today," she said as she settled in the passenger seat and fastened the lap belt. "You're the partner, after all."

"Hey, I told you what I—" He broke off as her tone sank in. "You're not angry. You're sassing me." He sounded astonished.

"Life is too short," she said. And how long would she be able to hold onto that attitude? Probably till some idiot cut her off on the freeway. That would last a bit, if the kids stayed at Woodcrest. She sat back, determined to relax and not let anything about Los Angeles bother her. "Well? Shall we go? I'm hungry."

Ogarkov grinned and gave her something between a Boy Scout salute and the military version. "Yes, ma'am," he said, and started the car.

So maybe, she thought, she'd be spared any more of his guilt trips. She hoped so. She liked him rather well, as a colleague and casual friend. It would be a good thing if they could go on on that basis.

The Mexican restaurant was always a busy place. Today it looked as if a good part of the firm had decided to step over there for lunch—and most of those hadn't, yet, got in their good wishes. By the time Nicole and Gary had been seated at a table, the procession was up to parade strength. Nicole would have enjoyed it a fair bit if her stomach hadn't been growling at her. It was a long time since breakfast, and this body wasn't used to being hungry.

Lunch was delicious. For one thing, Mexican food in L.A. was, not surprisingly, a hell of a lot better than in Indianapolis. For another, she hadn't tasted corn or tomatoes or chiles in all the time she'd been in Carnuntum. The Romans hadn't known about any of them. She hadn't particularly noticed that while she was there; she'd been too busy surviving. But now she had them in front of her, she was ravenously hungry for them.

"Thanks, Gary," she said as she set her fork down on an empty plate. "That hit the spot."

"Probably tastes like heaven after hospital food," Ogarkov said—again, doing her work of concealment for her. She nodded. She hadn't been thinking about hospital food, but he didn't need to know that.

Almost as good as the food in her estimation was that he seemed to have decided to lay his guilt aside. He was just as she remembered, good company, occasionally witty, willing to talk shop or gossip or whatever she happened to be in the mood for. Whoever said women were the worst gossips must have been a man; because when it came to dishing the very best and choicest dirt, the male of the species gave the female a solid run for the prize.

Nicole hadn't enjoyed a meal so much since she couldn't remember when. She went back to the office in a glow of good humor, all ready and set to tackle the papers Sheldon Rosenthal had slapped down on her desk. By midafternoon, after the interruptions had tapered off to one per hour, she was beginning to have a feel for the way the analysis should look. If there weren't any surprises in the rest of the documents or in the case law that pertained to them, she'd be on solid ground in her assessment.

That was a good feeling. A very good feeling indeed. She'd missed this: the exercise of her mind in the intricacies of a legal system she knew and understood. And no man was patronizing her for being able to understand it. She really was a lawyer here, a *woman* lawyer, and that was maybe not common enough yet, but it was getting there.

23

So, SHE THOUGHT. NO surprises. Or should she assume that? If she did, she could make a call or two of her own now without feeling guilty for wasting the time.

Before she reached for the phone book, she called up a file from the computer and printed it out. She wanted to be sure she had all the facts handy. As she read over the two pages from the laser printer's tray, she smiled grimly.

County Government Offices, the heading in the white pages said. The office she wanted was on Ventura Boulevard, only two or three miles away. She dialed the number. "Good afternoon, District Attorney's office," said the voice on the other end. "Family Support Unit—spousal- and child-support cases. How may I help you?"

Nicole steadied herself. Here it was. Moment of truth. She said it baldly, in her best and crispest professional voice. "My ex-husband has been late on a good many child-support payments, and he's missed a good many others altogether," she said. "I badly need the money, and I want help collecting it."

"Please hold," the voice said without expression. "I'll put you through to the Child Support Enforcement Section."

For her listening pleasure, or lack thereof, the FSU offered 101 Strings—soothing enough if you weren't the sort who preferred acid rock. Nicole, whose taste ran to Top Forty when it ran to anything at all, lived through it until a new voice came on the line: "Child Support Enforcement. This is Herschel Falk. I understand you have a collection problem. May I have the details, please, Ms.—?"

"Nicole Gunther-Perrin," Nicole said. His silence had an interesting quality: like an open door, or an open mind. She gave him the details he'd requested. All of them, with scrupulous exactness, from the date and number of the child-support order to the dates of Frank's checks that had come late to those of the checks that should have come but never had.

"Well, well," Herschel Falk said when she finished, and then again, a moment later: "Well, well. You certainly have all that at your fingertips, don't you, Ms. Gunther-Perrin? I wish everyone who called here were so well prepared."

"I'm an attorney," Nicole said with a hint of tightness. Her teeth had clenched while she ran through the list of Frank's delinquencies. She couldn't seem to pry them loose.

"I see." Falk sounded like a man who'd heard everything at least once, and most things a lot more often than that. "Now you've had it up to here with your ex, and you're going to hit him up for everything you have coming to you."

"Mr. Falk," Nicole said, "that's exactly what I'm going to do. Let me give you Frank's—Frank Perrin's—work and home telephone numbers, too, while I'm at it."

She heard the scratch of pen on paper as she read them off. Then he said, "If I don't get him, I will leave a message at both those numbers this afternoon. Let me put the figures into the computer, so I can tell him how much he owes to the penny. There's ten percent interest on delinquent payments, you know."

"Now that I had forgotten," Nicole said with a grin Frank would not have been happy to see. "I'm in corporate law, and I really thought he would keep up after we divorced. I didn't pay as much attention to the regulations as I should have."

"That happens," Herschel Falk said with every evidence

of sympathy, and a degree of relish that she took note of. This was a man who enjoyed his job. Not a nice man, oh no, but a very good man to have on her side. "We'll take care of it from here," he said. "Some people find a call from the District Attorney's office amazingly—mm, maybe *therapeutic* is the word I'm looking for. It doesn't work on everyone, but it does for a good many."

"I thought that might be the case," Nicole said. "Frank wouldn't even think of holding up a bank, and God forbid he should walk off with a wallet someone dropped on the sidewalk in front of him, but when it comes to stiffing me— well, that's not *really* a bad thing, is it? I've got my job, after all. It's not like I'm starving. And it's so difficult to come up with the money some weeks, what with the trips to Cancún and the payments on the Acura. And it really gets inconvenient, you know?"

Herschel Falk laughed shortly. "Believe me, Ms. Gunther-Perrin, I do know. And we'll do our best to teach him that one doesn't just obey some of the laws some of the time." He added dryly, "And, of course, we'll do it for nothing: your tax dollars at work. Quite a bit less of a bite than your own attorney's two hundred dollars an hour."

"Two-fifty," Nicole said. "Yes, that does enter into it. Ironic, isn't it? If he'd been paying up, I'd be able to afford the fees."

"Life's little ironies, yes," Falk said. "All right, then. I'll call and see what Mr. Perrin has to say for himself. If he doesn't dispute the facts, we'll go from there. If he does . . . well, we'll see. May I have your number, please, so that I can reach you when I have something to report?"

Nicole gave him her office and home numbers. "I don't think Frank will dispute the facts," she said. "He's in computer science—he knows what's real and what isn't. Sometimes he just does his best to ignore it."

"Maybe this call will do some good, then," Falk said in a neutral tone. "We can but hope. Good day, Ms. Gunther-Perrin."

"Good day," Nicole said, and fought an urge to giggle.

His slightly old-fashioned style had infected her. It was appealing, really. Even though, as a confirmed governmental cynic, she wasn't sure he really would do as he promised, or do it in any kind of timely fashion, she still felt good about the call. Finally she was doing something about a long and frustrating problem.

She went back to her analysis with a lighter heart, and a sense that she should have done this a long time ago. There *were* legal mechanisms in place here, and they *would* work in her favor, even if they took a while. She wouldn't have to beard an Emperor in his den, and then rely on his goodwill, to get what was rightfully hers.

The calls from well-wishers had tapered off, but they still kept coming. Her patience was wearing thin by the time Frank added himself to the list. Obviously he hadn't heard from Herschel Falk, or he'd have been screaming in her ear. The good Mr. Falk must have been operating in lawyer time when he promised to call this afternoon. No doubt he meant *some afternoon this week*, or possibly *some afternoon this month*.

Then, at about a quarter to four, Cyndi rang in to report, "I have your ex-husband on the line, Ms. Gunther-Perrin." Her tone had a slight hint of question, and an edge of warning.

Nicole smiled and shoved the environmental impact report to one side. "Really? Good, then, I'll talk with him." She waited for the small click that meant the secretary had transferred the incoming call, then spoke in her sweetest, most reasonable tones: "Hello, Frank."

"Nicole!" Frank sounded neither sweet nor reasonable. "What the hell are you doing? I just got off the phone with this crazy bastard from the DA's office, and he says—"

"What am I doing?" Nicole broke in. "I'm doing what I'm legally entitled to do, and what I should have done the first time you missed a payment. You're violating a court order, Frank. It's just as much against the law as knocking over a liquor store."

"Oh, give me a break," her ex snarled.

"I've given you too many breaks already," Nicole snapped. "So many breaks that I'm broke. I need the money you owe me. If you pay up, Mr. Falk goes away. If you don't, he goes after your assets. I can tell him—I *will* tell him—where a lot of those are, and I'm sure he can find any I'm not aware of. People in the District Attorney's office have all sorts of interesting connections, and their software is getting better all the time."

She didn't know how true that last was, but it certainly rattled Frank's cage. He howled a suggestion that sounded a lot like Falk's last name. Then he calmed down a bit, or at least got his voice under control. "That bastard says I owe you some ridiculous amount. I may have missed once or twice, but—"

"Shall I e-mail you the dates of all the checks you missed?" Nicole asked sweetly. "You can add them all up and figure the interest due on each one. If your number doesn't match the one Mr. Falk gave you, I'm sure he'll be happy to discuss the discrepancy."

Glum silence on the other end of the line. At length, Frank said, "I find Woodcrest for you, I pay for the first month, and you go and do this to me. Thanks a hell of a lot, Nicole."

"You're welcome," she said. "You can take that off the total; fair's fair. Now, suppose you tell me when I can expect the rest. If it's later than Thursday, I expect you'll be hearing from Mr. Falk again."

"Thursday!" he howled. "Do you have any idea how much money that bastard says I owe?"

Just about enough for a nice vacation in Cancún, and a couple of payments on the Acura, Nicole thought. She elected not to say it. "I'm sure Mr. Falk will be pleased to discuss the matter with you," she said.

"He can talk to my lawyer," Frank snarled.

"That's perfectly all right with me," Nicole said equably. "You can pay me, or you can pay me and your lawyer both. I'm sure you can figure out which one is cheaper."

"Bitch."

"Thank you. Remember—Thursday. Send it here to the

office, so I can get to the bank on the way home. Now that the kids are at Woodcrest, that will be a lot easier," Nicole said.

Frank had to be on his cell phone. There was no satisfying slam of receiver into cradle. Just a prissy little click. Nicole threw back her head and laughed. Oh, that had felt wonderful! And the beauty of it was, he would pay. She was as sure of that as of sunrise tomorrow. Sunrise in West Hills, what was more—not in Carnuntum.

Cyndi popped her head into the office, wide-eyed and reminding Nicole vividly, just in that moment, of Julia. "What's so funny, Ms. Gunther-Perrin?"

"Not *funny*, really," Nicole said. "But you know what?" She waited for Cyndi to shake her head. "This is a pretty good place."

"What, the office?" Cyndi sounded amazed. But then, Cyndi had no idea how much she automatically accepted as the physical and mental furnishings of her place and time. Nobody did. Nicole certainly hadn't, not till she got her nose rubbed in it.

She leaned back in the comfortable padded chair, glanced at the computer screen and the color photos of her children next to it, and took a long breath of clean, odor-free, air-conditioned air. "It's not so bad," she said. "It really isn't."

Nicole started to wonder about that as she pulled into Woodcrest's godawful excuse for a parking lot. If Kimberley and Justin had turned out to have a difficult day, she'd be back to square one again. But *this* time, for absolute certain, she wouldn't be whining to any gods or goddesses. She had every intention of staying right where she was.

The preschool building was much better than its parking lot, though it had a tired, end-of-the-day feel to it. Kimberley let out a squeal and did her best to tackle her mother. Justin was right behind her. Nicole braced automatically and took the brunt of the double blow, and smiled down at them. They smiled back. From the look of those smiles, they'd had a good day.

Kimberley got hold of her hand and dragged her toward the four-year-olds' cubbyholes. "Mommy, come here! Look at the picture I made!"

A heavy weight of worry dropped from Nicole's shoulders. It was all right; the kids were happy. As she initialed the sign-out sheet, Miss Irma appeared from the depths of the room to say, "Kimberley was a very bright, well-behaved girl today. I think we'll enjoy having her here."

Justin hadn't tried too hard to tear the place apart or burn it down, either, from Miss Dolores' account of his day. For a two-year-old, that was moderately high praise. Nicole left Woodcrest in a warm glow. She'd forgotten how good that felt—and how good it felt to feel good.

Getting home was dead easy, once Nicole escaped that miserable parking lot. *Small price to pay,* she thought as she did her best to keep her car from getting clipped coming out. If this was the worst she had to do to keep the kids happy, she'd take it.

"We had tacos for lunch today," Kimberley informed her. "Chicken tomorrow, and hotdogs the day after. That's what Miss Irma said." If Miss Irma said it, Nicole gathered, it must have come down from Mt. Sinai with Moses.

"Hogs!" Justin agreed gleefully. He couldn't say *hotdogs* very well yet, but he loved to eat them.

Too much fat, Nicole thought automatically. She couldn't get as exercised about it as she used to. It was *food*—something she'd learned to appreciate, deeply, when she hadn't had enough of it.

Dinner went as well as dinner could with a pair of rambunctious kids who were tired from a long and exciting day. When she'd got them both bathed and put to bed—so clean and sweet-smelling, and no nits to pick, not even one—she did a little work with reference books and notepad. Then, yawning, she put herself to bed. Just as she turned out the light, she slid a glance at Liber and Libera on their plaque. "It was a good day," she said. "It was a very good day."

* * *

She slid back into the routine of her late-twentieth-century life almost as easily as if she had in fact been away for only a week. Everyone's assumption that she'd been away only that long helped a lot; if she slipped up, they attributed it to her illness, and brushed it off.

She didn't slip up much, at that. Old habits died hard. Her life in Carnuntum began to fade, to seem more distant than it actually was, like an intense and vividly memorable dream.

On Wednesday morning, she went to see Dr. Marcia Feldman. The doctor wasn't any happier to see her than she'd been before, or any happier to report, "By all the tests, Ms. Gunther-Perrin, you're still perfectly normal." Her eyes on Nicole were accusing, as if she suspected there was something Nicole wasn't telling.

Nicole wasn't about to tell it, either. No matter how tempted she might be to share her experience with someone, this meticulous medical scientist was not the person she'd have chosen. She fit her response to one of the things Dr. Feldman must be wondering. "No, I didn't take any drugs you couldn't detect. I don't do that kind of thing."

"Everything I was able to learn about you from your co-workers and your ex-husband makes me believe that," the neurologist said, "but it leaves what did happen a mystery. I don't like mysteries, unless I'm reading one." That was meant to be a light touch, but it fell flat. She shrugged. "Under the circumstances, I don't know what I can say, except that I hope it doesn't happen again. Everything's been all right since you went home?"

"Everything's been fine," Nicole answered truthfully.

"All right." Dr. Feldman sighed. "In that case, all I can do is give you a clean bill of health and tell you I do not know whether it will last and how long it will last. Just that, for this moment, you are as healthy and normal a specimen as I could hope to see."

"Thank you," Nicole murmured, quashing the small jab of guilt. The truth would upset this good doctor a whole lot more than her current uncertainty. Nicole had to remember that.

"Good luck," the doctor said at last. "That's not very scientific, I know, but it's the best I can do for you."

"It's good enough," Nicole said. "Thank you, Dr. Feldman. Really. You did your best for me; I do appreciate that."

Dr. Feldman didn't look exactly pleased, but she had the grace to see Nicole out, and to shake her hand at the door of the waiting room. Feeling oddly as if she'd been given a blessing at the church door, the kind of thing a priest did to equip a parishioner with some small defense against the big bad world, Nicole made her way back to the office.

Cyndi was at her desk, trying hard to look busy. She raised a questioning eyebrow as Nicole came in. Nicole gave her a thumbs-up. Cyndi silently clapped her hands. Nicole grinned and sailed past her, and tackled that analysis. She'd hit her stride there. No matter what Sheldon Rosenthal had done to her, she was going to give him the best piece of work she could. She had her pride, after all. And if she wanted to show him up just a bit, well, who could blame her?

Thursday was D-Day: the deadline for Frank to pay up. Nicole twitched all morning and all through lunch. By midafternoon she'd made the sanity-saving decision to call Herschel Falk first thing in the morning and find out what, if anything, was happening.

But late that afternoon, a little before she had to pack up her work for the day and head out to fetch the kids, a FedEx deliverywoman set a cardboard envelope on Cyndi's desk. Nicole resisted the urge to leap out and grab it. Properly, as an attorney should, she waited for Cyndi to bring it in to her for signature and release. Only after both secretary and FedEx driver were gone did she rip open the envelope.

Inside she found a certified check, a receipt for her to sign and return, and a note. *I've taken out the cost of the microwave along with the first month at Woodcrest,* Frank had written. *If you don't like it, call the damn DA.*

Nicole grinned like a tiger, and called Falk—but not to complain about that. It wasn't too unreasonable, considering. 'Good," the attorney said when she thanked him. "I wish hey were all that easy. Most people these days don't have any respect for anything, let alone law or authority."

"I thought my ex would," Nicole said. She turned the check over in her fingers. It wasn't enough to get her all the way out of the hole, but it would help quite a bit. "Now, if he just keeps up from here on in, I'll be in fairly decent shape."

"If he doesn't," Herschel Falk said, "you know where to call."

"You bet I do," Nicole said. It wasn't going to be or stay easy, particularly if Frank got hardened to hearing from the District Attorney's office if he got behind in his payments. But it wouldn't be easy for him, either, if he got slack. With luck, he'd be smart enough to figure that out for himself. Without it, she'd remind him—as forcibly, and as often, as necessary.

Nicole finished the analysis Friday afternoon, saved it and printed it and checked it over before she took it upstairs to Rosenthal's office. That would gain her points: turning it in early.

But as she read it through, prepared for the flush of achievement and the satisfaction of a job well done, her mood crashed into the barrier of the first paragraph. It was written in lawyerese. Eye-glazing, brain-numbing lawyerese. Half of it was deliberate obfuscation, which was part of the game. The rest could have read a lot better, too.

She hadn't written her petition to Marcus Aurelius in lawyerese. Chiefly because she didn't know the exact formulations of Roman law, but also because she wanted to be as clear as possible. She'd *wanted* him to understand exactly what had happened to her and why she was demanding restitution.

What was it Tony Gallagher had said, just after he hit on her? She wasn't cooperative enough—by which he meant that she hadn't been obliging enough to come across for him. But maybe he'd been trying to tell her something more, something important.

She reached for the phone and punched up Gary Ogarkov's extension. "Gary," she said when he picked up, "I've got an analysis here that I need to give to Mr. Rosenthal on Monday. Any way you could help punch it up so it reads better?"

"I'll be right there," he said with every appearance of willingness. "If I can't do it all now, I'll take it home and do it over the weekend."

"You don't have to do that," Nicole said. She tapped a finger on her desk as she pondered what he'd said, and what he'd left unsaid. He was still feeling bad about the way things had gone. If he wanted to atone for it this way—why not? As long as he didn't try to lay another guilt trip on her.

By the time she came out of her meditation, she was listening to a dial tone, and Gary Ogarkov was saying hello to Cyndi at her desk outside the office. He breezed in just after Nicole had dropped the receiver into the cradle, all ready and set to go. "Okay," he said. "Let's see what we've got here."

Nicole handed him the analysis. He skimmed it, then slowly nodded. "It's not bad at all—I didn't think it would be. Here's what I'll do. I'll break up these sentences here, and here. There's some passives I can turn into actives, and shorten up some of these fancy jawbreakers you've got here—see? Not too hard, is it?"

Nicole shook her head ruefully. "Not hard at all, if you paid any attention in English class." *Or if I'd stopped to notice what I was doing with my Latin, either.*

"English class is a good thing to pay attention to," Gary said.

Nicole didn't argue with that, but neither was she going to let him take control. "I don't want the meaning changed," she said. "Just the way it's written."

"Of course," he said cheerfully. "But you win a cigar if you can tell me how *utilize* is different from *use*."

"It's longer," she said. "And cigars are gross."

"Unlike some other things," Gary said, "when it comes to readable prose, longer is not necessarily better." He grinned at Nicole's foreboding expression, and pulled a pen out of his pocket. "How about I get started? I edit better on paper. I'll pass you each sheet as I get done with it, and you can key the changes into the computer. If you don't like 'em, just leave 'em off."

Nicole nodded and, after a slight pause, thanked him. He didn't notice. He was running down through the first page—scribble here, slash there, swirl and jot and flip, on to the next page. When the complete page flew her way, it looked like one of her freshman English professor's slash-and-burn specials. But she had to admit, as she typed it in, that it read a whole lot better and more clearly than the original version.

They finished a few minutes after five. As Nicole was making the last revisions and deletions, Ogarkov said, "This is a hell of a piece of work, by the way. I should have said that sooner. If it doesn't knock Mr. Rosenthal's socks off—"

"Then it doesn't, that's all," Nicole said calmly. "But I didn't do it for him. I did it for *me*. You know what I mean? And you helped make it better. I appreciate it."

"Hey, no problem," he said. "Any time." He saluted her as she typed in the last couple of sentences, scanned them, then set them to print. "Good luck," he said, "and have a great weekend."

"You, too," Nicole said sincerely.

Then he was gone. Cyndi had left just as the printer started. The rest of the office was emptying with Friday quickness. Nicole tapped her foot, starting to lose patience with the printer's deliberate speed. At last, however, it was done, slapped into a folder, and ready to take upstairs.

As she'd expected, Sheldon Rosenthal's secretary was still there, clacking away at that antique of a correcting Selectric. Nicole could just barely remember when it had been state of the art. She could also remember when state of the art had been a reed pen and a sheet of papyrus.

"Good evening, Ms. Gunther-Perrin," Lucinda said in her cool, genteel voice. "What can I do for you?"

"I finished the analysis Mr. Rosenthal asked for," Nicole said, setting the folder on the secretary's desk.

Lucinda's expression didn't change in the slightest. "He's with a client right now," she said. "I will see that he gets it." That part of her duty done, she went back to her typing.

Salaried attorneys got efficiency, no more. Cordiality, she reserved for partners and clients.

Nicole wasn't about to let it irk her. Umma's sisters in Carnuntum had been a lot sniffier. She'd got her point across, and she'd got the work done. She had a whole, free weekend ahead of her—and an empty one, once Frank and Dawn came to pick up the kids Saturday morning. She'd get them clean tonight, and see that they were packed and ready to go.

She sighed at a memory: Lucius going off to the baths with Titus Calidius Severus, the small dark boy and the sturdy dark man, both of whom she had, in her way, come to love. Whatever had happened to Lucius, he'd lived long enough to have at least one child of his own who'd lived to grow up and . . . and in seventy or eighty generations, here was Nicole, hurrying toward the elevator on the way to her car. She hoped he'd had a long life and a happy one, not too heavily touched with sickness or sorrow.

And what would a descendant seventy or eighty generations removed from her think about the life she was living? Considering what she'd thought of Carnuntum, ignorance was probably bliss.

Frank was none too cordial when he and Dawn came to get Kimberley and Justin. "I should have taken half my plane fare out of that check, and Dawn's, too," he grumbled, "seeing how you screwed up Cancún for us."

"That wasn't my fault," Nicole said: not strictly true, but Frank didn't need to know that. "And I did need the money." She glanced at Dawn, who was French-braiding Kimberley's hair. Kimberley looked pleased with herself. "I'm going to be so pretty, Mommy," she said.

"You already are, sweetheart," Nicole answered. It wasn't a bad thing that Kimberley liked Frank's girlfriend. Really. She made one more gesture toward civility: "Thanks for getting the money to me when I asked for it," she said to Frank.

"That's okay." Frank caught himself; she must have taken him by surprise. It certainly wasn't her usual approach. "No, it's not okay, but it's done. The . . . heck with it." That wasn't civility for Nicole's sake. He'd always made an effort not to swear when the kids could hear.

With Kimberley and Justin out of the house, the place felt empty and much too quiet. Nicole tackled it with vacuum cleaner and duster, scrub brush and plain old elbow grease. She hadn't given it that good a going-over since well before she woke up in Carnuntum. By the time the place was spotless and all the kids' toys picked up and put away, she was bone-tired. But it was a different kind of tired than she knew after a long day in the office.

It felt good to sit down to a solitary dinner: a small steak, pan-grilled with garlic and cracked black pepper, and a baked potato—no potatoes in Carnuntum. She ate this miniature feast in front of the TV, with the VCR running her tape of *The First Wives' Club*. She howled all the way through it. She'd got even, too, by God. It felt wonderful.

Frank and Dawn brought the kids back Sunday evening, putting an end to a long, lazy, surprisingly pleasant weekend. Nicole had idled through the Sunday paper with bagels and cream cheese and lox, watched another video, even spent a little time drowsing in the cool and familiar quiet of her bedroom. She was awake and refreshed and able to smile at the kids as they burst through the door—minus their father and his girlfriend, who, true to form, had dropped them off and sped away for a night of, Nicole could presume, relentless debauchery. Or else they were going to buckle down to a little extra work.

Kimberley's mouth was going even before the door was fully open, pouring out her latest news: a trip to the zoo. "We saw lions and tigers and chimpanzees and elephants and flamingos and meerkats—meerkats are *so* funny, Mommy— and we ate hamburgers and French fries and pink lemonade."

"Elephant make big poop," Justin added. He laughed. Bathroom humor and two-year-olds went together like ham and eggs.

"He sure did," Kimberley agreed. She made a face. "It was dis*gust*ing." Then, with a giggle, she stuck a finger in front of her nose and trumpeted. So did Justin. They ran around being elephants, at impressive volume, till Nicole snagged them and pitched them into the bathtub. They splashed enough water to turn the rest of the bathroom into a swamp. That might have been fine for elephants; their mother was not amused.

When Monday morning came, the elephants were magically transformed into preschoolers. They were eager preschoolers, as eager to head to Woodcrest as they'd ever been to go to Josefina's house. That was good news—very good indeed. So was the trip to the office, short, sweet, and simple. She was definitely getting to like that part of her day.

This Monday's return was rather different than her last one. The outpouring of good wishes had stopped. And yet there were still greetings, smiles, welcoming waves: a friendliness and sense of being wanted that she couldn't remember from before. Was it new, or had she been too harried to notice it?

She took a warm feeling into her office with her. It helped as she tackled the mountain of work she'd neglected in favor of Sheldon Rosenthal's analysis. More had come in while she was doing that, and some was urgent. The fact she hadn't heard from Sheldon Rosenthal didn't concern her too deeply. Word would come down from Mount Olympus, or it wouldn't. There was no point in worrying about it.

By the time she came up for air, it was Thursday. She had a vague memory of the week, including at least one food fight between Kimberley and Justin—the kitchen curtains would never be quite the same—and a birthday lunch for one of the other women associates.

By Thursday morning, she was beginning to think she'd reach the bottom of the pile some time in the not too indefinite future. She was so pleased to realize that, she didn't even snarl when the telephone rang. Cyndi's voice said, "Mr. Rosenthal's on the line, Ms. Gunther-Perrin."

"Put him through," Nicole said—strictly pro forma, of course. One did not, no matter how wickedly tempted, put the founding partner on hold.

"Good morning, Ms. Gunther-Perrin," Rosenthal said in his smooth, polished tones. "Could you come up, please, to discuss the analysis you prepared for me?"

Could you come up, from the big boss, meant, *How close to yesterday can you get your fanny up here?* "Of course, Mr. Rosenthal," Nicole said with what she hoped was suitably bright willingness—and no apprehension. "I'll be right there."

The seventh floor was as hushed and august a place as ever. It had, now she had a basis of comparison, a certain Roman feel—but she doubted very much that the decorators would have been pleased to be informed of *real* Roman taste in decor, including the nauseating color combinations and the gaudy, and X-rated, statuary.

She was keeping her spirits up rather well, she thought. Not stressing out. Not letting herself imagine horrors, or flash back too strongly to the last time she'd answered a summons from on high. She'd come up with such lofty hopes, and gone down like a soul into Hades, all the way down the helix of time to a tavern in Carnuntum.

Lucinda was sitting as always in the outer office, door dragon par excellence. She nodded as Nicole entered. "Go right in," she said. Was that cordiality? It couldn't be. It was just—a touch more than her usual civility. Maybe it was Nicole's nice gray suit. Power dressing had its uses. "He's expecting you."

The office hadn't changed at all—but it had only been three weeks of this world's time since she'd seen it. Rosenthal stood up to greet her. She couldn't read his expression. "Coffee?" he asked, just as he had when he'd dropped the bomb on her.

"Yes, thanks," she said, and let him pour her a cup. There was a subtle protocol in that, and she was as well aware of it as he was.

It was excellent coffee. She sipped at it for a moment, admiring the view from his window, before she sat down across from that battleship of a desk.

She couldn't tell what, if anything, he was thinking. Her

gray suit, her cream silk shell, and her understated professional makeup wouldn't offend his eyes, she didn't think.
Maybe she was a little more confident than she'd been, or a
little less worn down by the world in general. She was definitely happier, now that she had a basis of comparison.
Historical perspective, she thought, *is an amazingly under-
rated thing.*

Sheldon Rosenthal studied her for a moment, a scrutiny
she endured with what she hoped was suitable equanimity,
and tapped his forefinger on the analysis. "You think a challenge to developing this parcel, should one occur, would be
likely to succeed."

Nicole's heart thudded, but she calmed it down. She nodded. "Yes, I do. Anyone who takes a look at that environmental impact report will find plenty of ammunition. I've
outlined a couple of possible strategies, with citations."

"Yes, you were most thorough." Rosenthal tapped the top
page again. "Most thorough," he repeated. Nicole wondered
if he meant it for a compliment. He coughed, then said, "I
notice you credit Mr. Ogarkov with assisting you here."

"That's right," Nicole said. *And what do you intend to
make of that, Mr. Founding Partner?*

"And why did you seek his assistance?" Rosenthal asked.
"Did you not consider that, since I gave the assignment to
you, I might have wanted it to come from you and you
alone?"

"I did consider that, yes." Nicole spoke with great care.
"But I also thought you would want the analysis to be as
good as it could be, no matter how it got that way. Mr.
Ogarkov writes better than I do"—*you drove that home with
a sledgehammer*—"and so I asked him to polish it before I
gave it to you. He was kind enough to oblige."

"I see." Sheldon Rosenthal coughed again. Nicole couldn't
help remembering what a repeated cough had meant once,
in Carnuntum. But this was lawyerly pose, not pestilence.
"He made a point of telling me that polishing, as you put it,
was all he did: that the legal analysis is entirely yours."

"That's true," Nicole said, cautious still. Of course Rosenthal had checked in with Gary before he summoned her. It was good of Gary not to try to take more credit than he deserved. But then, he didn't need to hog credit now. He'd already made partner. Whereas Nicole—

I've got a job, she reminded herself firmly. *It could be worse. I know how much worse it could be.* She could hang on here till she got some resumes in the mail. If she found something better, she'd take it. If she didn't, she'd keep hanging on. That was all she could do. All she needed to do, really. As long as she had food, shelter, and means to pay the bills, that would be enough.

"It is, I think, an excellent analysis," Rosenthal said.

"Thank you," Nicole said. He'd praised her work before. It hadn't meant anything then; it needn't mean anything now. Nevertheless, she couldn't stop her heart from speeding up again. *Just drop the bomb and get it over with.*

He coughed once more. In another world and time, she'd have been waiting for him to break out in a rash and collapse. Instead, he plucked at the neat tuft of hair on his chin. Was he nervous? Of course not. He was playing a game of some sort, and she, it appeared, was the spectator. Or, perhaps, the target?

"Not long ago," he remarked, "Mr. Sandoval informed me that he was resigning to accept a position with a firm in Sacramento. He has, I believe, ambitions of working closely with the State Legislature." One of his eyebrows twitched microscopically, as if to say he found such ambitions unsavory.

Nicole had been prepared for a number of things, but this particular change of subject took her by surprise. She didn't know Sandoval past the occasional greeting in the hall, but she could say honestly enough, "I hope he does very well."

"I have no doubt that he will. He is able and personable and, as I say, ambitious. That, however, is not why I mention the matter to you." Rosenthal got up, refilled his coffee cup, and Nicole's as well, without waiting for her to nod. More power games. More odd resonances. He sat down, sipped, and resumed: "I mention it because, with Mr. Sandoval's departure, we are left with a vacancy in our partnership structure. Would you by any chance be interested in filling that vacancy?"

Nicole sat in what felt, just then, like a perfect vacuum. He'd said words. The words meant something. What they meant . . .

She was sitting, she realized, and staring blankly at the founding partner's face. It had blurred into an abstract, a pale oblong of features, two dark dots for eyes, and a grayish smudge of beard. Slowly, though perhaps not as slowly in real time as in the eons inside her head, she found the rags of her professional demeanor and put them on. The first thing that came to her, she didn't act on. A shriek of *Yee-haaaa!* was hardly appropriate in the founding partner's office.

The second response, the one she selected, came out rather well, she thought, and rather calmly, too: "Thank you, Mr. Rosenthal. I would like that very much."

Was that the wintry ghost of a smile on that austere face? She let herself suppose it was. "Well, splendid," Rosenthal said. "I know I must have disappointed you in our last, formal meeting. After this truly outstanding piece of work you've done here, I'm doubly pleased to make this offer."

She might be half blind with joy, but she could read between those lines. He must have taken more flak than he'd expected when he named Gary and not her. He'd given her the analysis as a test of sorts. If she'd done it badly—maybe even if she hadn't thought to ask Gary to help with the prose style—he would have had the ammunition he needed to prove he'd been right. If she did well, as she'd done, he had justification for promoting her. How long had he known Sandoval would be leaving? Had he by any chance encouraged Sandoval to leave just then?

She couldn't ask, and she wasn't about to try. If she hadn't lived in Carnuntum while her body spent six days in a coma, what would have happened? If he'd just dumped the analysis on her in the state of mind she'd been in after she lost the partnership, she'd probably have told him to put it where the sun didn't shine. Or she'd have given him a half-assed, halfhearted job, the work of an obviously disgruntled employee.

For all she knew, that was exactly what he'd expected of her. If so, he wasn't showing it, and he wasn't likely to. If she'd surprised him, he'd never admit it. Nor would he ever confess to disappointment that she'd proved him wrong and her supporters—the whole amazing number of them—right. *Thank you, Liber,* she thought. *Thank you, Libera. But for you, I'd be out on the street right now.*

Rosenthal was waiting for her to say something. She couldn't let him know exactly what she was thinking, but she came as close as she dared: "Sometimes things need to work out at their own speed."

Thanks again to the god and goddess whose answers to her prayers had taught her so much, and shown her how to conduct herself in two worlds, she'd said the right thing. "A very mature attitude, Ms. Gunther-Perrin," Rosenthal said, nodding with more vigorous approval than she'd ever had from him. "Commendably mature. The proper attitude for a team player. Yes, I think you will be valuable to the firm in your new role."

She heard everything he didn't say—everything he'd said to her in this office three weeks ago. Would he attribute her change in attitude to her six-day coma? Or would he just assume that she'd taken time to rethink her priorities?

It didn't matter. He'd changed his mind about making her a partner. She *was* a partner. She'd broken out of the trenches; she had a future in the firm. Life was good. Life was very, very good.

This descent from the upper regions was far different from its predecessor. Nicole kept a deadpan expression, which must have been convincing: people glanced at her, some with curiosity, but for all they knew, she'd just gone up to get the feedback on her analysis. If the office grapevine had been humming, nobody was showing it.

Cyndi was making a point of being busy, no doubt to keep from noticing any new disappointments. Nicole thought of striding on past, but that wasn't exactly fair to Cyndi. She let go her deadpan expression, let it go completely. What

Cyndi must have seen out of the corner of her eye was a high-grade idiot grin.

She looked up from her keyboard and got the full blaze of it head-on. Her eyes went wide. "Did you—?" she asked. "Did he—?"

"Yes!" Nicole's answer was all-inclusive.

Cyndi leaped up with a complete disregard for proper secretarial demeanor, and threw her arms around Nicole in a bruisingly tight hug. Nicole's jaw ached with grinning, but she couldn't seem to stop. When Cyndi whirled her in a little dance of joy, she went along, and let it spin her right into her office. She fetched up next to the phone.

She was aware, peripherally, of Cyndi setting the grapevine going at top speed. And why not? She picked up the phone and punched a particular extension. "Okay, Gary," she said when he answered. "Today *I* buy lunch."

He couldn't have helped but hear the jubilation in her voice. "Does that mean what I hope it means?"

"You better believe it," she said.

He let out a war whoop right in her ear. It was still ringing as she set the receiver down and tried to get back to work. Futile as that was: between Cyndi and Gary, within ten minutes the news had traversed the entire sixth floor. The seventh had probably known for hours, if not for days, which way the decision would go.

It was all she could do to get away for lunch, with all the people streaming in to congratulate her. She caught herself noticing who seemed overjoyed and who eyed her speculatively—women associates, many of those last. They'd be seeing the crack she'd made in the glass ceiling, and contemplating ways of making it wider.

More power to them, Nicole thought. She had to drag Gary away, finally, which probably started a whole new spate of gossip.

So let people talk. Today, at least, she didn't give a damn.

Gary chose Yang Chow for lunch. That seemed fitting. Nicole had eaten there when things looked their worst. It was only right she should go back now that they were looking as good as she could ever remember. She even ordered the chili shrimp again, to take the curse off it, and to make it a good-luck dish. Then she sat back in the cool open space with its white tablecloths and its candy-pink napkins, and looked out through the blinds at the green-lined street, and indulged in a moment of great contentment.

"It's a shame you don't drink," Gary said. "You should have one to celebrate."

"You have one for me," she said, "since I drove. I don't *think* I want to begin my drinking career"—which, in this body, it would be—"by drinking and driving. A 502 on the day I made partner? No, thanks."

He laughed ruefully and agreed—and ordered a double Scotch on the rocks, in her honor. Watching him drink it, she didn't think she was ready for that yet, even if she wasn't driving. What she *was* ready for, however . . .

She got hardly any more work done the rest of that day than she had when she came back from the hospital. She didn't worry about it a bit. Sooner or later, she would catch up. In the meantime, she'd enjoy herself. She'd earned it.

And if that wasn't a change in attitude, she didn't know what was. *Seize the day,* the Romans had said. *Eat, drink, be merry. Tomorrow you may die.* It wasn't macabre at all, or particularly pessimistic. It made a great deal of sense, as worldviews went.

On the way home with the kids, she stopped at Cost Plus Imports. Kimberley and Justin loved the place. Among other things, Cost Plus had weird toys from all over the world—and imported candy bars, too. Nicole wasn't ready quite yet to corrupt them that far, though she almost yielded to the temptation. Instead, she bought Kimberley a child-palm–sized frog with bright green, satiny skin, and Justin a red-and-blue lizard. They were delighted with their prizes.

And she bought herself a bottle of red wine. She didn't know anything about wine; except in Carnuntum, she'd never had anything to do with it. The brands had changed a bit since then: no Falernian in stock here. She hoped it would be good. It certainly had cost enough, even at a steep dis-

count. If it wasn't as upscale as its pricetag, she could only
hope Liber and Libera would forgive her.

There was a certain comfort in the routine of a Thursday
night at home: dinner she actually cooked, fried fish and
mixed vegetables and, as a treat, a package of curly fries;
then baths and bedtime story and bed for the kids. They
didn't understand why Mommy was so happy, or just what
a partnership was, but they were glad because she was glad.
It mattered more to them that there were two new additions
to the population of stuffed animals. Nicole was amused to
hear Kimberley explain to Scratchy the stuffed bobcat,
"Now, remember, Scratchy, you can't eat Ribbit, even if he
is a frog. You have to be friends."

Justin protested loudly: "Lizzie! Lizzie too!"

"Lizzie, too," Kimberley agreed. "You hear that, Scratchy?
You can't eat Lizzie, either. Except," she added with calculation worthy of both her parents combined, "if Justin is
naughty—"

"No exceptions," Nicole said, exercising parental veto.
Kimberley glowered, but for that particular sentence, there
was no court of appeals. She sulked for a minute or two, but
she'd survive it. Nicole kissed her good night and left her
clinging tightly to both the much-mended and much-battered
Scratchy and the shiny new Ribbit. Justin was already asleep
in his own bed. Nicole kissed him on the forehead, too lightly
to wake him, and went back to the brightly lit and newly
quiet kitchen.

She had to rummage through the drawers before she found
a corkscrew. She'd never used one before, or paid much
attention to anybody else who did—she'd been too busy being censorious about the evils of alcohol—as if good red
wine and rubbing alcohol were the same poisonous substance.

She managed to push the cork down into the wine instead
of pulling it out of the bottle. Her mouth twisted in chagrin,
but really, it didn't matter. She found a goblet deep in a
cupboard, one of a set of crystal she'd been given as a wedding present, and filled it nearly full of wine that looked like

the Falernian she'd sold by the cup in the tavern. It smelled much less sweet, but no less rich; a richness that felt, somehow, very modern, very spare and contemporary. That was fitting, when she thought about it.

She picked up the goblet and a dishtowel, and carried them into the bedroom. The bedside lamp was on, shedding a soft glow on the plaque from Carnuntum. She folded the dishtowel at its base and poured a little wine, first over Libera's face, then over Liber's. Whatever the deities didn't drink ran down the limestone surface and soaked into the towel.

"Thank you," Nicole said to the god and goddess. "Thank you, thank you, thank you." She set the glass in front of the plaque as a second offering. But there needed to be more. She lifted the glass again and, for the first time in her modern life, took a sip of wine.

It wasn't nearly so sweet as Falernian. The flavor, like the smell, was richer, and more complex. After several sips and some moments' thought, she decided she liked it better. She could hope Liber and Libera did, too.

However they felt about it, they weren't saying. She set the cup down half empty, leaving it for them if they wanted it, and turned out the light. She'd sleep well, she was sure. Whatever worries she had, for this night at least, none of them mattered.

In the dark silence of the bedroom, Libera's stone eyes swung toward Liber's. The god was already looking her way. They nodded. The wine had been a little on the sour side, but it was the first formal offering they'd had in a long, long time. They were both well pleased.

They were also both amused. They were gods; they could read a human soul as easily as a man could read letters on a parchment. Nicole had not simply been thanking them for returning her to this time—which she, for incomprehensible mortal reasons, preferred to their own. She was thanking them, too, for all that had gone well in her life since.

And that, Liber and Libera knew, was foolishness. How could it be anything else? She'd done those things, every one of them, herself.